THE ENERGETICS
PARANORMAL ROMANCES
BOOKS 1-3

ELLEN BARD

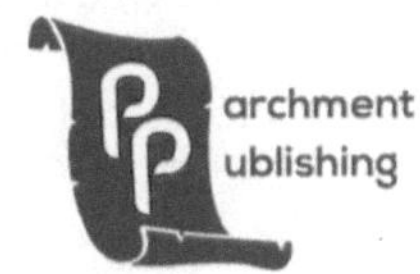

ISBN: 978-0-9934394-6-9
Published by Parchment Publishing.
ParchmentPublishing.com

THE ENERGETICS, BOOK 1

BLAIZE AND THE MAVEN

ELLEN BARD

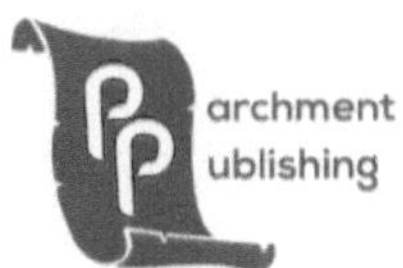

Dedication

To my mum, Mary, and sister, Sarah, who support me in all my crazy adventures. And in memory of my inspiring and loving dad, Chris Bard (1952-2007).

The Chakras and their Energies

 **Muladhara:** The Root Chakra – Earth Element
The energy of nourishment and home, family and safety.

 **Svadisthana:** The Sacral Chakra – Water Element
Fluid and adaptable, the energy of movement and connection, of practical and physical creativity. The energy of pleasure, sexuality and sensation, and emotions.

 **Manipura:** The Navel Chakra – Fire Element
The energy of the individual; of confidence, of proactivity and of drive and passion. Playful and proud.

 **Anahata:** The Heart Chakra – Air Element
The energy of healing, and of balance, located in the middle of the body and the seven Chakras. The energy of love, of relationships, of devotion. Of compassion and empathy.

 **Vishudha:** The Throat Chakra – Ether (Space) Element
The energy of communication, of conceptual creativity, and of truth. Of expression, and of listening.

 **Ajna:** The Third Eye – The Mind
The energy of imagination, of visualizations, and insight. Of clarity and wisdom. Of dreams and intuition.

 **Sahasara:** The Crown Chakra – None*
The purest of all the energies. Only experienced through the Grace of the Source (the energetics' name for the creator, the divine).

---

*Neither a dominant nor auxiliary Chakra for energetics

1

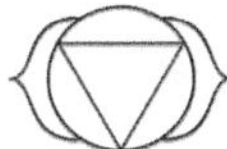

Blaize stood in front of the Three.

They looked back, their faces impassive.

Blaize needed to wait, to show patience; everything about today was part of the ritual. Even the waiting was a test—a gentle test compared to what was to come—but a test nonetheless, of her self-discipline.

But her skin itched with the need to do something. Dominant Manipura energetics like her often suffered from a lack of patience. Manipura—the energy of fire, of passion, of willpower. But also of pride, arrogance, and a quick temper.

She pushed the impatience down and willed herself to stand in front of them without action. The sand was warm under her bare feet, and the harsh heat of the sun bit even at this hour of the morning. The quiet of the jungle temple provided little to distract her from the waiting.

They stood like this in silence for thirty minutes. She kept her gaze steady and held each pair of eyes in turn as they studied her. None of them moved. *What are they thinking?*

It was unusual for an Adherent to fail the trial at such an early stage, but it could happen. Her stomach contracted and she held herself rigid to keep her face neutral. *Stay confident.*

One of the three stepped forward slightly. "Blaize Blackfire, of the Blackfire clan, you come before us on the recommendation of your Maven,

Fai Sweetwater. After a scant five years of teaching, she believes you are ready for your Practitioner trial."

The speaker's robe draped her strong, lean body, and her silver hair cascaded down her back like a waterfall. The only markings on the white robe were the three red stripes across her upper left sleeve, which denoted her Master status in the Manipura Guild. The tiny owl symbol next to the stripes showed she was also a Maven.

"We represent the Manipura Guild, one of the six energetic Major Guilds. Based on your performance today, we will decide whether you are ready to move from Adherent to Practitioner." Her grey eyes held Blaize's. "First, we must ask you. Do you attempt this trial of your own free will?"

Blaize nodded.

"State your answer so the record is clear." The woman's voice was kind, but firm in her admonishment.

"I do."

"Are you aware that if you fail to reach the standard required you must wait a full year before you attempt the trial again?"

"I am." Blaize tried hard not to wince as she said this. *I'm ready. More than ready.*

"Has your Maven taken you through the dangers that await you within the trial? That even death is possible?"

"She has." Blaize's gaze met Fai's, and Fai gave a small smile and an even smaller nod that hinted at their relationship.

Fai. The woman who had been her Maven for the last five years of her life—and had always been her aunt. Blaize was so grateful to Fai, for her love, her support, her discipline, that the idea of failing—of letting her down—was unbearable. Blaize tried not to shiver, but her shoulders twitched anyway. Today Fai wasn't here as her aunt, or even her Maven. She was here as one of the Three.

"Do you consider yourself ready to face the trials that are ahead of you?"

"I'm ready." Blaize squared her shoulders and lifted her chin. She was confident. She was. She'd been pushing for the trial for months, certain she could pass. Fai had finally agreed, and now here she was. Her stomach was a tight ball inside her, and she was grateful that the preparation involved fasting, as she wasn't sure she'd be able to hold food down. *I'll be fine when we start.* Blaize liked action. *It's just this waiting that's killing me.*

"Then we will begin." Serafina, the Italian Maven, stepped back after she spoke. Blaize felt she was being judged, and hoped that Serafina didn't find her wanting at this early stage.

"Your trial will begin with a test of the strength of your energetic power. You must conjure and create Warrior fire, and hold it for one hour. During that hour, we will challenge the strength of the fire that you create. If the fire is extinguished, you will fail," Huo, the male who made up the Three for the trial with Serafina and Fai, said. "If the fire has dimmed at all, you must bring it back to full strength, or you will fail. The fire must be contained within the circle of sand in the temple. If you lose control, and your fire spreads further than this, you will fail. Do you understand?"

Blaize forced her voice to ring out. "I do."

"Then we will begin." The male's near-black eyes were steady and neutral. He was the only one of the three she'd never met before the trial. He was Chinese, and as with the other two Mavens, had the same three red stripes and owl symbol on his white robes. As a male Maven, his stripes were on the right, the Yang side.

An energetic was born a 'Dormant.' Once the energetic started to train in one of their energies, they were given the title 'Adherent.' After many years of training, they faced their Chakra Trial, as Blaize did now, and after successfully completing the trial, they became a Practitioner. After this—and many decades—they might become a Master. Most energetics remained at Practitioner level in their Major Guild, as it took a great deal of power and focus to become a Master.

Only Masters could become Mavens—a title outside the energetic hierarchy, given only to those who helped other energetics develop their own powers.

The Three, all experienced Mavens, moved to worn stone seats at the edge of the sand circle Blaize stood within. This circle had seen many trials in its time. It was the heart of one of Manipura's most important temples, an open-roofed stone sanctuary on a quiet island to the west of Thailand. Hard to find if you didn't know where to look, the temple was surrounded by twisted green jungle, rough terrain, and the clinging wet heat that was the typical climate of the island at this time of year.

With the nearest habitation several miles away, Blaize could use her energy as she liked without any humans knowing.

Blaize stepped into the circle and closed her eyes. She made an effort to loosen her shoulders and took a few deep breaths to saturate her system with oxygen. In her mind, she visualised the shape and size the fire she wanted to conjure would take. There would be time for more showy stuff later. This trial was all about strength, power, and protecting her fire against the challenges that the Three would test her with.

She drew on her energy centre for Manipura Chakra, at the core of her body, where her belly button would be. This was her link to what her people called the etheric plane, or ether, where Blaize needed to draw the energy from to the terrestrial plane, where the energetics lived alongside their unknowing human neighbours.

All energetics had two active Chakras, one dominant, one auxiliary. For most, the dominant was considerably more powerful than the auxiliary.

Blaize's dominant Chakra was Manipura, fire, and her auxiliary was Ajna, the power of the mind. She was still an Ajna Dormant, with little interest in her power in that area, as all her energy to date had been spent training her Manipura. Refining it, honing it, ready for today.

She used her Manipura energy centre to pull energy through from the ether in a steady stream that fizzed and sparked inside her. She shaped and created the fire in front of her with her eyes closed, not needing them to know what she was doing. The flames were strong, powerful and burned from the floor in front of her higher than the top of her head. She could create fiercer, taller flames, but that wasn't required. The trial would also test her pride, another weakness of hers. She always wanted to be the best, the biggest, the strongest. In this particular test, that could easily be her downfall.

Each energetic had their own natural limit for pulling energy that determined how strong they were. Her limit was high; she just didn't know whether it would be high enough.

The fire burned hot, but she kept it within the circle.

The first attack came a few minutes later, from Fai, whose auxiliary Chakra was Svadisthana, the water Chakra. Rain fell on Blaize's fire. At first the rain was playful and fell lightly over the fire. The mix created steam in tiny 'pfts' as each drop sizzled in the fire. But moments later it changed into a deluge that targeted Blaize's flames, and she had to concentrate hard to draw enough energy through to keep her fire burning.

It flickered and dimmed, but Blaize had faced this attack from her Maven many times before in all its variations. Blaize raised her flames high above her head, seeking the source of the rain, and used the fire energy to nullify the water energy. There was some resistance, but in time the rain slowed to a stop, and her fire returned to its previous height, just above her head.

The next attack came before she had centred herself after the first. This was from Serafina, the Italian Master whose auxiliary Chakra was Anahata, the Chakra of air.

Wind whipped around Blaize, and her hair snapped against her face. The wind aimed to drive her fire out of control, and out of the circle. The fire's wild flames danced, and part of Blaize wanted to dance with it, to lose herself to the power and the energy. She exulted as Serafina's air fed the fire more oxygen, and it rose and rose.

Blaize stopped herself just before the fire crept over the edges of the circle. She was now at the centre of a furnace, and she delighted in the heat on her skin. She forced the flames in towards her and lowered them to neck height, so that she stood in a much smaller circle of flames, a witch burning at the stake. But she wasn't burning. The opposite in fact. The more she drew on the power, the better she felt.

The air continued to dance around her, but it could no longer find a way into her tight circle of flames. Fire and air licked at each other, each darting around the other energy, deadlocked. Blaize sighed in pleasure and drew energy through, feeding her flames. A weaker fire energetic might find this air attack a challenge, but for Blaize, air was just fuel for her fire.

After an indeterminable time, the dust and sand that had been caught up in the air drifted back to the floor, and the wind calmed. Her fire was still strong, and sweat ran down the sides of her face and her back from effort and the hot sun.

The next attack surprised her. It was from Huo, whose auxiliary Chakra was Ajna—the Chakra of the mind. Rather than attack the fire itself, he spoke inside her mind, an unusual power even among Ajnas.

<*That's enough, Blaize. You've passed. You've done well. It's time to rest.*>

His tone was soft, persuasive. Blaize frowned. She was sure an hour hadn't passed yet. The trial wasn't over. This must be a trick. She kept her fire burning.

His voice was insistent. <*Relax. Let go of the energy. Sit down. Rest…*>

She shook her head involuntarily and tried to block his voice out. Her flames wavered as she heard the voice persist.

<*You don't need to prove anything to us. You're strong, proud. You know your powers are as good as a Practitioner; why do you need our approval?*>

Her eyebrows drew together, a crease forming between her eyes. That sounded like a thought she'd had once or twice. Had he taken it from her mind? His powers were an exact match for hers—his dominant energy Manipura, and his auxiliary Ajna, the energy of the mind. Did that connection make it easier or harder for him to speak in her mind? Blaize was a bit murky on what Ajna could and couldn't do, despite it being her own auxiliary power.

<*Rest, Blaize. Let the flames die down.*>

The insidious voice became harder and harder to block out. For the first time in the trial, she opened her eyes to check her fire. Her eyes widened as she realised it was suffocating. The other two Mavens had joined the assault, creating an environment of damp air in which it was hard to sustain the flame.

Blaize bared her teeth in a fierce grin. He might have taken some stray thoughts from her head, but he didn't know her. She thrived on competition.

The challenge just makes it more interesting.

She tipped her head back and closed her eyes. She focused on the energy she pulled through and tugged harder, using the energy to make her flames burn brighter and hotter, maintaining their height. It took some finesse to keep everything balanced, but she could do it.

For the next ten minutes, she fought off more attacks from the Three, the attacks stronger and more complex each time they renewed their assault. But her flames burned, her focus steadfast.

The attacks ended, and there was quiet. Blaize judged it about the right amount of time for the trial to end, but she wouldn't take any chances. She kept the flames at head height until Serafina said aloud, "This trial is complete. You may rest for a short period before the next trial."

Blaize drew in a shaky breath and opened her eyes.

"It is done," Fai and Huo's voices spoke as one.

Blaize breathed out and let the energy subside. The first trial was over.

Her body buzzed and hummed, and she felt energised, ready for anything. She knew all too well that this could be a trick of her body and mind, and that if she weren't careful she could find herself with an 'energy high,' unable to judge if she was close to burning herself out. So she folded herself cross-legged on the sand and breathed deeply. *In and out. In and out.* She focused on the air she breathed in and out through her nose. She steadied the energies, and grounded and stabilised herself. Waiting.

There were still two tests to go. All three would contribute to her success — or failure. She had completed the test of strength. The next were the tests of stamina and finesse. She was most worried about the last, but both held their traps and dangers.

Huo stood, his hands clasped together in front of him, his face distant. "The next test is of endurance. Use your defensive abilities while we call Warrior fire against you."

She nodded her understanding.

"You may not use your offensive abilities. If you use offensive energy, you will fail. If you step out of the circle, you fail. In this trial, you can end it before time should you wish, by calling stop. This will mean you fail the trial immediately."

Source, there are a lot of opportunities for me to fail. Blaize tried to keep her face as serene at the Three, but inside she winced.

"Do you understand?" Huo finished.

"I understand." Blaize rose to her feet.

"You may have a few moments to prepare." Huo remained standing, and Serafina and Fai joined him, arranging themselves in a line, gaps of about a yard between them, much further apart than the stone chairs. Each of the Mavens closed their eyes and made their own preparations.

Blaize shut her eyes and drew on the energy she still felt within her, and took yet more from the ether. It was almost impossible for your own energy to be turned against you, but an energetic could be hurt by energies wielded by another energetic. This trial was about defending herself from some of the most powerful members of her Guild. As before, she'd had practice. A lot of practice. And over time, she'd had a lot of burns. But it had been a while since Fai had been able to touch her with her Warrior fire, at least without taking her by surprise. Blaize felt confident if they attacked her one at a time she could defend herself.

I hope I can manage all three at once.

She spooled power inside her. She built a defensive wall around her and snapped shields she'd spent years working with into place.

She extended her energy out a little into the temple.

She felt Fai's energy—fire and water—hot but almost fluid. Serafina—fire and air—was warm and light. And then there was Huo, the most mysterious of all, whose fire and mind powers were sharp, laser-like. *Will my powers ever feel like that?* Blaize wanted to learn about her Ajna powers, her mind element, but she could wait. She loved the energy of fire too much to want to focus on anything else right now.

Without warning, the attacks began. Huo slashed fire across her face. Blaize drew in a breath—and her throat burned. As she sent energy to repair the weakness in her shields that Huo's Warrior fire had created, another slash came. And another. She spooled energy, and her breathing increased. She was keeping up so far, but each slash caused her pain and depleted her energies. Her whole body shook with the effort of defending herself.

Fai added to the attack with a fluid fire that flooded the area around Blaize's legs as if she stood in hot water. Though the fire didn't come close to penetrating her defences like Huo's, she knew that if she didn't pay attention to it, Fai's Warrior fire would erode her defences, scraping them away until she was cooked.

Blaize threw a wash of defensive fire along her body and reinforced her shields. Which was lucky, because at that moment, a blast of heat hit her and she staggered from Serafina's attack.

None of the three moved from their solid stances. Blaize was closer to the stone wall behind the circle now, and she used this as another tool, a shield at her back. She parried attacks rather than absorb them, with no time to intellectualise and analyse, just respond.

Attack. Parry. Slash. Parry. Strike. Parry.

She drew more and more energy from the ether, and her body expended huge amounts of energy to keep her shields up. Sweat ran down her body. The drops tracked through the dust that Serafina's wind in the first trial had thrown at her body.

One of Huo's attacks whipped through her defences and created a thin red burn across her shoulder. She shook off the pain and turned up her defences once more.

Blaize was hit by another wave of heat from Serafina, followed in quick succession by several slashes from Huo. Blaize lost her balance and fell to one knee. Burning sand penetrated the thin material that covered her legs. She strengthened her shields. The attacks continued, fast now, so fast she didn't have time to get up. She parried, defended and deflected, and burned through energy at a blistering rate. *How long can I keep this up?*

Huo's insidious whisper crept into her mind once more. <*You can call time on this, Blaize. Just say stop.*>

Source knew, Blaize was tempted.

C H A P T E R

2

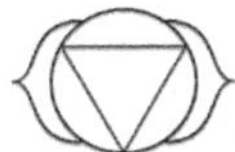

Huo's barbs kept coming, and his voice inside her head was louder now. *<Your defenses are weakening. You're going to let your Maven down.>*

Blaize stiffened, and her body shot to attention, giving her the energy to push up on her foot, teetering as she stood. *He's wrong. He has to be wrong. I will not fail this test.*

<You're weak, Blaize.>

A wave of heat flushed through her body that was nothing to do with her energies. *How dare he?*

<You're going to fail. You're going to end up just like your parents.>

At this taunt, Blaize's vision misted, her nails dug into her palms and she stepped towards Huo. But as she did her shields wavered, and she staggered and fell back to her knees, pain smashing through her kneecaps as they hit the rough sand.

Huo sent a flurry of strikes and slashes through the weakness in her defences that had opened when she'd been about to attack him. Each hit left a raised red welt. Blaize's vision cleared and she caught Fai raise her eyebrow very slightly.

Blaize drew her defences around her, keeping them in tight to her body as she knelt on the sand. *What the hell was I thinking?* If she used offensive fire, she would fail. It had only been the shock of Huo punching through her shields that had stopped her from lashing out at him. Her stomach gave a lurch and she swallowed, her mouth dry.

I need to focus. How can I keep him out of my mind? Can he read mine? She tried to use the same kind of shields of fire energy she used on her body to protect her mind. The energies twisted and pain shot through her head. *Ouch. Okay, so not exactly the same principle.* But the voice stopped. For now.

Her thoughts were slow, but her movements and instincts remained fast. She'd been hit a number of times now, and there were new burns on her shoulder and hip. Her cotton trousers and white cotton T-shirt were torn and covered in dirt and sweat. *At least burns don't bleed.*

She winced as another of Huo's attacks snuck through her defences. She felt lightheaded; the extensive energy use had taken a toll on her body.

She. Would. Not. Call. Stop.

The stone wall behind her gave off heat as it reflected Fai and Serafina's Warrior fire. Blaize protected her body, back and front, with defensive fire. She drew a deep breath in and centred herself even as she pulled a massive amount of energy. The defence she created was almost impenetrable. The attacks no longer reached her skin, and she put all her energy into maintaining the shield and nothing else.

Time stopped. There was nothing but her defences.

She didn't have much left in her. She needed to rest. *How long will this go on?*

She maintained the shield from the floor. She knelt and attempted to ground herself. Managing her physical body as well as her energies was almost beyond her.

And then, nothing.

The attacks stopped.

"It is done," said Huo.

Serafina and Fai echoed his words and the Three stepped back to their stone chairs.

"Rest again. The final trial will begin in one hour." Serafina's words soothed Blaize. She really needed that rest.

Blaize wanted to cry, her body limp and her arms hanging heavy by her sides. There was still one more trial to go. *Did I pass the first two?* It felt like it, but judges were capricious, and they had the last say on her performance.

She got to her feet, feeling like a newborn fawn. She needed a drink. She gestured to the door, and Serafina nodded.

Blaize walked out of the circle and down the stairs that led to a dark, familiar storage room away from the Three. She grabbed a bottle from the fridge in a hidden cupboard. She drank the cool water down, the liquid a balm for her throat, which was rough from breathing in the heated air of the trial. She drank another and washed her face in the sink. She leaned on the edges of the basin and stared into the mirror. She looked dreadful. Her hair hung in wet curls around her face, and her normally bright green eyes were shadowed.

The water helped. She rubbed her hands over her face and sat on the hard wooden chair that sat in the corner of the room. She closed her eyes, relaxed her body, and sank into meditation. She would repair as much of her energies as she could within the hour's rest period.

Blaize had fasted for the last twenty-four hours. She'd taken a ritual bath, and had spent time in meditation, focusing on the fire in her mind, in her body. When she'd come to the temple that morning before sunrise, she was as clean, as purified, as she could be, physically, emotionally, and mentally.

She tried to get back to that state as she meditated. The hour passed quickly – *too quickly* – and soon it was time to head back upstairs. She walked back into the circle with her game face on.

Serafina stood. Her eyes were grave as she held out a solid goblet, as smooth and worn as the stone seats in the temple. "The next trial tests your finesse. You must drink the poisonous liquid held in this goblet. Use your energy to burn every trace from your system. If you do not, it is probable that you will die. The poison is fast-acting. You will have about five minutes from drinking the poison before you feel the effects."

Serafina offered the goblet to Blaize.

She had tried this exercise successfully many times, but never with a substance that could kill her. The worst had been the liquids that made her sick, which Fai believed acted as a definite incentive to learning.

Blaize clung to the conviction that she had enough experience to get her through this trial, and tried to stop her stomach from jumping into her parched mouth and throat.

She cupped her hands around the heavy goblet and looked down at the green liquid inside. Serafina had sunk into the third stone chair without a sound, her face immobile. All of the Three were now still as statues. Blaize met each of their eyes in turn, Fai last.

I can do this. I will do this.

Then she tipped up the base of the goblet and the liquid flowed into her mouth and throat. The taste was bitter and somehow floral, and she gagged, her throat convulsing as she battled to keep it down.

Gah! That was disgusting.

Her throat burned, and her heartbeat sped up, her pulse a physical drumbeat in her body. She fought to keep the panic from overwhelming her as the poison flooded her system and began to do its work. She felt cramps in her abdomen and wherever the poison had passed.

Adrenalin surged through her body as she realised she'd made a major error by not spooling more energy before she drank. *Stupid.* She hastily drew energy from the ether, sending the energy inside her body rather than outwards as she had with her shield in the previous trial. She opened her consciousness up as deeply as possible to her own body, and the stone temple faded to the background of her mind. Her energy raced around her form like wildfire, in corkscrews and spirals. Wherever it encountered a molecule of the poison, it incinerated it before any more damage could be done.

The task was a difficult one. Finding every trace of poison as it coursed through her system was no easy matter. To burn the poison from her throat and stomach was straightforward enough, but the few seconds' head start the poison had was enough to give her some cramps. Her muscles were tight, and she gulped convulsively as she sent more and more tendrils of energy through her system to attack the poison molecule by molecule.

Perhaps the cramps she felt were psychosomatic. *Serafina said I had at least five minutes…*

Blaize tried to ensure her inner turmoil wasn't visible to the inscrutable eyes of the Three. But after a minute or two, sweat beaded at her temples, and her breath had quickened.

She found fewer molecules of poison. *Is there enough left to kill me? Perhaps if there's only a small amount left, it won't kill me even if I miss the five-minute deadline. Hmm.* Not really a chance she wanted to take.

Her stomach cramped again, tighter, and she was grateful it was empty as the spasms turned into a retch. Her right arm throbbed.

The poison saturated her system, a spider-web of pain throughout her body. She could no longer manage the multiple streams of energy around her body. *I'm not going to make it through this in one piece.*

The pain in her stomach, one of the areas where the poison had been at work the longest, was agonising. She made a split-second decision to focus on her vital organs and pushed her energy as hard as her strength would allow into her viscera and away from her arm.

A cramp like multiple stab wounds gripped her organs, and she couldn't breathe. She could think of nothing but her stomach, and she dropped once more to her knees.

The pain worsened.

She was going to run out of time.

3

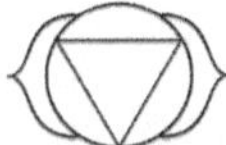

"It's not possible." Cuinn gripped the phone receiver in his hand and forced himself to keep his tone even. He kept his eyes on the stunning green view from the window of his workroom.

"Cuinn, please, reconsider. She has spectacular energies," Marius said. Fai's husband, he had called Cuinn from Thailand. Again. "Her Manipura is one of the strongest her Aunt has trained, and we think her Ajna energy is almost as strong—it's unusual for an auxiliary energy to be that powerful."

"I know." Cuinn's reply was dry. His own energies were also abnormally strong. He was one of the strongest Ajna energetics in the Guild. And much good had it done him. He rubbed his face, feeling the stubble that had grown there while he'd been immersed in his books yet again.

"You'd be a perfect Maven for her Ajna. She needs someone strong but grounded. It's hard to find a Maven with Ajna and Muladhara." Marius's Irish brogue had been dulled by time and travel, but could still be heard by Cuinn, also born there, many years ago.

"You know better than most that I can't take an Adherent. I've told you and Fai both for months. Why are we having this conversation again?" Cuinn felt a wash of heat across his chest and put a palm against the cool glass of the window. *Why are they still pestering me about this?* If his friendship with Marius hadn't been so old—and Marius and Fai were two of the small number of people in the world he cared about—he wouldn't have even taken the call. As it was, the temper that others rarely saw was now close to the surface. He took a deep breath to slow the pulse that had sped in reaction to Marius's harassment.

"Her trial's going on now. She'll pass, but her anger is still strong. She can be hasty, proud, quick to flare up. Rogues, in particular, have an ... incendiary effect on her."

"It's understandable, given what happened to her parents." Cuinn knew the girl's history. It was a hard one, and he of all people knew how tragedy could change and influence a person. He didn't blame her, but that didn't mean he wanted anything to do with her.

"It was fine when she was young, a Dormant, but she'll be a Manipura Practitioner after the trial. If her Ajna isn't well developed by a grounded Maven, she could easily go off course. She may be a straightforward Warrior now, but one day she could be a Guild Leader. She needs to develop the power of the mind, especially her farseer powers. It may seem as though her leadership won't be required for many years, but the death of her parents shows us that even the most experienced and longest lived of us can be taken by surprise. We want to be prepared."

"Her grandmother is strong, cautious, and adaptable. She's going nowhere. And the girl would have to be voted in by her Guild, which is unlikely. She's ridiculously young for the politics that would be involved. Which is something I can't teach her." *And wouldn't want to even if I could.*

"Please. For us. We need your help." Marius wouldn't budge.

Cuinn sighed. If this was a competition for the most stubborn energetic, he was happy to oblige. And it wasn't as if he was pretending, either. His plate was full. His brain buzzed with the glut of information he'd been taking in recently in an attempt to decipher the prophecies. "There are other things going on. I have things that I'm working on for the Circle."

"You'll always be busy. Your work ethic and your sense of duty determine that." Marius hesitated for the slightest moment. "But it's time for you too. Time for you to take another Adherent."

"That's for me to decide." Cuinn's tone became clipped. The heat now washed through not only his chest, but his neck and head. His forehead joined his palm against the window. "I value your friendship, you know I do, but don't presume to discuss matters with me that are my business alone."

"It's not only your business. You've cut yourself off for too long. Just because you won't take a leadership role for the energetics, doesn't mean you can't do important work elsewhere."

Why won't the man take no for an answer? "I *am* doing important work elsewhere."

"Part of being strong is working with others."

"That's enough." Cuinn's voice had a dangerous edge now. All he wanted was to be left alone, and Marius knew that. Surely that wasn't too much to ask after more than two hundred years of service to the Guild?

He kept silent, reining in the anger, kept staring at the green view, and Marius didn't break that silence.

At the back of Cuinn's mind lurked the debt he owed Marius. A debt that he gratefully acknowledged; Marius had brought Cuinn back from the brink of madness after Cuinn's horrific experience with his last Adherent. But surely Marius would never call in the debt in this way? He of all people knew how unsuited Cuinn was to be a Maven.

After a handful of moments, Cuinn relented, shaking his head. The girl was unlikely to pass her trial this fast. And even if he simply managed to postpone this conversation, at least he'd be able to get back to work now.

"She has to get through her trial first anyway. It's never a given. It would be rare for an energetic to pass their dominant energy's trial with only five years of training. Come back to me when—if—she passes, and we can discuss it again."

Cuinn hung up, slung the phone onto the desk and strode back to the window. His hands clutched the windowsill as he stared out, willing the view to ground him as it usually did.

The gentle hills, at this time of year still dusted with snow, reminded him of the Ireland he'd left many decades before. This kind of view was less common in Canada, his adopted home. But he'd found it in this area to the south east of Vancouver, Fraser Valley. Of course, Ireland didn't have the huge, white-capped mountain that was Mount Baker behind the valleys, but that just added to the view.

Not in the least soothed, he spun around and paced across the spacious room, stepping around the piles of books heaped on the floor.

Damn him. I don't want an Adherent. And not because he wasn't prepared to be responsible for a beginner's mistakes like many Master level energetics who chose not to become Mavens.

My reasons are far more important.

Cuinn's Ajna energy, the energy of the mind, gave him the power to dreamwalk. To visit the ether, and to use farsight to see slivers of the future. His recent dreamwalks had terrified him. So much so, he'd already reported them to his Minor Guild's Circle member. Over recent weeks, day and night, he'd explored the prophecies to try to understand more, but they were patchy, and the feelings of fear and trepidation that came with them had increased.

Cuinn stopped pacing and sighed. He pushed his hair back from his face. He hadn't been sleeping and his body felt as if it had gone three rounds in the practice ring with Adam, his extremely well-muscled and well-trained cousin.

Cuinn didn't want to have to deal with some fiery Adherent on top of everything else. He wasn't cut out to teach. Time had shown that.

He opened the door and went downstairs towards the house's huge kitchen, where, if he was any judge of the smells wafting down the corridor, Tierra, Adam's sister and Cuinn's other cousin, was baking. Adam and Tierra were all the family he had left – he didn't count his father – and they were the two most important people in the world to Cuinn.

He came through the kitchen door and saw her, humming along to the mellow sounds of a saxophone coming from the radio. Her dark hair hung around her face as she bent over the oven and took a mouthful of something from a baking tray. She looked up when he came in, eyes wide, guilt on her face.

"I was just having a taste!"

"Good?" He frowned. Had he missed something? *What was she talking about?*

"It was a small taste. It doesn't count against my diet." She had a smear of chocolate on her forehead. He walked over to her and wiped it off.

"You're on another diet?"

"Yes, yes, I want to lose a few pounds. I saw this beautiful dress in town, and I'm between sizes at the moment. I need to lose a few more pounds to get down to the next one."

"Why don't you enjoy whatever you're eating and go up a size?" He pinched a bit of brownie from the baking tray for himself and tasted it. Hot, a bit squishy, but good. Very good.

Her mouth dropped open. "What's wrong with you?"

"What's wrong with you?" He poked her in the arm and grinned at her.

She smiled back, shaking her head, and he gave her a quick one-armed hug. "I will never understand women. You'd have to go a long way before you found a man who wouldn't appreciate your curves."

"Not much chance of finding a man to ask given the luck I have in that area." She pushed the brownies back into the oven. "They need a few more minutes anyway. What have you been up to today?"

Cuinn tried to keep his tone casual. "I just got off the phone with Marius. He's trying to push his niece on me as an Adherent."

"You're talking about taking a new Adherent? That's big." She shut the oven and straightened.

"I'm not talking about it, he is. I'm not taking her. I told him no. Again."

Tierra rubbed her forehead and smudged more chocolate on her butterscotch skin. Cuinn suppressed a smile.

"Maybe it's time," she said. "It's been decades since …"

He stopped smiling. "I know how long it's been. There are others who can help her. It doesn't need to be me."

She leaned one elbow on the counter, resting her chin in her palm. "Hmm. It doesn't have to be, but it could be. Have you talked to Adam about it?"

He shook his head. "I haven't heard from him for a few days."

Tierra sighed. "The last message he sent said his team took a contract hunting some Rogue in Russia, so he's probably off the grid. I hope he looks after himself. And you, too—how's your work going? Have you made much progress with your dreamwalks? Are the prophecies any clearer?"

"Yes, and no. They're blurry, much blurrier than my farsight is normally." He shook his head and realised he was grinding his teeth. He relaxed his jaw and circled his head. "All I can tell is, trouble's coming, and it's coming for all of us. The energetics. But I don't know how, who—even when. I have only fragments, not enough to piece together yet."

"When did you last get a full night's sleep?"

"I don't know. A while." *Weeks. But she doesn't need to know that.* "I'm spending all the time I can on this. When I'm dreamwalking, my physical body's lying down, so it's a sort of rest."

"It won't help your farsight if you don't stay healthy."

Cuinn gritted his teeth and tried to change the subject. "How's your work?"

Tierra wrote nationally syndicated gardening and agony aunt columns. "Good. I sent off both this week's columns early. Let's have a proper dinner tonight, at the table. I'll cook something you like. Stop working by six, and come help me set the table."

Tierra was always ahead of her deadlines, whereas Cuinn felt like he could never catch up with his. "I don't have time."

Tierra waved a hand. "You can stop for an evening. Another good reason to get an Adherent—an Ajna will make a perfect assistant—she can spend her time with all of those dusty books of yours."

Cuinn raised his eyebrows. "Those 'dusty books' are the history of our race. And probably the future too, if only I can decipher the farseeings of those who've gone before me."

"The books can wait for you to have a good meal and a proper night's sleep. You're too thin, you'll waste away."

"You've been saying that for decades, and I still eat twice as much as you. It's my metabolism. My energies. But," he put up a hand to forestall yet another argument, "I'll keep you company at supper. And I'll only do a couple of hours afterwards before I go to bed. How's that?"

"I'll take it. You can tell me all about this Adherent of yours when we eat."

"She's not ..." Cuinn gave up as Tierra chuckled and pushed him out of the kitchen. He shook his head and gave a small smile, and as always, he felt lighter after spending time with his cousin, whose combination of earth and heart, Muladhara and Anahata, made her one of the most nurturing people he knew. He was lucky to have her in his life.

When Cuinn came back down again to dinner a couple of hours later, he was in a more relaxed mood. He'd found reference to a text that he thought might provide some suggestions about a way forward with the prophecies. He felt he had made some progress for the first time in days. He shut the door of his study area behind him for the night and took just the one book with him to read in the library after supper with Tierra.

As he walked towards the kitchen, he heard Tierra scolding someone who answered back in amused, lazy tones, "Don't pretend you're not pleased to see me, T."

Cuinn's eyebrows rose at the faint European accent that told him who she was scolding.

Cuinn came through the door and grinned. "Fintan! Why didn't you let me know you were coming?"

A tall, broad-shouldered, strawberry-blond man stood talking to Tierra's back. He turned. "What, and miss the opportunity to piss off your cousin here by adding an extra person to dinner?"

There was a 'hfft' from Tierra, who slapped at Fintan's hand, which was reaching for the spoon in her pot of sauce. It did smell great.

Cuinn walked to Fintan and they hugged like brothers—which was the way Cuinn felt about him. Fintan wasn't family, but after growing up in Scandinavia, he'd spent decades with Cuinn in Ireland when they were younger energetics, just as Marius had.

Marius. Of course. So that was why Fintan was here. He was backing up his phone pestering with a personal visit.

Frowning, Cuinn pushed away from Fintan.

"Marius sent you." Cuinn didn't have time for these games.

Fintan fidgeted and avoided his gaze. "What do you mean?"

"You know exactly what I mean, brother." He emphasised the last word. "Marius sent you, didn't he? Don't tell me he and Fai have gotten you involved?"

Fintan didn't meet his eyes, and shifted, moving over to where the crockery was waiting to be put on the table. "Let's have some of this delicious supper your cousin's cooked first, eh, Cuinn? Time enough to catch up about old friends afterwards. I hear there are brownies."

Cuinn could just hear the edge of Tierra's muttered "... brownies for Cuinn, not for thieving Scandinavians ..."

"Don't tell me you've already managed to upset Tierra? Watch how you go on this Maven issue, or you'll make it two for two." His tone was light, but Fintan's wince showed he knew Cuinn meant it.

"Come on, let's set the table and we'll talk after dinner. Surely there must be some gossip you've brought us back from the Guilds. That dreadful woman Maya, for example. What's she up to these days? You know Tierra loves her gossip."

At Tierra's huff he turned to her, giving her a gentle poke in the side. "I don't know what you're upset at, it's not your life he's come to turn upside down. I thought you wanted me to stop working? I'll never get anything done with this chatterbox around."

Tierra rolled her eyes but smiled, and some of the tension in Fintan's face disappeared. He put the crockery out and came back over to Cuinn, slapping him on the arm as he grabbed for the cutlery.

Cuinn put his unease and everything else that was on his mind aside for a couple of hours. "So, what did you bring us to drink? Something suitably expensive, I hope?"

C H A P T E R

4

Blaize tried hard not to regret drinking the foul green liquid. She knelt on the sand, bowed over with pain and eyes squeezed shut, as she concentrated on chasing every last trace of poison from her system. She was close but was reaching the end of her energy reserves, and her limit on how much more she could pull from the ether.

It was a strong poison.

The pain in her arm was agonising. It burned as if acid was eating her from the inside out. She'd left it till last, had focused on her vital organs rather than her extremities. She swept her energies around her viscera again, before she breathed in and out once more and concentrated her attention on the pain and poison in her arm. *Don't think about what could happen.* She could lose the ability to hold, to touch, and feel in her arm.

She liked her arm.

But she was so tired. The fact that she'd had no food in the last 24 hours might be good for purification, but was less good for strength and energy. The last two trials had brought her close to exhaustion, and she'd struggled to bring herself back to full strength in between. She opened her connection to the ether wider. She needed to pull more energy to burn the final grains of poison out. Her head span.

A last burst of effort, and tiny threads of energy like the finest lace spread throughout the inside of her arm. *There. I'm done.*

With lead in her legs, she got back to her feet, determined to finish as she'd begun. She consciously slowed her breathing to pretend it hadn't been such a close call.

"It is done." She lifted her head to the Three, and again, met each of their eyes in turn, and if her gaze wasn't quite as steady as before, she didn't think anyone would blame her.

Once again, she met Fai's eyes last. Although Fai's face was still impassive under her cropped black hair, as Blaize watched, Fai's lips parted and she let out a soft, deliberate breath.

Blaize couldn't believe that just minutes had passed. She was drained.

"It is done." The Three intoned the phrase in unison.

How did they do that? Did they practise? Or did Huo mind speak to the other two so they knew when to say it? Who knew?

Huo spoke again. "We will confer. Remain in the circle until we return." They rose and walked out.

Blaize sank to the ground, all attempts at grace gone.

She gazed at the star-salted sky. *How insignificant we all are.* A million stars ... an infinite galaxy. Her efforts to pass the trial were pretty small stuff when compared to that.

Her eyes were as gritty as the sand beneath her, and she blinked away some of the tiredness before she closed them, and opened her energetic connection. She didn't pull any energy from the ether, but sent gratitude, and vowed once more to Source to be aware, conscious, and mindful in all her actions, whatever happened.

The link with Source calmed her. She hadn't even realised she was still anxious until her heartbeat slowed with the prayer and connection.

Blaize could sense the different energies as the Three filed into the circle once more. Their bare feet padded on the sand and stone—no one wore shoes in the temple—but Blaize continued to sit with her eyes closed until they were all settled. The evening sounds of the jungle grew, the noisy chorus of crickets a background of white noise.

She opened her eyes. The sun was going down and the night had cooled the air. Until now, Blaize hadn't felt the difference because of the energies she had raised. One of the benefits of fire energy. She didn't get too hot and she could keep herself warm when it was cold. Though she much preferred hot climates when she had a choice.

Once the temple was silent again, she shakily rose to her feet. She stood in front of the Mavens, unable to read their faces. They were as poker-faced as ever.

"Blaize Blackfire, we greet you." Serafina took the lead.

"We greet you." The others followed the ritual salutation.

"I greet you." She intoned the words back. This was the moment. She thought she had passed, but these trials were never predictable. But she was too tired to be anxious. She had given her best today, and it had nearly killed her. *What more could they ask?*

"You have purified body and mind, and passed the trials of Strength, Endurance and Finesse," Huo said. "You have completed the Manipura Trial in front of three Mavens. We, the Three, have weighed and judged you. Our opinion, representing the Manipura Guild, is that you are ready for the title of Practitioner."

Blaize's shoulders sagged. Something inside her opened up, and she looked down at the sand.

"We have a concern that we wish to share with you, however."

Blaize's stomach dropped, and her eyes snapped back up to meet Huo's dark stare. His gaze was unblinking and held her with an almost physical weight.

His voice was silky, but in the manner of liquid metal, his words capable of engulfing the listener and burning them up in an instant. "We rarely remove Practitioner status, but it is possible. This is a warning to you. Your anger, pride, your desire to be the best have the potential for harm as well as good. Practise safely. Do not take inappropriate risks, whatever the goal. Do not let others trigger you over things that are history. Be in the present where your actions count."

Blaize slowly nodded. *Not exactly rousing support. But I passed.* She knew she was proud, but she had her drive, her anger, under control. *And I'm only competitive about the important things.*

"Thank you for your faith in me, Mavens. I will do as you say. I hope to bring honour and pride to my Guild."

"Then kneel, Adherent. Take the Manipura oath," Huo said.

Blaize knelt in the hot sand. Her body felt as if it had been pelted with stones, her clothes were tattered and dirty, and she wasn't sure if she'd ever manage to get up again, but none of that mattered in this moment.

"I honour the power within me. The fire within me burns through all fears. I can do whatever I will to do. With these words I recommit myself to the Manipura Guild as a Practitioner. To uphold our precepts. To strive to conduct myself for the honour of Guild and energetics race."

She bowed her head and shuddered as the energy of all of the Three entered her. The heat was just the wrong side of painful, and she clenched her teeth. The fire had different undertones depending on their auxiliary energy, but it was still fire.

The skin on her arm burned, and she felt a new tattoo form on her left arm, the pain coalescing and hanging there for a white-hot moment, like the flick of a whip. As quickly as it had come, it was gone, adding a second band to the one she already had, a mark that couldn't be faked. Two bands was the mark of a Practitioner, and although for formal occasions she would wear a robe with the two red stripes on her left sleeve, from today she would bear the marks on her body as well.

The pain had gone, leaving a numb after-image like the negative from an old film camera, the lack of pain as surprising as the pain had been. She resisted the urge to rub the area to wake it up, her body and brain enlivened as the energy of the Three spun around her system.

"We use the energy of the Three to break the binding between you and your Maven, Fai," Huo said. "As a Practitioner, you are released from the need for a Maven in Manipura. You are independent, and the Guild treats you as such."

Another rush of energy and a sharp pain in her belly, the seat of Manipura Chakra, and the energetic bindings that tethered her to her Aunt were severed. She felt a wave of sadness along with the triumph. *Does Fai feel the same?* The pain faded though the absence of her bond with Fai remained.

"It is done," Huo said.

"It is done." Serafina's voice was lighter.

"It is done." Fai's voice held suppressed pride.

Blaize stood again, for the final time in the ritual. "It is done."

And if she never heard that phrase again, she'd be just fine.

She waited as the Three left. It was her job to clean up the temple. She blew out the candles and picked up fallen petals from the sand. She took the petals and threw them into the surrounding jungle, then found the broom in the cupboard. She felt her body, mind, and spirit settle as she erased the footprints and other evidence of the ritual, to leave the temple clean and ready for the next visitors.

Outside the temple, and alone, she pulled out a pair of shorts and a T-shirt from her scooter's storage compartment and swapped her once-white clothes for the new ones. She took a moment to stretch out the kinks in her neck and back before she swung a leg over the little scooter she used to get around the island. Since Fai would need to entertain the visiting Mavens a little longer, Blaize could deliver the good news to her cousin Nixie first.

The peace Blaize felt now might just be the calm after the storm, but she wouldn't analyse it too deeply. She'd done well today.

She had the right to be proud.

The elegant man, dressed, as ever, in a tailored suit, was visiting Indigo in the suburban house in Vancouver where she lived, and which he paid for. He sat on a hard chair in the basement but looked as relaxed and unruffled as usual. He was a man in total control of himself, his environment, and her.

Indigo felt a trickle of sweat down her back. Why had he come here today? She hadn't expected him till later in the week. She hadn't been ready. She liked to prepare. She wasn't prepared.

"Would you like a drink or something?" The words felt awkward in her mouth, but she knew it was what people did in this kind of situation.

He smiled at her, an indulgent smile, like a father whose child had done something clever. He had white hair, discerning grey eyes, and looked a well-preserved fifty, though Indigo knew he was many hundreds of years old.

"No. Sit," he said, and gestured to the concrete floor in front of him. There were cushions and even other chairs in the room, but she sat at his feet, and looked at his knees. She didn't want to meet his eyes.

He was her Maven, the man who'd seen something in the lost girl she'd been and moulded her into a woman. The first man who'd ever wanted her, though he'd never touched her sexually.

Their Maven-Adherent bond had never been broken despite the fact she had become a Practitioner many years ago. But although he did still—sometimes—use the bond to teach her, to protect her, usually he used it to control her.

"Things are coming to a head. An ancient prophecy has been set in motion. But as ever with these things, the prophecy can be changed at certain pivotal points. At this point, the prophecy is against us. But we have six chances to ensure it can never come true."

Indigo looked up at his serene face. "What happens if it doesn't?"

"Then, my dear Indigo, we have the chance for the kind of power you can't even dream of. Power that will mean we evolve past even the most powerful energetics you know. Power that will give us the opportunity to destroy our enemies and repay our friends. Power that will change our race forever."

She nodded, understanding now why he was here. He had a job for her. "What do you need me to do?"

"How's your energy?"

She licked her lips and tried not to glance behind her. "F-fine."

"It's time for you to branch out on your own. I've found an energetic match for you who just happens to be someone who has the potential to cause me a lot of problems. If you can take her, you can have her."

Indigo's foot started to twitch. "Who? Where?"

"I need you to move to a town called Merrow and wait. In the meantime, I'm going to share with you the prophecy I've seen so far."

She tried not to whine. "You can just tell me. I don't mind if you just want to tell me."

He smiled again and spoke gently. "It's better if I show you, my dear. You know that."

He beckoned her forward and she shuffled towards him and bowed her head. He put his hands on her hair, and she closed her eyes and braced.

Agonising pain shot through her head, as images were forced into her mind.

She saw twelve energetics shining in front of her, their faces as bright as the sun.

She saw a red-haired woman tied to a bed, an IV drip coming out of her arm.

She saw a tall, dark-haired man fall to his knees in a forest, his face agonised.

She saw, in her own Haven, her safe space on the etheric plane, the red-haired woman tied to a chair.

His hands left Indigo's head and she slumped down. Her head lolled and she felt something wet come out of her nose.

He clucked his tongue and put his right hand under her chin, lifting her head up. He put his left hand in his pocket and pulled out a pristine handkerchief, and wiped away the blood under her nose.

"The red-haired woman is your target. You're to move to Merrow, and to dreamwalk yourself to find what else you can of the prophecy. At the moment there is a possibility that the man and woman you saw may not even meet, in which case I will have other work for you. You will stay in touch." He let go of her head, which wobbled but she kept it upright. Her gaze was fixed on his knees again.

He picked up a black briefcase at his side, and pulled out a plastic wallet filled with papers. He leaned down and placed it by her side. "This is the information you need."

He stood up and looked down at her. "Now, get your mat. I'm going to make it so that no other energetic can recognise you with protection wardings. I don't want to spring the surprise early, after all."

She cringed, but got up and pulled her mat into position, and concentrated hard on ignoring the dead body that lay in the corner of the room. The blood from the corpse's nose had dripped past his chin and onto his chest but was now brown and dried.

"Lie down and relax," the man instructed. "You know it hurts more if you're tense."

She lay on the mat and screwed her eyes shut. This time, she tried to make her limbs slack as his energies—and the white hot pain—seared her every muscle and nerve.

It was for her own good, after all.

5

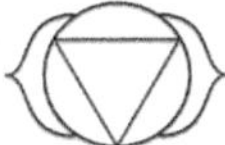

"Must you ruin a pleasant evening?" Cuinn kept his voice amiable, but the warning was clear.

He and Fintan had retired to the living space, and as expected, Fintan had continued the argument on Marius's behalf.

But Cuinn had had enough.

"The answer is no, Fintan. I don't want another Adherent. I'm working on the prophecies. It's too important to be distracted by some inexperienced girl."

Fintan looked sombre, unlike his usual playful self. "I understand. Tierra tells me you've taken a sabbatical from the university to work on deciphering the prophecies you've seen. But it's time."

He sprawled in an armchair, his gaze on the fire that Cuinn had lit to warm the chilled room. Fintan raised and lowered the flames as rhythmically as some people stroked a cat.

Cuinn stood, his gaze on the fire, his posture stiff and unyielding.

Fintan's relaxed voice ignored Cuinn's reaction. "You're the right candidate. For her, and for you. The level of control that's needed to manage one's own energy plus an Adherent's is difficult, and you have the energy, the power, to manage someone who has strong potential but no training. It might be a hard experience at first, but you need it to heal. What happened to Sophea wasn't your fault."

Cuinn's fists balled, but the anger was drowned in a bleak guilt that lay like ice water inside his chest. "I don't want to talk about that."

"I know you don't. You never have. You've kept it inside you, where it's eaten away at your personality like a poison. You're becoming someone quite different from the Cuinn I knew of old. You were always serious, but at least then you had the capacity for a little spontaneity and play. That's been leached away by the burden you carry about Sophea. A new Adherent, and a more positive, successful relationship will heal you more than you know."

Cuinn was shocked by this speech though he tried not to let it show on his face. He took refuge in anger instead, sneering at Fintan. "If I'm not the person you want me to be, then piss off back to whoever's bed you're warming at the moment. I'm fine on my own. And anyway, I have Adam and Tierra keeping me company. I'm not alone."

Silence stretched between them.

Fintan played with the fire.

Cuinn crossed his arms over his chest. *This is none of his business. They should all just leave me alone.* He didn't want another Adherent, didn't deserve another chance. And the girl certainly didn't deserve him. She was better off somewhere else.

He closed his eyes and memories assaulted him. An ethereal woman, her face lit up as they discussed philosophy and literature. Watching her Ajna energies blossom and develop. Her Haven in the dreamscape a labyrinth of books. Keeping up with her as she switched languages depending on the topic, from English, to Latin, to Greek, to her native Italian when she was truly excited. The moment she had shown him the hidden room in her Haven, and his wretched handling of the situation.

He swallowed to reduce the thickness in his throat, and fought to keep the feelings off his face.

But Cuinn wasn't trapped yet, whatever Fintan thought. The cage door still had to close.

One word would determine whether it would.

He asked the question he had been dreading since Fintan came through the door. "Is Marius calling in my debt?"

Fintan looked grave. "Yes."

That's it. With that one word, the cage door slammed shut, and Cuinn felt light-headed.

"I need some time alone, Fin. We'll speak tomorrow." He spun around before Fintan could answer and left the room.

Marius calling in his debt was the last straw. Cuinn could no longer refuse.

He would have to become a Maven again.

6

Cuinn walked through the door of his workroom and shut it behind him. He leaned against it, limbs heavy with fatigue. The idea of taking another Adherent made him feel sick to his stomach. His last experience had ended in horror, grief, and shame, and he couldn't face that again.

After the conversation he'd had with Fin, Cuinn's energy was unstable, and the room felt too dark. He pulled the armchair to the windows, which he opened as wide as they would go. The light of the moon relaxed him, and he added some candles to supplement its gentle light.

He pushed hair away from his face and sat in the worn and comfortable armchair. He leaned back and tilted his head towards the sky. With few artificial light sources such as street lamps or cars, there was little light pollution and it was easy to see the stars.

Ah, Tierra. He felt a stab of guilt. One of Fintan's best placed blows had been a claim that Tierra was lonely. Tierra was loving and sociable, and Cuinn had thought that with himself, Adam, and visits to and from her best friend Cara, who lived on an island off the west coast of British Columbia, Tierra had enough interaction to nurture her. And she seemed to enjoy looking after Adam's Husky, Argus, when Adam travelled to a country where foreign dogs weren't welcome.

But Fintan had told him the last time Tierra had seen Cara had been months ago. Adam seemed to be away more than usual at the moment, taking Argus with him, and Cuinn was locked in his rooms more often than not.

Tierra herself had never mentioned feeling lonely, though she wouldn't. She was kind, good-hearted, and meant the world to him. She was the sister he'd never had, and since his mother had died long ago, had been the main woman in his life for decades. Since … the last one. Sophea.

His hand worried at the arm of the chair, at a worn patch his nervous gesture had created over years. The feel of the material under the pads of his fingers comforted him. Cuinn's gift sometimes meant he was ungrounded, and reconnecting with the environment around him brought him back to the physical world.

His energies also meant he spent a lot of time in his head. He blew out a breath, and closed his eyes.

Perhaps the girl wouldn't be too useless, and could help him. Dreamwalking and prophecy work was a critical part of mind training—it might be that he had to train her in a rather unusual order, but he could work it out.

He fell asleep in the chair minutes later, halfway through rearranging the typical Ajna training in his mind to suit his new purpose. But at the back of his mind, one thought kept intruding.

His world was about to change again.

7

Blaize arrived at her family's cluster of traditional-style bungalows and parked underneath her own wooden-framed raised house. Instead of going inside, she walked across the hard-packed earth to Nixie's bungalow and shouted her name.

As Blaize started up the stairs, Nixie appeared on her balcony, wiping her hands on a towel. "Hey! How'd it go?"

Nixie's dominant energy was Svadisthana, or water, the energy of fantasy and imagination—and sexuality. Combined with her auxiliary energy of Vishudha, or ether, the energy of communication and creativity, it meant that Nixie tended towards sexy, a little spacey, and loved to chat.

A year or so younger than Blaize, Fai's daughter, Nixie had the petite frame, dark hair and eyes of many Thai women, combined with her father's Gaelic paler skin. Her looks were striking, and many men—and sometimes women—fell over themselves to talk to her.

Blaize, who saw Nixie as a sister, didn't notice her sexuality. In their teenage years, there'd been a time when Blaize had been unsure why the boys in their class flocked to Nixie, but seemed scared of Blaize. Nowadays, Blaize had her own share of attention, and just found men's regard amusing.

Blaize reached the top of the stairs and held out her arms to Nixie for a hug. "I passed! I'm officially a Practitioner of the Manipura Guild!"

She took Nixie in her arms and spun her light frame around.

"I knew you'd do it." As Nixie's feet touched the floor again, she stepped back and wrinkled her nose. "Put you through your paces did they? You need a shower."

"I haven't slept or eaten for nearly two days. A shower's on my list, but I want some food first. I feel too buzzed to sleep."

"Do you want a fruit shake? Or I could put a fruit salad together? You don't want to eat too much too quickly after a fast."

"A fruit salad would be great, thanks." Blaize eyed the light blue hammock hanging in the corner of the balcony. "Mind if I hang out here?"

"Of course. But you have to tell me all about it as you do—and don't fall asleep." Nixie went into the kitchen and asked over her shoulder, "Did Mom manage to keep a straight face?"

Blaize settled into the hammock. "Pretty much. She didn't change her expression even when I was almost poisoned to death."

"What?" Nixie ran back onto the balcony, a mango in one hand and a knife in the other.

Blaize laughed. "I'm fine. Now, anyway. It was harder than I thought it would be. I don't know what they used, but it was difficult to dig it all out of my system. I managed it, but it was closer than I would have liked."

"I don't know how Mom stayed impassive through that." Nixie shook her head.

"I don't think she'd have let me die ..." Blaize's brow wrinkled, "but it doesn't matter anyway. It's done."

Blaize rocked herself in the hammock, one foot out and balanced on the floor to give her a little momentum. She filled Nixie in on all the details while she worked her way through two bowls of fruit salad.

An hour or so later, when Blaize's eyes felt heavy and she and Nixie had hashed through every detail of the trial, Blaize heard the soft crunch of tires on sand. The car's headlights raked the balcony as it parked under a larger house nearby.

"Mom's back. Are you going to talk to her? It doesn't look as if she has anyone with her. She must have dropped the others off at their hotel after supper."

"I should probably have a shower before I speak to her."

Nixie shook her head vigorously, her silky black hair flying around her face. "Don't be silly! She's your Aunt as well as your Maven. She'll want to talk to you straight away to discuss how it went."

"And give me some feedback no doubt." Blaize winced. She loved her Aunt, but Fai didn't make any allowances in their Maven-Adherent relationship for their family connection.

"Off you go. Pop back later if you feel like it." Nixie poked Blaize in the side.

Blaize rolled out of the hammock and stretched. "Okay. I'll see how I feel once I've had a chat with her. I'm pretty desperate for a shower and some sleep."

Nixie put her hand out to squeeze Blaize's, but Blaize pulled her into another hug. Usually, Nixie was the demonstrative one. This time, Blaize was more than willing to share her happiness.

Blaize walked to the main house and caught sight of herself in the car's windows. She winced at her tangled hair and the crumpled clothes that had been stored in the scooter's seat compartment. But Nixie was right, Fai would want to see her as soon as possible. And Blaize wanted to see Fai and thank her again for the long years of training that had finally paid off.

Blaize rang the cowbell that served as a doorbell. Its resonant sound vibrated through her, and she took a deep breath, still a little spaced from the last couple of days.

When the door opened, Marius stood before her. He smiled and took her in strong arms. As he hugged her tight, he said, "Blaize, love, congratulations. I knew you could do it. Not an easy crowd to impress but you managed it."

He squeezed her again before he let her go.

A big man compared to Fai's slight build, he had several inches on Blaize, who at five feet ten inches wasn't small for a woman. He had a broad chest, with an imposing bulk when he chose to wield it that way. Which he rarely did. He was one of the kindest men Blaize had ever known—a man who had acted as a father to her since her own had died when she was nine.

She realised she was still standing there. "Sorry, Marius. I'm exhausted. I was miles away. Thank you."

He grinned and nodded. "After my first Chakra trial, I slept for two days straight. Of course, you're shattered—but I'm so glad you came over. Fai and I need to talk to you."

Blaize wasn't too tired to catch the seriousness in his tone. "What's the matter? Is everything alright?"

She hoped there wasn't a problem. She didn't have the energy for an important discussion.

"Everything's fine. Come through to the living room."

They moved into a spacious room on the right, with big open windows that let in the cool night air. Cushions were scattered across the floor, with low tables next to them. Fai sat near one of the windows but rose to her feet when they came in. She put her hands on Blaize's shoulders and looked into her eyes, examining her deeply. Blaize shuffled, and Fai sighed and opened her arms. Blaize stepped into them and put her arms around her aunt.

When she looked up at Blaize, tears shimmered in the corners of Fai's eyes.

Blaize's eyes widened. "Aunt Fai, what's the matter? I'm fine, I made it; you should be happy."

She put her hand up to the other woman's cheek and wiped away a tear.

Fai nodded. "Blaize, darling, I'm so proud of you."

Blaize's throat tightened. *Huh.* She wasn't sure she'd ever heard Fai say that before. Blaize drew away, and said, "Let me get you some water."

Marius, who'd watched till now in silence, shook his head. "Sit down, both of you. There are things to discuss. I'll get the water."

Blaize frowned. Something was going on. Fai returned to her seat and beckoned Blaize to follow. Blaize sank down onto a soft, flat floor cushion from India. On the walls were Chinese and Thai wall hangings, their only common ground bright colours and strong prints. As most energetics did, Fai and Marius had moved around in their long years together, and their house was a showcase of the best of all their travels.

What does Fai need to tell me? A small spike of anxiety hit Blaize, chasing away some of the grey fog in her brain.

"You did well," Fai said. "You worried me with the poison, but your finesse with the energy on the first task was beautiful."

"Thank you, Aunt Fai." Blaize's chest loosened.

"But your drive and competitive nature was noted by the judges. You must keep your ambition and anger under control. Your power is too strong to be combined with any kind of aggression. Huo was able to get under your skin too easily." Her voice was gentle, but the rebuke still stang.

"It's under control. I just wanted to pass the trial and make you proud."

Fai pursed her lips as Marius came back into the room with a jug of water and some glasses. He put them down on the table before he levered his body next to Fai. He leaned against the wall next to the window and put his arm around his wife. Her posture didn't change, but she inclined her head towards him a fraction.

"Fai, Blaize knows to be careful with her power—you trained her, after all. And her power can only help her in her journey," Marius said.

Blaize looked at him. "What journey?"

His face was innocent. "Your journey through life."

She narrowed her eyes. The spike of anxiety grew. There was no tiredness now. "What do you want to talk to me about?"

"Your Ajna Chakra training," said Fai.

Blaize frowned. *That has to be a joke.* She kept her tone light. "It's a bit soon for that isn't it? I've just passed Manipura."

Fai and Marius exchanged a glance. *Not a joke.* Blaize was confused now, as well as anxious. Energetics always had a break between their dominant and auxiliary training. She'd been looking forward to spending time on the island, and then working as a Warrior, capturing Rogues.

"You can have a month off to relax and recharge," Fai said. "But we want you to continue with your training soon."

"A month? After five years of training? You want me to have a month off and then spend another five years training? I want—I need—more." Blaize's voice rose. She took a breath and closed her eyes. "Maybe this isn't a good time to talk about it. I'm really tired."

She could barely think straight. She wouldn't win an argument with Fai feeling like this.

"The decision is made." Again that soft tone, with undertones of steel. "You're a strong energetic, and your control is good, as you've shown in the last twenty-four hours. But you're still ruled by the emotions of Manipura—and yet you have access to Ajna. When you harness the power of your mind, you could be one of the greatest leaders we've ever seen. Perhaps even a Circle member one day."

Blaize blinked. "There's no rush for that. Grandmother's tough. She won't be going anywhere for years."

"Child, Grandmother is one of the older energetics. She's tired and ready to step back from her leadership role. There's no rush—for her, another ten, twenty, thirty years is nothing, but we need to push you along more quickly than we discussed when you were young. You are her chosen successor, and the family supports that choice—but only if you have the best possible grip on your power. Until now you have focused on your dominant Chakra, Manipura. Your personality and attitudes are shaped by this. You are passionate, vibrant, and powerful. But," she held up a hand to forestall any comment from Blaize, "you can also be quick to anger, volatile, stubborn, and you love to have the last word."

Blaize scowled, and then tried to wipe the scowl off her face as she registered the content of Fai's words. *Damn. Boxed in.*

"I've loved training with you, Aunt Fai. Well, mostly," she corrected herself and her lips quirked up. "I've learned so much from you. And I'm proud to be an energetic, a member of our family, and now a Practitioner member of Manipura Guild. But I wanted some time to do other things. To be out there, using the powers I've developed, without someone looking over my shoulder all the time."

Fai's face was impassive, Marius's sympathetic. Neither looked as though Blaize's arguments were changing their minds. She tried again.

"To go from you to another Maven means going from one person being responsible for me to another. Plus, who would it be?" She struggled to keep her voice even given what Fai had said to prompt it, but with those last words it rose and cracked a little. "It's not as if there are loads of Ajna

Mavens. It's got to be a very short list. And none of them are based on the island, or even in Thailand. … Are you sending me away?"

"Of course we're not sending you away, Blaize, my darling. But if you'd worked in the human world again, or as a Warrior, you would have left us," Marius said.

"I could have come back whenever I liked. If training for Ajna's anything like Manipura, I'll be too busy to come back for a while, won't I?" The idea hurt. The island was her home. And after so many years of intensive training, she'd looked forward to time to relax. Time to recharge.

Fai nodded.

"So it's like sending me away."

"A very old, good friend of mine has offered to train you," Marius said.

Fai seemed to wince at this, but Blaize wasn't sure why. Blaize's growing sense of confusion told her there was still more going on here than she was being told, but she didn't have the energy to think of the right questions to puzzle it out.

"His name is Cuinn. You met him when you were young. You may not remember. I grew up with him in Ireland when I was a young man. We had some good times together, he and I, and Fintan later on."

Fintan, she knew—first as an honorary Uncle, and then when she'd been training for her Manipura—as a colleague with whom she'd been on several Rogue runs. But she'd never heard of this other man.

"Quinn? With a Q?"

"It's spelled with a C. He was born in Ireland, same as me, a couple of hundred years ago," said Marius. "That's how we know each other."

"If you were so close, how come he hasn't visited for a decade?" demanded Blaize.

"He had some challenges in his personal life about fifty years ago, and he hasn't been very sociable since then. He's a powerful Ajna-Muladhara mix. He could have been Guild Leader if he'd wanted, and he's been a Master for many decades. He's been Maven to several energetics."

Blaize's lips flattened. He didn't sound like much fun. Powerful but uninterested in people. He was probably arrogant to boot. "But he's feeling sociable again now?"

"Something like that." Marius gave a slight cough. "He lives with his cousins, Tierra and Adam, a couple of hours outside Vancouver, Canada. Adam's not there much of the time, as he travels with his job, but Tierra keeps house and makes it a home. She's wonderful, Muladhara-Anahata, and loves to look after people. I think the two of you will get on."

Blaize was less sure. She was an action-taker. The things she enjoyed most in life were physical—sports, martial arts. She loved setting goals and challenges. She didn't think that she'd have much in common with a homebody like that.

"So it's already been decided? And everyone knows but me?" Blaize struggled to hide her hurt feelings and got to her feet.

"Blaize. We're trying to give you the best possible chance to develop your energies, and evolve and grow to be a truly great energetic. To fulfill your potential as a leader. You'll be part of safeguarding the future of our race, and you owe it to yourself as well as everyone else to take every opportunity to harness your powers." Fai spoke from the floor, but Marius got up as Blaize had. He leaned down and stroked a hand over Fai's dark hair as he stood beside her still, seated form.

"And I will … but I thought I had more time," Blaize said. More time to spend growing in other areas before I committed to the intensity of training again." She wasn't going to win this argument. She saw no cracks in either Fai's determination, or more unusually, in Marius's. Usually, she was able to persuade Marius to her point of view, but he appeared just as committed to this future as Fai.

"Go back to your bungalow, take a shower, and get some rest." Marius moved over to her and took her hand. "Have you eaten anything yet?"

"Some fruit, with Nixie. Wait. does Nixie know?"

Marius shook his head. "No. Do you want to tell her, or do you want us to tell her while you're sleeping?"

Blaize closed her eyes briefly. "You can tell her. I'll speak to her when I wake up. I'm so tired."

She got to her feet and headed out of the door, too tired for further conversation. *More training. Another Maven.* Her throat ached, and her eyes were damp. If she stayed in the room with her Aunt and Uncle, she might cry.

She really hated to cry.

Cuinn came to, cold and stiff, on the floor of his workroom. He'd decided to try a quick dreamwalk, and had lain on his ritual mat, and sunk into the light trance that enabled him to go to the etheric plane.

He'd been out all night.

His body cramping, he sat up and stretched out to grab the nearest paper and pencil. He needed to capture every possible detail of what he'd discovered.

As always, the details were sketchy. In previous dreamwalks he'd seen various shadowy figures, and he wasn't sure if they were humans or energetics.

They were accompanied by a sense of foreboding, of something off, something beautiful and good perverted for illicit ends. This dreamwalk had been the same as all the others—the presences were taunting him as he stood in front of the race of energetics, knowing he was all that stood between this evil and his race, his people.

As before, there were five male energetics to his right, and six female energetics to his left. He usually couldn't make out much about any of them apart from their genders, and some kind of coloured bracelets on each wrist—the right wrist for men, the left for women.

But in this dreamwalk he'd gathered some new details.

One of the females had stepped forward in front of the other energetics—and in front of him. She'd raised a sword of fire, and run towards the shadowy figures. Watching, he hadn't been able to move, shout, or do anything to stop her from sacrificing herself. And it had been agony to watch. Her energies shone, but the figures soon surrounded her, and their darkness absorbed her light like blotting paper.

He came out of the trance with a queasy feeling in his stomach, and a deep sense of unease. The female figure was important, as were the line of females and males he stood with in the dream in front of those shadowy figures. And he also had a role. He just didn't know how, or against what. The frustration made him feel scratchy and irritable.

He sighed, noted the date and time, and put the pencil and paper down. He would file it with the others later.

C H A P T E R

8

"Did Fai talk to you?"

Nixie bit her lip. Her eyes welled up and tears overflowed as she sank into a cross-legged position next to the hammock where Blaize was lying, and rested her head on Blaize's leg.

Blaize had slipped home the night before without calling on Nixie, but Nixie had shown up on Blaize's balcony soon after she was up and about.

Blaize's anger and upset of the night before had turned into sadness and resignation this morning. She'd go to Vancouver. And if she was honest with herself, a part of her loved the idea that she would get to push on with her training this fast. Most energetics would need a year or more between trainings to let one side of themselves settle before they started working with the next. Fai must be very confident of her abilities to ask her to start training in her auxiliary this quickly. But Blaize had been looking forward to more of a break from learning, and time to actually use her abilities as a Warrior.

"I'm the one going, Nix, not you." Blaize bent and touched Nixie's cheek. "It'll be fine. We'll call; you'll visit."

Nixie nodded. "I know. But … I'll miss you."

"You managed when we were at university, and then when I lived in Singapore and you were doing your Chakra training."

Nixie had taken a different path. She had started as an Adherent directly after leaving university at twenty-one, so she'd completed her training in her dominant Chakra, Svadisthana, the water element, a while ago. She'd decided to take a break before starting her next Chakra training—just as Blaize had intended to do.

"Yeah, but it's been a good few years since we've both been back here and able to hang out together. I like it. Friends and family close by." Tears leaked onto Blaize's leg. As a water element, Nixie had a tendency to express herself with tears—happy and sad—a lot more frequently than Blaize, but Blaize was used to it, and just ran a hand over Nixie's glossy hair.

"How do you feel?" Nixie said.

Blaize lay back and looked up at the sky. "Like I'm not just tired today, but tired more generally. The Manipura training was tough, and I so wanted to do well. I feel like I did, but I also made mistakes. I'd have liked a break before I start studying something new."

She paused, looking out at the dense green jungle at the edges of the large plot their houses stood on.

"I love it here too. I love you, Fai, Marius, the people we know, our friends. The energetics community here and the humans. I love the pace of life, being able to go out trekking in the jungle or lie on the beach. Singapore was so built up, so many people, so many buildings, vehicles. I don't want to go back to a place where there are that many people."

"Cuinn doesn't live in a busy place; he practically lives out in the wilderness, way outside Vancouver towards the Rockies. It's pretty beautiful, but the sea is hours away." Nixie shivered in mock disgust.

Great. He lives in some country backwater. Not much chance of using her Warrior training, or helping out on Rogue runs there.

"You know him?"

"Yeah. He's a Professor at Vancouver University in the human world, and super smart. Some kind of brain science, which helps with his energetic work around the mind. I guess all Ajnas are pretty clever—apart from you, of course."

Blaize smacked Nixie gently on the top of her head.

"Ouch. Yeah, bright, a thinker. He does a lot of dreamwalks and prophecy work for the Major and the Minor Circle. He's maybe two hundred? Two twenty? He grew up with Dad. Not married or anything though. Which is not because of what he looks like—he's pretty hot." Nixie pretended to swoon. "And Maven-Adherent pairings often become romantic; it's part of working closely with someone for so long."

"Not a factor. You know my views on relationships."

"Well, it doesn't hurt if the face you have to look at every day is attractive, right? And anyway, you don't have to marry him, just, you know, have a little fun."

Blaize rolled her eyes but smiled. "Do you ever think about anything apart from sex?"

"Love?"

The energy of Nixie's two Chakras meant she almost always had a boyfriend. And Nixie was quite happy to audition men for the part for as long as was needed, though she never settled for long, always looking for 'the one.' Blaize guessed Nixie's parents also influenced her view, as they were still a solid partnership after over a hundred years together.

Blaize had a direct approach to sex, like most Manipura energetics, but she didn't romanticise it. She didn't see the need. She'd seen what love could do, and it wasn't always hearts and flowers. She wasn't interested in a relationship.

"What's he like as a person?"

"Well … he can be a bit … stern. Focused. But because of his earth auxiliary he's very grounded, which makes a good contrast for his Ajna. Practical. Disciplined. Works hard."

"Hmmmm." Blaize wrinkled her nose. "Doesn't sound much fun."

Nixie shrugged. "He's fairly senior in the Ajna Guild, so should be a good teacher at least."

Just what I need. A strict, joyless Professor that I'll be stuck with for the next few years. Yay.

She shook her head and turned the conversation away from her departure. There was time enough for that.

Indigo lay on her mat and stared up at the water-damaged ceiling.

The prophecy was in motion. Blaize and Cuinn would meet soon. And Indigo would get her chance to repay her Maven for his teachings and support.

There was little furniture in the dark and dingy bedroom, and yet although she had the whole house to herself, the meagre possessions she'd brought with her from Vancouver were all contained in this room. She travelled light.

She got to her feet and took her cell phone out of her bag. She switched it on and dialled his number. The man she'd been with as an Adherent and beyond.

She walked to the window and looked out while she waited for him to answer. The property was at the end of a lane, a twenty-minute drive from Merrow. There would be no one to interfere when she had Blaize here.

A click at the end of the line. "Indigo."

"Another piece of prophecy is confirmed. She's coming. He's agreed," she said.

"Get a job in town. Get more information on Cuinn and the set up at their house. Keep seeking more of the prophecy." The man's warm tones were deceptive. Underneath the velvet, there was a dark brutality in the voice that expected her instant obedience.

"And she's mine?" Indigo tried to keep the need out of her voice.

The silence echoed down the line, and Indigo shifted, pressing her palm against the window. The cold bled into her bones.

"I'm sorry," she said.

She was left with silence as he hung up.

She felt jittery, wired. She strode over to the door and threw it open. She ran down the creaking stairs and went out the old house's back door without pausing to grab a jacket. She was burning up, her energy keeping her warm. Too warm.

She went to the back of the overgrown garden where she'd set up a rough area for energy practice and stood in the centre of the charred circle. She took a deep breath. She pulled energy and forged the hottest fire she could between her hands. She put all her hate and shame into the flames. Then she spun and threw the burning sphere as fast as she could at the metal target fifty yards away. Sparks flew as the fire engulfed the metal, and it glowed a dark, angry red.

Her body trembled like an addict's. She panted and her sides heaved as she sucked in deep breaths. She needed more energy, and these days, she struggled to draw on the ether without help. The impetuous burst had tired her out. The chill damp of the spring morning drained the heat from her, and the trembles in her limbs intensified. She trudged back towards the house.

She needed to conserve her energy, not waste it. Her Maven had promised her Blaize, which would solve a lot of Indigo's problems, but only if she was able to catch her, physically or energetically. If Indigo wasted her chance, he wouldn't forgive her. And he was unlikely to give her another opportunity. He'd punish her, or watch her suffer withdrawal symptoms.

Either of which could kill her.

9

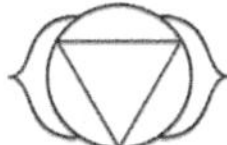

Five weeks after her Manipura trial Blaize found herself on a plane.

Time spent meditating in the energetics' temple had helped her process her feelings of being abandoned, or sent away, by her family. Exploring and examining them despite the 'ouch' feelings they brought her, she was able to realise that she had total confidence in Fai and Marius's love for her, and their attempts to do the right thing.

Now, on her way to her next Maven, she didn't feel exactly enthusiastic, but she managed acceptance. Her journey gave her more time to centre herself, with several flights and a bus that took her from the hustle and bustle of Vancouver airport to a bus station at the edge of a small town.

She hadn't spoken to Cuinn directly yet—they'd emailed a couple of times before Cuinn had directed her to Tierra, who'd helped Blaize with practicalities. Tierra had been friendly, and her emails managed a lively and welcoming tone.

Cuinn on the other hand … he was a bit of a mystery. His communication was terse, signed 'C,' with no niceties, and always focused on the factual information. There were no questions about herself, which Blaize didn't mind. Well, OK, she did mind a bit, but then he hadn't responded to her probes about him either.

Maybe it was a guy thing. She'd been used to working with her aunt, a woman and a family member, on her dominant Chakra, and Blaize wasn't sure if working with a male Maven would be different. Or whether she would like it.

She sighed as she got down off the bus and stretched out the kinks, trying to shake off a sense of apprehension. She reminded herself of her promise to be positive—after all, she could be here for years.

She looked around the deserted bus station. A lone woman stood waiting at the exit gate, reading from a tablet. Given that no one else was in sight, Blaize assumed she must be Tierra. *Cuinn's delegated again.*

Cuinn certainly gave a good impression of someone uninterested in her. How would that work when he was her Maven? The bonding ritual would create a link between them that would be long-lasting. Perhaps he was giving her space until then, when there would be a lot less choice about the two of them interacting.

She walked to the petite, curvy woman, who looked up and smiled. She radiated an earthy femininity—warm and natural. Blaize faltered, intimidated by her despite the fact that Blaize could probably take her out in seconds. Blaize was good with violence. She was less good with unconditional acceptance.

Tierra was quick to close the gap between them, and Blaize's hands were already half-raised in a defensive gesture before Tierra had thrown her arms around her. Tierra was a good few inches shorter than Blaize, with a soft, long skirt the colour of pine needles, and a fitted white sweater.

Tierra stepped back and met Blaize's gaze with dark-chocolate coloured eyes.

"Pleased to meet you! I'm Tierra. Of course I am, who else would I be? It's so exciting you're here! Your boxes have already arrived; I've put them in your cottage. You'll love it; it has privacy but is close enough to the main house that you can pop over whenever you need. And for meals! It will be great to have someone else to cook for. I just love cooking."

Blaize let the words stream over her, and considered interrupting but decided there was no need. Tierra kept up her chatter all the way to the car, and for most of the half-hour journey back to the house. She peppered Blaize with questions, but rarely gave her the opportunity to answer them, which was fine with the weary Blaize. Despite that, Tierra was extremely likeable, a nurturing and agreeable presence.

Eventually Tierra said, "Almost there. It's spring now—a few weeks ago we still had snow, but it's starting to warm up. I guess still a lot colder than you're used to."

Blaize nodded. She was wrapped up warm—a lot more warmly than Tierra, who'd thrown her jacket and scarf into the back of the car once they got in. Blaize had taken her scarf off, and put it on her lap, tucking her hands snugly into it, but was still wearing her jacket, and even so was cold enough to consider using a little energy to warm herself up.

They pulled off the main street onto a route that was little more than a dirt track. Setting aside the vegetation and the weather, it was the kind of road Blaize was at home with, the kind she used to speed along on the island on her scooter.

The rough road continued for a couple of miles. They crested the gently rolling terrain, which revealed an elegant slate-and-stone house that fit into the green bowl of the landscape as if it had grown there.

Blaize stared. She'd never seen anything like it.

Tierra laughed. "Yeah, that view used to get me like that too. Still does sometimes, especially if I've been away. Welcome to Cathair Cuinn. Cuinn designed most of it himself, using Irish stone and working with the architect. And when Adam, that's my brother, and I moved in later, Cuinn had additions built for us. Plus, of course, there're a few cottages, bungalows, in the grounds for visitors. You'll have one of those for privacy."

Tierra spoke so quickly it was hard for Blaize to keep up after what felt like weeks of travelling. She was jet-lagged and dropping with fatigue. She focused on one thing. "What does the name mean?"

Tierra laughed. "It's a joke. Cathair means castle in Gaelic. Fintan—he's a friend of ours, I think you know him—named it as a joke when Cuinn had it built, and it stuck."

They parked on the drive, and got out of the car, and Tierra helped Blaize bring her luggage in. Blaize thought Tierra might ring the bell to bring Blaize's new Maven down, but Tierra unlocked the sturdy wooden door instead and pushed it open, gesturing with her head for Blaize to come on in, as her arms were full of Blaize's things.

Blaize followed Tierra through the door into an imposing hallway. A large wooden staircase led up to the left, and she counted at least seven different doors off the hallway.

Tierra put Blaize's belongings in the hall.

"You'll be in Garden Cottage. Your boxes are already there, but let's get you some food first, then you can settle in and sleep." Tierra looked at her watch. "If you can give it another hour or so, then you should sleep through the night and reset your internal clock."

Blaize nodded. She was almost too tired to sleep, and she wasn't sure she wanted to eat anything. She followed Tierra through a corridor to a huge room split into a kitchen and an eating area. The latter had a big farmhouse-style table and chairs, and huge windows looking out onto the lawn.

"This is the kitchen. We eat most of our informal meals in here. We only eat in the dining room when we have guests."

Tierra pulled out a chair and steered Blaize into it. Blaize's head was fuzzy, and she heard Tierra's words without really taking them in. Tierra talked as she poured Blaize water, and then brought over fresh bread, cheese, butter, and some ripe tomatoes to put together a snack.

Blaize tried to nod and smile in the right places, but she knew she was being unresponsive. She drank the water, which helped wake her up a little, and then her stomach growled, telling her she was hungrier than she thought. She murmured a quiet "thank you" as Tierra pushed the food towards her, and ate.

It didn't take her long to demolish the sandwich. "That was amazing, thanks. I will have another glass of water, if that's okay. I think I got a bit dehydrated on the plane."

"Of course." Tierra jumped up, took Blaize's glass, and refilled it. "I'll take you to the cottage now, and you can get some sleep."

Blaize frowned. "What about Cuinn? Is he here? I'd like to meet him."

Tierra looked away, her usually constant smile wavering for a second. "He had to go away for some Circle business. He'll be back in the next couple of days. Sorry, I'm sure he wanted to see you. He gets called away sometimes. In the meantime you can hang out with me and get settled. Come on. Let's take you over."

Blaize felt a stab of disappointment. She hadn't even met the man yet, and he was annoying her.

Tierra cleared the table while Blaize fetched her luggage from the hall. Tierra led her to a back door, and they headed into the gardens.

The weather was sharp, cold and biting. Blaize was glad of the token warmth from the scarf she'd thrown back on. They walked a short way before a small cottage appeared out of the falling dusk. It was next to the woods, but the other three sides looked out onto the main house and the view respectively. Not that there was much of a view at this time of night, but she could see the lights of the big house from here, which was comforting in this foreign place.

Tierra pushed open the door and tugged in Blaize's big suitcase. Blaize trailed in behind her, laden with everything else. The cottage had a small hallway, and Blaize was surprised to see that it was a proper self-contained house. It had one large room downstairs, with a toasty looking fire—lit and smouldering, the fire guard up—a comfy sofa, and a table with a couple of chairs. The front window even had a window seat, which Blaize immediately fell in love with.

At the back of the big room was a galley kitchen. A microwave, a small oven, a hob with two rings, and a tiny fridge.

Tierra went ahead of her up the steep stairs. The doors of the two rooms on the first floor were directly off the stairs, opposite each other with barely a square yard between them.

Tierra plumped up the cushions on the bed, brushing imaginary fluff off the duvet.

"It's small but it's cosy, and it means you can have privacy when you need it. But I hope you'll join us for meals whenever you like—I'm so excited to have someone else here to chat to and spend time with." Her tone was a little wistful.

Is she lonely? Tierra was a gentle, warm person, with a curvy but strong body—she'd managed to lift Blaize's suitcase after all. Earth energetics needed people around them to nurture and look after. "Does Cuinn often go away?"

"Sometimes. He's been here a lot more recently. He's a good man. But he gets rather caught up. And his work is important."

Blaize nodded. She built a picture of Cuinn in her mind. Stern, cold and aloof, indifferent to his cousin's problems. And most probably indifferent to Blaize as well. After all, he wasn't here to meet her, so she couldn't be that big a priority for him. Thank Source for Tierra.

Cuinn was in Athens, sitting in front of Minh, the head of Cuinn's Minor Guild, Ajna-Muladhara Guild, and two of the other Ajna Minor Guild Leaders.

These energetics together were highly skilled in understanding and predicting prophecies, these were the farseers of Ajna: Past, Present and Future.

Three of the most powerful energetics alive.

"Minh, I'm concerned," Cuinn said. "These prophecies feel unlike any I've come across before. They have a sick, twisted quality to them. There's danger coming for all of us, and I can't tell what it is."

Minh's dark eyes appraised him. "At the moment you are the only one receiving such prophecies, and you know we have our eyes open in many areas. We have spoken to all the strong Ajna dreamwalkers, and nothing has struck us as unusual. We three, also, have tried specific dreamwalks to see if we can pick up any of the strands of the prophecy. We have found nothing that matches what you say you have seen."

Cuinn was frustrated. He and Minh had a difficult relationship because Minh couldn't understand why anyone with Cuinn's power—which both of them suspected was stronger than Minh's—wouldn't want to be Guild Leader. Cuinn had the power, but no desire. It made for an uneasy tension between them, and Cuinn tended to avoid him if he could. But this prophecy was too important to involve personal issues. He needed to make Minh understand. Believe.

"It's not a full prophecy at the moment, not while I can barely put words to half of it. But it is a warning of some kind." Cuinn leaned forward in his chair.

"Continue your dreamwalks, your research into the area. See if you can link what you've seen to anything we know. Take more books from the library." There was a hint of impatience in Minh's tone. "When do you start working with Marius's girl? I heard she did well in her Manipura trial."

He leaned back in a wide, high-backed chair, and tapped his fingers on the formal wooden table they sat around.

"She'll be there when I get back. Although I don't really have time for it. I'll start her on theory first, and reading, while I carry on with this task." Cuinn shrugged.

Damanea, the Ajna leader representing the future, whose gaze had been turned inwards until this point, appeared to refocus on the others in the room, and shook her head. Her eyes met Cuinn's with a surprising intensity. "Blaize Blackfire's destiny is bound up with yours, Cuinn. This I have seen. You must train her quickly. Troubles come before we ask for them. Have you looked into her future?"

Cuinn shifted in his chair. "I tried, but it's hazy, blurry. I thought that might be because she wouldn't stay long with me ..."

He felt a trickle of power in the room, like static along his arms, where it raised the hairs to attention.

"You're too close to her to see," Damanea continued, her voice low and forceful. "And there are many possibilities. But in all of those that turn out well, you need her. She is the female Warrior. You are the male Sage. You will also need the Protector, Creator, Healer, and Communicator. Male and Female elements. You have seen the troubles coming, and you are correct. They are not what they seem. Six smaller challenges will come, and be overcome, before the final battle is faced. The success of the small challenges will determine the last. Balance and harmony may depend on all."

She closed her eyes and bowed her head for a moment, taking a breath. "Work wisely and well with Blaize, Cuinn. You must lead, connect, unite."

Cuinn felt prickles of ice down his spine, and he shivered. He hadn't been involved personally in many others' prophecies. He'd seen his own, which had had implications for others, and sometimes implications for himself. But for him to be mentioned in this way in a prophecy—for that's clearly what this was—by Damanea, of all people, was disturbing.

Minh raised his eyebrows. "This is a personal prophecy, Cuinn. We will scribe it for you and you can review it to see if any of the elements resonate with your own dreamwalks and prophecies. Perhaps there is something to your own dreamwalks after all. For now we support you taking the girl as an Adherent. But be careful. You must provide stability. An anchor to her pride. Come to us again if you think you have more dreams of note. We will discuss this further between ourselves."

Minh stood up, as did Damanea.

Kenji, the past farseer rose more slowly. "Your history is weighing you down. It is a millstone around your neck. Be confident now that you have come through that experience wisely. There is no need for the past to be repeated in the future."

10

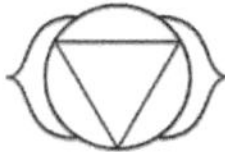

Cuinn arrived home after a long night of travelling and very little sleep. He'd stocked up on coffee at the airport, knowing he would drive home tired. When he arrived at Cathair Cuinn, he wanted nothing more than a shower and bed. But before he could head upstairs to his rooms, Tierra appeared from the direction of the kitchen. She gave him a warm hug, then took his hand and led him back to the kitchen. "You need food. Sit there, and I'll get you something. Toast okay?"

Cuinn nodded and sat on one of the stools at the breakfast bar. There was an easy silence between them for a couple of minutes before Tierra asked sympathetically, "How'd it go?"

"It's been worse, and it's been better." Cuinn's tone was bleak, and he glanced over at Tierra's back, hesitating before telling her. "They gave me a prophecy. About me."

"What?" Tierra turned with a mug dangling from one hand.

"I know, I know. It didn't make much sense, but it was official. They want me to see if I can reference it with any of my prophecies. The small but nasty set of puzzle pieces I'm unable to work out."

"You'll figure it out." She put a plate and a mug of tea in front of him and went to tidy up. "And Blaize arrived yesterday, so you'll have some help. She seems smart."

"I tried to get rid of her again with Minh and the others." He spoke around a mouthful of toast. "It's the last thing I need right now. I'm exhausted and I'm not in the right space for teaching, but even the farseers seem to think it's important I take her. I don't want to risk it again, but I don't have any choice. I owe Marius for his help with the Sophea situation. And the worst of it is he thinks it's for my own good. They have no idea what we're messing with."

She coughed but he ignored her, ploughing on, "It's such a bad idea. For all I know she's not even capable of using Ajna energies anyway. What a waste of time."

"Cuinn. Please." She motioned urgently to something behind him.

He swivelled in his seat.

Blaize stood in the doorway, mouth open.

None of them spoke.

An eternity of seconds of tense stand-off passed as their eyes—his appalled, hers mortified—connected across the cheery kitchen.

Blaize shook her head, colour in her cheeks, pivoted on her heel and left the kitchen.

Cuinn put his head in his hands.

"Shit."

Blaize didn't quite run back to her cottage, but it was close.

Her brain felt muddled from jet lag and tiredness, but her cheeks burned. *How dare he?*

She reached her front door, threw it open and headed up the stairs in a few bounds. She pulled her case out from under the bed where she'd stashed it neatly just hours ago, and gathered her clothes, scooping them from drawers and dragging them off hangers. She heaped them into the case, dumping socks, underwear, pants, dresses, and shirts in together. Her eyes darted around the room, trying to remember everything she had tidied away into cupboards and drawers earlier, but she couldn't focus.

The noise as the front door opened and shut made her screw her eyes closed and wince. She pressed her hands to her cheeks to cool them down, and shook her head, trying to clear it.

Measured footsteps sounded on the stairs. Her face hot and her pulse hammering, she stepped from her bedroom door across the square yard of hall at the top of the staircase to grab more of her stuff from the bathroom. Her throat felt thick and it was hard to swallow.

She gathered her possessions from the bathroom and spun back around to the door. Exiting, she flew across the narrow space at the top of the stairs back to the bedroom, her arms full.

And slammed into a wall.

She had a split second to see that she'd run directly into Cuinn's back as he faced into the bedroom, his tall frame taking up most of the small space between the rooms, and then, thrown off balance, she toppled backwards and down the stairs.

The shampoo, soap, toothbrush, and everything else she was carrying fell as she threw her arms out to catch herself. Her stomach hitched in a burst of adrenaline as she pitched into empty space, managing only to slow her progress by grabbing the rail. But her head still slammed into a step, her feet ending up towards the top of the stairs and her head closer to the bottom.

"Blaize!" The voice seemed to come from a long way away. "Blaize, talk to me. Please!" But before she could answer, the dizziness took her, and she heard no more.

11

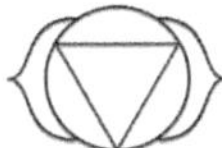

Cuinn scooped Blaize into his arms, and twisted his body to get them both down the slender staircase without bumping her again.

As he sped out of her front door, he kept up a constant stream of pleas and questions, his insides clenching at her lack of response. Energetics were usually pretty hardy, and long-lived, but it wasn't impossible for them to be hurt, injured, or even killed. He might not have wanted to be her Maven, but it was nothing personal.

His guts roiled as he carried Blaize to the main house.

As he went in through the kitchen door, he shouted for Tierra who ran in and quickly assessed the situation, then directed him to the living room.

Once there, he lay Blaize down on a sofa. Moments later, Tierra hustled through the door with a damp cloth.

"Did you need to move her?" Tierra leaned over the sofa to take Blaize's pulse.

"She was lying upside down on the stairs." Cuinn fidgeted in place.

Tierra's eyebrows rose. "What happened?"

"She walked into me at the top of those stairs, fell, and hit her head. I didn't push her if that's what you're thinking."

"Don't be silly." Tierra examined Blaize as she spoke. "Where did she hit her head, do you know? In one place, or more?"

"Where it's bleeding. Only once." Cuinn stood a few feet from the sofa, clenching and unclenching his hands, while Tierra used the cloth to gently wipe the blood and inspect the injury.

"It's probably not as serious as it looks. Head injuries always bleed more than they should," said Tierra, absently.

"What if there's internal damage? It was a pretty hard knock on the head."

Tierra didn't answer immediately. She lifted up the girl's eyelids to assess her pupils, and did some other fast checks.

"I'll look energetically to see if there's any damage to her brain. If there is, the nearest energetic facility is Victoria Island, so we'd need the chopper to get her there or maybe Cara here, but I don't want to do that unless I have to. Can you get me some ice and a clean dish towel?"

Cuinn nodded. He bolted out of the room and barrelled back through the door moments later, coming up short as he saw Tierra on the floor next to the sofa where Blaize lay. Tierra was massaging her own forehead. She used the chair to pull herself up and rubbed her wrist.

His heart jumped in his chest. *What the hell ...*

"What happened? Are you okay? Is she?" His gaze flickered wildly between the two of them.

"Calm down Cuinn." Tierra sent out a calming thread of safety, security, and comfort from her earth energy towards him though it lacked her usual strength.

"She was protecting herself, and managed to kick me just as I was withdrawing. If that was Blaize harnessing Ajna energies without training, she'll be a force to be reckoned with when she's trained."

"But is she okay?" Cuinn persisted.

"I've checked her, and I think she's fine. I couldn't see any energetic or physical disturbances in her energy. There's some swelling; she'll have a killer headache and a bump. And we should keep an eye out that there's no concussion. There's no need for the chopper."

Cuinn's shoulders dropped from where they'd been up next to his ears and he let out a long breath. He sank to the floor near the sofa. Tierra touched Blaize's pale skin and did another fast scan, and then leaned back, nodding, her own body seeming to lose some of the tension of the last few minutes. "We need her to wake up now and keep her awake for a while. I'll bring her round, and you can sit with her for the day. It might be an opportunity for you to talk."

Cuinn hunched his shoulders. "Sure." He had an unpleasant cocktail of emotions inside him—shame, guilt, and mortification. And he didn't think it was going to get any better for a while. Tierra wasn't someone who shouted or got angry, but her disapproval of his actions was clear.

His cheeks burned. Blaize's body lay on the sofa like a reproach. He hadn't given her a chance. It might not have been personal to him, but it was to her.

Tierra placed some of the ice in a tea towel and held it against Blaize's injury. "Can you hold this while I wake her up?"

Cuinn shuffled over and put a hand out to hold the makeshift ice pack in place. Tierra dipped one of the other tea towels into water and wiped it around Blaize's face. Tierra closed her eyes, and Cuinn felt a shimmer at the edge of his consciousness as she sent a little soft energy into Blaize to gently bring her back to wakefulness.

After another minute, Blaize groaned.

"Owww. What the hell happened?" She didn't open her eyes. "Can someone turn the lights off in here? My head feels like a nuclear device went off."

Cuinn watched her, more relief pouring into him, along with more guilt at how pale she was, and at the shadows under her eyes.

Tierra walked to the curtains and closed them, blanketing the room in an artificial dusk. "Blaize, it's Tierra. You fell and hit your head. I've checked and you're going to be fine apart from a nasty headache. But we also need to make sure you don't have a concussion, so Cuinn will stay with you for the day to make sure you don't fall asleep again."

"Cuinn? Awesome." Blaize mumbled it, but her meaning was clear enough.

Cuinn took a breath to speak, to apologise, but Tierra held up a hand to stop him. Blaize still hadn't opened her eyes.

"Blaize, I'm going to put a cool cloth on your forehead and eyes, which should help with the headache and the light. You need to just stay where you are. I don't think you're going to want to eat for a while, but you only need to let Cuinn know when you do."

Tierra moved Cuinn's hands away from Blaize, and put a fresh cloth over her eyes and forehead. "Cuinn, move one of the armchairs over to the sofa. You should stay close."

Cuinn did as he was told, and then slumped down into the chair.

"You can't go to sleep, either," said Tierra, as she turned to Cuinn. "I'll pop in and see you both once an hour or so, but I think you should use this time to get to know each other a little better."

Blaize heard Tierra's footsteps leave the room. There was silence. Blaize stayed still, the pain in her head immense, an inflating balloon squashing her brain against the walls of her skull.

"Blaize?" Cuinn spoke softly, in a deep baritone.

"Cuinn." Her answer didn't invite further conversation. She had no wish to speak with him at all, and especially not with this pain in her head.

"I'm sorry," he said. "I just came back from seeing the Ajna Guild Leaders. It was a rough and tiring trip. I shouldn't have said what I said, and I'm sorry you overheard it."

She kept silent. The pain and anger mixed inside her skull in an ugly headache. She hated feeling like this, and she especially hated the fact he had created the situation. She wanted to curl into a ball on the sofa, but she knew if she moved her head at all, the pain would just increase. She was grateful for the cool, wet cloth across her eyes and forehead, which provided some measure of relief.

"I know you're angry with me. But I don't want you to leave." Cuinn said, his voice low but persistent.

"You don't want me to leave? Or you can't get rid of me?"

Blaize's eyes were still closed, and it took some effort of will to string that many words together, but her anger cut through the pain like a laser, forcing the words out with a deadly precision. *I won't stay where I'm not wanted.*

Of course, when she was no longer focused on talking, the pain rushed back. She gingerly put her hand up to her head to feel the damage. There was a bump the size of a robin's egg on the back of her head, and her hair was matted with water from the melting ice and something stickier, which she assumed was blood.

"Ouch." She tried to keep her exclamation under her breath, but Cuinn responded immediately.

"Can I get you anything? Let me know when you're ready to sit up."

Blaize kept silent because of the pain that had pulsed through her skull like thunder when she'd touched the bump.

Stupid. Never press a bruise.

"Blaize?"

Maybe if she ignored him, he'd get bored and read a book or something. Although his voice was nice to listen to and didn't increase the pain in her head too much. Though the fact it didn't hurt just irritated her more. *Gah.* She gritted her teeth and resolved to wait him out.

She didn't have to wait long.

"I think you can help me." He was hesitant.

"Really? You want my help? After the morning we've had?" Her mouth dropped, and she pried her eyes open only to find the cloth blocking her view. She put a hand up and pushed it to one side, blinking in the gloom. She saw Cuinn's silhouette next to her. What in Source's name made him think she'd help him now?

"Let me tell you what's going on." He spoke haltingly at first but gained strength as he gathered pace.

He finished, "Something's coming, something very bad, that threatens the whole of the energetic race. And right now, I don't know enough to stop it. Yet I'm somehow involved. And honestly, I'm conflicted about you."

Blaize snorted. Softly so her head didn't move too much.

He scrubbed a hand over his face. "I don't have a lot of time right now, and I hadn't planned to take on an Adherent. But I'd be a fool not to take all the help I can get."

His head dropped and he gazed at the space between his feet. "This is a challenging project, with far-reaching consequences if the prophecies are right.

Oh shit. She hated it when she had to feel sorry for her enemies.

"How do you think I can help?" She really hoped she couldn't. Cuinn was a rude idiot, but he clearly had a lot on his plate, and she could see that adding a new Adherent to the mix might be a bit much for him. *But then why did he agree? He should have just said no and we could have avoided all this.*

"If I'm training you in Ajna, then you'd have to understand dreamwalking and how prophecies work. It would include prophecy research. We could work together and you could help review previous prophecies for relevant information." Cuinn's head came up and his eyes brightened as he outlined the possibilities.

"Grunt work, you mean?" She was better than that. He didn't need an Adherent; he needed a servant.

"No," Cuinn sounded surprised. "You'd be doing this anyway. At the moment I'm doing it, which would probably continue, so I'm not asking you to do anything I wouldn't be doing myself. And maybe, if you show some talent for working with Ajna energy, you can support in dreamwalking too."

He told her about the personal prophecy he'd received from the Ajna farseers.

She listened, feeling her stomach squeeze at his mention of a personal prophecy. She'd only heard about one of those, and it had turned out badly for all involved. She put a hand up to her eyes and rubbed them, trying to clear the cobwebs so she could think as he talked.

When Cuinn finally went quiet, he sat in the armchair next to Blaize's head, his body rigid and still.

She considered his words. It sounded as if the problems he was dealing with were greater than him. And he was pretty senior in his Guild if he could get in to see the Guild Leaders. *I really need to find out more about him.* She hadn't been in the mood to discover much about him before she came.

And if she was honest with herself, she was intrigued by his story. Some kind of threat that affected everyone she knew and was close to? The Warrior in her, her Manipura energy, rose up ready to protect.

"What do you think?" he asked.

How bad could it be?

"I think … it sounds interesting. Now, for Source's sake, let me rest."

12

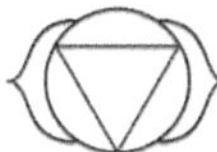

But Cuinn couldn't let Blaize rest.

Instead, he talked at her for what felt like hours, but she wasn't listening. She was too tired.

Tierra came in to relieve Cuinn. She brought hot tea and freshly baked muffins. They smelled pretty good. For the first time in hours, Blaize turned her face away from the sofa cushions and back into the room.

Tierra put the food down and bustled around the room adjusting cushions and straightening things as she went. Although as far as Blaize could see, the cosy room was already spotless.

Blaize cautiously raised her upper body until she was leaning back with her head upright. Tierra made a pleased noise when she turned and saw Blaize's efforts.

"Well done. I think you should get some food into you as you didn't have breakfast," Tierra said. "I've sent Cuinn off to do whatever he needs to do. And I'll try not to babble at you like I did last night. I'm glad you and Cuinn have sorted out your differences and you'll be staying with us. It's a pleasure to have you here."

Blaize managed a weak, but genuine, smile. Tierra was easy to be around. She gave off a sense of strength and solidity, comfort and care. And the muffins smelled good. Blaize took one and asked, "What are they?"

"Ginger and chocolate chip." Tierra placed a muffin on her own plate on a small table between them. She poured the tea.

"I'm sorry that your introduction to Cuinn went so badly," Tierra said. "He's avoided meeting new people for a long time. Usually it's just myself, Adam, and him here."

"Adam's your brother?" asked Blaize. *Anything not to talk about Cuinn.*

Tierra beamed. "Yes. He heads up a security team that hunts down difficult Rogues."

Blaize raised her eyebrows. *Now that sounded like a man she could talk to.* "Sounds interesting. When's he back next?"

Tierra deflated a little. "I'm not sure. He comes and goes depending on how the hunt goes. You'll like him. He's quiet but thoughtful."

"Hmmm … a hunter and tracker, works in a Security team but thoughtful …related to you and Cuinn—I'm guessing Muladhara-Ajna? Muladhara for protecting others, and Ajna being where thoughtful comes from?"

Tierra's smile was back. "Yes. He's the reverse of Cuinn. Adam and I share Muladhara from our parents, and our mother and Cuinn's mother were sisters."

Tierra sighed and switched topics back to Cuinn. "Give Cuinn a chance. He's a good man, really. It's just he has a lot of balls in the air at the moment. It's not easy for him, having another Adherent. It's been a while. I hope he'll tell you about that sometime."

"What do you mean?" Blaize leaned forward slightly.

"It's not my story to tell. But, please, don't see this morning as typical behaviour. He can get very focused, that's true, but it comes from a good place."

Blaize had known Cuinn had had Adherents before, but no one had mentioned any problem with one in the past. She leaned her head back against the top of the sofa again and sighed. Was she involved with a Maven with a difficult past? When she was feeling better she was definitely going to ask more questions. And not only that, get answers.

Cuinn sat at his desk in his workroom. After Tierra's efforts over the last couple of weeks, the room was a lot tidier than before, with actual space on his desk and only a small number of books around the room—and most of those on shelves. He was still tired. He'd lain down after his first 'watch' over Blaize, but he hadn't been able to sleep.

Damn it, she infuriated him. He couldn't think about her without his jaw muscles clenching. Frustrated, he flipped through the pages of a book in his lap without taking any of the information in, realised, and went back to the start.

But his irritation was also laced with guilt, because although it was true he hadn't actually pushed her down the stairs, he had certainly been the cause of her fall. His heart had raced as he'd carried her downstairs, as he'd focused only on getting her to Tierra's sure and healing touch.

He hadn't noticed her thick red hair, soft and touchable against his chest, or her strong, spicy scent.

Except he did.

He shook his head and scowled. Where had that come from?

He hadn't had female company that wasn't related to him for a while. It was probably just a reaction to that.

He thought he'd persuaded her to stay, but he sensed it wasn't a given. He rested his head on the back of the chair and closed his eyes. Marius wouldn't be happy if Blaize returned home, whether Cuinn sent her, or Blaize went of her own accord. And Fai … well, he would have to avoid Fai for another fifty years if that happened.

The door creaked open, and his head snapped around. When he saw it was Tierra and not Blaize his face relaxed, and Tierra laughed. "It's only me—don't look so worried. I brought you some food. You need to eat. And something healthier than cake and muffins."

Cuinn looked at the plate and his stomach rumbled.

"Fine. Thanks." He put the unread book down and took the food.

Tierra angled a chair to face him at his desk and sat. "She's a nice person. And as I said earlier, smart."

He nodded, then slipped a forkful of pasta into his mouth.

"You need to get to know her. There's no way you can do any kind of binding ceremony right now. Neither of you trusts the other. You need to have a week or so where you just do stuff together—show her the grounds, take her to the sea, the mountains, anything. Just spend time together, talking and just being."

Cuinn stopped eating and stared at her. "But what about my work? The prophecies?"

"You need some time off too. Let the dreams and the information that the Ajna Circle members gave you percolate in your brain. Some of the best connections between ideas come when you're not trying."

Cuinn frowned but went back to the food. He speared a baby tomato on his fork, then pointed it at her. "You just want me to get out more."

Tierra smiled. "Of course I do. And in the company of an intelligent, strong woman—what could be better?"

Cuinn was horrified. "She's here to learn, nothing else."

But damned if he couldn't get that spicy fragrance out of his nose.

13

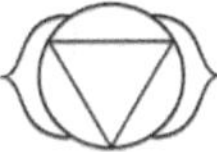

Cuinn woke early. Much too early. He was finding it harder and harder to sleep even when he wasn't working. It was taking a toll on him. Wearing him down.

He decided he might as well use the time productively. Given his half-awake, half-asleep state, he decided to dreamwalk.

But it was a short and discouraging excursion into the ether. The only new scrap of prophecy he'd seen was a woman in trouble. He couldn't tell who she was, or what the danger was, but he hadn't been able to do anything about it, and he'd woken with a dry mouth and a neck like a block of wood.

Brow creased, he went down to the kitchen. Time to address the next problem.

"I'm going to apologise to her," he said, as he came through the door.

Tierra looked up from the sleek silver laptop she was using. "Good. I'm just working on a column about spring plantings for next week's newspaper, but I'll be done in about twenty minutes. Ask her to breakfast, but don't push it. She might want some time alone."

She cocked her head as she examined him, then jumped up and went over to where more muffins were cooling on the side. "Take her a muffin. A peace offering. Oh, and Cuinn?"

He nodded, waiting.

"Smile."

He rolled his eyes and went out the back door, walking over to Blaize's cottage. He would wait to tell her about the getting-to-know-you week when Tierra was there to chaperone them. He and Blaize seemed to get on a lot better when Tierra was there.

He knocked on the door of the cottage. No answer. He stepped back and looked through the downstairs windows. No one.

He tried the door, but it was locked. He went round the back. That door was also locked, and pressing his face to the glass of the back window didn't show him any signs of life there either. The cottage was dark and empty.

He pushed a hand through his hair. Surely she couldn't have gone home already? Left under her own steam?

Or was the head injury worse than it seemed—was she wandering outside, hurt or in pain? The memory of his dreamwalk, still fresh in his mind, came back to him, and he ran back to the house.

"She's gone," he panted.

"What do you mean?" Tierra raised an eyebrow as she looked at him.

"She's not in her cottage. I'm worried. Can you track her?"

Tierra nodded, and closed her eyes. He felt the ripple of her earth energy as she connected to the grounds.

After what seemed like forever, Tierra spoke. "She's in the woods. She's using Manipura energy."

"What? Why's she doing that?" He didn't wait for an answer, but pelted out of the door into the forest. His heart beat erratically, and his stomach churned. What if she was in trouble? What if the woman in the dreamwalk had been Blaize, now?

The run to the woods took forever, and images played out in his mind as he pounded through the trees. He saw Blaize as she'd looked yesterday, pale-faced and crumpled at the bottom of the stairs. He imagined her now, lying on the floor of the woods, injured and signalling to them with her Manipura energy, trying to get their attention.

How long has she been out here?

Blaize missed using her fire energy. She'd woken very early, her body still not adjusted to the new time zone. She had first used the opportunity to place a video call to Nixie in Thailand, for whom it was late in the day. They caught up about Fai and Marius, and then Nixie asked about Cuinn.

"What's he like?"

"He pushed me down the stairs." At Nixie's horrified look, Blaize relented and told her the whole story.

"Hmm. Doesn't sound very promising." Nixie frowned. "What do you think of him?"

Blaize shrugged. "He's annoying."

"Does he have any redeeming features?"

Blaize thought for a moment. "He has a nice enough voice."

"And?" Nixie pressed.

"And he does seem to be dealing with a lot." Blaize hesitated. She wasn't sure if the prophecies were common knowledge. She guessed not. "He's working on a project for the Ajna Guild, which seems important."

"What kind of person is he?" Nixie was more interested in the person than the project.

"Arrogant. Proud. Works hard."

Nixie smiled and raised her eyebrows. "Huh. Do we know anyone else like that?"

Blaize scowled. "He's also conflicted. One minute he doesn't want me to work with him, the next minute he does."

"What do you want?"

"I want to help. And I want to learn about Ajna from an expert, which he does seem to be. But I hate the idea that I'm not wanted." She looked away from Nixie's picture as she said this last. It burned to admit it.

"He'll soon see you for who you are," Nixie said firmly.

"Who's that then?" said Blaize, amused.

"A confident, competent energetic who's going to learn fast and be of help in no time."

Blaize shook her head and laughed, and turned the talk to other things.

The conversation lasted another thirty minutes, and refreshed, Blaize went outside in the cool Canadian morning. She walked into the dense and damp woods, and played with a fire droplet, scattering it into many tiny drops that looked like a burst of fireflies around her head.

She started working—or playing—in earnest.

Strings of light dipped and twisted like thread, creating a fabulous pattern, the lightest and most delicate of lacework in fire in the sky. She played like this for another hour or two, and the day gradually got brighter and her creations more complex. She experimented both with power and delicacy. She revelled in playing with the energy in a way she hadn't done for years. For the last few years, it had been all about work, work, work as she practised for the Manipura trial.

She tried to hold a creation that involved several different aspects, a tableau of her aunt, uncle, and Nixie.

"What are you doing?" a male voice asked from behind her.

The voice startled her, and her creations wavered and disappeared as she turned in his direction. She groaned. It was Cuinn.

"I wanted to connect with fire again after my accident yesterday." She kept her tone level.

Something flashed across Cuinn's face and he scowled. "Anyone could have seen you."

"Anyone who, exactly? You live in the middle of nowhere. There's no one for miles." Blaize put her hands on her hips.

"You should have left a note to tell us you'd be outside."

"Why? Are you my keeper? I thought I'd be back before you were up." She flicked a glance at her watch and looked away from his glare. It was much later than she'd meant to be out. But she wasn't going to apologise to this idiot.

She passed by Cuinn as she walked towards the house. He caught her arm and turned her none too gently to face him.

I don't think so.

She travelled with the movement, deftly ducking under his arm and breaking his hold. She grabbed his arm and put it in a lock, forcing him to his knees.

"Don't touch me like that again." She looked at him flatly.

He stared up at her, eyes wide, but said nothing.

She released the lock on his arm with a little push and stalked back to her cottage.

Cuinn stayed on his knees in shock while moisture seeped into his pants.

When he'd come close enough to Blaize to see her playing games, he'd lost it. He'd been worried she had been using her energy to call for help, and instead, she'd been messing about like a child.

He hadn't meant to reach for her like that, but he'd just wanted her to stay in one place so he could tell her off. The feeling of relief he'd felt on seeing her had made him want to touch her, a feeling he'd shaken off even as he had made contact.

And then suddenly, he had been on his knees, and all the light and laughter had left her face, revealing the fire Warrior she was. He'd forgotten the physical training that went into Manipura, the many hours of martial arts practice. He'd forgotten that Manipura energetics were often—to the extent any were ever needed—the 'soldiers' of their race, the enforcers, those who captured Rogues and returned them to the Healers for rehabilitation.

And on his knees, he had looked up and into her cold eyes, eyes that so far he'd only seen run hot. This blank face, empty of emotion but with a terrible strength behind it, had been disturbing in the extreme.

He wanted to run after her and apologise, and felt confused about the emotions she'd stirred in him. The muffin he'd brought as a peace offering lay in the dirt next to him.

It had been many years since he'd encountered physical violence. As a dominant Ajna, he solved his problems with words, with logic, with argument.

Not violence. Never violence.

His mother had been far too close to the fighting in World War II because of her healing gifts. She'd been working with her sister, Adam and Tierra's mother, also a strong Anahata, in a Polish hospital when she'd been killed. Her death—and the violence of it—had driven him and his father apart. Despite the fact he and his father shared Ajna energies, his father had refused to talk to him about it and had blamed Cuinn for supporting his mother's decision to help in the war. Of course, when Cuinn had supported her, he hadn't really understood what it might mean.

He blamed himself too.

He walked to the house and into the kitchen to see Tierra. She sat at the table drinking a cup of tea. When she saw him, she raised an eyebrow. "What happened? And where's Blaize?"

He looked down at himself, mud and grass stains on the knees of his stone-coloured pants. "She's gone back to her cottage."

"Why? I thought you were going to ask her to breakfast."

"I didn't get around to it. I was too busy getting up from the ground where she tossed me."

"What are you talking about?"

He reluctantly explained.

She sighed. "Cuinn, you need to get a grip on yourself."

"Me? I'm the one she pushed over." But he avoided her eyes as he said it.

"You grabbed her. That's both inappropriate and out of character. What's going on with you? I thought you'd feel a bit more stable after a good night's sleep, but you still seem all over the place. What happened to the new plan of getting to know her?"

"I'd say I got to know a different side of her, that's for sure." He shrugged.

"Of course she'd react like that. She's a Manipura energetic. And remember what happened to her parents."

Cuinn's body felt heavy, and he sat down at the table with a thud. Tierra shook her head and poured him a cup of tea.

"Do you think that me grabbing her reminded her of her parents?" he asked, the weariness seeping deep into his bones.

"There's a chance. Plus, she only came out of her training a month ago. There's a lot of fire there. And you say she was playing with her element when you went out? If she was deep in fire, then it's no wonder it turned to anger when you touched her—you were lucky she had such strong self-control."

When any energetic used their element, the qualities of that energy were likely to be more potent within them. Manipura was dominant, proud, and controlling. There was a reason why Manipura was the energy of the Warriors of the energetics race. He rubbed the heel of his hand on the table, using the smooth wood to ground himself. He was reasonably sure he could have controlled her if she'd attacked him. Assuming he'd been conscious. Mentally, she was no match for him. Physically, he was no match for her.

"I have to apologise again, don't I?" Cuinn kept his gaze on the table, misery in his voice.

"Yes. But this time I'll facilitate it. She'll never trust you if you behave like this. Cuinn, words are your gift. I'm not sure why this situation is making you lose your balance like this, but you've got to focus. Maybe you should go up to your room and meditate for a while? Find your centre? I'll talk to Blaize. Come back down for lunch and be prepared to grovel."

He grimaced. "I told you all I couldn't be a Maven again. Looks as if I was right."

"Don't be silly." Tierra's voice was brisk. "You just need to get over these initial … bumps in the road, and you'll be fine."

"Bumps? They feel like mountains to me."

14

When Cuinn came back down to the kitchen a few hours later, he felt refreshed and considerably calmer.

Tierra and Blaize sat at the table, Blaize leaning her head in her hands and Tierra with a hand placed comfortingly on the other woman's shoulder.

Cuinn winced.

The two women looked up at him as he stood in the doorframe. There was a moment of silence and then Tierra twitched an encouraging eyebrow.

"Hi." Cuinn, for all his power with language, was feeling a bit lost. This was a different type of woman than he'd been used to—more volatile than the steady and peaceable Tierra. There had been no fire in either his own parents or Adam and Tierra's parents, so it was an element he wasn't used to. Perhaps he could appeal to her underdeveloped Ajna instead.

"Blaize, I apologise for my behaviour." His tone was formal, clipped.

Her eyes were a bright, hard jade and he had to steel himself not to flinch under their stare. He had no desire to end up on the floor again. But, he reminded himself, she was both fire and mind. He needed to engage with the latter.

"Let me give you some background." He talked her through his most recent prophecy image, and why he'd reacted as he had. With Tierra's encouragement, he managed a reasonably eloquent apology. The fire in Blaize's eyes dimmed.

He offered her the opportunity to get to know him outside the Maven-Adherent relationship, and showed her the itinerary he'd put together. A very logical itinerary.

And they agreed to start now.

15

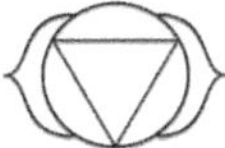

They started with a picnic, which was … okay. He couldn't really say much more about it than that. She'd told him about her education in the UK, and later working in the human business world in Hong Kong and Singapore, and, as part of her training, as a Manipura Warrior all over Southeast Asia. She'd certainly travelled a great deal in her short life.

All while he'd locked himself up in Cathair Cuinn for the last fifty years.

The girl seemed smart enough, but she had no concept of Ajna Chakra and the energies it contained. She was too steeped in her fire energies. Not unusual considering the short time between training in the two Chakras, but it might make things harder if she wasn't a fast learner.

Cuinn was back in his rooms now, still unsettled after their tempestuous morning. It was rare he had to apologise, and yet he felt as if that was all he'd done since she arrived.

He decided to try another dreamwalk. He'd use the energy of the morning to encourage more of the prophecy to emerge.

He made his preparations. He lit a candle at each corner of his mat and eased his long body down onto it. His body supine and still, he faced the white ceiling and took some deep breaths, clearing his mind.

He had to let go of the anxiety he felt about the prophecy. To forget Blaize, their arguments, and the fact she was now a millstone around his neck for the next however many years.

He had to be totally focused on the present moment. Mindful only of his breathing. To let everything around him fade away. He took another deep breath, and his body relaxed, some of the tension leaving him.

There was a rap at the door.

The noise jerked him back from the calm, empty state he'd been in, and confused, it took him a moment to place the noise.

There was another sharp crack, knuckles on wood.

He rose from the mat and went over to pull the door open. Blaize stood in front of him.

What is she doing here? "Yes?"

"You said to pop up later and you'd show me around the house. And your working area. It's late afternoon now." A slight crinkle appeared on her forehead, and she tilted her head a fraction.

Cuinn looked at his wrist, at what turned out to be a non-existent watch. "Oh."

He didn't remember saying he'd take her around the house. It didn't seem like him. And he really needed to get back to the dreamwalk. It felt as if she was at the end of a long tunnel, and half of him was with her, and the other half was still preparing for the ritual. He couldn't concentrate on what she wanted.

There was a beat while they looked at each other, her expectant, him unsure.

"So ... can you show me around now?" She spoke slowly.

"Oh." He paused, processing what she'd asked. "No, not now. I'm in the middle of something. Maybe tomorrow."

"Right. Of course. I'll ask Tierra then, shall I?"

"Fine." Cuinn was distracted. The meditative state was fading fast. He'd have to start again. He frowned.

"Right. So ... see you at dinner?" Blaize was backing away from the door and shaking her head.

"Fine." He shut the door and she was gone; he could get back to the ritual.

He lay back down, the girl disappearing from his mind, and breathed deeply until his body felt weighted and heavy. He relaxed more, his breathing slowed, his body still as death.

After some minutes, his body no longer felt heavy, but like nothing at all, as if he was no longer tethered to it. This wasn't literally true—some Ajna Masters could project their spirit, their energetic body, out of their physical body and move to other places on the Earth, but his movement today was all in the energetic world, and not on the physical plane.

He was now in a sleep state of sorts. But a lucid, conscious sleep state, where he knew he was dreaming and could act in the dream. He was on the energetic, the etheric, plane.

But his actions could have consequences for the real world.

He opened his eyes and looked around. The energetic plane was a wondrous one, where the mind could create a different reality—the energy that the energetics were able to pull through into the physical plane was all around here, and could be shaped and moulded as long as they knew how. There was some danger—unprepared energetics could kill themselves with the almost unlimited energy here.

When he visited this plane, he always began in his Haven, the name Ajnas used for their 'safe place' on the energetic plane. His Haven was a tower of thick stone walls, stretching up several stories, with one good-sized room on each floor.

To get into Cuinn's Haven would take an energetic of enormous strength if they could even find it in the first place, which was doubtful without an invitation or a previous visit.

Though much of his work on the etheric plane could be done from his Haven, for his dreamwalk today he needed to go to one of the unclaimed places in the energetics world. One of the places that was unshaped by energetics, full of untamed energy that might show him a glimpse of the future. It was dangerous because of who or what he might meet, and because the energy itself was so wild it could almost be said to have a mind of its own.

But that itself was a risky thought. Sometimes in the dreamscape, the energy reacted to your thoughts—good and bad—and created a reality from your mind. Which, given how jumbled and confused most people's minds were, could go very badly indeed.

His Ajna training had taught him how to keep a clear mind, how to focus, and how to be in the wild energy but keep his mind on the question he wanted answered. And sometimes, just sometimes, the wild energy would bring him answers.

The first inklings of this prophecy had been six months ago, and had been strange. He hadn't sought out the prophecy but been drawn by a feeling to one of the places of wild energy, where he had been gifted with a confusing jumble of images and feelings.

The few images made little sense, but the feelings that came with them hit home.

Despair, loss, destruction, emptiness—he'd woken up pale and sweating in his workroom at home, thrown from the dreamwalk without the usual decompression in his tower, and had staggered to the bathroom to throw up. He'd shared the images with Adam and Tierra, and later with Minh.

Since then, the prophecies had continued to come—some, unasked for like the first, powerful and exhausting in their intensity, and some, actively sought, usually clearer, but also much lighter in detail. These latter were like tiny shards of glass—whatever you could see in them was crystal clear, but only a very small part of the whole. The unasked-for visions were like opaque windows—a much bigger picture could be seen, but at the cost of clarity.

Both had an impact on him. Sometimes he woke up utterly drained. Tierra, Fintan and Adam all knew about his dreamwalks in search of more information on the prophecy, but as none of them were farseers, none of them knew quite the toll each dreamwalk took on him.

A dreamwalk involved not just a visit to the etheric plane – which could be taxing at the best of times, even when he stayed in his Haven, his safe place – but once there, a trip out into the wild energy on the etheric plane, a world that would react to his very thoughts. That he could shape to his will— if he was powerful enough. 'Thoughts become things' wasn't just an inspirational saying in the dreamscape.

But the effort, the control needed, could be exhausting and dangerous. He'd been hiding the impact on his mental and physical condition as much as possible, fearing that Tierra, in particular, might try to stop him. And he knew he couldn't let her do that.

His health was nothing compared to the survival of his race.

Today, emerging on the energetic plane in his Haven, he walked downstairs and to the heavy wooden door that provided access to the etheric plane outside the tower. He breathed in and out, using the familiar energy of the tower to create a shield to protect himself as much as possible outside his own Haven. Some of the grounds were warded – energetically guarded by him – too, but his strongest protections were in the tower itself.

With the door open, he stared out onto the flat grassland that he'd surrounded his tower with and was his preferred terrain—all the better to see something coming. Everything within his boundaries he had created, by drawing on the energies of the etheric plane. Beyond his boundaries all he could see was what looked like mist, fundamentally grey, with the occasional spark of colour.

Pure potential.

He strode to the edge of his Haven's limits, where he paused for a moment to take a deep breath – and then stepped into the mist.

He experienced weightlessness, vertigo, claustrophobia, and agoraphobia all at once. His energetic essence on this plane was untethered, and he needed to ground it or he'd never manage to focus enough to gather more shards of prophecy.

He reached for the energy, which responded to him like a very sticky, resistant toffee. It took great amounts of effort to shape his own body and some of the environment around him. Eventually, after much work, he found himself standing on a barren, rocky plain with little but scrub in either direction. The horizon was formless, and even the sky was an unrelenting grey, with no sign of the sun. There was no life to be seen.

Now came the dangerous part. He'd managed to define a small slice of reality, and he needed to let some of the wild energies back in, but in a controlled, focused fashion, that might help answer his question.

He opened himself very slightly to the wild energy. He focused his mind on the image of the twelve energetics facing the threat. He wanted to know who they were, and the part they would play.

Holding his focus, as well as holding the environment steady took huge amounts of mental and energetic effort. He breathed deeply.

The image blurred, shifted, changed. Eleven of the energetics disappeared, till just one woman, the one who had been standing closest to him, was left.

Blaize.

The picture of her shifted. Her eyes, a dull olive, looked at him from a face that was bruised, with a smear of dried blood under her nose. She was tied to something underneath her, and her energy was fading, though he wasn't sure why or how.

As always with a dreamwalk, he couldn't alter the vision, just watch in despair as her energy drained, and her green eyes turned glassy.

As the life left her face, the image of the twelve energetics came back to his mind.

But even as he watched, the vision changed. In it, Blaize turned to meet his gaze, smiled sadly, and faded from the vision.

This change was accompanied by a desperate sadness, a longing, and a deep emotional pain. The wrench of her disappearance shocked him like a sudden blow, and he felt himself thrown back into his body in the physical plane.

He barely had the energy to open his eyes, let alone the energy to sit up on the mat. His eyes and cheeks were wet, and he realised he was crying.

He lay like that, empty, silent, tears falling, until dawn.

16

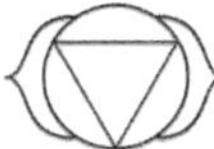

Blaize had an unsettled night. Dreams came and went, slipping though her mind like stagnant water down a drain, leaving anxiety behind like a bad smell. But she couldn't catch any details as she swam in and out of consciousness, and when she finally woke, she felt as tired as she'd been the night before.

She put it behind her, as today Cuinn was taking her to the local town. He was already belting up as she opened the passenger door and got in beside him.

Blaize admitted to herself she'd been a little disappointed at Cuinn's choice of car for their trip, a tricked out charcoal Land Rover Discovery. He'd told her, uninterested, that Adam chose their cars, though they did have several in their garage. Given Adam was a Muladhara energetic, it was unsurprising that the cars turned out to be brutes, built more for safety than for speed. And logical, she supposed, given the terrain. But her own penchant was for sleeker cars, cars that were powerful and fast. *At least he didn't choose the pickup.*

She belted up as he put on some kind of highbrow classical music. Very Ajna, she thought. Not much rhythm in this. But she settled back in her comfortable seat and watched the scenery pass by, as it was clear that Cuinn wasn't—yet—in the mood to talk.

The landscape passing by was, like Cathair Cuinn, showing signs of spring. Trees had some pink or white blossoms, still tightly in bud, but there. There was plenty of mud in the fields around them, but also green peeking through at the sides of the roads.

Cuinn's hands were neatly in the ten and two positions on the wheel, and he drove with minimal effort and movement, his eyes more blue than grey in the morning light. From the side she could see his eyes were fringed by thick lashes that made her a little jealous.

"So, assuming we agree to work together, and be joined as Maven and Adherent, how do you like to work? How have you worked with Adherents in the past?" As the words came out of her mouth she saw his lips tighten, and felt the car jerk, presumably in reaction to him pressing a little harder on the accelerator. She could have kicked herself. Tierra had told her there had been an issue with a previous Adherent. She needed a fast change of subject.

"Me, I like room for spontaneity. Some structure, some goals, but also the possibility to read about a topic and explore anything that's interesting. Sometimes I can get really involved and consumed by an idea if I get really into it." She gabbled out the words, trying to make sure he didn't clam up again.

There was a pause. Blaize sipped the coffee she'd brought with her and looked fixedly out of the window, pretending that this kind of long gap between contributions was completely normal.

She turned back to him when he finally spoke. His face hadn't lost the pinched look. In profile he had a strong face with an aquiline nose and a firm chin. His skin was pale—*presumably because he never leaves the house.* "With Ajna there must be some planning, some looking ahead. We'll start out with a plan for what we do with our time. But I'll try and ensure you have time to explore your own interests within the topic. Over time you'll need to find your own speciality areas. Your own specific talents within the mind."

Intrigued, she asked, "What are your talents?"

There was another pause, smaller this time. His mouth relaxed a little. He was a lot more attractive when he wasn't annoyed with her. Which so far was about one percent of the time.

"I have a talent for prophecy. And I'm strong. I can dreamwalk, and work on the astral plane as well as the physical."

Blaize raised her eyebrows. "What's your Muladhara energy like?"

"These days I don't use it as much as Ajna, but it's helpful. It … grounds me. It helps keep the lighter energies of Ajna stable. We'll need to be careful of your own fire energies. Fire combined with the mind can mean speed of thought, burning curiosity, laser-like focus—or it can mean being consumed by your own power, being possessed by intellectual pursuits above emotions or relationships with others, or even being burnt out too soon." His glance flickered over to her, and she met his eyes, now as opaque as fog, before he turned back to the road.

She shivered. You really didn't want to hear someone with the gift of prophecy say something like that.

The powerful vehicle ate up the miles to the town, and after passing only a handful of other cars, with about the same number of words between them, they arrived.

Driving into the small town, he told her a little about it. "There's not too much in Merrow—officially it's called Merrow Mount, but everyone just calls it Merrow—but it's the biggest town around. There are a couple of guest houses, a handful of places to eat, some grocery stores."

He pulled into a space on what seemed to be a reasonably busy street, and Blaize watched as a passerby waved at Cuinn, who lifted a hand and returned the greeting. Blaize's eyebrows rose. *Interesting.*

"Shall we go and get a cup of coffee?" he asked.

They were both out of the car by now, and this time Cuinn caught her raised eyebrow.

"I thought you might want a drink, and I can introduce you to the best coffee shop in town." He remained polite.

"Of course," Blaize murmured, proud of her own restraint in not mentioning she'd just finished a cup of coffee. She caught up with his long strides as he made his way across the road, watching him wave to two more people. She was fascinated by how different he seemed away from Cathair Cuinn.

Entering the warmth of the coffee shop, Blaize inhaled the aroma of fresh pastries and coffee. The café and shop, 'Sugar and Spice,' was doing a roaring trade. As she and Cuinn approached the counter to order, the motherly woman behind it caught sight of Cuinn and made a pleased sound. "Cuinn, how lovely to see you. It's been a while. Working hard again?"

Cuinn smiled at her. "A little. This is a family friend who's moved here to help me with some research. Blaize, meet Rosa, who makes the best cakes and coffee in Merrow."

Rosa dipped her head in acknowledgement and thanks, and said "Coffee for you, Cuinn? With a little sugar? And a scone? It looks like you could use a few more calories in you again—does Tierra know you've been starving yourself?"

"I'm fine, Rosa, and Tierra does her best to feed me. You're lucky she doesn't set up a bakery in town—she's one of the few people who might be real competition." Cuinn smiled at her again, and Rosa laughed.

The woman was human, but she appeared to have an activated Muladhara Chakra, very unusual in a human. She, and those around her, would be unaware of it, but the energy and her natural warmth would draw others to her. Humans and energetics were different races, but every living being had

Chakras within them. The energies were the foundation of all life on the planet.

"Hi," Blaize offered. "Can I get a cappuccino?"

"No problem, lovie. What would you like to eat? No, let me guess." She narrowed her eyes in thought. "Hmmm. I know. I just made some chocolate chili cupcakes. They're mainly chocolate, but have a little kick to them."

Blaize's eyebrows rose again, and she was starting to feel they might as well stay up near her hairline given the surprising turns the morning kept taking. "That sounds perfect."

"I'll send Indigo over with it all in a minute. Take a seat. And Cuinn, don't stay away so long next time."

He smiled back at her, and led the way to one of the smaller tables with two comfortable armchairs on either side.

"I can see why you like it here." It was interesting to see Cuinn in this new light. Perhaps he wasn't so bad if someone as warm as Rosa was fond of him. He folded his lean, rangy form into the soft and well-used cushions as she watched. She sat opposite him, perching herself on the edge of her chair rather than sinking into a soft, sagging seat.

He nodded. "Rosa's like a mother hen. Although what she doesn't know is that I'm nearly two centuries older than her."

He leaned back in the chair, his knees close to the table. "I like this town. We've managed to live harmoniously here for a long time. Not too much mixing with the town, some judicious ageing, and a little reincarnation. When I arrived here I wasn't feeling too friendly anyway, so that made 'coming back' a second time easier. Adam's been through several incarnations, partly because he enjoys it, I think. Anyway, it works."

Blaize nodded, and then shivered. *What the...?* She felt a trickle down her back, and turned, craning her neck to look around the coffee shop. She sensed a threat. But there was nothing in the scene before her that matched the menace that flooded her body with unease.

Mothers and their children, and students with books and laptops sat around them in the cosy space, knees against tables in squashy armchairs in reds, oranges and browns. Those rushing in and out to get their mid-morning coffee were dressed in work clothes. More often than not, Rosa would suggest to them a pastry or piece of cake, and though some managed to resist, the majority walked out with baked goods as well as their drink.

But there was something off here. Something wrong.

The twisted energy she normally associated with a Rogue.

Indigo put the grey-haired woman's order gracelessly on the table, baring her teeth at the two elderly ladies having tea and sandwiches. They didn't notice. She was invisible to them, just another service industry drone.

For a moment, her hate turned towards them and she narrowed her eyes, imagining pulling the hair of one and exposing her neck so she could slash it with a knife. She'd watch the blood pour out, covering the table and those repulsive sandwiches. The other woman would look at her in fear, and she'd know who was in control. Who had the power.

The woman looked up at her. "That's all, thanks." She smiled and turned back to her companion.

A hiss came out of Indigo's mouth. The woman looked back, confused, and Indigo pressed her lips tightly together and turned away.

She walked to the other side of the café to take the order of two irritating students so she wouldn't launch herself at Blaize, just yards away.

She'd been working at the café for over a month, to try and pick up town gossip about the reclusive family who lived just outside Merrow.

She'd chosen the café because Cuinn and Tierra seemed to have a relationship with the over-friendly proprietor though Rosa had been annoyingly silent on the subject so far.

Indigo refocused on the students in front of her and took their order on autopilot, uninterested in their cake and coffee. Indigo didn't eat much these days. She took the details back to Rosa, forcing a smile as she handed the bit of paper over.

"Everything okay, love?" Rosa asked.

"Fine thanks, Rosa. Just a bit tired. I was up late studying last night," Indigo lied. In fact, she'd spent her two days off in Vancouver, with *him*, and driven back the night before. She shuddered slightly.

She went back to the kitchen to take another order out and passed scant feet from Blaize's back. Indigo's eyes filled with anger. It would be so easy to set this whole place alight. To watch them all burn.

She and Blaize were an energetic match. Indigo was a Manipura-Ajna energetic, just like Blaize. But that was the only place where their lives matched.

Indigo hadn't had Blaize's opportunities. Her chances. No fancy university for Indigo. No family and friends who'd support her choices.

And now, Blaize and Cuinn were sitting in the café in a window seat watching the world go by.

They hadn't seemed to notice Indigo's energies. Indigo's Maven had both energetically warded her and given her his protection, and taught her to keep her energies hidden. In addition, Rosa herself was a human with some natural energies. Earth energies, which Indigo had little interest in, but energy nonetheless that masked Indigo's own power.

Indigo went back to the kitchen. She knew she couldn't attack them here, in public. Her role was to watch, and to gather information only. Her fists clenched. But she really, really wanted to.

'Table three," said Rosa, placing a cup of coffee on a tray that already held a chocolate chili cupcake, scone and cappuccino. "They're friends of mine. Introduce yourself."

"What's the matter?" Cuinn said.

Blaize didn't reply, still scanning the room. A waitress approached them with their order.

"Coffee and cake." The waitress put their order down and looked into Blaize's eyes.

Is she the threat? Their gazes locked. The waitress was very thin, with jet black hair and dark eyes. There was a hum in the air. The woman had energy, but Blaize couldn't tell if she was a human like Rosa, or an energetic. Either way, she didn't seem friendly.

All Blaize's instincts were on alert now, and Cuinn was looking at them. He half rose, but Blaize waved a hand at him.

If the woman was an energetic, she would surely indicate it. *And what would an energetic be doing waitressing in a town like Merrow?* But there was nothing. Blaize addressed the waitress. "Is everything okay?"

"Of course," said the waitress. "Enjoy your cake."

She strolled away, confident, and still Blaize wasn't sure. The sense of threat remained. The waitress paused a moment to chat with Rosa, who smiled at her.

Blaize frowned and pursed her lips. There was something here, tickling her consciousness. Her Manipura instincts had flared, and she just needed to concentrate enough to find out what it was. She closed her eyes and drew a little power. *Focus.*

She felt a warm pressure on her arm. "What's the matter?"

Her concentration broke and the trace of threat dropped away. She opened her eyes again and pulled her arm away from Cuinn's hand, irritated. *I nearly had it.*

"I don't know. Something's not right here."

Cuinn sat back and looked around. "Are you sure? I don't sense anything."

Her lips thinned into a line. "Yes, I'm sure. But it's gone."

She tapped her fingers onto the table. The waitress had disappeared back into the kitchen.

"Do you know that waitress? The one who brought us the coffee?" Blaize was looking past the counter of the café into the kitchen, straining to see the woman.

"Indigo? I've met her once or twice. She's new."

"Do you get a sense of energy from her?"

Now Cuinn frowned. "Energy? No."

"Nothing?"

He shook his head. "From Rosa, yes. Maybe you're feeling energy from her?"

Blaize pushed a hand through her hair. "It doesn't feel like Muladhara. I'm not even sure what energy it is. But it was a threat."

"There are no other energetics who live here," said Cuinn. He picked up his coffee and sipped it, leaning back in his armchair. "You're jumping at shadows."

Blaize stayed on alert. "I'm just going to use the bathroom."

She got up, movements abrupt, and stalked towards the door in the back. She'd touch the waitress and read what she could. If there was a threat, she needed to know.

But when she reached the back, sticking her head into the small kitchen, there was no one there but a young man with blond hair putting a sandwich together. "Can I help you?"

"Is Indigo here? I just wanted to ask her a quick question," said Blaize.

He shook his head. "She's stepped out for a minute as it's her break. Sorry. Do you want me to pass a message on?"

"No. Thanks." Blaize went back to their table, disappointed. The uncomfortable feeling had gone. *Am I imagining things?* Then a thought struck her. *What if the threat was from Cuinn?* Her stomach lurched.

She sat down opposite Cuinn, assessing him as a threat. He was strong, she knew that, despite having shown her nothing of his power. And strong Ajnas could project thoughts into others' heads, like Huo had at the trial. He hadn't mentioned that gift, but she knew very little about him.

She shrugged. *It's not like I've got anything to lose by asking him.* "Are you threatening me?"

17

"Are you serious?" Cuinn put his coffee down. If there had been anything unusual in the coffee shop he'd have known it, and he sensed nothing. *Now she's accusing me?*

He didn't have the patience for this. He hadn't told Tierra or Blaize about his vision of the night before. He was convinced he'd interpreted it wrongly. The idea of this irritating, possibly crazy girl as a part of the prophecy disturbed him.

The vision had affected him too deeply. He'd known her less than a week, and he'd shed tears after seeing her disappear from the vision. *Dammit.* He was losing it.

And now this.

"I'm not threatening you, Blaize. Far from it." He pushed his chair out from the table and stood up. "Let's go back to the house. It sounds like we could both do with some space."

"It's fine. I'm sorry." Her cheeks were flushed. "Whatever it was has gone."

"Maybe it was the sugar or the caffeine going to your head. Or jet lag. Or you're oversensitive to Rosa's energy."

Her lips flattened and her eyes sparked. "No. I sensed something, and it felt like Manipura."

Unlikely. The nearest energetic was in Vancouver as far as he knew. Energetics weren't territorial, but in an area with a population as small as this, they tended to ask permission before settling in.

Was she getting confused about her own energy? Either way, they needed to head home. Perhaps he'd start her off on some grounding meditation exercises.

She could do those in her own cottage, and he could get back to work.

Blaize walked along Merrow's Main Street filled with shoppers, mothers and babies, and even the odd tourist, and felt a shiver run across her back. Cuinn was back in the café paying, and Blaize had come out for some air, regretting the impulse that had caused her to accuse Cuinn.

She stopped and turned around, surveying her surroundings, but saw nothing out of the ordinary. She frowned and was moving on again when someone shouldered her out of the way, knocking her off balance. She staggered and span around, tensed, looking for who'd bumped her.

The most likely culprit was a dark head moving quickly away from her. A dark head that looked familiar. Blaize began to jog after the figure, who she was almost certain was the waitress from the coffee shop. *What was her name?*

"Indigo? Indigo. Wait, I want to talk to you." Blaize pitched her voice to carry to the woman, ignoring the glances from those around them.

The other woman glanced back and started to run in earnest. That only made Blaize more certain that she was right. All her instincts were screaming at her to catch the woman, human or energetic. Just because Cuinn didn't believe Blaize's gut about the woman being dangerous didn't mean Blaize shouldn't check for herself. He wasn't her Maven yet. And the woman had been stick thin. No match for Blaize's own training and honed muscle.

She would find out what was going on without any help from Cuinn.

Blaize sprinted down the street, dodging strollers, and small dogs being towed behind smaller children. The gap between her and the figure was closing. It might have been a week since Blaize had last trained, but she was fit, agile, and very motivated.

A ripple in the air, and Blaize sensed energy being used. *Shit.* She didn't know what energies the other woman had, but at least now she knew she was dealing with an energetic and not a human. Though she must be a well-shielded energetic not to have triggered Cuinn's nose for power, and to have set off Blaize's own instincts only a little.

Blaize span around a corner and came up sharp. She was in an alley between shops that was sheltered from the street. There was nothing in the alley but garbage cans—and the energetic.

"What do you want?" Blaize said. She put her arms up in front of her in a defensive crouch, and pulled a little energy from the ether, spooling it inside. She was as able to defend herself physically as energetically. And she was ready for either.

The woman didn't speak, but closed her eyes for a second before bringing up her arms fast and shooting a stream of fire at Blaize.

Blaize staggered back, throwing up her own defensive shields to protect herself. She hadn't expected the other woman to attack so quickly, especially so close to humans.

"What do you want?" Blaize said again. She wasn't ready to make a move, though at this point, if she saw an opportunity to restrain Indigo, she would. She'd dump her in Cuinn's lap and not say "I told you so." *Well, maybe just a little.*

It was against all energetic laws to use energy close to humans, so Blaize had reason enough to hold the woman. But Blaize needed to keep Indigo in this alley until she could either calm her down enough to have a rational conversation or she could take her down.

"Indigo, is it? What are you doing in Merrow?" Blaize kept her tone reasonable though the fire in her blood was itching to get out. She tried another tack. "What's your auxiliary Chakra?"

It was obvious enough that the woman's dominant was Manipura, just like Blaize's.

Indigo's eyes were hard and burned with emotion. She still said nothing. She was angry. Not just angry, raging. But Blaize had no idea why, which meant she wasn't sure how to address it.

Blaize took a step closer. "Why don't you come with me back to my home? There are several energetics there, and we can help you if you're down on your luck."

Energetics were rarely on their own. The family and Guild structure meant that energetics were linked like the warp and the weft of cloth. And energetics always, always offered hospitality to each other. It was a fundamental part of their culture. If Indigo turned it down, it would be an insult unless there was a very good reason. Which she would need to provide.

Not that Blaize expected her to accept given Indigo had just thrown a fireball at her. You didn't get much ruder than that. But you never knew.

If anything, Indigo's eyes went harder. The rage in them burned, and power shimmered in the air around her. If Blaize hadn't been sure in the coffee shop, she'd have needed only a second of seeing Indigo like this to know she was an energetic, and a powerful one. A Practitioner like Blaize, or maybe even a Master.

This time, when Indigo threw the fireball, Blaize was ready for her. She caught it with her own energy and absorbed it, ensuring it didn't get loose into Main Street behind her. But even as she did, she ducked and crossed the few feet between them. She kept her head down and propelled herself into Indigo's stomach. The air went out of the other woman in an 'ouf,' and she fell backwards, thumping into a large trash receptacle.

Blaize grabbed the woman to keep her upright, and put her right arm like a bar across her windpipe. The other woman clawed at Blaize's arm, clutching it to bring it away from her air supply.

"Really," said Blaize. "Why are you here?"

Blaize was aiming for cool and composed, but her blood was up. A week at Cuinn's without proper physical or Manipura training and no way to take out her frustrations with him, Blaize was left with a lot of pent up energy, despite regular sessions of meditation.

"Now's not the time for this," said Indigo. She was holding onto Blaize's arm, pulling on it to keep the pressure off her throat. She was starting to go red.

"Are you ready to come with me? You know you can't use power like that in public."

"I couldn't help myself. You're just so … irritating." The woman rasped the words out through a constricted throat.

"What?" Blaize loosened her arm very slightly in surprise. Indigo took the opportunity to wrench Blaize's wrist away from Indigo's neck and down. Indigo, still holding the wrist, stepped forwards, which broke the arm lock so Indigo ended up behind Blaize. Indigo had now reversed the situation so Blaize's arm stretched out painfully, Indigo's hands on her wrist in a lock that held Blaize in place.

Blaize could no longer see Indigo. She craned her neck to see what Indigo was doing, but Indigo jabbed her arm down, pulling at the shoulder joint. Blaize winced. *Ouch.*

"Much as I would love to spend more quality time with you," Indigo spat, "now's not the time for us to meet properly."

She bent Blaize's arm and forced her against the wall, using her other hand to push Blaize's neck into the rough surface. It was a classic control arm lock.

But Blaize knew Indigo would have to break the hold at some point unless she had an accomplice or some kind of restraints.

Blaize was ready for the transition. She just needed a little movement to get out of this. She kept her head twisted to make eye contact with Indigo.

"There's no need for this. Please. Let's talk. I have no idea what your issue is with me. I don't know who you are or what you want. Tell me. Maybe I can help."

Indigo snorted and just pushed Blaize's cheek harder into the wall. The irregular surface grazed Blaize's face, stinging like a thousand tiny whips.

Indigo leaned closer to Blaize, still shoving her into the wall. Blaize was trapped, her arm held tightly up and out behind her back.

"You can still walk away from this, Indigo," Blaize tried. "Don't let it become more than it is, or you know I'll have to report it to the Guild."

It was likely both of them knew that she'd be telling the Guild anyway, just as soon as she could, but there was no need to escalate things further. Blaize drew power to build defensive shields. She would have to work fast against another Manipura, but it could be done. She could heat her way out of the situation. She drew in a breath.

Indigo leaned her weight on Blaize's arm, and bent her head forward so her obsidian eyes looked into Blaize's. They were magnetic. Blaize couldn't look away.

"I'd love to leave you something to remember me by, but I'll get in trouble if I damage you this early in the game." Indigo's tone was conversational, but the hate was still there.

"So relax. Take a breath." Indigo's voice softened, and she almost crooned the words.

Blaize felt her muscles go lax, and she stopped drawing power. She felt … odd. The alley blurred a little and she blinked.

Indigo stood, sparks flying from her hands and hair. She drew Blaize upright as she did, easing the pressure on Blaize's shoulder.

Blaize came to a standing position. Her head felt fuzzy. Confused. *There's something I'm supposed to be doing. What is it?*

She looked around. Indigo was watching her, a smirk on her face. Indigo stepped back towards the entrance to the alley, Blaize staring at her. *Why can't I remember what I'm supposed to be doing?*

"Okay. Maybe just a little something." Indigo's smirk grew wider.

Blaize felt as if her brain was full of fog. She shook her head, trying to clear it.

"Blaize bitch?" Indigo waggled her fingers.

Blaize turned her head slowly back towards the voice. Indigo's voice. There was a haze in the alley and it was hard to make out the details of what she was seeing. Was Indigo an enemy? *No. Yes. What?*

Indigo whirled towards Blaize, snapping her foot out and into Blaize's stomach. Pain blossomed in her abdomen, and she crumpled forward.

"Teach me," Blaize demanded of Cuinn. "I need to learn what she knows. She took me by surprise today. It won't happen again."

They were home in the kitchen. Cuinn had insisted they report the incident to the police and to Rosa, who had been shocked to hear her waitress had attacked Blaize. Neither report to the humans had involved any mention of energy, and it had gone down as an attempted robbery. Cuinn had asked Rosa to let him know if Indigo returned but had made her promise to call the police first.

Cuinn stood leaning against the wall while Tierra dabbed at the scratches on Blaize's cheek. Blaize held ice to her stomach to bring the bruising down. She'd refused Tierra's healing Anahata energy, saying she wanted to feel the pain so she'd be prepared next time.

"You think she was an Ajna. That she controlled your mind," Cuinn stated. He hadn't believed it at first. How could the woman, someone he'd met two or three times, be an Ajna strong enough for mind control? *How didn't I sense her?* The vision of Blaize, beaten and tied up, was still fresh. Seeing her bruised and scratched wasn't helping him stay calm.

"Of course she was. How else do you think I got these?" Blaize waved at herself.

"Perhaps she was just faster than you. Better trained." Cuinn kept his voice mild.

Blaize growled. "She was better trained. In Ajna. There's no way she was better trained than me in fighting physically. She had no muscle tone. And I'm pretty sure I was the stronger in Manipura. No. She did something to me. Held me in position. I got confused during the fight. I didn't know what was happening, whether she was a friend or an enemy. Everything went foggy like there was some kind of mist in the alley. She kicked me in the stomach while she was controlling me with her mind."

Blaize gestured sharply, still clutching the ice pack. Tierra put her own hand on Blaize's arm and gently pushed it back down. "Keep holding the ice, lovie."

Blaize was confident, he'd give her that. But today, it seemed, overconfident. He couldn't afford that. She couldn't afford that. She needed to be more careful. He needed to remind her that she wasn't as good as she thought she was. "Then how did you get the scratches on your face?" Cuinn asked.

There was a pause.

"She had some training," Blaize admitted sullenly, "but not enough, and not to take me down with a kick in the stomach. I was ready to break her arm lock. All she needed to do was transition out of it and I would have had the upper hand again. But she did something—"

She broke off in frustration.

Cuinn walked deliberately over to the sink and poured himself another cup of coffee. He set the full cup on the side and gripped the sides of the sink for a moment, looking out of the window, his gaze on the gardens outside. He took a few deep breaths. It had been decades since he'd felt the kind of anger and frustration that Blaize managed to bring out in him. She was so unbelievably stubborn. She'd been in a fight with an unknown energetic who was potentially an Ajna and/or a Manipura Master, and here she was, raging to go another round. *Does she have no fear?* Tension contracted his back muscles and he put a hand up to rub his jaw, to release some of the tightness there.

When he walked back to the table, his tone was still calm. "I didn't say I didn't believe you. I just wanted to explore all the possibilities."

"So we can begin training?"

Cuinn sighed. *This is a bad idea.* "Be at my room at 9.30 a.m."

18

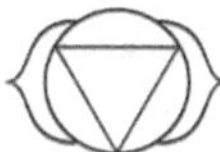

Cuinn was ready and waiting for the sound of knuckles on the wooden door at 9.30 a.m sharp. He trudged to the door and opened it. She stood in front of him radiating a strange mix of eagerness and distrust.

"This is the room where I work." He gestured around him.

Blaize nodded. The room was less clear and tidy than it had been after Tierra's efforts a couple of weeks before, but he'd managed not to completely fill it with books again. There were only a few on the floor. A few piles, that is. He coughed and her attention came back to him.

"I bought you something."

Her lips flattened, the eagerness leaving her face, leaving only distrust behind. "What?"

He reached behind his desk and brought out a large cloth bag, handing it to her. She opened it and pulled out some heavy fabric. "What is it?"

"It's a meditation mat. We're going to ward it, energetically guard it, so that you can use it to dreamwalk. It's easier to have something familiar that you use every time. That way your energies seep into it—it's like seasoning a wok."

She blinked and he hastened on, sensing the example hadn't worked that well.

"When we dreamwalk, we're open and unprotected in a way we're not on the physical plane. We need to protect ourselves. Most Ajna energetics, rather than drawing chalk circles all the time, use a warded rug or mat that they can carry with them. It doesn't have the drama of a physical circle, but it's a lot more comfortable when you're lying on it." He tried a smile.

She stood back to shake open the rug. As the folds fell out and it hung in the air from her outstretched arms, she looked at it with a smile, pleased. "It's lovely, Cuinn, thank you."

Cuinn relaxed, and his own smile became less tentative. He'd picked the rug up in Merrow, before the incident with Indigo, when Blaize had been in the small sporting goods shop. He'd chosen it carefully.

He felt something shift inside him as she touched the finely woven strands with unreserved happiness, her face soft. Perhaps he didn't give enough gifts, if generosity could feel as good as this.

"I want us to spend some time meditating together. To get a feel for each other's energy. Before we can even think about dreamwalking, we need to become used to each other."

"I'm a fast learner." Blaize took her gaze off her rug for a second to meet his.

He kept his sigh internal. "I know. But this isn't about intelligence. It's about getting a 'feel' for each other. It's nothing intellectual, or cognitive."

She nodded slowly. "How will we know when we've got this 'feel' for each other?"

"We'll know." He walked to the large windows, throwing them open, letting cold, damp air flood the room, along with the low morning light.

Blaize wrapped her arms around her. "Is that really necessary?"

"You'll get used to it. Be grateful. When I did my Ajna training, my Maven made us do all our work outside. He said it was more conducive to the energy of the mind."

"And when was that?" Blaize asked, her eyebrows raised, her head cocked.

"It was … some time ago." *Okay, two hundred years ago.* "I don't think we need to go that far, but I do think fresh air helps clarity of mind and meditation. You can set up."

Cuinn cleared some of the piles of books to the sides of the room to make space for her mat. Blaize leaned down to help and he stopped her. "I know what's in each of the piles. It's better if you don't touch anything."

Blaize's face tightened. Cuinn looked away and moved some of the piles closer to each other, keeping the books in the right order.

He cleared enough of the smooth blond wood floor so that she could put her mat down next to his, still out from the night before. When the two rugs were laid out lengthwise next to each other, he gestured to Blaize to sit on hers. She frowned.

"What's the matter?"

She hesitated for a moment. "I don't like sitting with my back to the exit. No Warrior would."

He forced himself not to shake his head in frustration. "You're in my heavily warded rooms, in a heavily warded house, on a heavily warded property. Any danger you encounter isn't going to come through that door. It's what's in your head that you need to worry about today."

He continued, trying to relax his jaw. *Why can't she just do what she's told?* "As Adherent, and student in the process, you sit with your left side—your receptive side—towards the window, the light, and the air. As Maven and teacher, I sit with my right side, my emissive side to the window."

She pursed her lips, but dropped into a crossed-legged position facing his rug, her left side to the window—her back to the door. His back was to his desk as he sank down in front of her.

He held his hands out, palms up. "Rest your palms face down on mine, parallel to the floor. Then our little fingers and thumbs slot into each other."

"I know how to behave in a meditation like this. I've just come from my last Maven, remember?" Blaize's tone was polite, but her words had an edge of irritation to them.

"It's better if we start from scratch. There'll be some things your aunt and I might do in the same way, but given the very different energies we're focusing on, I'm sure there will be things we do differently too. And when the consequences of a mistake can be madness for one or both of us, it's worth being certain."

Blaize's eyes narrowed, and she gave a grudging nod.

I guess working with a fire energetic's never going to be easy.

They joined hands. Hers were warm and dry against his own cooler fingers. There was a curious sense of rightness as her hands fit into his, smaller than his own, but equally slender and fine. Neither of them had hands that had seen much manual labor. Despite his affinity with earth, it had been a long time since he'd tilled the land.

"I'm going to take us through a guided meditation. As you get more experienced, you'll need less ritual and preparation, but for now I want you to close your eyes, listen to my voice and follow my instructions. We'll keep it simple, and get a sense of each other."

"A feel."

"That's right. You'll see what I mean. It will be different from working with your aunt, someone you've known for a long time, and both of you having the same dominant energy. For you, Ajna is your auxiliary energy, and not strongly developed."

Again she took a breath, leaning towards him, and he added, "I didn't say not strong. You may have a great deal of potential; I don't know. Just not strongly developed."

She settled back.

The cool spring air had refreshed the room, airing it out as they'd settled on their mats. The room smelled of new growth and the earth after rain. The sun, still gentle at this time of the day and year, touched Blaize's hair, giving it natural highlights of burnished fire. She shook her head to remove a strand that had fallen too close to her eyes, and he was distracted as sun and strands danced.

He rarely got distracted. He was more tired than he thought. Her small but pert chest rose and fell, unconsciously echoing his own deep inhalations, and he realised he was staring when he caught the slight crease between her eyebrows.

Damn.

He needed to begin.

"Close your eyes." His voice was soft, persuasive, and her eyelids fell obediently.

His own breath was rhythmic, and he consciously deepened it, making his exhalation a fraction longer than his inhale. After a few of these, his thoughts steadied.

"Breathe, Blaize. Relax your shoulders, your neck. Your jaw, and all the tiny muscles in your face." Her breathing slowed. Her hands relaxed in his.

He lowered his voice further, keen not to disturb her as she focused. His aim was to put her into a very light trance state, a practise session for later dreamwalks. He expected she'd need to practise many times before they got anywhere near that. Today was just about relaxing and seeing if she could feel his energy. He could already feel hers.

He wanted her to use a little of her energy so he could see how visible it was to him when he made a conscious effort, but didn't want to tip his hand. So instead he pulled some of his own energy and sent a tiny and delicate tendril to touch Blaize's aura, the natural energy that every energetic, and in fact, every life on the planet had around them.

Whilst the auras of most life on earth were faint even to the eyes of energetics, the auras of energetics—at least to other energetics—were palpable. His energy brushed lightly against hers, and she shivered.

He pulled back quickly, stunned at her receptiveness and the sensation the touch had created within him. The heat of the contact seared him and he tried to keep his breathing steady as the hair on his arms stood on end.

Hmm. Perhaps more caution was warranted.

CHAPTER

19

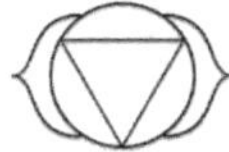

What was that?

It was several hours later and they were still working.

Whatever it was, Blaize couldn't hold onto the vision. She fell out of the light trance and her eyes snapped open as the images slipped away from her. When she focused her eyes she found Cuinn staring into them. She flushed. What had just happened? She wasn't sure if she wanted to ask, but Cuinn spoke before she had a chance.

"Good. You created a safe space in the dreamscape, a Haven, which for you was a garden. Your energy, which was all fire at first, was able to brush against mine and shift to a more Ajna energy. Did the smell, taste, or even 'feel' change? What could you see?"

He'd had her imagine herself in a place of positive memories, and to imagine him there with her. They'd no longer been in his Haven. He'd had her interact with his energy. "It changed colour. Well, sort of. It kept flicking between red and blue, with purple and all the colours in between. It was intense. ..."

She hadn't been able to hold on to the feeling. It had been too much.

"That's good. Did you see my energy as blue?"

She nodded. She didn't want to tell him what a beautiful blue it had been. She'd been drawn to it, and to him, and when she'd reached out with her own energy to touch his, she'd only been able to do it for seconds before the delicious intensity had slipped away.

"Your energy adapted to the touch of mine, and it brought out some of your own dormant Ajna energy. Great start. Let's break for lunch."

"But we've only just started," Blaize protested. She was here to work. And she had been surprised to find she'd been enjoying it. Even enjoying spending time with Cuinn. He was a good teacher, calm and helpful, providing useful feedback but letting her find her own way.

"It's one p.m.; Tierra will kill me if I keep you up here and we miss lunch."

Blaize shifted and felt the fatigue in her body, her limbs stiff. Several hours had passed. Where had the time gone?

Several sessions later, Blaize was still trying to trust the process.

"Try to call your own Ajna energy. Use the sensations you felt when you touched mine to guide you."

They were back in her Haven and she felt clumsy, with no idea of what she was doing. She'd forgotten what it was like to be such a beginner and she found herself wanting to impress Cuinn.

I can do this.

She opened herself up wider than normal to see what else was out there that might be different from fire energy. What else could she draw on? She reached out, seeking the blue energy that had surrounded Cuinn to see if she could call up her own.

Instead, she touched something very different.

A dirty, oily blue energy that came into the garden fast and began to attach itself to her.

Suddenly, Cuinn wasn't just watching her. He shouted and moved towards her, his face filled with fear.

But it was as if he was moving in slow motion.

She turned to him, puzzled, as the oily blue began to replace her own red fire energies, turning them a dull brown. She felt heavy, her heartbeat loud in her ears. Her hands shook, and her eyelids fluttered. She wanted to ask Cuinn what was happening, but she couldn't form a single word.

This was not going as planned.

Something … else, something more, had come through. Cuinn had leapt to protect them both against it, trusting his own defences would hold against whatever was intruding where it didn't belong. But before he'd managed to get to Blaize, she'd fallen unconscious, and he'd found himself thrown out of her garden and back in his Haven.

He'd jumped out of the etheric plane and back into his own body as quickly as he could, wincing as he moved between planes too fast, only to find her lying on her mat in his study, a trickle of blood under one nostril in a hideous echo of the prophecy.

He slid from his mat to hers and shouted for Tierra. Then he turned back to Blaize. "Blaize? Blaize. Wake up. Wake up, now!"

As Tierra rushed through the door, she appraised the situation and gestured to him to move aside as she knelt down beside Blaize. "What happened?"

"I'm not sure. Something tried to get through and I was kicked out of her dreamscape and into my own. When I got back, she was like this."

"I don't like the blood." Tierra checked Blaize's pulse and felt her forehead.

Cuinn rubbed the back of his neck, all traces of the relaxation he'd felt in the dreamscape gone. *What the hell had happened?* Was Blaize alright? Was he responsible for this?

Tierra sat back on her heels and closed her eyes to examine Blaize energetically.

Blaize was horribly pale as if the red smear under her nostril was the only blood left in her lean body. Tierra was motionless, hands in her lap, but he had no doubt her mind and her energy were working furiously. Cuinn wiped away the blood on Blaize's face, at a loss as to what else to do while his cousin worked.

He waited a few more seconds before he broke. "Tierra. What's going …"

She shushed him. A few more minutes passed. Cuinn's neck muscles got tighter, and he rubbed the heel of his palm in a repetitive motion on his thigh. He was considering calling an ambulance and involving the human medics when Tierra finally opened her eyes. "She's okay."

His body sagged a little and he pressed his palms into his eyes for a moment. "Why hasn't she woken up then?"

"She will in a minute. She seems to have had the energetic equivalent of a knock on the head. Another one."

A sound came from Blaize. Not loud enough to be classed as a moan, it was definitely a sound of pain. Blaize's hands flexed, and her head lolled a little to one side.

"Cuinn?" Her voice was soft, not at all what he'd been used to hearing over the last few days.

"Blaize." He put his hand out and when they touched, her hand closed around his like a drowning woman holding a life preserver. "Blaize, you're fine. Tierra and I are here."

"Where are we?"

"In my study again. Something happened and you were knocked unconscious and back into this plane."

Blaize's free hand came up to her face, which started to get some colour back. He stared into the now murky-green depths of her eyes and saw confusion, mixed with a little fear. He was sure his eyes held the same emotions—though with a lot more fear.

Seeing her like this brought back a lot of memories he'd tried to forget. It was one more reminder of the reasons he hadn't wanted to take on another Adherent from the start. He rolled his head, stretching out his neck, still almost unbearably tight. Tierra looked at him, concern in her eyes. She knew what he was thinking. He couldn't deal with that now. He shook his head before turning back to Blaize.

"Blaize, you're okay, you just need to rest. Tierra, can I sit her up?"

Tierra nodded. "Carefully. Blaize, sit up slowly. I've checked you over, and you don't have any lasting damage."

"Just another bump on my head," Blaize muttered the words, but Cuinn caught what she said, and looked away.

"There won't be a physical bump this time." His words were sharper than he'd meant them to be, and Tierra frowned at him.

He moved behind Blaize, and with Tierra's help lifted her so that her head was propped up on his lap. Blaize's eyes were open, but unfocused. She winced as she put her hand up to her head and rubbed her forehead. "Ouch."

Tierra moved and left Blaize's weight solely supported by Cuinn.

"I'll make you something warm to drink. Cuinn will look after you." Tierra shot Cuinn a warning look. "Help her into the chair when she's ready. And remember, slowly."

She put her hand over Blaize's and gave it a short squeeze. "You're going to be fine, I promise."

"Yeah, until the third time." The words were quiet but stopped Tierra as she was getting to her feet.

"What?" Cuinn wasn't sure he'd heard correctly.

"The third time. When you knock me unconscious a third time. Three's the charm, so they say."

Tierra smiled and walked out. Cuinn moved Blaize up his body so she rested in his arms. Her body was as supple as it looked, and he could feel the toned muscle under her clothes.

"Umph." Blaize scowled. "No big moves yet. Please."

"Sorry." He shifted his weight so his position was more comfortable, and sat back with his legs outstretched, Blaize resting warm against his chest. "I'm sorry. There won't be a third time. Really. And this time it wasn't me."

Blaize's eyes had closed again. "Whose fault was it then? Was it mine? Something I did?"

He had to lean down to hear her voice, which faded as she spoke the words. As he did, he could smell her fragrance, light and exotic, a hint of jasmine and something else.

His breath quickened, and his arms tightened around her. Blood flooded his groin and he almost dropped her in his haste to hide his body's betrayal.

What the…?

It had been a long time since he'd touched a woman he wasn't related to. He obviously needed to get out more if he was aroused by a woman with whom he did nothing but argue. *Focus, idiot.*

"You didn't do anything. Well, you did, but nothing you shouldn't have. You started to pull energy a little strongly, and something happened. Something tried to piggy-back on the energy you were pulling through. I don't know what. We were both kicked out of the etheric plane before I could discover what it was. You were doing well—some people take weeks to create their Haven, their safe place. You did it in a day."

"It wasn't that safe." Blaize's hands came up to rub her face again and she opened her eyes.

Her face flushed and she grimaced, as she realised she was leaning against Cuinn. She placed her palm flat on his chest as if to push herself away.

He put a hand over hers. *She mustn't get up too quickly.*

"Just rest for a while. Tierra will be back with a drink in a minute. There's no rush." He tried for soothing in his own voice, but could hear a rough edge in it from the arousal he was still fighting.

"There's no need to sound so cross about it."

He cleared his throat.

"I'm not cross. Not with you, anyway. I don't know what happened, and given how much in the dreamscape I'm unable to explain right now, it makes me edgy."

"Crabby."

He smothered a smile. "Maybe."

"You're always crabby with me. Except when you're not."

"I'm sorry for that." His voice was gentler now, and he gave the hand under his a little squeeze. Her hand was over his heart, and he tried not to consider whether she could feel his heart rate pick up the longer it stayed there. He shifted again, restless, and when his hand let go of hers to cradle her body, the simple movement put her hand on his face. He looked at her.

As his face tilted down, hers turned up.

"You could be kinder," she whispered. He felt her warm breath on his lips.

It seemed the most natural thing in the world to close the gap between them and brush a careful, gentle kiss over her lips.

Her mouth opened with an "Oh," and as it did so, his tongue slipped inside as if someone else was directing it. She tasted sweet and tangy, and as enticing as her perfume. Her tongue curved over and around his, matching his soft exploration.

He smothered the sound of desire that the kiss drew from him against her lips, his arms going around her as if he did it every day.

And that movement, that movement, which had happened without a thought, without a decision, stopped him dead.

He never, ever, went with instinct alone.

20

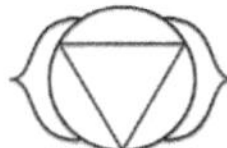

Several hours later, Blaize lay on the sofa in her living room, a blanket draped over her, and everything she needed within reach. The spring rain had returned, and she was glad she had made it back to the cosy cottage before it had started or she felt sure Tierra would have kept her in the main house overnight. As it was, Blaize had strict instructions to call if she felt unwell in any way.

She wasn't certain if she felt unwell exactly, but she certainly didn't feel like herself. In fact, all aspects of her were tired—mental, physical, energetic, and emotional. Her hand strayed to her mouth, touching her lips gently. As gently as Cuinn's kiss had begun.

Why had he stopped? He'd moved his hand to cradle her skull and pressed her closer to him. She had felt as if she might combust at any moment, the adrenaline melting the headache she'd been fighting. But she'd felt him falter. He'd rested her head back on his chest.

Tierra had found them soon after when she returned with a cup of spicy herbal tea sweetened with honey, and, Blaize suspected, brandy and healing energy.

Tierra had looked at them with her head tilted and her eyes narrowed. She'd tapped her bottom lip with her fingers. Blaize felt her cheeks heat as she wondered if Tierra had realised what they had been doing moments before she returned.

Blaize really hoped not.

Cuinn wouldn't think about Blaize.

He'd gone with instinct, something he never, ever did. He was a thinker—a decision-making style perfectly aligned with his energy. Every choice he made, every action he took, was planned and considered. And that kiss had definitely not been in the plan. Any plan.

It had been a bad idea to agree to another Adherent. Today was a reminder of the terrible events that had happened last time he took on an Adherent.

He went to the library and pulled out a heap of books that might have references to something trying to come through when an energetic pulled energy. What had it been? And had it been connected either to his farseeing of Blaize dying, or to the prophecies in general? So many questions and so few answers.

He worked late into the evening, sorting his way through books with very little to show for it. He needed to go back into the dreamscape himself to see if he could find any trace of the presence that had tried to invade Blaize's dreamscape. But if he was going to track it, he needed access to Blaize's Haven, and he needed her for that.

It was already late, and she needed the rest. He'd put it off until tomorrow. He sat in his chair by the window, and looked out into the dark, wet night. He needed the time too.

He needed to distance himself from that damn kiss.

C H A P T E R

21

Indigo hummed as she walked around her Haven. A fairytale castle, it glittered and shone. Her Haven was her most precious, safe place. A place where she could have whatever she wanted, and do whatever she wanted. Where she was free. A huge four-poster bed sat in one corner, a dressing table fit for a princess against a wall. She had a closet full of clothes, and more possessions here than any girl could need. Not to mention the room full of weapons.

She curled up on a window seat in the castle and played with the crystals hanging down from one of the lamps. She watched the light dance as it hit each individual drop. It had been satisfying to attack Blaize in the ether. She'd been waiting for days for Cuinn to take that bitch into the dreamscape. She couldn't understand why he'd waited so long. But her own slivers of the prophecy had told her that a chance would come if she was patient, so she'd waited.

And Indigo had nearly had her. She wasn't sure why she hadn't been able to destroy Blaize. Take her. The bitch was untrained and shouldn't have been able to fight Indigo off. Twice now, once on the human plane, and now on the etheric plane.

I'm a Practitioner. She's not even an Adherent. She shrugged the thought off. She'd get her eventually. She'd seen it. She'd have her here, in this very room. Indigo looked across the wide expanse of the main room of her Haven. At the heart of her castle a chair sat in the middle of the space, chains neatly stacked underneath it. Ready.

There was a brief ripple in the energy of her Haven, and she looked up, her muscles tensing. There was only one person who could get in here without Indigo providing a bridge. Only one person she'd introduced to her safe space. She cowered in the window. She pressed herself into the cushion, pulled her legs into her body and hugged them tight.

The energetic locks and chains that Indigo had created fell away from the door and the tall, elegant man came through.

"Indigo, my dear. How are you?" His voice was a pleasant baritone that caused shivers down her spine.

"Fine. Just fine." She didn't want to upset him. Say the wrong thing. But it was so easy to say the wrong thing with him. In fact, it was hard to say the right thing.

"You failed to capture Blaize."

She stifled a whimper. "Yes. But I will. The prophecies say I will. It's just a matter of time."

She wanted his approval. Wanted him to think she'd done well.

"Indigo, didn't I train you better than that? You learned that the future is fluid, pliable, in your Adherent training. A prophecy is seen, the most likely of futures, but not the only possible future." He walked closer, his steps light. "We must do everything we can to ensure that our version of the future wins out. I want Blaize here in your Haven before the month is out. She must be destroyed; Cuinn damaged."

She nodded. Her back was against the window now. There was nowhere to go. He was still coming closer. He was unpredictable. Would he hurt her? Or help her? She was tired. Energy low. He could help with that. *But will he?*

The sparkles in the room had dimmed. Her beautiful knickknacks dulled and discoloured in his wake. It amused him to tarnish some of her glitters when he came in. It always took her days to clean them again.

He was standing in front of her now. She looked up at his clean-cut jaw, his kind face. Should she stand up? She couldn't. He was blocking her way.

"We will. I will. She'll be here before the month is out," said Indigo, the words falling from her lips like a mouthful of bad food.

"Hmm," said the man. "Because bad girls get punished, but good girls get rewarded. Don't they, Indigo?"

She nodded.

"Should you be rewarded or punished, I wonder?" His hand rubbed his chin.

She closed her eyes. It was a trick. It was always a trick. Whichever she said, he'd punish her. *I don't want to be punished.* She hunched down, trying to make herself as small as possible.

He put his hand out, and she reared back. She hit the window behind her hard, and it cracked with a loud bang. She pulled energy without thinking, repairing the damage. But she was weak and didn't have much energy to spare. Her head ached. She attempted to pull some energy from the ether. The headache grew worse.

He watched her, his mouth twitching in a smirk. "I can help."

She shook her head. *No.* His help always came at a price.

But his hand reached out, and clamped down on her shoulder. His grip bit tight, his fingers grinding against the bones. She suppressed a cry.

Energy bled from his fingers into her body. At first, it was blissful. A cooling balm. It replenished her energy and soothed the headache.

But he pushed too hard. Too much. His energy was so powerful. So strong. It began to burn. She moaned aloud. "Enough. Please."

He laughed. "Until you have Blaize here, you need this."

His energy invaded hers. She fell to the side, her body tightening into the fetal position. She looked up at him, eyes pleading for him to stop. A tear fell onto the cushions underneath her. He looked down, dispassionate.

Eons later, the pain stopped. He stepped back. She looked up at him through bleary eyes.

"That was necessary. I want you to search in the dreamscape for more of the prophecy. We need to increase what we know." He walked back towards the door.

She couldn't speak, though as the pain faded her body rallied, electrified by the energy he'd shared with her. She began to shake.

He opened the door to exit. "And you're done with the waitressing job now. Burn those bridges."

"What happened between you and Blaize yesterday when I was out of the room?" Tierra asked Cuinn as he joined her for breakfast.

He shrank down in his seat and huddled over his coffee. "Nothing."

"Ha! Don't be ridiculous. I know something happened, I just don't know what. It looked to me like you smooched. Am I right?"

Cuinn was amused enough at the word 'smooched' to sit up. "We didn't smooch. Whatever that even means. We might have ... touched lips. Briefly. Accidentally. It won't happen again."

Tierra came round the table and sat next to him. She placed her hand over his hand, which was still clutching the coffee as if his life depended on it.

"She's not Sophea, Cuinn. Sophea's gone. Blaize is strong in body and mind. And this time, the attraction isn't one-way."

"There's no attraction. And I know she's not Sophea." His words were flat, and he ignored her hand on his. "I'll give Blaize another opportunity to back out today. But if she doesn't, I'll do the binding ritual this week."

Tierra's eyebrows rose. "Really? So soon?"

"I need access to her Haven in order to find out what happened yesterday."

"Cuinn! You can't do a binding that could last for years just for research! You know this is a lasting commitment—you can't go into it half-heartedly."

"I know." He sighed. "It's not that. I can protect her better if we're bound. And I'm not half-hearted. I've spent most of the night thinking about it. I can see she's strong, Tierra. But the energy that knocked her out yesterday, it was … malevolent. Nasty. And I have no idea what it was. If we perform the binding, we'll have access to each other's Havens, and I can protect hers with wards as strong as mine. Nothing will be able to touch her."

"But you're going to give her the chance to back out."

He nodded.

"You know she won't. She's too proud. She doesn't have that aspect of Manipura fully under control yet."

He shrugged. "I can't force her either way. It will be her decision. But our energy recognised each other yesterday. And I have a … feeling about this. I'm worried about her now, as well as the prophecy."

Tierra flinched. "What do you mean? Have you seen Blaize in your dreamscape? Is she involved in the prophecy?"

He still didn't want to tell her. He might have made a mistake. Tierra would only worry. He hedged. "Maybe. I don't know. I still don't have enough information. But it's hard to believe that whatever happened yesterday isn't connected in some way."

"I agree. But Blaize doesn't understand what she's signing up for. You need to tell her more about what's going on. All the details." She rose. "I'll check on her. I'm not sure she'll be up to lessons today."

"That's fine. I need to do more research anyway. I just wish I had more to go on."

"Is there anything else I can do?"

"I don't think so." He stood and engulfed his cousin in a long hug. "Thanks. I'll let you know if you can do more. For now, looking after Blaize helps."

She hugged him back. "I love you, cuz."

I'm lucky. Even with all that's going on, I am lucky.

And I'd do well to remember that.

Blaize had woken several times in the night, each time coming to from some kind of weird dream. In every one, there was some reason to pull energy, to pull power, and each time, she had resisted—but then the dream ended badly for her. She fell from great heights, was hit by cars, drowned, and had been bitten by a poisonous snake. When she woke up at dawn, she felt just as tired as when she'd gone to bed.

An hour or two later, Tierra knocked on the front door and came in. She put her hands on Blaize's shoulders and assessed her. "Did you sleep?"

Blaize nodded.

"Just not very well. A lot of bad dreams." Blaize tried to shrug it off. "Want some tea?"

Tierra's mouth twisted in sympathy. "I'm sorry, love. What were they about?"

After a long exhalation, Blaize said, "I think something is trying to get me to use my power. I keep being sent dreams where people I love are put in danger, and a voice I don't know tells me that all I need to do is use my power, my energy, to save them. And I feel if I draw on my energy, then something bad will happen. I don't know why I don't just use power to stop it—after all, it's not really pulling power in a dream, is it?"

Tierra was frowning and biting her lip. "Your auxiliary is Ajna, and sometimes those who have Ajna as one of their energies can make things happen in dreams. It's just another version of the dreamscape. We need to tell Cuinn about this urgently. It's bound to be connected to what happened between you yesterday."

For an embarrassing moment Blaize thought she meant Cuinn's kiss, which showed just how off her game she was. Heat touched her cheeks and she turned to the kettle to pour hot water over a tea bag.

She spoke over her shoulder. "You think? I just assumed that yesterday was because I wasn't very experienced."

"What did Cuinn tell you happened?" asked Tierra.

Blaize brought the cup of tea over to the sofa where Tierra was perched and sat at the opposite end, her legs curled under her, the tea on a table beside her.

"I'm not sure. Something about me pulling power too strongly? I don't really remember." She avoided Tierra's eyes as she said this last, her hands worrying at the edges of a cushion.

Tierra frowned. "The two of you need to have a proper conversation. Considering what's going on, there are some important gaps in your education."

Tierra leaned forward. "I understand why Cuinn's doing it this way, to help give you the choice about whether you want to enter into a Maven-Adherent relationship. But I don't think it's helping."

Blaize thought that the slow speed of their relationship was more a result of Cuinn's reluctance to take her on as an Adherent than him protecting her from making a bad choice.

"By taking you into the dreamscape yesterday without the two of you being bonded, he opened you up to danger. Did he tell you that?"

"No." There had been no suggestion of concern as they'd been working together. Had he really been trying to protect her? *I hate it when people do that.* A trickle of annoyance ran through her.

"The risk was low but still, as a beginner you had no idea how to ward yourself on that plane, and without being properly bound, it would have been harder for him to protect you. And as you saw, split seconds in the dreamscape can make a big difference."

Tierra got to her feet. "Leave the tea. I'll make you something in the main house, but you need to come with me. It's time for you and Cuinn to talk. Really talk."

C H A P T E R

22

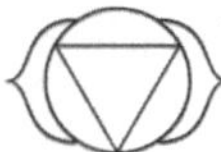

Cuinn was in the library, books strewn about him. He'd moved to the floor so he could spread the books out in a bigger space, and the room looked unlike its usual tidy self.

Tierra barged through the door. "You and Blaize need to have that talk earlier than planned. There've been some new developments."

Cuinn glanced at the door behind her, which had bounced on its hinges, and then looked up at Tierra's serious face. "What? Why? Is Blaize okay?"

"She's fine, for now. Come down to the kitchen, and the two of you can share your secrets." She started walking back down the hallway. "There's hot chocolate on the stove if you want some."

Cuinn scrambled to his feet, trying not to dislodge the piles of books with their many bookmarks. *What now?*

When he strode into the kitchen, Tierra was already at the stove stirring a fragrant liquid that he assumed was hot chocolate. But his attention was drawn to Blaize, who was sitting in a chair at the big wooden kitchen table, her gaze focused down, and her hands wrapped around a glass of water.

When her eyes rose to meet his, he saw that the green was faded, and the colour of her hair was in sharp contrast to her pale skin. She had been so vibrant when she'd arrived. She had still had some colour from the Thai sun, and her spirit had been so alive.

Now she looked drained.

"What's happened? What secrets do you need to tell me?"

"I think you should start with a few of yours first." Tierra's tone dripped disapproval as she brought mugs, the pan, and a ladle over to the table. "You should have been clearer with Blaize about what taking her into the dreamscape yesterday actually meant."

"I didn't want to inhibit her. She's a natural." Tierra's impassive face made him shift his weight on the chair. He stared down at the floor. "I wanted to see what we could do in that session. The danger was minimal."

"And yet," said Tierra.

Harder to argue against that. He met Blaize's gaze. "I'm sorry Blaize. I had no idea there would be any danger."

He couldn't tell what she was thinking and he didn't like it.

"She's right, you should have told me. I make my own decisions; I don't like to have those choices taken out of my hands." Her tone was even though dulled with fatigue. Had the experience the day before taken so much out of her?

"I wanted to see whether our energies were compatible before we did anything rash and went through a binding ceremony that's almost impossible to undo. It might have been years before your own energy was strong enough to release from mine."

"Don't make this about me, Cuinn." A little of the fire was back in Blaize's eyes, and he took a perverse pleasure in seeing it there, even at his expense. "You haven't wanted me here from the start, you've made that clear. I just wish I knew what I'd done to deserve that kind of reaction."

Cuinn stayed silent, not ready to give up all his secrets. But Tierra rapped his hand with a teaspoon. He jerked. "Ouch."

She stared at him, her usual good-natured gaze now a steely glare. *Damn.*

"It's not all about you, Blaize. I had a … bad experience with my last Adherent." The words were hard to say. What was she going to think of him when she knew the truth? He hadn't exactly made a sterling impression so far. This might be the last nail in the coffin.

Blaize's arms were crossed, and she leaned towards him, waiting.

"My last Adherent, Sophea, was a Vishudha-Ajna mix. She was a bit … um, otherworldly. I wasn't used to her combination of energies. My Muladhara keeps me grounded most of the time despite my Ajna. With her Vishudha, the element of ether, of space, combined with the Ajna, she was very abstract. She loved to talk about the concepts and ideas of energies. She loved learning, knowledge. We had some fascinating discussions."

He paused again, his throat congested as he forced the words out. "What I didn't realise was that she was falling in love with me."

Blaize was getting some colour back in her cheeks.

"Sophea had been here about a year. One night, we were alone in my rooms, which wasn't uncommon. We'd been discussing a particular aspect of the dreamscape, she wanted us to go there to experiment with the theory I'd been teaching her about. It was late, and we were both tired, but her enthusiasm was infectious." He rubbed his face with his hands, feeling that same tiredness now. He put his hands around the mug of hot chocolate that Tierra had passed to him, and gripped it as if it tethered him to the earth. "She'd been planning it for a long time. She'd created a special room within her own Haven, a bedroom I'd never seen. She'd scattered flowers and lit candles. When we reached her Haven, she took me there. And then she tried to seduce me."

Blaize held his eyes, but she was very still. He couldn't read her. *What is she thinking?* This was his darkest secret. It had coloured everything— everything—in the last fifty years of his life. He felt cold.

"I didn't react well. I hadn't seen it coming, I'd had no idea she felt that way. I didn't see her as a romantic or sexual partner. And she saw it on my face. She slammed her defences in place against me and took me enough by surprise that I was thrown back to the physical world."

Cuinn didn't look at Tierra, who knew this story as well as he did. Even after decades, her face would still show supportive sympathy. She'd been one of the rocks in his life since the tragedy of Sophea, and without her practical help, looking after him and forcing him to eat and live a normal life, he would also have been lost. But he didn't deserve her sympathy.

"I waited for her to come back. Our mats were side by side and hers was as powerfully warded as mine. She was a strong energetic and knew what she was doing."

He fell silent, unsure if he could bear to tell the story's ending.

Minutes passed like eons.

"What happened?" Blaize whispered.

"She lay on her mat, face peaceful, and I paced around my study, waiting. I was agitated and didn't want to go back to the astral world immediately in that mood." His fingers twining and untwining as he repeatedly rubbed his hands together, the agitation of that night echoed here.

"After an hour, I returned to the dreamscape to find her. I wanted to talk about what had happened. I went back to my own Haven and tried to get across to hers. When you complete an Ajna binding ritual, your Havens are linked and you can move between them." He shook his head. "She'd managed to block me. I don't know how—I'm very powerful. But I couldn't get to her. It was as if her Haven had become untethered from mine, lost."

"What do you mean?"

"She never returned. Her body remained as she had left it, essentially in a coma. But her mind was lost somewhere in the astral realm. Her mind had become untethered from her body, and she either couldn't, or wouldn't, return."

Blaize's eyes were wide, and she hugged herself tightly, her arms wrapped around her body. "That can happen?"

"Of course. It's one of the reasons why we spend so much time training and why the binding is so important, because even if your Haven becomes untethered from your own body, your Maven can find you and bring you back. She shouldn't have been able to sever the connection between our Havens. I still don't know how she did it."

"Where is she now?"

"She's in a Rogue rehabilitation centre on an island to the west of Canada. Tierra's friend Cara works there and gives me updates. And I go and see her when I can. I still hope …"

"You think she might come back?"

"It's possible." He glanced away as he said it.

"Is it … likely?"

"Possible is enough. And if she does come back, I'll be there. Sometimes I look for her in the dreamscape. Our paths might cross. It's feasible." His head dropped. He'd had hope at the beginning, fifty years ago, but while he said the words, he no longer felt them. But he couldn't let her go.

Her body, still youthful as energetics aged so slowly, lay as if in stasis in the rehabilitation facility, hooked up to machines to help her eat and expel waste. And she could stay like that for hundreds of years. It was a terrible fate for an energetic. His stomach curled inside him.

"So, now you know my darkest secret. I killed my last Adherent."

Blaize's fatigue had lessened as she'd heard Cuinn's tragic story. And her heart had wrenched for both Cuinn and for the young woman who had tried to give him her love.

Energetics lived a long time, but tended not to talk about their past, living with the mantra of 'live for the now.' It wasn't that the past was taboo, it just wasn't seen as relevant or necessary, and it helped to iron out sometimes huge age gaps between energetics, who lived, worked, and loved together.

Blaize, who'd studied psychology for her undergraduate degree, wasn't so sure that it was possible to always live in the now. Here was a case in point. In this case, Cuinn's past explained a lot of his reactions to her over the last week or so. Including why he'd pulled away from their kiss, and why he had seemed so against having her as an Adherent. It had nothing to do with her personally, and everything to do with him. And Sophea.

"You didn't kill her, Cuinn." Her voice was sharper than she meant it to be.

He took a small sip of his hot chocolate.

"What happened was terrible, but it wasn't your fault. Sophea made her own choices." Immature choices, from Blaize's point of view, but she knew love could affect people in different ways. Most of them bad. Another good reason to avoid it.

"I looked for her for months afterwards. I spent all the time I could in the dreamscape trying to find a trace of her. But it's an infinite place. I could look forever and not find her." She had to strain to hear him. "Your uncle, Marius, helped me keep my sanity when I thought I would go under. And Adam and Tierra's earth energy kept me grounded and made sure I didn't disappear. But I was tempted at times."

Tierra got up and stood behind him. She put her arms around him and rested her face on his shoulder. "Drink the hot chocolate."

Blaize shook her head. "I'm not her. Manipura energy is very different from Vishudha. The only similarity between us is that we're both your Adherents, and we both have Ajna as an auxiliary energy. That's it. Right?"

Blaize turned to include Tierra in her appeal.

"Yes, love. You're very different." Tierra lifted her head from Cuinn's shoulder and sat at the table between them. "And Cuinn, you think you're the same person as you were then, but you're different too. But you should have prepared Blaize better for the dreamwalk yesterday."

Cuinn half-shrugged, and he leaned heavily on the table.

"I told you both, I thought it would be easier if Blaize approached it naturally. She's powerful, and gifted. I didn't expect her to create her own Haven so easily. I'm sorry, Blaize. You don't want to be my Adherent. It's not safe. I'm not safe."

That was practically a compliment. Tied up in a rejection. "I can make my own decisions. But only when I'm given all the information."

She was almost too tired to be angry, but there was a spark to her words. She hated being kept in the dark.

Tierra nodded briskly. "I agree. And Blaize, you need to tell Cuinn about your dreams. No more secrets on either side."

"This wasn't a secret," Blaize protested. "It's only just happened."

"Tell me," commanded Cuinn, a touch of imperiousness back in his words.

The room was dark, and when Blaize glanced out the skies outside were overcast, heavy with the promise of rain. She got up and flicked the switch on the lamp in the corner of the room. It cast a gentle light over the three of them, and the room instantly became cosier.

She took a breath as she sat back down, waiting a beat before she launched into a fast and concise retelling of her dreams. Tierra listened more calmly this time, but Cuinn's face had the same look of concern Tierra had shown on the first telling.

"Why didn't you tell me earlier?" He was no longer slumped.

Her eyebrows rose. "Earlier when? In the middle of the night? Four a.m. when I woke up the second time? I thought they were just nightmares. I was hardly going to get you out of bed for a bad dream. When another one came this morning I told Tierra, and here we are." There was something going on here. *Why is he so bothered about a bad dream?*

"How do you feel now?" Cuinn's tone was gruff.

"Fine thanks." She crossed her arms over her chest again. "Apart from the lack of sleep and the sense of impending doom."

Tierra subdued a smile as she put a hand out to touch each of them. "Relax, both of you."

Blaize let out a shaky breath. "Okay, I'm sorry, Cuinn. Let's start again. For some reason, you wind me up the wrong way. But if you could try to remember that a) this isn't my fault as far as we know, and b) I'm doing my best here, I'd appreciate it."

She looked across the table into eyes that echoed the grey of the sky outside. They met hers, and for a moment, all three of them were still. Connected. Energy shivered through them, balm on physical and emotional hurts. Tierra removed her hand, and Cuinn moved his gaze to hers. "Thank you."

She nodded. "I know you don't love me using energy on you, but the two of you need to calm down. Neither of you has had much sleep recently, and as I've said, we all make bad decisions when we're sleep-deprived. You're on the same side. Really."

The energy Cuinn had shown as she'd told him about her dreams had gone. His usually upright spine was bent, and his gaze was on something unseen out of the window. He shook his head, and looked back at her. "I'm sorry, Blaize. There's so much going on here. And I need to tell you something else."

He described the newest slivers of prophecy he'd collected. About seeing her injured and restrained. How he'd recognised her in the group of energetics who stood with him in the first glimpses of the prophecy.

She couldn't believe this. She'd been there for days, and he'd said nothing. Her body felt as taut as a violin string. *How many more secrets were there?* "You should have told me earlier."

"I know."

"If you had told me before, I'd have come straight to you with the dreams. Source, I'd have woken you at four a.m."

"I know."

She stood and paced around the kitchen. She felt sick. He'd seen her brutally beaten, but perhaps also ready to save their world. How was she supposed to handle all that?

He sat quietly, watching her. After a few agitated minutes, she put her hands on the back of the wooden kitchen chair she'd been sitting on and stared into his eyes again. "No more secrets, Cuinn. Seriously. No more. You have to tell me everything. Is there anything else?"

Cuinn and Tierra exchanged a glance. Tierra's look seemed pointed.

"My Guild Leaders told me I needed to work with you. That my future and yours are bound up together. That I would need you."

Blaize felt overloaded by all the information. She wanted to stomp around, to smash things. More, she wanted to break something over his pigheaded skull. Some of the most powerful farseers in the energetics race had told him their futures were linked, and still he fought taking her as an Adherent?

Tierra rose and gave Blaize a quick hug. "That's everything. Why don't you help me prepare some lunch, and we can talk about it more when we've all had some food? You—both—need time to process this morning."

Blaize wasn't sure that preparing food was going to help in terms of saving the world, but she'd use the break and be grateful for it. She felt frazzled from the intensity of the emotions in the room. She put a hand up to rub her temples, to soothe the headache she could feel lurking.

"I agree." Cuinn pushed his own chair back from the table and got up.

Tierra stepped in front of him as he moved towards the door to the corridor. "I don't think you should go back to your room, Cuinn. You need to replenish your connection to the earth. Go outside and walk for an hour while Blaize and I cook."

He gave her a cool look, but he went to the utility room and grabbed his jacket. "Fine. But if it rains and I catch cold, I'm blaming you."

23

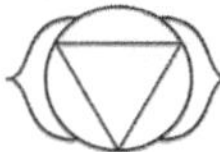

"Talk to me," Tierra said to Blaize once Cuinn had left.

"I feel … a bit blank. It's hard to imagine featuring in a prophecy. My only —" Blaize fumbled for the word "— experience with them has been negative."

Tierra tilted her head a fraction, eyebrows furrowed. "What do you mean?"

Blaize so did not want to go there. She was already raw from the last hour. She wondered whether she would get away with a diversion, but Tierra stayed silent. Expectant.

This was a dark part of Blaize's past, and one she rarely discussed. But she wanted to explain her strong reaction to Cuinn's latest information. She hadn't thought about the connection between Ajna and prophecy when she'd been told she was to start training, but it seemed there was no getting away from it as a part of the Ajna energies. She'd keep it brief.

"My parents were given a prophecy when they were married. It hinted at what eventually did happen. They ignored it. And they both died." Blaize kept a tight rein on the emotions that bringing the topic up raised. She was proud there was no break, no hitch in her voice. *It was a long time ago. I barely knew them.*

"I didn't realise." Tierra's voice held anguish. "You need to tell Cuinn that. This situation is bad enough, but both of you are carrying a lot of baggage from your past. You need to share everything and get past that."

Blaize nodded and let out a breath, trying to relax but stay in control.

"Is Sophea why I hadn't heard of Cuinn? Now I'm here, he seems as powerful as any of the Master energetics I've met, but I didn't know who he was before Fai told me about him. Yet I know all thirty of the Minor Circle's names, even if I haven't met them."

Blaize traced patterns on the table as she thought aloud. She had a lot of questions. "Is it because of what happened with his previous Adherent?"

"Yes, but not in the way you think." Tierra got up and went over to the kitchen island. She motioned for Blaize to follow her and sit at the breakfast bar. "Cuinn's always been involved in Circle business. He would have been a good choice for his Minor Guild's Circle seat when the last energetic who held it passed away. Many energetics in his Guild—and outside—were keen for him to take it, but since Sophea, he's resolutely refused any formal position. He'll help out based on his sense of duty, but he doesn't trust himself to be in a position of responsibility."

Tierra brought over a bag of potatoes and a peeler. "I hoped you could help him move past that. By taking on a new Adherent, a new responsibility, he would regain the confidence he lost. It was a big deal for him to agree to take a new Adherent, and to be honest, we—Adam and I, and some of his other friends—pushed him into it when the opportunity arose. He has so much to offer. And as I told you at the start, he's a good person who's lost his way."

Tierra hesitated for a moment. "And as you'll have understood from the story about Sophea, he's also not that great with women. Sometimes his book smarts get in the way of his people smarts."

Blaize rubbed her face to hide her blush. When she thought the colour had died down again, she took out a potato and began to peel it, concentrating on the task as if it was brain surgery. "Cuinn and I still have some talking to do, I guess. And we should perform the binding ritual as quickly as possible."

"Really?" Tierra looked surprised.

"Our energies work together, and there's danger ahead—not just for us, but for the whole energetic race. I've trained to be a Warrior, Tierra. It would go against everything I've trained for up to now to back off because of the personal consequences." And in saying that, Blaize felt a kind of peace settle over her. She was someone who liked to have a goal, and the more stretching the better. This definitely fitted the bill. Maybe she'd be able to use her Manipura training sooner than she'd thought. "But I need to start physical training again. Will you open up the gym for me after lunch?"

"Of course. But are you sure about the binding?"

"Yes." And the simple word resonated with the total confidence of a Manipura Warrior.

Cuinn spent an hour walking his land and renewing his connection with the earth. The day had remained dry despite the clouds above. He moved through the woods, smelling the damp, peaty earth, and paused in a clearing bathed in one of the few patches of sunshine he'd seen that day. He sat on a fallen log, closed his eyes and leaned back on his hands, the rough bark digging into his thighs, grounding him.

Tierra had been right, he'd come almost to the end of his resources. And while he could see that the secrets he'd been keeping from Blaize needed to be shared, exposing himself like that had been one of the hardest things he'd done in years. He couldn't bear to see the condemnation in her eyes. Or worse, pity.

But when he'd been brave enough to look at her, he hadn't seen either. He'd seen empathy. Compassion for the man he'd been, and acceptance of the man he was now.

Blaize was also unsettled, and he didn't blame her. Her dreams were worrying, along with her sense that she shouldn't draw on her power—which had persisted after the dreams had ended.

He had just told her about a prophecy where she was terribly injured. That tended to put a crimp on someone's day. He hadn't been able to bring himself to tell her he'd seen her die. That wasn't keeping a secret; it was holding a little something back. Something that might have pushed her past her reserves.

Should we go ahead with the binding? He wasn't right to be a Maven. His arrogance and ignorance had caused the last tragedy. And if he was honest with himself, really honest, his feelings for Blaize had become—complicated.

He hadn't allowed himself to think about the kiss until now. He'd taken advantage of her when she was barely in her right mind after being thrown from the etheric plane by Source knows what. He groaned. *What an idiot.*

He couldn't repeat the strange behaviour, the impulse that had overtaken him. She was desirable, an attractive woman, but he could control himself better than that.

Anyway, it had probably just been his own stress reaction to seeing her lying on the floor, bleeding. He'd been terrified. When she'd come around, his relief had been so great, it had translated into the kiss. In fact, when he thought of it like that it was almost as if he had hugged her. Sort of like a sister.

But he then thought, ashamed, of the reaction of his body. The lascivious heat that had spread through him like honey as he'd kissed her. Heat that was firmly centred around his groin. That hadn't been the way he reacted to female family members—in fact, it wasn't the way he reacted to women at all these days.

He wasn't a man who went in for brief, uncomplicated sexual relationships. But right now, he wished he did. A night of healthy sex with a woman who had the same understanding might have gotten rid of these complicated feelings he had for Blaize.

His body reacted to the thought of Blaize and sex in the same sentence with its own opinion, his cock throbbing, and he adjusted his pants. It seemed that some parts of him were quite strongly in favour of the concept.

He groaned again.

This wasn't helping. He and Blaize couldn't get involved sexually; it would just complicate things further. The feelings would probably fade as they got used to each other.

He'd just take plenty of cold showers until they did.

Blaize and Cuinn helped Tierra set the table, then sat to eat.

"I have one more secret. Well, not so much a secret, as something I didn't think was relevant." Blaize took some salad and passed the bowl to Cuinn. "But Tierra thinks I should lay out all the pieces for you."

He nodded and added a veggie burger to his plate.

"My parents." She stopped.

"I know what happened to your parents, Blaize." He bit into his burger.

"Yeah. I guess the story got around." She flared for a moment, angry. She gritted her teeth and stabbed at a potato. "There's more that not many people know. And I'd like to share the whole story with you."

"You don't have to. And I know because of my friendship with Marius, nothing more."

She shrugged. "If we're going to be bound, you need to know it all. It's the last secret. I think, anyway."

"And are we?" He'd stopped eating, his eyebrows high. Her anger died as she saw that he had been genuine about his offer to release her from their agreement to be Maven-Adherent.

"Yes. It's the right thing to do. If I—we—can help to protect our whole race, why wouldn't we?"

"You have the right to say no."

"I know. I'm making a choice, don't worry. But you'd better help me train as quickly as possible so I can protect myself. I'm a Warrior—I don't like it when others have to protect me." She really hadn't liked the experience in the alley. She was proud—justifiably—of her fighting abilities. To be beaten like that had been a difficult experience. She needed to know how to beat Indigo when she next came up against her. To bring her in so she couldn't do that to anyone else.

"You have a great deal of Ajna power. I could sense it when we were in your Haven. It won't be long before you're able to create barriers and protect yourself with energetic wardings." He leaned in towards her, sketching walls in the air with his hands. "But, you can still change your mind. We'll provisionally schedule the ritual for a couple of days' time. But promise me you'll sleep on it. You can still back out. It's not something to be taken lightly."

"Fine by me. But the answer will be the same." She took her own small forkful of food. Her stomach felt tight, knotted. She chewed. She would learn. And she would take Indigo down.

Tierra put another spoonful of fried potatoes on Cuinn's plate. "Eat."

He did so, digging into them. "This is great."

Tierra nodded. "Blaize, love, carry on."

Blaize drew in a deep breath and put her own knife and fork down. "My parents ... my parents were Aria McCarthy and Aden Blackfire. A couple very much in love. Eyes only for each other, they were together many decades before they had me."

She shifted in her chair. "When I was nine, my mother went on retreat as she did most years. I was left with her brother, Marius, and my father. One night, I overheard them arguing, and my father stormed out. That was the last time I saw him."

These were her blackest memories. She'd had a good childhood, before and eventually after this. But this tragedy still incited her anger. She just didn't know how her father's energy could have twisted so badly. That he could have committed those terrible actions.

And whether that potential is in me, too.

"Later, Marius told me what happened," she said. "My father's jealousy had got out of control. He'd made up his mind that my mother wasn't on retreat, but with a lover. He left the house to find her and bring her back to where she belonged, with him."

Her pulse sped a little. *Breathe.*

"Without her Anahata energy to ground him, his energy overpowered him, and he went Rogue. He found her on her retreat, alone, as she'd said she would be." Another breath. "A few days later, Marius found the two of them, dead."

"I'm so sorry, Blaize," Tierra murmured.

"None of this is the point." Blaize pushed her chair out and stood, adrenaline washing around her body as if she was about to defend herself to the death. *I want to run. To move. Or to fight.* "I'm telling you this because before they were married, a Seer gave them a personal prophecy that not many people are aware of. The prophecy said their marriage was likely to be the source of both great good and great harm. That they would suffer, but that that suffering would bring about a greater positive change in the world. That they still had a choice as to whether or not they married, but the odds weren't in their personal favour. And that a man would come between them in some way.

"My Father, never that interested in Seers, ignored it, but my mother felt the greater good was worth her suffering, and felt her love for my father would be enough. But, as is often the way with prophecies, the seed planted by the Seer that a man would come between them stayed with my father. Eventually, it was what tipped him into a Rogue state. He was convinced that there was a man. But in fact, the words just meant that the idea of a man would come between them. There was no man."

She walked over to the back door and threw it open. She stood in the cold draft, breathing deeply.

"So I'm not sure how I feel about prophecies. They caused a lot of damage in my own life. And destroyed my parents. They're twisty things. Slippery, hard to pin down, and cause as much harm as good."

Silence.

"I'm sorry, Blaize. I had never heard about the prophecy." Cuinn looked at her with compassion. She rubbed her arms and blamed the cold air for the fact that her body was shaking. She held her elbows and looked away from the cosy scene inside the kitchen. She had a feeling none of them would eat much this evening.

"Thankfully, Marius and Fai adopted me into their family without question and always showed me just as much love as they showed Nixie, their own daughter, and my cousin. You'd love her, Tierra. A gorgeous spirit." She smiled briefly. "And so here we are. With me still wondering, thirty or so years later, what exactly the greater good was that came out of their deaths. Because it all seemed pretty senseless." She took one hand away from her body, and gestured, palm down. Tiny sparks flew from her hand, her energy making its presence known. She felt a sense of unease and spooled the power tightly inside her. She hadn't shaken off the dreams yet, and she wasn't ready to use her power.

"You can never know." Cuinn's words were quiet but gentle. "The butterfly effect is a simplistic idea that explains something very complicated—how one tiny action can leave traces on all kinds of other things. It's hard to know what the greater good might have been—it could have been something small that affected many people, or perhaps it's still to come."

He and Tierra exchanged a thoughtful look, which Blaize caught as she turned back into the kitchen, no longer shaking, some of her adrenaline burned away. "Yeah. Grandmother thought that I must be the greater good. It's one of the reasons she wanted me trained to be a Guild Leader. But it seems pretty unlikely to me."

C H A P T E R

25

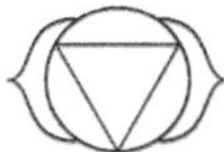

Later that afternoon Cuinn went down to the gym to see what Blaize was doing. She was trained as a Manipura Warrior, and he wanted to see her in action.

He told himself it was to see what her skills were like, and whether she might be able to translate some of them into the dreamscape. *Yeah, right.* The thought of that strong, toned body had intruded one too many times on his consciousness in the last few days.

He pushed the door to the gym and it opened smoothly, letting a little of the stale air-conditioned air out. He felt the temperature drop as he moved into the space. The sound changed too. The underground gym was soundproofed, and opening the door let out a blast of some kind of alternative rock, high energy and angry.

Blaize pounded on the heavy bag with a number of sharp elbow strikes and punches that looked like some kind of martial art.

Dressed in a black and red sports bra and some kind of tight workout pants that came half-way between her ankle and knee, she moved like danger. Her power was sleek and deadly, and she flew through the moves in a blur. It was a completely different side to her.

He thought she hadn't noticed him, but after a few minutes of watching her, fire in motion, she stopped. She wiped the sweat from her face with a small towel and turned to him. Her mouth moved, but he couldn't make out what she said over the music.

But even if he had, he wasn't sure if he'd have been able to answer. He'd only seen her back as she had been facing the bag up to now. Getting a front-view of her in her workout clothes had given him a punch that was just as effective as any she'd given the bag.

She dripped with sweat, her flame-red hair slicked back in a rough pony tail, and her workout gear showing off every curve on her lean body. He was transfixed. She stepped closer to him, and he wanted to pull her towards him by her hips and press her up against the door behind him.

He was still possessed by the idea when she waved a hand in front of his face in puzzlement. "Cuinn?"

He had an image of pushing the sports bra up and licking the sweat off her stomach and breasts. *Where the hell did that come from?* He shook his head and turned away from Blaize. He reached for the music volume knob on the wall behind him.

His cheeks hot, he turned back to her and pushed his hand through his hair.

"Is everything okay?" Blaize held the towel in one hand and her water bottle in the other. "Did you need something?"

"I just came … to check that you were alright."

Blaize's frown deepened, and she touched the base of her neck. That drew Cuinn's eyes down again to the trickle of moisture running down from her neck until he realised and snapped his eyes back up again.

"Thanks. But Tierra showed me around when she turned everything on earlier." She took a drink from the bottle and wiped her face again. "Really, are you okay?"

"I'll leave you to it." He turned quickly—and walked into the door.

"Bollocks." Luckily he'd been leading with his shoulder, so the damage wasn't too bad. He checked his arm, but it all seemed fine. Apart from the bruise he'd probably have tomorrow, as well as the gaping wound in his pride.

A muffled laugh came from behind him. "Still okay?"

"I'll be fine." *Just as soon as I get out of here.*

"Maybe you should do some exercise. You seem to be a bit off. More grounding needed?"

"Thanks. I'm fine." He turned back to face her. She was much closer than she had been. So close, in fact that they were almost touching. He could smell her, very faintly, spicy with hints of sandalwood. He looked down at her, and she put one hand up to touch his face.

"Really? Because I have to say, Cuinn, you don't seem … fine." That lilting laughter was still in her voice, and he closed his eyes for a second as skin met skin. As always, she was hot to the touch, and his whole being focused on that one spot on his cheek, his bruised shoulder forgotten.

When he opened his eyes again, her other hand moved up to his face, and before he could form any words, she'd drawn him down to her mouth.

And then, all thought vanished. There was just sensation. Her soft lips. Her mouth, sweet and spicy at the same time. Her scent, the sandalwood much stronger now.

At first he just dipped his head as her fingers guided him, and let her lead the kiss. And then her tongue flicked out, gently insistent, and he parted his lips to give her access. Their tongues danced, coiling around each other in a heated sensual tangle.

And he lost his mind again.

He brought his arms up swiftly and pulled her in towards him. She gasped, and he took the opportunity to explore her mouth more thoroughly.

She put one arm around his waist, and rested it just above the jut of his hip, and pressed their bodies close. His hands roamed around her back, especially the damp and naked skin between the waist of her workout pants and her top.

She moaned. The sound was erotic, and he wanted to worship her, to lay her down on the floor and praise every inch with his tongue and fingers. He wanted to hear her moan again, more frequently and with renewed volume.

And just as he was considering doing exactly that, her hands swept down his back, below his hips, and he lost his reason again. But as quickly as she'd shifted them down and brushed his ass, she moved her hands again, and pushed and spun him at the same time. It left him a few feet away, dazed and confused, with her now between him and the door.

This time she didn't stifle the laugh.

"I thought I'd better help ground you. I'm going to shower now. See you at dinner." And with a grin, she blew him a kiss and disappeared through the door, leaving him staring after her.

Perhaps Cuinn was right, and Blaize needed to think more about strategy. It probably hadn't been that clever to kiss him. She was starting to think she might be quite comfortable having a sexual relationship with him without any other complications, but somehow she doubted a casual relationship would be enough for him.

And then there was the issue of Sophea. She hadn't been thinking of Sophea when she'd kissed him, and Blaize was damn sure he hadn't been either. But he was certain to afterwards. It had been one of the reasons she'd decided to eat alone this evening. That, and she thought Tierra had some kind of radar for this kind of thing, and Blaize wasn't ready to discuss it.

There had been so many confessions between her and Cuinn today that she'd barely had a chance to think about the horrible dreams of the night before. She desperately needed a good night's sleep. Maybe she should have asked Tierra for something dosed with her earth energy to help her sleep.

As if she didn't already have enough on her plate, she still felt a lingering sense of worry about using her power. The dreams had unsettled her, and the discussion with Cuinn had only heightened her anxiety. She would keep her power controlled until she'd gone through the binding ritual with Cuinn. At that point, she'd have his protection in the astral world, which was where she felt the real danger was.

But all the emotions of the day had left the energy churning inside her, stirred up by the confessions and subsequent feelings. She wanted to use it, to let it loose. *But I have more control than that.* She was impulsive, sure, but not stupid.

So tomorrow she'd go over to the house for breakfast, confirm that she was going to take part in the binding ritual, and spend the day in meditation. She wasn't sure if there was any other preparation needed; she'd have to check with Cuinn. He'd continued to be close-mouthed about the ceremony itself, but she thought that was probably due to the fact he'd thought it would be way off in the future rather than because he was keeping more secrets from her. They were beyond that now. Weren't they?

Her Manipura ritual to bind herself to Fai had been a long time ago now but she remembered it clearly. Knowing Fai so well had helped. The element of fire was about change and transformation. Fai had given Blaize instructions to bring something dear to her, something she needed to let go.

She had chosen a toy that her mother had given her, which had grown moth-eaten and ragged. At nine years old, old enough to understand that her parents weren't coming back, the big-eared bunny had been the thing she'd clung to at night in the strange house, trying to fit into a family that wasn't her own.

But by the time she was ready for the Manipura binding, and truly a part of the very happy family that was Fai, Marius and Nixie, it was time to let go of the toy. And let go she did, because as part of the ceremony Fai had required her to sacrifice it to the flames, in order to help power the energy of the binding. It had been hard. But change, courage, transformation, were all part of what she was embracing.

She wondered what, exactly, she would be embracing with the power of the mind.

26

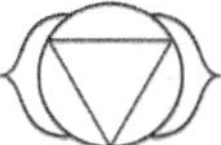

Cuinn cleaned his rooms on the physical plane, and then needed to clean the energy of the room. The space was already protected because of his work there, but he still performed a short cleansing ritual to refresh the room itself. He drew a new sacred circle and placed his and Blaize's mats in the middle. They would draw the circle together later, over the top of the work he'd already put in, strengthening its protection still further.

He also redrew the protection symbols he had at the windows and both the door to his bedroom and the door to the hall. The symbols flared in the air each time before disappearing from normal vision, though if he drew on his Ajna energy he'd be able to see them there.

When finally satisfied with how everything looked, he sat down on his own mat, ready to move to the astral plane and begin again there.

He went directly to his own Haven, the tower. Though it was heavily protected by hundreds of years of his wardings, the last few weeks had made him wary and extremely cautious.

He went down the thick stone stairs of the tower to the heavy door, using energy to redraw the wardings on this as on every other opening of the tower before heading outside.

They would enter Blaize's Haven from his own. But before that he would construct a connection, a gate between their Havens that would ensure that as part of the binding he could extend some of his own wardings to her. He looked around, considering the landscape.

His tower was surrounded by open land and plains. It was the basic protection mechanism used by his ancestors in Ireland who built their houses and castles on them so that they could see enemies approaching. But it meant he wasn't sure where to create the connection to Blaize's Haven. This connection was important because it would be a weakness in his own defences—a place someone who wanted to get into his Haven would choose, rather than other much more heavily guarded areas.

He chose a piece of land near a small stream. Just because water wasn't part of his own mix of energies, didn't mean he didn't find the sound soothing. He sat on a boulder with his back to the water, and he drew power.

He wanted to create a doorway between parts of the astral world, but a doorway that wouldn't be activated until the ceremony with Blaize. He deliberated a minute, then concentrated. Something began to grow a few yards in front of him. Two things. Two shoots came out of the grass about a yard apart. They grew steadily and swiftly until they were about six feet high. Ash trees, supple and strong. The trees bent towards each other at an unnatural angle and grew. Their branches touched with a shudder, and tiny buds exploded into a riot of leaves.

He stood, pleased with his work.

He put his hands on the trees, connected with them, and thanked them. They shivered under his touch, responsive. He curled energy around them, the power of earth and of the mind.

His many years of experience meant that he was able to use the power of both of his energies on this plane, not something everyone could do. He didn't need earth energy to do what he had just done on the astral plane. The power of the mind was enough. But enhancing it with the energy of the elements made it somehow stronger, more real.

The door was now energetically warded, if not activated. No one could use it at the moment, and even when it was opened, only he and Blaize would be able to activate it. He would make sure of that.

Blaize had also spent the day preparing. A long yoga practice in the morning, stretching her body into impossible poses, had expanded her body and mind at the same time. She'd taken it slowly, holding the poses for a long time, sinking into each one to connect to the energies it aroused, working her way through the seven Chakra energies, at the end opening herself up to Source.

These seven energies enabled life; and each of the energies brought something different to the world. All energies were present in every living thing, though only energetics were blessed to have an 'activation' of two of their Chakras.

Yoga was one way in which energetics—and humans—could get in touch with their energies, balancing all of the energies that were present within them, even those that weren't 'active.' Yoga helped to ensure an energetic was in balance, harmonious.

But only six of the energies could be active in an energetic. The seventh, the energy of Sahasara, was the energy of Source. The Crown Chakra. It was the purest of all the energies, and could only be experienced through the Grace of Source, a Grace that few experienced. Source was the energetics' name for the creator, the divine, the supreme being. The other six energies were distributed among the energetics' race much as they were through the body.

Each energetic manifested the two energies that would become their 'active' energies in childhood, mostly during puberty. For Blaize that had meant some unfortunate fires and a strong ability with puzzles. But since then, it had been Manipura that Blaize had concentrated on. Immersed herself in.

She was about to change that.

She'd spent the day preparing herself, body and mind, and she felt as ready as she thought she'd manage. It was time to focus on her Ajna for a while. She wasn't as comfortable with it as she was with her Manipura. Well, of course. She'd spent years on her Manipura, her dominant Chakra, whereas Ajna was just her auxiliary.

She walked in bare feet across the grass between her cottage and the main house. The woods and plains around her seemed hushed, everything waiting for the ritual's start.

She paused at Cuinn's door, checking herself one more time. She loved the dress that had been a present from Tierra that morning. The material was soft and gauzy, and Blaize enjoyed the way it moved around her. With her height, Blaize rarely felt delicate, but the dress had done the trick.

She knocked on Cuinn's door, and took one more deep breath. When he opened the door, they both stopped. She took him in in a rush.

He wore loose white trousers that hung from his hips, and a classic fitted white shirt that emphasised his lean, compact frame. The shirt had the three indigo stripes across his right shoulder that showed he was a Master, and a tiny embroidered symbol of an owl in royal purple thread that indicated he was a Maven. He was freshly shaved and his hair was tied back neatly, and seemed darker than usual against all the white.

She dropped a curtsey to break the tension, her white dress pooling on the ground around her. She stood back up again with a mischievous smile. "I guess we both scrub up well then?"

"I guess so." He moved out of the way. "Come in."

His workroom had been transformed. He'd put up fairy lights, and the ritual sacred circle around their mats was beautiful. Something flickered at the corner of her eye. She squinted and caught a hint of purple at the windows. She stepped closer. "Are these warded?"

He smiled. "I strengthened the wardings today. It's a good sign that you can sense them. It means your Ajna is waking up."

He shut the door behind her, and she felt a tingle as he pulled a little more energy to protect and ward the door and seal them in. He turned back to her. "Are you ready?"

"As I'll ever be."

"Don't worry, I'll guide you through. Let's draw the circle."

He went to the small altar, took two candles, and gave one to Blaize. The room grew darker, the fairy lights growing more distinct.

"We're going to light the candles." He held up a hand as she took a breath. "Don't use your Manipura energy. Tonight you need to focus on Ajna alone."

They lit their candles from the candle he already had burning on the altar, and both blessed the ceremony in their own words, taking their time to connect to Source. They then moved to their mats, faced each other, and placed their candles in front and to the side—both the same side, his right and her left.

She was aware of her body, her every movement, her heartbeat. The anticipation was almost unbearable. There were no nerves now. Just excitement.

He took a canvas bag of rock salt that was next to the altar. "I've blessed this already. I'll cast the circle first, then you, then we'll draw it together, so we've cast it three times."

They cast the circle individually, then he took the bag of salt from her, and cupped her right hand in his. He poured salt into her hand, and steered her hand to drop salt around the circle for the third time. She shivered a little at his touch, feeling his breath on the back of her neck as they moved clockwise in the flickering candlelight.

He paused and she half turned in his arms, looking up at him. His gaze captured hers. His eyes changed from dove grey to almost charcoal, the iris blending with the pupils. She couldn't look away.

He broke her gaze and gestured down. "The mats."

She pulled away and sank down onto her mat, a puppet with the strings cut. She could still feel his arms around her, missing the feel of his skin against hers. The infuriating man really did have the strangest effect on her. She sat cross-legged, and closed her eyes. The air moved as he sat opposite.

"We have drawn the sacred circle and are protected for the night," he said formally. "Breathe deeply, and focus inside. Consider the infinite power of the mind. Centre yourself."

He fell silent, and they sat, immersing themselves in meditation. Blaize enjoyed meditating, but her mind—like most people's—had a tendency to wander. She focused as much as possible on the mind, using her breath to draw her back when she got distracted.

"Blaize Blackfire, you come to offer yourself as Adherent in the Guild of Ajna," Cuinn said in a lower tone. "Stand now as we offer our binding to the elements."

Blaize stood. His voice seemed different as it took on the power in the room. She opened her eyes. He almost seemed to shimmer in his white clothes, a commanding presence.

"Offer yourself to the North."

Blaize turned to the North. "I offer myself to the North."

"May you be blessed by the element of earth. Of strength, stability, and a strong sense of self."

At his instruction, she offered herself to each direction, and the circle itself, as he asked for a blessing from each of the elements: earth, water, fire, air, and ether.

"Thus we petition the elements to support our binding ritual." He drew in a deep breath, and there was another tingle, the air shimmering between them. "Hold out your hands."

Blaize did. They trembled ever so slightly. He took her hands and turned them over gently so both faced upwards, then crossed them so her right arm was on top of the underside of her left wrist. He turned his arms so that the palms faced down, crossed them, and grasped hers.

"Our hands join together in the sign of infinity, eternal renewal. We commit ourselves to be linked until Blaize Blackfire reaches the level of Practitioner in the Guild of Ajna."

He looked deeply into her eyes, unblinking. A heap of purple silk thread on the floor moved towards their wrists. Cuinn's gaze didn't waver from hers as he directed the thread with his energy to loop around their joined wrists, binding them. "We are bound in fact. Let us be bound in blood."

His grip on Blaize's hands tightened, and a sharp pain pricked her palms. Drops of blood fell from their joined hands.

"Our blood mingles; our energy mingles." A tingle started through her left palm, moved around her body and then through her right palm until her whole body was alive with energetic power. Goosebumps rose along her arms and she shuddered. The power was cool, and felt different from her Manipura energy.

Ajna energy.

Her left arm burned with a sudden, blinding pain. She turned her head to see an indigo Ajna mark, a band around the top of her arm, a little above her Manipura bands.

She was an Adherent on the physical plane.

"We stay bound as we move to the astral plane. Let's sit together."

They sat opposite but close to each other, their legs crossed and their hands now resting, joined, on their knees.

"Close your eyes, Blaize, and follow the sound of my voice."

She did. He talked her into the light trance she needed to get to the astral plane, taking her to his own Haven.

They stood in his tower.

"So this is your Haven?" Blaize, fascinated, drank in the scene. They were in a large airy room that, given the view out of the window, seemed to be fairly high up. "Lucky I'm not a psychologist, or the fact that your Haven is a great big tower might make me think—"

He shot her a look that was almost an eye roll, and she smiled.

"You did well to follow me here. Your Ajna energy is strong. Can you see my energy again?"

She tried to see the streams coming out of his body that she'd seen last time. It took her a little longer, as if they were at the edges of her vision, and she could only see them from the corner of her eye. But after a while, she caught the trick of it again and suddenly he was surrounded by purples. He shone with it. This was nothing like what she had seen in the village garden, in her own Haven. The streamers had become a mass.

She gasped. "Wow. There's a lot more than before."

He nodded. "Good. That's because this is my Haven—the place I created on the astral plane. It's the centre of my power on the astral plane. It's almost impossible for anyone to come here unless I want them to.

"We're going to build a connection from my Haven to yours, so you will be welcome here all the time we're bound. This will effectively be a binding on the astral plane."

"How?"

"No hesitation?"

"Once I'm in, I'm in."

"Good. The door we'll build is in the gardens of the tower. So you don't have to worry about being contaminated by any phallic symbolism." He laughed. "But first I want you to get used to this place. The more you can visualise it, the easier it will be to return. So, have a look around."

She raised her eyebrows. "You're giving me permission to poke around?"

"Well, I wouldn't put it like that exactly, but yes, I want you to get to know it. There are a few floors with different rooms. Be my guest." He sat on a chair, crossing his legs elegantly at the ankle.

She walked around the room they were in first, going out to the balcony to look out. "This is a wonderful view. But it's all from your head? How does it work? Is what I can see real?"

"Hmmm. Sort of. If you go closer it will probably become real. Although it could also change depending on what I wanted or needed it to be."

Blaize frowned. What he said didn't make sense.

"It's hard to explain, easier to show you."

27

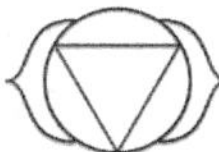

Cuinn hadn't realised that Blaize would be quite as interested in every nook and cranny as she was. He shook his head as she picked up every object and opened every door and cupboard.

He finally managed to draw her out of the room, and led her down the solid stone stairs to the heavy tower door. They went into the gardens and to the archway that Cuinn had created.

"That's beautiful." Blaize walked around it. "How does it work?"

"It doesn't—yet. We have to activate it together." He took her hands again in the same crossed-wrists position they'd held in Cuinn's physical rooms, and tugged her to stand so that the archway was in between them, hands directly under it.

"We're going to create the doorway to your Haven. This door will open if you need it." He changed his voice to the more ceremonial tone he'd used in his rooms in Cathair Cuinn. "Blaize Blackfire, do you agree to link your Haven with mine for the duration of our binding as Maven and Adherent?"

"I do."

"You're already on the astral plane this time. All you need to do is visualise your Haven, and will yourself there. This archway is a door designed to follow and capture the movement between spaces. Will your Haven to be the other side of the archway, and when we step through we will be in your Haven. Does that make sense?"

A small crease appeared between Blaize's eyes.

Cuinn smiled. "Don't worry, you have more than enough power. You just need to believe in it. Can you see your streams of power?"

Blaize looked down at herself, trying to see her own power in the way she had Cuinn's. Her eyes roamed the space around her body as she sought to do as he asked. After a moment, she shook her head and met his gaze, chewing her lip.

He tipped his head, asking her wordlessly to try again. She did, and he saw the moment when she caught sight of her energy. Her mouth fell open and her eyes grew huge, their green luminous.

Unlike last time, when it had been mainly Manipura she had been manifesting, this power was mainly Ajna. The purple was purer, less red, more blue. And it shone. She was powerful.

She blinked.

"Good. That will help. With Ajna, a major part of being able to use the energy involves believing you can."

Blaize shook her head. "I'm still not sure I understand."

"That's okay. You don't need to understand it to use it. Sometimes understanding comes through use. So, can you visualise your Haven again?"

"I think so." Her voice was anxious, and her breathing had speeded.

"There's no danger this time. Don't let go of my hands—physically in the 'real' world, here in my Haven, or when you visualise yourself in your own Haven. I'll come with you that way, and I am heavily warded." He didn't tell her he'd also done what he could to energetically protect, or ward her in each situation.

Her own Haven was the weakest spot at the moment, but there was nothing he could do until she took him there. As soon as they arrived, he would energetically protect the space until there was no possibility of anything getting in to hurt her, ever again.

"Okay."

"Trust me, Blaize."

"Do I need to close my eyes?"

"Whatever's easier. All you need to do is visualise your Haven. Think of the garden, the river. The flowers and the bees. It's a beautiful day. ..." He made his voice as hypnotic as possible and her eyes closed involuntarily.

A few minutes later, she opened her eyes again. And her grip on his hands loosened as she was distracted by the sight of her Haven. He tightened his, terrified she might slip out of his grasp at this crucial point. All the time they were joined, he could protect her. Shield her. Ward her. If she let go with the binding incomplete, her Haven unguarded, and her energy and magics unleashed and enhanced by his own, she would be a shining target for every malevolent being in the ether. As it was, it was still possible for anything to enter her Haven until the binding, and wardings, were complete. They needed to get this done.

"Ouch!"

"Sorry. But you can't let go until we've finished this." He kept his voice calm, though his mouth had gone dry.

"I wasn't going to let go," she grumbled. "I was just surprised, that's all." She glanced around her, and he did the same. The Haven was alive with tiny details—brightly coloured flowers, the buzz of bees, and the feel of the grass underneath their feet.

They stood under a mirror image of the arch that he'd created in his Haven, their hands still clasped in the middle of the arch, their bodies either side.

"We've made the link. Now watch me while I set some wardings up. I'm going to draw on the energy of the etheric plane and create shields that are anchored to the boundaries of your Haven. Eventually I'll teach you how to ward on this plane, but for now, I'm just going to secure the space as much as possible. You'll also grow and develop your Haven, just as I have. But that takes time."

He closed his eyes, and pulled more Ajna energy. He had been pooling it all day, carefully building his reserves, as well as building his strength in case he needed to pull more unexpectedly. This time, he would be prepared. Nothing was going to harm her. All he needed to do was finish the warding and complete the binding.

He opened his eyes and warded the area, creating more delicate trellis work around the pretty garden to set some boundaries, and using the river as another. Blaize watched. "They're beautiful."

"Hmmm?"

"The roses you just grew out of nowhere."

"I'm setting boundaries so you know not to go further than that in your Haven at the moment. Eventually, as your ability to pool Ajna energy grows, you'll expand your Haven, and move the boundaries back with your own power."

"How big can my piece of Haven real estate be?"

Cuinn frowned as he tried to focus on his task. "As big as you like. Although usually it's related to your power, as you need to be able to hold the territory with wardings, like this."

Blaize watched Cuinn, and each time he drew a new symbol with Ajna energy, she would lean a little more towards it, attempting to see exactly what he did. Each symbol would hover in the air for twenty seconds or so, glowing with power. They were mainly purple, but other colours came and went in ripples, creating a rainbow anchored by violet.

Finally, he finished and her Haven was as warded as he could make it. It was time to test the wardings and the link.

He caught her gaze again, and she stared back solemnly, unblinking.

"Blaize Blackfire. We are now bound, you and I, as Maven and Adherent. I pledge to protect and guide you, teaching you to harness the power of your Ajna energy for as long as it takes for you to be ready for the Ajna Practitioner trial.

"Do you agree to follow my teachings and guidance? To study until you are sufficiently proficient with Ajna to take the Ajna Practitioner trial?"

"I do." Her voice was firm.

"Then we start a new chapter, you and I, this night here in your Haven." He stepped through the archway, but she didn't move back, and he found himself inches away from her. He could feel the heat coming off her body. She tilted her head up, her breath feather-like on his neck.

He wanted to kiss her. For a moment, he couldn't think of anything apart from the shape of her mouth, the curve of her cheek.

"The first thing I'll do is teach you to move between our Havens. Watch."

With a grateful exhalation, he stepped backwards through the trellis, towards the spot he'd so recently vacated.

And disappeared.

28

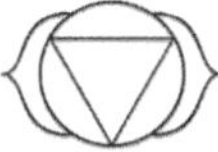

Blaize blinked. One minute, Cuinn stood in front of her, glowing with power, and the next minute he was gone.

Although given she'd had to prevent herself from kissing him again, perhaps a moment of space between them was for the best.

She examined the trellis door, which had a sort of shimmer effect inside it. She thought she could see his garden through it, but the image wasn't still. It was like the heat haze you sometimes got from hot sun on tarmac.

Should she step through? Would that take her to his Haven? She assumed so, but what if she needed to draw on her power to get through it? She hadn't used her power since the dreams had started and wasn't sure if now was the time to start.

She cautiously moved her leg forward when Cuinn popped back—and stumbled straight into her, knocking her to the ground.

Stunned, she lay beneath him.

"Third time's the charm," she mumbled, still dazed.

"What on earth were you doing standing there? Didn't you move at all?"

"No … you didn't tell me to move."

"Oh, so now you're obedient?" He shifted his weight and put one hand on the ground to push himself up. She felt his muscles flex and the warmth of his breath on her cheek. There was a flash of heat in her groin.

He stopped pushing himself upright and put his hand under her head, cradling it. He raised and tilted her head until they were staring into each other's eyes, scant inches between them. "Are you okay? Blaize?"

She sighed, and gave in to the inevitable. She loved a man's hand on her neck. She snaked her arms around his neck and pulled. He fell to his elbows, one hand still supporting her head.

She closed the gap between them, and pressed her lips softly to his, her nerves overstimulated, on fire.

At first, he resisted, mumbling something against her lips, but she used the opportunity to bring him closer by slipping her tongue into his mouth, and opening her own to invite him to do the same. His mumbling turned into a moan that vibrated through her.

His body pressed tightly against hers, pushing her into the earth. She didn't mind the hard ground against her back, but they'd have to do this again in bed one day. Her body hummed, tingled with energy and power. She wasn't actively pulling power, but it was as if she was swimming in it.

She wrapped her legs around his hips and moved her hips to rub his hardness against her softness. He returned her kiss, and she sighed and poured passion and need into the kiss.

She shifted her hip and put her foot on the floor so her leg was bent. Then she pushed and used the force of the movement to flip them both over, so she was on top. As she did, she caught sight of something in the garden, something that hadn't been there a minute ago.

She sucked in a breath and stopped halfway back to Cuinn's mouth.

He was instantly alert. His eyes snapped open and he took her with him as he sat up, his arms encircling her so she sat in his lap. He had gone from lover to fighter in seconds. "What?"

She pointed a finger at the object that had appeared in the garden.

Cuinn followed the finger with his gaze, and the tension in his body flowed out of him. He laughed. Big belly laughs, coming from somewhere deep inside him. He hugged her to him, his body heaving with amusement.

"W-what the hell?"

"You must have created it. Because I know when I create something on the astral plane, and that wasn't me. We're definitely going to have to teach you how your Ajna works, or your subconscious is going to be stripping you bare all over the place."

"What?"

"You wanted a bed. Or some part of you wanted a bed. And so, your energy gave you—a bed." He gestured towards the object that had appeared out of nowhere as they'd been kissing. It was, indeed, a bed and a glorious one.

The bed of her dreams.

It was big, and both solid and delicate. Gothic-looking, black ornate iron scrollwork danced towards the sky in straight lines and curls. Two smooth, hard posts reached upwards from each side of the bed, joined by another black rod that went between them. The rod supported gauzy red curtains that looked like living flame. Serving no purpose other than decoration, the curtains dropped gracefully from the rod down past the headboard made from iron scrollwork to the floor.

"Wow," Blaize said.

"Yeah." Cuinn stood and took her with him, her legs around his hips, his hands cupping her buttocks. She wriggled with desire, trying to move her hands closer to the space between his legs. He hadn't stopped smiling.

He walked the few yards to the bed and released Blaize onto the soft red sheet that covered a firm surface. He drew his own shirt, pants, and boxers off before following her onto the bed, pinning her arms above her head with one hand. He used his other hand to shimmy her dress up over her head, leaving it between her head and her elbows to hold her still.

His heated gaze raked over her body, catching on her slight white underwear, and her nipples peaked in response. She shifted on the bed, urging him to touch her. His skin was pale and his hair fell scruffily around his face, the dark of it contrasting with his ivory skin. An indigo shimmer surrounded him, his Ajna aura flaring, pulsing in and out of existence. He was hard and ready. She wanted him inside her.

Cuinn kissed her again, licking the flesh surrounding her collarbone. She moved her hips restlessly, trying to get him to shift down on the bed and move against her. *Why doesn't he use his hands?* Her blood pumped hot around her body, pressure building between her legs. She jerked her wrists, meaning to take back control, to free herself from the dress. She needed to remove her underwear, and she urgently wanted to touch him. To take all that male firmness inside her body and pleasure them both.

She noticed too late the red silk that seemed to be growing from the ironwork at the top of the bed. He pulled the dress free as the silk flowed towards her and trapped her wrists in a strong hold that left Cuinn free to use his hands in other ways. Cuinn threw the dress out of harm's way, then dragged her underwear down her legs, and scraped his teeth and tongue after them. "You're out of your depth here, Blaize. I've been using Ajna for centuries." His grin was wicked now. "Play nicely or who knows what I'll conjure up."

Her eyebrows rose at this new side of Cuinn. *It was always the quiet ones.* But that was her last coherent thought for a while. She tugged against the bonds—bonds she could burn away in an instant—not because she didn't like them, but because she relished the unusual feeling of someone else being in control. It was a measure of how much she'd come to trust Cuinn, despite everything, that she found the silk wrapping her wrists added to her excitement rather than anything else.

Her body craved the pleasure that Cuinn was now bringing with mouth and hands. His skin was smooth on hers. Droplets of sweat from both their bodies mingled and minimised friction. His teeth were a dull rasp as he dragged his mouth down from her breasts, over her belly, and to the hot flesh between her legs.

Here was relief from her worry about how to find Indigo and how she was going to develop her Ajna quickly enough to beat her. Here was a beautiful distraction, strong and masculine. Here were cool hands that traced her curves and ran over her hips.

And here finally, *finally*, he drove two fingers inside her.

The shock of it sent adrenaline coursing through her body and she gasped, raising her hips higher, driving them against his fingers to push him deeper. Her breath came in short pants, her heart beating like a hummingbird's.

He slid his fingers out, and stroked her, urgency compelling them both. His shaft was taut, and she wanted all of him inside her, not just his fingers. She shifted her hips again, and he rolled eyes the colour of granite up to look at her, his gaze fierce and possessive.

He was magnificent.

When her orgasm crested, she grabbed the bonds and clenched her fists around them, her body bowing, as she pushed herself into Cuinn's palm, his fingers and tongue dancing in and on the hot flesh at her core.

Tension she hadn't even known she'd been holding onto released, and her body lay limp beneath his, endorphins chasing pleasantly around her body in the after-glow.

He paused a moment, eyes still locked on hers. The savage desire in his gaze made a shudder run through her. But he wasn't finished. He worked his fingers more deeply inside her, stroking the spot that made her cry out with the violence of the feeling. She made breathy sounds as she tried to relax into it, but her body instinctively twisted away from the intensity that hovered on the edge of too much.

"Blaize." His voice was a low rumble.

She could take more. She would take more.

He'd conjured a condom from somewhere, and she moaned a little as she watched him roll it over his impressive dick. He slid up her body so he lay on top of her, skin pressed together. He kissed her neck and replaced his fingers with his dick, thick, hard and ready. He entered her liquid heat with a gentle push that quickly turned into something much more forceful.

She welcomed him in. Had she ever wanted anything so much?

"Oh." He drove the shocked noise out of her as he changed his angle and penetrated her more deeply. She made a long, low sound as the visceral feeling transformed again. It hurt a little, but it also felt good. Really good.

She felt a hot flush move across her chest and climb up her neck. He kept his movements rhythmic and constant, and she curled her legs around him, digging her heels into his buttocks to draw him in closer. They moved in time, and her head fell to the side. She wasn't sure how much longer she could straddle the fine line between ecstasy and too much. She paused and looked up at him.

"Relax, Blaize. Trust me and let go." He growled out the words, seeming to read her mind.

As their eyes met, some final barrier lifted, and their energies bled into each other's. His power raced through her, the light mystery of Ajna, and the heavy grounding of Muladhara. He captured her body and mind.

Her own energies smashed into him, the fire of Manipura dominating, but threads of Ajna woven through. She wanted to burn him up from the inside, to consume them both in an orgasmic fire. He was hers.

Stars formed and exploded inside her, and her whole body was suffused with energy and light.

Cuinn groaned. He held himself over her, one hand on the bed, and the other grasping her head and holding it firmly in place under his. He covered every inch of her with his body and kissed her again. Their mouths formed another conduit for the power that now span and mingled around their bodies.

Cuinn's long strokes deep within her continued, drawing out the experience, her core rhythmically clutching and squeezing him to his own explosion, causing her in turn to crest another peak.

The aftershocks rippled through her body as she shuddered beneath him, her body trembling, eyes closed, head lolling to the side.

Cuinn.

At some point, he'd released her arms from their silken shackles, and she brought them around him now to hug him as close to her as possible.

He relaxed against her, and burrowed his face, his hair hanging around it untidily, into her shoulder. He nipped at her neck, and she wriggled underneath him. "Cuinn! Enough! I've got nothing left."

His head came up, and he smiled at her again, his face relaxed and open in a way she hadn't seen before. It was as if all the troubles that were weighing on him had fallen away.

"I do." He raised his eyebrows. "And I'm sure I can re-energise you. ..." He drew away from her and sat up, straddling her waist. As he did so, his attention focused on something behind the bed. He froze, and his jaw dropped. "Um ... Blaize ...? I think you need to see this."

29

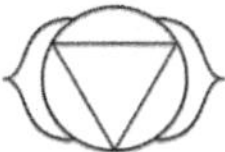

Sex with Blaize hadn't just been amazing because it was Cuinn's first time in a while. There had been an … intensity in his connection with Blaize. Deeper than the physical.

And if he hadn't already thought that, the scene that greeted him when he raised his head would have been evidence enough. The previously simple space, the pretty English garden with grass, some wooden tables and chairs, and a few trees providing shade had blossomed.

If that was the word for it.

The warding boundaries were thickly covered by climbing roses, with pink, red, white, and yellow blooms in full flower.

Blaize propped herself up on one elbow and gazed at the garden around them. As well as the roses, the grass had also blossomed with wildflowers, a riot of colour with the bed at the centre.

Ajna energy responded to the creator's thoughts and desires. The bed had given him the confidence to respond to Blaize's kiss, a clear statement of what she wanted from him.

And this time, unlike Sophea, he wanted it too. They were equals. Blaize was strong. More than a match for him. He wasn't going to hurt her as he had hurt Sophea.

The explosion of flowers said that he wasn't alone in his feelings about the sex they'd just had. It also said that Blaize had a great deal of power waiting to be tapped. "I see you've started creating."

"I did this?" Blaize looked as though she'd been hit over the head. Again.

"Correct. Unconsciously, perhaps, but these are your creations. And you were certainly shining with energy at the, er, end there. The power needed an outlet, and it found it here." He gestured around them. He sat up next to Blaize and put an arm around her, drawing her into the crook of his shoulder. She complied, unresisting, and drew in a breath.

She frowned. "Why can't I smell the flowers?"

"Well noticed. That quirk is the way you can tell you're in the dreamscape. Nothing has a scent here. If you're ever unsure, all you need to do is sniff."

"Why?"

He smiled. Her curiosity was still present and correct, despite the slightly stunned look on her face. "I don't know. Just one of those things."

He glanced towards the garden, and closer to the river where what looked like a stone altar had appeared. There was something on it.

He raised his eyebrows. *Strange.* He got no sense of threat from the new addition, but he'd also never seen anything like it manifest in an individual's Haven though similar objects were in every energetic temple. He gently disentangled himself from Blaize, and got up and went to check it out. Blaize wasn't far behind.

They both stood, unselfconsciously naked, over the altar, which held two objects.

"What are they? And where did they come from?"

"Good questions." Cuinn put his hand out to touch the objects. They were similar: two tightly corded bands, one slightly larger than the other, made of purple, red, yellow, and white silks. The colours were interwoven. He considered them, and the context. "I think it's the colours of our Chakras. Purple for Ajna, red for Muladhara, yellow for Manipura. And white for the divine, for Sahasara, the crown Chakra. They're bracelets. Probably one for each of us."

He picked them up carefully, and measured one against his own wrist and the other against Blaize's. A perfect fit. Which didn't mean they should put them on. *I know these. I've seen them somewhere.* He searched his memory to find where it had been.

"Did I create these too?" Blaize's voice was soft and hesitant.

Cuinn shook his head slowly as he realised where he knew them from. "This is Source's altar. I think these are gifts from Source. And, Blaize—I've seen us wearing these."

She looked from the stone to him, tilting her head, confused. "What do you mean? I've never seen them before."

"In the prophecies. You, I, and the other five men and five women were wearing similar bracelets in the prophecies. And you were wearing it when …"

"When I was beaten." She looked away from him, and her hands curled into fists by her sides.

He nodded.

She snatched hers up. "Easy. I just won't wear it on the physical plane then. In fact, it probably won't even exist there. Will it?"

"I don't know. It's my first 'gift' in this way." He fingered the larger of the two. "There's energy here." Gifts from Source could grant the recipient power or other blessings, but they always came at a price.

She slipped hers over her left wrist. "It's lovely. But I'm going to leave it here."

As she said the words, the bracelet moved on her wrist, and she gasped. Before Cuinn could do anything, the bracelet wrapped tightly around her wrist, not so much that it would have hurt, but too tight to pull it off.

Cuinn didn't hesitate, and placed the other bracelet over his right wrist. It span and when it stopped, it rested in the same way on his wrist, snugly bound.

"What did you do that for?" Blaize had frozen in place, eyes locked on his wrist.

"I won't leave you alone in this." Even if it meant another snap decision. Another decision without thinking it through.

"In what? We don't even know what's going on. That was a stupid thing to do."

He hoped she wasn't right.

"Perhaps it's just another symbol that Source approves our binding. We just created powerful energy. Look around." He waved at the new additions to the garden. "And we added an extra layer to the binding by making love here."

Blaize put her arms over her chest and frowned. "Making love?"

"Would you call it something else?"

"Yes … no … maybe. I don't know. So we're bound even tighter now?" Blaize's voice was a little higher than usual.

"You agreed to the binding, Blaize. And you certainly seemed keen on making love. Where's the problem?" He put his hand out to cup her cheek, but she shifted out of reach, her eyes not meeting his.

"We had great sex, amazing sex, in fact. But it's not the start of some great love affair. Sex between consenting adults is a beautiful thing, but it doesn't need to mean they have to become attached. You don't know enough about me, Cuinn." She stalked to the bed and pulled her underwear up her long legs. Cuinn tried not to be distracted.

"I agree. And I want to know more. But I know enough to know I want to explore this relationship—"

Blaize's eyebrows shot up.

"This relationship," he emphasised the word, "with you properly. The binding's complete, anyway, so whatever happens we need to work through the sexual side as adults, because we're going to be spending a lot of time with each other in the coming years."

He walked to her, more quickly this time so she couldn't move away, and put his hands on her face, tilting it up to meet her eyes. He tried to imagine what Tierra would say. How she would empathise with Blaize. What was it that Blaize was worried about? He thought back to their conversation of the day before and thought he had it.

"You're not your father, if that's what you're worried about. Just because you have your dominant Chakra in common doesn't mean you're anything like him."

Blaize's chin went up, and her cheeks flushed an angry red. "Can we go home? Is the ritual done?" Her tone was empty.

Was that too close to home, or nowhere near? *Why was she so bloody stubborn?* Women, again a mystery to him. Cuinn sighed. "Yes, the ritual is done. More than done. I'd like to see what happens to these bracelets when we get back to the physical plane. If they come with us, then the prophecy involving you has come a little closer and we're going to need to step things up."

She was dressed now, her arms at her sides. They clenched into fists and her mouth flattened into a thin line. "I can protect myself."

He gritted his teeth. *Add proud to stubborn.* "Yes, but there's always more to learn. And there's no shame in having others help you. Plus, we're bound now, you and I, so we work together. Don't forget you agreed to my teaching you in the binding ritual."

She scowled.

One thing at a time. The priority now was to make sure her Haven was secure. He needed to know she was safe when she was here. "I want to check you can travel between our Havens before we go back. It's the point at which you—and our Havens—are most vulnerable."

He'd approach the relationship issue again on the physical plane. Perhaps after he asked Tierra for some advice. He wasn't sure what was happening between them, but the sensible thing was to explore it. To plan ahead and to decide what to do with a little thought.

He pulled his own clothes on, and showed her how to guard her mind using a protection technique, before they moved to the arch.

"All you need to do is walk under the arch, protecting your mind as I showed you. You're vulnerable only for a split second, so there's not much danger, but given the situation, I'd rather be safe. Eventually it will become second nature to you to guard as you change locations in the dreamscape—and later, when you dreamwalk outside our Havens, you'll start your protection with this first technique, though you'll add others too."

She was all business now, body relaxed but alert. There was no trace of the wild abandon he'd seen in her a short while before. No trace of the softness, or the surrender. Her body language said she'd listen to him, but she'd make her own choices. Do it her own way.

"I'll walk through first. Follow me. Don't take long, or I'll be back looking for you," he said. He felt a sense of unease, but wasn't sure if that was down to Blaize's switch in behaviour, or a premonition. He didn't sense any potential danger, but he'd scan thoroughly as he stepped through to his Haven.

He proceeded through the archway, and moments later, he materialised in the gardens of his own tower. His heart thundered in his chest as he waited. Another few seconds, and she appeared. She looked a little disorientated, but she seemed fine.

"Great," he said, as his heart dropped back to its normal pace. "We'll return to your Haven and make sure you feel comfortable in both directions, then we'll head home." He waited until she nodded, then stepped back through the arch.

Cuinn took a second to look at the beautiful, rumpled bed. He hardened slightly as he saw an image of Blaize's lithe body writhing in the red silk. He turned his attention back to the arch. Where was she? What was taking so long? He dug his nails into his palms. Should he go back through? But what if he did and she came through at the same time?

Another minute passed.

Then movement and a shimmer in the arch, and he stepped forward with a sigh of relief.

Blaize fell through the doorway, bloody and unconscious, into his arms.

30

Blaize woke up in her own bed, a strange woman by her side. The woman offered her some water, which Blaize accepted gratefully, her throat dry and scratchy. As she tipped her head back, she felt a pull in the back of her hand, and looked down to see an IV drip attached to her. The woman's heart-shaped face exuded warmth and was surrounded by a honey-blond bob.

"Who are you?"

The woman smiled, and Blaize felt a little more at ease.

"I'm Cara, a good friend of Tierra's. I'm a Healer."

Blaize's heart turned to ice, the ease draining away. Her chest tightened and she raised her torso up a little. "You work at the Rogue Rehab centre."

"Yes."

"Have I …?"

Cara tilted her head then laughed. "No, no, love, you haven't turned Rogue. You're fine. Sorry, I shouldn't laugh. But you're in no danger of that. You have an iron grip on your energies."

The ice in Blaize's chest melted, and she relaxed back against the pillows.

"We think you were attacked in the astral world, when you went between Cuinn's Haven and your own. You fought with something. But you made it back to Cuinn, and he brought you home. They called me because they wanted help, not because you were going Rogue." She looked at Blaize, assessing her. "Can I get you anything else? How's the pain?"

Blaize tested the various muscles in her body carefully. "I don't feel too bad. What're the bandages for?"

"You had a deep scratch across your arm. I stitched it up and it's covered while it heals. I've given you a lot of healing energy. I'm glad it's working. We have drugs too, if you need them, but we didn't want to add anything else into your system before we knew the effects of the attack." She went to Blaize's side and felt for her pulse. "The drip's just for hydration. I've been with you for a couple of days—it's good to see you awake and okay."

Blaize's eyes widened. "Days?"

"I'm afraid so. You were badly hurt. But you're on the mend now."

Blaize blew out a breath. "Thank you. You're a Healer? You have Anahata as your dominant Chakra?"

It was Cara's turned to nod. "Yes, and Manipura as my auxiliary. Not the typical Healer combination, but helpful at the Rehab centre."

Satisfied with Blaize's pulse, she plumped her pillows and helped her to sit up.

"I'll get Cuinn. He's been here as much as he could over the last couple of days, and spent the rest of his time trying to work out what happened."

She swept out of the door. Blaize was tempted to pull the drip out but thought she'd better wait. Cara didn't seem like someone to mess with.

Blaize rested her head on the pillows and looked up at the spotless white ceiling. She wasn't looking forward to seeing Cuinn. After they'd had sex—*great sex*—she'd been taken aback by his leap to a relationship. She hadn't expected that. *Wasn't our antagonism beforehand part of the reason the sex had been so great?* That didn't seem like a good basis for a relationship to her.

She frowned. She hadn't had any real long-term relationships in her life. She'd always been focused on her own goals. Developing her energy. Being the best at whatever she was working on. Her longest relationship had been a year, and she'd been the one to end it when she'd started training in Manipura. Since then, she'd only had the odd fling, which had been more like getting a workout partner than a relationship.

Could she persuade Cuinn to have more fabulous, sweaty sex to keep them both fit? She gave a small smile while she prodded the area around the bandage on her arm, trying to see where the scratch started and ended.

The binding ceremony had been magical. And white certainly suited Cuinn. He'd looked so ... powerful. Masculine.

She winced as she hit the start of the scratch. *Ouch.*

The door burst open and Cuinn rushed through, Cara and Tierra following at a more sedate pace. Cuinn sat in the chair by the bed, and took her hand.

"Blaize." He dropped a kiss on her palm.

Blaize felt something warm and liquid flare in her at the touch, but at the same time wanted to pull her arm away. She didn't want a relationship, and she didn't want him to think she did. There was nothing wrong with healthy sex between consenting adults—*lots of amazing, healthy sex*—but relationships led to trouble. She need look no further than her mother and father to see that. She was attracted to him, sure—*wanted him, badly*—but that didn't mean they were going to date, let alone get married. She needed to step back.

"How do you feel?" Cuinn asked.

"Stiff and achy, but not too bad. Not bad enough to need a drip." She looked at Cara. "Can you take it out?"

"After we've gotten a bit more food and liquid into you. Not long."

"Blaize, can you tell us what happened?" Cuinn leaned towards her, his focus locked on her as if she was something precious that was his to protect. His voice held a world of worry.

She found herself both wanting to soothe him, and at the same time, annoyed and guilty that her actions could be responsible for the pain in his voice. *I don't need this.*

"I'm not sure. I stepped forward to follow you through the gate, and instead of it taking a few seconds like the first time, something seemed to—to catch hold of me, and pull me in a different direction. I fought it—I'm not sure exactly how, or with what, and even though I know it must have been in the astral world, I felt it physically. But ..." She focused on Cuinn, puzzled. "How did I get these injuries? I thought that what happened on the astral plane wasn't real on the physical plane?"

Cuinn's weary gaze told her he knew her question also referred to what had happened between them.

"No. What happens in the astral plane is as real as what happens on this plane."

Well, that explained the need for the condom.

He held up their joined hands and she saw the bracelets from the dreamscape on their wrists. Her stomach lurched. *What the hell?* But she couldn't think about that now.

"It doesn't always translate into action on the physical plane, as it depends on the strength of the energy, but it's no less real either way." He put her hand down and sat back. "In your case, the Rogue, which is what we're assuming it was, was strong. Strong enough for your injuries to show up here too. But that may also come from your own strength. You were almost drained when you came through the portal, and unconscious. You must have expended a lot of energy in a short time to have that happen."

"I don't remember much more. I don't know how I managed to get through the portal. I tried to focus on my Haven, but it was blurry. I focused on you as well. I could sense your energy."

Tierra and Cara exchanged a surprised look.

"That's because we're bound as Maven and Adherent. It's rare that we won't be able to find each other." He frowned at the other women. Blaize made a note to ask Tierra what that was about next time they were alone together. But Blaize had other priorities right now.

"Was I really out for days?"

"Yes. And you seemed to be having bad dreams," Cuinn said. "Do you remember any of them? The dreams might help us with the prophecy. Or even just with what actually happened."

"The prophecy!" Blaize half sat up, then winced as her muscles protested. "I'm injured—this must be the prophecy that you saw fulfilled. And I'm fine."

She felt a sense of dread lift that she hadn't been aware of. *One thing less to worry about.*

Cuinn didn't say anything.

"Cuinn? I'm out of the water now. You can stop worrying." She stretched out her good hand to him, touching him lightly on the forearm.

"Maybe. I'm not sure. There may still be more danger. It doesn't match what I saw exactly—I need to do more research." Cuinn didn't move.

"You always need to do more research." Tierra came over to him and put her arms around him. "Right now, you need to take a nap. What with checking on Blaize and your own dreamwalks, as well as research, you've barely had any sleep in three days. Or a shower. Go, take a nap, and Cara and I will put some food together for us all."

Cara glided over to the two of them, and placed her hand on Cuinn's shoulder. Blaize was surprised by a bitter taste in her mouth. She drew her own hand quickly back.

"As your Healer, I agree," said Cara. She was elegant, composed, and feminine. "You need rest. If Blaize remembers anything about the dreams, she can write it down and we can share it later."

The advice was sensible, but Blaize was distracted. Really distracted. An annoying thought had lodged in her brain, and wouldn't get out.

Had Cuinn and Cara ever been lovers?

31

Blaize wanted to be out tracking Indigo. Instead, Cuinn had disappeared, and she was under orders from Cara to rest.

Three days after waking, she was reading through prophecies in the library when a car drew up outside. Her heart lurched uncomfortably, and she walked downstairs, where she found an athletic blond with amused eyes, whose stubble-kissed look added to the overall picture of a surfer on his day off.

"Fintan!" Blaize smiled a real smile and gave Fintan an enthusiastic hug.

"Hey, Sparks." A friend of her Uncle's, Fintan had called her that since she was a teenager, as she'd loved the sparkles he'd created for her in the tropical night, distracting her from her nightmares soon after her parents had died. Her own personal fireworks show.

Cuinn followed a little way behind the others, looking bone-weary, and as if he'd lost another seven pounds since she had last seen him.

She stood awkwardly in front of him, Fintan's arm loosely around her shoulders. Cuinn looked at the two of them and smiled grimly.

"It's been a long few days, but I think we have a way forward. Fintan, you might as well fill Blaize in. I need a shower."

He didn't wait for an answer but disappeared back out of the door. Blaize took a half-step after him, and then shrugged, and turned back to Fintan. "Want to fight?"

Blaize squatted and kicked out with a low roundhouse sweep, and Fintan jumped back just in time.

"Nice."

"So what's the plan? Are you and I going hunting?" Blaize was eager to hear what Cuinn had agreed as a way forward with Minh, the Ajna-Muladhara Minor Circle member. Anything was better than hanging around the house. Thank Source Cara had agreed Blaize could train again, as long as she didn't overdo it. *Though it's possible we have different ideas of what overdoing it means.*

"Not exactly. You're going to be bait." Fintan sent a right hook towards Blaize's head. They were both sweating now, even though Blaize had turned the AC up high as soon as they'd hit the house's gym.

Blaize smiled as she darted backwards. "Sounds like my kind of plan."

"Cuinn's been at the books pretty hard since your attack. He found some references that seem relevant in an ancient prophecy that goes back to the fall of Atlantis, where a great evil was predicted that would upset the balance of the world and threaten our race. The prophecy says 'a full complement of Chakras' is needed to fight the evil."

Blaize struck him in the side of the leg with a kick, but he caught her foot and twisted, throwing her hard to the ground. *Ouch.* She landed face down and flipped herself, fast, to face him and at the same time kicked out with both legs. She hooked his ankle with one foot and slammed him in the knee with the other, and brought him down to the ground with a thud.

But he was quick to recover and scrambled up Blaize's body to sit on her in a Jiu-Jitsu mount.

"How can we use a full complement of Chakras when we only represent six? How would we include the Crown Chakra?" Blaize panted only slightly as he sat on top of her chest, his legs pinning her arms, his hands at her throat.

"The prophecy was put aside as incomplete centuries ago because of that very concern." Finn shifted to sit more firmly on her lungs, making it harder for her to breathe. "Whatever Cuinn's dusty books say, we need to capture the Rogue."

He put a bit more pressure on her throat, and she felt the blood build up in her head. Her cheeks heated, and tiny spots appeared in front of her eyes.

"For some reason, the Rogue wants you." He smirked. "Though if she could see you right now, she'd probably change her mind."

Blaize hefted her lower body, and dislodged Fintan enough so that he slipped slightly. It was enough for her to shift her hips again and twist her body so that he was knocked to the side, his hands away from her throat. She heaved a breath and coughed.

"Enough?" he asked from a horizontal position next to her. They'd been sparring for an hour now, and both were sweating with exertion.

She shook her head and pushed herself off the floor. She loved this. "Let's add energy. Protect the room."

He stood, and after a moment, a wall of fire caged them. It would keep any energy they used between them. She spooled a little Manipura energy, cautious.

"The plan is to get you to shine in the dreamscape like the tasty morsel of energy you are. When the Rogue comes for you, Cuinn will capture her on the astral plane, will find out where her physical body is, and Cara and I will go find it and take it to the Rehab centre. Simple."

Blaize frowned. "I need more time to learn about Ajna. She kicked my butt the other day. It was embarrassing."

Fintan's torso burst into flame. Out of the inferno, a handful of tiny daggers of fire flew through the air towards her. She dodged one and spread energy in front of her to absorb the rest. She created her own defensive fire and began to heat the ground under Fintan's bare feet.

His voice came from behind the wall of fire. "You have two days. We don't want to wait too long."

Her frown deepened. "Fine."

She'd be ready.

Fintan's flames disappeared and he danced on the spot as the heat seeped into his bare feet. "Tierra doesn't like it."

He ducked and rolled past Blaize and threw a fireball at her back from the floor.

She fell forward, the heat absorbed, but the strength of the hit pushed her to the floor, and her defensive fire flickered and went out. Her voice was muffled. "What?"

Fintan came up behind her fast, and before she could push herself up, he grabbed one of her arms and wrenched it up her back. *Ouch.*

"Using you as bait."

Blaize tried to shrug, but her arm was tight up against her back and she couldn't move. She heated up her own body hoping to dislodge Fintan.

"We can't leave the Rogue out there, or every time I draw power the Rogue could attack," she said. "And who knows what damage it might be doing at the moment? We can't leave it out there to ruin another family's lives."

"I agree."

The pain in her arm brought tears to her eyes. She used her feet against the ground to move her body forward, which took the pressure off for a moment, and was all she needed to twist her body around. She was still on the floor, but her arm was no longer trapped.

Fintan made a grab for her. "How are you getting along with Cuinn?"

She hesitated for a second, and he used the moment to catch her and pin her, one knee on her arm, the other arm secured by his hand.

"Fine. We're fine." She struggled to free herself, but he was well-built and drove all his weight down. She couldn't move either arm.

"And the binding went well?" He smirked at her.

She stopped struggling and scowled at him. "What did he tell you?"

"Nothing. But you just did." His bright blue eyes sparked with mischief.

His weight was high up her body, and her legs were free. She scissor-kicked, bending her body at a right angle, and caught his head between her feet. She yanked backwards, and he tipped back off her chest though he didn't let go of the wrist he'd been holding.

"There's nothing going on. We slept together, it was fine, he wants a relationship. I don't do relationships, you know that."

There was a brief struggle until they were both on the floor, limbs entwined. Fintan was on top, though by a slim margin. Neither of them had much wiggle room. The wall of fire around the room had gone.

"Maybe you should." Fintan sounded a bit out of breath.

She scowled harder and shoved her fingers into the notch in the centre of his collar bone, at the bottom of his throat, and forced him back.

"Not. Going. To. Happen." She struck him with each word, each blow driving him back off her. She kept hold of one of his arms, and stretched it tight, until he laughed and yielded defeat, tapping the floor with his free hand.

Cuinn knocked at Blaize's door. He'd told himself he wanted to check on her safety. That he needed to ensure that Fintan had briefed her properly. But what he really wanted to do was ask her exactly what her relationship with Fintan was. They'd seemed so … natural together. Without any of the antagonism that he and Blaize seemed to share.

He scowled just as she opened the door. She narrowed her eyes and made no attempt to invite him in. "Yes?"

"I came to check Fintan had filled you in on the plan." He pushed past her and walked into the living room.

She turned, watching him, her arms folded. "Yes."

"And you're okay with being used as bait? Even though we can't be sure the prophecy I saw about you has been completed?" He swept a glance around the room as he waited for her answer. Blaize had only been here for a few weeks but she'd already put her mark on the house. The fire smouldered—he suspected given her fire energies it rarely went out.

A striking picture he'd never seen before hung on the wall, of a beach—but a beach very far from the usual tourist postcard version of a beach. In black and white, it showed an angry sea, where jagged lightning forked down from the sky to meet it.

A couple of her scarves were hung over the end of the sofa and the room smelled like her. Woodsmoke and … what was it? Whatever it was, it sent a tiny jolt of arousal through him, which he crushed. He'd been away for days, in tiring meetings and lost in books and research. He'd looked forward to seeing her. But when he'd arrived, he'd come through the door behind Fintan, whose easy intimacy with Blaize had inspired pangs of both envy and hatred.

Cuinn turned around to see Blaize standing in the doorway still watching him. He met her eyes and raised one eyebrow.

"I'm fine with it." She shrugged.

He didn't see what she had to be annoyed about. He was the injured party here. "We'll start your training again tomorrow. But carefully. You can't overdo it. Mind energy is just as exhausting as any other kind."

"Good." She was polite, but wary. The heat that he'd seen in the dreamscape had gone. But he knew it was there under the surface, smouldering like the fire in the grate.

Ah damn. She's beautiful.

The night was hushed around them.

"I thought I'd examine the house's wardings and protection. To make sure you're safe."

Blaize frowned, but shrugged again. "Sure. Better safe than sorry."

Her body language was taut, her shoulders stiff, her arms still crossed tightly over her chest.

He walked through the tiny living room, checking that the back door in the kitchen was still locked, and taking a look round. He touched the wardings at the back door and windows. Each time he touched them with his energy, there was a flash of indigo. Satisfied, he came back into the living room. She hadn't moved. "Shall I check upstairs?"

Again, the shrug. It was starting to annoy him now. He was feeling very out of his depth. He brushed past her, her scent becoming stronger the closer he got, and his arm skimmed her soft burgundy sweater as he walked towards the stairs.

After a few seconds, he heard her footsteps on the stairs behind him.

What was he doing? What did he want to happen? He had promised himself he would give her time, time to realise how good they were together, how right. And not just for sex—though that was out of this world—but for so much more than that. She'd bewitched him, and although he wanted more than almost anything to consummate that relationship in the physical world, he'd decided that nothing else would happen between them until the Rogue was stopped.

So what, exactly, did he think he was doing, climbing up her stairs with an excuse as flimsy as any schoolboy's?

CHAPTER

32

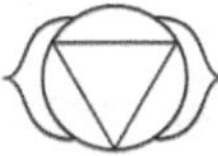

Blaize was confused. Well, not confused exactly. She knew what she wanted, and what she didn't. She wanted hot sex with the gorgeous man climbing her stairs.

She did not want a relationship.

Unfortunately, his interest in the latter meant the former was probably a very bad idea. Not that you'd know he felt like that from the way he'd barged into her house. He'd been striding around her living room like he owned the place. Which she supposed he did. *But still. Rude much?*

And yet here she was, following him as if drugged. Although, of course, she was drugged. Did mild healing energy count as behaviour-altering? Perhaps she could blame that for what was about to happen.

She stood in the doorway.

They looked at each other, less than a yard separating them physically, but it felt like miles.

"We need to talk," he said. The scowl that had been on his face since she'd opened her door was still there. And something else. A dangerous edge she hadn't seen in him before. She didn't want to talk, though. If he was interested in more discussion, then he could piss off back to the house. She just didn't have the energy.

"Not tonight, Cuinn. I'm too tired. And you don't look so great yourself."

She went to the tiny dressing table, turned her back to him, and took her jewelery off. She was killing time. If she ignored him, he might go away and take that tempting body with him. She felt a tug low down in her body when she thought of it.

"About what happened in the dreamscape," he said.

He wasn't going away then. She turned back to face him and found him closer than before. This time only inches separated them, his breath warm on her face. She went on the offensive. Perhaps she could annoy him into leaving. "A lot happened in the dreamscape, Cuinn. Including me almost getting killed."

"One of the most frightening moments of my life."

"It wasn't great for me, either." She put a hand on one hip, and raised her chin. But the angrier she got, the more he seemed to relax, the scowl melting away to leave a more thoughtful expression on his face.

He reached for her, and with nowhere to go, her back against the dressing table, she couldn't dodge him without looking like a child. But he only took her hand in his.

"We're connected now, Blaize."

"I know." His hand felt cool, dry, and comforting. She wasn't sure whether to wrench hers away or to grab him with her other hand and pull him in tight.

"It's more than just the Maven-Adherent connection."

"Sexual attraction's a powerful connection, true." She refused to give an inch.

He moved a little closer. *Too close.* "It's more than that, Blaize."

His breath rifled through her hair. His scent was musky and male, and she felt light-headed. *To hell with it.* She'd made her intentions clear. If he wanted to pine for a relationship, that was his problem. And anger made for heat. And she was in her element in hot weather.

She licked her lips, and looked up at him. She slowly reached to put a hand on his hip. His hair, messy as always, cast shadows on his face in the dim evening light of the room, and his eyes, almost lost in darkness, fixed on hers. Her hand slipped around to his lower back and dipped to touch the skin underneath his black chinos. He took an audible breath. His hands went to her head, cradling it in his hands. She shivered as one of his hands cupped her neck and drew it towards him.

She was transfixed. Hypnotised. Her nerve endings were on fire with anticipation. His body lined itself up against hers. He leaned down towards her mouth, and she closed her eyes and tilted her face up, ready. It was going to be a wild ride.

He dropped a light kiss on her mouth … and then, nothing. She opened her eyes in confusion. He'd gone. She heard him call back up the stairs, "We will talk, Blaize." The front door shut and the lock snicked behind him.

She was still in the same place minutes after his footsteps had died away. *What the fuck?*

The next morning Cuinn concentrated on work, despite the fact that all he really wanted to do was talk to her about their relationship. Because, despite what she seemed to think, they were going to have a relationship—if they weren't already in one.

"We're going to stay in the room today; we're not going to dreamwalk," he said. "I'll put you in a light trance, and we'll see what you can remember about the Rogue. Any information we can pick up is helpful at this point for dealing with the Rogue later. But we'll go into your memories, and not into the dreamscape."

She nodded, one professional to another. He was impressed that she didn't seem to feel any fear for what they were about to try. It was unlikely to be easy.

"Just tell me what to do." She sat on the floor opposite him, both once more on their own mats.

"Lie down and relax." He kept his tone light and impersonal. He could do professional too. Though it had taken all the willpower he had to walk out on her last night. Right now he wanted to grab her, to shake and argue her into a relationship with him, but he kept those emotions locked down. She shot him a suspicious look, but followed his instructions, and lay back on the mat and closed her eyes.

Once she was relaxed, he said, "I'm going to ask you some questions. However those questions make you feel, remember I'm keeping you safe. Let any emotion wash over you without absorbing it. You don't need to take it on. Do you understand?"

"I do." Blaize murmured the words.

"Take yourself back to my Haven." He brought her mind back to the moments before she went through the portal and the Rogue attacked. He drew a careful breath. This was delicate work. He couldn't let any of his own fear or frustration show, because if she sensed it and became afraid herself, they could get nothing.

"You wait a minute or so, and then you step forward through the portal." A breath. "What do you see?"

Fear flickered across her face, and she shook her head slightly. Her hair pooled about her shoulders, and blended into the red tones of her mat. Her eyes remained closed and there was a tightness that hadn't been there before. But her voice was steady.

"I walk through and at first, there's—nothingness. I know it's only a breath between portals, so I take another step to get to my Haven. But as I lift my foot, I'm wrenched backwards. Strong arms are around me. I'm fighting them." A shallower breath. "She's a match for me here, where I don't know what's up and what's down."

"Remember, you're safe here, Blaize. Nothing can hurt you now."

Blaize's face was twisted though he wasn't sure whether it was in distress or anger. It smoothed some with his words.

"Can you feel her energies?" He sat crossed-legged at her side and leaned in closer, his elbows on his knees and his chin propped in one hand.

"I'm not sure. Her arms are squeezing me. I'm bending over, trying to throw her off me. Bear hugs should be easy to get out of. But she has me with something more than just her arms. And she's hot. Or at least, she's the same temperature as me, which is hot in this vacuum.

"I turn in her grasp, and her fist comes up and hits me in the face. It hurts! I fall backwards. She kicks me. The pain feels greater than just a physical blow. Each kick or punch has an energetic resonance. It's as if each time she touches me, I lose a little energy."

Cuinn's stomach twisted and he felt sick. He knew what the Rogue was. Something forbidden. Taboo.

Blaize came to the same conclusion and her eyes snapped open seconds later. "Oh, Source. She has the same energies as me, and she was feeding from me." Her gaze as it met his held a storm of emotion behind it.

"She's a Leech."

33

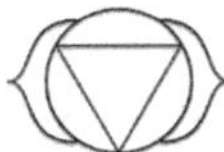

Once Indigo had been bound to him as Maven and Adherent, a binding almost unbreakable, he'd introduced her to leeching. To help her be strong, he said. To live up to her full potential.

Her desire to please him had ensured that her initial shock at the forbidden practice had easily turned to curiosity. And then she'd experienced the almost sexual ecstasy of taking energy from another energetic. The fine line of pleasure-pain as you pulled energy not from the ether, but from another person.

And the power. Oh, the power.

Watching that other person, terrified, open before you.

Their face as you took more and more, and you became more energised, more powerful, while they wilted like a bloom picked days ago.

Indigo's body reacted to her thoughts, and even as she lay on her hard bed in the bare room on the outskirts of Merrow, she felt a thrill course through her, a pleasure almost sexual igniting her nerve endings. She let out a breath.

She longed to leech again. To take energy from an unwilling victim. To see the pride in her Maven's face as she drained that victim in front of him. It was worth every moment in this shitty town, in this shitty house.

Indigo still needed her Maven's help, or drugs, to overpower another person for leeching, and her Maven had been stingy with opportunities so far.

So far.

The trance had been unpleasant, despite Cuinn's efforts to make it as easy for Blaize as possible. The two of them had joined Fintan, Tierra and Cara for lunch afterwards, but Blaize only picked at hers, pushing food around her plate.

"Do you think it's Indigo?" she asked no one in particular.

"It could be. But geography means nothing in the dreamscape. Whoever it is could be anyone, anywhere in the world. It's likely, but we can't count on it," said Cuinn.

"The Rogue is probably an addict if she's leeching off Blaize. And it explains why she chose you Blaize, if you're her energetic match. It makes more sense now," Cara said.

Blaize leaned back in her chair and sipped at a glass of water. "So it might not even be anything to do with the prophecy. If she's just an individual Rogue who's addicted to energy and leeching from others to get it."

"Except that you're involved in the major prophecy," Cuinn said, as he put his knife and fork down. "You were in the line up with the other eleven. And if you were hurt, or worse, then it would still stop the prophecy from coming true, even if you were hurt through something else."

Blaize frowned. "I guess so. So we carry on as before? Especially now we know that I'm the best bait we have for this Rogue?"

Blaize wasn't sure about the major prophecy. Cuinn had refused to take her out into the wild energy in the dreamscape. He'd been adamant, saying she'd need a lot more training for that. But Blaize believed that the piece of the prophecy where he'd seen her hurt had been fulfilled by the Rogue's attack in the dreamscape, and she was itching to come up against the Rogue again.

Except that this time she'd be prepared.

But although Cuinn had agreed to using her as bait, he still wasn't keen.

"Maybe we should change the plan." He shoved away from the table and went over to the kitchen, coming back with another full mug of coffee.

He sat back down and his foot tapped against the floor under the table. Blaize thought maybe he'd had enough coffee for today. She decided not to comment on either his words or his behaviour, and silently congratulated herself for her unusual tact and diplomacy. She smothered a smile.

Fintan clapped Cuinn on the back. "Let it go. The plan's fine, and Blaize will kick the Rogue's ass. Blaize won't even need to charge herself with as much energy as we'd planned because the Rogue is looking specifically for her."

"Blaize is already powerful, considering she's only just started training. Especially as Ajna is her auxiliary, not her dominant energy." Cuinn took another sip of coffee. "I've seen energetics with Ajna as a dominant who were weaker than her."

Cuinn didn't look at Blaize as he gave her what was probably the first compliment he'd paid her. *Huh.* It boosted her confidence. If he thought she was strong, she had a solid chance of bringing the Rogue down.

"We'll spend the afternoon meditating and charging both your energies, Manipura and Ajna. And we'll spend the rest of the week practising for your trip outside our Havens on the astral plane. By then you should be almost well enough." Cuinn held up a hand to forestall Blaize's inevitable comment that she was already well enough. Blaize just wanted it done. But unfortunately, she wasn't in charge.

Cuinn was. "Cara gets the final say on when you're ready."

34

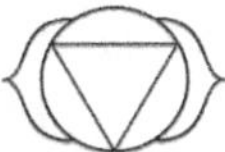

Cuinn was in Merrow with Tierra. She'd needed to stock up on supplies for the house, and he hadn't wanted her to go alone.

His cell phone rang, the discordant sound jarring. Very few people had his number. He held the phone up to his ear.

"Yes?"

"Mr. Ahern, it's Detective Davis. I'm sorry to tell you that the woman who attacked your friend came back. She broke into Sugar and Spice after closing and assaulted the owner. We've just sent Rosa to the hospital."

Cuinn grasped the cell tightly. "Rosa? Is she alright?"

"She'll live. The cafe's been pretty badly damaged. The assailant set some kind of a fire."

A wash of adrenaline hit him. One of a very small number of people he cared about had been attacked. He needed to find out what had happened, and see for himself if Rosa was ok. But this could be the break they needed. If they could follow the Rogue's trail, there would be no need for Blaize to act as bait. *No need for her to put herself into danger.*

"I'm in town. I'll be there in five minutes." He flicked the phone off and bolted out of the bookstore he'd been browsing in to find Tierra. He strode to the grocery store he'd left her in and stopped in front of her. She looked at him, surprised, a bag of cashew nuts in her hand.

"Rosa's been attacked by the Rogue. I need you to find out what Rosa can tell us about Indigo while I talk to the police."

"Whatever you need." Tierra, her eyes wide, followed him outside. "Shall I call Blaize?"

"Let's find out a bit more first. We can call her then. There's nothing she can do from home."

Everything was in position. The male and his weak sidekick were in town checking on Indigo's old boss. Indigo hadn't meant to hurt Rosa quite as much as she had. But it had been fun to burn down the café where so many patrons had looked down on her. Treated her like nothing.

Indigo looked around the clearing, which was about thirty yards across. The corpse of a homeless woman lay like a bundle of rags, propped against a large log. Indigo had burned the foliage a little to enlarge the clearing, so she had a good view on all sides. She was confident no one would be able to sneak up on her.

All Indigo needed to do was to get that bitch here. She got out her cell phone. Her Maven had given her Blaize's number – he had ways and means far beyond anything Indigo knew how to do. She dialled the number now.

As soon as she had Blaize's mind within reach, she was going to play a little game. She'd soon teach Blaize how little she knew about Ajna. That she couldn't trust her own senses. She was going to make the bitch feel like she'd won—and then bring her world crashing down around her head.

Because no one had ever told Indigo not to play with her food.

Blaize was in her cottage, working her way through a pile of combined prophecy books. Each collected the prophecies from farseer energetics in a particular place and time, and included such interesting titles as "1702: British Crown Colonies," and "1868: The Canadian Confederation."

Despite their boring titles, she'd been surprised to find herself captivated. They were like puzzle pieces. Each book was a collection of prophecies, and came with a handbook that was a commentary containing any thoughts on the individual prophecies other farseers had had. Blaize wasn't entirely sure what she was looking for, but Cuinn had suggested she use some of her downtime, before it was time for her to play bait, to get used to the feel of prophecies. She could see now that they were rarely clear cut.

Each prophecy came to a farseer energetic as a series of pictures. Some had audio, but not all. They might be a static picture or more like a film. It was different for every farseer. The stronger you were energetically, the more likely you would be to use all your senses to receive a prophecy.

And then the farseer had to describe the prophecy. This wasn't easy. Farseers were trained in observation, in noticing detail. She winced. That wasn't usually her thing. She was a big-picture person, though after spending the last few days training with Cuinn, she was learning, a little, how to notice more, and how to describe the world around her in richer detail.

They drilled the plan with the group at lunchtimes and supper. The work with Cuinn mainly focused on how she could shield her mind from Ajna attacks. But, as Blaize had admitted to Nixie that morning in a video conference call where they'd gossiped and caught up, it didn't come naturally to Blaize, which was just one more annoying thing about Ajna. Nixie had been more interested in the fact Blaize had had sex with Cuinn, and had teased that Blaize did seem to remember a lot of detail about that.

Blaize flushed a little.

The more detail the farseer noticed and was able to describe in a way others could understand, the more likely the farseer would be able to interpret the prophecy, alone or with others. Many of the Ajna farseers worked together at the Guild in Athens in order to connect prophecies together.

Even Cuinn had worked at the Guild, once upon a time. Apparently he even spoke fluent, if archaic, Greek. These days he wasn't an active farseer for the Guild and the prophecies he saw were almost accidental. He visited the Guild when he needed to, which was why he was away so often at the moment to discuss the prophecy that he believed put them all in danger.

She was deep in late 18th Century England when her phone rang, her mind full of the politics of war and revolution, and the prophecies that had tried to guide the energetics through the wars safely, while saving as many humans as possible.

She was jolted out of the book by the cell phone ringtone she used for unknown numbers. She frowned. She rarely received calls. Her family and friends overseas sent texts or emails, and the only people she knew in Canada were the energetics she was living with.

Her heart beat faster. What if there was an emergency at home? If Nix, Fai, or Marius were hurt? She grabbed the phone. "Blaize here."

Silence. Puzzled, after a few seconds she said, "Hello? Is there someone there?"

"I thought we might dance, you and I." The woman's voice had a sharp edge, along with suppressed delight. It was an unpleasant combination and Blaize's skin crawled as she realised who was speaking. "I have Rosa, your friend from the café. She's not feeling too good. Catch me if you can. You have thirty minutes to get here, or I start burning her. If you bring anyone with you? She's dead."

She ended with a map reference, a laugh, and the phone disconnected.

Blaize stared at the phone in shock. The Rogue had called her. How had she gotten Blaize's number? She needed to go find her, now.

But everyone else was out, and way more than thirty minutes from that map reference. Even if she called them, they wouldn't make it in time.

Fintan and Cara were in Vancouver, he following up a potential lead, and she checking in on an energetic patient. They were a couple of hours away at least.

Tierra and Cuinn were in town. Closer, but not close enough. She'd call them on the way and hope they'd be there in time to help. She seized her jacket and flew out of the front door. She couldn't waste any time. Indigo was clearly not in her right mind—who knew what she might do to Rosa, the friendly human from the café. Plus, this was an excellent opportunity to capture the Rogue. If Blaize waited, then she might miss it.

She ran out to the cars, chose an SUV at random, and shot off down the road. She plugged the map reference Indigo had mentioned into the GPS, and gunned the engine. She dialled Cuinn's phone as she shot onto the lane that led to the highway, juggling the steering wheel and the cell phone as she did so.

Voice mail. *Shit.* She left a message, the map reference, and a plea to come urgently. She tried Tierra. The same. Where were they both?

She called Fintan, who answered in his usual laconic drawl. "Yeah?"

Blaize filled him in on the call from Indigo. She really wished he was here.

"Sparks, under no circumstances go on your own," he ordered.

"What choice do I have? Tierra and Cuinn aren't answering their phones. Plus, I think I can take her now. I've been working on protecting myself from mind control attacks with Cuinn, and that was how she beat me last time."

"We don't know enough about her. Or who she's working with. What if she's not alone?"

Blaize frowned. She hadn't considered that. Why hadn't she considered that? She had a moment of self-doubt, then shook her head. "I don't think she's working with anyone."

The SUV purred, swiftly eating up the miles. She was less than five minutes away.

"Based on what exactly?" Fintan snapped.

"Uh ... a feeling?" Blaize squirmed in the driver's seat, but she kept her eyes on the road. She glanced at the GPS. Nearly there. "Okay. I'll scope out the situation and wait for Cuinn to get here. I won't engage."

"Good. We're on our way back now. We'll be with you as soon as we can. I have the map coordinates. Stay away from the Rogue. Visual contact only." Fintan's voice was a little softer, but it was still an order.

They hung up, and Blaize pulled over to look at the map on the car's GPS. She was close to the coordinates Indigo had given her.

Will Indigo know this terrain any better than me? She had no idea if the woman was a local. Just because she'd been new to working at the coffee shop in Merrow didn't mean she was new to the area.

Blaize sat in the car and navigated around the area using the GPS, shifting the picture on the screen so she could get a good sense of where she was. There were some woods and a couple of barns marked. Not much in the way of housing, just a few cottages here and there. This wasn't well-travelled land.

Blaize checked her phone once more. Nothing from Cuinn or Tierra. She texted Cuinn: "Going to scope out the situation. Won't engage. Come ASAP."

She waited a moment, then switched the phone to silent and put it in her pocket. Her deadline wasn't far off. She got out of the vehicle, her body and mind now on alert. Indigo could be anywhere—and this was almost certainly a trap.

But Blaize was confident. Catching Rogues was what she was born to do. She decided to loop round and approach the meeting site from the opposite side. She didn't want the Rogue waiting for her.

She walked away from the car and into the woods that rolled over the land like a carpet. It was darker there, but she loved the smell of damp earth.

She picked up the pace, and breathed in deeply, her feet hitting the soft ground with gentle thuds. The pleasure of the physical activity was wonderful, despite her concern about what was waiting for her. Her chest lightened. She was finally taking action.

She slowed when, deep in the woods, she saw a clearing and something slumped against a log in the centre. But Blaize was too far away to tell if it was a body, let alone if it was Rosa. She crept closer, staying low and hidden.

Blaize checked her cell. Still no message from Cuinn. She squatted on her haunches to wait. She trained her eyes on the body, glancing around every now and then to ensure there was no one else around. If nothing else happened, she could wait Indigo out here until Cuinn arrived. And then Blaize would meet the Rogue on her own terms.

Blaize breathed in and out to still herself, and put in place the shielding Cuinn had been teaching her for her mind, just as she might lock her Manipura shields over her body. This new type of shielding was harder to hold in place than her fire shields, but Cuinn had assured her that was just practice. And she had been practising. Practising until she was sick of it.

She had been there only a few minutes when she caught movement across the other side of the clearing. A thin figure with stringy black hair, wearing dirty jeans and a pink top, strode towards whatever was against the log. *Indigo.* Blaize managed to stop herself leaping to her feet and attacking. Just.

She gritted her teeth and watched the tableau play out. Indigo gave the pile a kick, the thud persuading Blaize that it was a body. But Blaize still couldn't tell if it was alive or dead.

Should she show herself? *What is Indigo doing?* Indigo seemed to be talking to the body on the floor, but there was a strange haze in the gap in the forest, and Blaize struggled to see clearly. *Is Indigo using fire?* Was smoke causing the scene to blur? *Is she burning Rosa?* Blaize shook her head to clear it. There were no flames, and she couldn't smell any smoke. Something wasn't quite right here, but she couldn't put her finger on what, exactly.

There was a movement to her side, and she tensed, ready to spring, to attack.

And then her whole body relaxed as she saw Cuinn, who crouched down next to her, his eyes on the clearing.

"What's going on?" he asked.

She filled him in. He stayed expressionless, listening. When she'd finished, he nodded, speaking in a harsh whisper.

"We can't take any chances. We'll go in from different angles. I'll work my way around the clearing. When you see me attack, follow me. I'll hold Indigo with my mind and you get Rosa. When Rosa's safe, I'll incapacitate Indigo, if I can."

"Surely it's better if I attack her?" protested Blaize in a low, urgent tone.

"You're not strong enough. She's too powerful." He moved off without another word through the forest.

Blaize felt a stab of disappointment in her belly. He hadn't even considered that she could attack the Rogue. And Blaize was a Warrior, not Cuinn. He was just a … a bookworm.

She scowled into the thick foliage between her and the gap in the woods, waiting. But following on the heels of annoyance was anxiety. He needed her to help him fight Indigo. He wasn't a fighter and had no wish to be. She was surprised by the thought that followed on from that: this was her opportunity to show him she was independent. That she wasn't Sophea.

She squinted across the clearing, which shimmered, the figures of Indigo and Rosa flickering in and out of sight. She tried to keep her focus on them despite the headache that pinched at her temples. Uncertainty filled her. What did she need to do? Confusion blurred her next steps.

Long minutes later, Cuinn broke through the woods the other side and shot towards the Rogue, rushing her in a physical attack. Blaize narrowed her eyes, the haze thicker now. Cuinn and the Rogue swam in and out of view, sometimes entirely obscured by the smog. Alarmed, Blaize exploded into action, and ran towards the body. If Indigo was going to burn the area, Blaize needed to get Rosa out now.

But as Blaize approached the struggling figures, the Rogue smashed Cuinn across the face with a hammer fist, and Cuinn fell to his knees, Indigo towering above him. The Rogue drew a knife from her hip, and slashed it across his throat. Blood sprayed across the clearing and spattered across the Rogue, whose triumphant gaze met Blaize's horrified one. Cuinn fell without a sound, his body disappearing into the thick haze.

Blaize sprinted the last few yards, torn between Rosa and Cuinn. But the scene was blurred, and Blaize's head felt fuzzy. She missed her footing as she got close and stumbled on a stray root.

She put her arm out to break her fall, and gasped as she hit the ground. On her hands and knees on the floor, she started to push herself upright, but confusion filled her and she couldn't remember what she was supposed to be doing. There was something urgent, she knew. Something life or death. She swayed on her hands and knees, her head drooping.

A strong arm grabbed her from behind, and pulled her head backwards and up by the hair, which stretched her neck out painfully. She felt a sharp prick where her neck and shoulder joined, and then—oblivion.

35

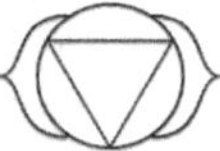

Cuinn didn't spend long with the police. After a short conversation, he left the police station and walked towards his car, pulling his cell from his pocket to text Tierra he was on his way back to pick her up.

The police, with whom he had a reasonable relationship, had let him read Rosa's statement. Indigo had come to see Rosa as she'd been closing up. Rosa had been worried about the other woman, explaining Indigo had looked even thinner than usual.

Rosa—*always too softhearted*—had invited Indigo in for something to eat, wanting to broach what had happened with Blaize. Rosa had told the police she'd never felt any need to be afraid of Indigo before, and she didn't intend to start now.

Rosa didn't remember much after that. An attack, pain, and then to her surprise, the arrival of the police. No one knew who had called the attack in.

The address the Rogue had given in her application form to the coffee shop had been false, and they had no way of tracking her down. The police were still making inquiries – which Cuinn felt was just another way of saying they had no idea where she was.

Cuinn had his hand on the car door when he saw the missed call from Blaize. His stomach gave a lurch, and he shook his head. He was jumping at shadows—the uneasy feeling would be nothing.

But once he'd listened to the voicemail and read her texts, Cuinn's stomach churned, and he gripped the phone in his fist.

What the hell was she thinking? Blaize was impulsive. Unpredictable. And the danger could be specifically directed towards Blaize—there had been a reason that Indigo had attacked Blaize and Cuinn still wasn't sure what it was. Until he understood if the leeching was the only purpose, or whether there was some darker purpose for choosing Blaize particularly, he wanted to keep her out of it. And, he admitted to himself, to protect her.

If only he'd answered the phone, he could have told Blaize that Indigo didn't have Rosa. That there was no need for her to go. By now the churning in his stomach had turned to a cold, hard rock.

He dialled Tierra on his way to the hospital, and her shocked voice said she would wait for him outside.

When he picked up Tierra, her face was paler than usual. He pulled away as soon as she shut her door, heading for the map reference at the northeast end of Kanaka Creek Regional Park. They'd both had messages from Fintan as well, who was well on his way back with Cara.

Tierra updated Cuinn on Rosa as they drove; she had been surrounded by white sheets and bleeping machines. The last thing that Rosa had said to Tierra had chilled him right down to the bone.

"She's damaged. She was like a junkie seeking a fix. I don't know what she's addicted to, but she's unpredictable. I've never seen anyone so out of control."

Cuinn and Tierra found the SUV Blaize had used and called Fintan and Cara to direct them there. There was no sign of Blaize or anyone else. Tierra had to threaten Cuinn with an energetic fight if he didn't wait for Fintan and Cara before he headed off into the woods to find Blaize. She closed her eyes to seek and track Blaize while they waited.

"She's not close by. I don't feel her within my range," she told him.

Cuinn paced up and down, grinding his teeth with impatience until Fintan pulled up almost an hour later, and he and Cara tumbled out of the car.

Cuinn updated the newcomers, and Fintan nodded before he spoke. "Okay. Tierra, can you work with me to track her? We can start from here and see where she went."

"Of course." Tierra pulled a coat from the car.

Fintan stopped Cuinn from joining them. "I think you should go back to the house. Check her Haven and the dreamscape. We'll take the cell phones in case she's injured. If she is, we'll call you. But the more of us out there, the more likely we are to obliterate any tracks. Tierra's our best tracker energetically and physically, so you need to let her work."

Cara nodded. "I'll stay with Cuinn until you need me."

Cuinn ran his hands through his hair. "I need to come."

"You'll do her more good at home, Cuinn. I promise. Now let us go and do what we're good at," Fintan said.

Cuinn could see the logic of his argument, but the emotions inside him threatened to overwhelm him. Cara put a hand on Cuinn's arm, and Tierra gave him a fierce hug. "You know I can do this, Cuinn, but Fin's right, I can't do it if there are too many distractions. It's going to be tricky enough when it gets dark. It's already six o'clock"

Cuinn nodded reluctantly. Tierra was good at finding things, but it wasn't a skill she had much use for these days. He hoped she'd had enough practice recently. "We'll stay at the car. But we're not going home immediately. You might need us. I'll see if I can find her mind in the physical area before I go to her Haven."

Fintan sent him one last sympathetic look and then he and Tierra were gone into the woods.

"Do you need anything else to be able to search for her?" said Cara.

Cuinn shook his head and got back into the car, putting the seat back so his long frame could lie down as much as possible. He relaxed and searched for her mind in as wide an area as he could. But he could find no trace of her. She was either unconscious, or she'd been taken out of his range—a range that was further than Tierra's. Neither was good. His stomach was a knot of tension, and all his muscles were tight. He couldn't stop thinking about the image from the prophecy, of her tied up, bloody and beaten.

After a couple of hours, with full dark outside the stuffy car, Cara's cell phone rang.

The noise felt shrill, intrusive after the quiet he'd been working in, but he welcomed it nonetheless. His eyes snapped open, and he put the seat back up as Cara spoke. Her end of the conversation didn't give anything away, and after a few "Okays" she turned the phone off.

"They've tracked her to a clearing where it looks like her trail ends. They think she's been kidnapped."

Cuinn wouldn't accept that. He opened the car door. Fintan had created a bobbing light with Manipura energy for them to follow. It led them to where Fintan and Tierra waited. A grave Tierra showed him the tracks they'd followed from Blaize's car to an overgrown area at the edge of a clearing where it looked as if someone had waited. The four of them then walked the tracks of someone heavy who'd left the clearing—possibly someone carrying another person. Those tracks went to a dirt track road, where Tierra thought a car had parked, before turning and leaving.

"Cuinn, I think we should call Adam. He can get us what we need to help us find her. Most of his work is tracking down Rogues," Tierra said. Her brother, Adam, Cuinn's cousin, was in a security team that worked across the Guilds to protect them from internal and external threats. He had access to tracking resources as well as being a powerful energetic tracker in his own right.

Cuinn felt sick. All his worst fears had come to pass. "They could be anywhere by now. They have hours of lead on us."

They would never find her.

Fintan nodded at Tierra, and she went to the side of the clearing to phone Adam.

"We'll find her Cuinn. If it's the same Rogue who leeched in the dreamscape, there are more of us, and we're smarter. We'll find her."

Cuinn punched a fist into the nearest tree. "I knew that the vision wasn't fulfilled by what happened on the astral plane. But I didn't want to believe it."

Slam. Slam.

"I wanted to believe it was over. I should have said something. Guarded her. Stayed with her. I've failed her, just as I failed Sophea."

Slam. The pain felt good. He deserved it.

Fintan grabbed his arm and gave it a shake, forcing Cuinn to give him his attention. "We'll find her. But you have to stay focused and present. We need you."

"Okay." It was easier to agree. He'd do what he could to help. The nausea in his stomach had stopped and everything felt numb. Switched off.

He couldn't bear it if he lost Blaize too.

36

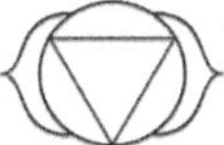

Blaize woke up, groggy and nauseated. Where was she? She tried to stretch her aching joints but found herself shackled, unable to move more than a few inches. That woke her more quickly. What had happened? She remembered the clearing. A haze. Rosa. Cuinn.

Oh, Source. Cuinn. He wasn't dead. He couldn't be dead. She refused to accept it as a possibility. She needed to find out what had happened, and now. But before that, she needed to get out of here.

She looked around her. She lay on a dirty bare mattress, in a small, dark room. It seemed like a basement, as there was only one window, high up in the wall, and a rickety metal staircase on the other side of the room, leading up to a solid looking door.

She had no sense of where she was, whether she was still in the woods or if she'd been moved.

She tried to use the power she had stored. But as she drew on it, she felt nauseous again and stopped. She gasped, and leaned her head to the side, not wanting to be sick while she was lying down. The nausea receded after a few minutes, leaving her shaky as well as tired.

After an indeterminable amount of time, the door opened. Blaize shifted, ready to defend herself as much as the shackles allowed.

It was the Rogue.

Now thin to the point of emaciation, she had a hollow look around her eyes.

She sneered at Blaize.

"Good morning. For me, anyway. For you, not so much. And for Cuinn?" She laughed.

Blaize strained against the metal chains. She needed to get free. But how the hell could she do that without access to her energies?

Indigo laughed and ignored her struggles. She checked the bonds that held Blaize. "Didn't try to burn your way out yet? Shame. As soon as you pulled power, you'd have been sick. I was looking forward to seeing what you'd look like after you'd tried to call Warrior fire."

Blaize twisted her wrists as far as they'd go, trying to find some give in the chains. The sick feeling she'd had when she'd tried to pull energy earlier suggested Indigo wasn't lying about that, so Blaize would need to get free physically.

"Still, seeing you lying here surrounded by your own vomit would have been fun, you stuck-up bitch."

"Why are you doing this? And what did you do to Cuinn?" Blaize's body was no longer aching, the adrenaline energising her. Her heart tripped in her chest as she tried to understand what was going on. She was shocked by the poisonous ire that Indigo was directing at her.

"Cuinn?" Indigo shrugged. "He was nothing. To me, anyway. Others might say different. But I need what you have. Your energy. Tasty energy. You're just … well, food basically."

The woman stepped away from the bed and closed her eyes. Energy swept over Blaize and her gut roiled. "Hmmm. Yes, you're still ready. Charged—you seem to have even more power than when we last met."

Indigo shook her head.

"I nearly took you then, in the dreamscape rather than here, but we—I—wasn't ready. I tried to get you to pull power in your dreams so I could tie you to me. But persistent thing you are, I couldn't make you though I had fun killing you over and over." She smiled.

"But that's in the past. I enjoyed our little game with Rosa and Cuinn. That made up for it a little. And now," she clapped her hands together, "now we're going to take a trip back to the dreamscape together where I can taste you properly, and I'm going to have me another snack. And that's really what life's going to be like for you for the next little while."

"Don't do this." Blaize tried to make her voice firm though she wanted to be sick. "We can help you, rehabilitate you. My friend works at the Rehab centre on the West Coast; she can get you over this addiction. There's no need to hurt me."

Fear mounted inside her as the woman talked. Indigo wasn't in her right mind. *How am I going to get out of this?* All her muscles were tight as she heaved against the chains at her hands and feet. Could she loosen any of them? Or was there enough give for her to strike Indigo when she came close again? Even a few inches might be enough to stun Indigo if Blaize was fast enough and put enough physical power into it.

"Why would I want to get over it?" Indigo's voice was amused. "It's such fun. And the taste … the taste of an energy like yours? It's hard to even put into words. It makes me feel … invincible."

She leaned over, and Blaize waited until the woman's face was inches away before thrusting her clenched fist towards it, putting every ounce of physical power she could into the movement. But Indigo was too quick and swerved easily to the side. Blaize caught a glimpse of something metal in Indigo's hand. Blaize flinched away, but where could she go?

"That's enough talking. Let's take a trip." Indigo grabbed Blaize's arm and shot something sharp into it.

Blaize winced at the stab of the needle, and then her eyelids became heavy as the drug took her under. Ignoring the nausea, she pulled power to try to burn it away, but the drug was faster than she was, especially in her current condition.

"No … wait."

And then, she went under.

When Blaize opened her eyes again, she was in an ornate room with a grand chandelier. She drew in a breath through her nose. No scent. She was in the dreamscape, though not Cuinn's Haven or her own. Her throat tightened. *Don't think of Cuinn.*

She was still tied down, but the chair and the chains were fancier. She shook her head, trying to dislodge some of the fatigue that had come over her. She didn't feel at all as she had previously on the astral plane. She felt dizzy, and it was hard to focus. Her vision swam.

Indigo appeared in front of her.

"No, no, don't get up." She laughed. "Really, all you need to do is sit there. I'll do all the heavy lifting."

Indigo stood behind her, hands on Blaize's shoulders. Blaize tried to shrug her off, but Indigo's bony fingers dug unpleasantly into her muscles with a bruising grip.

She felt ripples of power on her shoulders as Indigo leeched from her. At first it was just odd, like someone running her hand the wrong way along velvet. But then the feeling intensified and became painful as Indigo took more and more power.

And Blaize felt herself getting weaker, lassitude spilling into her limbs until her head lolled to one side, falling onto her shoulder.

Fintan and Tierra stayed in the park to see if there was anything else they could find. They'd agreed to go into Merrow at first light in case anyone had seen Indigo in the last couple of days and they could get a lead that way. Tierra hadn't been able to get through to Adam, who was still somewhere deep in Russia. Cuinn and Cara went home for Cuinn to work in his own environment.

He wanted to dive straight into the dreamscape, but while he was setting up the room, warding it with energetics shields one more time, Cara disappeared and came back with an energy drink. She handed it to him wordlessly, and although he grimaced, he took it and drank it.

Cara settled herself in the armchair, her eyes alert and watchful, and Cuinn sank onto his mat, arranging his position so he lay on his back.

Cuinn closed his eyes and took a few deep breaths before pulling the energy to go into the dreamscape, starting in his own Haven. He strode around the tower quickly in case there was any trace that Blaize had managed to come back here. He saw nothing.

Outside, he looked around before walking over to the green bower that held the portal between their Havens. The grass was soft underfoot and delicate roses had bloomed around the gate. His mouth twisted, and in response to the strong feelings and energy he was putting out, the sky started to boil. Thunder cracked and lighting streaked down. He nodded viciously, satisfied as the rain poured down on him, soaking him to the skin.

He stood in front of the portal for minutes, hoping when he stepped through he might find her there, and terrified that she wouldn't be.

Eventually, he gathered the courage to go through, the moment of disorientation before he stepped into her Haven making him blink. He scanned her garden, but she wasn't there. He paced over to the bed she had created the last time they were here, and dropped onto it, his hands grabbing the red silk. His breath came in heaves.

He tried to think what to do next. She wasn't in either of the two safe places for her in the astral plane, that was clear. He would need to go outside and seek her. Just as he had done fifty years earlier, seeking Sophea's mind.

He took one last look around her Haven and headed to his own to prepare for going out into the wild energies.

Many hours later, he opened his eyes in his own body. He was shaking. He had over-taxed himself on the astral plane, and for nothing. Cara was still sitting opposite him, watching him from the chair. She came over, lifted his head, and put a cushion under it. She offered him some water. He drank and let his body settle.

Cara looked at him questioningly. He shook his head.

"You need to rest. Still a few hours until Fintan and Tierra can go into town, and they're getting some sleep until they can leave."

He opened his mouth to protest, wanting just to replenish his physical energy with some food and then go in again. She caught his gaze. "There's no way you can go back in again straight away. You need sleep first, then food and drink. You can try again first thing in the morning. But you need a few hours of rest or your body will burn itself up."

Cuinn got to his feet with her help, and realising how exhausted he was, agreed. "But wake me for breakfast with the others. I want to talk strategy and see if there's anything they found that was unusual in the woods. Four heads are better than two."

She nodded, and helped him into his bedroom.

"I'll leave a note to ask the others to wake us."

"Thank you, Cara."

"Tell me what you found last night," Cuinn said, addressing Fintan and Tierra through a mouthful of toast early the next morning.

"Not much," Fintan said.

"We thought we'd go and talk to Rosa again. See if there's anything else she remembers." Tierra hesitated. "Do you think we should share more with the human police about Indigo? The non-energetic aspects?"

Cuinn shook his head, adamant. "It's too dangerous. Indigo's too volatile. She could hurt humans, or expose us. But see if you can find out anything else from the police as to what they have found out about the attack on Rosa. Fintan, you might have more luck there. Get Tierra to introduce you and play on your military background," Cuinn said. "I'll go back into the dreamscape."

"I'll stay with you. I can keep an eye on both you and the house," said Cara.

"Fine," said Cuinn.

"We'll stay out as long as we need to." Tierra addressed Cuinn directly. "Don't forget to eat."

37

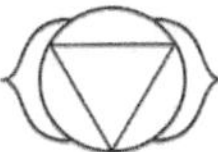

Blaize was woken by a persistent pain. She turned her head groggily to see a narrow plastic tube leading from a stand towards her arm, a nasty bruise forming around the entry point.

She tried to stay conscious. But flashes of memory, or dreams, kept intruding. Were they in her head, or was she in the dreamscape? The scenes were like pieces of a mosaic, flashes of colour that hurt her head, and nothing that she could focus on for more than a few seconds.

But the fragments, and the haze and fog that came with them nagged at her, trying to get her attention. There was something she was missing, something important. She moaned and shifted on the bed in an attempt to get comfortable in the restraints. She tugged on her wrists, and thought of a happier time when she had been willing to give up her control to an infuriating, rude, and inhospitable man who had gotten under her skin in a big way.

Her consciousness drifted over her accusation that he was the threat to her in the café. How wrong she had been. Her mind swam as snapshots from the fight with Indigo drifted through. How Indigo had beaten her. How hazy and confused she had felt.

How there had been a haze around them both, and how difficult it had been for Blaize to see clearly. A haze. Smog.

Blaize's eyes opened wide as she put the pieces together. Cuinn wasn't dead. The Rogue had torn through Blaize's mental shields like tissue paper and showed her an entire tableau that didn't exist. Anger warred with relief. *Cuinn was alive.*

The relief gave her some true sleep. But she soon woke again and drifted between fragments from the ether and consciousness.

Every time she woke up back in the basement, the renewed hope drove her to pull enough power to burn away the drugs that were being fed into her body through the drip. But they built up each time while she slept, and it was like trying to drain the ocean with a teacup.

As time passed, she became more and more agitated. Her fire energy was looking for a way out. Whatever combination of drugs and energy Indigo used had trapped Blaize's energy in her own body.

If she used energy, she'd be sick. If she didn't use it, eventually it could twist into a darker form, the sinister form that some energies could take when they had nowhere to go. She could become the thing she most hated: a Rogue.

She needed to get out of there. *Think. What are my options?* Her brain was mushy and fogged.

I need to contact Cuinn. And that was best done in the dreamscape. If he were alive—not if, there was no if; he was alive, she knew it—he would try to find her there. She just needed to send him a signal so he could locate her.

But she wasn't able to access the dreamscape with the level of drugs in her system at the moment. The only way she accessed the dreamscape was with Indigo. Blaize was trapped in the dreamscape just as much as she was trapped on the physical plane.

Her thoughts swirled round and round, and she fought against hopelessness as she swam in and out of consciousness.

What was her first priority? Get rid of some of the drugs in her system.

She burned them in tiny increments, increasing the amount in the moments of clarity she had and making her feel nauseous. She'd rest, then burn a little more, then rest.

After doing this for what seemed like hours, she passed out again. This time, it was a more healing sleep.

Blaize jolted awake with a sharp pain on her right cheek, which rocked her head to the side. When she opened her eyes, her face burned and she caught the movement of Indigo drawing her hand back. This new pain quickly blended into all the other pains in her body.

"Yeah, wake up bitch." Indigo's angry tones were back. "Thanks for supper." Blaize could see the hollows on Indigo's face were a little less pronounced than the day before. Blaize's energy clearly agreed with her.

Blaize stared back, exhausted. She aimed for a defiant sneer on her face. "I know what you did."

Indigo cocked her head. "What …"

She laughed. "Oh, you figured out my little game? Took you long enough."

"Why?"

"Why not? It was a good way to keep you occupied so I could catch you. And the look on your face when you thought your precious Maven was dead? Worth a little of my energy." She shrugged and put a box containing a greasy pizza on the bed next to Blaize. It smelled disgusting. "You need to eat."

Blaize stared at her.

"To keep your energy up," Indigo said. "You're pretty strong, but if you don't eat something—even with the drip—it will be hard to keep you alive. As I take your energy, your body will burn itself from the inside out. You'll lose weight and eventually your organs will fail."

Blaize blinked, and shook her head. She'd never been this close to her own death before. *I need to do something.*

"Why don't you just stop taking my energy?"

"Good one. You'll eat eventually. Because now you've worked out that Cuinn's still around, you have romantic notions of rescue. So I'll keep you alive and get to enjoy you for longer, and you'll lie there hoping someone will come and get you. They won't, of course. No one knows where you are except me and—" she stopped and put a hand to her mouth. "Except me. So, eat. Keep your hopes alive."

Blaize had to contort her body to reach the pizza box because of the chains on her wrists and ankles. But she managed to grab a slice of the pizza. The oil from the pizza made her stomach roil in protest. But Indigo was right. She wanted to stay alive. And she wanted to be rescued.

Well. No. She wanted to rescue herself.

But with horrible clarity, she realised that her pride, her extreme self-reliance, and her focus on doing everything herself, had played a huge part in getting her into this mess in the first place.

She might **want** to rescue herself, but she **needed** to get help. And she had an idea of how to do it.

She kept her eyes on Indigo as she ate, nervous of the strange energetic's unpredictability.

"Good work," Indigo said, once Blaize had eaten the slice of pizza.

Indigo walked towards the top of the bed, and Blaize flinched. But Indigo just checked the drip.

"I'll leave you with the rest." She went over to the door. As she opened it, she looked back. "You've been in training your whole life to be my battery, you know. You shine with power. And it's mine now. We're going to be spending a lot of time together. And don't worry, we're going to move to more comfortable conditions soon. We're still a little too close for comfort to that idiot, Cuinn."

So we're still close by.

Blaize felt relief and anxiety at the same time, and was unable to stop the conflict of emotions chase across her expression. Indigo cackled. "Ah, you still think he might find you and save you? I've been stalking you all since you arrived, and the only time you saw me was in the café. And he didn't even notice me then, did he? I'm protected. I'm not worried he'll find you. And even if he did, with the amount of energy I have from you, I think I could take him. You weren't hard, after all."

Indigo looked around the room, and her gaze stopped on a rickety wooden bookshelf in the corner of the basement, with a few damp books lying in piles on it. She narrowed her eyes, and the bookshelf burst into flames.

The heat was intense, and Blaize contracted her body on the bed and strained against the chains. The adrenaline from the fear burned more of the drugs in her system away. *Will she burn me to death?*

Blaize looked around the room, desperately searching for something she could do to protect herself from the fire. But the fire burned hard, and after minutes, books and bookshelf were just a pile of stinking ash on the floor.

"I don't think he'd have much of a defense against that, eh? Anyway. Enough fun. Eat your food." She turned away, and went to the door, and slammed it behind her.

It took Blaize several hours, but she managed to get the pizza down, no easy thing, given her bonds. Her neck ached by the end of it, and she lay back down again with a sigh of relief. Perhaps now, with a little rest, she would be able to burn away more of the drugs, which were just another poison, after all, from her body.

If she had less of the drugs in her system, the next time Indigo took her back to the dreamscape, into Indigo's Haven—which was what she assumed the trashy mansion was—she could break out and reach Cuinn with a message. He could then follow her and find her physically.

Cuinn was going to be very, very angry. Blaize had wanted to save Rosa and she'd rushed off, sure if it came to it, she'd be able to beat Indigo. Her impulsive and proud nature had gotten her into trouble again.

But with Cuinn, she'd held back. She'd kept her feelings under a tight rein. She'd been ready for spontaneity and impulse in terms of sex, but she'd been the opposite when it had come to a relationship.

She had thought she was like her father. That if she fell in love, her energy might twist, and she'd end up in a similar tragic situation. And she couldn't have borne it if that had happened to Cuinn.

If she survived this—when she survived—without her energy twisting, she would do things his way. They'd try a relationship. She felt a flutter in her stomach at the idea, and a new resolution fill her.

She closed her eyes, ready to try again for the dreamscape, but the door opened, and Indigo walked in with a fresh bag for the drip and another syringe.

"Don't get too comfortable, bitch." She changed the bag on the drip, giving it a satisfied tap, and then raised the needle.

Blaize, more alert this time, tried to flinch away, but the chains kept her well within Indigo's reach. "There's no point trying to get away. There's nowhere for you to go." She stabbed the needle into Blaize's tensed arm, and blackness crept over Blaize's vision. As she faded back into unconsciousness, Indigo said, "This is your life now. You, me, and the energy."

Despair flooded her as the drugs pulled her under.

38

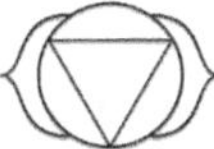

Cuinn had spent most of the day in the dreamscape with nothing to show for it. He was exhausted. Cara had eventually forced him to come away from his rooms for a short period, making him eat. He was burning his own resources because of the amount of energy he used, and he already looked pounds thinner.

As he sat at the kitchen table with Cara, chewing listlessly on some stir-fried rice that Cara had put together, the front door opened. Tierra came in, her face tight, Fintan following behind her.

"Everything okay?" Cara asked them.

"Fine," Tierra's answer was terse, "but we didn't find much."

Cuinn's face focused on her. "But you found something?"

"Just a better sense of the Rogue's energy at the café." Fintan sat down wearily, and Cara put a plate of rice in front of him. "There was no question she burned the place, and Tierra didn't sense any other energetics there."

"We tracked the Rogue to where she must have had a car parked." She hung her head. "I'm sorry, Cuinn; I couldn't track it any further."

Cuinn put an arm out and touched hers. "No one could. I need to go back into the dreamscape." Cuinn stood. "That might be our only chance of finding her."

Tierra looked him up and down. "You're burning yourself up. You'll do yourself permanent damage if you don't rest a little. I wish we could track down Adam; this is much more his area."

"I can find her. There's no time for rest."

Tierra opened her mouth but hesitated.

"What's the matter?" Fintan said.

"I've had an idea. It's pretty ... unusual, and I don't think you're going to like it, but if you're going to keep searching in the dreamscape, then I don't think you have much choice."

Cuinn frowned. "What?"

"Promise me you'll hear me out."

"Get on with it, Tierra. We don't have time for games," Cuinn said.

"Let's blend energies. You can take some of my energy."

Cara gasped, and Fintan's eyes narrowed.

"It's an unusual situation, and I know you won't take too much," Tierra said quickly. "And no one else ever needs to know. I'm the only one here who can share energy with you; the others don't share either of your Chakras. It has to be me."

"This is a very bad idea," Fintan said. "Blending is forbidden other than between Mavens and Adherents. For good reason. People get addicted doing it. That's how you get Leeches in the first place."

"Cuinn and I are strong enough to do this. He's a Maven with experience of sharing energy."

"With his Adherents, maybe, but it's not the—"

Tierra gestured with a hand and cut across Fintan. "No one is going to get addicted. We can't stop him from going back to the dreamscape, but if he goes as he is, he either won't have the strength to deal with the Rogue when he finds her, or he'll harm himself. Cara's a Healer—as am I—and she can make sure we stop in time."

Cara nodded slowly. "I can do that."

Fintan jerked his head round to look at Cara. "You approve?"

She winced. "If the two of them want to do it, then I'll support them. I don't think it's the world's best idea, but I'd rather help them than have them do it unsupervised."

"Let's do it," Cuinn said. "Anything that helps me to search is good right now."

Fintan shook his head again but appeared more resigned. "Tierra, a word?"

She huffed, but the two of them went out of the kitchen together.

"Eat more rice," Cara said. "You need anything that will support your energy."

Cuinn took another mouthful. After a few minutes, Tierra and Fintan came back into the room, a frosty silence between them.

"We'll do it in a couple of hours. I need to prepare, as it's been a while since I worked with my Maven and shared energy with anyone. And you should rest, Cuinn."

"I'm too wired to rest."

"Well, you need to relax then. Wired isn't a good state to be in for the energy transfer."

"And you're sure you're okay with this?"

"You know I am." She took a forkful of rice and a drink of water. "Now, eat."

The four of them gathered an hour later in Tierra's workroom. The usually cosy room felt crowded to Cuinn with all of them present. He paced while Tierra prepared her sacred space. She had opened her glass doors to the evening air and surrounded her mat with plants. Cuinn had brought his own mat down from his room, and Tierra put handfuls of earth in the corners. He'd protested at first, but she'd reminded him he most often used the mat for Ajna work, and that this was Muladhara. She grounded his mat as best she could.

"You also need to get grounded," she said to Cuinn. "You need to relax."

"I don't feel relaxed."

"Sit and do some breathing exercises. This will be harder for both of us the further away from the earth you feel. At the very least, pace outside in bare feet so you connect with the earth."

Cuinn turned on his heels and stalked out of the glass doors. He shucked off his shoes and socks on the stone patio and stepped onto the cold, wet grass. At first the sensation was unpleasant, but as he dug his toes in, he felt his connection to the earth revive. He breathed in moss and damp soil. The garden was dark, the soft candles from Tierra's ceremonial setup behind him was his only light. He forced his breathing to deepen. He connected to the woods, to the earth, to the environment around him.

"The earth supports me, and it meets my needs." He repeated this mantra as he stretched out his arms, and thought of family, home, safety, security, and boundaries. And trust. Trust for the cousin who was more like a sister, and was prepared to break an energetic taboo to save another's life.

He grounded himself in his body, pulling a little energy from the earth around him. By the time he caught Tierra's shadow as she stood between the doors, he felt more himself.

A few minutes later he sat opposite Tierra in the space she had prepared. She took his hands. Fintan sat behind her, angled so he was able to see both her and Cuinn, and Cara was sitting behind Cuinn. They were energetic 'spotting'—making sure Cuinn didn't take too much energy and damage Tierra, or become addicted—both real possibilities, and the main reason that sharing energy between energetics who weren't Maven and Adherent was forbidden by the Circle. All of them could get into trouble for taking part in this activity, even if it went perfectly. For Cuinn, it was a risk he was willing to take for Blaize, but he felt a stab of guilt at involving the others.

Tierra had put on some low drumming music in the background, and the beat was rhythmic, hypnotic. He closed his eyes and centred himself in the element of earth, in Muladhara Chakra. Pine incense floated around him, further connecting him.

Each type of energy was shared in a different way. For Ajna elements, it was in the dreamscape. Fire energy was shared through an intense, unblinking gaze. For earth, it was through the power of touch.

He focused on his hands, and on the connection between himself and Tierra. After a few minutes of concentration, he could feel her energy like a prickling heat in his hands. This was an unusually fast connection, probably because of their relationship and the fact that they knew the feel of each other's energy so well.

He opened himself up to her energy, which pushed at him, eager to move from Tierra to him. He pulled a little, just as he would when pulling energy from the environment and astral plane, but this time he pulled from Tierra herself. He could almost see the strands of energy looping between them, replenishing his own dwindling stores.

The feeling created an endorphin rush, which was the reason it was easy to get addicted. It wasn't like pulling from the environment, which normally topped out at what each individual energetic could handle. When you drew from another energetic, there was no limit to the power you could take— until the other person died.

He tried to maintain his own Ajna activation while focusing on the Muladhara energy, a fine line to balance. But keeping his mind energy alert would give him the discernment to say stop.

It didn't take long for the rush to turn into a high, a euphoric feeling that had an unwilling smile edge across his face, though his eyes were still closed. The smile, more than anything, brought him back to the moment. He'd never felt less like smiling in his life.

The line between pain and pleasure at this point was delicate, and the connection between his hands and Tierra's smaller, more delicate hands felt intense. He could almost feel every individual whorl and line of her fingers.

"I think … we should stop," he said, over the drumming. But he didn't break the connection, unwilling to let go of the rush quite yet.

Cara stood and touched Tierra and Cuinn on their shoulders, and closed her eyes briefly. When she opened them again, she nodded. "I agree. Enough, Tierra."

Nothing happened for a moment, and then Cuinn felt Tierra's energy cut off. He held back a groan as the pleasure left him. He rubbed his hands together, his eyes still closed. The incense hung heavy in the air around them, the drumming continuing. Everything felt suspended in time.

He opened his eyes just as Tierra let out a gasp, and Fintan moved forward to support her. Fintan scowled at Cara and Cuinn.

"She's fine, Fintan," Cara said, that hint of amusement back in her voice. "Help her into her room to lie down and get her to eat something light."

Fintan nodded and let Tierra rest in the crook of his arm for a while as Cuinn got up and stretched. He felt amazing. "I'll go back into the astral realm and see if I can make contact. She might be sleeping, so there's the possibility I might be able to connect to her dreams."

Cara rose. "I'm right behind you."

39

Blaize woke up. And almost wished she hadn't. She was still trapped in the disgusting room, and her arms and legs ached from lying down for the last twenty-four hours. She felt better than the last time she'd been awake—perhaps the pizza had helped after all though she could tell she had already lost some weight. Indigo was right; taking her energy was draining her physical body quickly. She'd have to eat more if she wanted to keep herself going.

She lay, staring at the ceiling, trying to work out what to do. What she could do.

Part of her felt shame—shame that she had been captured so easily. Cuinn would be so angry with her. She winced, remembering Indigo's sharp comments about her own 'romantic notions of rescue.' *I have to hope. It's not naive to think I'll get out of here.*

She was strong, stronger than Indigo. But while Indigo was weak, she was also unpredictable, addicted as she was to the energy.

All Blaize needed was a moment. She didn't think she could break out of the shackles she had on, but if she could get control of herself in the dreamscape, she thought she could contact Cuinn.

And that had all better be done fast. Indigo was already talking about moving her.

The door opened again.

"Good morning, bitch." Indigo sang out the words. She walked jerkily to the end of the bed. Her eyes darted around the room and over Blaize, the pupils pinpricks.

Is she still high? Blaize shivered. It was hard to see how Indigo could be even more disturbed. She was already unpredictable enough.

"How are we today? A little thinner, I see. Ooops!" Indigo covered her mouth with a hand. "I took more than I meant to yesterday. But you, Blaize-bitch, are dee-licious. I'll have to keep myself in check in the future, or there won't be enough of you to go around, and I'll get into trouble!"

"What do you mean, go around? Are you working with someone?" Blaize's voice was scratchy.

Indigo froze for the smallest of moments, then laughed. "Just me, BB."

She put a can she'd been carrying next to Blaize.

"I brought you a protein shake. One of those meal replacement thingies. Enough calories to keep you going." She turned on her heel and walked out.

Blaize needed to drink it if she was to be well enough to take advantage of any chance that arose to get a message to Cuinn. She took a sip, grimaced, and started working on a new plan.

When Blaize hit the astral plane this time, she didn't wait. She knew what to expect, and as soon as her eyes opened in Indigo's tasteless Haven she focused the hottest fire she could create on her chains and broke them.

Indigo stepped back a pace, and her eyes widened. Blaize was able to land a backhanded blow across Indigo's gaunt face before she recovered from the surprise. But Indigo had the advantage health-wise, and even as her head snapped to the side from the blow, she came back with a hammer fist that just missed Blaize's cheek, catching her on the shoulder as she moved out of the way. Pain blossomed across Blaize's upper arm, and she staggered.

They fought in earnest, but Blaize had thought about this already. Physical fighting was only part of the tactics that could be used in the dreamscape. After a handful more blows were exchanged, she drew back from Indigo, bending forward slightly as if she was getting exhausted, but, in fact, creating space and distance between herself and the other energetic. She drew on the energy that she saw around Indigo, weakening her. The energy felt tainted, giving Blaize strength but also making her feel nauseous, so even as Indigo staggered, Blaize wobbled on her own feet.

Indigo fell onto her hands and knees and looked up at Blaize, hissing through her inky hair. She pushed off the floor and launched herself at Blaize, flying through the air with more height than Blaize could have managed in the physical plane. Her hands were grasping claws and the force of her landing pushed Blaize to the floor.

"You're nothing," Indigo hissed into her face. "You think you're somehow special. But you're nothing. You shouldn't have even been born."

Blaize was on her back with Indigo's hands around her neck and was perilously close to losing consciousness. But Indigo's words penetrated her brain. *What the hell?*

"You know nothing about me," Blaize panted out.

"I know your parents were told to stay apart. And look what happened to them. Your father became a Rogue, who killed your mother and himself."

When the anger washed over her body, Blaize didn't fight it, but she did hold on to her focus. She wouldn't let the anger control her this time. She would use it.

Blaize planted her feet firmly on the ground. She shifted her hip, ready, and took hold of Indigo's right arm. Blaize shoved and pushed her hips up at the same time, which tipped Indigo to the side, and Blaize used the momentum to switch places with Indigo.

Indigo fought under the influence, whereas Blaize fought for her life.

Once Blaize was in a sitting position she pinned one of Indigo's wrists with her knee, and the other with her hand. She held Indigo there while she took another moment, and then she pulled at Indigo's energy, which was flickering and weak.

Instead of absorbing the energy herself, she used it to build a cage around Indigo, throwing herself backwards as she closed the front of the cage. She then put a blindfold on the woman, pulling enough of Indigo's energy to render her unconscious.

She had the woman's astral body trapped. But for how long, Blaize didn't know.

She closed her eyes and focused everything she had on Cuinn's Haven. She sent out a pulse of energy that was as strong as she could make it, an energetic cry for help.

She repeated her message over and over. But her strength was limited. And it was failing.

Indigo stayed unconscious in her cage, her body stretched out on the floor. The prison Blaize had created for the woman's spirit held. For now.

40

Cuinn was in the dreamscape, out in the wild energy. He was close to having to go back to at least his Haven, if not the physical plane, to rest. His fists clenched at the thought.

He wouldn't lose her.

He wouldn't let her down.

He moved his astral form through the untamed places, making and remaking the world as he proceeded through it. He sifted through pieces of dreamscape like an archeologist seeking shards of pottery from the past, looking for any trace of Blaize's distinct energy.

The inhospitable environment tested his strength, as he kept his own mind as focused as possible.

He especially didn't want to think about the vision of Blaize in the prophecy, dying.

He focused his mind on one thing only.

Finding her.

Staying receptive to any indications of her energy while broadcasting his own signal as a beacon and enclosing his mind in a strong shield, sapped his energy.

He would have to go back. He would be no good to Blaize if his own mind was caught in the dreamscape, lost to the influence of other, unknown energies.

He followed his trail of reality to his Haven. He was cautious, taking no chances, but his bitter anger at not finding Blaize infected the trail, his emotions changing reality as he jogged back.

A snarling dog appeared in front of him, and he stopped, using his black feelings to quickly shape some of the energies around him into a bigger dog. A hellhound. It sat at his side for a moment, before it threw itself towards the other dog—which didn't hesitate, but turned and ran.

Cuinn called his dog to his side.

It looked at him, eyes glowing, fierce teeth dripping saliva. He called it to heel and used the hellhound to chase away anything that tried to injure him.

He was close to his Haven when he felt something. A tug. A pulse of energy that felt familiar. It felt … like Blaize. He span in place, trying to read where the energy was coming from. How had it reached him?

He put his hand on the dog, drawing the energy and the emotions that had created it back inside him, the hellhound disappearing like smoke.

He drew on the energy of the emotion, every single feeling that Blaize had ever caused him to feel. Anger, frustration, annoyance, irritation. Amusement, contentment, fun.

Love.

He wove this complex mix into an arrow. He created a bow and drew the string back, the muscles in his back and arm tense and straining. He released the string and shot the arrow into the air.

Find her.

The arrow disappeared from sight, and Cuinn followed its energy trail into the ether.

The wild energies flickered past him. Invisible hands grabbed at him as if he was being dragged through brambles and bushes, their sharp thorns scraping his skin and leaving him covered with long bloody scratches.

But finally the arrow connected to Blaize's pulse of energy in a stranger's Haven.

The Haven was warded, of course, he could see the energetic protection that surrounded it, but the wardings were as irregular as the Haven was misshapen. It had the appearance of a castle in a fairytale, but it was subtly wrong. Off.

He held up his hand, and the arrow flew back to his palm. His body shook from the efforts he was making. But he wouldn't give up now.

He hauled on his emotions again, putting everything he had into the arrow.

He drew the bow.

And released.

The arrow shot out, and twisted and turned, spinning in the air, a golden blur.

It found one of the weaker wardings and pierced it. Cuinn followed it in, expanding the weakness into an entrance.

And once he was in, he could feel her.

But her energy was faint. Fading.

He ran through the strange corridors, crystals and gold flickering at the edges of his vision.

He found a huge room and slammed through the doors. His gaze darted around the room until he saw her lying on the floor, her back propped up against the side of a bed.

Thank Source.

He got closer and saw she was battered and bloody. Next to her was an energetic cage. Holding the unconscious Rogue.

Blaize saw him and sagged in relief. "Can your energy follow me back to the physical plane? See where I am? Come find me? Indigo, the Rogue, said I'm not far from Merrow. But she'll move me as soon as she wakes."

Blaize started to fade, losing her connection with the dreamscape.

He clung to her energy and travelled back with her to her body. Once there, he looked around, trying to gauge where the property was. Blaize and her captor were unconscious in the basement, but he was unable to do much physically.

After what seemed like an eternity, he found a heap of abandoned junk mail thrown on a shelf. They all had the same address. Bingo. He noted the address and fled back to his Haven, gathering his strength and then dropping back into his own body.

It would be critical to reach her before the Rogue woke up. Source knew what damage the Rogue would do to Blaize when she did.

He'd never associated Blaize with the word 'fragile' before.

It was breaking his heart.

All four of them piled into Cuinn's rugged 4x4, Tierra to keep Cuinn calm, and Cara with medical supplies to help Blaize and restrain the Rogue. Fintan drove. On the way, Cara called the medical facility where she worked to request backup transport for the Rogue.

Each minute Cuinn spent in the car was agony. His body was rigid and stiff, and his every breath rasped from him like the noise of a saw blade. There was a metallic taste in his mouth.

He needed to get to her. Desperately. He couldn't let her down like Sophea.

They reached the address. Fintan dimmed the vehicle's lights and turned off the engine to coast onto the property as quietly as possible. They parked far away from the house and Fintan sketched out a plan. Despite Cara's Healer status, she'd also trained in Manipura and had fighting skills akin to Blaize's, so Tierra was the only one of them without any offensive training.

But Tierra's training meant she could spot any energetic shields the property had. "I'll walk around the house and check for wards."

"We don't have time for that," Cuinn said. "Blaize is in there, and who knows what shape she's in."

Fintan had a hand on Cuinn's arm, a reminder to stop him rushing off.

"It's more dangerous if we don't check first," warned Fintan.

Cuinn felt desperate. "See what you can find Tierra, and then we'll decide. Hurry."

He was so close, and still being held back.

They were crouched in the shadows of a thick set of bushes at the side of the house. Tierra drew in a breath and closed her eyes, and Cuinn felt the prickle of her Muladhara seep out. After a few interminable minutes, she opened them again.

"It's warded with Manipura and Ajna only. Cuinn, you should be able to get through the Ajna, and Fintan, if I show you the wards for Manipura by flaring them with my energy, can you destroy them?" Tierra said.

Cuinn went to work immediately. He opened up his energetic awareness and drew on his store of energy. The wards were sophisticated, but nothing Cuinn couldn't get rid of. He burned all three away, leaving nothing but Manipura. He gestured to Fintan and Tierra. *Hurry.*

Tierra closed her eyes and a ward flared over to the right. "Again, please," requested Fintan. It flared again, bright as a small sun.

A moment passed, and the ward exploded.

"One more. To the left." Tierra pointed. Another ward flared, and this time, Fintan was ready. The ward disappeared in a shower of energy.

"Now. For fuck's sake, let's go," said Cuinn, already moving. He went directly to the worn back door. It was locked. Fintan gestured to him to move and stepped back to give the lock a kick. The old wood shattered and splintered, the door slamming open but leaving the lock in position.

In the dirty kitchen, Cuinn looked around for the door to the basement he'd seen in the dreamscape. It was easy to spot, and he tried it. Locked again. Fintan came over. This time he put his hands on the door, and simply burned the lock out. Cuinn went through the door at a run, and threw himself at the bed, leaving the others to restrain Indigo, who thankfully hadn't yet regained consciousness.

Blaize lay shackled to a dirty bed, a tube coming from a needle attached to her hand. *Thank Source. She's alive.* He cradled Blaize in his arms while Fintan undid her chains. Cuinn felt sick, and he kissed away the tears drying on her face and wiped the hair from her forehead. He had nearly lost her. That wouldn't happen again.

She opened her eyes. "You're here."

He nodded. "I'm so sorry, Blaize. We found you as quickly as we could."

"Rescued myself, didn't I?"

He nodded, unable to speak because of the thick emotion that clogged his throat.

"But I thought I'd let you help. Now we're a team and all," Blaize finished, with some effort.

Cara looked at Cuinn, drawing his attention away from the exhausted woman in his arms. "The Rogue's fading. I don't know if she'll make it. Her body's okay, but her mind is—unstable."

"We could call a human ambulance; would that help?" said Tierra.

Cara shook her head. "I don't think so. It's her spirit and her mind, not her body. Not that that's in great shape, but she won't die from it. It's the addiction; it's eating her up."

"You need to check Blaize before you do anything with … that." Cuinn's tone was flat.

Tierra came over to Blaize. "I can check her. But you'll need to put her down."

Tierra stepped over to the bed, gesturing for Cuinn to move out of the way. Cuinn reluctantly and gently lowered Blaize onto the bed. Her hand came up and clenched around his, as Tierra softly touched her and checked her for injuries.

Cuinn could see a little colour return to Blaize's face as Tierra mended some of the worst injuries. Cara looked up, her eyebrows drawing together. "Tierra, be careful. You don't have much to spare yourself yet." Tierra nodded and stepped away, wobbling slightly. Fintan caught her. She frowned and tried to push him away. He settled himself more carefully around her. "Just until you get your balance back."

Cara was still working on the Rogue.

"How long do you think the evac team will be?" Fintan asked.

"Not soon enough. She's nearly gone. Her pulse is thready, and her energy is unstable."

"I want to talk to her," said Cuinn.

"I think Blaize's dreamscape cage is holding her mind. You'd have to talk to the Rogue on the etheric plane, and you'd be exposed if she got free. It's her Haven. She's strongest there," said Cara.

"She won't. I'm stronger. A lot stronger." Cuinn's firm stare dared Cara to disagree with him.

"It's a risk."

"It's not worth it, Cuinn." Blaize's voice came weakly from the bed, her fingers gripping his more tightly. "She'll live, or she won't. I'm sorry for it, but I wouldn't trade my life for hers. Or yours."

"Nor would I, but I still want to talk to her." He needed to find out what was behind her attack on Blaize—if it was anything more than a Leech who had found the perfect energetic to draw from. He needed to know if it was linked to the prophecy. It was worth the risk of going into Indigo's Haven once more.

He lay on the revolting bed next to Blaize and relaxed his body as fast as he dared.

He followed the energetic trail that he'd created earlier, and entered through the hole he'd torn in the Rogue's wardings.

Once inside he looked around at the decor, and pitied the Rogue. The environment was so far from the surroundings of the abandoned property where her physical body now lay, it was ridiculous.

He stood in front of the energetic. She lay on her side, restrained and caged. Her body seemed skeletal, her black hair hanging around her face like a shroud.

He nudged the cage. "Rogue. Wake up."

"No. No. I'm sorry. I'm hungry. I'm tired. Let me sleep," she muttered, and he had to strain to hear the words. She didn't sound rational.

"Rogue. Tell me if you were working alone or with someone else." He spoke louder, squatting so he was closer to her head. She opened her eyes slightly and squinted up at him.

"Indigo, I'm Indigo. Where's my tasty dinner? I kept her alive, the redhead." Her face shifted quickly to anger. "The bitch. Thinks she can Queen Bee me. I'm the queen of the castle here, I am."

"Blaize is far away from here where you can't hurt her any more." Cuinn resisted the urge to kick the cage. Instead, he gripped the bars and put his face to hers.

She spat at him, and he jerked back, wiping at his neck where the spittle had landed. The Rogue was out of her mind. But he needed to be sure that she was the end of this. That this wasn't related to the main prophecy. That Blaize was safe once the Rogue was dead. As he could see she soon would be.

"You are Queen Bee, I can see. Queen of the flowers and of your beautiful Haven."

She laughed. It was an unnerving sound. Her face rubbed against the floor like a cat.

"Hmmm. I love my house I do. Safe here." Her face turned sad. "Usually safe. Not today. Not today."

"Indigo, were you working with someone else? Was anyone helping you?"

"Secrets, secrets. I know some secrets. Secrets about your friends. Friends now, and future friends. Prophecies come to all with Ajna you know, not just the good ones."

His frustration built, and one of the jewelled lamps across the room exploded.

"Naughty boy! A temper on you despite your energies. You're not the only one with a temper either. Your cousins have challenges ahead. Did you know they're part of the prophecy? And that friend of yours. He has a temper on him too, the blond one. Likes to play. Ah, so many of you caught up in the web. Some you know; some you don't. Surprises in store." She laughed again and more glass broke.

Adrenalin pumped through Cuinn's tired body as he looked around him. *She knows about the prophecy.*

"What are you talking about? What prophecy are you talking about?" He wanted to shake her.

Her Haven was starting to break up as she lost control of her mind and faded.

"Nothing's set in stone," she sang, her voice grating. "Thought I'd win this one; didn't. Maybe you think you'll win the next one; won't. Who knows? Whoknows? Whoknowswhoknowwhoknows?"

The room was breaking, falling and exploding around him now. He put up a shield to protect himself from the flying pieces. He needed to get out of there.

"What else do you know, Indigo? Who were you with?"

Her eyes opened and fixed on his. "More than you, smarty-pants. More than you. Send my love to your father."

The life went out of her eyes and her head slumped, blood trickling from her nose. Wild energies seeped into the room, savage and unpredictable.

He fled.

41

He sat quietly on the patio of the large house far from the city, staring out at the countryside around him. The earth was green and fertile, but no birds sang, and no insects chittered. The air was paused around him. Waiting.

The destruction of Indigo and her Haven had affected him badly. No matter how much power he had leeched from the flotsam and jetsam of the energetics—because no matter what the Guilds said, not every energetic was part of a happy family—no Maven could lose an Adherent and not suffer.

He clenched his fists. *Indigo should not have failed me.*

It took him a moment to rein in his anger, but he was a practical man, and his anger took energy from him that he could ill afford.

He breathed in and out, slowly, carefully, and drew on a little power from the ether each time, replenishing himself.

A tall, graceful blond woman came out from the house and stood next to him. "How are you feeling?"

"Fine," he said. "I just need to rest."

"If there's anything I can do, let me know." She played with the silver teardrop necklace that she favoured.

"I will. Perhaps you could send Dagon to me at some point. I need him to attend to some business. We'll visit the house in the city in a day or so too."

"Do you think you'll be well enough?" She sounded concerned.

"I'll be fine." At least he would after he'd had a chance to leech from the energetic match that Dagon would procure him.

She patted his arm and walked back to the door. "Just shout if you need me."

He didn't move when she had gone. He sat and thought for a long while. About Indigo, Cuinn and Blaize, and the prophecies. They chased the same prophecy, but he had more clarity about the stakes than them.

Unlimited power was within his reach. All that prevented him from gaining it was twelve energetics. Not only that, but they needed to be in six very specific couples. All he had to do was prevent one couple from bonding, and the prophecy would fall apart.

Prophecies were tricky things. They mattered—but they could be changed. Nothing was set in stone.

So he'd been unsuccessful the first time. That was fine.

He had five more chances.

Blaize woke up with a gasp. She snapped her eyes open and checked her surroundings. She was in a bright, clean room. She breathed a sigh of relief as she realised she wasn't in the vile basement.

But where was she?

The pristine white room seemed to be in a high-class hospital. Had she dreamed about the rescue? Had she been taken somewhere else? Her stomach clenched.

The door started to open, and she tried to sit up, but the change in pressure caused dizziness to crash over her, and she fell back onto the pillow.

"Blaize, Blaize, honey, it's okay; it's me, Cara. Everything's fine." Cara hurried over to her and stroked her forehead. "You're fine."

"Where's Cuinn? What happened to Indigo?" Blaize shuddered.

"Cuinn's fine. He's in a different room. He tried some heroics of his own and only just escaped in one piece, so he's resting too."

"Where are we?"

"We're in my Rehab centre out on the West Coast. It was the best place to bring you and Cuinn. And the Rogue."

Blaize shifted in the bed. If the Rogue was here, then Blaize was going to prepare herself for another fight. Just in case. *Although*... "Did she ... Did she survive?"

Cara shook her head. "She was a long way down the addiction path—you weren't the first energetic she did this to. I'm sorry."

Blaize breathed a guilty sigh of relief. "I'm not. I'm sorry I killed her, but I'm not sorry she's dead."

"I understand. We'll talk more about it later. My experience says this won't be the last time you'll think about her I'm afraid." She poured a glass of water and handed it to Blaize.

The water was cool and refreshing.

"Do you think you could eat something?"

Blaize's stomach shifted and growled. She laughed. "I guess so. But no fast food. I won't be eating any more of that for a while."

As the days passed, Blaize became more and more suspicious that Cuinn was avoiding her. *Why isn't he here? If he loved me, wouldn't he be here? I nearly died, for Source's sake. But I survived. And I didn't turn into a Rogue.* She was safe to be around.

Her heart broke a little bit more every day he didn't visit her. She'd been ready to agree to his terms, but hadn't had the chance to tell him.

Eventually, she was allowed to move around a little in the facility, going outside for the first time, and standing in the gardens, which overlooked the pebbled beach and restless sea.

"You're seeing it at its best," said Cara, coming out to sit next to her and passing her a cup of hot tea. "It's nearly summer now, and the weather's good. It can be a real bitch in winter when we get snow."

"Where's Cuinn?"

Cara sighed. "He's back home. Tierra, Adam, and Fin are with him. Something came up that he needed to deal with. Once you're ready, you can go back there and see him."

"I'm not sure I want to." *Lie.*

"He didn't leave because he doesn't want to be with you, Blaize. He has a strong connection to the energies there, and we thought it would help him recover more quickly. And other information came up when he was interrogating Indigo—"

Blaize flinched at the name.

"And he's gone back to look into that too."

Blaize was sure Cuinn had realised she was a liability, her impulsive nature one that would put them all at risk, time and time again. And yet her confinement and ordeal had made her see that Cuinn was the most important person in her life.

Cuinn felt empty. Despite the infusion of energy from Tierra, he'd overextended himself to break into Indigo's Haven, and it had taken him a while to recover.

But Indigo's final words had galvanised him to get back to his books and dreamwalks—as soon as Tierra and Cara had allowed it.

He had told the others he had more information, but despite their probing, he hadn't yet revealed to them that he suspected several of them were also involved in the prophecy. He needed more information before he dropped that bombshell.

His single-mindedness was all designed to keep Blaize, and his family, safe. That was what he told himself. As he returned this time from seeing the Circle members and filling them in on what had happened with the Rogue, he forced himself to admit there was more to it than that.

He'd made a mistake when he'd compared Blaize to Sophea. When he'd seen how Blaize had caged the Rogue and called to him in the dreamscape, he'd realised Sophea and Blaize were nothing alike.

Blaize was independent. Self-sufficient. She was a grown woman who was a match for his own inner strength, while her passionate nature balanced his own logical calm. She had enough power to protect herself. She was going to be a hell of an Ajna energetic once she'd been trained.

Seeing her lifted him. She made him laugh. She annoyed the hell out of him.

He was in love with Blaize.

And he didn't know what he would do if she didn't love him back. He could wait if he had to, but every moment of the coming years would be a living hell, being Maven and Adherent and not lovers. She pushed his objectivity, the stability that usually came from his earth energies, to their limit. What if she never admitted she loved him? He was sure she did. Sure of it.

But he was worried—terrified—that he had messed things up irrevocably. He'd let her get taken, for Source's sake. She hadn't been in contact as she recovered, and he'd respected her privacy. But now she was at the house, and he was heading home to see her for the first time since her capture.

Cuinn's dreams had changed as well. Thankfully, he'd stopped dreaming the prophecy of Blaize's death, and now he dreamt of her with him, but just out of reach.

In his dreamwalks, more of the twelve had faces.

Tierra and Fintan were there, as well as Adam and Cara. Other figures were still shadowy. The fact that some of his family and friends were involved had made him work even harder on the problem.

He opened the front door to the sound of voices in the hub of the house, the kitchen. He walked to the room, feeling as if he was on death row. In a few minutes, he would find out if Blaize returned his feelings.

There were five of them in the room: the three women, Fin, and Adam.

But he only had eyes for one person.

Her hair curled gently around her face, and her green eyes looked at him. Her face seemed pale, and she hadn't put back all the weight that she'd burned off through Indigo's leeching. Still, she was beautiful.

Cara moved in front of her, greeting him warmly, and the room filled with the sounds of people. He took his place at the table. Tierra filled his plate, this time with pancakes, fruit and a lot of syrup, and handed him a cup of coffee.

As he ate, he was acutely aware of Blaize sitting quietly opposite him. She still seemed so fragile, as if something in her had been damaged by her experience with the Rogue. Which, of course, it probably had. He wanted to take her in his arms and hold her against him.

It seemed like hours before everyone had finished eating and started drifting to other parts of the house. Blaize stood, saying she was heading back to her own cottage for some peace and quiet.

He jumped at the chance. "Let me walk you back."

She tilted her head and frowned. "Don't be silly, Cuinn. It's a hundred yards. Indigo's gone."

"I insist." He put out his arm for her to take. She sighed and took it, her hand in the crook of his elbow. He swallowed as he pulled his arm in toward his body, her hand hot against his side.

They reached her door with no words yet exchanged. He felt tongue-tied, but as she opened her front door, he had to say something.

"I'm so sorry, Blaize."

She turned to him. "For what?"

"Everything."

Her eyebrow rose. "Everything?"

"You getting kidnapped, me not managing to save you sooner. Your injuries. Everything."

"I'm sorry I got caught. I was careless. Stupid. Proud." She looked away. "She took me by surprise."

"But it's not your fault," they said simultaneously.

They regarded each other in silence.

"Huh," said Blaize. "Where have you been? Why didn't you call?"

"I thought you would want some time alone to heal. Without me."

"I wouldn't want to see you?"

"Did you?"

She didn't say anything for a while, as she examined his face with a scrutiny that made him feel as if she was examining his soul.

Finally, she sighed. "I did."

His stomach flipped, and a tiny spark of hope flashed inside him. He stepped forward slowly and took her hands.

C H A P T E R

42

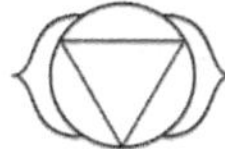

Blaize was afraid to move. Cuinn was in front of her, living, breathing. She could smell mint on his cool, sweet breath, and the mixed male scent of his sweat and deodorant. It reminded her of moss and recently chopped firewood.

She breathed him in, as his cool, dry hands took hers. She loved the feel of his long fingers as they wrapped around hers. His firm but gentle grip gave her butterflies as he pulled her towards him. She didn't lift her eyes from his chest as he brought her slowly closer.

One of his arms snaked around her, and his hand came to her chin to tilt her head up. Her gaze trailed from his chest up, past his strong collarbones to his elegant neck. His five o'clock shadow added to his usual aura of rumpled geek chic. She felt a surge of tenderness, delighting in his touch.

As she finally met his eyes, which today were dove grey, she saw a hint of vulnerability. Vulnerability that she suspected would be reflected in her own eyes. This was the start of something different. Something she'd never allowed herself before.

She put her hand on his cheek, enjoying the roughness of his facial hair, and rubbed her hand backwards and forwards. He tipped his head to one side, resting it more fully on her hand and placed his hand on the back of her neck.

"We have a lot to talk about." His voice was pitched lower than usual.

"But perhaps we should talk later? I've heard we both need a lot of rest." She stepped back into the house, pulling him inside with her, their hands still in place, locking them together.

"I agree. You can't take chances with the injuries we've had."

"A lot of bed rest." She advanced up the stairs but stopped when she was a step above him, his hands now on her hips. He cocked an eyebrow at her, which shot higher as she stripped off the sweater she was wearing and dropped it beside her.

When she put her hands on his hips and tugged at his sweater, he raised his hands above his head, his eye contact solid. She smiled.

She drew him after her, and they stumbled up the rest of the stairs, eyes locked and their hands keeping contact with each other's bodies.

When her legs hit the bed, she fell backwards, taking him with her. Their mouths met, tongues tangling in a passionate joining.

They struggled with each other's clothes, laughing at their efforts to strip each other as quickly as possible.

She threw an arm out to grope into her bedside table for a condom, barely taking her lips off his as he used his own hands to remove her delicate underwear.

Finally, they were skin to skin, their bodies moving together in time.

<Blaize?>

Startled, she looked up at him. She frowned, figuring it out. Huh. *<Yes?>*

He grinned as their connection deepened further.

<Great, now we discover this! Would have been useful last week> she sent with her mind.

<You should have had sex with me on the physical plane before>

She narrowed her eyes at him, and then reached down between their bodies to add her hands to everything else that was going on, and he stopped talking in a hurry.

Much later they lay together, sheets and limbs entwined, in her little cottage bedroom. She felt happier than she had for a long time as if her two energies had blended as she relaxed. She was warm and confident from her Manipura, but also insightful and perceptive from the Ajna.

She propped her chin on her hand and looked down at him. Her other hand traced circles on his stomach; then she trailed her fingers through the arrow of hair that led from his belly button down to other, more fascinating things.

"To be clear," she said. "I'm not going anywhere. I'm with you now. Whatever's to be faced, I'll face it with you. I don't need protecting. Or, sometimes I will, and sometimes I'll protect you."

He nodded. "I know. I also know that's a very distracting view." His gaze flickered to her breasts, which given their respective positions were presented quite close to his face.

She laughed.

"I also know that I love you, Blaize Blackfire."

She flopped down next to him and snuggled into the crook of his outstretched arm. "Well. I still think this is all a bit fast, but hey, who am I to fight it? I love you too, Cuinn Ahern."

He let out a relieved breath, and with his free arm he groped for a condom where she'd left them the night before. He slid it on and rolled on top of her, causing her to gasp. He moved again, slowly and smoothly, and the next sound she made was a moan.

The two of them spent the rest of the day making sure each of them got a great deal of bed rest.

Cuinn didn't leave Blaize's cottage that day or night, and they were late to breakfast the next morning, coming in holding hands. Blaize met the other women's eyes, a hint of colour in her cheeks, and they smiled back—Tierra with love, and Cara approvingly. Fintan opened his mouth to say something, but Cuinn narrowed his eyes at him and shut him up before anything came out.

After heaping his plate with food that Tierra and, to his surprise, Fintan, had put together, Cuinn got everyone's attention. He made eye contact with each of them.

"I need to share some information with you all. But it has to stay in this room for now. It's incomplete, and I don't yet know the meaning of it."

He talked them through Indigo's last words, and what he thought the implications were—mainly that most of them in the room appeared to be involved in the prophecy. There was silence for a while after this, as each of them digested the information.

"I spent much of the day yesterday back at the house where Blaize was held, because my team had suggested some disturbing findings when they went through it the first time." Adam, a large, solid man, with the same dark hair and eyes as his sister, had no problem commanding the room.

Cuinn frowned. The situation was already bad and Adam wasn't prone to exaggeration. Cuinn braced for more bad news.

"I don't think Indigo was working alone. And worse, I believe the other person was the driving force. Indigo was just the patsy."

Blaize squeezed Cuinn's hand tightly, her face sombre. "You're probably right. It's hard to remember everything clearly, but a couple of times she seemed to hint that there was someone else involved. And one time, she looked almost frightened by the fact she'd implied it."

Adam nodded. "There's someone else."

"This attempt to take Blaize was almost certainly tied into the prophecy. And now, so are all of you." Cuinn met each of their gazes again. "I need your help. This prophecy is a threat not only to us as individuals—because, make no mistake, Blaize's experience tells us there is personal danger here—but to our whole race. The enemy, whoever that is, seems to know more than we do. We may be the only thing standing between our race and its extinction."

The others around the table looked at him after his speech, their serious faces reflecting back his words. He was sorry to put this burden on them, dumping them in this mess without asking.

Despite the guilt, he was also glad, glad to share the burden with the people he trusted most in the world.

"I'm here. I'll see this through with you. Where you go, I go." Blaize lifted his hand to her soft lips and kissed it.

Tierra was next. "Whatever you need, I'm here."

Her brother just nodded his head, as if it were a given.

Fintan, his face graver than Cuinn had seen it in many years, the usual mischievous twinkle in his eye absent, said, "Whatever you need, Cuinn."

Cara's warm, soft voice added her assent.

Something inside Cuinn relaxed. With the people in this room, he had a much better chance of working through whatever was to come. He hated putting them in danger, but he couldn't solve this puzzle on his own. Their combined energies and efforts would give them a real advantage in whatever was to come.

He hoped that it would be enough.

END OF BOOK 1

The Guilds and the Circles

The energetics' power structure is Guild based.

There are six Major Guilds, one for each of the six Chakras:

- **Muladhara** (The Root Chakra – Earth Element)
- **Svadisthana** (The Sacral Chakra – Water Element)
- **Manipura** (The Navel Chakra – Fire Element)
- **Anahata** (The Heart Chakra – Air Element)
- **Vishudha** (The Throat Chakra – Ether (Space) Element)
- **Ajna** (The Third Eye – The Mind)
  (Sahasara, the Crown Chakra, does not have a Guild.)

Each energetic has two activated Chakras, one dominant and one auxiliary, and it is the combination of these that influences their power, and to some degree, their personality.

Because of the huge differences between an energetic like Blaize, who combines her Manipura dominant with Ajna auxiliary, and one like Fintan, who combines Manipura dominant with Anahata auxiliary, a system of Minor Guilds also developed. There are thirty Minor Guilds representing each combination of powers (for example, Manipura-Ajna is a separate Guild from Ajna-Manipura).

Each individual energetic therefore belongs to two Major Guilds, and one Minor Guild.

For example: Cuinn has Ajna dominant, and Muladhara auxiliary. He therefore belongs to the Ajna Major Guild, the Muladhara Major Guild, and the Ajna-Muladhara Minor Guild.

The Major Circle is the highest form of government with one powerful energetic representing each Major Guild, making decisions on behalf of the race. The Minor Circle, the second tier of government, is made up of the thirty energetics who lead each of the Minor Guilds.

List of Minor Guilds:

- Muladhara-Svadisthana
- Muladhara-Manipura
- Muladhara-Anahata
- Muladhara-Vishudha
- Muladhara-Ajna
- Svadisthana-Muladhara
- Svadisthana-Manipura
- Svadisthana-Anahata
- Svadisthana-Vishudha
- Svadisthana-Ajna
- Manipura-Muladhara
- Manipura-Svadisthana
- Manipura-Anahata
- Manipura-Vishudha
- Manipura-Ajna
- Anahata-Muladhara
- Anahata-Svadisthana
- Anahata-Manipura
- Anahata-Vishudha
- Anahata-Ajna
- Vishudha-Muladhara
- Vishudha-Svadisthana
- Vishudha-Manipura
- Vishudha-Anahata
- Vishudha-Ajna
- Ajna-Muladhara
- Ajna-Svadisthana
- Ajna-Manipura
- Ajna-Anahata
- Ajna-Vishudha

What's Next?

The story of the energetics continues in Tierra and Fintan's story, **Tierra and the Warrior**.

To get it, and for updates, giveaways and inside information, visit my website:
EllenBardAuthor.com/sign-up

Discover Your Energetic Profile!

Want to know what your Dominant Chakra would be?
Which Guild you would belong to? What your archetype is?

Take the Chakra Quiz, and find out!
EllenBardAuthor.com/chakra-quiz

Help Spread the Word

If you loved the book and have a moment to spare, I would hugely appreciate it if you had time to leave a short review where you bought the book, and/or on goodreads. For instructions, go to the link below.

EllenBardAuthor.com/how-to-leave-a-review

Your review will help other readers discover the series, and is greatly appreciated in spreading the word. Authors like me rely on amazing readers like you.

Thank you!

About the Author

Ellen is a fiction author who writes paranormal romance full of enchantment, intrigue and action. Her writing blends a background in psychology and her experiences travelling the world with a love of magic, fantasy and a (mostly!) happy ending.

She's also an entrepreneur and has a website where she shares actionable advice about personal development to support readers in making small changes so they can shine a little brighter in the world.

She's a Chartered Occupational Psychologist with the British Psychological Society, and continues to work as an international management consultant, which she has done for the last 15 years. She's worked all over the world including far-flung places such as China, Saudi Arabia and Malaysia.

Her passion for other lands and cultures helps inform her writing, as does her desire to try new things – from art classes to Krav Maga, the self-defence system.

She's a passionate and dedicated reader, working her way through between 100-150 fiction and non-fiction books a year – find her on goodreads to read her reviews.

Born in the UK, she currently lives in a tiny house in Chiang Mai, Thailand where the main feature is a hammock.

Connect with Ellen:
Facebook: facebook.com/EllenBardAuthor
Twitter: twitter.com/ellenbard
Pinterest: pinterest.com/ellenmbard/
Goodreads: goodreads.com/ellenbard
Instagram: instagram.com/ellenbard/

Acknowledgements

I feel so incredibly lucky to have wonderful family and friends who have supported me in plenty of crazy endeavours, this book being just one!

Mary Bard, my mum, has especially gone above and beyond, acting as alpha reader, first editor, cheerleader, and so much more. I can't thank her enough for all her love and efforts to support me on my journey. My sister, Sarah, is an incredible beta reader with great attention to detail, and is also a huge support on the artistic side, helping with websites, visuals, graphics and many other things.

My sprawling family – Dunnes and Bards – thank you all for your support and love over the last few years.

My developmental editor, Lynnette Labelle, thank you for such constructive advice on bringing the story to life. My copy editor and friend Angela Anderson, who did a great job at American-ising ('-izing'!) my usually very British style! Erin Dameron-Hill, thank you for such an amazing job with the cover – I love it. Simon Hartshorne, thanks for your help bringing the visuals of the archetypes and the Chakras to life on the website.

NaNoWriMo 2013 was the event that clarified I wanted to write fiction, and I'm grateful to the Thailand group for getting me through that first book, but I got so much more out of the month because Nyla Nox, the Thailand moderator, became a friend who I have had many 'writing races' with since. She was at the other end of Skype writing her own books for a number of the pages of this book. I hope we continue to motivate each other through future works.

So many elements from things I've learned in life have gone into the book. My Krav Maga teacher, Matt, is a hero of mine, for all the things he has taught me – resilience, inner strength and just never-give-the-f**k-up. I hope I never have to use any of his teachings in practice, but it's been fun to use them for Blaize and the gang. He also checked over the fight scenes for me – all mistakes are my own!

For Professor Cowie, who taught me self-hypnosis and Jungian theory – I never thought that the tower would come in handy quite in the way it has, but I love exploring my inner world and bringing a little of that to life has been fantastic.

I'm grateful to all the yoga teachers and meditation teachers over the years, especially my most recent community in Thailand where I've spent two seasons so far, and will probably return again soon. There are too many to mention here, but Amitayus, thanks for brainstorming archetypes with me in our little island café, and Grace Bryant, who was both a beta reader and has worked with me on many other behind the scenes activities, thank you.

My other beta readers and friends, Laura Quinn, Catherine Bedford, Katie Bullas, John Mansfield and Debbie Hantusch, thanks for the great suggestions and support. I'm so grateful to you all for taking the time to read the book and give me your feedback – I think it's very courageous and was a great help. Thanks also to my aunt, Ellen Dunne, who helped do the final proof of the paperback version of the book.

Caroline Leon, who was instrumental in helping me to change my life by encouraging and supporting me in Thailand, thank you – keep being amazing.

Justin Morgan and Ed Clarke – I love you boys so much, thank you for always being there for me. Graham Morley, thanks for helping to keep me sane and grounded. Helen Blackie, Ray Glennon, Sam Blackie, Ann Curtis, Alan Gardner, Samia Khan, Ian Newcombe, Tom Sandman, Sally Gold and Tessa Kelly, thank you all for your support, accommodation, meals, coffees and chats as I wrote sections while in the UK.

Finally, Dad, I miss you every day and I wish so much you'd been here to see this happen. Cuinn's golden arrow was for you (it was a longbow).

Ellen Bard, September 2015

THE ENERGETICS, BOOK 2

TIERRA AND THE WARRIOR

ELLEN BARD

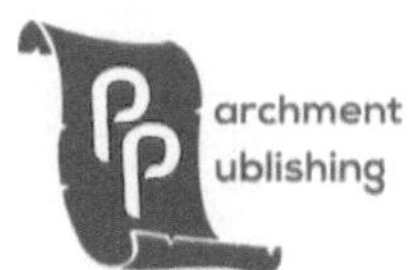

Dedication

Sarah, Mum, Fox.
Three core pillars of both my life and my writing.
Thank you.

The Chakras and their Energies

 **Muladhara:** The Root Chakra – Earth Element
The energy of nourishment and home, family and safety.

 **Svadisthana:** The Sacral Chakra – Water Element
Fluid and adaptable, the energy of movement and connection, of practical and physical creativity. The energy of pleasure, sexuality and sensation, and emotions.

 **Manipura:** The Navel Chakra – Fire Element
The energy of the individual; of confidence, of proactivity and of drive and passion. Playful and proud.

 **Anahata:** The Heart Chakra – Air Element
The energy of healing, and of balance, located in the middle of the body and the seven Chakras. The energy of love, of relationships, of devotion. Of compassion and empathy.

 **Vishudha:** The Throat Chakra – Ether (Space) Element
The energy of communication, of conceptual creativity, and of truth. Of expression, and of listening.

 **Ajna:** The Third Eye – The Mind
The energy of imagination, of visualizations, and insight. Of clarity and wisdom. Of dreams and intuition.

 **Sahasara:** The Crown Chakra – None*
The purest of all the energies. Only experienced through the Grace of the Source (the energetics' name for the creator, the divine).

---

*Neither a dominant nor auxiliary Chakra for energetics

1

Tierra prowled through the messy, dank garden at the back of the dilapidated property, all senses on alert. She was fully tapped in to her Muladhara energy, the magic that enabled her to track people, but what it told her about her environment made her skin crawl.

There was darkness here, in the energetic traces that she sifted through. The house itself was barely a shack, a few rooms and a musty, water-damaged basement, surrounded by weed-infested grounds that seeped into an overgrown piece of forest.

The property was isolated, twenty minutes from the pleasant, if small, town of Merrow a couple of hours east of Vancouver. This location was in total contrast to the bustling community there. Here, there was a sense of foreboding. She shivered. A sense of danger.

Tierra halted her slow progress and squatted. She rested a palm on the ground and closed her eyes. She drew on her energies, and a tingle of cool earth centered her. She breathed deeply. Her skills in this area were rusty. She needed to focus.

What could she sense?

Great anger had been expressed here. Manipura-fueled rage and violence. The negative emotions were almost overwhelming, and she wobbled on the balls of her feet. It had been so long since she'd done this, she wasn't sure she could protect herself from the negative effects of using her energies in this way. She frowned. No. She fisted her hand in the soil, and grounded herself. The ghostly storm of feelings whirled around her, and she tried to observe without being caught up, but her breath quickened despite herself.

She had been a homebody for the last few decades of her long life, enjoying a respite from the world, looking after her reclusive but brilliant cousin Cuinn and his huge house, Cathair Cuinn.

That had all changed in the last month or so. Blaize, Cuinn's new Adherent, had burned her way through Cuinn's self-imposed isolation and barriers, and into his heart. Her intelligence and passion challenged him, and brought him out of his seclusion. At the same time, he had seen a horrible prophecy that somehow involved all of them.

Tierra squeezed sticky earth between her fingers, and attempted to sift the emotional traces around her to discover something useful: people, place or thing. Anything concrete. She screwed her face up in concentration, attempting to become one with her environment.

Tierra's earth abilities allowed her to draw power and connect to anything natural in the environment around her, and sense the whereabouts of people. As part of the earth energetic training, Muladhara energetics were also trained in how to hunt. They were encouraged to tap into their primal energies and read an environment, to empathize with others and imagine what they might do and where they might go, and sense the emotions and lies in people's words. But combined with Anahata, as Tierra's energy was, she could become too sensitive.

Grim scenes whipped through her, and she gritted her teeth to stop herself crying out. A furious and broken young woman who Tierra recognised, throwing energy balls at a smoking target. That same woman hustling Blaize's drugged body into the house. Tierra shuddered at what had almost happened.

Another scene and, ah, another presence. Much fainter, but, oh, the power.

The other personality – male, from the energy – hadn't spent long on the grounds. Tierra would need to enter the house to learn more. She wasn't looking forward to that. Source knew what was in there.

She relaxed her hand and attempted to let go of the difficult feelings she'd absorbed, ready to stand. Her nerves were stretched thin.

"Can we talk?"

Tierra sucked in a breath, her pulse attempting to escape, and whirled round. But the crouch she was in wasn't made for that, and she slowly, excruciatingly, toppled over.

She lifted her head up to see the owner of the masculine drawl with a hint of Scandinavia, and groaned.

"Fintan. Don't do that when I'm concentrating." She pressed her lips together, hoping the heat in her cheeks was internal and didn't show on the outside. "I'm a bit busy at the moment. We can talk later."

Fintan's blonde-with-a-hint-of-strawberry hair was messy, and as usual it had been a while since his face had seen a razor. He wore ripped jeans and a tight T-shirt that showed off his well-muscled torso. The T-shirt had a picture of a VW van on it, and matched his twinkling sea-blue eyes.

"You're tracking. You can talk and track." Fintan stepped in front of her and stretched his clean hand out to take her muddy, sweaty one.

Tierra had hoped that volunteering to see what clues she could find at the scene of the kidnapping would give her some sorely needed peace and quiet.

When they'd rescued Blaize, Cuinn had called the friends he'd identified in the prophecy and asked them to gather at Cathair Cuinn. At first she'd been in her element. She loved looking after people. But after a few days she'd remembered she also loved her space. Her home was her safe place, her nest, and it had been decades since she'd had to deal with so many people at once.

"Tierra, c'mon. I'm bored, and I've been wanting to talk to you about something anyway. You can multitask." He sounded puppy-dog-hopeful. Fintan was easily bored, especially in times when not much was happening.

Tierra ignored his hand and pushed herself up. "I don't know why you came, anyway. This isn't your thing. There's not going to be any action here."

"I didn't think you should be alone in the house." He shrugged. "It's a nasty place."

"There's no one here. And I need to focus."

"I know you're scared."

She sniffed. "There's nothing to be afraid of here. I've tracked plenty of times before."

That had been the other reason she'd come out here. She wanted, needed, to contribute to the work the others were all doing, trying to find out who had been behind Indigo, and what the prophecy really meant.

He cocked his head. "I didn't mean of anything here. Though…it's been a long time since you've tracked anything. You're pretty out of practice."

Oh, the man was infuriating. She shook her head, trying to dismiss his comment without actually lying. After all, the prophecy had her terrified down to her bones.

He looked nothing more than a beach bum on his day off, so why was he so perceptive? She sighed. Appearances were deceiving. Fintan was a Manipura-Anahata energetic, one of the energetic race's Warriors. Battle-honed, with a keen sense of duty. Unlike Blaize's Manipura, which manifested in passion and drive, Fintan's Manipura tended towards play, risk and mischief. For all that, he was loyal, and cared deeply about family and friends. Initially friends with Cuinn, Fintan had been around for centuries.

And she'd been in love with him for nearly as long.

For most of her life, that hadn't really bothered her. It was a distant, unreciprocated love, and Tierra got on with things by ignoring it. But recently, something had changed. She wasn't sure what, exactly, but she no longer wanted to be his confidante. To hear about his numerous romantic trysts. He always fell in love with them, of course. His Anahata wouldn't stand for anything less. Unfortunately his Manipura, his fire, meant he also had a tendency to crave new things, so he usually fell out of love with them just as fast. Or, at least, in love with someone else.

She didn't need this right now. "I need to go inside the house. Someone was here with Indigo, and I want to see if I can gather more perceptions of him. It could be a lead."

"Alright." He examined her face. "Why don't we take a walk off the grounds first? You're not looking all that great."

She closed her eyes and sent a prayer to the Source for strength. "Thanks, Fintan. Just what every woman wants to hear."

Although she could do with a break. She'd opened up to the atmosphere around the house, and it clawed at her. If she was going to do good work inside the house, she needed to move away from the energetic traces here for a few minutes. Fintan was annoying, but his presence was familiar, and his energy was steady and comfortable. "Fine. I need to wash my hands. Give me a minute."

She walked around the corner to where she had seen an outside tap and rinsed her hands. Spring had definitely sprung, though the temperature was still chilly enough to wear a coat. It was the season for earth energetics. Let the fire energetics have summer – this time was all hers. From the quietness of the winter months, the earth was suddenly alive. Flowers and trees had started budding, and there was some sunshine at times. The soil was still damp enough to smell of growth and change, the breeze soft.

She tried not to drag her feet as she walked back to Fintan. When she reached him, she didn't pause, just kept moving. He, light on his feet as ever, easily caught her up.

"I thought you might want to talk," he said.

She shrugged. "Not really."

"You're the heart of the family, and Adam and Cuinn see you as unshakable," he said. "But I know what happened to Blaize scared you, and the prophecies that Cuinn has uncovered so far frighten you too. And that the danger is still out there."

"It's been a difficult month." If that wasn't an understatement, then there would be no flowers this summer.

"You don't like change. So no matter how much you enjoy playing hostess, new people in the house for this long is bound to unsettle you."

She shrugged again. *How dare he know me that well.*

"Everyone's scared, Fintan," she said, her words brittle. "Except you crazy fire energetics. And Adam. My brother has an entirely too casual attitude to danger."

"It's our job. We deal with this kind of thing more often than you know." He caught her hand in his and tugged her to a stop. "We'll deal with this threat just like we do every day. It's just another day at the office, T."

She pulled her hand free and kept marching. They'd have to walk a few minutes more for her to be out of range of the atmosphere of the house. "Well it's not my job. I've barely written a word in the last few days because of the cacophony of noise that comes with six energetics – and a dog – under the same roof."

"Well, you're trying to take care of everyone. Everyone apart from yourself." He matched pace with her again.

"Someone has to make sure the washing is done and there's food in the cupboards. Who else would do it?" Tierra was being unfair. Her brother, Adam, another earth energetic, took turns in the kitchen, and she never had to clean up. If she asked, others would help run the house. But…she didn't want to have to ask.

"It's not because we don't want to help." He attempted to put a hand on her arm, but she twisted out of his way. "No one wants to disturb your systems. I can make up a schedule when we go back if you'd like."

She wanted to shrug again, though knew she was being petulant. He was right. She was channeling fear into her housework, but wasn't taking enough time to rest and ground herself. Her sense of home, of rightness, of safety, had been shaken to the core.

Tierra's pace put her curvy body in front of Fintan again. He wasn't sure what the problem was between them, but he didn't like it. It had been a month or so now since their usual easy relationship had taken a strange turn. She'd been snappish. Irritable.

It was strange because Tierra was one of the most stable energetics he knew. Few things fazed her. She was always the rock at the center of the storm. He could count on her. They all did.

He'd have understood if she'd just been like this the last week, given how their lives had been turned upside down. It had to be affecting her. Whereas Fintan had dealt with Rogues for centuries, though it wasn't often you got a case that was as close to home as this one had been. Thank fuck Blaize was ok. He had known Blaize all her life, had been friends with her father – it wasn't uncommon as an energetic to know several generations of a family when your life span was hundreds of years.

It had been a long time since Tierra had been involved in anything so ugly. The last time was probably World War II, when Tierra's mother had been one of that war's tragic death count.

But the change in Tierra's behavior had started before Blaize had arrived. One day Tierra no longer seemed to find his jokes as funny. They'd always sparred—that was part of their dynamic—though normally she was so easy going, she never got annoyed with him. Until now.

"Let's talk about the fight." He tried once more to take her arm, which she shook off.

"What fight?" she said.

They were deep in the woods now, sunlight dappling the ground around them in short bursts, most of the forest shaded and dark. The ground smelled peaty, and flowers in early blossom were scattered across the floor of the forest, in greater density near those patches of sunlight.

"Our fight about you sharing energy with Cuinn."

"Hmph."

"I know you're still annoyed with me." he said. "But I don't know what you were thinking. It's illegal under energetic law, and it was very unlike you to volunteer. It was a crazy idea, and someone needs to watch out for you, if you won't do it yourself. You could have been seriously hurt."

She turned towards him, her dark brown skirt rippling and flowing as she turned. She could have been part of the woods, she seemed so at home in that environment. It was so unfair. He took risks all the time. "You think that's you?"

"You're like a sister to me. I don't want you to get hurt. There are times when you give too much to others, and you don't keep enough back for yourself." He struggled to explain himself under her unrelenting brown eyes.

She blinked. "A sister. Right. Well, Fintan, I might not be a trained Warrior, but I can take care of myself if I need to. I'm a strong enough energetic in my own way. I was there in World War II along with the rest of you, healing *and* protecting."

"I know. This is different. If Cuinn hadn't controlled himself, you could have been drained like the Leech was draining Blaize. There are reasons sharing energy is forbidden unless it's between Maven and Adherent. Plus, if anyone else found out, we'd all be in huge trouble."

"Given it was only you, me, Cuinn and Cara there, I don't think anyone else is likely to find out. No one else needs to know. Even if they did, I'd do it again to save Blaize." Tierra's face was set, but her foot scuffed at the floor, displacing leaves.

Fintan shook his head, frustrated. "Who'll save you from yourself?"

"It's not your job, Fintan." Tierra's tone was flat. "This little sister can look after herself. Let's walk back now. I have work to do."

They turned back. Fintan sidled next to her, body at a right angle to hers, trying to catch the attention of her chocolate eyes. Her gaze stayed focused in the far distance, and his body itched with frustration.

"I don't want to fight with you. I hate it," he said. "What's going on? Why are we arguing?"

Tierra frowned. "Not everything's about you."

They were nearly back at the house. Not especially sensitive, he could mostly ignore the disturbing energies that wrapped around the property, and anger helped drive the traces of them away. "Great. Then stop fighting with me."

"I'm not fighting," Tierra yelled, her hands in balls by her sides.

A slow smile spread across his face, as Tierra reluctantly realized what she'd said, and how she'd said it.

"Fine." She blew out a breath. "You're annoying. I've been annoyed. I *am* annoyed."

"Why am I annoying you? What am I doing that's different?" He wouldn't let this go. She was too important.

"Nothing. Everything. You're right. I'm finding things challenging with everyone here. I'm trying to keep the house going, and I don't know how to make everyone happy."

Finally, something he could fix. "You don't need to. I'll draw up a schedule for some of the key tasks for this week when we get home. Adam will probably return to his team soon if nothing else happens – though I think if Argus had his way, they'd stay. That dog loves it here. Cara will go back to the Rehabilitation Center. So it'll be back to Cuinn, Blaize, you and me."

"When are you going?" She played with the wooden beads at her throat.

"I'm not sure. It depends what Cuinn needs. And if any more snippets of prophecy come through that we can use, or if we find anything here. He and Adam are discussing it today, so we'll see where they get to after dinner. Cuinn's been a bit…caught up, with Blaize." He grinned. "Nice to see."

Tierra lifted her head and smiled. "They make a lovely couple – they're good for each other. And I'm glad he has someone helping him with the prophecies. Doing it alone was really taking a toll on him."

Blaize's training had got off to a rocky start, but she was powerful and smart, and she had taken to her training like a duck to water.

Fintan nodded. "Any progress they can make is good. It feels strange to be involved in a prophecy and only know we're involved, nothing more."

Tierra shivered. "Yes."

She put a hand on his. "We're fine, Fintan. I'm a bit, well … off, at the moment. Bear with me."

The last of the tension left him and he took a breath, then put his arm around her and hugged her close, her scent made from delicate violets and earth. She smelled like home.

She stiffened for a moment, then leaned into him and sighed.

"Okay, Fintan. Let's go inside the —"

There was a loud noise and a clod of earth exploded next to Tierra's foot. Fintan leapt to put himself between Tierra and the direction the projectile had come from. They were under attack.

CHAPTER

2

Tierra yelped and reared back.

Fintan pulled her towards a dilapidated shed on the edge of the property. Things were happening so fast she couldn't understand the sequence of events.

Another noise, another clod of earth. Hot pebbles hit her in the shin. Fintan pushed her behind him and peered out from the cover of the shed. She shook her head in bewilderment.

"Fintan, what's going on?"

"Someone's attacking us. A Manipura energetic of some kind given the fireballs. I assume something to do with Indigo. Do as I say." Fintan ducked his head out and then jerked back as another fireball flew past him.

Tierra's breathing was erratic as her brain finally took in the scene.

"I can only see one person, but there's no guarantee she's alone," Fintan whispered.

A stream of fire hit the shed, sparks exploding. The building creaked. Tierra trembled, her stomach roiling.

"This isn't going to protect us for long. Can you shield us at all?" Fintan asked. He seemed as relaxed as ever, limbs loose, his shoulders free of the tension that was building up in every part of Tierra's body.

Her heart beat faster. The last time she had been in battle it had all gone so horribly wrong. She wasn't good at this.

"I'll…try," she said. Her hands shook and she wrapped her arms tightly around herself.

No. She could do this. She could.

She let her arms hang loose at her sides, and pulled on the Muladhara energy she had drawn in earlier. She wrapped herself and Fintan in a protective bubble, thin at first, then layering on more protection like an onion. Another stream of fire came at them, and the heat seared her back. Her bubble popped, and she staggered.

Fintan dodged the stream and sent return fire. His attacks were much smaller, like bullets made from fire. "Quickly T, we need to get out from behind this shed before it's destroyed, but we need cover."

Sweat prickled along her spine. The atmosphere of the grounds, the energetic traces she had picked up earlier, and this attack were all combining to overload her system. She wanted to retreat, to hide.

Fintan appeared so competent and in control. *There are people firing at us!* she wanted to scream.

He glanced back at her. "Anytime now."

She bit her lip and tried to still the shaking. As she made her next attempt, three balls of fire smashed into the shed, one blowing the door off with a bang that made her heart jump, and another catching Fintan's arm. He swore.

Her mouth dropped open, and she stared at the nasty burn on his arm. Apart from the curses he had dropped, Fintan seemed to be ignoring the injury for now, but Tierra couldn't see anything else. The skin was an angry red, and it needed treatment.

She stepped forward in a daze. She could heal it. He'd fight better if it was fixed.

Fintan stepped back so he was sheltered by the bulk of the building, still seemingly unaffected by the wound.

She put a hand up, and he seemed to catch sight of her. He took her by the shoulders.

"Oh, T. Okay, breathe. Breathe, T."

She struggled limply, her gaze blurry. More fire streamed past. Her breathing hitched. What was wrong with her? She needed to focus. Protect them. "Your arm."

He gripped her shoulders, and the pressure helped to ground her. She concentrated on his voice.

"My arm's fine," he said. "We'll sort it later. T, if you don't think you can do this, it's okay. We'll get out of here another way."

Her chest heaved, but she shook her head.

"Okay. How can I help?" he said.

He already was.

She tried again to pull on her energies. They came more easily this time, earth responding. It had been a long time. She should have practised. Kept up her skills. But she hadn't thought she would ever be in this position again. She wasn't a fighter.

He grasped her by the chin, tilting her head up to meet his gaze. "T. You can do this."

Her bubble grew and stretched and thickened around them. She connected the bubble to them both, so Fintan could fire out of it, but nothing could pass through to reach them.

"Great job. Can you hold it while we move?" he asked.

She nodded, and prayed to Source she could.

He let go of her, and moved to the corner of the shed. She winced and pushed power into it so the bubble would stretch. He glanced around the corner.

"The best thing I think is for us to get to the car and get out of here. If I was alone I'd try and capture one of them, but I want to get you to safety." He grimaced. "But I'd like to know if the firebrand is alone or has someone with them."

She held the protection around them, but hung her head. She was a liability in this situation.

She swallowed. And then her eyes widened. She was an idiot. She could use her earth energies to see if there was anyone else on the property. The time she had spent tracking on it so far had given her a solid sense of it. She'd know if there was more than one person. But…she'd need to drop their shields for a minute. She didn't think she could do both actions at the same time.

Fintan darted his head from the cover of the shed to look. She didn't want to bother him. A moment later, fire smashed into him, and Tierra gasped. But the flames skidded harmlessly off her shield. He turned back to look at her, a wild grin on his face. "Great work!"

Her mouth dropped open. Surely he wasn't enjoying this? "I need to drop the shield for a minute. I think I can work out how many of them there are."

He quirked an eyebrow. "That'd be helpful. You're sure?"

She nodded. "I need you to stay safe though. Don't get hurt. It's distracting."

She couldn't tell him how distracting it really was. She'd been paralyzed when his arm had been hit. She moved until her back was against the wooden shed. Then she slid down so her butt and her hands touched the earth. The more natural surfaces she could touch that were part of the grounds the better.

She closed her eyes. She sent her energies out in streaks that bounced around the ground under the house and its gardens.

The Manipura energetic was easy to spot. Tierra had no energies in common with the woman, who held Ajna as her auxiliary energy. The woman's energies were twisted, and dark, her Manipura full of rage and bitterness. Tierra shuddered. The woman was a Rogue, using her energies in a way that wasn't congruent with the Source. In ways that upset the balance of the world, rather than supported it, which was the energetics' sacred duty from the Source. Not all Rogues were killers, but given who this one was associating with, she probably wasn't there to offer them cake.

The woman was inside the house, and sending her streams of fire through a window that she had smashed.

Tierra found no one else in her fast sweep of the grounds. She needed to do the same for the house. It wasn't big, and there was a great deal of wood in it, which she found easier to send energy through. The concrete was harder.

She could hear Fintan and their attacker, though neither of them cried out. A tree near them had been set on fire, and burned brightly. She would mourn it later.

Pressure on her shoulders made her eyes snap open. She gasped.

"The house is on fire," Fintan said, urgently. "When you do your sweep, can you also track? See if there's anything else you can find? This might be our only chance if the house burns down."

She nodded, but inside her body the adrenaline was draining her faster than she could use her energies.

She tried to recenter herself. Her hands balled into fists in the earth. She could smell burning wood, and the crackle of the flames emphasized how desperate their situation was. If there was anything to find in the house, now was the time.

She sucked in a breath, and coughed on the smoke. They couldn't stay here much longer, either way.

She let her shoulders relax and sank back into herself, and the earth. She aimed her energies at the house. She passed the fire energetic without pausing, and pushed energy into the wooden frame of the house.

There! There was another person. She nudged at him. Another energetic, yes, this one with more familiar energies. Very familiar in fact, though she wasn't sure why. He was a match to Tierra, with Muladhara-Anahata.

But, Source.

Bile rose up in her throat. It had been hard to touch the presence of the first Rogue, but to touch someone who had your own energies, but had twisted them into something so corrupt, so contemptible, so evil, was horrific.

She wavered. She felt him stop what he was doing. He could tell something wasn't right. Could he sense her? He'd have to make the effort to do so, just as she was.

She wished she could read minds.

"There's two people – another one inside. Searching, I think." She squeezed the words out. Fintan flung back an affirmative.

She moved off the repugnant man and sifted through the house. The energetic traces were full of desperation, especially in the basement, where Blaize had been held, and Tierra could feel the shining traces of the presence of her friend. She had been leeched by Indigo. But there were traces of that other presence in the basement, traces that were stronger than they had been in the grounds.

The charred floorboards of the basement contained the echo of a man, his energies twisted even more darkly than the two currently in the house. It was strange, but the presence reminded her of someone. Perhaps it was the combination of energies? But twisted, and strong. Her skin crawled. If she came across him again, she'd recognise him.

She moved her energies through the rest of the house, fast. There was only the one other person currently in the building. If they could get past the woman who was attacking them, they could get out of here. And right now, she wanted nothing more.

Her mouth twisted. Was she really going to leave, having gone through all this, without any further information? Her stomach soured. If they left without making a last try for clues, by the time they came back, these two would have stripped the place of anything useful.

Her fear could have consequences for everyone.

Her body was weak, and she was shaking consistently now. She had no idea how she was going to get out of here when they needed to.

She rubbed her hands back and forth in the soil, the repetitive action soothing her body while her mind and energy focused on the house.

Could she pick up a sense of what the man in the house was searching for? She concentrated and honed in on his presence again. He was in the bedroom, low to the ground. What could he be doing?

She probed, with fragile tendrils of energy she hoped he wouldn't notice. Despite them being thirty feet from the house, she could hear the crackle of flames as it burned, warm air drifting across her skin. She could only imagine what it must be like to know that the fire could bring the house down any minute. Whatever he was searching for must be important. But all she could sense were his feelings, not his thoughts.

Moments later, his energy flooded with triumph, and he moved at speed out of the room. Whatever he had been looking for, he'd found it.

"The energetic in the house is coming out, Fintan!" she yelled it, and rose unsteadily to her feet. If their attackers came after them, she would need a clear head.

They didn't. The assault on them stopped, and an engine roared into life. Fintan shot out from their cover and headed towards it. She staggered after him.

By the time she had skirted the harsh heat that billowed out from the blazing house to follow Fintan, he had already reached the lane. A vehicle headed away from the house at speed.

"Should we follow?" She had to raise her voice to carry over the crackle of the house fire. She really wanted the answer to be no.

Fintan shook his head and gazed down the road, mouth a flat line. "Are you okay? Get anything from the house?"

"Not really." She turned back to face the collapsing building, to see if there was anything else she could pick up. Her stomach was tight. He wasn't following the Rogues because of her, and she hadn't managed to pick up anything useful. Her attempt to help had had a negative impact.

"We need to call this in to the fire service. I'll tell them we were driving past and saw it from the road." He pulled out his cell and moved away from the noise of the fire.

She nodded miserably, her gaze downcast. She drew on what was left of her energies, and tried for one last energetic examination.

But the rooms she'd searched just minutes before were turning to ash, any natural materials that might hold traces being consumed by the fire. She pulled her threads of energy back towards her – and they snagged on something. She frowned.

She couldn't get much of a read on it with her energies, only that it was a disturbance, something energetic, but not natural. It wasn't anything she could read with her magic – was there something physical there?

She took a step, but the heat was intense. She gritted her teeth. It was only another handful of feet, but the smoke from the house covered the way so she couldn't make a visual inspection.

Whatever it was was on the ground. She would need to feel for it.

She glanced behind her, but Fintan was on the phone, facing in the opposite direction. She wrapped her scarf around her mouth and nose, and dropped to her hands and knees and began to crawl towards the house. She held the strange object in her energetic perspective even as her vision was obscured by the smoke. A few more feet, that was all. It was just inside the doorway of the house.

By the time she got to the item, she was coughing, acrid smoke burning her throat. She tried to keep her inhalations short. She reached out and grasped the item, small enough to fit into the palm of one hand.

It burned.

She gasped, and then choked as smoke filled her lungs. Dizziness filled her. She gripped the hard-edged object. The burn wasn't the heat of the house fire behind her, but a cold burn.

She turned on the spot, to crawl away, but after she'd progressed a few feet, she realized that the flames and noise of the house were hotter and louder. She'd gone in the wrong direction. Tears streamed from her eyes. She shook her head, dizzy. Which way was out?

She couldn't get a grip on her energies, and the smoke wrapped around her. There wasn't enough oxygen to sustain her, even this low to the floor, and sweat poured off her from the heat of the blaze.

"Fintan!" she tried to shout, but his name came out in a croak. She dragged herself a few more feet, trying to move away from the house, but the heat seemed to surround her, and she couldn't tell whether she was moving closer to the source of the flames or away to safety. Her head drooped.

She couldn't breathe.

Couldn't make her body do what she wanted.

Couldn't get to Fintan, and safety.

And she wasn't sure how real the touch of that reassuring Warrior energy was as the smoke became too much for her.

C H A P T E R

3

After a fast but necessary shower had dulled the edge of the aches and pains from the afternoon's unexpected entertainment, Fintan joined the others in the spacious living room. Its cathedral ceiling with exposed wood beams helped the room feel uncluttered despite the fact there were five of them and a dog scattered around it. Someone – probably Cara, given Tierra's current state – had pulled together some cookies and hot drinks, and the room smelled of sugar. Fintan grabbed a cookie from the plate and took stock of the room.

He loved Cathair Cuinn. It, and the people who lived there, had been a home to him like no place of his own had ever been. Its thick stone walls (so like Cuinn) and comfortable textiles (so like Tierra) had provided comfort and stability for decades. Despite his tendency to change where he lived on a whim, he knew he could always return here and be welcomed.

Adam, Cuinn and Blaize argued in the middle of the room while Tierra lay on the sofa, Cara checking her over. Adam's husky, Argus, sat with paws and nose on Tierra's legs, and gave her the occasional lick. Tierra grumbled at Cara's ministrations, her skin sallow, and her eyes red from smoke.

Cara, who had a striking combination of blonde bob and unusual bronze eyes, was Tierra's best friend, an Anahata-Manipura, and she worked as a Healer in a Rehabilitation Centre off the west coast of Canada. She looked after others without complaint – but her Manipura auxiliary Chakra meant she didn't take any shit while doing it.

Fintan gazed at her with relief. The exhilaration of the fight had nearly been wiped out by terror that Tierra might have been injured, or worse.

Fintan headed over to her and caught Cara's gaze. He lifted an eyebrow and she gave him a slight nod. His chest loosened.

"What the hell happened out there, Fintan?" Blaize glowered. "You're supposed to protect civilians."

"It wasn't his fault," Tierra rasped.

Guilt clutched at his insides. Yes, it was. He should have kept Tierra safe.

"Let him speak, Blaize," Cuinn said.

Fintan swallowed, and filled them in on what had happened with the Rogues. Then he squatted down next to Tierra. What he wanted to say was, what the fuck did you think you were doing going into a burning house? He'd turned around to call the fire service, and when he'd looked back, she'd disappeared. His heart had stuttered.

He restrained himself. "What I don't understand is why you went into the smoke in the first place."

Tierra put a hand into her pocket and brought out a bright, white stone, that seemed to glow. "I went to get this. I think they dropped it."

Cuinn's eyes narrowed. He walked over and plucked it out of her hand. He turned it over in his palm, then his gaze became unfocused as he checked it at an energetic as well as at a physical level.

When he raised his head, he looked ill. He sank down into one of the wing-backed armchairs. "This shouldn't exist. It's a white sapphire, and it contains stored Ajna energy."

He placed it on a small table in front of him and shuddered.

"Doesn't everything natural contain energy of one kind or another?" Blaize asked.

"Yes, but that's not what I mean. This stone has been used like a battery. Someone has drained an energetic and stored their magic in this stone."

There was a horrified silence.

Fintan rubbed his forehead. "I didn't think that was possible."

"Neither did I," Cuinn said, his face set. "And yet there it is."

"Are you sure?" Adam rumbled.

"There are some more checks I need to do. But I'm pretty certain, yes."

"Did the energetic they drained survive?" Cara asked. Her hand rested on Tierra's hair.

"I don't know," Cuinn said.

Fintan paced back and forth. "We have to stop this happening again. We need to find those Rogues."

"No shit," Blaize said.

"Where are we on the prophecies?" Adam said.

"We haven't made much progress since rescuing Blaize, I'm afraid," Cuinn said. "The only change we've seen is that Blaize now stands with us, rather than dies, so I'm confident that part of the prophecy has been diverted."

Cuinn, an Ajna energetic, had gone into the dreamscape at no small cost to himself to find the prophecies. He'd shared them with the rest of the group as he'd realized they were all a part of them – and now they were all in it together.

Blaize stood, and ran a hand through her hair in agitation. "This explains the jewels in the prophecy, doesn't it?"

Cuinn's mouth twisted. "Probably, yes."

"What are you talking about?" Fintan said. His body was full of adrenaline, ready for a brawl, but there was nothing and no one to fight.

"The last prophecy image that Cuinn found contained a heap of jewels, surrounded by bones. We thought it referred to some sort of treasure," Blaize said.

Cara's nose wrinkled. "The bones – it suggests the energetics probably don't survive the process then."

"We don't know that," Tierra protested softly from the sofa. Cara patted the other woman's hair comfortingly, and Argus whined.

"It's not a great sign," Cuinn said.

"Where do we go from here?" Fintan asked. He hated this helpless feeling.

"Difficult. Cuinn and Blaize can do the most." Adam turned to them. "Prophecy and stone research."

Cuinn was still gazing at the stone on the coffee table. "I need to find somewhere to store this."

"I'll go to Vancouver," Adam continued. "Follow the diner receipts we found during the first search of Indigo's place. For you, Fintan, and Cara, business as usual."

"Business as usual?" Fintan balled his hands by his sides. "Are you serious?"

"You have work. So does Cara. And we're probably going to need to pull you away from that work again in the future. So for now, we use our resources wisely."

Though Adam was a pretty senior energetic Protector, and he and Fintan had worked together often, it was unusual to see this more commanding side of him at Cathair Cuinn. Cuinn might be the person who understood the prophecies and the ether the best, but Adam, Tierra's brother and Cuinn's cousin, was the group's leader in terms of strategy and tactics in the physical world.

Adam turned from Fintan to Cara. "That reminds me. You said that the Rehab Center has had an abnormal number of Rogues this past year. Can you tell us more?"

"There's not much more than that really," said Cara. "We're the Rehab clinic for the Pacific north west of North America, and western Canada. We take a few other cases too, but that's our usual area. We're probably getting about fifteen per cent more than usual." Cara smoothed her skirt over her legs. "No links I can see. Very few have been significant – some of them have already been rehabbed and released. I don't believe we've had any cases of a Rogue being an energy Leech apart from this one."

Cuinn cocked his head. "That time frame is about the same period as for the prophecy dreams. Do you know if any of the other Rehab Centers have also experienced an increase?"

"I don't, but I can ask. Actually, has the Minor Circle been updated? I might get in touch with the Anahata Minor Guilds and ask them. They might have an overview. I'll start with mine."

There were thirty Minor Guilds, representing each combination of dominant and auxiliary powers, for example, Anahata-Manipura which was Cara's, but also Manipura-Anahata, for energetics with a dominant Manipura and auxiliary Anahata, because the two blends could be so different. Thus each energetic belonged to three guilds – their Minor guild, and two Major Guilds (Anahata and Manipura, in Cara's case). The Minor Circle consisted of a representative of each of the thirty Guilds, just as the Major Circle had a representative of each of the six Major Guilds. Since Sahasara, the crown Chakra, and Chakra of the Source, was neither dominant nor auxiliary for energetics, it didn't have any Guilds.

"Good idea." Adam nodded. "If anyone spots anything else similar, let Cuinn and Blaize know. Cathair Cuinn is our base of operations. Questions?"

Tierra sat at her workbench in her private living room. A handful of scented candles she'd made needed their wicks trimmed before they were ready to use. This recent batch was lavender scented, from herbs she'd collected and distilled.

Normally her answer to difficult feelings was to cook or clean, but she didn't have the energy for either. She was glad she had her own space in the huge house. She really needed it.

She held the scissors listlessly, and snipped the first wick. Then put the scissors down and stared out of her large windows at her little garden.

She'd tried to help, and she'd messed up. Because Fintan had had to protect her, Indigo's house had burned, and they'd lost the opportunity to find further clues. Without Tierra, he might have been able to catch the Rogues, but he hadn't wanted to leave her.

And now, everyone had a job to help with the prophecies but her. Adam hadn't even mentioned her in his summary. She was a glorified housekeeper. She was a hindrance, not a help. She snipped another wick, more viciously this time.

There was a knock and her door opened.

It was Cara. "How are you feeling?"

Tierra shrugged.

Cara walked over and put a hand on Tierra's brow, checking her temperature. She frowned, walked to the glass doors, and let in the smell of damp earth and growing things.

"Physically, you're going to be fine. But I don't need to sense your feelings to see you're sad. So what's up?"

Cara pulled up another chair next to Tierra's. A petite woman with a heart-shaped face, she was a strong Anahata, and could intuit a lot from using her energy around feelings, though it wasn't usually considered polite to do this. Tierra could sense moods when her own emotions were stable, and was fairly empathetic in the human sense, but she didn't have the strength of gift that Cara had.

The two women had got to know each other while working for a period in Anahata Guild in Cairo in the late 1800s, Tierra in Records and the Archive, Cara managing the Major Guild's relationships with some of the Minor guilds. Learning to belly dance together had cemented their friendship, which had endured to this day.

"I wish I was more useful," said Tierra.

Cara's brows drew together. "I don't understand. You're one of the most practical people I know. Look at these candles you're making."

She gestured at the pretty glass containers with their purple wax.

"I want to do more to help with what's going on, but I've barely left Cathair Cuinn and Merrow in decades. Today made me realize how scared I've become." She swallowed a lump in her throat. "I fought alongside you all in World War II. And look at me now."

Cara studied her. "You did, but it was tough on you. You needed time to heal."

"I think I took too long. I thought I was doing Cuinn a favor, coming here to look after him all those decades ago. But I got stuck. I used to travel all over the world. Now the furthest I go is to visit you on the other side of Vancouver."

"Is that a problem?"

"I froze today." Tierra swallowed. "I forgot my training."

"That's not the role you need to take," said Cara. "You have a good job in the human world, and you do provide huge support for all of us, but it's a different kind of support. Don't think we don't need it just as much though. Cuinn wouldn't have survived the last few decades without you."

Tierra glanced at her, then away. She bit her lip.

"What you do with this house baffles me," said Cara. "I could never manage to run it in the way you do. You make all of our lives better."

"But I don't want to sit at home. I want to help."

"Most of us are going back to our day jobs, like you."

Tierra, slightly mollified, rubbed a hand over her face and rested her chin on it. "I guess so. But I think Adam sees me as the little sister who's only good to look after the house."

"I wouldn't say he thinks of you as 'only' good enough to look after the house. He's as grateful as the rest of us. When there's an opportunity to help, you will."

Tierra sank down on her chair. She knew Cara didn't mean to sound patronizing, but that was how it felt. "Maybe."

"Sleep some more." Cara got up, and ran a hand lightly over Tierra's hair. "Fintan said to tell you he'll make dinner."

Tierra started. "Fintan?"

"Yes. Fintan." Cara cocked her head and gazed at Tierra assessingly. "Is there anything you want to talk about?"

Tierra's eyes opened wide. Why would Cara ask that? "No. Nothing. Why do you ask?"

"No reason." She walked to the door. "I'll call you when it's time."

The door shut behind her, and Tierra straightened in the chair, and snipped another wick. She gazed outside. Fintan was cooking? She couldn't remember the last time he'd taken charge in the kitchen. She'd like to see it. But she didn't want to get in the way.

She groaned and covered her face with her hands. *Get a grip, Tierra.*

Enough of this self-pity. She mentally shook herself and got up. She spotted her slim silver laptop on a shelf and grabbed it. She tugged a blue scarf, dotted with pretty pink flowers, from a hook on the wall, and wrapped its softness around her neck.

She'd rest, sure, but she'd also work, she thought as she stepped into her garden, leaving the glass doors that led to it open. She reminded herself that she was gainfully employed, in a job where people needed her and enjoyed her writing. And that although what she did might not be saving the world, it did help make the world an ever-so-slightly better place each week.

Outside was a shady wood, cool at this time of year, with a wooden table and chairs where she sometimes worked. She opened up the laptop and found the reader email she'd been thinking of.

"Dear Tierra,

Thank you so much for your wonderful advice column in the Vancouver Daily, which I always find helpful.

I'm having a tough time at the moment. I'm 24, and I work in an office job and still live with my family.

I know it's time to branch out and leave home, but my parents are protective, and I'm scared. They don't want me to go, and I'm finding it hard to make the leap when they see me this way.

How can I help them understand that I need this for my own independence? And how can I get the confidence to be more self-sufficient?

Yours, Debbie."

Tierra started typing, her fingers flying over the keys.

Dear Debbie,

Thanks for your letter, and I'm glad you enjoy my column.

I can certainly empathize with your issue. Sometimes we can get stuck in a situation without realizing it, and it can be hard to make a change, especially when others see us a certain way.

There are two things here.

The first is to sit down with your parents and tell them that you're old enough to look after yourself, but you're happy to set their minds at ease by talking them through your move to manage any worries they have. Ask them for their objections, and then logically present the evidence to them that you have tackled each one. Keep emotion out of it.

The second is to develop your own self-confidence. Consider what, exactly, are you afraid of? What's the worst that can happen? What measures can you put in place so that doesn't happen? Face your fears head on, but in a way that's kind to yourself.

Either way, it's your life, and while you need to be aware of their feelings, you also need to set boundaries about what is your decision to make, and not theirs. You earn your own money, you're an adult, and it's okay to make your own decisions.

Take care,
Tierra

Tierra sat back, satisfied, though her fingers ached from hitting the keyboard harder than normal.

There was another knock at her door, and she turned towards it, squinting through her open doors from the garden to see who had come into her room. Cara was back.

Tierra glanced at her wall clock, where each number was a pretty bird. "Dinner already?"

"No. Adam's had some kind of call from the Circle and he's being sent to sort out some urgent problem. We need a new plan."

Fintan studied Tierra as she and Cara entered the room.

Petite and shapely, she seemed even smaller than usual. Her dark hair was pinned back, and her brown eyes were serious. She was usually more bouncy, and her enthusiasm for life infectious, but still, she seemed more relaxed than when she had left them. He'd been worried about her. She'd been injured physically, but she'd also folded in on herself, and was swathed in a rich purple cardigan. He wanted to engulf her in his arms, to hug her worries away. He grimaced. Whatever they were facing was going to take more than a hug to make disappear.

"What's going on?" Tierra asked. Her eyes were still red from the smoke, and there were smudges underneath them. She sat on the sofa, her legs curled under her. Cara perched next to her.

"Something critical's come up that the Circle needs Adam to deal with," Fintan said. Adam was highly skilled at his job. He'd taken personal time for what was going on, but without telling the Circle and the Guilds what he was doing, and as his employers, they wanted him back.

"Someone else can handle it. I'm not their only Protector." Adam wrinkled his brow, his arms crossed over his broad chest. Argus huffed at his feet. "This situation is as urgent."

"What's going on with the Circle?" Blaize asked Adam.

"I'm not sure. A problem in London. Sensitive," said Adam.

"You need to help the Circle. Our situation will have to wait until you're back. Or Fintan can go to Vancouver," Cuinn said. He didn't have his usual upright posture. He sat on the edge of one of the armchairs, Blaize behind him on one of the arms. Her hand was on his shoulder.

"Not the right skill set." Adam's voice was matter of fact. "Needs a tracker with earth energy and instincts to follow her trail."

"We're not out of options yet," Cara said. She glanced at Tierra, who narrowed her eyes.

"What do you mean?" Cuinn absently stroked Blaize's hand on his shoulder.

"Well, we have more than one tracker," Cara said. She put a hand on Tierra's arm.

Tierra sighed. "Me."

"You?" Adam frowned. "After earlier?"

"Absolutely not." The words were out of Fintan's mouth before he'd really thought them through. But, really, what a ridiculous idea. He'd seen today what Tierra was like in a defensive situation. The last thing they should do was send her out again. She'd be scarred for life.

"I don't think it's your decision to make." Cara said, her tone warm, but firm. She caught Tierra's gaze. "It's your decision. This is something you can do. If you want to."

"If I'm brave enough," Tierra muttered. "But yes. I can do this."

"We're all involved in this," Fintan argued. "I have a say."

What the hell is Cara thinking?

"Only as much as anyone else," Tierra said. "Let's vote. All those who think I should go to Vancouver, raise your hand."

Tierra looked around the room, meeting everyone's gaze in turn, daring them not to raise their hands.

All the women raised their hands immediately. Blaize nudged Cuinn, and his hand followed, albeit slowly. When Fintan looked at him, mouth open, Cuinn said, "I don't love the idea, but she has the experience. Don't be sexist."

"I'm not being sexist. She's not a Warrior. You weren't there today. It affected her badly." *Was the world going mad?*

Tierra scowled at him.

"I'll take Blaize or Cara with me," said Tierra. "Either way, I'm going. I'm the right person."

Argus whined, and trotted over to stand next to Tierra.

Adam glanced at him, and then around the room, and he rested his hands on his hips. "Huh. Alright. You can, but not without protection. Unfortunately, Blaize is needed here, and Cara is needed at the Rehab Center." Adam's gaze moved to rest on Fintan. "You can go with her. I'll square it with the Circle."

"Haha," said Fintan, wincing at Adam's unexpected and terrible attempt to lighten the mood. "This is still a bad idea."

His whole body was tight. Tierra didn't track killers. She was the heart of Cathair Cuinn, the only real home he had.

Tierra looked torn, presumably at the idea of him accompanying her. It didn't feel great, but she'd be safer with him. She looked at Adam mutinously.

"You can track," said Adam to Tierra. "But you're rusty. You haven't defended yourself for decades. You need someone with you and Fintan is the only Warrior here who doesn't have another pressing job. And he can work with you on your defensive skills in the downtime." He shrugged. Decision made.

Both Fintan and Tierra were scowling now.

"Okay?" Adam had already moved on.

"Fine," said Fintan.

Except that it wasn't even close to fine.

Elrian stood in his closet. His crisp white shirts hung neatly in a row, several pairs of black pants pristine beneath them. Shiny black shoes were lined up on the floor. He reached and took down a shirt, and pulled it on one arm at a time. His movements were calm and measured. Deliberate.

Today would be a good day.

It hadn't been a good couple of weeks. His Adherent, Indigo, who had been with him, helped him and served him for many years, had been killed. Through her own stupidity, of course. He frowned.

As her Maven, her death had hit him hard. Her Haven—her 'safe place' in the dreamscape—had been destroyed when she died. As it had been tethered to his own Haven, he had needed to shore up his defenses in the dreamscape. His power had been severely depleted.

He took a pair of suit pants out of the closet and shook them, hard. He hated creases. After all, outer order created inner calm. Ensuring things were neat, tidy, and in their proper place helped to quiet the tangle of voices inside his dreamscape.

It wouldn't do for Cuinn to find him. Not yet, anyway. Indigo's death had also meant Elrian had lost his opportunity to hurt Cuinn's partner, Blaize. Now that would have served a two-fold purpose, breaking the prophecy and devastating Cuinn.

Elrian took a breath as he shut the wardrobe door, then smoothed his shirt down over his chest. There were other chances coming.

He was confident he was still ahead of the game. His work in the dreamscape meant he had more pieces of the prophecy than Cuinn did. Elrian had been working on it longer, after all.

But Cuinn and the others were seeking Elrian out. They would follow Indigo's trail back to Vancouver. He had prepared for that. They were unlikely to find the upscale house where he was right now. They should find the nasty motel she had spent most of her time in. Despite the fact he had set her up in this affluent community, she hadn't wanted to spend time here, preferring the fire of the metropolis to the suburbs, which she had considered lifeless. But he would limit his time here anyway, and soon jettison this place. He had no attachment to it, and it was one of a number of places he moved between for work.

The prophecy slivers he had picked up that morning suggested this was a turning point. Cuinn's people had choices about who they set on Elrian's trail, and whoever was sent would determine the next of the six possible couples that he needed to derail.

They had two trackers, the brother and sister.

Adam and Elrian had never gotten along, and Adam was strong enough that he could be a problem, especially when you added in that mutt of his. Not every Muladhara energetic needed an animal. That kind of bonding with a lower species had always seemed unsavory to Elrian.

His sister, Tierra, on the other hand, was weak. The intelligence he'd gathered told him she had fossilized in that pretentious house of Cuinn's. She wouldn't be a challenge.

Elrian hoped they'd send Tierra.

4

There was silence in the car as they left Cathair Cuinn behind them. Tierra shifted uncomfortably in her seat and took a sip of the coffee in her travel mug. Fintan's vehicle was fast and powerful, a Chevy Corvette – red, of course. Their overnight bags were in the trunk; his worn khaki duffel bag, and Tierra's small, barely used wheeled suitcase.

Fintan reached down and switched on the radio, finding a soft rock station that Tierra couldn't really complain about. Even though she wanted to. She was scratchy today.

She had mixed feelings about this whole situation. When Cara had suggested she go to Vancouver instead of Adam, Tierra had realized she didn't have a choice. She'd complained she didn't have a way to contribute, and Cara had offered her one. So she could make up for the day before.

Yet at the same time, there was an icy core of terror inside her. There wasn't any question she wanted protection. Yesterday had shaken her up and reminded her how vulnerable she was.

But, Fintan? He would protect her, there was no doubt. But would he also try and control her? He hadn't wanted her to come. Hadn't supported her need to play a part in the hunt for Indigo's co-conspirators. And that had hurt more than she'd wanted to admit.

Tierra needed to step up and show she could protect herself. And that didn't include a nanny.

Then she caught sight of the burn on Fintan's arm, and hunched her shoulders, remembering how he had looked after her the day before. She blew out a breath.

What had she replied to Debbie? *"Ask your parents for their objections, and then logically present the evidence to them that you have tackled each one. Keep emotion out of it."*

She'd take her own advice and address this awkward silence between them head on.

"Why don't you want me to do this?" She kept her gaze on the road as she sipped her drink.

The music filled the car with lyrics about love, holding on, and being a small-town girl. She turned it down.

"I was with you in World War II, T. I saw how much the violence affected you, the deaths of your mom and aunt especially," he said. Concern layered his tone. "How long it took you to recover. Yesterday was like turning back the clock. You were in shock last night."

"We're not at war. We're going to Vancouver to find out where Indigo was staying. We're looking for leads, not fighting an army. Those thugs have no idea we're going to Vancouver." She made an effort to relax her hand around her coffee. *Keep emotion out of it.*

"We don't know what we'll find, but the signs yesterday weren't good. There are at least two of them, and they're not afraid to use violence." He took a turn to the right onto a main road, heading towards Vancouver.

"So we track them, and then bring the others in when we've found them. We don't need to engage." Tierra kept her voice level. "If we do, you take the lead. But don't forget, it was my bubble shield that helped us escape yesterday. I'm not without resources. I just need to blow away the cobwebs on that aspect of my energies."

Right?

They sped along the highway, a road that followed the glittering ribbon of the Harrison river. Tierra loved the scenery in this part of the world. It had helped in her transition from the Mediterranean, where she had lived for many decades before relocating to Canada. She'd moved because Cuinn had needed her, but she'd also welcomed the break from Europe after the wars that had ravaged it.

Energetics tried to live in a place lightly, given that they often had to leave a location to prevent their long lives being discovered, but their connection with their natural environment went deep. She'd had a lot of self-healing to do after the wars, and her sorrow had been over the land as well as the people. Canada had been clean and fresh, with few people and a great deal of open space.

"We need to bring your training up to date," Fintan said.

"What training?" Tierra frowned at the change of topic.

278

"Your offensive and defensive abilities."

Oh. Not such a change. Tierra's shoulders slumped. He was right. But she wasn't enthusiastic.

"It's okay, you know," said Fintan.

"What is?"

"You're not suited to combat. Not everyone is. Source gives us all different aspects, different gifts. Violence isn't one of yours." He shot her a glance. "It's not a bad thing."

He was right again. So why was there a tight ball in her chest? Why was it hard to swallow? Why was she feeling so angry? It was as if all the emotions from the last twenty four hours were being squeezed into a tiny hollow between her breasts, making it hard for her to breathe.

"Let's talk about what we're going to do when we get there," said Fintan.

"We'll go into the diner on Hastings that was on the receipts. Have some food. Look around. See who we can talk to." She stared out of the window and rubbed the spot just above her heart Chakra.

"I should take the lead," he said.

"Oh, you have tracker training, do you? Know how to get inside someone's emotions? Because if so, you haven't been demonstrating that much lately." *What is wrong with me?* Tierra wasn't usually someone who made sarcastic comments. Or not with the angry edge that had made those words slice at him. She took a deep breath in a futile attempt to calm herself and slow her pulse, which hammered in her chest.

"It's better if I draw their focus. And I don't think you should go anywhere alone. If we're together it's much less likely you'll have trouble." Fintan's tone was oh-so-reasonable, but Tierra had had enough. The thin veneer of control she had clung to since the first fireball the day before splintered and fractured.

"Stop the car." If she didn't get into some open space, she was going to explode. Her energy, her magic, demanded that she connect to the natural world before she burst her skin.

"What?" Fintan's forehead wrinkled, but he didn't take his foot off the accelerator.

"Stop the car. Now." She was going to prove to him — and more importantly, to herself — that she could do this. That she didn't need to be wrapped in cotton wool.

"Why?" said Fintan.

Tierra drew a little power, and sent energy through the tires, asking the land to grip them and slow the car. She realized as she did how rusty she was — it hadn't even occurred to her to do the same the day before when the Rogues were leaving.

Fintan grappled with the wheel as the car skidded. He applied the brakes. Within seconds he had pulled the car over to the side of the road. "What the—"

Tierra threw her door open, and headed for a glade of trees on the right. After a few strides, she ran. The freedom of the forest surrounded her, and she drew deep breaths of fresh air into her lungs. She could have blended with the forest, hidden herself from him, but that wasn't the point of this exercise. She wanted him to follow.

Fintan stumbled out of the car and shouted her name, but she had a good lead. She stopped a minute or so later, in the middle of a thick glade of pines, and pulled power, waiting for him to catch up with her.

He entered the clearing and walked cautiously towards her. She sent tendrils of her power into the earth, stirring roots, branches and vines. She riffled through them as if she was looking for a file in a cabinet. She chose the vines.

Before Fintan had taken more than two steps, she'd caught him. Her vines, thick, strong and supple, reached out of the earth and wound themselves around his muscled calves. He glanced down at them, his eyebrows raised. "Tierra, what the hell are you—"

The vines grew quickly, and she drew them up his body, and wrapped them around his skull, so his jaw was bound. His eyes narrowed, though he seemed merely irritated, not angry.

She, on the other hand, was furious. The tight ball of emotion that had sat so heavily on her chest exploded through her body, and the earth shook. Fintan, his legs tied by vines, fell. She wrapped more vines around him and he made a stifled noise, struggling. He glared at her as he tried to speak.

"I'm showing you I can protect myself!" The words burst from her. "I'm not helpless. I was surprised yesterday. I can do this, Fintan!"

He stilled, and cocked his head, considering her from his position on the ground. He nodded once, and she felt him pull his power, Manipura, fire energy. She forced panic down. Was he going to defend himself? If so, she needed to show him she knew what she was doing. Because she did, didn't she?

She did a fast scan of the environment. What might he do? Ah. He could burn through the vines.

She used her power to lower some of the longer, higher branches, tying the vines to them and lifting him high, high up in the air. He'd be a lot less likely to set alight the branches from up there, where he'd fall if he freed himself.

She tipped her neck to stare through the boughs. He wasn't struggling, but watched her with the patience of a hunter. The pleasant glade hummed with power, the animals and birds hushed. She bit her lip. Having that assessing gaze directed at her was disconcerting.

She wanted to talk to him, explain, before he did anything rash. She sent her power into the trees, and several branches bent towards her, their leaves whispering gently. She stepped onto one, held on to another, and lifted the branches up so she was close enough to Fintan that he could hear.

It had taken less than a minute, and she'd neutralized him.

"I. Can. Protect. Myself." She shook a little with the aftermath of the adrenaline that had flooded her system. "Stop seeing me as the little sister you need to control, and treat me as an equal. A partner. Because that's what we are for the next day or two. If we don't work together effectively, we waste time, not just for us, but for everyone. What's at stake here is a lot bigger than the two of us. Do you understand?"

She released the vines that bound his jaw.

"You made your point. We'll train later, and I'll show you exactly why you do need me. Let me down." A vein pulsed at his temple. Okay. Perhaps he wasn't so relaxed about what she'd done.

"I wouldn't have needed to do this if you weren't such an arrogant idiot." She moved her branch a little further away.

"Arrogant? Me?" His hands, down by his hips as he was still wrapped in the vines, balled into fists.

"Yes. You. Just treat me as if I was any of the others. And let's move on." She drew on her energy to take them both back to the ground and release him.

"Okay. I'll treat you like any other Warrior who tried a trick like this," said Fintan, grimly.

The hum of power around them intensified as he pulled energy. A heartbeat later, he burned through his bonds, and he propelled himself over to her branch, his weight sinking it, and them, to the ground at an alarming rate. Oh. Apparently being up high wasn't the deterrent she'd thought it would be.

He, anticipating the landing, took it in a graceful roll, whereas she tripped as she landed, and had to put an arm out to catch herself.

As he came back up to his feet, he dived and snaked his arm around her throat, lifting her head up at an awkward angle. Fire rose up around them, heating the air.

Oh dear. She was trapped in a circle of fire with an angry fire energetic.

Her back and butt were pressed into him, and his solid arm was hot against her neck. She could hear the rasp of his breath in her ear. Her brain fogged over.

And then her anger was gone, chased away by a pulse of something that was one part fear, and – disturbingly – three parts arousal.

Fintan's blood was up. Tierra was being so, so, irritating. When, exactly, had that happened? All their lives, she had been the sweetest, most loving of energetics. Since running Cathair Cuinn, she'd always been welcoming, always been supportive. She always listened to him. Provided an ear.

So who was this?

She had attacked him. What had she been thinking? There was no way she could best him, as he'd just shown. There was a move she could make to get out of the stranglehold he had her in, but he doubted she'd remember. Perhaps this could serve as the first of Adam's suggested lessons. Though he wasn't sure this was exactly what the big man had had in mind.

Tierra moved against him, and he got wind of the scent of her hair. Which smelled of flowers. She was soft, and the curve of her back, and, Source help him, her ass, was pressed into his groin. She tried to twist in his arms, and that movement stirred something in him.

Something that had never noticed Tierra before. His groin twitched.

He let go of her as if she were hotter than the flames he had conjured.

She yelped and fell towards the circle of fire around them.

"Shit!" he said, and dropped the flames and grabbed for her at the same time.

She flailed as she fell, and ended up awkwardly in his arms, off-balance, clinging to him. Her fingers dug into his forearms and they stared at each other.

He righted her as if she were made of glass, and let go. He stepped backwards, putting some distance between them. She had a dazed look in her eyes.

The silence stretched uncomfortably.

The forest air suited her. Sunlight through the forest canopy made her hair shine dark and glossy, and her skin was once again smooth butterscotch rather than the yellower color it had been the evening before. Her Latina genes were highlighted by the browns and greens of the woods. She was a curvaceous dryad, apple-cheeked and innocent.

Whatever insidious part of him had woken up when she had been pressed up against him wasn't going away. He growled, and her eyes widened.

Damn.

He'd never seen Tierra as anything other than family. An honorary sister, as Cuinn and Adam were like his brothers. Part of him craved a sense of family, a sense of home, and while his many-years-dead biological family hadn't been up to much, his chosen family was vitally important to him. The love that she'd always provided him with was crucial to his wellbeing, to his purpose. It gave him the strength to carry on when things were tough and he had moments of emptiness, or loneliness. Not that those happened often. He was someone who could always find a beautiful woman to keep him company. After several centuries, even the most inept of men had a better understanding of seducing women, and he had never been inept.

Tierra was different though. Her love was steady. Constant. It was part of his foundations.

And he wasn't going to fuck that up just because of a brief and weird moment of sexual desire.

They needed to get out of this forest, where some kind of wicked magics were at work.

"You need more work on your self-defense," he said.

She bit her lip and nodded. "You need work on your social skills."

He raised his eyebrows slightly, but decided discretion was the better part of valor.

They walked back to the car. He hoped like fuck she hadn't noticed anything. What the hell was going on with him? Adam and Cuinn would kill him if they knew what had crossed Fintan's mind as he'd held her in that chokehold.

At his car he hesitated again. "Do you want to drive?"

She smiled. "No thanks. But I'll choose the music."

"Okay."

They drove the two hours to Vancouver, breaking their silence only to discuss the best place to park. Fintan suggested—carefully to make sure it didn't seem like a command—that they park some distance from the diner and walk.

She agreed, and he parked a few streets away.

"Will you put a protection warding on the car?" Fintan said. "This doesn't seem the safest of areas to leave it."

She nodded, and looked around the dull concrete environment. "There's not much here for me to draw from."

Muladhara energetics didn't enjoy built up environments. He needed to remember that. He pointed towards a spindly looking tree that stood in a patch of dry earth, part of some previous gentrification project that hadn't taken. She nodded, and after a few moments, said, "I've warded the car to appear less expensive, and less flashy."

She raised her eyebrows at him, and he rolled his eyes. And those childish gestures of teasing did a lot to resettle him.

The drab and dirty diner was no improvement on their surroundings, the smell of bacon fat and the cleaning agent used to wipe tables down assaulting his nostrils as they entered. A sullen waitress gestured to the mostly empty room behind her, to indicate they should seat themselves.

Fintan scanned the other occupants before choosing where to sit. An old man in his eighties sat hunched over a newspaper and a greasy looking all-day breakfast in a booth near the windows. A tired mother, her two children squabbling opposite her, picked at a plate of fries. And a handful of teenagers, most of them sporting piercings and tattoos though none of them looked a day over eighteen, were draped over the booth furthest from the door.

He weighed up the room, and judged none of these to be a threat. That didn't mean he wouldn't take his usual precautions, and he chose a seat where he had his back against the wall. One of the teenagers made a lewd gesture about Tierra behind her back, but a look from Fintan, and the kid's hands fell to his sides. The teen muttered something. Fintan smiled.

Tierra sat, and looked around. "Poor Indigo. Adam said from the receipts she ate here almost every other day for a month."

"Poor Indigo?" Fintan gave Tierra an incredulous look. The woman's heart was uncontainable. "She leeched from Blaize. She'd have drained her dry if Blaize hadn't stopped her."

"Who knows what her background was? Maybe she didn't have our opportunities. Our families. No one would choose to spend so much time in a place like this if they didn't have to," she said. The corners of her mouth turned down.

Fintan picked up the laminated menu from a plastic stand embossed with a perky tomato. "All families have their issues. Cuinn's father isn't exactly a peach, for example. Do you want something to eat?"

"Not really. But we'd better have something. Otherwise, it'll look a bit strange. Plus my stomach is unsettled. Food might steady it." She craned her neck to see what others were having. "Omelet and hash browns? They have to cook that from scratch, and there's not that much that can go wrong with it. And coffee."

Fintan gestured to the waitress, who ambled over on her own schedule.

"What?" The waitress drawled the word.

"Two omelets with a side of hash browns each. And two coffees."

"Whatever you say." The waitress walked off to the counter. She ostentatiously repeated their order to the cook, who, given he was only a couple of yards from them had probably heard it the first time. She returned with a stained coffee pot in her hands, and two mugs.

She poured coffee for each of them, pointed to the creamer and sugar on the table, and walked off again.

"I guess Indigo didn't come here for the service." Tierra tore open a couple of sugar packets and tipped some creamer into her mug, and slid the condiments towards him.

"What's the plan?"

"Can you pick up any energetic traces?" he said.

She glanced around the room. "It's mostly metal composites and manmade things in here. Plus this is highly trafficked. I'll scan, but it's unlikely I'll pick anything up."

"Sure. See what you can do," he said.

She leaned down and looked under the table and made a satisfied noise.

"The table's made of wood under the laminate." She put her hands underneath the table, touched it, and drew in a breath.

She pulled power, and the air shimmered around her. He watched and waited while she worked, her eyes shut. Her long lashes rested on her cheeks. Her face was serene — and bewitching.

He grimaced. It was like a switch had been flipped inside him, and he was suddenly seeing a completely different Tierra.

He was someone who had a lot of relationships. He enjoyed the company of women. He liked cuddling, and he liked sex. But his relationships never lasted that long — for an energetic, anyway. A handful of years, max. His schedule, away from home for long stretches, usually frustrated women after a while. He got bored easily, too. There weren't many people he could spend long periods of time with without wanting more variety.

Though he'd never felt that with Tierra.

He shoved his hands in his pockets and leaned back, his eyes widening in alarm. He needed to nip this in the bud, now. Tierra was the heart of his adopted home and family. That was far more important to him than her being some sort of sexual conquest. His mouth twisted in disgust at the thought. She deserved better than him. He snorted. Way better.

Her eyes popped open. "Everything okay?"

"Fine. Anything?" He winced internally at how curt he sounded. They'd just made up, he didn't want to upset her again.

She frowned. "No. There are some energetic traces here, and I would say they fit Indigo and the male presence I found in the basement, but they're too diluted for me to get much off them. So no progress."

She took a sip of coffee and stared despondently at the table.

"You confirmed this is a place that Indigo came to. That's progress." He reached over and squeezed her hand. "Next step is to offer the waitress cold, hard cash. She's not exactly the friendly type. You can read her if she gives us any useful info."

He opened his wallet under the cover of the table, and checked to see what he had. "But we eat first."

"Let's see what it looks like when it comes." She traced invisible patterns on the table with a finger. "About earlier—"

"Forget it. I was an idiot, you were angry. We're definitely going to refresh your self-defense skills soon though."

"Okay." Tierra's answer seemed meek considering the emotions she'd displayed in the woods. "Just treat me like a partner, and we won't have any problems."

Like a partner. Yes. He tried to blink away the sensory impression of her body tight up against him, his arm around her smooth throat, and took a swig of coffee to distract himself.

"Euhhh." He tried not to spit it out. He forced himself to swallow it, grimacing as it went down.

"I told you it needed sugar."

"There's not enough sugar in the world." He tipped in several packets anyway. Maybe as sweet tar it wouldn't be so bad.

The waitress, whose nametag said 'Betty', brought over two plates and put them on the table with poor grace. As she was about to walk away, Fintan said "Betty."

She turned, eyebrows raised.

"We're looking for a woman," he said.

Betty's nose wrinkled. "I may not be much, but I'm not that desperate, thanks."

Tierra's lips pinched together and she shook her head. "Sorry, that's not what he means. We're looking for a friend of mine. We heard she's been in here a lot recently. In her last phone call home she told us how much she liked the place."

A small 'oof' came from Tierra as he kicked her under the table to prevent her from overdoing it. He added a $50 bill to the table to help her out.

The waitress caught sight of the money, and stopped in her tracks. "What's her name?"

"Indigo. She has dark hair, and she's thin. Pale."

"Maybe I know her. Maybe I don't. What's she to you?" Betty asked.

"A distant cousin. She's been in some trouble recently, but she was planning on coming home. We haven't heard from her in a month or so." Tierra clasped her hands in front of her. "We really need to find her. We're worried."

The waitress thawed a little, though whether in response to the money or Tierra's doe-eyed pleading, Fintan wasn't sure. Betty slid the money from where Fintan had wedged it under the grimy container of creamer, and slipped it into her apron, her gaze never leaving Tierra's.

"I can't tell you much. She was in here every couple of days for about a month, then she disappeared. I thought she was a druggie to be honest. She had that thin, desperate look that junkies get when they're looking for a fix."

"Did you hear where she was staying?"

Betty shrugged. "Probably at the Motel 72. There's not much else around here. It's down the street."

Tierra nodded. "We'll try it. Thank you."

Before the waitress could walk away, Fintan added one last question. "Did you see her eat with anyone else? We'd like to find her friends. They might know something."

"She met up with a guy a couple of times, they left together. Older man. If he hadn't been dressed so fancy, I'd have thought he was her dealer, because she always looked better after they met."

Fintan tried not to seem too interested. "Can you describe him?"

The waitress turned away. "White guy, fifties maybe. Like I said, well dressed."

She walked off to another table.

Tierra let out a breath, and poked her omelet.

"Pretty good." Fintan raised his eyebrows. "And you told no actual lies. Apart from the one about Indigo being your cousin."

"She is, in human terms. She's an energetic. I said distant." She gave up on the pale and greasy omelet, and ate a fry. "That seemed to go well."

"Yeah. Time for our next delightful stop on our tour of Vancouver's finest establishments, Motel 72."

5

Tierra rolled her shoulders uncomfortably as they walked down the road towards the motel. All around her were the signs of a deprived area. Angry graffiti, broken windows, boarded up shops. The smell of trash because it was heaped in piles of garbage bags rather than in a dumpster. Passers-by avoided eye contact. She hooked her hand into the crook of Fintan's arm.

Then wished she hadn't.

She'd forgotten, for a moment, their strange encounter in the woods. She wasn't quite sure what had come over her. It was so unlike her to behave in such a crazy-person way. But Fintan was incredibly irritating.

And gorgeous.

Putting her hand on his bicep, the muscle flexing as he walked, was giving her some very inappropriate thoughts.

It was odd. She'd loved him for centuries. But she hadn't lusted after him in the way she had since the moment he'd looked down at her, anger in his eyes, flames around them, his arm stretching her throat out like an offering.

She could let go of his arm. She really didn't want to though. Alright. Time for a change of topic.

"How do you want to play it at the motel?" she asked.

"The cousin thing worked well. It'll probably be a guy on reception though." He scratched his chin and narrowed his eyes thoughtfully. "So…why don't you open an extra button on the cardigan?"

Her mouth fell open. "What?"

"Nothing too much. Just…encouragement. It might distract him enough to let his guard down. Your figure is pretty captivating."

She gaped at him. He'd called her body captivating. And possibly insulted her at the same time.

"That ok? You don't have to. You did a great job with the waitress. Wow, she was a piece of work."

She pulled her arm out from his, and stopped. She used the dirty window of a car to redo her lipstick, a subtle rose color, and undid her scarf, stuffing it into her shoulder bag. An amber pendant hung above her cleavage. She popped another button on the nut-brown cardigan, and turned to Fintan.

"How's this? Slutty enough?"

"You look lovely." There was a strange look on his face, a look that didn't match his words. A slight wrinkling of his brow. And was there the faintest hint of disapproval in his voice? She sighed. *Oh well.*

Tierra kept her hands well away from Fintan's biceps as they continued on. He held the door for her and scanned the street to see if anyone watched them enter.

In the motel foyer, an unpleasant dank smell struck her. Like clothes that had been left in a washing machine for too long, and had started to mildew. She headed to what could loosely be called the reception desk, behind which, as Fintan had guessed, was a scrawny man watching a TV. He barely looked up.

"Rooms are \$30 for an hour, \$70 for the night. Reductions for longer stays. Whaddayawant?"

Tierra leaned over the desk, putting her cleavage in the man's line of sight.

"We're looking for my cousin, Indigo," Tierra said in her best sultry voice. Well, her first ever attempt at a sultry voice. "She was staying with you for a month or so. Dark hair, pale skin, thin. We haven't heard from her in a few weeks, and we're worried."

The man, drawn to her cleavage like it was a magnet and his eyes iron filings, appeared to have been rendered senseless. *Not entirely unflattering. If only I could capture Fintan like that.*

"Maybe. Your cousin, eh?" The man's cynicism was strong enough to get past the view, though his gaze didn't shift.

"Distant cousins. You remember her, then?" Tierra leaned towards him.

"Maybe. What's in it for me?" He leered.

Tierra stepped backwards into Fintan. She could almost feel his eyes burning into the man's face.

Fintan waved \$50. "Eyes up, dickwad."

The man mumbled an apology. Fintan put the money on the counter, and it disappeared into the guy's pocket.

"She stayed here about a month. Left a few weeks ago." The man avoided eye contact.

"Do you know what she was doing?" Fintan asked.

"It's not like we had long conversations, Mister. Most people come here for privacy." He snickered.

"You might have overheard something. A man in your position hears a lot of secrets I'd imagine." Fintan gently moved Tierra to his side so they stood next to each other. He leaned a casual hand on the desk, and bent over the counter. It forced the weasel-faced man to look at him, though he had to tilt his head to meet the much bigger man's eyes.

"Maybe, maybe. I might've heard something about research a couple of times." The man leaned back in his seat, putting distance between him and Fintan as casually as possible.

"What kind of research?" Tierra jerked in excitement, the amber pendant swinging.

The man's eyes followed the pendant's path, hypnotized. "No clue. Something about a man? Irish name maybe? It sounded like she was trying to get information about some kind of hippie commune to the East. Talk about dreams and earth, fire, that kind of thing."

That sounded like energetics. Thank the Source, they were on the right track. But who was Indigo researching? Blaize? And who was this other man? What was his relevance to the prophecy?

"Did anyone come here to meet her? Or did she get any phone calls?" said Fintan.

"She had a cell. Didn't make or take many calls from her room." The guy shrugged.

"She had some? Can we see the phone records? Her final bill?"

The man narrowed his eyes and assessed Fintan. "Not strictly legal, that."

Fintan held up another $50 and the man smirked. And did nothing.

Fintan glared at the man, but held up one more $50 bill.

The manager got up and went into a back room. Tierra turned to Fintan. "There's no need to act like my bodyguard. Partners, remember?"

He eyed her and lifted one eyebrow. "It's part of the act. Just like your new and improved voice."

Not much she could say to that.

The man came back out, a piece of paper in his hands. "Here's her bill. There's not much on it. A few phone calls. She didn't use much here apart from the room. We don't have food, or many extras. Just a bit of pay-per-view porn."

"Of course," said Fintan.

Tierra rolled her eyes.

"But she didn't use that."

"How was she? How did she seem mood-wise?"

"Moody's a good word for it. You'd never know whether she was up or down. Not my place to say, though if you ask me, she was doing some kind of drug. High as a kite one day, then a grumpy bitch the next." He caught Fintan's gaze, and said, "'Scuse my language."

Tierra took the paper and beamed at the man, while her skin crawled. "Thank you for your help."

"Sure. Next time, come alone with the money, and maybe I can help you a little more." He sniggered.

Tierra hunched her shoulders, and Fintan growled. A jolt of panic went through her at his face, and she took him by the arm and dragged him out of the motel.

Back in the blessed fresh air, Tierra shuddered. "I need a shower."

"It's probably a good idea to book in somewhere for the night now we have a couple of leads to follow," said Fintan. "I'll text the numbers to Adam and he can check on them for us."

His gaze was on his phone, and his fingers moved as he spoke. He didn't see one of the teenagers from the diner sidle up to them.

Thin and bedraggled, she had three piercings in one ear, one in the other, and her eyebrow and nose both sported rings. She looked to be Asian, and wore heavy biker-style boots, ripped jeans, a white t-shirt with a unicorn on, underneath which it said 'go to hell' in rainbow bubble writing, and a battered leather jacket over the top.

"I heard you wanted Indigo." The teen glared at them both.

Fintan tensed. Tierra put an arm up to stop him moving. The girl's demeanour was a front. Anxiety came off her in waves. She wasn't a danger.

"Yes, that's right. Do you know her?" Tierra kept her voice gentle.

"Do you have money?" The girl brought her chin up.

"We can pay you a little for information." Tierra hesitated. "Why don't we buy you a meal?"

The poor girl was slender to the point of too thin. And she could have valuable information. Maybe.

"You can buy me a drink." The glare softened slightly.

"Okay. Where do you want to go?" *Not the diner, please.*

"I know a place." The girl shoved her hands in her jeans pockets, and, head down, strode away.

Tierra followed her, and she heard Fintan sigh behind her, but he'd joined her side within a few strides.

"What's your name?" Tierra asked.

"What's it to you?" The girl mumbled from ahead of them.

Tierra had to strain to hear her, she was so quiet.

"Just something to call you," Tierra said.

"Whatever. I'm Ai."

A couple of blocks later, the girl stopped at the entrance to a bar.

Fintan whispered to Tierra, "This could be a trap. Stay alert."

She nodded, and kept watchful. Fintan's eyes moved constantly, scanning for trouble. Despite all Tierra's confident words of the last twenty-four hours, she was glad of his presence. While talking to the waitress and the guy at reception in the horrible motel had felt like a game, Ai's demeanor made her uncomfortable. Something was very wrong, though Tierra had sensed no threat from Ai herself, despite her angry tone. It was a puzzle.

Ai pushed open the door and went in, without any indication that she was bothered if they joined her.

"Let me take the lead." Tierra put her hand on Fintan's arm to pause him following Ai.

"You think she'll listen to you?"

"Maybe," said Tierra. Hopefully. "There's something about her. I'm not sure exactly, but yes, let me take the lead. If anything happens, you can take over."

Her tracker instincts were on alert. She hoped they would get something from Ai that would move the investigation forward. Then Tierra would have done her part and they could go back home.

Fintan nodded, and led the way through the door. There were a few steps down to the dingy bar, which held more customers than the diner. The floor was grimy, but the bar was well polished, if worn. A few of the patrons drank in a focused fashion, and many of them looked like they had been here for a while. This was a place for serious drinkers, not socializing, and there was little conversation between the customers.

She scanned the room, and found the girl sitting in a booth. Tierra slid in across from her.

"What do you want?" Fintan asked.

"Soda, please," Tierra said.

"A beer." The girl traced circles on the table in old beer with a slender finger.

"How old are you? You're not old enough to drink." Fintan raised an eyebrow.

"Old enough to give you information about your *cousin*. So old enough for a beer. Or two."

Fintan shrugged and went to the bar, leaving the girl and Tierra together.

There was something unusual about the girl, but Tierra couldn't put her finger on what, exactly. Tierra considered reaching out with her energy, but even humans could sometimes feel that, and Tierra didn't want to upset her. At least not until they'd had a proper conversation.

Tierra wrinkled her nose. She was starting to think like Fintan.

"What do you do, Ai?"

"Not much." The girl's chin was still up and her defensive glare held a lot of anger. What kind of life had the girl had, to have such rage in her eyes for strangers? "This and that. Some errands. Whatever needs doing."

"Do you live around here?"

"You could say that."

Tierra gave up, relieved, when Fintan came back with the drinks.

He sat next to her in the booth, his muscular thigh pressed against hers, the heat of it burning through her dress. She frowned, and turned her attention to the girl. "So. Ai. How do you know Indigo?"

Fintan divided his attention between Tierra and Ai's conversation and the room. This would be a good place for an ambush. There were only two exits, the door where they'd come in, and another that appeared to lead to a backstage area. If Ai had set them up, he would be ready.

"Met her in the diner," Ai said. "A couple of months ago. She offered to buy me a burger. I told her I wasn't into funny stuff, and she said that wasn't what she wanted. Said she recognised herself in me. After that we hung out in the diner a few times."

What had Indigo seen in this young woman? They both seemed to have had a shitty deal from the world. Maybe that was it. And street smarts – they reminded him of urban foxes, feral creatures that could turn on you at any time.

"Did she tell you what she was doing?" Tierra asked.

"She said she was working for a guy. And looking for info on another guy. I couldn't help her there." Ai took a sip of beer.

"What else did she tell you? Or do?" said Tierra.

"She met with a few people in the city."

"Do you know who they were?" said Tierra.

"One of them. Said she'd introduce me to a guy who needed a kid to run errands. The money sounded good. We went along to a place in Upper Delbrook. Fancy place. House in north Van. Plenty of glass and wood."

She took another sip of her beer.

Fintan willed his impatience down. The girl was enjoying the attention.

"Trippy from the start. He was weird. And I know weird. He had the same vibe as the girl. I thought they were both on drugs." She shifted in her seat. "Though he was less wired than she was. More in control. He said he could always use people like me. Then they both laughed. Something was off. I decided to disappear. Waited till they were in the other room. Went out a window."

"What made you leave?" said Fintan. He sat back in the booth and stretched an arm out along the back of the seat. The stink of stale beer hovered in the air. Was the weird guy the man who had been in Merrow?

"Just a feeling. I'm good with feelings. Learned to listen to them. Helped me out of bad situations a few times." Her mouth twisted. "The one time I didn't listen, things got ugly. Learned my lesson. Don't take chances now."

Tierra's hands were flat on the table, and she was practically vibrating with excitement. What was she seeing he wasn't? "What happens when you get a feeling, Ai?"

"Not much. A tickle in my brain. Feeling in my gut. Heat."

"Do you ever get dreams? Dreams about real life? And the dreams come true?"

Oh. Surely not. If it was what he thought, then this mess had just got even more complicated.

Ai's eyes widened slightly, and met Tierra's gaze for the first time since the street. "Why?"

"I have ... a feeling."

"That's what Indigo asked me. Said she had them too." The girl had stopped clutching her beer and had begun to scoot towards the edge of the booth.

"You're free to go at any time, Ai," said Tierra. "We're not like Indigo, you know that. Because your gut, and the tickle would tell you if we were. And it hasn't, has it?"

Ai shook her head slowly. "Do you have dreams?"

"No. But both of us have gut feelings. Like you."

Sacred Source.

The girl was an energetic.

6

Tierra's heart raced. Lost energetics were few and far between. She and Fintan needed to be careful, as the girl seemed skittish at best. Tierra refused to lose her. They needed her to find out what was behind the situation with Indigo, but Tierra also wanted to bring the girl home.

The name Ai, which meant love in Chinese, indicated she'd been named by energetic parents, as all energetics' names had some kind of link to their dominant Chakra – Tierra came from the Latin for earth, while Fintan was Irish for 'white fire'. An energetic's dominant chakra was usually evident right from birth, though their auxiliary could take a while to settle.

Ai hadn't moved away from the edge of the booth. She was poised to run.

"I'm not crazy. Neither are you. We're cousins too, in a way," Tierra said.

"Like you and Indigo?" Ai snorted.

"Sort of. Indigo was in with some bad people. We're trying to find them, to make sure they're not taking advantage of any other kids, like you."

"I'm not a kid." Ai crossed her arms over her chest, her beer bottle held in one hand.

"You can help us," Tierra said.

"If you show us where the house was, we can tell you more about yourself," Fintan said.

Ai narrowed her eyes, but she settled back into the booth. Tierra's heart rate slowed. Fintan's appeal to Ai's self-interest had worked.

"What else can you tell us about the man she met?" Tierra asked.

"Tall. Thin. But wiry-strong, rather than thin like Indigo. As I said, in control. He was the boss-man. Not her. Grey hair. Looked like a lawyer off a TV show. Rich."

"Anyone else there?" Fintan said.

"I didn't see anyone. But maybe. The house felt wicked strange. I didn't stay to find out." Ai rolled her shoulders back and thrust out her chin. "What do you know about me?"

"Did you know your parents?" Tierra asked.

"No. I was in the foster system. What do you know about me?" she asked again, insistent.

Tierra spread her hands out, palms up. "I think … I think you've always known when something bad was going to happen. At first you told people. But they ignored you, and bad things happened anyway. Sometimes they blamed you. So you stopped telling them. But you didn't like to get close to people because of it."

Ai turned her head away, her arms wrapped tightly around her slender body. "How do you know that?"

Tierra's heart squeezed. Ai's name and her 'feelings' indicated Anahata. The tickle in Ai's brain, the dreams? That was Ajna. The energy of the mind.

She was an Anahata-Ajna energetic, who had somehow fallen outside the world of the energetics. Both Chakras were dormant, but untrained energetics were dangerous. Volatile.

They needed to get Ai to a teacher as soon as possible.

"Because we're like you," Tierra said. "We get those feelings too. And we know a lot more people like us."

"Where's Indigo?" Ai asked.

Tierra blinked at the change of topic, and bit her lower lip, hesitating. Now wasn't the time to tell her that Indigo was dead. They needed to win Ai's trust.

"We're trying to find her, and we think the man you met might know where she is," Tierra said. "How about this. We'll check into a hotel, and you can meet us again later. In the meantime, listen to your instincts about us."

The girl relaxed her arms and took another sip of her beer. She put the drink down, and slid out of the booth. "Fine. Seven p.m., Gabrielle's. You can buy me dinner."

She disappeared out the door.

Tierra let out a breath. It had been like handling a wild animal, which at any point could have turned on her. "Don't say it."

"What?" Fintan cocked his head.

"That I let our best lead go."

"I think you did great."

Tierra lifted her head and looked at Fintan, her eyebrows raised. "Really?"

"You figured out she was a Dormant long before me, and she responded much better to you."

Tierra swallowed, her throat dry. The compliment was appreciated. She picked up her soda and took a sip. "The poor girl. I wonder who her parents were, and how she slipped through the net. The Circle is usually so good at keeping tabs. Her parents must be dead, surely, for her to be in the human foster system. Do you think she'll come back?"

She really hoped she would.

"I do. Letting her go was a stroke of genius." Fintan patted her hand. "It'll show we can be trusted. Let's find a place to stay."

Fintan drove them to a nearby hotel. Tierra fiddled with her necklace the entire journey, her face drawn. He hoped she wasn't worrying too much about Ai. Sometimes her compassion got the better of her.

It wasn't long before they were in their room – one room, two beds. Thankfully, it was a lot nicer than the motel they'd visited earlier in the day, with fabrics in soft pastels and more cushions than any man knew what to do with scattered around every surface. As he threw his bag down on the bottom of his too-soft bed, the thought triggered the memory of the softness of Tierra's body against his own hardness in the forest.

Sister. She's like a sister to me.

Tierra headed straight for the bathroom. "I need to wash the diner off me."

After a few minutes, the shower started, and fragrant steam leaked out under the door.

He tried hard not to think about her, the soap, water, and bubbles. He shook himself, and called Cuinn, which had the same effect as reciting algebraic equations.

"How's it going? What have you found?" Cuinn sounded tired.

"We have a lead – apparently Indigo met with a man a few times, and a girl has told us she can take us to the place he lives."

"That's great news. Should I send reinforcements?"

Cuinn always had his back. "Not yet. We'll scope the place out and see if he's really there. If he is, we'll find out what he's doing, and who he is. Then Blaize and Adam, or whoever, can come and help us if we want to go in."

"Okay, if you're sure. I trust your judgement. How're you and Tierra? I hope you're not still arguing."

"We're good." *Apart from the fact that I've started lusting over her.* Fintan ignored the feminine scents coming from the bathroom and filled Cuinn in on Ai, and after a bit more conversation, they hung up.

The walls were a uniform cream, with pictures of British Columbia's impressive scenery.

Scenery like that which had surrounded them in the forest. He shifted on the bed, reached for the remote for the TV, and turned it on, flicking through the channels to try and distract himself from the thought of Tierra in the forest, or, perhaps worse, in the shower.

After what seemed like an age, she came out, already dressed, her skin flushed from the heat, in a cloud of the musky perfume she always wore. Fintan's cock hardened slightly, and his eyes widened. Shit. He focused his mind on Cuinn and Adam. *They will kill me. And they would be right to.*

She wore a long skirt that swirled as she walked, and a tight-fitting vest top that showed off every delicious curve.

"Are you going out like that?" It came out of his mouth before he'd thought about it.

She looked up, frowning. "What? Like what?"

"With just that vest top on. You'll freeze." While he, on the other hand, might overheat.

Her forehead creased. "Of course not. But it's a bit hot in the bathroom to wear cashmere."

She searched through her suitcase as she spoke, and pulled out another of those soft, touchable sweaters.

She tugged it over her head, and as she raised her arms, a little of her stomach showed.

A little more of his blood diverted into his groin. *No, no, no.* He tore his gaze away. "I'm going to shower."

"Sure." Tierra tugged the sweater into place. "I'll email a few people to see if they know which energetics were in the Vancouver area, what, about seventeen years ago?"

"I'd say more like fifteen to sixteen."

"Really? Okay. See you in a bit."

She leaned down, looking into the bottom of her bag as she poked around to find her laptop. This stretched her skirt tight over her bottom. Thankfully, that also meant she didn't see the now very visible bulge in Fintan's pants.

He went into the bathroom with a sigh of relief. *This isn't acceptable.*

He stripped off his clothes, his erection jutting from his body. He flushed, and turned the shower to cold, and stepped in with a shudder. He'd wash away the lust. Freeze it out. He'd focus on their plans for the evening, and getting Ai to trust them, and following the leads.

He definitely wouldn't think about the fact that Tierra's warm, soft, naked body had been in here and covered in soap suds minutes before.

7

Sitting on her bed, Tierra sent emails to five energetics who had been in the BC area between fourteen and eighteen years ago. She, Adam and Cuinn had also lived here then, though she couldn't remember anything that might be relevant. Maybe one of the boys would. She emailed them both.

Then she put the laptop down, and sighed. Why was this hotel room so stuffy? Why did windows never open in these places? She wished she'd thought to bring one of her homemade candles with her.

Then she forced herself to examine the real reason she was feeling a bit suffocated – what was she going to do about her feelings for Fintan?

Truth, integrity, and being open and honest were core parts of her being. Her values. She drew her knees up to her chest, and hugged them. She hated lying, and she felt as if that's what she was doing. She put her head on her knees.

She wasn't acting in accordance with her values when it came to Fintan.

She'd told him that her grumpiness towards him was to do with the situation they were in, which was only partly true.

When Cuinn had first started having the prophecy dreams a few months before, Fintan had been one of the few people Cuinn had confided in. The unshakable loyalty that Fintan had shown to his friend, and his genuine offer of 'whatever Cuinn needed' had reminded Tierra that there was more to Fintan than the couldn't-care-less persona he usually projected. Tierra's love for Fintan, love that she had always been able to put into a box in the back of her mind, had started to shift into something new.

Something uncomfortable.

When Blaize had been kidnapped, Tierra and Fintan had worked together. Tierra had used her rusty tracking skills to see if they could trace the whereabouts of either Indigo or Blaize.

They hadn't been successful, but working with him had given her another glimpse of a different, more professional Fintan.

Fintan the Warrior.

Her carefully managed love for him wouldn't pack back into the box she'd contained it in. It scratched and prickled and frustrated her, and it was harder and harder to ignore.

When she'd given energy to Cuinn in a highly illicit and taboo ceremony so that he could find Blaize in a dreamwalk, Fintan's protectiveness of Tierra, and his care for her afterwards, had shattered the box entirely.

But it had still been love. Something she could consider pure, and unsullied.

That moment in the forest had destroyed that illusion too.

She loved him. She also lusted after him. When she was with him, her emotions were muddled, and there were times when it was hard to put thoughts together. It wasn't ideal.

So what was she going to do about it?

She rubbed her hands over her face. She knew what she needed to do. She needed to tell him the truth. Or she needed to find a way of dealing with her emotions without affecting their friendship. She grimaced. She was a very open person. She needed to tell him.

How would she approach it? She should be good at this stuff. She did it for a living, didn't she? She could pretend she was advising one of her readers. *Let's see.* She pulled her laptop to her. What would the letter read?

Dear Tierra,

I need your help. I've been in love with a friend for years. It's not reciprocated. He's someone who falls in and out of love all the time — he needs variety. He's just not a one-woman man.

I thought I could live with it — I have for years, but recently something's changed. I've started to lust after him as well as love him. I don't want to hear about his latest conquests.

It's affecting the way I treat him, and I don't like the person I am when I'm with him. He doesn't understand what's happening, and it's upsetting him.

What on earth should I do?

Yours,
Anguished of BC

That was about it. She drummed her fingers on the bed cover. So, pretend she'd just got the letter. What would she write?

Dear Anguished,

I'm so sorry to hear of your problem. That sounds tough. Have you been able to tell any of your friends about your problem? Sometimes it can help to share things, get them out in the open.

It sounds like it might be a good idea to have a conversation with your friend. Have you ever told him how you feel? People can sometimes surprise us. Even if he doesn't reciprocate your feelings, you can ask him to be more sensitive in his conversation with you — I'm sure he can find other people to tell about his conquests.

Find a quiet moment, and just let him know how you feel. Don't make too big a deal out of it. Something like: "Can we have a chat? I have something I want to share with you. I don't feel very comfortable saying this, but I have romantic feelings for you, feelings that go beyond the friendship we currently have. Nothing needs to happen, but one thing I find challenging is when you talk about your lovers, or your feelings for other partners. I wanted to ask you if we could stop having those conversations until I move on."

Now, that probably sounds a lot harder than I made it seem.

If you tell him the truth, you'll feel in integrity with yourself, you'll have explained why you've been unhappy with his company lately, and he can change his behavior so he's not upsetting you.

Try not to dump it all on him. He has feelings too. Let him respond.

And perhaps once you've let go of your secret, you can start thinking about moving on — how often do you get out and about and meet new men? Just a thought.

Wishing you luck
Tierra x

Tierra sat looking at the screen in surprise. Where had all that come from? She met new men all the time, didn't she?

Did she?

Ah, heck.

She hadn't thought about that aspect of hiding in Cathair Cuinn all these years. When you were long-lived, like the energetics, sometimes decades passed before you realized it.

Tierra tended to keep her dating within the smallish energetics community, given that relationships with humans usually meant a lot of secrets and heartbreak. But she hadn't run out of new energetic males to meet yet.

She nodded, resolved. She'd tell Fintan, get that over with, and then when they got back home, she'd suggest to the also-single Cara that they go out and meet some new men.

She'd be over Fintan in no time.

Elrian opened his eyes, then smiled. He was on his mat, and had been in the dreamscape, searching for the latest on the prophecy.

Searching through the tangle of voices and the….mess that his dreamscape could sometimes be, it was still easier for him to navigate than it was for Cuinn. Elrian knew what he was looking for, had been working with this prophecy for years. Cuinn flailed about blindly, hoping to stumble across information.

Though it was true that something had happened in the last day that had tipped the scales against Elrian – something which made it a fraction more likely that Cuinn and his friends could beat him, though he hadn't been able to work out the specifics – at the same time, Elrian had found his next target. And she was no match for Elrian. No match at all.

Tierra.

When Fintan came out of the shower ten minutes later, he found Tierra sitting on her bed, as still as a statue. Not wanting to disturb her meditation, he crept around the bedroom to hang up his towels and put his dirty clothes in his suitcase. In a room this small, with a neat freak like Tierra, he wasn't going to leave them in a heap like he normally would.

Eventually Tierra opened her eyes, more cheerful than she had been when he'd gone into the shower. Relief saturated him and tension he hadn't realized was there melted away.

They headed out. At the front door, he looked up and down the street to get his bearings. "If we want to go through a park so you can recharge some, it's this way. We have an hour or so before we need to be at the restaurant with Ai."

She nodded, and they walked in comfortable silence till they reached the entrance to the park. Tierra stopped for a moment and took a deep breath. He could feel her pull a little energy, and she seemed to brighten.

She let go of his arm, and danced into the park. It might be in the middle of Vancouver, but there was a reasonable amount of plant life, green and natural materials. Fintan looked around to check no one was watching, because if you didn't already know she was something supernatural, you'd guess from her reaction to her element after only hours with concrete and glass around her. No wonder she didn't live in a city. Manipura energetics didn't get drained in the same way, as long as they spent time in the sun every day. He mainly preferred hot countries, with plenty of sunlight and heat, but growing up in Scandinavia, with short days in the winter, had toughened him up.

He wandered along the path behind her, as she appeared to be greeting every tree and flower in the park. Finally, she sat in the middle of a patch of grass, and he dropped down beside her. He took off his jacket and enjoyed the gentle breeze on his skin.

The sun started to set, and dusk grew around them. The evening felt intimate, the two of them together without the hassles and demands of others. A bubble of tranquility in their currently difficult lives.

"Fintan, I wanted to talk to you about something."

"Sure." He leaned back on his elbows. Clouds floated through the sky above him. He was at peace for the first time in a while.

"It's no big deal, but I want to get it off my chest." His brain caught up with the words, and, confused, he twisted his head to look at her.

"What?"

"You remember you said that you love me like a sister?"

He nodded, and reminded himself that not only had he said that, but it needed to be true, despite his strange reaction to her recently. Because Cuinn. And Adam. And family.

"I love you too. But it's not very sisterly." She bit her lip. "I've been in love with you for a long time."

A slow second passed, and a thousand times a thousand choices of response whistled through his mind. He was stunned, exultant, terrified, and complete. In his mind, he said yes, he said no, he reasoned with her, and swept her into his arms and kissed her thoroughly.

The strangest thing was that none of the responses was disinterested.

Nonetheless, there was no way they could be together. They were entirely wrong for each other – that is, he could never be good enough for her. She needed someone with a deep and true Anahata, their heart Chakra full. That would never be him. And he didn't feel the same way about her.

At the same time, he tried to put out the nascent and unexpected spark of something, something he couldn't identify, that her words had roused.

He opened his mouth to speak, though what he would have said, he had no idea, but she put up a hand to stop him.

"Nothing has to change. I just needed to tell you. But I'd rather you didn't talk to me in such detail about your love affairs any more. It seems to make me cranky. One day I'll have hearts and flowers of my own, but right now, that's not my path. I know it's not very enlightened of me, but I get grouchy when you talk about all the girls." She rested a hand on his arm.

His mouth remained open, and his brain had stopped functioning. "Ah … what?"

"I don't want to make a big deal of it. But if you could just keep your adventures in that area to yourself, that would be great." Her brown eyes were wide and trusting.

"Of course, I'm sorry that – wait, I'm sorry, what?" He shook his head to try and clear it, and catch up with the conversation. She'd just said she was in love with him. As in, 'in' love. Not love in a more general way. Right? Something inside him quivered, expectant.

But at the same time, she didn't want them to be together? The only reason she was telling him was to ask him to stop sharing?

She'd already risen, and was brushing off that damned skirt.

What did she want from him? His brain wasn't responding, conflicting feelings chasing around in there like an out-of-control pinball machine.

"Thanks. I'm so glad I was able to be honest with you. I feel better."

He scrambled to his feet, and she put her arms around his waist, and laid her head on his chest. She looked natural there. He put his hands gingerly on her upper back, but before he could really connect with her, she pulled back.

"Let's go see Ai." She walked in the direction of the park exit. He walked several paces after her before he remembered his jacket was still on the ground. He turned back, picked it up, and then had to run after her, as she marched to the gate.

What. The actual fuck. Had just happened.

He caught up with her and got into step. "What you said, back there."

It was a smooth opening. And he had no follow up.

"Yes? I hope Ai comes today, don't you? Poor girl. It would be great if we can take her back to Cathair Cuinn. We have plenty of space."

"Tierra, I'm not quite sure…what do you want me to say?" He was entirely at a loss. She'd dropped a bombshell, one that could explode their friendship, and now was carrying on as if everything was the same.

She looked at him, puzzled. "Say? What do you mean?"

"To what you said, in the park. Although I don't understand, exactly, what you said."

"I'm in love with you, is what I said." Her voice was just on the tart side of apple pie. "But, that's ok! In fact, it's fine! What wasn't fine is the fact that I was keeping it a secret. Which is never good between friends, hmmm?"

She patted his arm, and continued walking.

He stood still for a few seconds, before he realized she wasn't stopping. He hadn't lost control of his energy in centuries. Not when he'd been in a ten person bar brawl over his ex, when some country bumpkin in 19th century England called her a doxy. Not when a human business associate he'd invested with in 18th century France had gambled much of Fintan's savings away. And yet now flame appeared around his fists, which hung clenched by his sides. Tierra looked back over her shoulder and paused.

He drew on his heart center, limited as it was, and tried to be calm. His Manipura, the fire, was far too close to the surface right now. The flames flickered and went out.

"Tierra. You've just told me you're in love with me. And that, apparently, you have been for a long time. What do you want me to say?" He tried to stay reasonable.

"Nothing." She looked surprised. "Weren't you listening? I just needed to tell you. Now it's out in the open, we can move on."

"Move on? Move on?! I haven't even caught up." His whole body had begun to heat up. His skin seemed to burn.

She stepped in close again, and put her hands on his arms, then took them off hurriedly. "It's ok. Really. I've told you, and assuming you're okay not to talk about your, um, flings with me, then we're fine. I know you don't feel the same way. Let's meet Ai and see if we can find out who this energetic is, and where he's located."

She smiled, but it faltered as she caught his gaze.

He needed time to process this. Time to work out what the hell he was going to do. He was not nearly as sure as she was that 'nothing' was the answer.

He pulled Anahata energy to cool himself. After a few moments, when the heat had subsided, he held out a still-not-quite-steady-arm for her, and they walked to the restaurant in silence.

8

They entered the restaurant just before seven p.m. A perky waitress showed them to a table. There was no sign of Ai.

Tierra wasn't sure what to make of Fintan's reaction to her words, but now she had dealt with that difficult business, she was relieved and ready to talk to Ai. He might need some time – he had seemed a little more taken aback than she'd expected.

She squirmed in her seat as the waitress poured them iced water. Was the idea of her loving him so difficult and unpleasant? She wasn't using any energy when she talked to him, but he'd emitted an onslaught of emotions that she couldn't help but pick up. Emotions that were so muddled, however, she hadn't been able to decipher them. She grimaced. They needed to focus. Maybe she should have waited. She hadn't thought it would matter that much to him. Perhaps she hadn't thought it through enough. She'd just wanted to get it off her chest. Get it out there and over with. She hadn't really thought through the consequences. She shifted again. She couldn't get comfortable in her chair.

Ah. She'd forgotten to let him respond. Okay, not her finest moment maybe. But they had other things to focus on now. They needed to get back to normal.

"It's too soon to worry," she said to Fintan.

He fiddled with his napkin, smoothing it out again and again. He looked across the table at her. "Too soon? Source is right it's too soon. You only told me five minutes ago. I haven't even processed it yet, let alone worried about it."

What? "What?" Tierra said.

They stared at each other blankly.

"Where our pierced teenager, Ai, is?" She persisted.

Comprehension dawned on them both a few seconds later, but only Tierra smiled. "Put it aside for the minute, Fintan. We need to focus on Ai, and what she has to tell us."

She took her phone out of her pocket and checked the time. "Assuming she comes. Which she will, because we're buying her dinner. And because her gut will tell her she can trust us."

They couldn't deal with the personal stuff now. Tierra felt a twinge of guilt as she glanced at Fintan. He looked a bit, well, wild. And the flames on their candles were a lot taller than those on other tables. Surely that couldn't be because of their discussion?

"Fintan," she hissed. "You need to control your energy. You're affecting the candles."

She blew them out. They lit again, and the smell of hot wax and smoke wound around them. "Stop it. We're out in public. With humans. We're not at Cathair Cuinn where you can play. Settle down."

"I'm not feeling very stable right now." The words came through gritted teeth. She could practically hear them grinding.

"We're going to have a teenage girl with us any minute. One we don't want to scare." The flames increased in size. Tierra bit at her thumb, worried now. "Fintan. Please."

He looked her dead in the eyes, and her stomach churned. His Manipura Chakra was burning, and the energy was starting to twist.

Twisting energy, eventually, was how someone became a Rogue. Energetics were alert to any sign of it, as it could be the start of a negative progression – though many energetics had come up against tests of self where their energy had wavered, due to a lack of control, or to intense negative emotions, most were able to catch themselves. Having healers around while energetics were in physical adolescence, and also while they were learning each energy as an Adherent, was helpful for grounding and to mitigate the risk of twisting. Energy twisting didn't mean one automatically went down the path to Rogue, but a person whose energy had twisted once had a tendency to seek out the darker side of emotions, which could eventually corrupt the person into a Rogue, someone who had given up their connection to Source.

This is not good.

She made a decision to earth him. Literally. Trained as a healer, she could stabilize him with her energy, take some of his within her, and ground him. Which, given she seemed to have been responsible, she felt she should. She'd missed a trick here. She hadn't considered his reaction to her news – well, she had, and she'd assumed it would help him understand why she'd been cranky recently, and there might be a smidge of embarrassment between them, but that it'd soon pass. She hadn't really counted on him … being actually affected by it.

She put her small hand on top of his large one. It burned. She winced, and knew her hand would be pink when she pulled it back, but there was no help for it. She pulled a little energy of her own, and spooled it, weaving together a lot of earth energy with a little air energy.

He was deep inside himself, looking at her as if he didn't know her. Also not good.

She squeezed his hand, and took a breath. And pulled. She drew the excess energy from him, the twisting energy, like a poison. It caught in the net she created for it, but still it burned. She captured it, and dissipated it, and he shuddered, his eyes closing. She sent a pulse of pure Anahata, healing energy, into him.

"Stop." His voice was hoarse, and she took her hand away from his to pass him his water glass. He drank, fast. She poured him another when he held his glass out. He drank that too.

She watched him glancing over to the door every now and then to look out for Ai. This wouldn't be a good time for her to come in.

Fintan was pale and looked more believably like his Scandinavian roots than he had for decades. "Are you ok?"

"Sorry." His voice rasped, despite all the water.

"That's fine. I guess we should probably talk a bit more after all." Yeah. She had probably messed that up.

He opened his mouth to speak, and she hurried on with, "Not now. Because Ai will be here at any minute, and we can't afford for you to burn this place down to the ground before she even gets here. Okay?"

He pressed his lips together.

"More water?" she asked.

He shook his head, and they sat there. Tierra wasn't quite sure of the way forward. She wanted to help him – and clearly he wasn't feeling as sanguine at her information as she was – but she couldn't afford to upset him again. Especially when she wasn't completely sure what had set him off in the first place. Was he angry that she was in love with him? That didn't seem fair.

Ai came through the door, her face a mix of swagger, apprehension, and awe. She ignored the coat check girl, and headed over to their table, the maitre d' following. When the maitre d' realized the girl was with them, professionalism won over her disapproval, and she pulled out the chair for Ai.

Ai was made up to look years older than she actually was, with a sweep of black eyeliner at the corner of each eye. She wore a long black skirt that was slit all the way to the top of her legs, and the 'fuck you' t-shirt was gone, replaced by a charcoal vest top. Over the top she had a black trench coat, which despite being somewhat battered, looked amazing. She didn't remove the coat.

"Thank you for coming." Tierra said.

"I'm here for the food." The girl didn't meet her gaze.

"We're happy to be buying. Have a look and see what you'd like." She pushed the menu in Ai's direction.

Ai picked it up as if it might contain something nasty inside. Or explosive. She opened it, and couldn't keep the deadpan look on her face at the many different menu items – and their chichi descriptions – inside.

Tierra knew how she felt. She loved food, loved cooking. Few things gave her greater pleasure than sharing food she'd just put together with those she loved. And it usually meant she didn't have to be the center of attention in other ways. She turned her focus back to the menu.

"There's a lot of choice," Tierra said. *Well, duh.*

"Yeah. What's up with him?" Ai gestured at Fintan with her head. Fintan hadn't spoken. Hadn't stood when Ai arrived, hadn't acknowledged her presence other than with a nod.

"Nothing. We've just had –" What could she say. "We've just had a difficult afternoon."

This seemed to satisfy Ai. But Fintan spoke. "I'm fine. Sorry Ai. It's good to see you."

She nodded, and went back to her menu.

Tierra looked at Fintan, putting a question in her eyes. He nodded back, if perhaps a little less vehemently than she might like, and started to read his own menu.

Fintan stared down blankly at his menu. He couldn't make out a word, whatever his reassurances to Ai and Tierra.

He couldn't remember the last time he'd lost control of his energy.

He ground his teeth in a mix of humiliation, outrage and shame.

Tierra had had to rescue him. To ground some of his energy, which had to have taken a toll on her. And now they were sitting at the table, choosing their dinner as if none of the last hour had happened.

What was he supposed to do with her words at the park? Did she really think she could drop that kind of information on him, then move on? The candles at the table flickered, and Tierra flashed him a warning glance. He gritted his teeth again. *Get back in the game. Idiot.*

"How was your afternoon, Ai?" Tierra asked.

The girl shrugged, though he sensed she was pleased to be asked. Had anyone ever taken an interest in her like that before? Without an agenda. Although he supposed they still had an agenda.

The waiter came over, and they ordered. The girl tried to hide her satisfaction at being called 'Madam'. Fintan had to hand it to the man, he wasn't fazed by the girl's dark attire and multiple piercings.

Once the waiter had left them, their water glasses refilled – Fintan wasn't ordering beer for the girl again, not twice in one day – Tierra asked her how she was feeling.

A loaded question.

Ai was smart. She knew exactly what Tierra was asking when she talked about 'feelings'. "I'm here, aren't I?"

Ai's gifts had told her she would be safe with Fintan and Tierra.

"How do I know what you're saying is true?" said Ai. "What you're saying, what you're talking about – it's magic, right? How do I know you're not just talking shit?"

"We have…other talents," said Tierra. "As you will, with a little training."

"What?" Eyes narrowed, arms folded.

Tierra hmmm'ed, then reached out to take a stem from a pretty posy of white flowers in a vase on the table.

She held the flower, still in bud, low in front of her. "Watch."

Fintan felt Tierra pull earth energy, pushing it into the flower. The flower's tight bud rippled, and slowly, gradually, unfurled. There was a strange tug in his chest at the sight of Tierra, prettier than any flower, concentrating on this tiny piece of loveliness in front of her.

Ai's eyes got bigger in proportion with the flower's opening. By the time the flower was fully in bloom, they were huge. Tierra, with just a hint of glow around her, handed Ai the flower.

The girl cradled it in her hands, examining it from every angle.

"We call ourselves energetics," said Tierra. "We're like humans, but we evolved from a more…elemental source. Have you ever heard of the Chakra system?"

It probably wasn't the time to tell the girl about their homeland, Atlantis, and its mysterious destruction, Fintan supposed.

The girl shook her head.

"It's known in some Eastern philosophies," Tierra continued. "Essentially, it says that there are seven 'Chakras' or energy centers, in a person. In human beings, these tend to be very underdeveloped. Occasionally a human is born with one activated, or manages to activate it in their lifetime, but their energy is still weak."

Fintan hadn't seen Tierra in teaching mode for a long time. She was patient and relaxed. He enjoyed watching her.

"Energetics, on the other hand, originally evolved from this energy." Tierra was leaning forward, and moved her hands as she talked. "Our existence helps maintain the energetic balance of the earth."

As Tierra continued her lecture on the basics of the energetics, Ai's posture loosened. When Tierra introduced the idea of Dominant and Auxiliary Chakras, Ai's eyes gleamed.

"What am I?"

Tierra smiled. "We think you're Anahata-Ajna. That links to air and mind. You must be strong to have coped for so many years on your own, with no one to guide you. And to keep your energy pure, and not twisted."

"What do you mean, twisted?" Ai's forehead creased.

"Sometimes in our community there are those who become 'Rogues'. This, I'm afraid, is what Indigo is. Her energy has twisted, and she's using it in a negative, rather than positive way."

The girl's cheeks had spots of color, and she looked down at the table. "What do you do with those whose energy is twisted? Do you kill them?"

"That's not our way." Tierra shook her head firmly. "There are few we can't help in our Rehabilitation Centers, given time."

The girl toyed with her starter, which had arrived a little while ago.

"How do you know if someone's energy is twisted? And what if someone did something with their energy that wasn't good, but they didn't mean to? Maybe they were protecting themselves?" The girl's face was a picture of misery. Fintan was glad that Tierra was handling this and not him. The girl was clearly worried about something, and he had an inkling of what it might be, given her background.

"What kind of thing?" Tierra asked. "If it wasn't her fault, we'd help her sort it out, and make sure her energy was kept untwisted."

The girl shrugged, and stuffed some of her garlic bread in her mouth. She addressed Fintan through the mouthful. "What can you do then?"

Fintan leaned over and blew the candle out.

"Watch." He held a fist up to his mouth, and blew it open, as if he were blowing a kiss. The palm unfurled in the direction of the candle – which sparked to life.

Ai gasped.

He grinned and took another mouthful of pasta.

They spent the next hour eating and explaining some of the energetics' history and background to Ai. She was intrigued by the possibilities of her powers, and keen to try them out.

"How old are you, then?" Ai asked.

"Hmm. Well, think in terms of centuries, rather than decades," Tierra said.

"Woah. You only look in your thirties. How long will I live?" Ai asked.

"No reason why you wouldn't live as long as us," Fintan said through a stolen mouthful of Tierra's dinner. "Your Guild will help you manage the details of pretending to age normally. One of our Guilds, Vishudha, whose powers include communication, have expertise in creating new identities. It's much easier to move to a new city or country and start again, though it can be tiring. And we do age, it's simply slower than humans."

Tierra scowled at him and poked him with the fork. "Some of us should be old enough to know better."

Fintan smirked at her. He felt a bit better, teasing her. It seemed more … normal.

"And do you get like, a black belt in it?" Ai asked.

"How d'you mean?" Tierra said. She was eating more defensively now, an arm around her plate, which made Fintan smile more.

"Do you take magic exams or something?" Ai said.

"Er, no. But there are different levels. You're a Dormant, which is how all energetics are born. Usually their parents can tell the Dominant chakra of their child very early, and that's how names are linked to chakras. Once you train with a Maven, you're an Adherent. Eventually you do a Chakra Trial, and you become a Practitioner, and then eventually, after many decades, your Guild can affirm you as a Master."

"Huh," Ai cocked her head. "How long does it take? And what are you two then?"

"Anything from five to twenty years per Chakra. I'm a Master in Manipura, Practitioner in Anahata," Fintan said. "Tierra, though, is a Master in both her energies."

Tierra flushed. "Yes. Well. I'm a bit rusty these days."

He wondered why her usual sense of self was letting her down. The current dangers they all faced were really affecting her. His mouth flattened into a line. That was fine. He would protect her, and keep her out of trouble. No one would hurt her while he was around.

Ai ate every scrap of her food, and seemed to enjoy it. But he could see something still nagged at her. He thought he knew what it might be. Perhaps he could help.

"I grew up in a remote part of Scandinavia, and trained with a Maven called Gunhild for Manipura, my fire energy. She was a good woman, but tough. She trained new energetics by tiring them out physically so they had better control of their energies."

He tried to speak casually, but the story brought up a slew of memories. Friends and family who were gone, and growing up as a youth in a difficult era.

"Each day I would muck out the various stalls of the animals with a shovel and barrow. It was hard work. Though I loved the animals."

He paused to sip at his water, his throat still sore.

"I was an angry young man – the dark side of Manipura. You don't have to turn Rogue for your energy to slip and twist a little."

He tried not to look directly at Ai as he said this, but he could see he had her attention. Tierra had grown up in a happy family. She had a lot of empathy, but she couldn't know what it was like to live every day with that anger inside you.

"Anahata can use others' feelings against them – manipulate or humiliate them,' he said. "Some can even cause illness – purposefully, or, if we're not in control, the very force of our feelings can cause sickness in others. Just as our joy is perhaps more infectious than others' might be."

Tierra was watching too, listening, lines on her forehead. He wasn't sure she had ever heard this story before. He hadn't considered that. He hoped it didn't affect her view of him.

"Anahata's element is air, so we can cause winds. Hurricanes even, if we're powerful enough."

He blew another kiss at the candle on the empty table next to them, and it flickered and went out.

Tierra shook her head.

He shot her a quick smile to reassure her, and continued.

"So, angry young man. Isolated, because Mavens are responsible for the damage their Adherents do, so most Mavens live a little away from any human community. Lots of feelings I couldn't understand, not being the well-adjusted, emotionally mature man I am today." He didn't feel he could meet Tierra's eyes on that one.

"One hot summer day, I'd been cleaning out the barn for hours. The animals were in the fields. Gunhild came into the barn, and pointed out, very matter-of-factly, several spots I hadn't cleaned properly. My energy leapt inside me. I couldn't contain it. I started to burn."

He had Ai's full attention.

"Luckily, it's rare for us to harm ourselves with our own energy. I didn't even realize I was alight. My Maven smelled my clothes burning, swept me up with her air energy, and dumped me in the stream. But half the barn had burned down before she was able to douse the flames. Thankfully, none of the animals was hurt."

Even centuries later, the story still caused him shame. He hated the fact he'd lost control to that extent, even as a youth.

"She wasn't happy, though she understood it was a mistake. She upped the intensity of the physical effort, but changed the direction of my training. She explained what had happened, and we talked about ways to manage it."

"Were you in trouble?" Ai asked.

"A little. She made me rebuild the barn. Without my energies." He winced. "I can still remember the blisters – in the days before power tools, it was quite the job."

Ai looked thoughtful, and gave her spoon one more lick before putting it down. "I'll take you to his house. The guy's. The weird one. But I'm not coming inside."

Tierra put her arm out to touch Ai. "Thank you. We'll keep you safe, don't worry. You're part of our extended family now."

The girl shrugged. But didn't move her hand away.

9

They went their separate ways outside the restaurant, with plans to meet up again the next night to scout out the house of the 'creepy guy'.

Tierra and Fintan walked back together to their hotel without much talking. They didn't go through the park this time, Fintan's gaze just glancing over Tierra as they passed the now-locked gates. He didn't bring up their conversation. He hadn't quite decided what he was going to do about it.

She had dropped a bombshell. One that he had no idea how he was supposed to respond to. The only thing he did know was that however he did respond, it would probably be wrong. And not only wrong in the eyes of Tierra, but Adam – oh hell, Adam – Cuinn, and Blaize too.

The other, more humiliating, part of the evening had been his own loss of control. He didn't understand where that reaction had come from. Before he brought it up again with Tierra, he needed to work out exactly what this was about.

The person he'd usually talk to about this kind of situation was Adam. *So not an option.* Cuinn would usually be a close second – again, not an option.

Perhaps this was one he was going to have to figure out on his own.

He looked at Tierra, who was walking next to him, her smaller size meaning she had to take one and a half steps to his one stride. He slowed his pace to match hers, and she looked up at him. "Everything ok?"

"Yeah, just realized I was walking a bit fast for you."

She angled her head to the side. "No faster than usual. But thanks."

He shrugged.

They took a few more steps.

The evening darkness seemed to accentuate the intimate bubble they walked in, rather than conceal the fact he didn't know what to say to her.

Yeah, this was awkward.

"What's our plan tomorrow?" Tierra said.

A plan. Okay, he was on more familiar ground here. "We meet Ai at ten p.m. and then drive to wherever she says we need to be. We leave her somewhere safe, and you and I go and scope out the house. We should probably give her Cathair Cuinn on speed dial, just in case, but if we're only checking things out, there shouldn't be any need for back up."

"Sure. So we have the day to kill? What do you want to do? We'd better sleep in if we're going to be up late," she mused.

A flash of Tierra waking up, her hair messy and loose, and her chocolate eyes sleepy, hit Fintan's brain. Ouch. He was going to have to shield his feelings a little more carefully around Tierra if this was going to happen.

"What about a hike tomorrow?" he suggested. Physical exercise sounded good right now. A lot of it.

"Sure," she said.

"Okay. Sleep, breakfast, head to the park for a hike. Late lunch somewhere. Rest and recharge in the hotel room before the evening."

"Great. Less time for me to get nervous that way."

Tierra reached the doors of their hotel first, having bounced up the steps. As they walked through the quiet lobby, he said, "What are you worried about?"

She shrugged.

"All of it? I'm fine, but it's been a while since I've done anything like this. I'm totally capable, before you say anything –" he held his hands out, palms up, as if to suggest he had no intention of doing anything like that " – but like I say, it's been a while."

"We can talk it through again if you like," he said. "With some 'what ifs?' thrown in. What if he's there, what if he's not there, what if there are other people there, what if he's got someone else, just like Indigo had Blaize. That's what I do with my team. Worst case, or almost every case, planning. Of course, life always throws you a new curve ball, something you just didn't have on the list, but it helps to work through possibilities. Especially when you need to make fast decisions in the moment."

"Alright," Tierra said. "How do you throw your Anahata intuition into the mix? Your feelings?"

"I make sure I listen to my gut. I've had a few times when listening to a nagging feeling that something wasn't right about what seemed to be a perfectly normal setup saved my ass." He shrugged. "That's a good reason for us to spend a bit of time in meditation tomorrow afternoon, just tuning into our energies. We'll both need to listen to our feelings, and we'll also need our other energies."

"We might need your Manipura and your fighting skills, but what do you think we'll need earth for? We don't need tracking skills, we know where the guy lives."

"Maybe he'll have moved. Maybe there'll be a garden, grounds, and I'll want you to check if anyone else is there. There are plenty of uses for earth. Remember, I've worked with Adam a lot over the years, so I know how Muladhara can help."

"I'm not Adam." They were in their room now, and Tierra sat heavily on the bed, lines appearing on her brow. "I don't want to let you down."

"You won't let me down. We're on a scouting mission, we're not going to engage."

She nodded, though the creases on her forehead didn't disappear. He came over to sit next to her, and put his arm around her. She fit snugly into his shoulder. He gave her a squeeze, and dropped a kiss on her forehead. Her skin was soft, and she smelled good.

She tilted her head up, and a thousand thoughts swirled around his head.

Heat flooded his body, and he froze, his gaze on the sweep of her eyelashes, the curve of her brow. Her nose was so cute.

Without considering it further, he leaned down and gently bopped his larger nose against hers, squishing it. Their heads were so close together that her breath fluttered over his lips. His mouth watered.

Her eyebrows raised, her mouth open a fraction.

He bent his head at the slightest of angles, and an inch of movement brought their lips into contact.

His breath stalled as his mouth captured hers with the pressure of a butterfly's wings. His skin tingled and his brain went fuzzy, confused.

What was he doing? He couldn't change their relationship, especially after what she'd said in the park. He couldn't give her what she deserved.

But it was fine. This was a chaste kiss. No tongue, no touch.

He drew away from her, and wondered if he had a similar dazed look in his eyes.

"Let's go to bed."

Tierra woke up to the sound of the shower running. She was used to being first up. She wasn't feeling as perky as normal this morning.

Last night had ended in the strangest way. Fintan had given her a hug that had started like any other of the thousands of hugs he had given her over the centuries they had known each other.

It hadn't ended that way.

She couldn't remember him ever kissing her on the mouth before.

But the kiss hadn't been sexual. Not really.

Not…exactly. *I mean, it might have made my entire body prickle with sexual heat, but it didn't have any effect on Fintan.*

The kiss had been almost absent-minded. An after-thought. A kiss of a child before bedtime.

She frowned and sat up. She grabbed the hotel room's guidebook. She needed to take her mind off that moment. They'd planned to go for a short hike this morning around Burnaby Mountain, which was why Fintan was already up.

When the bathroom door opened, she looked up, and then blushed when she realized that Fintan only had a towel round his waist. His sculpted, manly waist. He was rubbing at his hair with a second towel as if he was in a shampoo advert. She went mute.

What did you say, after all, when the man of your dreams came into your room, all chiseled abs and wet from the shower?

"Hi." Start simple, and work up.

"Morning. How're you feeling?"

"Um, good. You?"

"Yeah, better than yesterday, thanks." He threw the towel, damp from his hair, down onto his bed, making his skin move over his chest muscles in a distracting – delicious – fashion. She hadn't seen him like this for a while. It would certainly give her something to think about on cold winter nights.

Fintan was lean and muscled. With some interesting scars. She knew where some of them had come from – had been with him for one of them in particular – but there were some she didn't remember.

She realized he was looking at her. "Is everything alright, T?"

"Oh, yes, sorry. I…I just woke up." She tried not to babble, and was glad that fire energetics couldn't read minds. And hoped his Anahata wasn't picking up the waves of lust his outfit – or lack thereof – was causing in her. Happily he wasn't a strong empath. Usually.

She scuttled in and out of the shower, feeling more together once she was washed and dressed.

"I assume we're staying another night here?" she said. "If we're only going to this house at ten p.m., we won't be back till the early hours of the morning."

Fintan nodded. "So you don't need to pack. In fact, why don't you leave your stuff untidy? Live a little."

She scowled at him. "There's no need for sarcasm. And there's nothing wrong with being neat."

He suppressed a grin. "Let's go get you caffeine and breakfast."

They headed to a nearby bakery, where the smell of bread and pastries wafted out and enticed patrons in. Tierra chose a window seat so that she could watch the passers-by on their way to work. There were still a few yoga bunnies here, but the crowd was mainly a work one, given it was a weekday in the city. She had a moment of gratitude that her job as a writer meant she could work wherever and whenever she liked.

Plus the fact that, as a long-lived energetic, money was never a problem. You lived long enough, it built up. Tierra had worked in a lot of roles over the few centuries she'd been alive – energetics hadn't had the gender stereotypes humans had – though as often as not, behind the scenes. She'd had a lot of fun running an Inn outside London in the late 1800s, on one of the routes down from London to the coast, in a market town called Kingston-Upon-Thames. Working in different professions helped to keep a long life interesting, and also was sometimes necessary given one had to move around so humans didn't realize you still looked about the same age at 60 as you had at age 30. Learning new things also helped the energetics' minds and attitudes stay flexible, a plus when you were trying not to get stuck in the last century's attitudes.

Her favorite job had probably been as an apothecary in the 1800s after her time as an Anahata Adherent. Being a nurse during the two great wars had been some of her most important work, and contributed to the energetic race's purpose of maintaining balance in the world. But it had been some of the toughest.

Fintan eyed her cautiously over his first croissant. His blond hair was tousled, and he was casual in jeans and a sweater, though his jeans had seen a lot more wear and tear than hers, and his sweater was a giant hoodie with the mascots from the 2010 Vancouver winter Olympics on it. Tierra's favorite was Miga, who was a combination of mythical sea bear, killer whale and spirit bear, and managed to be both cute and a little dangerous. *Much like Fintan.*

"We'll work on refreshing your self-defense moves while we're out today," Fintan said. "That okay with you?"

She was unenthusiastic, but given all the protesting she had done to get herself to Vancouver, she couldn't show it. "Sure."

"What you did in the forest wasn't bad. Now you need to keep your emotions under control when you engage. If you fight angry, your emotions can cloud your moves."

"What about scared?" She was only half joking.

"It's harder not to be scared. Better if you keep calm. It's like going into a meditative state, and fighting from there."

"Do you get scared?"

"Sometimes. Not too often. I know I'm big and bad."

She took a bite of her almond croissant, which she was eating in small bites to make it last as long as possible. Fintan had long since finished his first pastry, and was onto his second.

As she reached out to pick up her cup, Fintan's eyes flashed and he put a hand out to stop her.

"What? What's the matter?" She put the cup back down. "Did you see a bug in it or something?"

She peered into the cup to see if she could see what he was staring down at. He hadn't released her hand, and she let go of the cup, thinking he was trying to make sure she didn't drink anything.

When he just took her hand in both his hands, she tugged ineffectually, trying to make him let her go. But he held her fast. Her heart jumped. "What's going on, Fin?"

10

Fintan stared down at her hand, feeling sick. Her hand, the one that she'd grounded him with the night before, was burned.

He'd burned her.

He didn't know what to say. Sorry seemed so…inadequate.

He realized she was trying to get her hand back, and he dropped it. She pulled it back into her chest and cradled it against her. Oh hell, he'd hurt her again.

He stood up, his metal chair clattering on the stark black and white tiled floor.

"I have to go to the bathroom." He walked off, eyes averted.

In the small room, he glared into a mirror with a cheery 'Please wash your hands' sign with tiny hearts drawn around it stuck to the bottom of the glass.

He'd burned her, and she'd never mentioned it.

He leaned on the sink and bowed his head as her words from the day before came back to him. She was acting normally, as if having divulged her feelings for him the day before, she'd been relieved of a burden.

A burden that she'd shifted onto him.

He washed his hands for want of something to do. Running his hands through his hair rather than waste a paper towel, he made a decision. He wouldn't worry about Tierra's feelings today. Well, he would, of course, he amended, but not her, er, romantic feelings.

He walked back out into the cafe, teaspoons clinking against cups, mothers chatting, their children sleeping in strollers next to them, and the aroma of ground coffee beans scenting the air.

Tierra squinted at him as he sat down. "Is everything ok? Is there something wrong with your stomach?"

"I'm ok." He took her hand back, cupping his larger hands around it as if it was fragile and expensive.

Her face added puzzled to worried.

He turned her hand over and examined it. He took a breath, and pulled energy of his own. Air energy. Healing energy. He'd been too addled, and possibly, he thought to himself, too ungrounded, to think of it last night. And of course, she'd never waste it on herself.

She looked startled as his energy crept into hers, cooling, healing. The antidote to the energy she'd grounded for him the night before.

The faint pinkness of the skin on her hand, that had turned her butterscotch skin to a dusky rose, faded back to normal. Although her cheeks remained pink.

"I'm sorry about last night." He gave her hand a final squeeze between his palms before placing it on the table.

"That's ok." She sounded uncertain.

"Really. It won't happen again."

And neither of them was sure what, exactly, he was talking about.

Fintan drove them a little way out of Vancouver to Burnaby Mountain. In the car park, he got out a backpack containing water and some provisions, as well as light rain jackets that could be folded up tight and small. It was spring, and the weather was unpredictable. Although it was clear and dry at the moment, it could easily rain later. Perfect weather for hiking, though, if you liked that kind of thing.

They walked up the rocky trail, and he quizzed her on the ways she could use her energies to protect herself. She wasn't enthusiastic. She might be a Master in her energies, the highest level of Practitioner, but she wasn't keen on using them in that way.

They reached a plateau, and Fintan beckoned Tierra over. She went to him, caution in every step.

He slid an arm around her, and before she knew it, she was in a headlock.

"You know what you need to do to get out of this," he coached.

Tierra struggled to breathe, but was determined not to tap out too quickly. She croaked, "Yes, but knowing what to do and doing it aren't the same thing."

Tierra put both her hands on one of Fintan's, the arm currently locked around her head. She pulled down sharply on Fintan's hand, then stomped down hard on the earth next to his foot to simulate stamping on his foot. Then she moved her shoulder into Fintan's arm, breaking the lock. She twisted her body around to come up for air behind him.

"Good," Fintan said. "Now, don't forget, if you've broken out of the headlock you either need to run, or you do some damage to the person from behind, fast. You need to train for that. If you just train for the move itself, the muscle memory will stop there, and you'll just get caught again as you'll hesitate while you think what you should do next, and you'll just be standing behind them while you think."

Tierra's shoulders drooped. "Neither's a great option for me. I'm not exactly a runner, and I can't imagine hitting someone, let alone from behind."

Fintan turned towards her and put his hands on her shoulders. "If it's you or them, make sure it's not you. We're not talking about you attacking some innocent here, Tierra, but someone who's already initiated an attack on you, or someone you love."

Tierra shrugged off the feel of his warm, solid grip, off. "I know. It's just…hard."

She made as if to sit on the ground, but before she could, Fintan narrowed his eyes. "That's not the end of the practice. We need to step it up a bit. Make it more real."

He grinned at her, and Tierra's eyes widened, and she halted her progress.

He jerked his head, and a sheet of intense fire surrounded Tierra. She gasped, heart pounding.

Fintan grinned. "Let's play."

The crackle of fire burned close to her skin, but didn't touch it. She was pinned in place.

She looked around her, took a deep breath, and pulled energy. She gestured with an arm at the earth, and lifted it up, up, and then down again onto the fire, putting the fire out with the damp scattering of earth.

"There," she said. "Happy?"

Fintan's smile grew. A wind stirred her mounds of earth, blowing them out of the way.

How do I counter his wind?

A tree behind Fintan, with long slender branches, caught her attention. *That's how.* She made it move, its leaves and twigs like fingers reaching for him. She made a grab for him with the tree, aiming to tie him up like last time. But he burned the ends of the branches away. The tree drew back quickly, its leaves singed.

She sent an apology to the tree, then shot a pulse of energy into the earth, and made it ripple underneath Fintan. He staggered, and nearly fell. She did it again, keeping the ground under her own feet steady.

What now? Fire was tricky for an earth and air practitioner to counter. *Hmm.* She wasn't able to use the energy of water, but she could move it if she found it. She sent tendrils of energy into the earth, seeking a source of water near by.

Fintan drove a small whirlwind around her, which trapped her as effectively as the fire. She planted herself in the earth, letting it grip and hold her while the wind whipped around her. She struggled to suck enough oxygen to breathe, and concern flooded her. This was a game, wasn't it? He wouldn't actually hurt her, surely?

She pulled on air. It came into her body from the ether delicately, a very different feel from the solid earth energy which felt almost tangible.

Air energy was like pure love entering her. Her heart swelled. She channeled the love into the earth, combining her powers. Every buried, dormant seed in the ground germinated and grew.

In seconds, Fintan was surrounded by a meadow of flowers. But the flowers weren't the only seeds. Saplings sprouted and she wove the springy trees around him, a new prison.

She counted on the fact he wouldn't destroy the plants with fire when it wasn't truly necessary. Energetics supported life, they didn't destroy it, though those with Muladhara were the most connected to plants and animals in that way.

He didn't need to. He used air energy to lift him in a huge jump over the new growth on the clearing's floor and landed in front of her. He tackled her by the waist, and took them both to the ground.

She fell with a thud, and Fintan's weight pinned her there.

"You can't forget the physical," he said. "Just because we can fight with energy, doesn't mean we have to, or we will. How will you protect yourself from this?"

He levered himself up so he was sitting astride her waist, holding her left wrist with his right hand, with his left knee grinding into her right arm.

She struggled to move.

I can do this. Don't think, just do.

Her legs were free, and in one swift move she shifted her hips and bent her legs up at a right angle, hooking a foot around his neck. It didn't shift him off her, but it rocked him slightly as he reacted to the threat, and his knee slid off her arm. Without hesitation she thrust down with one foot and lifted the same hip, which shoved him further. Her free hand came up to catch his forearm, so every aspect of her body was concentrated on moving him to the side, muscles straining.

He pressed his weight down hard, but her movements dumped him from her body onto the dirt. She rolled away from Fintan, and got to one knee, ready to get up. She was trembling with the effort she had exerted, and sweat coated her back despite the cool day.

Fintan grabbed her ankle and slid her to him. Rather than trying to get away, she went with the movement, and when she got close enough, she kicked at his face.

It didn't connect, but he let go of her ankle, and she scrambled to her feet. He shook his head, rolled, and got up as smoothly as if he was tugged upwards by strings.

They faced each other, Tierra panting hard, Fintan balanced lightly on the balls of his feet.

Still grinning inanely, he seemed to be waiting for her next move. She wanted to growl. And she really wanted to wipe that smile off his face.

She sent energy into the forest to see if she could find any animals. She connected with a handful of squirrels. Tierra linked to them, and sent a silent request for their help. She didn't want them to hurt Fintan, she wanted them to disorientate him.

She gave the 'go' to the squirrels, and five of them scampered out of the trees and ran up his body, racing up and down his limbs. He batted ineffectively at them, and she ran forward and shoved him.

Blinded by the squirrels, he staggered back, and fell over the short earthen ridge she'd been building behind him.

She released the squirrels, and as fast as she could, she drew earth over Fintan and packed him in mud. He was horizontal in the earth, buried, with only his head out.

She drew a breath, pulse pounding, body shaking.

He laughed. "That was good. Creative."

She sat, keeping several yards between them. She could barely move. It had been the most concentrated use of her physical and energetic powers at the same time for many decades. *Damn him for showing me how out of practice I am.*

Branches rustled as the wind picked up. Leaves blew through the clearing, and the earth started to shift away from Fintan. Air loosened the packed earth, building to a whirlwind. She could no longer see him for the mixture of earth, branches and leaves that blew around where his head had been. She scooted away, her forearm over her face to protect it. She was too tired to create her own air shield.

Her eyes stung as particles of mud hit them, and she squeezed them closed. The air was warm and insistent. Pressure built around her, as the hot air compressed her. She opened her eyes to find him standing a few feet away, covered in mud, smiling. She tried to move, and hit what felt like a wall of heated air.

She was in a cage, and she had no idea how she would break out of it.

Elrian sat in the back of the luxurious town car and seethed.

Indigo's death continued to affect him, and it had made him sloppy.

He had taken the leeching of his most recent victim too far. The girl had managed to get under his skin. Elrian and the others in the room had taken too much energy, and the girl had died. He'd captured most of her energy in a Remnant stone, but some had been lost. And they needed twelve full stones for the next part of the prophecy. He cursed again for the loss of the Ajna stone at Indigo's shack.

At the same time, he'd been called back to the house in the country. There was an urgent problem there he needed to sort out.

They needed to move the body out of the Vancouver house. But a neighbor had had a break in – some mundane burglary – and there were more cop patrols than usual. He'd decided to leave the body where it was for the time being. They couldn't risk a body being found in the car right now, whatever the camouflage he could provide.

Elrian had put extra warding and protection on the suburban house, and Dagon was driving him to the place in the country.

Once there, Elrian would draw more Muladhara energy from the land, and supplement the Ajna energy he had taken from the girl. As soon as he was up to his usual strength, he would return to the city and clear things up.

And then it would be time to start again with a new victim. He would find the street brat that Indigo had brought to them before this current one, and this time, he would forget the niceties.

He would simply drain her dry.

11

"I think you need to remove some of the silver." Fintan had to hide his amusement at Ai's outfit. She'd really gone to town on the goth look for the evening, taking their suggestion to wear black in a completely different direction to his own black jeans and sweater, along with a black watch cap stuffed in his pocket to tuck his blonde hair under. "It kind of reflects the light."

Ai was wearing all black. And silver. A lot of silver. A pair of baggy black jeans, with a black belt and big silver buckle. Black Doc Marten boots – now those he approved of – and a tight black t-shirt that had strange holes cut out of the sides and around the top. It looked lopsided to his eyes, but what did he know about teen fashion?

She had silver bangles that clinked as she walked, as many rings, studs and other face jewelry as she had piercings, and what he could only call a collar – black and silver, of course.

She made quite the picture, and certainly didn't blend with the local environment as he'd hoped – even in the coffee shop they sat outside, she stood out. Tierra, with her earth training, was capable of blending into the background. His own more mundane military training helped him be capable of the same. But Ai had no training, and a lot of shiny.

"Let's go to the bathroom, Ai," suggested Tierra. She stood, and winced.

He shifted on the chair and averted his gaze. She was going to ache after their workout together, but it had been a useful day. Being in nature was good for any energetic, and he always enjoyed practising his own self-defense, drills, and attacks. He'd gone easy on Tierra today, but not that easy, and she'd fought till he called time. She might never be a Warrior, but with a little more training, she'd get back up to the skill levels she'd had in World War II.

He'd almost offered to give her a massage after she'd showered, had wanted to take care of her for a change, but the thought of his hands on her body had been too awkward. He had a lot of confusing feelings about her at the moment, and he couldn't afford to let them distract him. Tonight was a time for action. Careful action, but action nonetheless.

His phone bleeped. He turned it over, and Cuinn's name came up. A text.

"Progress on the prophecy from some of the older prophecy texts. Confirm the six roles the Ajna Farseer noted – Sage, Communicator, Healer, Warrior, Creative and Protector – are archetypes linked to each Chakra. Not much on the stones. Still searching there."

He texted back a thanks.

He was the Warrior, and he supposed, Healer if he counted his own pitiful Anahata. That was obvious enough. Tierra was both Protector for Muladhara, and Healer for her much stronger Anahata. But battles were coming, and she would need to fight. Or at least protect herself properly.

She always looked after others. Always. She'd handle the situation with Ai's outfit as kindly as she did every other. She'd talk to the girl in that soft voice of hers, and Ai would come out of the bathroom dressed more appropriately, self-esteem intact.

Not a skill he was blessed with. His fire was too dominant.

It was rare that anyone took care of Tierra. He'd tried to do it when Blaize had been captured and Tierra had offered her energy to Cuinn. Crazy woman. Not only was it forbidden by the Circle to share energy with anyone with whom you weren't in a Maven-Adherent relationship, but there was good reason for that. The taker could easily become addicted, and end up as a 'Leech', with the person who was providing the energy becoming drained, with the possibility of death.

He'd tried to dissuade her, and she'd held firm. He'd sat behind Tierra for those minutes when Cuinn had taken energy from her, and felt physically sick at the risk she'd taken.

He hated sitting around, and the days since he'd realized the import of Cuinn's dreams had been challenging for Fintan. Others might think that he rarely took anything seriously, with a temperament that contained a large amount of Manipura mischief and love of variety and change, as well as an Anahata's more dreamy distraction, but there was one thing that was sacred to him.

Family.

He didn't have any blood relatives alive. All energetics were related pretty much if you went far enough back, but his own immediate family, parents, grandparents, were all dead. And he and both parents had been only children, not uncommon in energetic families.

Their race had been a lot more populous when nature ruled the earth. But as the oily machines of the nineteenth century had come into being, fewer and fewer energetics had been born. Which made it all the more important that lost sheep like Ai were brought back into the fold. The other side of the noise-dampening glass, Tierra and Ai stepped back into the harsh fluorescent light of the coffee shop, weaving their way between animated patrons to the door.

Ai didn't catch the light in quite the way she had, but energetically, she was still an angry flame in the darkness. He wasn't sure how either he or Tierra had missed the fact that she was an energetic. He and Tierra seemed to be off their game.

"All good?" he asked. He pushed his chair back from the small table.

Tierra nodded. Ai shrugged.

"Let's go."

They took the black sedan car he'd rented that afternoon after their hike. The Camaro not only drew more attention than they needed this evening, but it only had two seats, so nowhere for Ai to sit. They'd park a couple of streets away and then walk to the house.

Ai had refused to give them any more detail than the general area, and he hoped this was because she wanted to feel useful rather than because she didn't remember the address. He still didn't completely trust her.

Tierra got in and gestured to Ai to sit in the front, so she could direct Fintan. They buckled up and he pulled away from the curb. A few miles after crossing the Ironworkers Memorial bridge, they came to the outskirts of an upper-middle-class neighborhood. Spacious houses set back from the road had driveways with one or more expensive cars. Doctors, lawyers and bankers lived here. Maybe consultants, psychiatrists and CEOs.

At Ai's uncertain direction, the car glided down the street. They passed a cop car, and Tierra made a thoughtful noise.

She pulled a little power, and the reflections in the car windows they passed no longer showed every detail of their vehicle. She had blended the car with their surroundings. They wouldn't be invisible, but they'd be less noticeable.

He should have thought of that.

Ai's face was pale in the moonlight, and her eyes were too white in the darkness of the car.

"Recognise where we are?" he said.

"Yeah. We're close." Her words were clipped.

"How close?" He kept a wary eye on their surroundings.

"A street away. Left at the end and then it's on the right. I think."

He nodded. Tierra put a hand through from the back of the car onto Ai's shoulder in support – a hand that the girl didn't shake off. Perhaps they were getting through to her.

"I'll go past it the first time. As slowly as I can without attracting suspicion. He'll have no reason to think anyone is coming, but there's no point in drawing anyone's notice. Then we'll park and come back on foot," he said.

He put his signal light on to turn left as they approached the intersection. The tick-tick-tick was loud in the car.

They made the turn.

His heart beat a little faster, but it was excitement rather than anxiety. This was a straightforward recon job, nothing more, due to the need to bring the girl.

"Say when Ai," he said.

"It's coming up." Her words were jagged.

Seeing only lights on in the driveway at the house she indicated, he slowed a little more. The house was contemporary, and he estimated four or five bedrooms. It had a vaulted roofline and huge windows, and there were no cars parked in the spaces that belonged to the building.

His brow furrowed. He'd expected there to be at least one car. That kind of house rarely had just the one occupant. And he didn't know any energetics who couldn't drive. They might not all love being enclosed in metal boxes, especially some of the really old energetics, but with the long timespans they all lived, most of them had learned in the last hundred or so years.

Why are there no cars in the drive?

As they passed it, he checked one more time. He gestured with his head towards the darkened house. "That one?"

"Yeah."

"We won't let anyone hurt you, Ai," Tierra's voice came from the back, low and soothing.

"Sure. Whatever." Ai shrugged the words off, voice tight.

Fintan drove a few streets away and parked. This neighborhood was more blue collar, with people working shifts. Less likely to pick up on a car coming and going after midnight.

"Okay. Suit up." He pulled the watch cap from his pocket, and the others also put on gloves and hats. The place they'd parked afforded them a quiet walk to the house.

"What did you notice?" he asked.

"No cars." Tierra's voice was still pitched low.

"Yeah. Strange. Makes it less likely anyone is there. Which is odd because...?" He was treating them like any new members of his team, seeing how they responded to the environment.

Ai stared at him, and Tierra put a comforting hand on her forearm and spoke. "The house was big. There should be a few people living there, even if some of them are staff."

"I didn't see anyone apart from the old guy and Indigo last time," Ai said.

"Yes. Though there could be a garage. Or maybe no one drives. More likely, no one is home. The last would be best for us. Ready?" They nodded, neither enthusiastic, and he started moving, continuing their discussion in a low voice that matched Tierra's. "Right. What's the plan?"

"We've been through it, 'Dad'." Ai's voice emphasized the last word with a sarcastic tone. "We know what we're doing."

He was glad to see a bit of spark in the girl, but made her talk them through the plan anyway. The most critical part of which was that Ai couldn't join them until they'd checked the house was safe.

"Which is stupid because I'm the only one who's been in the house." Ai muttered this, an argument they'd had several times already.

They ducked down a side alley and brushed through some scraggy bushes at the edge of a new housing development.

"We're coming up to a road where we don't have much cover. We should walk normally. As normally as anyone coming home at this time of night on foot would, anyway," he said.

He turned to Tierra and tugged off her hat. "Hey!" she protested, slowing.

"It's just for a minute. Take my arm. Keep walking." Puzzled, she did so. "And Ai, take my other one."

Ai, not nearly as obedient as Tierra, shook her head. But she sensed what he was up to, and slipped around him to take Tierra's other arm.

"Playing at happy families are we?" *Hmm.* The girl was sharp.

"Something like that. We're just a family walking home from our friends' house," he lectured.

"In the dead of night," muttered a scowling Ai.

They approached the street with the house. He looked around to see where Ai could hide.

He scouted out a likely looking place by some shrubs, where she could remain unseen both from the house and the street. When she was safely stashed he stepped away, Tierra pulled a little energy, and the bushes swayed slightly. When they were still, there was no longer any sign of Ai. He nodded his approval.

They approached the house from the rear, which meant cutting around the back of several other houses, which he hoped wouldn't have dogs or alarm systems. Tierra could calm dogs, but every one she had to reach out and connect with took a little of her energy, and he wanted her as primed as possible.

Going along the backs of the houses they passed several large lawns, a swimming pool, and one property which was entirely walled off. A good place for an energetic to blend in. Anonymous suburbia.

They arrived at the rear of the target property, marked by a line of trees and bushes. Tierra put out subtle tendrils of energy to check for wardings, and her eyebrows rose.

"This place has a lot of protection. It's going to take me a while to unpick. You want to take a walk and scope the rest of the house out?"

He frowned, unwilling to leave her.

"I'll be fine here," Tierra said. "I need to concentrate. The person who lives here is either a reasonably strong earth energetic, or they paid one to secure the home. Go get the lay of the land. See if you can get a sense of anyone in there physically. We don't think anyone is there, but you can check. You need to treat me like a real member of the team."

He nodded, and wished for the millionth time in his life that he had the Ajna power of mind speaking. It would come in really handy.

Fintan walked away. Tierra scolded herself at the millisecond she let herself be distracted by his very nice butt. She went to work.

These wardings were complicated. A sophisticated and powerful energetic had put them together. She hoped the house was as empty as Fintan thought it was, because whoever lived here would be able to tell she'd gone through the protection they'd created. She tried to slide through them gracefully but what she was actually doing was hacking at them with an energetic machete — which was taking a lot of power.

She traced one of the wardings that surrounded the house. They glowed with power. They were connected like knotted string. She tugged at one of the ends. It was like unraveling a knitted sweater, though one with the power to bite if you unraveled it in the wrong place. It was the type of guardian energy that stopped you getting in, not out, so she picked at it to make a hole where they could enter, and then they could leave anywhere.

After many minutes, she was sweating in the night air, and she was almost at the limit of what she could do with her earth powers. She hoped they wouldn't need them inside. Her body was high on adrenaline, hyper-sensitive to the environment around her, and to the task at hand.

But she was proud. She'd managed to make a hole big enough for the three of them to get through, and she'd deactivated three or four other wardings that connected to it.

There was no sign of Fintan. But there was no sign of anyone else either. The property was almost certainly empty.

Should she go in alone? Perhaps she should pop through the hole she'd made and check for other wardings. She wouldn't go into the house, but she might as well be thorough.

She used some of her air energy to tag the hole to Fintan so it would shine if he came by. The circle she'd made glimmered a white-blue color for a moment before it faded. That was as big a clue as she could leave. Not that it mattered, she'd be back by the time he returned.

She bent down and put her hand on the earth, and 'asked' the hedge to let her through. The branches moved out of the way, rustling as if the wind was moving them, but in a very specific direction. After a few moments there was easily enough room for her to creep through.

She moved through the hedge without incident, and stood on the other side. It was a big garden for a suburban house, a well-tended lawn with the odd flowerbed and some small trees. It wasn't a working garden – no vegetables, no herbs, nothing useful.

There was also very little cover. Anyone who was in the house and looking out at the garden would be able to see her if she moved across the lawn.

Except that she was an earth energetic. She pulled power, which had begun to be a strain, and wrapped it around her. She blended with the night, and moved across the lawn, sticking to the side of the garden, next to the hedge and going towards the house. She kept her energetic senses open the whole time, checking for more wardings.

She didn't find any.

She crept to the back door, her heart pounding. She'd investigate the house's protection, and for signs that there was anyone inside.

She put her hand on the brick and she sent whisper-thin tendrils of power into the house, seeking. She touched each room in turn, surprised at how big the place was. After a few minutes, she let out a breath. There was no one in the house. No signs of life at all, not even a cat or a dog.

It was safe to disable the last of the protection, and then she would get the others. She turned her attention to the house. She found another security warding linked to the house itself. It took her a few more minutes, and more energy, to disable it, but she managed it.

She needed a break. She sank down on the grass, her back against the house, and put her hands into the damp earth, seeking support from her element. It wasn't the same as rest and recharging, not with the amount of energy disabling the protections had needed, but it would help.

Somewhat refreshed, she got up and prowled around the house, checking for anything else energetic. She kept a hand on the house at all times, trailing it round behind her as she used every sense to see if there were more. She was more relaxed now she knew there were no people inside.

At a large window, she peered inside to see into the darkened room.

And reared back, her gorge rising.

Because she'd been wrong. Well, half-wrong. There was someone inside. But she'd been right that there were no signs of life.

A lump the size of a sleeping bag lay on the otherwise very tidy living room floor. She forced herself to step back and focus on the lump to check she was right. She squinted, and couldn't look away.

It was a dead body.

12

Fintan flowed between shrubs and trees, if not as quietly as Tierra, near enough. Certainly no human would come close to his stealth. He crept past several cats, a fox, and a squirrel, but none of them startled.

Once he'd circled the house, found nothing out of place, and checked on Ai, he returned to the place he'd left Tierra.

She wasn't there.

His belly squeezed. As he moved into the spot he'd last seen her, a shimmer of something touched him, and a faint circle of air energy appeared, surrounding a low gap in the hedge.

Bloody woman. This wasn't the plan.

It wasn't like this when he worked with other Warriors. They knew to follow instructions. He pressed his lips together and got down on his hands and knees to maneuver through the small hole in the hedge. He and Tierra were going to have words.

He got halfway through the opening, and slammed into something solid. He rocked back and moved into a defensive posture on his knees, unable to see anything as his head spun. The hedge's spiky thorns pricked and scratched.

He searched the dark to see what he'd ricocheted off, and a human cannonball barreled into him. Its momentum took him down to the floor with it. It took a moment more for the 'ouuff' noise the other body made to filter into his stunned brain.

And for him to realize that the warm, soft body he had in his arms was Tierra.

Tierra ended up on her back in the alley with Fintan on top of her. She panted hard from her short flight from the house, and her back and butt hurt from tiny stones digging into her.

She blinked and shook her head.

"Fintan? Fintan, get off of me," she said. She struggled to catch her breath.

He was as dazed as she, his cap askew so some of his reddish blond hair poked out at the side. "Fintan!"

She arched her torso slightly to nudge him off.

"Sorry." He moved to the side and put an arm out to pull her into a sitting position.

Tierra pressed a hand to her forehead. Her heart drummed in her chest. She didn't want to close her eyes in case the image of the still body came back.

"There's a dead person in the living room." She couldn't swallow over the lump in her throat.

He slid to face her, both of them still on their butts on the ground, and grabbed her by the arms. "Did you go into the room?"

She shook her head vigorously. "Of course not. I saw her through the window and came back out to get you."

She couldn't have gotten away fast enough, in fact. A blush of heat rose up her neck. Should she have done more?

"Did you sense anyone else in the house?"

"No." She wanted to be home, in her garden, where it was peaceful, there were no dead bodies, and no one tried to attack her. This was such a horrible mess.

"We need to get Ai." He stood.

She rubbed her hands over her face. If only her head would stop pounding. "We can't bring Ai in with a dead body in there."

His face was impassive. "The body means we need a new plan. And if we leave her outside much longer she might join us on her own — we're lucky she's obeyed up until this point. I don't trust her to follow orders. You didn't."

She closed her eyes, her face hot.

"Maybe she'll know the body, or have other information. Better to have her with us."

Tierra's nod was slow. She still reeled at the sight of the body. Should they really expose Ai to the same? But Fintan made a good point about her coming to join them anyway. Ai was a wild card. Tierra would just have to try and protect Ai however she could.

Fintan had already disappeared, and reappeared a few short minutes later with a pale and vibrating Ai.

"Did you tell her?" Tierra asked.

"It's not my first stiff," Ai's tone was flippant, but her hands clenched and unclenched.

"Tierra, can you open the back door?" Fintan said.

"I've ripped through a lot of the wardings. Given our lack of subtlety so far, I think you might as well burn through the back door's lock."

"There might be no other live humans, but we don't know what other nasty surprises might be hiding there." His hand rubbed his chin. "We do a sweep before we look at the corpse. No lights. Actually, give me a second."

There was a light buzz as he reached for the energy of fire. He shaped the energy into a small glowing ball that he kept muted.

"That should seem enough like moonlight that it won't be too suspicious in the unlikely event that anyone sees it from the outside."

"Can I do that?" Ai whispered.

Tierra shook her head. "Manipura energy."

Ai sighed.

"Are you ready?" Fintan said. "Understand the rules?"

"Yes." She wasn't going off-script again.

"As much as possible, try not to leave any traces of yourselves." He drew latex gloves out of a pocket and handed them each a pair to put on.

Too soon, they were ready.

"Let's go," Fintan said.

He gestured to Tierra to lead them through the hole in the hedge. She ducked down and wriggled through the space, coming up on the other side in the garden, where she waited for the others.

It was hard to believe that a body lay on the other side of the manicured lawn. The last corpse she had been up close and personal with had been in World War II, a lifetime ago. A bad time. Her mother and aunt had been two of the bodies, which Tierra had helped sift through the remains of a hospital to find and identify. The miasma of cordite that had hung around the wreckage, combined with the smell of wet burning and damp cement had blended together into a unique and horrible perfume that Tierra hoped she never had to smell again.

The sound of Ai coming through the hole was audible in the crisp night air. Tierra shook herself.

Fintan came through the gap without leaving a trace. "After you."

Tierra nodded, and set off towards the house, taking a circuitous route that kept them to the edges of the gardens. She could hear her heart thud in her chest, and sucked in deep breaths to attempt to calm herself.

When they reached the back door, she moved aside, and Fintan put his hand on the door handle. He traced a laser-sharp blade of fire around the lock mechanism, until he was able to open the door while the lock stayed in place.

He sent his energy-ball low into the room, its glow dull but helpful. Tierra took in a spacious kitchen, full of gleaming metal and marble. It looked like a show kitchen – everything in its place, nothing ever used.

She followed Fintan through the house, room by room. The rest of the house was just as impersonal. The pictures on the wall were bland art that could have come from IKEA, though had likely cost a great deal more.

Nothing revealed anything about the owner.

The house had been mostly cleared out apart from one room, where there were a couple of boxes stacked up by the door. Tierra pulled off the lid of one of the containers, and poked through the contents.

Ai, looking over her shoulder, let out a muffled noise.

"What?" Tierra turned to her. "Is everything ok?"

"I think this is Indigo's stuff." Ai moved forward and started her own inventory, pawing through the contents. "This is a necklace she wore, and I think this was one of her t-shirts." She yanked out a black shirt with the name of a heavy metal band on it. "Why's her stuff piled up? Do you think he's done something to her?"

They still hadn't told Ai that Indigo was dead. They hadn't gotten around to changing their original story that they were searching for her. But now wasn't the time.

"Hard to say," Fintan said. "Let's keep going. I don't think we should stay here long, and we need to spend some time with the body."

Tierra closed up the box again, and stared down at it. Poor Indigo, a woman whose life had ended up stacked into a couple of boxes, most likely to be thrown into the trash.

They worked their way through the rest of the house, finding nothing else, then approached the doors to the living room.

Fintan cracked the door, and held his hand up. "Let me go in first."

He slipped silently into the room, his light ahead of him, and left the two women standing in the hall. Ai moved closer to Tierra, and she put a hand on the girl's shoulder.

After a few tense moments, he came out again, his face grim. "Okay, you can come in. There's not much to see, but she's been dead a while. Don't touch anything if you can. Whoever did this is likely to come back to clean up."

"They'll have seen that someone has been here from the wardings I took down," Tierra pointed out.

"Let's keep it at a minimum. There's no point in letting them know who we are." He slipped back into the room.

Tierra took a breath, and followed him, Ai trailing after her.

The living room was stuffy, and the nausea that she had tamped down surged up again at the stink of the body.

She wasn't sure if she could do this. Her feet dragged on the plush carpet as she walked to the window where Fintan stood surveying the body.

It was a teenage girl, perhaps a few years older than Ai, with streaked blond hair and nails bitten down to the quick. She was thin and dressed in some baggy jeans, nondescript trainers, and a hoodie. Her face seemed pinched even in death.

Tierra's hands sweated in the latex gloves. She pushed up the sleeve of the girl's hoodie, left side and then right side. The girl had the look of a a junkie, but there were no track marks that she could see. She frowned and checked other possible injection sites. How had the girl died?

"Do you think she was…like us?" Ai's voice was thick.

Tierra mentally kicked herself. How had she not thought of that? She needed to examine the body from an energetic's perspective, not a human one. She really was off her game.

"I'm not sure," Tierra said.

"Can you read the room?" Fintan asked.

Reading a room was something only powerful energetics could do. Tierra could, but she rarely practised it. Emergencies only. It took huge effort.

"I'm not sure I have enough energy left. But I can try."

Fintan rubbed the back of his neck. The glow of the light showed up the shadows under his eyes. She'd barely thought about the impact of the situation on him, assumed it was commonplace for him, but he was still sensitive. Just because he could deal with it, didn't mean he welcomed it.

"Don't do it if you don't have enough." He glanced around. "Let's start with a physical exam."

He searched the room methodically, checking for hidden spaces, and examining every possible detail. Tierra stayed with the body, Ai looking on, her arms wrapped around her thin frame, bravado gone.

Tierra might not want to read the room, but she could have an energetic look at the body. Her Anahata energy was a healer's energy, and would let her see inside. She wanted, needed, to help.

She removed one of her gloves, and pushed up the girl's hoodie so her sunken stomach was revealed. The closer Tierra could get to the girl's own Anahata Chakra, even if it wasn't activated, the better. Not that Tierra had done this often on dead bodies.

She drew a breath, and pulled what little energy she had left. She'd mainly used Muladhara, earth energy on the house's protection, and so it was good that she was using Anahata here. She went inside the body, and sought out anything unusual. It didn't take long to see what the problem was.

Ai was right. The girl was an energetic. Her life's energy had been sucked away by a Leech, leaving her drained, with nothing to sustain her system.

Tierra drew her awareness out of the body, and opened her eyes. She rose to her feet in a smooth motion, but she swayed when she was upright. How could any energetic, sworn to protect the earth and its life, do something like this?

"She was drained," Tierra said.

Fintan turned. "Drained?"

"Yes. She was an energetic, an active one. I don't know her, but…" She pulled the girl's left sleeve higher, displaying a dark stripe of what looked like a tattoo. "She has an Adherent mark. She'll be known to one of the Guilds."

"Someone should be missing her. That's interesting. Which Guilds?" Fintan asked.

"Anahata-Ajna."

Ai's ears perked up at this. "Like me?"

"Yes. Like you. But she knew she was an energetic. She would have had what we call a Maven, which is someone who trains you in one of your energies. Most likely she was an Anahata Adherent as that's what her stronger energy was. It's hard to tell how developed it was given she's been drained like this." Tierra stood to face Ai. "Draining someone else's energy is one of our greatest crimes. It's a type of vampirism, cannibalism almost. It's extremely rare."

If Tierra got out of the house without throwing up, she would have done well.

"Yet we've seen it more than once in a matter of a month." Fintan mused.

"What does he mean? Where did you see it before?" Ai asked.

Tierra hedged, unsure of what to tell Ai, so new to their world. They would need to tell her about Indigo, and what had happened, if only to show Ai how serious things were. Later. "Let's talk about it when we're not in a room with a dead body."

Her stomach twisted. It wasn't a deception if she held off the full truth for a while, surely?

"The house doesn't look as if it's in use at the moment, but I need to talk to Adam about the best approach from here. We don't have infinite resources, but it's one of our best leads. We can also look into a paper trail for the property, which might give us another place to look." He took out his phone and snapped a few shots of the dead girl. "It's hard to know how long she's been here. And whether whoever did this intends to return and…dispose of her, or has left and doesn't care."

"A paper trail will help us there, as we might be able to track it to a person. Besides, they're likely to come and move the body. In which case we'll have them," Tierra said.

She couldn't imagine that person. Would that person be evil, or mad? How disturbed did you need to be to break the darkest taboos of their society? Her nausea returned.

"Either way, we need to get out of here," Fintan said. "We're not in a position to capture an unfriendly at this moment. We also need to find out who she was – I'll send the photo to the Anahata Guild when we get back to the hotel."

He took a final look around the room. "Let's go."

It had been four a.m. by the time they'd all hit the sack, and Tierra had insisted Ai stay the night, so Fintan had ended up on the floor.

He got up early and went for a run to help him think. He'd barely had a moment to himself in the last few days. He'd been with Tierra the entire time. Which hadn't been bad, but it had been different.

He spent that kind of time with his unit, but rarely with a woman. Okay, lots of those he served with were women, but Tierra was, well, a *woman*. A woman he didn't quite know how to interact with right now.

His feet pounded the pavement, as he built from a jog to a run. Sweat beaded his forehead. Physical activity had always been the way he'd processed difficult feelings or events, and the last few days had been as confusing as fuck.

He had a few issues he needed to work out: next steps on the investigation; the girl and what to do with her; and then, Tierra. His mind shied away from that last, and he sped up.

Investigation first then.

He hadn't expected the body at the house. He would never have brought Tierra – let alone the girl – to a house with a dead body. Tierra had seen enough of that in the war, and he didn't want to expose her to it again. She was softer, gentler than him, and she suffered more at other people's distress. He needed to protect her.

He hadn't seen the body coming, and neither had Cuinn predicted it in a dreamwalk. They needed to find the girl's identity, watch the house, and discover whatever they could about the owner. This was solid ground for Fintan, an area where he had plenty of experience. He knew how to run an investigation. Since the war, he'd been a trouble shooter for the Manipura Guild. He preferred to work alone – he didn't enjoy managing a team – but he had access to plenty of resources. As did Adam. They'd catch up, work out the details of the op and take it forward between them. Fintan had already sent the other man a few brief texts giving him a heads up, and there were people on the way to stake out the house.

He turned right at a corner with a huge steel and glass building. At this time of day he'd passed plenty of typical Vancouverites, with yoga mats over their shoulders and Starbucks cups in their hands. Fintan had dated a few girls like that in the past. They didn't seem as appealing now.

He picked up the pace, sweat pouring off him. Ai was a harder problem. She was untrained, and a liability in several ways. She was also, one way or another, family. They needed to find out who she was, and bring her in so she could learn about her magic and how to use it safely. Would she, though? Would she trust them enough to come in? Leave the world she'd known behind? He grimaced.

Tierra wouldn't want to let the girl out of her sight, for fear they might lose her. It would be easy for Ai to disappear in a city like this. It was important that the girl made her own choice. If they forced her, the chances of keeping her were slim. He hoped Tierra would be on board with that. Once they got her to Cathair Cuinn, he hoped she'd be intrigued enough to stay. The ideal would be to get her to one of the Guilds. She had a lot to catch up on.

The last problem was Tierra. He swiped at the moisture on his forehead with his forearm, drops falling behind him as he ran.

In the park Tierra had told Fintan – in the same way she might offer him a sandwich – that she loved him.

He groaned. What was he supposed to do with that?

Yet, she didn't seem bothered. She'd told him with her usual grace and warmth, and then seemed to move on. Surely if she was able to do that, she'd mixed up her feelings. She couldn't actually love him.

At the same time, he'd found himself having some disturbing feelings in relation to her. Disturbing, because it was entirely unthinkable that they could ever be together. They would be a terrible match. He couldn't give her what she needed – someone who was able to love with a full heart, and who was able to be a rooted presence for her at Cathair Cuinn. Fintan, on the other hand, had a role that involved danger and travel, unpredictability and change, none of which Tierra enjoyed, even by proxy.

What was the way forward here?

His usual approach was to face a problem head on. Should he talk about this with Tierra again? But what would that gain them? She'd said her piece, and he agreed the idea of them trying to date, whatever his willful dick said, was incomprehensible.

She was prepared to pretend it wasn't a thing, and so would he. Their attention right now needed to be on the prophecies, and whoever was draining young women. After that, he'd get back into his work in Europe for a while. Have a break from Cathair Cuinn. He gritted his teeth. Some space would be good.

He slowed his pace, more relaxed. His feet hit the pavement with satisfying thumps, and his breath puffed out in little clouds as he jogged back towards the hotel. Exercise always cleared his head.

He stopped at a coffee shop on the corner near the hotel and picked up a Caramel Macchiato for Tierra – her favorite – but hesitated over Ai. He went with a mocha as a balance of sweet and coffee. Though knowing her, she'd probably want a double espresso. He got a triple-shot Americano for himself and went to the room.

The room was warm and smelled of flowers and moss. Like Tierra. The beds were made, and the room was tidy, their bags packed.

"Keen to get back?" he asked.

She smiled. "Yes. There's stuff I can do there."

She stopped, her brows lifted. "Oh, you brought coffee! Thank you, Fintan. That was really thoughtful."

Fintan flushed at Tierra's disproportionate delight. He did nice things for her usually, didn't he? Why was she so surprised? He handed the drinks out quickly.

"Where do we need to go to pick up your belongings, Ai?" he asked.

She looked down into her mocha, one arm wrapped right around her thin frame. "Um, about that. I can't just, you know, pick up and leave. I need a bit of time, to sort things out. Say goodbye to some people. I can get the bus over in a few days, and we'll see."

Fintan rubbed the back of his neck. Not pressuring her to come back with them would help her to trust them more. Plus, she might need a bit of time to come to terms with the very different turn her life was about to take. Before Tierra could say anything, he spoke. "Okay Ai, that's fair."

She took a relieved sip of her drink and jerked her head in response.

"But please, keep in touch," Fintan said. "All you need to do is contact us, and we'll help you however we can. We'll see you within the week – there's plenty more to tell you when you arrive. Do you want a phone?"

He stated her arrival as fact, leaving her no room for argument. He might not know how to deal with teenage girls, but he had dealt with a lot of unruly subordinates. He was going to treat her like that from now on.

Ai shook her head. "I have one."

"Do you want us to drop you somewhere?" he addressed her, not hopeful, while wanting to see if she would trust them a little more.

She shook her head. "Nah. I can walk from here."

"Okay. I'll walk you downstairs." He caught Tierra's frown, but he had a couple of things he wanted to say to Ai in private.

They walked from the room to the elevator, and he checked around to see no one was watching before he pulled out $500. He stepped in with her.

"This is to get you to Cathair Cuinn. Get a case or something to pack your stuff into, and make sure you pick up some more clothes here in the city. There's probably not much in Merrow that will suit your dress sense."

She looked at the cash in his hand and to his surprise, paused. "I can earn my way you know. When I get to the house. You can give me jobs and stuff. I learn quick."

"I'm sure you do. And no doubt we'll have a fair few for you. Helping Tierra in the kitchen and garden, helping Cuinn and Blaize with research."

Ai didn't look thrilled, but she nodded anyway. "Whatever. But I don't need charity. Give me room and board? I can pay you back."

Fintan was hoping to find out who her parents had been, to see if they'd left an estate or anything valuable behind them. He'd quizzed Ai on what she could remember of them, and of her life with them – which wasn't much – and he and Tierra had agreed between them that this should be high on their list of priorities once they got back to Cathair Cuinn.

"We can work it out when you get to the house," he said. "Take this for now. One other thing. You asked how we know if someone's energy is twisted. Unless the other person is shielding, it's something we can tell by sending our own energy threads into theirs to check."

She had frozen, her face pale.

"I think you might have a personal interest in the answer. You've lived on the streets for a while. Probably faced some tough situations. I wanted to tell you neither of us picked up any sign of your energy twisting."

The girl's eyes welled up, though nothing escaped. She sagged back against the wall of the elevator. "Okay."

"Okay. Look after yourself, and make sure you're with us within the week – check in every couple of days so we know you're good. And please, Ai, don't go back to that house on your own. He's still out there somewhere and you may be a target given you've already had contact with him."

She shrugged one shoulder, feigning indifference – the tears unshed but still glittering. "Why would I? There's already one dead girl there. I'm not stupid. But if Indigo comes back, what should I do?"

"Let us know," said Fintan smoothly, without taking a breath.

Ai hadn't seemed to like Indigo especially, but he'd detected a hint of hero worship there, especially once Ai had found out about Indigo's powers. They'd tell her what had happened when she was safely at Cathair Cuinn.

He was happy taking the wheel of the Camaro again. He loved driving, and it was a good trip from Vancouver to Merrow. Plus there was no 'new car' rental smell in this one.

Tierra was silent in the car, unlike her usual chatty self. He was pretty sure what she was thinking.

"I didn't like leaving her either," he said.

"She's a child, Fintan! A child!" The words burst out of Tierra like a flood breaking down a dam. "And we just left her, again!"

"When did we leave her before?"

"Energetics did. And we're energetics. Should we have pushed harder? Showed we cared? Was it a test?"

"No. We did the right thing. She needs space to absorb everything. It's a lot." He hadn't liked it, but it was the best way to get her to come to the house.

"Why didn't you tell her about Indigo?" she said.

"It seems too complicated. We can tell her when she gets to the house."

Tierra shifted in her seat. "I suppose. I just don't like hiding the truth from her."

"It's only for a week," Fintan pointed out. "Then we can explain everything."

The urban sprawl of Vancouver transformed into the rich green countryside, the imposing mountains in front of them. Fintan cracked his window to let the air, with its hints of spring, into the car.

He put a hand over to touch Tierra's leg for comfort, his eyes not leaving the road. Her leg was warm through her jeans. The car felt smaller, and he moved his concentration back to the road, and his hand back to the wheel.

"Let's talk about something else." *For my sake as much as yours.*

"Like what?" Tierra wasn't too interested, her eyes on the landscape they were passing through.

"What's the most unusual topic you've had in your advice column?"

She looked back over at him at that. "What?"

"Your column."

"No one ever asks me about that." She was frowning.

"Why not?" This was not the reaction he'd been expecting.

"Because…it's not important. Not really. Compared to the jobs everyone else does." She shrugged.

"You don't believe in what you do?" He was baffled. She took care of everyone around her, and held down a job in the human world, and still she didn't feel she was worthy?

She didn't say anything, just picked at an imaginary thread on her sleeve.

"You might not be doing one of the high profile energetic jobs, but you're fulfilling your energetic role as much, if not more, than most of us. How many newspapers is your column syndicated to?"

"About two hundred and forty."

"So every week, across Canada, you bring comfort and support to many thousands of humans. You bring a little balance to their worlds. How can you say, as a Muladhara energetic, whose energy centers around safety, security, and grounding, that you're not carrying out your role?"

She was looking at him as if she'd never seen him before.

"What?" he said.

"I've just – that's not something anyone else has ever said." Her words were halting.

"How long have you been working for the newspapers?"

"A few decades I guess. Writing under different names, of course, so the non-ageing thing wasn't a problem. And sometimes I 'retired' and handed the column down to a protégé. Dealing with people digitally has helped a lot. It took me a while to settle here when Adam and I first arrived, and I needed to get the house properly set up. Cuinn had built it, but it wasn't a home. And then I was looking for something to do, and met one of the newspaper editors at some mixer of Cuinn's at the university. He wanted to add a female touch to his paper, and Cuinn convinced him to give me a trial." She shrugged. "And it built from there."

"And you do a gardening column too?"

She blushed a little. "Yes. I could do more to keep myself up to date. Attend more courses. I just never seem to get around to it. I'm happy in the house, doing my thing. Being part of the community here. And writing the columns."

"The degree in horticulture must help though," said Fintan, dryly. "Let alone your degrees in psychology and social studies."

She wriggled in her seat. "What does your role consist of at the moment? You always seem to be doing something different. Adam's had a similar role for decades now, or at least, he's been in the same area, just gaining seniority. But not you."

Her tone was curious, and she'd abandoned the view to focus on him, shifting to look at his profile. He felt bathed in sunshine.

"I'm more of a trouble-shooter. I help out in difficult cases where there's a Rogue issue. This situation with Cuinn is actually just the sort of thing I'd be assigned to. I have quite a lot of leeway as to what I get involved in. Sometimes the Major or Minor Circle will direct me to investigate something. It's rarely boring."

"What do you enjoy most?"

"I love the variety. And I love problem-solving. I like people, but I'm not necessarily a team player, so I like the autonomy that the role brings me." He paused to overtake a battered truck that was chugging along the road. The driver, probably a farmer, Fintan thought, raised a hand to wave at them, and Fintan waved back.

"I like the travel, too," he said.

"Where's home for you these days? I know you have the apartment in Italy, the cottage in Ireland, and the penthouse in Hong Kong, but which is home?" Tierra asked.

He ran a hand over the stubble on his chin. He couldn't tell her the first answer that had come to mind, which was that Cathair Cuinn was the place that felt most like home. He'd even given it its name – in jest, originally, as Cathair meant castle in Gaelic, Cuinn's original language – but the label had stuck. An answer that was as much a surprise to him as it would be to her. He made short visits there every few months. And he'd been coming to visit for as long as Adam and Tierra had lived there. It added up.

"I'm not sure. They all contribute different things to my life. I like the variety remember?" He realized she'd neatly turned the tables on him, and was now asking him about his life rather than the other way round. He wondered if she even knew she was doing it. Tierra was humble – she never put herself in the spotlight, and always found a way to get the other person to talk and share their secrets.

Luckily, we're nearly home. He turned the car down the long lane that led to Cathair Cuinn. *Otherwise who knows what other secrets – secrets I didn't even realize existed – she would uncover?*

Elrian stood on the threshold to his property, and glared at the broken wardings. He and Dagon had come back to the house to remove the body, only to find that Tierra and that good-for-nothing Fintan had found the house, and worse, discovered the body. The disgusting…taste of their energies was everywhere.

Elrian's manicured nails dug into his palm. This wasn't part of the plan. Indigo's stay at the motel should have ended the trail there. How did they find this house?

He stalked around the edges of the land, using his earth energy to see if there had been anyone with Fintan and Tierra. He was surprised Tierra was powerful enough to get through his protections, but she hadn't done it gracefully.

Dagon unlocked the front door, and Elrian walked into the house and headed for the back room where they had left the body. It was still there, and to the naked eye, at least, it appeared untouched. But Tierra's energetic traces were all over.

Discomfort crept along his shoulders and back, and he shrugged it off, annoyed. He couldn't shield as well as he would like when reading the house like this.

In the living room, he stared down at the body of the girl, ignoring the stink. He twisted the thick ring on his right hand. The ring contained a tiny chip of stone, a Remnant, that he had recharged from the girl's energies.

Elrian stood in the room and closed his eyes. He reached out with tendrils of earth energy and riffled through the energetic tracks in the room. There was Tierra…there was Fintan…ah ha. There was a third, who also seemed familiar. Was it another of Cuinn's friends? Elrian drew his brows together. He couldn't quite place the energy. Female, definitely. Was it Cara? No, though Anahata energy was present in the traces, hard to pick out because both Tierra and Fintan also had that Chakra activated. And…the auxiliary…was Ajna.

The energetic scent tickled the back of his mind. He knew it. Who was it? He tried to relax, to let the tracks settle so the name would come to him. He took a couple of deep breaths, his body motionless in the center of the room.

Ah. A loose end. His eyes snapped open and he gritted his teeth.

That little bitch, Ai. Indigo had brought her round as a gift for Elrian's lover and mentor. His nostrils flared. He needed to find that girl. Either way, if he found the girl, he'd likely find Tierra and Cuinn, and vice versa. And if he knew Cuinn and his family – and he did – then if they'd found the stray, they'd adopt her. But Elrian needed to get to her. She'd serve more than one purpose.

She knew things about Elrian he didn't want Cuinn's family to know – yet.

And she could be the exact bait that Elrian needed to destroy them.

13

In her living room, Tierra opened the glass doors that led to her garden. The peaty air would freshen the room up. She was so pleased to be home, in her space.

She had just put the kettle on when there was a knock at the door.

"Come in," she called.

Blaize's auburn hair appeared around the door, and Tierra smiled and took another mug out. "I was just making tea."

"Great." Blaize flopped onto Tierra's sofa. "So, I'm up to date on the difficult stuff, now give me the important stuff. What was Ai like? Does Fintan snore?"

Tierra had liked Blaize from the first moment she'd arrived. Young for an energetic – in her late twenties – she was confident, and her green eyes twinkled with fun as much as they were serious.

Tierra laughed. "No, he didn't snore. He was a good roommate actually, if a little messy."

"Huh."

Tierra brought their tea over and sat at the other end of the sofa. She tucked her feet under her.

"I had one interesting chat with him." She kept her tone casual.

Blaize perked up again. "Yes?"

"We went to the park for me to recharge." Tierra sipped her tea. "I decided it was a good time to share something."

Blaize's eyebrows rose. "What?"

"I told him that I loved him. And that I didn't need anything from him, but I felt I wasn't being honest with him by keeping it to myself. It was making me awfully cranky with him," she said, her tone confiding.

Blaize had almost choked on her tea at the first few words, and was still recovering.

"You told him – what?"

"That I loved him."

"And, how long … have you, hmm?" Blaize gestured weakly with the hand that wasn't holding the tea.

"A long time. As long as I can remember."

"But, Fintan? Really?" Blaize's forehead was furrowed.

Tierra frowned at Blaize's tone. "Yes, why?"

"Well…he's just so…unsuitable for you."

Tierra bristled. It wasn't that Blaize was wrong, exactly…but. Okay, but what? Why was she annoyed? She took a deep breath and let it out slowly.

"I realize we're not a good match," she said. "All I did was tell him, and ask him not to share details of his romantic life any more."

Blaize sagged back against the sofa. "Okay. Good call. I love Fintan, really, but he can be a disaster in relationships. He's always falling in and out of love. I remember my Aunt and Uncle teasing him about it when I was a teenager."

Tierra frowned. "It's not like he's fickle. He only ever has one relationship at a time, and he cares for them."

Blaize fidgeted, getting comfortable in the seat. "Well, sure, but you're so different. He loves travel and variety, you love stability and home. He loves to go skydiving and have sex outdoors. You love baking and snuggling up by the fire. You're chalk and cheese."

"It's not like opposites can't attract. Anyway, I like sex outdoors." Her words were very slightly defensive and she added. "Not that we're going to get together. Or we should. Or I want to."

"How long have you been crushing on him?" said Blaize.

"A long time," said Tierra. She wasn't sure she wanted to talk about it now. It was one thing for her to choose not to pursue something, another for Blaize to tell her it was crazy. What, she wasn't good enough for Fintan? He wasn't good enough for her? She was also embarrassed to say quite how long she'd pined after him. It had been back of mind as long as she could remember. It had faded when she'd done her training for her energies, fading from a burn to an ache. It wasn't like she hadn't dated or had relationships in the meantime.

Blaize's expression was sympathetic, which irked Tierra more.

"He's an attractive man," Blaize said. "I had a crush on him growing up. He always looks like he's just about to play a joke on everyone. And with those bright blue eyes and that surfer hair, well. He has that bad-boy-with-impulse-control-issues thing going on. It's pretty hot."

"Hmm." Tierra drank more tea. She wished she hadn't said anything.

"You're right though," continued Blaize, oblivious. "He falls for each woman head over heels, but they never seem to keep his attention. Not that any of them ever seem to hold a grudge. He must do the most charming break-up speeches in history. He could probably write an advice column of his own on it."

"I guess," said Tierra. She felt scrunchy, and she didn't want to talk about it any more.

"What did he say?" Blaize asked.

"Not much. Though it obviously annoyed him, because later on that night he lost control of his energy for a little while." Which had been weird, in retrospect. Perhaps Fintan also thought the idea of dating Tierra was unthinkable, horrible. Enough that the thought of it made him so ill he'd lost control. Tierra rubbed the back of her neck. Her muscles were tight.

Blaize's forehead wrinkled. "He did?"

"Yes."

Blaize smirked. "I bet that hasn't happened to him in a while. That's not the kind of impulse control issue I was thinking about. You should probably have told him that it happens to all guys at some point or another."

Tierra rolled her eyes.

"Have you talked about it since?" said Blaize.

"No."

"Why not?"

"I've told him the situation, what else is there to say?" Tierra got up and began fluffing cushions. She was done with the topic. "I don't expect anything from him. I just wanted to get it off my chest. Oh, and not have to hear endless stories about his latest conquest."

Blaize gazed at her thoughtfully, silent for a while. "When are we expecting Ai?"

"Another week or so." Tierra's chest loosened. She'd process her feelings about Fintan by herself in the future.

"You want help getting a room ready for her? Cuinn's had me reading through old prophecies for days. I'm going a little stir-crazy. If it wasn't for exercise – which I'm still not allowed to do at full tilt – I'd be going mad."

"I bet you get some exercise." Tierra's grin was teasing.

"What do you – oh. Well, yes, you're right, I do get some. That can be pretty exhausting." Blaize grinned in return.

"How are you and Cuinn doing?"

"Really well." The smirk on Blaize's face was a little self-satisfied.

"Enjoyed having the house to yourselves?" Tierra hugged a cushion to her chest.

"Well, we've had a lot of work to do. Of course. But yes, we did manage to explore a lot of the house I hadn't yet seen."

Cathair Cuinn was a sprawling residence, with several outbuildings, one of which was a small house in its own right where Blaize had stayed when she'd first arrived. Cuinn, Tierra and Adam had quarters of their own which had everything they needed – living area, kitchen, bedroom and work space, though each was decorated quite differently. There were guest quarters with the same, and other simpler rooms with bathrooms. Many of them were closed up, but the house could easily accommodate a large number of people. Tierra wondered, not for the first time if Cuinn had considered bringing more students here to teach, not simply in a Maven-Adherent role, but more like his day job as a Professor at Vancouver University, from which he was currently on sabbatical. Having decided to opt out of his Guild for a while, perhaps he'd thought one day he'd want to offer something and would need the facilities to do so.

"I'll help you with getting a room ready for Ai, ok?" said Blaize. "Don't do it without me. I'm sure you have your own work to catch up on, and you do a lot more than your share around here."

Disconcerted, Tierra frowned. Had Fintan said something? "I don't mind looking after the house. I enjoy it. And I can't help with the prophecies the way you and Cuinn can. It's what I can contribute."

"Hmm. You contribute in lots of ways, Tierra. It doesn't mean you have to be everyone's maid."

At supper a few hours later, Tierra and Fintan explained to Cuinn and Blaize what had happened in Vancouver.

The kitchen was cozy in the evening dark, the lamps were lit and the four of them were sitting around the sturdy wooden kitchen table together. Tierra felt able to relax for the first time in days. Cuinn opened another bottle of wine, and filled their glasses. "A night off for all of us. We deserve it."

He looked a little hollow around the eyes, but not nearly as bad as he had before Blaize had entered his life. She had managed to heal some of his old wounds, but he still carried the weight of the world on his shoulders.

The three men in Tierra's life – Cuinn, Adam and Fintan – were a study in contrasts. Cuinn was cerebral, conceptual, and scholarly. Adam was the opposite – not that he wasn't highly intelligent, more that he channeled his intelligence into a pragmatic, practical outlook that aimed to get the job done.

Where did Fintan fit? He was practical like Adam. A Warrior, so he'd have to be. He had the air element too, which meant he was also conceptual. He liked ideas, that was for sure. Though he didn't tend to stay serious in a discussion for long. She loved his mischievous side.

"When's Adam due home?" she asked. "Do you know why they needed him?"

Cuinn shook his head. "He knows you're both here though, so he wanted to try and come back within a couple of days."

"What are our next steps?" said Blaize.

"We need to follow the paper trail on the house," said Fintan. "Tierra's going to contact the Anahata Guild to see if she can find out who the victim in the house was."

Cuinn nodded. "Sounds good."

"What's the latest with the research?" said Fintan.

"The only new sliver of prophecy we have is: *The one you find at first shall not be the one you ultimately seek.*" Cuinn shrugged. "I don't think it adds much – apart from confirming that Indigo is only the tip of the iceberg."

Blaize reached out a hand and put it over Cuinn's slender fingers, which tapped the table, restless. "Confirmation is still useful, especially when it's as hard won as it is."

Cuinn's nod was a little stiff, but he thawed as she wrapped her fingers around his, lifted his hand to her lips and kissed it.

"We've found a few possible avenues in the prophecy books," he continued, "but nothing that we've been able to pinpoint with any certainty. We're pursuing the Archetypes, as we said the other day – Warrior, Sage, Healer and so on. And the stones. Though they're considered a myth by most."

"I could help more if I was allowed to dreamwalk on my own," said Blaize, wrinkling her nose.

"You need to strengthen your Haven first," said Cuinn. "It needs to be as real and as solid as this house before you can start wandering off. You need to be much more strongly tethered."

"I know, I know." Blaize turned to Fintan and Tierra, rolling her eyes. "I have training wheels on."

Cuinn opened his mouth to speak again, but stopped when he saw she was smiling. "I just want to keep you safe."

"And I, you."

Tierra looked down, moisture in her eyes at this intimate moment. There was an ache inside her chest. Would she ever have that? Perhaps now she had let go of this Fintan nonsense, she could. Her mouth twisted. She took a breath and raised her gaze to find Fintan staring at her in a peculiar way. She broke eye contact quickly and looked at the floor.

The conversation moved on. Eventually they got round to Ai.

"She needs a home, and some education before we find her a Maven," said Tierra. "I'm going to talk to Anahata Guild about that. In the meantime, we have a flexible household, with energetics in and out that she can learn from, and an extensive library. I want her here."

"I'm happy to teach her combat and self-defense," said Blaize.

"Okay,' said Cuinn, rubbing his chin. "We need to find out more about her parents too. Ask Anahata about that. Someone out there must have missed her. It worries me that she fell through the cracks. It shouldn't be possible."

Tierra was grateful for her family, then. That they would be open to taking in a child they didn't know, on Tierra's say so.

"Given all the things we want to ask them, you'd have better luck visiting the Guild in person," said Fintan.

"What, go to Egypt?" Tierra was taken aback. She hadn't left Canada for years. Actually, decades.

"Why not?" said Fintan.

"I can't leave Cuinn and Blaize again."

"Sure you can." said Blaize. "We're working on the prophecies – Cuinn barely lets me out of the work rooms. We can feed ourselves. And you can work on your column anywhere, right?"

"But – but I like it at home." Not a great argument, and she flushed, realizing she sounded like a child. But she felt like she'd been brave. Done her travels. Got out of the rut. Surely now she could stay at home a little while?

Fintan put a hand on her shoulder. "Maybe I can come with you, before I head back to the office."

'There's no need for that." His palm was distractingly hot on her shoulder, and she shrugged it off. "We're spread thin enough as it is."

"I don't mind,' said Fintan. "It might be fun. I haven't been to Anahata HQ for a long time. It's probably time I reminded them I still exist."

"I'm sure they haven't forgotten you, Fintan," Cuinn's lips quirked. "Didn't you nearly burn the place down at some point?"

"I was much younger then," said Fintan, affronted. "By several hundred years. I'm sure most of them have forgotten that."

"I heard that they warn young Anahata energetics about you as part of their training – and that they're especially wary of anyone who is a Manipura-Anahata," Blaize snickered.

Fintan threw a balled-up serviette at Blaize, who ducked and laughed. "Rumors aren't facts."

"That's settled then,' said Cuinn. "Tierra and Fintan, you leave tomorrow."

"But, what about Ai? What if she comes early? Who will take care of her?" Tierra protested.

"I think we can manage," Cuinn said, somewhat dryly.

"But she won't know you," Tierra said. What if Ai bolted before Tierra got back?

"You won't be gone long. Fintan said she wasn't likely to be here for at least a week, right?" Blaize said, with a brief frown at Cuinn, in a more gentle tone. "We'll let you know if she turns up. And we can operate the stove and the washing machine. It'll be okay."

Tierra's gut swirled and she bit her lip. It didn't feel okay. And if she admitted it, it wasn't only Ai she was worried about. Tierra herself could do with time at home to regroup. She wasn't ready to be out in the world again so soon.

But she was the one who had wanted to contribute. So it didn't look like she was going to have much choice. It was time to step up.

The flight to Cairo was straightforward, if long. Tierra insisted on driving from the airport to the Guild, citing Fintan's tendency to road rage when he was in Egypt.

He'd protested, but it was true he'd learned to drive early in the 20th century when there weren't many cars on the road. He loved driving places like Canada, where the traffic was orderly, but in Egypt the roads were obscenely busy, slow-moving collisions were an everyday occurrence, and every car they saw bore dents and scrapes. He had no problem dealing with this by yelling out of the window and beeping like every other driver on the road here, but Tierra had steadfastly refused to let him.

She rolled her shoulders and drove them out of the crowded airport. She seemed more relaxed in the car than she had in the airport, where the throng of people had jostled her petite frame. He'd tried to put himself between her and them when he could. Her passport worked fine – she'd kept her formal human-style identity current, as energetics were taught growing up. Vishudha Guild, responsible for communications, had a department responsible for keeping the papers of energetics from giving away their secrets. In the age of surveillance their longevity could be harder to manage, but when you could create perfect copies of country documents, you could 'belong' to any country, and be any age.

Dust covered many of the cars they passed, the close desert heat in the 90s as the long hot Egyptian summer began. The washed out yellows of the buildings were familiar to him, but there were many more structures than when he was here last.

When the Guild had re-located near Memphis, after the destruction of Atlantis and at the height of the Ancient Egyptian civilization more than four thousand years ago, the plains had been spacious and bare, with plenty of room for the energetics of air. Since then Anahata had moved buildings a number of times, but had stayed in the region, despite political and religious turmoil and an increasing population. The energetics had watched with dry amusement the excavations of the so-called Egyptologists of the early nineteenth century. They could have shed some light on a number of mysteries, had it not been their rule by then not to interfere with human progress.

He glanced back at Tierra's profile. He was glad to spend more time alone with her.

He'd realized that it was rare that it was just the two of them. Usually someone else was around. Tierra was most often at the heart of the household, visitors gravitating towards her. She always seemed to have plenty of time for everyone, despite her job.

It was because, he mused, she made everyone feel as if they were the center of the universe.

Whoever she talked to felt cleverer, nicer and more important just by the way she interacted with them.

She was humming to herself in between grumbles. She'd chosen the music for their trip. A mix of rock ballads, not what he'd choose himself, but he'd found himself singing along to an ancient Bon Jovi track, so he couldn't really complain.

He snuck another glance at her. Her focus was on the road, her speed not exactly sedate, but just a whisper over the limit. She navigated the traffic like a pro.

Her hair curled over her shoulders, loose today. He liked it loose. Its waves set off her body's soft curves. Her eyes were ahead. He'd obviously been staring at her too long when her glance shifted off the road and onto him, eyes narrowing. "What?"

"Nothing," he said, easily. "Just thinking."

"Hmph. That'll be the day." But she smiled as she said it, and her attention went back to the road.

An hour later they reached the Guild headquarters, the sprawling buildings in front of them. It was the hottest part of the day, and the sun baked the sandy ground. The buildings looked no different from other buildings in the area — the flat, middle-eastern style, in a pale yellow, a little off-color from age. Energetics didn't draw attention to themselves. The humans who lived in this area thought it was some kind of research institution, anonymous and boring.

The Anahata Minor Guilds were also housed in the midst of big cities. There were many Rogue Rehab Centers run by the Guild too, each one a hospital of sorts for energetics, as well as what might be considered a jail in human terms.

That wasn't how energetics thought. They weren't interested in retribution. Energetics who acted against the good of society — Rogues — were taken to a Rehab Center, assessed, and wherever possible, rehabilitated.

It was rare for an energetic to act against the greater good. Energetics didn't have the same kind of societal problems that existed in the human world. That was one of the reasons that Ai's case of abandonment had shocked Fintan and Tierra so much.

In the main, energetics were brought up in a strong family unit. The birth rate for energetics was low, their population barely maintaining over the millennia. Children were wanted and brought up knowing their heritage.

Fintan and Tierra stretched and got out of the car, Fintan grabbing their bags. Stepping through the front door was an odd experience. It had been a long time.

Tierra and Fintan were both auxiliary Anahatas, but still trained as healers. They used these skills in different capacities – Fintan often did double duty in his unit as the unit medic. Tierra had worked for a few periods over the years with different Rehabilitation Centers, and was currently on call for emergencies at the center off the coast of British Columbia where their friend Cara worked.

Energetics weren't exactly considered second class citizens at their auxiliary Guild, but it was definitely easier asking for favors at the Guild of your dominant energy. Always hard to put your finger on, perhaps it was just more the energetic resonance – by definition, an energetic had a stronger resonance with the energy of their dominant Chakra. Fintan wasn't sure. All he knew was that sometimes, all the love and peace of the Anahata Guild was a bit much for his Manipura side. And some bad experiences here in the past meant he didn't have much love for this place.

It had seemed like a good idea to come with Tierra, a way to protect her, but he was less sure now.

Tierra seemed comfortable enough as they checked in and headed to their rooms. "Don't look so grim. I set us up an appointment with a friend, Jebediah. He's been here a few decades, and has a good handle on who's working with whom. He'll give us somewhere to start."

"Lunch first?" he said. An army marched on its stomach, after all.

She laughed again at the hopeful look in his eyes. "Yes, lunch first. Who knows who we might meet in the hall."

They had a two-bedroom suite with a living room between the bedrooms. Tierra had perked up when she'd seen they had a bathroom each.

Fintan threw his duffel in his room, and himself onto the sofa. "Ready."

Tierra, who was opening all the drawers and cupboards, gave a tut of annoyance, and said "You'll just have to wait. I want to freshen up. Didn't that plane journey tire you out at all?"

"I'm used to it. A lot of traveling. You need more practise," he said, and flicked on the television. He found a sports channel after a bit of hopping around, and slouched down on the sofa to watch two Asian nations play some kind of handball.

14

Tierra showered, pulled on a blue summer dress patterned with tiny woven daisies, added sandals, and was ready to go. When she went back into their living area, Fintan was in exactly the same place she'd left him.

They walked down the hallways out of the accommodation area to the main living quarters. Anything between fifty and one hundred and fifty energetics lived here at any one time, and so the buildings were flexible enough to account for that, with parts that could be shut off or opened up depending on need. Just as at all the other Major Guilds, a large library was housed here, and many of the Guilds' most experienced Masters and Mavens came to share teachings or to learn.

It was easy to tell when they were close to the hall, as the noise level increased. Usually seventy-five percent of the inhabitants of Anahata Guild would come down for meals. People could be heard chattering to each other, with laughter and the clanging of cutlery against plates.

Lunch was a buffet system, with food at the side of the room, and a free table system of long benches, where you could sit with whoever took your fancy. A great deal of networking and swapping of information – and gossip – took place here, and Tierra's gaze ranged over the hall to see if there was anyone she knew.

Well, anyone she knew and wanted to spend an hour with.

She'd lived a surprisingly solitary life in recent years for someone of her energies and nature. She grimaced. It was time to push herself out into the world again. She walked over to the buffet and picked up a tray, handing a second to Fintan. Scooping up cutlery and a napkin, she moved along the buffet table taking small portions of various tasty looking dishes.

She didn't see anyone she knew, so moved to the closest table with spaces and put her tray down. A striking blonde woman already at the table gave her an assessing look. "Hi."

"Do you mind if we join you?" Tierra asked.

The woman nodded slowly. She wore a lightweight cream skirt suit, perfectly pressed. Her face was beautiful in a sharp way, like the glint of sun on a blade. "Be my guest. I won't be long. I'm teaching a class shortly. Have you just arrived?"

"Can you tell?" asked Tierra, self-conscious. The woman was gorgeous, and Tierra wondered if jealousy was the reason she had a sudden chill.

"I don't remember seeing you around." The woman ate a delicate mouthful of salad.

"We've come to use the libraries. It's been a while since I was here." Tierra sat opposite the woman.

"I'm sure it hasn't changed much." She shrugged.

Well, this was awkward. It was rare that Tierra's social skills weren't up to the task, but she wasn't doing well in this interaction. Where was Fintan?

"What are you teaching?" said Tierra.

"A course on weather manipulation."

"Sounds interesting. I'm Tierra, by the way."

The blonde jerked her head in acknowledgement. "I'm Maya. You were one of Jebediah's Adherents, correct?"

"Some time ago, yes." More than a century, in fact.

"He uses you as an example sometimes when he teaches, as one of the stronger auxiliary Masters in Anahata. He said you were 'remarkably balanced', your energies almost as strong as each other." Maya put her palms face up and moved them up and down as if they were weighing scales.

"Maybe you have me mixed up with someone." Tierra frowned. Fintan walked over, his plate laden with food, and at the sight of the woman next to her, stopped.

"Maven Maya." He gave her a short nod.

"Fintan. It's been a long time."

Tierra glanced between them. They knew each other, clearly, but where was the tension coming from? Her stomach clenched with unease. She hated friction. She patted the bench next to her, and he grimaced and slid onto it reluctantly.

"You know each other?" She'd address things head-on.

"We did, a long time ago. Fintan was a student here in one of my previous phases of teaching."

Interesting. To all intents and purposes, Fintan had had a difficult time as a student here, though he didn't talk about it much. Perhaps this woman was a reminder of a different time.

Fintan stuffed a forkful of food in his mouth and gave a short jerk of his head in response to Maya, who responded with an amused eyebrow lift.

"I was saying that Tierra – who appears to be modest as well as talented – is still talked about by Jebediah, in his lectures to new and prospective Mavens."

Heat crept into Tierra's cheeks. There was something in the woman's tone that was almost mocking. Was she…smirking? Okay, this was strange. Tierra wasn't sure she resonated with this woman.

"That sounds like a surprisingly accurate statement." Fintan waved his fork at Tierra's plate. "No need to be embarrassed, T. Eat something."

She picked at her fried rice. Fintan focused on his food. Was Tierra being oversensitive? "We're here to see Jebediah actually. We have a couple of mysteries we think he might be able to help with."

"Oh yes?" Maya finished the last couple of mouthfuls of her salad. "Sounds intriguing. Maybe I can join you all for supper tonight. Get to know you both better."

It wasn't like Tierra could say no, whatever vibe Maya was giving her, and whatever Fintan's odd reaction. The woman was clearly a senior member of the Guild, and she might be helpful in their search even if interpersonally she was difficult.

"Sure," said Tierra, weakly.

"Have a great afternoon." Maya strode off.

"Hmph." The noise escaped Tierra before she could stop it. She waited for the women to get out of earshot, and turned to Fintan. "Who is she?"

Fintan was still shoveling food in his mouth as if they were about to ration it. He shook his head.

Tierra hesitated. Something about the woman was off, but she had nothing concrete to back that up. She'd sound snide if she said anything without something more solid. She gazed into her food, thinking.

"Don't get caught up in the flakey day dreaming they all do around here," commented Fintan.

Tierra looked at him in surprise. "You don't really think that about Anahata do you? It's your auxiliary energy too."

He shrugged. "My Manipura's stronger. I never really fit in here. It's not a big deal."

"Okay. Seems strange, that's all. It's been a long time since you've been here, right?"

"Yep."

"So, give them a chance. It was Caradoc who was the Major Circle member then?"

He nodded.

"I think the culture's changed a lot since Aiko became Guild Leader. Different leadership styles."

"Damn straight," said Fintan. "Maya worked pretty closely with Caradoc."

Caradoc, who had been the Anahata Major circle member for an unusually short time of about a decade, had been more of a broadcast empath than a receiving empath. He was a highly skilled healer, but he had also tended to broadcast his feelings – which because of his auxiliary Manipura, had at times had a hot edge to those around him. *Had Fintan and Caradoc had a run-in of some kind? How was Maya connected?*

"Anyway," said Fintan. "Tell me about Jebediah. I don't think I remember him."

"Um, sure. Probably one of the longest serving Mavens in Anahata I would think. Kind, smart, strong. He's currently the go-to person for new Anahata Mavens, sort of a Maven's Maven. Skilled in both healing and empathy, with great instincts. Sometimes almost too sensitive for his own good – he can read others' emotions like you'd read a book."

Fintan nodded. "And he was yours?"

"Yes. I was lucky, he was a great teacher." She smiled. "Now, my own intuition tells me that you want another helping."

Fintan watched as Tierra knocked on Jebediah's heavy, old-looking door, the nails and studs even darker than the knotted sycamore. It was a door with a lot of character.

Fintan was intrigued to meet Jebediah. Tierra seemed to have a lot of respect for him. Though he'd sounded a bit like a boy band singer, the way she'd described him.

He hoped to the Source that the guy had a sense of humor. That wasn't always – necessarily – the case with Anahata energetics. Fintan wasn't usually a fan.

Tierra had told him that Jebediah had been sequestered in the Anahata headquarters for a long time. After the Second World War, he'd been almost drained by the amount of healing energy that he'd expended, as well as having been surrounded by the horrors of the war, even when it was just in others' minds, for so long.

"A kind of PTSS, we'd call it now," Tierra had said. "He's a lot better than he was, but he's chosen to stay here to keep himself out of the world. He finds other people – intrusive."

After a 'Come in,' Tierra pushed open the door to reveal a large, pleasant room, much lighter and brighter than the door had indicated. A slender, though solid, man was standing next to a desk in the same rich wood as the door. He shook Fintan's hand, and took Tierra in his arms. The man's looks were unconventional – his cheekbones sharp, his eyebrows dark slashes despite hair that was a lighter brown with some bronze hints. His features indicated mixed heritage of some kind, though predominantly Caucasian. It was hard to pin down, but the man was striking, certainly.

They hugged for a long time. Fintan suppressed a twinge of – what, exactly? protectiveness? – as the man's face showed an unalloyed happiness as he held her close. And Fintan could appreciate the man was attractive, and his combination of stability and the intuition that Tierra had told Fintan about was bound to make him a hit with women.

They settled themselves in comfortable chairs that were in the lightest area of the room, in front of several large windows, black lead crisscrossing them. One pane even had ancient-looking stained glass in it, though Fintan couldn't make out any detail. The room was a study in blues and creams, the only dark notes being the door, the desk, and the shelves on which the books were placed. The sofas and chairs were modern, though very much in keeping with the style of the room.

"Tierra. I'm so pleased to see you. It's been a while." Jebediah's voice was deep. *What was his auxiliary energy?*

"It's Svadisthana, Fintan." Jebediah smiled, and Fintan narrowed his eyes. He hadn't sensed the energy of Svadisthana at all. Perhaps it was a weak auxiliary. He didn't love mind readers though.

"I didn't read your mind. There's no Ajna here. Just your emotions. I usually remind people early on in the conversation that this is part of my talent. Not everyone's as comfortable being an open book as Tierra here. It's easier to get it out of the way, rather than accidentally shock you later by answering a question you didn't ask." He kept smiling, but Fintan could sense weariness behind the words, which had clearly been repeated many times.

"It's not an easy gift, for me or the people around me." Jebediah shifted in his chair, his hand resting on his abdomen, but his dark blue eyes were steady. The guy didn't seem to be hero material, but there was something engaging about him, almost like a charisma he was reining in. Fintan wanted to like him, despite the annoying head stuff. Hmm.

Tierra put a hand on Fintan's arm, though whether in support or in warning, Fintan couldn't be sure.

Jebediah offered them a drink, and they got down to business.

"Thank you for seeing us. We have several things we'd appreciate your input on. We've found an unattached energetic, a teenager, in the Vancouver area. She didn't know anything about our world, and she's an Anahata-Ajna.

She's been caught up, peripherally, in a problem that Cuinn's investigating for the Minor Circle." Tierra filled him in, but kept the detail light.

"We want to know which energetics might have been in the Vancouver area about ten to fifteen years ago. Probably a couple with either Anahata or Ajna as their linked energies."

Jebediah was rubbing the multi-hued stubble of reds and browns and blonde on his chin, eyes gazing into the distance as he thought. 'Okay. We can look into that. You can try Records. And I'll have a think as to who was in the northwest of the Americas then. It's not that long ago, someone will know."

Fintan's attention wandered to the room around them. It was a study, so there were a number of books – that was common with most Mavens. It wasn't a role that Fintan had ever sought out himself.

As well as the books, there was evidence that Jebediah had had his lunch at his desk, a laptop propped open and an empty plate beside it. There weren't any photos on the desk, or any evidence that the man had any family himself. The study had a reclusive feel, isolated despite being at the heart of the Guild.

Fintan tuned back into the conversation.

"There is another area we'd like your help with Jeb." Tierra hesitated. "This is – darker."

"Darker than an abandoned child?" Jebediah questioned.

She nodded and reached down and picked up her bag, rummaging through it to pull out an envelope. "Fintan and I tracked a person of interest in one of Fintan's cases to a house in Vancouver. We found a body."

Jebediah's lips thinned, but his voice was gentle, a rumble in the hole left by the words. "I'm sorry, Tierra, love."

Her head made a shallow acknowledgement. "I did a reading of the body."

Before she could go on, Jebediah leaned forward, his brow creased. "And I'm sorry again. What did you find?"

"She was an Anahata-Ajna mix, just like Ai. That's how we met Ai, actually. She'd also been to the house, but ran before anything happened."

"Did you get a reading on how the girl died?" Jebediah asked.

"She was drained."

There was no shock on the man's face, just a deep sadness, the lines on his face becoming even more pronounced. Fintan wondered just what the man had seen and endured for this to be his reaction to such a violation of energetic law. Perhaps it was better not to know.

"We were hoping you might be able to help us find out who she was." She hesitated again. "I have her picture, and I hoped you'd take a look for us."

They stared at each other for a long moment. "I will, of course. But I need to recharge my energies first. Tomorrow? You can talk to others and search in the records in the meantime for Ai's origins."

Tierra nodded. "Thank you, Jeb. I really appreciate it. I wouldn't ask if I – if we – didn't think it was important."

"I know." The words were simple, the emotions complex. *I'm missing something.*

15

"Blaize had a great idea." Cuinn's voice came over Tierra's cellphone's speaker, tinny and far-away.

Fintan and Tierra were back in their suite, sitting at either end of the sofa. A lazy breeze blew through the open wooden shutters. They had both been around heat enough in their lives to be comfortable without air conditioning. Fintan was sprawled out once again, and took up at least two thirds of the long, comfortable piece of furniture. Tierra sat with her arms around her knees, chin resting on those same knees. Fintan tossed an apple in one hand.

She was trying to focus on the conversation, but she was still thinking about Jebediah, and how he seemed so much more muted than before. She knew he still had an injury, sustained in the war, something that she didn't know much about but seemed to still be there, decades later. The war had affected them all, she thought. They'd paid a high price to help the humans.

"What idea?" Fintan prompted, when Cuinn's excited voice didn't continue, clearly expecting some reaction. "Tell us and we'll get excited, I promise."

"We've been working on sharing mental images. Blaize isn't quite up to sharing words with anyone apart from me yet, but she's able to send a picture to someone she's close to and resonates well with, as long as they're physically close. She's a fast learner." His tone was animated.

"So is it just the fact that Blaize is amazing that we're pleased about, or is there something more?" Fintan's voice was lazy. He took a bite of his apple.

"No, no, that's not it. I mean, you should be, because she's brilliant –" that was all pride "– but she had an idea about how we could use it. We've seen the face of another energetic in the ether, and I don't recognise him. Blaize suggested she could share the image with Nixie and Nixie could draw it. That way, we can show it to people, and we don't have to just rely on my own memories."

Nixie was Blaize's best friend, living in Thailand. Tierra hadn't met her in person, but she seemed to be a fun, vibrant personality who didn't take life too seriously, quite the contrast to Blaize's confident intensity.

"Great idea," Tierra enthused. "The more visuals you can get of everything in the prophecy dreams the better. You never know what detail one of us might spot. Don't just draw faces, do every aspect."

Fintan nodded. "Definitely."

"How are things at your end?" said Cuinn.

They shared their plan to work with Jeb the next day, and to visit the Records department again, which so far had yielded nothing, but there were many more relevant Records to review. They were likely to spend another couple of days in the Guild.

"I don't need you to be here," Tierra pointed out, when Cuinn had signed off. "I'm fine on my own. Jebediah can help if there's anything I need."

"It looked like he was the one that needed help," said Fintan. "What's the deal with him and the photo? Why did he need to recharge? Is his energy really that weak?"

Tierra's eyebrows rose. "Not at all. Did I not explain?"

"Explain what?"

"His gift."

"I thought his gift was mind-reading, or whatever it was."

Tierra shook her head as she got up and put the kettle on. "No. I mean, yes, but he has more Anahata gifts than that." She took out two white mugs from a small cupboard underneath the kettle. "He's a sensitive, and able to do psychometry."

"He can read objects?" Fintan crunched the last bite of the apple and tossed the core at the garbage in the corner. It hit the back of the container and dropped in with a thunk.

"Yes. He needs to touch, then he can read them."

"We only have a photo. He can't read that, surely?"

"He can, if someone who was there when the photo was taken is with him. So, us."

"That's extremely unusual." Fintan frowned.

"Yes, it is." She poured the water into two cups. "And it takes a great deal of energy to read from a photograph. And the kind of photograph we're

372

asking him to read from? He wouldn't usually take it on." She sighed. "I wouldn't ask him if I thought there was another way. But we have no idea who she is, or who killed her, and we can't afford to involve the human police at this point, it's too risky. And with the kind of darkness that Cuinn's foreseen? We need to know what we're dealing with."

Her stomach squeezed. Jeb was her friend, and she was asking him to do something that could harm him. At the very least, he'd have the images of the dead girl in his head, to add to the many sad scenes he'd read over the ages. At the worst, they might bring trouble in the form of the prophecy to his door.

Was she being selfish, asking him? Did he have the strength to do this? Was there another way?

Jeb, always more serious but once the sort of man at the center of romance era sagas, had turned into a tragic hero after the war. He considered himself fallen, she knew, and had closed a part of himself off because of that, but his sexuality could be glimpsed in brief moments if you knew where to look. He was a magnetic, even seductive, man who tried to hide that fact as much as possible.

She brought the mugs over to the coffee table where her phone was still resting, and nudged it aside to put them down.

"Thanks." Fintan looked into his cup and back at her. "Peppermint?"

"We had enough caffeine earlier." She ignored his eye roll. Though maybe she was fussing over him some.

"And I didn't get any sense of Svadisthana energy at all. Is he, well, is he ok?"

And that was the heart of the matter.

She settled herself back down on the sofa. "You don't get a sense of Svadisthana? Really?"

Svadisthana, the energy of creativity and sexuality.

"No. Why, you do?"

"Yes. His voice alone…" There was no doubt in her mind about Jeb's sexual energy. It was there. He was holding it in check, dampening it somehow, that she would agree with, but he was a deeply sensual being. "But you're right, his Svadisthana isn't as strong as his Anahata. He hasn't had a partner in many decades. He's moved from eros to agape, he says."

She frowned and wrinkled her nose. "It's all very well to forego sexual love for brotherly love, but I'm not sure it's healthy to shut down part of yourself."

"I see." Fintan studied her face. "Then what are you worried about, T?"

Tierra sighed. "He's such a good man. He's been like a brother to me. I'm scared this reading might hurt him. And he's already injured."

"Injured? How?" Fintan asked.

"I'm not sure. His stomach perhaps? It happened during the war, and it was part of his reason for retreating to the Guild. He needed to recover."

"I'm not sure he has. Is that why he was holding his abdomen?" Fintan said.

"He was?" She felt bad she hadn't noticed.

"Why doesn't he just heal it? Seems odd. Anyway, don't feel guilty for asking him. He's an adult." said Fintan.

"Why do you think I'm feeling guilty?" She flushed. Every time he showed an insight into her thoughts or emotions, it threw her.

"Because you always worry about other people more than yourself. Reading the body took a toll on you, yet you did it." Fintan rolled up to a sitting position, reached out and cupped her cheek. There was comfort in his touch, and she leaned into it, despite telling herself it was a stupid thing to do. "You're not asking Jebediah to do anything that you wouldn't do if you could. And there's probably only a handful of energetics who can even do this."

"I'm aware. But it doesn't mean that I have to accept danger to my friends without regret. I'd feel the same if it was you." No. She'd feel worse. Despite the fact that Fintan was a Warrior, the idea of him in danger made her nauseous. She shuddered.

He slid his hand round to rub her neck. "It's going to be okay. He'll help us, we'll find out who killed this girl, and take them down."

She nodded, her throat tight. She wanted, for a moment, to believe him without argument, to pretend that he was right, and all would be well. He massaged the nape of her neck, and some of the tension seeped away. Her shoulders relaxed.

His words would be comforting – if only she could believe it would be that simple.

Fintan showered, and toweled off roughly. He ran his fingers through his hair, considered it brushed, dismissed the idea of shaving, and pulled out one of the shirts that Tierra had made him pack. It was a pale blue. He scowled. *A very Anahata color.*

Dressed, he left his room. There was no sign of Tierra in the living area of the suite, though the scent of lavender lingered, as Tierra seemed to have brought some of her candles from home. She really knew how to make temporary digs more cozy. He looked at the clock on the TV. They were dining with Jebediah and Maya in a private room shortly.

He was not enthusiastic about eating with Maya. She'd seemed keen to have dinner with them, though he wasn't quite sure why, considering their history. She was attractive in a hard sort of way — all diamond edges and sharp points, but he had no interest in her. At this moment he yearned for something softer. Warmer. He frowned.

Perhaps this prophecy business was taking more of a toll on him than usual.

He texted Adam a quick "What's up? Any news?" and received a typically terse reply. "No. You?" He sent back "Met Jebediah. You didn't tell me he was a hermit. Doing a reading tomorrow. Is he strong enough for this stuff? Health doesn't seem the best. Nothing from Records so far."

He looked around the room as he waited for Adam to reply, or Tierra to come out. *Maybe I should call her?* But, no. He'd known Tierra through centuries of women's clothes and fashions, and she wasn't a woman who took ages to get ready. She pampered at times, yes, but she didn't primp.

Sitting down, he flicked on the TV. Fifty-seven channels and nothing on. He switched it off and considered Maya some more. Bitch. They should have said no to her for dinner. They could have been freer with conversation with only Jebediah. Tierra, open-hearted as ever, hadn't wanted to say no.

His phone vibrated. "Jeb's a hero. Tougher than he looks. Deserves to be relaxing on a beach somewhere, not the politics of Anahata."

Fintan raised his eyebrows. That was high praise indeed from Adam, whose idea of tough was very tough indeed. The guy must have some hidden steel in his spine. He'd have to ask Adam about Jebediah next time he and Adam had a beer. Though the likelihood of that happening any time soon wasn't looking that great.

He couldn't figure Jebediah out. Fintan was pretty puzzled why a guy living in the Guild of the Healers had a wound so bad it wasn't healed in over half a century. Something was up there.

The door to Tierra's room opened, and he forgot about Jebediah as Tierra appeared in an elegant green dress that hugged her curves and flattered her petite frame. It also showed a lot more cleavage than usual. The discomfort in his body that had been building since he'd got dressed stretched across his upper back. He stood and rolled his shoulders.

"That's a nice dress." It really was. These days he only saw Tierra in casual clothes. It was strange how a dress could change her appearance so much. She was so elegant. But he wasn't sure if he liked it, if it was his Tierra that was standing there. She looked like someone new. Someone different. Someone who might not be interested in a friend like Fintan, who was casual down to the very bone. Why had she dressed like that? Was it for Jebediah? He wished he'd shaved after all.

She was scowling. "Don't be sarcastic."

"I wasn't." He kept his tone mild, and hid his alarm at the idea of Tierra changing and growing away from him. "It's a nice dress. And you look nice."

"Hmmph." Tierra muttered as she walked across the room to open the door. "Okay. Let's go down. Nicely."

He raised his eyebrows as he got up and followed her out. What was that about? "Hey, what about me? Don't you think I look nice? We men like to be appreciated too, you know."

And to his surprise, he found he was only half-joking.

Nice. Pah. Tierra hated herself for bothering to dress up. She'd made the effort knowing that if she didn't, Maya would hopelessly outclass her. Maya's casual daytime dress was more stylish than Tierra's evening wear, for Source's sake.

And Fintan's response was that she looked nice. Nice! Who wanted to look nice? She wanted to look sexy, like a goddess. A movie star. She bet Maya didn't look 'nice'.

Screw nice.

They passed through corridors and halls until they reached the main dining hall. Tierra headed to one of the rooms off to the side. It was a paneled, high-ceilinged room that spoke of age and history. Jebediah and Maya were already there, chatting in low voices. Jebediah's seductive rumble was easy to place, even before they got to the room.

She gave Jebediah a quick hug, unable to resist the love he radiated. It was always so safe, being held by him, and it melted a little of the spikiness she'd been feeling. Though she'd seen many women become infatuated with him, she'd never had any romantic or sexual feelings about him — he was like a brother to her. She'd been grateful for that, as she'd seen energetics get distracted by his magnetism in the past. That would have made it hard for Tierra to be his Adherent.

He'd been there for her to support her through the growth and development of her auxiliary Chakra, as it had grown almost as powerful as her Muladhara. She'd been scared of her own power. She hadn't the maturity then, she thought, to be a powerful enough vessel for the energies. They'd spent eight years together as she'd developed not only her power, but her confidence. It had been towards the end of the Spanish Empire, and she had travelled with Jeb around what was now Mexico, where the culture of Europe mixed with the ruins of the Aztecs and other native peoples of the Americas.

Tierra herself had been from a family of energetics who had left Egypt, where the energetics had based themselves immediately after the destruction of their home, Atlantis, in 200BC, to live in the city of Teotihuacan. Like many energetic families, the occasional mixing with humans — generally not approved of, but not forbidden – had given rise to her family's eventual Hispanic appearance.

The travel, meeting so many new people, keeping their powers hidden while still using them to do the good needed to maintain the region's balance – especially after some of the horrors the Spanish inflicted on the native people – had built her experience and confidence. Tierra's shoulders drooped. Somehow, since the 1940s, she had lost some of that confidence. She frowned as she walked to her chair. Well, she was traveling again now. It was time to get it back.

They sat at the formally laid table. Maya wore a pair of hip hugging pants that flowed around her legs as they fell from the waist. They had a slit down one side that showed glimpses of pale flesh as she moved. She topped that with a turquoise corset that put her breasts front and center. It was an unconventional and striking outfit, especially against the simpler decor of tile floor and wooden furniture.

"What are we having?" Tierra asked.

"Pumpkin soup, Eggplant couscous, summer pudding for dessert. Or cheese. As you like," said Jebediah.

"I ordered white wine," said Maya.

Anahata's Major Guild had a small core of permanent staff to keep up with the ever-changing group of energetics who moved in and out. Many energetics took a turn to help out in their Major Guild, and Anahata was no different. Energetics who came to take courses here would take their turn in the kitchens, or cleaning up. Anahata energetics like Tierra, with earth as their auxiliary, tended to enjoy roles cooking, cleaning and serving best.

So the staff wasn't as large as one might expect. This evening, a dark haired young male energetic entered, carrying their soup on a tray. His eyes widened slightly as he caught sight of Maya.

Jebediah greeted him by name, speaking Arabic. "Good evening, Darrell. How are you today?"

Speaking many languages was one of the side benefits of living a long life. Tierra had learned Arabic herself while studying in Egypt.

"I'm good, Maven Jebediah." Darrell rested the edge of the tray on the table as he took their plates off one by one. The tray only shook a little. Tierra helped him by passing Fintan a bowl, and taking one for herself. The boy sent her a grateful look.

"Have you been practicing your defenses?"

The boy nodded, his dark eyes wide. "Yes, Maven."

"Well done. Let me know if you have any trouble with it."

The boy nodded again and hurried out of door.

"Sweet," Maya drawled, switching them back to English.

What was up with her? She was supposed to be a teacher here. Was that how she interacted with her students? Tierra was starting not to like this woman. Tierra bent to take a mouthful of her soup to hide her annoyance.

"He's a good lad," said Jebediah. "Shows promise. We're experimenting with new pre-Maven-Adherent schooling now. They come and spend time here, to be exposed to other Anahata energetics, and we teach them some basics."

He sighed. "The nature of Anahata is that many of them are so sensitive. And I don't mean with a capital S, just empathic to the point that they take on other people's feelings and issues, and worry so much. We try to build them up before they start working with a Maven. It's also enabling me to place Mavens and Adherents together in a more matched way. While matching to a Maven used to be haphazard, and based on who was local, or who the parents knew, now we focus more on matching personalities."

Tierra was impressed. "That sounds great. Not everyone is as lucky as I was. And it's a long time to spend with someone who rubs you the wrong way, for the Maven and Adherent."

Jeb nodded. "It is. It's still experimental, but it seems to be working."

"Aren't you exposing them to other people's feelings more by putting them in this environment?" Fintan questioned.

"To some degree. But it's contained. We keep them in small classes — there aren't huge numbers of energetics who are ready for the Guild each year. They've all completed normal human schooling at least, that's a prerequisite. That means a little of the tumult of adolescence has passed. We encourage them to go to human university too, if they have the aptitude. Gone are the days when energetics could get better schooling from their Mavens than the human system."

"Anahata is a powerful energy," commented Maya. "But don't you think it's odd that in the last hundred years or so we've seen more Anahata energetics' energy twisted and turn Rogue than almost any other energy?"

Fintan raised his eyebrows. "Really? I hadn't come across that statistic."

"Ask Adam. Or Blaize Blackfire," said Maya. "I heard she was training with Cuinn these days, is that correct? She'd know about the twisting of Anahata with what her father did."

How did the woman manage to make it sound like Blaize's fault? Tierra bristled.

Jebediah studied Maya. "You're right. I've been researching the phenomenon, and trying to understand it more clearly. We have a team of Healers here working on the problem of how Rogues are created, how they're formed."

"I thought we knew how they were formed?" said Fintan. "Their energy twists and becomes the opposite of itself. Anahata, love, becomes jealousy, or hatred. Manipura becomes anger or pride. Muladhara becomes lethargy, exhaustion, laziness. And so on."

He ticked them off on his fingers.

"The Rehab Centers report that some of the Rogues, especially recently, have been very strong," said Maya. "What do you think of the theory that they're simply harnessing others' negative emotions for their energy? And that they're doing those from whom they take them a favor?"

Tierra's spoon hovered in mid-air, her eyes widening. She couldn't believe her ears. Anahatas were trained to bring balance, but that didn't mean stealing emotions. It might feel hard at times, but everyone had the right to feel both sides of emotion, positive and negative, and be in balance themselves. Negative emotions could get out of control, but they didn't need removing, the individual needed training in how to bring that pain and discomfort back into balance. What Maya had suggested, that what Rogues did was acceptable, was…unthinkable.

Jebediah leaned back, one hand spread on the table. "I think, Maya, that it's a damaging idea, spread by a few heretics who want to cause trouble."

"For some energetics, harnessing negative emotions can mean they are more potent though? And surely it's a way of rebalancing energies, by siphoning some off?" Maya persisted, one perfect eyebrow arched.

Fintan had finished his soup, and studied Maya, his head to the side. Tierra considered him in turn. Did he think Maya was attractive? Well, she was attractive, clearly. Rather, was he attracted to her? Tierra's nose wrinkled.

"Individuals as well as the earth need to be in balance. But they have to find that harmony themselves. We can help them, but the answer comes from inside, not outside," said Jeb. He didn't waver, and was as polite as ever – though perhaps firmer – and he watched Maya carefully. Despite Tierra's unease – and disgust – at the topic, she was glad to see him braced.

Maya laughed, bright and quick, the sound more like breaking glass than bells to Tierra's ears. "I'm playing devil's advocate, of course. But it's always good to know what the man at the top thinks, so I can refute any misguided students who come to me with thoughts on it."

Jebediah's eyes narrowed. "Have any? And did you mention it to Aiko?"

Aiko was the head of Anahata. Maya shook her head. "Just being prepared."

There was a taut silence that stretched out, almost unbearably long. What was the relationship between Jebediah and Maya? And who was she? Did she believe any of the dangerous ideas she'd proposed? Tierra found herself twisting her napkin in her lap. The benefit of not spending much time with people was a lack of conflict in her life. She'd never enjoyed it, unlike more fiery Manipuras, who enjoyed nothing more than a good, rousing argument. Perhaps Maya was Anahata-Manipura?

Fintan caught her eye, and cocked his head. Checking on her. She gave him a weak smile. He pressed his lips together.

"So what's your research about, Jebediah?" said Fintan.

"There's still much to learn about Rogues," said Jeb. "For example, why do some go Rogue, and not others – what triggers it? Are some energetics more susceptible? Does energy, family history, environment, or any other factor make a difference? These are just some of the questions we're exploring."

"That sounds fascinating and useful. How far have you got?" Tierra pushed away the rest of her soup, though what she had eaten had been delicious. This conversation was putting a damper on her appetite.

"The Guilds didn't like sharing their records. Still don't, really. Anahata, as the energetics' healers, has a lot of data, but we need the Guilds to share their records more openly. While most Rogues come through a Rehab Center, not all do. When we get the data, we enter it into a database. Everything we know about Rogues goes in there, each individual case."

Maya toyed with her wine glass. "Will you share your results?"

"Of course. We're nowhere near that yet though. Maya, what are you working on at the moment?"

Tierra tuned out Maya's answer. The other woman had expressed some strange ideas, and Tierra wasn't quite sure how she felt about them all.

16

When they arrived at Jebediah's room in the morning, Tierra's stomach was queasy. Her memories of him were colored by a time when his psyche was strong, her role model and mentor.

She hadn't been involved in his rescue, or helping him to recuperate after the war, but she'd heard about it. A little from him, a lot from others. His mind was stronger than it had been then, but there was still a sense of precariousness, as if he could snap at any moment.

She just had to hope his strength was like spider silk, and could hold more than its own weight.

She knocked at the door.

"Come in," the low voice said.

They entered, and this time, Jebediah didn't immediately turn to them. He was looking out of the windows, and Tierra could see only the back of his head. A sadness surrounded him.

"Are you ok?" Tierra kept her own voice soft.

He turned, and there was a moment when he seemed to expect someone else. He shook himself with a visible effort, and smiled, though it was a pale imitation of what they'd seen the night before.

"I'm fine. I didn't sleep well. Let's do what you came to do. The sooner I help you, the sooner you can get moving on the case.

Tierra hesitated. "We could try someone else. Or come back another day."

He shook his head, and held out a hand. "No. Give me the photo."

"You don't want to sit down?" Fintan said.

"Would it make you more comfortable if I did?"

"It would, actually. I understand it's an intense emotional experience from your perspective." Fintan gestured at the seats they'd sat in the day before. "We'll join you. Do you need anything?"

"No." He moved across the room to the armchair that seemed to have seen the most use, and he seated himself with neat, efficient movements, though he winced almost imperceptibly as he did so. It seemed that Fintan was right, and his injury was still somehow active.

He held out his hand again.

Tierra dug into her bag for the photo. She held onto the envelope for a few seconds longer, reluctant now to hand it over. Were the answers to the girl's death worth impacting Jebediah's sanity and health? Was that what she was risking?

Jeb's gaze was implacable. His eyes were deep blue pools that showed nothing of what he was feeling. He was good at shielding his own emotions from others. You couldn't work in a place like this and broadcast without inviting trouble – you only needed to look at what happened with Caradoc's leadership of the Guild to know that.

She took a breath. And handed the envelope over.

The silence in the room was tangible. Jebediah's fingers closed around the innocuous flat white rectangle, and he sat back in his chair, holding it in his lap. He didn't need to hold it, any skin contact would do. It was why she'd kept it in her bag, to avoid any chance happening.

She'd tried to understand it once, how his gift worked – how it could work – but he'd talked about energetic resonance echoes, and then eventually admitted that it wasn't as clear as it was with objects, where the energetic imprint was still held within the object, in the same way a holograph held every piece of information about the whole picture within every single aspect of that picture.

Today, she didn't need to know how it worked, she just needed it to work.

Jeb was sitting in the chair, and he slowly pulled the photo of the dead girl from its protective wrapper. He let the envelope float to the floor, and held the photo loosely in his fingers, his eyes closed. His eyelids fluttered rapidly without opening, as if he was watching a film on the inside of his eyelids. She and Fintan watched intensely, monitoring his vital signs.

He paled steadily, sweat dewing on the stubble on his upper lip. After a few more minutes, a tear began to form at the corner of his left eye. It beaded, slowly gathering weight, until after what seemed like an aeon, it trailed slowly down his face, slowing its pace when it reached the stubble on his cheek.

Tierra itched to comfort him.

She could see Jeb's thready pulse. His systems were performing as normal, and he seemed to be experiencing more of an emotional, than physical, impact.

After about five minutes he froze for a long moment, and then, without Jeb visibly moving, the photo slipped from his fingers. It caught an updraft for a second, and seemed to hover in the air, the girl's face upturned, pasty and staring.

Tierra almost reached for it, but she knew not to disturb Jeb in this processing stage. He needed time to make sense of the emotions and impressions that the photo had given him.

To her surprise Fintan reached out, and took her hand in his. His larger hand folded over hers in a warm, firm grip that spoke volumes. She nearly burst into tears. She was glad he was here.

After many more long minutes, Jeb spoke without opening his eyes. They had agreed with him that they'd record what he said, and Fintan held his phone ready on his lap to start recording. At Tierra's look, he tapped the button for record.

"They met by chance, I think. She knew him, a family friend, perhaps. An older energetic male. There was no sense of threat at first. A little awe, perhaps, or at least respect."

Jeb's voice was almost inaudible. He gained force as he got the first couple of sentences out, and Fintan relaxed back with the phone, which he'd been holding out to catch the words.

"He took her for a hot drink. The feeling is safe. He asked her back to his home. She agreed. She still felt safe. And honored."

Neither Tierra nor Fintan said a word, despite long pauses between sentences or phrases.

"At the house – the house where this photo was taken, as she never left that house again – she feels uneasy. Uncomfortable. Not scared, not yet.

"There's another young woman there. Our girl's confused. I'm not sure why. She's disturbed by the girl. She also feels, I think, the sort of anxiety-fear-respect you get from a less popular adolescent when a more popular student comes along. Intimidation perhaps.

"I can't tell the timelines on all this. But quite soon after the other young woman comes along there's a great deal of fear. It's sudden. Something happened. Something that burst open our girl's feelings of safety, and security. Her bubble of trust is not just burst, it's exploded.

"There was physical violence."

There was another longer pause. The color had not yet returned to Jeb's cheeks, and his deep, usually melodic voice had become flat in the telling.

Tierra realized she was holding her breath. She opened her mouth slightly and released it, the warm air rasping like a saw inside her head.

Nothing else moved in the room.

"After this, fear colors every other emotion. It has peaks and valleys, but it's always there. She didn't live another moment of that too-short life without fear."

A dust mote floated down in front of Tierra, the sunbeams coming through the windows showing its out of place movement in the quiet stillness of the room.

"The violence, and the fear, were only the start of the girl's torture. You were right. She was drained. Repeatedly, over a long period, by several energetics. Her energy was put into Remnant stones, and also used by individuals. There was a casual violence to the way she was treated.

"Sometimes it's just one of them. Eventually, it's always just one of them. The girl is desperate. Desperate to die."

Another pause. Another tear grew at the corner of Jeb's eye.

"She has barely any resources left, but she seeks a vision, to find some way, anyway, out. Instead, it tells her of her death – and something more. She moves through the emotional spectrum at that point. Anger a little. Until finally, acceptance. She accepts her fate.

"She wants to die on her own terms. There's a feeling of … determination, almost. Though it's faint. So faint. The male comes back, and she says something to him, baits him, and it pushes him over the edge. He takes too much from her. And her final feeling is satisfaction."

His eyes still closed, he bowed his head. "I'm glad it was satisfaction."

Fintan moved his hand with the phone slowly back into his lap. He looked grim, muscles tensed and ready, though there was nothing to fight. He was still holding Tierra's hand, and he squeezed it now, once, before letting go.

Jeb hadn't finished. "When her killers moved the body from the basement, they found she had scratched something on the stone floor underneath her. It said 'Balance and harmony depend on all. 12->6->1.'"

Tierra sat for a moment, wondering why she couldn't see.

Before she realized that her eyes were full of her own tears.

Fintan had been shaken by the session they'd spent with Jebediah. The man was talented. He could be doing so much more than moldering away in this heap.

But seeing the man after the session, barely moving, exhausted, wrung out, he'd understood how much the activity had taken out of him.

Tierra had given him a little earth and air energy, the most healing and nurturing she could draw on. And still, it had barely put color back into his cheeks.

He'd just sat, his head resting on the back of his chair, his hands in his lap, as still as a statue, until they'd left. Tierra had made him a cup of tea before they'd gone, and Fintan suspected she'd also dosed that with healing energy. He hoped to Source the man drank it.

Back in the room, neither was ready to talk. After a short period of this, Fintan was going crazy.

"Come on," he said, tugging her by the hand.

She eyed him. "I don't feel like going out."

"Me neither. But it's that or sit here. And I don't want to sit here either. So let's go out. It'll be good for both of us. This place has huge grounds."

She'd acquiesced, although he thought more because she didn't have the energy to disagree or argue with him than because she'd been persuaded by his argument.

Cairo at this time of year was hot. But Fintan liked that. It also, once they'd walked a little way away from the buildings, had a view.

The huge pyramids dominated the flat desert landscape from any high building or hilly vantage point in Cairo. The heat shimmered in the thin haze of pollution that covered the city in the modern age.

They stuck to the shade, and walked away from the Guild's buildings. Fintan found a bench underneath a huge and ancient sycamore tree, and pushed Tierra, who'd followed him like a zombie, down onto it.

"Sit." She turned her face, that expressive face, up to him, and there was such a depth of grief in her eyes, that he sat next to her and pulled her roughly into his arms. "Tierra."

She crumpled against him. He could smell her delightful musky perfume, and her hair tickled his nostrils. He didn't care. All he wanted to do was to wipe the sadness from her eyes.

What could he say, after all? *Everything will be alright,* was facile. *There there,* seemed meaningless. *I'm sorry,* wasn't quite right either, as it wasn't his fault.

So why do I feel so responsible?

Why did he feel the need to turn the world upside down in his quest to make it alright again for her? He wished, for a moment, that he was a man worthy of her. That he could be someone that Adam and Cuinn would be proud to see their sister and cousin with.

He hugged her more tightly, as her grief turned into wracking, wet sobs that tore from her body. He cursed himself for not being a handkerchief man. Cuinn would have had a handkerchief. And Adam wouldn't have had a handkerchief, but he'd have had something manly that he could turn into one, like a bandana.

After several long minutes, her sobs subsided, and she just lay against his chest, quiet. He could hear her gentle breaths, no longer hitching. She radiated grief.

He tapped into his own healing energy, the energy of air, of Anahata. In his mind, he drew it into a sort of energetic balm. And he sent it to her through his hands and his arms.

She gave a small laugh. She knew what he was doing – after all, she was the mistress of stealth healing herself. She was always sharing healing or soothing energy with her family when they were tired or ill. She'd dose drinks, food, or her own hugs. Rarely did any of them use it on her, mainly because it wasn't necessary.

He could feel the balm settle on her, despite her laugh. She hadn't blocked it, or turned it away. So that was good.

She gradually disengaged from his arms, pulling away and sitting up on her own. Her face was streaked with tears, and her skin was blotchy.

She had never seemed more beautiful to Fintan.

She cared so much. Her depth of empathy for a girl she'd never met. Her ability to open her arms without judgment to the girl Ai. Her open heart and optimism.

He realized he was entranced. But Tierra was looking out at the ancient monuments in the distance, her gaze far away. When she brought it back to his own eyes, he could see that the effects of the last few days had caught up with her.

"So we know more about what happened to her. And how she felt." Tierra's voice was flat. "But we didn't get more than that. He couldn't see who the man was. And we don't know where they took her from. We're no further along."

"We are," he told her, firmly. "We didn't know the stones Cuinn mentioned had a name, Remnant stones, and we can connect Jeb and Cuinn to pool their resources on them. We know that the girl liked and trusted the Leech, and that he's an older energetic, which will hopefully reduce the number of suspects once we know who she is. And we have the numbers."

"Numbers which could mean anything. How do they help us stop this?" Tierra's tone was forlorn. He found the lack of her usual optimism disturbing. He hated to see her like this, and would do almost anything to fix it.

"We will, T, we will." Fintan wasn't just reassuring Tierra, he was doing it for himself. They needed to stop this man and send him to a Rogue Rehabilitation Center. This was a nasty, nasty business.

The cold rage that had been building in Fintan since he first heard of Blaize's kidnapping had blossomed into a true anger. *If we catch the man, and he doesn't make it to a Rehab Center?*

I can live with that.

Elrian, still not strong enough to leave his country house after the psychic and energetic injuries that Indigo's death had caused him, gritted his teeth. He spent a lot of his time in his Haven in the ether these days, venturing out into the wider dreamscape to collect and hoard slivers of the prophecy.

His latest venture had shown him the prophecy had moved forward another fraction – in the wrong direction. His own goal had been pushed a little further away due to the ridiculous pairing of the layabout Fintan and the coddled Tierra, which had somehow become a little more likely.

His eye twitched. He wanted to destroy them all, but he had to be more subtle. He needed them to destroy themselves – or to thwart the prophecy by splitting the five potential couples up before they got anywhere near love.

On the plus side, the impetus was now with Fintan. A guy whose relationship style wasn't exactly long-term, and whose external confidence hid surprising issues around his own worthiness to be with a woman he considered to be of any consequence.

Really, what were the chances of Fintan not screwing it up?

17

An hour or so later there was a knock at Tierra's door. She sat in the armchair by the window, and watched a group of birds dart and wheel in the bright blue sky above. The poor young girl who'd died would never enjoy that freedom. Tierra, on the other hand, had had the freedom to do whatever she wished, but had barely used it the last few decades, shutting herself at home with Cuinn. Guilt weighed on her.

"Come in," she said.

The door opened slowly, and Fintan put his head in. When he saw her in the chair he entered, carrying a sandwich. Tierra's stomach growled. She hated her body at that moment. Her needs seemed so basic and irrelevant compared to the problems they were working on. Fintan's caution in opening the door also irritated her.

"What were you expecting to see?" She tried for amused at the way he'd crept through the door, and instead heard annoyance in her tone. He raised his eyebrows, and she wrinkled her nose. *Gah*. "Sorry. Thanks for the food."

She took it from him, two fresh falafel and hummus wraps that smelled delicious, arranged on a plate, a knife and fork wrapped in a blue cloth napkin with them. "Looks good."

He perched on the bed. "How are you feeling? Did you sleep?"

Of course she hadn't slept. How could she sleep? She shook her head. "I spoke to Cara. I'm already out of synch enough from the travel. A nap would only make it worse."

He leaned towards her. "Are you going to be okay? Really? Can I do anything to help?"

She took a breath, and poked at the lettuce on her plate. She was about as un-alright as she'd been for a long time. And then on top of that, she was annoyed that she wasn't alright. That she couldn't take everything in her stride like the others seemed to. Reliving the young woman's death with Jeb had hit her on several levels – empathising with the poor, betrayed girl, and at the same time feeling for Jebediah who had to experience it so viscerally.

"I think…" She made her words slow and deliberate, "that a lot has happened recently. And I'm out of practice dealing with so much in so little time. And I didn't realize how out of practice I was, and that's upset me."

"Can I do anything?" Fintan looked so downcast, Tierra gave an almost-smile.

"No," she said. "Thanks for trying though. It'll pass. I need to get grounded."

"Do you want to work on your self-defense again? They have a gym here; we could go and train."

She gave a quiet snort. "No. Training's your way to ground, not mine. I might do some work on my column for a bit if you go down to the gym. Then we could hit the archives again to see if we can find anything else on Ai's parents?"

"Okay, that sounds good. I'll be back in ninety minutes or so." He hesitated. "And then maybe we could have dinner, just the two of us? And talk?"

She looked up and met serious cornflower blue eyes. She blushed a little. "Sure."

Fintan sweated in the quiet gym, running on the treadmill. He had never seen Tierra this off-balance. The feel of her tears soaking into his shirt when he held her wouldn't leave him. He upped the intensity of the run, letting the treadmill's computer include more inclines and sprints than usual to run off the worry. It made a small difference, and when he stepped off the machine, panting, he was more himself.

He switched to weights, and thought about their next steps. He ticked them off in his mind. First, they'd go back to the archives, and get to the bottom of the Ai situation.

Then they'd go to the dining hall for supper, and see what other connections they could tap for information on either of the situations. Both were somewhat delicate, but he trusted Tierra's intuition to know who the right people were to share with, and who weren't. And, he winced, they'd probably need to touch on what had happened in Vancouver. It was like a cloud hanging over their interactions, and they needed to get past it.

They also hadn't talked yet about Maya. Fintan disliked her as much as ever. She hadn't changed. Though it had been a while since he'd come up against anyone proposing openly that encouraging the darker side of emotions, or even creating situations to make others feel them, was positive. It was a dangerous philosophy to hold.

He'd put most of those who did into Rehab Centers.

Should he report her views to anyone in Manipura Guild?

No. Jebediah was a smart guy, and Fintan wasn't exactly objective when it came to Maya. Fintan frowned as he finished his last set of reps. Or maybe not. Jeb was smart, but also a bit, well, unworldly. Did he keep some of himself back because of his gifts? Undergoing other people's worst experiences in the way he had with the photo must take a toll.

Perhaps he'd drop by and check in on the guy, and bring up Maya. They could chat about Tierra too, and maybe see if anything else had come to mind about the photo.

Fintan's initial suspicions of Jebediah had been lessened, although Fintan still felt the guy was too good to be true – and that he was somehow deliberately minimizing his Svadisthana energy rather than it being naturally more slight than his Anahata as Jeb claimed. Which made Fintan wary, as he could see no good reason for it. Fintan was a practical person, and he didn't love mysteries.

Hitting the gym – which was quite basic compared to the one at Manipura Guild HQ, and only had one other person working out – had helped his mood. He'd have liked to go a few rounds of hand-to-hand, but there was always a lack of people to spar with in this Guild.

He had a quick shower and strode down to Jebediah's room. He tried not to think about whether Tierra would approve of him visiting Jebediah on his own.

He knocked, and at the acknowledgement, went in.

Jebediah had more color in his cheeks than previously, and greeted him graciously, gesturing at a chair the other side of his desk. "How can I help?"

"I wanted to see how you were doing." Fintan dropped down onto the seat. The study was a calm but cool place.

"I'm fine, thanks. It takes a great deal of my energy, and can be rather unpleasant. But food and rest and meditation all help me get back to normal." He waved a hand.

"It looked it. It was good of you to help us."

"I'd do a lot for Tierra," said Jeb. Fintan believed him. "The situation you've discovered is a nasty one. And Rogues are of particular interest to me at the moment, with my research, so perhaps the awful situation might lead to a new understanding."

"Have you worked much with Leeches?" asked Fintan.

"They make up a big part of the Rogue population, along with unstable energetics." Blaize's father, whose energies had been unstable, had eventually gone mad and killed her mother in a horrible murder-suicide. "But at the moment I'm examining trends, and I haven't dug into any one area in too much detail. Getting the data has been the initial challenge."

"If I can put in a good word at Manipura, I will."

Jebediah stroked his chin. "I might take you up on that at some point. For now, I'm working on the Svadisthana Guild. What does your work at Manipura involve?"

"I'm a troubleshooter for the Circles. So I have credit with some Circle members. I might be able to help out."

Fintan had started as a Warrior, after training. It had seemed simple at the time. There were bad people, and he fought them. His training in Scandinavia had been harsh, but it had suited that time, and that bleak and barren snow-covered land. His own parents had died one tough winter, when even their own magics hadn't been enough to heal them from a pandemic that had swept the region.

He'd taken longer than most to be ready for his Anahata Practitioner test, and had passed by the skin of his teeth. Anahata had left a bad taste in his mouth for more than one reason. It had been another sign to him that he'd been meant to be a Warrior.

He'd gone to Ireland to help support both the Warriors and the Healers there, and the people fighting against the English Crown to retain some semblance of independence. He'd met Cuinn there, and Cuinn's gentle mother and distant father, as well as Marius, Blaize's uncle.

He'd earned his stripes, risen to Master level in Manipura, and learned to help defuse conflict as well as fight in it. He'd fought in wars, and he'd worked alone to hunt down Rogues and dispatch them to Rehab Centers, until finally he'd started working for the Manipura Guild in his current role.

Jebediah nodded. "Do you enjoy it?"

"Life's rarely simple. My role allows me to color outside the lines more than most of my Guild. Though I belong with Manipura." It had been one of the reason he wasn't a Warrior anymore. As he'd got his hands bloody, he'd grown up, he'd understood that it was rarely as easy as good against bad, right against wrong.

"If you don't mind me saying, you strike me as a man who feels like he fits everywhere, and belongs nowhere."

Fintan tried not to bristle, and sat up straighter in his chair. Where had that come from? And who the hell did he think he was? "What are you talking about?"

Jebediah regarded him steadily, leaning back slightly behind the desk. "What's going on with you and Tierra?"

Fintan scowled. This was none of his business. This was just one of the reasons he hated this Guild. Everyone always wanted to talk about their feelings all the time.

"Nothing. And it's going to stay that way, don't worry."

"Why would I worry?" Jebediah made an open handed gesture. "You seem like you would make a good partner for her. Someone who would have her back, and make her laugh. Someone who'd help her be the best version of herself."

"You know nothing about me," stated Fintan, flatly. Heat rose from his belly.

"You think she can do better."

Of course she fucking could! He ground his teeth. The heat grew in his Manipura Chakra and spread through his torso.

Calm. He needed to be calm. He wasn't usually so on edge.

"What's your relationship with Maya?" he asked. Jebediah was a nice enough guy, but he had no right to ask Fintan about his personal life. He would shut that shit down.

Jebediah shrugged. "She and I get along, while not really being close. Why?"

"The ideas she was floating at the table are subversive." Maybe subversive was stretching it a bit, but they were certainly…troubling.

"I'm aware. She's caused some issues in the past. For you, too, I believe?"

Fintan flushed. Okay, so somehow, Jebediah knew. He'd been around Anahata for a while, after all. And it wasn't like it was a secret. His body tingled.

"I'm sorry. I didn't mean to upset you," said Jebediah.

Dammit, the man was too sensitive for both their goods. That was enough.

"It's fine. I don't mean to pry –" okay, maybe he did "– but are you injured?"

Jebediah's calm was ruffled for the first time since Fintan had entered the room. "Yes."

There was an awkward silence. *Okay.* Fintan pushed his chair back with a scrape and stood up. "I need to go meet Tierra. We have more records to go through."

And he needed to be out of this room. He'd had enough of Jebediah, well-meaning though he was, poking at Fintan's sensitive spots, keeping his own strange secrets, locked away in the Guild.

Jebediah nodded. "I'll keep an eye on Maya."

Fintan grunted, and headed toward the door, and tried to ignore the knowing look he saw in Jebediah's eyes.

Still. He was pretty sure the guy was okay on balance, and this thing with his Svadisthana energy, and his injury, whatever was happening, was his business. Surely someone in the Guild could heal him. And there were greater reserves of Svadisthana energy in the guy than he was displaying, Fintan was sure of it. He was suppressing it, whether consciously or unconsciously.

Personally, Fintan couldn't imagine going without the company of a woman for more than a month, let alone decades.

Perhaps that was at the root of Fintan's own issues. His last date had been a while ago. He shrugged. Easy enough to rectify, after this current business was done.

In the meantime, though, he needed to take care of Tierra.

18

"Ready to hit the archives again?" said Fintan. "Another scintillating couple of hours poring over old paper and trying to puzzle out who Ai's parents might have been?"

"I'm ready. How was the gym?" She walked ahead, along the corridors of the Guild, her big purse over her shoulder.

"Fine. Do you really need that bag?" He needled her as they walked towards the archives, trying to get a rise. He knew she liked to be prepared for everything – was always the one with sun cream, a band-aid, a snack or a hairbrush, so he didn't really need to ask, but anything was better than her sadness. He'd take annoyance or irritation directed at him if it bumped her out of this passive despair. "Or are you going to stash all the archives in the library in it so we can do our research in our room?"

She heaved a sigh and rolled her eyes.

Pleased, he darted ahead to open the heavy wooden door to the archives for her with a flourish. If he could make her laugh, perhaps all wasn't lost after all.

True, sometimes his flippant sense of humor got him into trouble, and there were those who couldn't see through his beach-bum looks and relaxed attitude, to the committed Guild member that he was. Though that element of surprise had helped him more than once in fights, where opponents hadn't appreciated his speed and his understanding of human psychology and tactics.

Tierra though, knew him inside and out. And still laughed at his jokes.

A couple of hours later, in the archives, neither of them was laughing. Their research had netted them nothing. As at many of the Guilds, the archives here weren't yet digitized, and consisted of books and papers loosely categorized according to whatever the system of the current Records Keeper was.

They stood at a high table, papers and books of all ages spread across the green felt surface. Both of them wore gloves to protect the records. Tierra's piles, naturally, were neater.

Tierra knew the current Records Keeper – of course she did, she knew everyone, even one of the most introverted energetics in the Guild. He was an Anahata-Ajna of Chinese origin called Feng, who Tierra had somehow managed to build a relationship with when she had studied in the Guild, a century or more ago. Fintan would have to get that story from her sometime. This short, thin man had slender fingers, and a distracted look, although he seemed to know where every record in the library was kept. Which was both a help and a hindrance.

Fintan knew Feng had numerous advanced degrees from Universities in a number of languages, but, delighted by Tierra's presence in the archives, he kept bringing her more and more books and papers, heaping them on her desk with all the adoration of a puppy bringing toys to its mistress's feet. When Tierra smiled and thanked him, the man looked like he'd died and gone to heaven.

Every time he brought something new, Fintan had to suppress a groan. *We'll never get out of here.*

They'd been working their way through the birth records of energetics in North America between fifteen and twenty years ago. And it was taking them a long time. It wasn't that Fintan couldn't do this kind of work. Much as he had found himself enjoying the time with Tierra, he preferred action, and being out in the field.

He was starting to think they should make an appointment to see Aiko, the current Anahata Major Circle member, to get her take on things. He wasn't sure how much the Ajna Circle members, who Cuinn had been updating, had shared with the other Guilds. Or whether Jeb would share details with her.

Fintan really didn't want to get involved with the Anahata leadership. This trip hadn't been as bad as he'd expected, but he preferred to stay off the radar. Unease spiked through him and he sighed.

Tierra had gone to use the bathroom when Feng skittered up to Fintan, his forehead wrinkled, mouth a worried line.

"What's the matter?" Fintan said.

"I think…there's a book missing." Feng hunched his shoulders, stricken. He spoke in a permanently low voice that meant Fintan had to strain to hear him.

"What book?" asked Fintan. There could be a hundred thousand books in the archives, all as dear to Feng as children. Feng had to have some kind of magical affinity with them.

"The one that contains the recorded deaths in North America among the Anahata members in the last twenty years. I thought it would help as it's a shorter list than the births, but I can't find it," said Feng.

"It's been misplaced?" That was annoying. They needed all the information they could get, and on the chance Ai's parents had died in the area, it would have been helpful. The sooner they got out of here, the better. He rolled his head, stretching out his neck.

Feng shifted from foot to foot, agitated. "No, not lost. I don't lose books."

Fintan tried to keep the disbelief from his voice. "Feng, there are a lot of books here. Misplacing one happens. Do you want us to help you look for it?"

"It's not lost," Feng insisted.

"What happened to it then?"

"It's been stolen."

Ah, hell. Feng was quite the neurotic. Maybe Tierra should handle this when she came back. Though she probably didn't need that right now.

"Perhaps another energetic needed to consult it and took it?" Fintan suggested, trying to keep his voice soothing.

"No! We have a system. Everything is checked in and out. And there are wardings around the library. I'd know."

"So it couldn't have been taken from the library?"

Feng shook his head firmly.

Fintan wasn't sure what he was supposed to do. Offer again to help look for it? Feng knew his books, but who would have stolen it? It was more likely it had been taken for a project and not been returned to the right shelf. It was probably in here somewhere. "It will turn up. We have other sources to consult."

In fact, it had given him an idea, which he should have thought of previously. He'd take the names of all those who had been born during the approximate period, and see if he could track them down. If there was anyone they couldn't find, they'd see if the child might be Ai.

When Tierra returned, Fintan shared the idea with her.

"That might work for identifying the dead girl too," she commented. "Just increase the age range by another 5-10 years."

"I'm going to hit the phones. I think the administration here might be able to help with tracking some of the energetics down." Fintan straightened, feeling better with more purpose, and action to pursue. He grabbed their notes of possibles from the table.

"Sure. I'll keep working with the paper records," said Tierra. She bent back over the papers, her glossy hair obscuring her face. He stared at her a moment longer, struck by a feeling he couldn't define, then shook it off and headed back to their suite.

Several hours of phone conversations later, his long list of possibles had been whittled down to four. These were all couples who had had a girl child in the right time period, they had the right mix of energies to produce Ai, and he either couldn't track the couple down, or the couple were dead and he couldn't find out where the child was now.

He checked his watch. Nearly dinner time and there was no sign of Tierra. He'd have to go and haul her out of the library.

Back in the Records he was surprised to see her talking to a solemn-faced Jeb who stood by the table, hand on Tierra's arm.

Fintan hastened towards them. "What's happened?"

"Jeb knows who the dead girl is," said Tierra. She didn't meet his eyes, her shoulders drooping.

"There's a girl who attends Vancouver University, and is missing. I looked up her photo, and it's the girl."

"What did you tell the parents?" Fintan's tone was sharp. Tierra looked at him, eyes wide. He tried to soften his tone. "We didn't recover the body, and we haven't made it known that we found it. If he told them we had her, we'd have some difficult questions to answer."

Jeb nodded. "I know. I didn't speak to them. I'd asked a colleague who deals with such matters to let me know if anyone went missing in the northwest area. When the notification came in, he called me. I didn't say anything about my suspicions, and it took me a while to find her on the system. But when I did, I knew."

"Who is she?" Fintan sat down on the bench that Tierra was perched on, her body tight as a bow string. He put an arm around her.

"Aimée Fortin. A 20 year old medical student who was in her second year at the University. She was living in human dorms, and two of her friends called her parents after she was away for a few days without letting them know. They said she'd gone to visit a family friend, but never came back. The parents knew not to get the human authorities involved until they'd spoken to their Guild, so they haven't – yet. They're desperate."

"Complicated." Fintan said. "I better let Adam know."

"We can't let her parents think she's still alive." Tierra's voice was soft. "We need to tell them what's happened."

"I want to speak to Adam. We need to do a check on the parents, the friends – and then we need to rediscover the body. But we have to do it

quietly. We can't lead the human authorities into what is an energetic death."
Fintan pushed his hair out of his face and sighed.

Jeb nodded. "Whatever you think is best. But talk to Aiko. This business
has to be brought to her attention without delay."

Fintan's heart sank. Dammit. Exactly what he'd tried to avoid.

Fintan went off to call Adam and Cuinn, and Tierra tidied up the papers
she'd been reviewing. She loved the smells of the library. She'd spent a lot of
time here in the past. It was a comforting place for her, which she was
grateful for at this moment.

She gestured to the stool next to her. "You should sit, Jeb. I'm so sorry to
have brought this to you."

"It's okay. Perhaps it's time that I engaged a little bit more with the
world."

"You already engage. You run the Maven program. You're doing great
work here," Tierra attempted to reassure him. Though she was hardly one to
talk about engaging with the wider world. She had been just as hidden at
Cathair Cuinn as perhaps Jeb was in the Guild.

"But there's more I could be doing." He stared down at his feet.

"There's always more all of us could be doing," she said. "But we can all
only do so much. What you're doing is enough. More than."

Was it?

"Those poor parents," murmured Jeb.

Fintan returned. "I couldn't get Adam. But I spoke to Cuinn and Blaize.
Adam still has a watch on the house where we found the body, a couple of
trusted members of his team. They're keeping it quiet. They haven't seen
anyone come or go since they arrived. The house seems deserted. They've
been trying to chase up who owns the house, but it's a rental, under false
documentation."

"So what are we going to do?" said Tierra. This was such a mess.

"The parents are on their way to Vancouver. They live in Montreal. Blaize
and Cuinn are going to talk to them, to tell them what's happened, and to
work out a story to tell the human authorities. The body needs to be
discovered, but not in a way that leads them to the real crime scene. Cuinn
and Blaize are going to work with members of Adam's team to retrieve the
body and move it someplace else."

Tierra shuddered. "That's just horrible."

Fintan looked at her. "Yes. But we walk a line here. The body needs to be
found, and the parents need to be told. But we could lose our only lead on
the case, and that would endanger other energetics."

He shook his head. "I didn't really think someone would be back, but I hoped. We'll keep a guard there, just in case, but it seems unlikely now. We don't think that the parents are involved, but there's always a possibility –"

"No, surely." Tierra looked at him aghast.

Jeb nodded his head slowly. "It's the kind of question that has to be asked."

"And I don't know the answer," said Fintan. "That's another reason why Blaize and Cuinn are going to see them. It's unlikely – to all intents and purposes they haven't left Montreal in months, but looks can be deceiving. They're also going to try and find out why this girl, specifically, was taken. And explore the family friend connection a bit more, as that's the best lead we have at the moment."

Jeb nodded again. "Because if you combine that piece of information with my vision, where the girl felt safe at first, she was almost certainly taken by someone she knew."

"Her name was Aimée." Tierra's voice was dull. Her head was empty and slow.

"What, Tierra?" Jeb asked.

"Aimée. Not 'the girl'."

"Are you okay?" Fintan's voice sounded unsure.

"Now she has a name…a family…friends, it all seems so much worse. And I didn't think it could." Tierra remained staring at a wall of books. "She had a future. And it was taken from her, at twenty. Not just taken, but torn, in fear and in pain."

She felt like a statue. Rooted to the bench. Still as a stone. There was a low-level buzz inside her head.

Both men moved. They paused, and Jeb gestured for Fintan to go ahead. He put an arm round her shoulders. She didn't stir, her body as tight and as motionless as it had been since Jeb had told them the news.

"The best thing we can do is to get her justice. And we will." Fintan promised.

"Can I go and help Blaize and Cuinn?" She muttered the words. She needed to help. To do something. To take action and get out from under this crushing sadness and regret for a life lost so young. The Records were suddenly suffocating her.

"We need to find Ai's parents. Ai is alive, and she's alone. You can help her more by finding her parents than you can Aimée right now." Fintan spoke in low, soothing tones.

Movement flowed back into her face and limbs and she lifted her chin. *Yes.* "I can."

She focused on this new path. "Jeb. We found several possibilities for Ai's family. Can you take a look?"

"Of course."

"Do you have them, Fintan?" said Tierra.

"Yes." Fintan handed the paper on which he'd scribbled them to Jeb. "We think she could be the daughter of one of these families. They match the parameters. Can you rule any out?"

Jeb looked at the paper for a long while. "I know one of them. She's alive and well and living here. There are two more I want to check on my computer upstairs. If I can't find out, then you can try Aiko. Ask her if she'll check the Guild database. The other families should be on that, and what's happened to them. Assuming we know."

"There's a Guild database?" Fintan was incredulous.

"Yes," said Jeb. "It's all part of the work we're doing around the Rogues. We have a lot of paper records, as you'll have seen, but Aiko's forward thinking. She wanted to see what we have in the Guild in terms of combinations of dominant and auxiliary Chakras, where we tended to settle, what people are doing, and the birth rates."

Jeb rubbed his forehead. "The Healers in Anahata have always been interested in the birth rates of energetics, as keeping them stable helps to ensure the world remains in balance. Every energetic counts. But Aiko hasn't made the project public. She hopes to encourage the other Guilds to do a similar thing, but given the trouble she's had over cataloguing and understanding the Rogues, she's put the full records on hold for the minute."

"There would be a lot of energetics who wouldn't like the idea of being on a database. Even for the good of the race," remarked Fintan. His voice didn't betray his feelings, but Tierra could tell he'd probably be one of those who weren't happy about it, though she wasn't sure why. Perhaps his own less-than-positive experiences with Anahata Guild.

"Perhaps." Jeb was noncommittal. "But there is much to be gained. And much of the information – as you've found – is in the paper records anyway. Why not put it onto a computer?"

"There's something different about having 'Archives' of the past, compared to a database of the present." Fintan frowned. "Haven't you read any George Orwell?"

Jeb smiled. "Of course. But that's not what this project is about."

"Anyway." Tierra, distracted for a moment by the potential for argument that was hovering in the air, stood up. "We've made a lot of progress today. Let us know what you find, Jeb, and we'll try and get an appointment with Aiko either way. I hope she can fit us in."

"I might be able to help you with that. She's in residence at the moment. Let me call her. I'll get back to you if I can help. Otherwise you'll have to go through her office." Jeb's emotions were locked down so tightly Tierra found it hard to get a read on how he was feeling. Her gut twisted again for getting him involved in this mess.

They went to dinner, but the talk Fintan had suggested didn't happen. They ate in silence, Tierra's head full of anxiety about all the balls they had in the air.

They headed back to their suite. Fintan's cell pinged as Tierra put her bag down.

"Ah," said Fintan. "Jeb's set us up with Aiko. She'll see us in the morning, first thing. Eight a.m." He didn't look that pleased, and she wasn't sure why. "He's also ruled out another one of the families. Two possibilities left."

"Alright. Helpful on both fronts – I thought Aiko might be too busy. There must be other people who can use the database. She can't be the only one," said Tierra.

"I expect it's more about making sure that we've got a good reason to check it," said Fintan, "rather than the actual checking itself."

"Oh. Yes, of course." Why did she always feel so naive?

"Do you know much about her energies? What's her dominant-auxiliary combination?" Fintan asked.

"She's Anahata-Vishudha."

"Interesting. Heart and the throat Chakras. Air and space as her elements. I wonder how she stays grounded enough to run a Guild?"

"I've met her a couple of times over the years, but not since she's been Anahata's Major Circle member. She's a great communicator. Quite the change in style from Caradoc's reign."

"Let's hope she can help us." Fintan frowned. "There's something not adding up with Anahata."

"What? Why do you say that?"

"Gut feel," he said.

She narrowed her eyes. "That's not good."

That meant Fintan's intuition was sparking.

Fintan slumped on the sofa. "It's really not."

19

Fintan and Tierra were in the living room area of their suite. Night had fallen, and the faint smell of shisha tobacco floated through the room from outside.

To say Fintan's feelings for Tierra were complicated would be a huge understatement. He'd wished for Cara, or even Cuinn, to talk to about the unexpected confession in the park, a hundred times or more. His embarrassing and unprecedented loss of control over his energies had been a stone in his shoe since then.

Fintan tended not to dwell on things. He preferred action to endlessly talking things over. And yet he'd barely stopped thinking about Tierra since that morning in the park.

Today, throughout his time in the gym, archives, and discussions with others, Tierra had popped into his mind multiple times. And how much he'd wanted – needed – to make it better for her.

Her confession in the park had taken him by surprise. He'd thought he saw her as a sister. As a friend, despite the odd moment of sexual attraction he'd felt recently.

Since then, he'd been watching her. Watching her curves, and how touchable all the material she wore seemed to be. How it draped over her body in a way that both hid and enticed. How she moved her hands when she got excited when she was talking. How still she'd seemed when she was holding in the sadness in Jeb's study.

And he'd realized that he could see her as a lover – and it had stopped him cold.

Whatever Jeb said, Fintan knew Tierra deserved more than someone like him. Which meant he needed to be cruel to be kind. He would have to knock any idea she had of them being together romantically on the head. She might be angry at him in the short term, but she'd see it was for the best, later, when she was free to be with someone who was right for her.

Some guy who could be relied on. Who was steady, and stable, and had his own family and friends. With a smarmy smile maybe – he growled as he imagined it – but someone who would always be there for her. Not a rootless loner like Fintan. He ground his teeth as he envisaged Tierra in the arms of the nameless man.

He'd decided to wait till after dinner for conversation, wanting to make sure Tierra ate properly. She needed to look after herself. He'd brought an extra bottle of wine with him back to the suite to help the conversation. He didn't think she was going to like what he was going to say. Even if it was for her own good.

He poured them both a glass now, the pale gold of the wine sparkling in the simple room.

Tierra sat on the sofa, her feet tucked up beneath her as usual. He handed her a glass, and sat on the couch next to her, leaving a careful distance between them.

He began. "I've been thinking about our discussion in the park."

She swirled the wine around in her glass, and took a sip, eyes downcast. "Hmmm?"

"It was flattering. But we're not suited. I don't feel that way about you." His face flushed. It wasn't a lie, exactly. His feelings for her had changed, but it was true he thought they weren't suited.

"Right." She clutched her wine. No eye contact yet. Is that all she was going to say?

"I'm sorry."

She shrugged, lightly. "Thanks. But I didn't ask anything of you when I told you. Well, apart from to stop telling me about your many women."

"It's important," he said. Had she really listened to what he said? She didn't seem bothered at all. Maybe her feelings had changed. There was a twist in his gut at the thought. Which was stupid, because that would be the best thing all around.

He needed to see her eyes.

He reached out and put his hand under her chin, tilting her face up.

"Tierra." Then he stopped, uncertain how to continue. Why was this so awkward?

"What do you want me to say?" She jerked her head back away from his touch, irritation in her tone, and her dark eyes sparked, the wine casting gold flecks into them.

She's beautiful. He frowned. He knew she was attractive, but he'd never really considered her in that light.

Her eyes narrowed as she saw the emotion flit across his face. "What?"

"You're stunning." The words fell out of his mouth without censorship, without thought. "You deserve someone who is worthy of you. I'm not that man. I can't be that man."

She narrowed her eyes and hunched her shoulders, wine held protectively in front of her. "I don't need empty compliments, Fintan. I knew you weren't attracted to me. I told you because it felt wrong to keep a secret like that from my best friend. But I know I'm not the kind of woman that men flock to. I don't have someone like Maya's glamor, and I don't have the kind of model looks you go for. And that's fine."

Anger burned his chest and his muscles clenched. How could she think he could find someone like Maya, who had no substance, who was brittle like glass, who was nothing, *nothing* compared to Tierra, more attractive than her?

"It's not an empty compliment," he said. His fists balled.

She'd backed into the corner of the sofa, her body curled into itself, and she'd put the wine down. Her chin trembled, even as she held it up defiantly.

A desperate need gripped him, a need to show her that she was beautiful, exquisite, wonderful.

He shifted towards her, and she held up a warning hand, even as moisture gathered in her eyes. His body filled with heat, with anger and desire and despair combined.

He took the hand she held up in his own, and gently moved it to the side. She hung her head, hand limp in his. He wanted that spark of defiance back. Wanted her to realize how amazing she was.

He used his free hand to raise her head up, and to gaze into her eyes, eyes that didn't want to meet his.

He leaned towards her, his chest against her knees, and dipped his head, as slow as honey flowing from a spoon. He gave her every opportunity to stop him.

His lips touched hers gently, sweetly. Her mouth was so soft and full. His lips clung to hers, and he moved his hand from her face to cradle the back of her head. He opened his eyes to see that hers were closed, her dark lashes resting on her cheeks, which had a blush of color to them. He butterflied another kiss on her lips, and pulled back.

His breath came a little faster. Her eyes opened, surprise and sexuality battling in them.

"Never think you're not beautiful. Desirable. I'm the one who isn't worthy of you, not the other way round."

He released her gently, an ache in his chest, went into his room, and closed the door.

The next morning, Tierra and Fintan waited in embarrassed silence outside Aiko's office.

Tierra wore a light gray skirt, soft brown sandals that wrapped around her ankles, and a subdued pink top that flattered her skin tone. Pink eyeshadow echoed the pink of the top, and a lick of mascara and some lip gloss completed the look. She was erratic about make up, but today she'd felt the need for it – and she looked every inch a woman in total control.

She did not feel it.

There was a tension between them that Tierra didn't know how to break. She didn't know what to make of last night. On the one hand, he'd been firm that he wasn't interested in her. On the other, he had kissed her like she was the only woman in the world.

The kiss had stunned her. It wasn't the asexual kiss of the hotel. This had contained a hunger, and a wanting, but also a sorrow that she couldn't interpret. Had it been a consolation prize? In bed she had puzzled over it for hours, replaying it in her mind, and trying to sort out the mess of emotions that had come with it.

This morning they'd been polite to each other, but it had been the forced politeness of strangers, not their easy familiarity. Something had broken between them, and she didn't know how to fix it. She swallowed. What if she was never able to?

This part of the Guild still had the exposed beams and historic look of the rest of the building, but instead of beds and wardrobes in the rooms, there were filing cabinets and desks. This early, there weren't that many people in the offices, at what was clearly the administrative heart of the building.

She considered saying something, anything, to try and mend things, but they weren't alone. Aiko's Executive Assistant, Sajan, a tall man with dark hair and eyes, sat at a desk outside Aiko's office, behind a sleek laptop.

A few minutes later, at an unseen signal, Sajan disappeared through a door, and Tierra clutched at the opportunity to fill the silence. Maybe something related to the meeting might get them back on track. "Do you know if Aiko is in the loop on Cuinn's prophecies?"

Fintan startled, in his own world. "Yeah. The Major Guild leaders are aware of Cuinn's prophecy dreams, and the Rogue incident with Blaize. I imagine it's not high on Aiko's radar though. Ajna has a lot of prophecies, and with something as amorphous as this, even the Ajna Guilds aren't putting resources into it until there's more to go on. And it's not like Anahata is the most…diligent of Guilds."

She frowned, unsure of what he meant. She'd thought the tension in him was about them, but was there something around Aiko, too? He'd seemed okay about their time in the Guild so far, seemingly relaxed about being there as they'd stayed under the radar, but perhaps this opportunity to look the Guild full in the face was causing him more agitation that she'd realized. She grimaced. She needed him to help her in this meeting, not to hinder her.

Sajan returned and gestured for them to follow him. The door led to a small hallway, where another door opened onto a spacious office. Aiko was sitting behind a large desk, signing papers. A small, delicate woman of Japanese ethnicity, she sat behind a desk which dwarfed her. Tierra could see a foot rest under the desk on which the woman's feet perched.

Aiko rose and came around the desk. "Welcome, Tierra, Fintan."

She greeted them in the traditional Japanese style, bowing to them with her hands on the tops of her legs. When she rose again, she smiled, and came over to each of them.

"But let us greet each other in the way of the Guild." She opened her arms and hugged each of them in turn, deeply. Every fiber of her being was contained in the hug, and calmness and love flowed into Tierra from the embrace.

"Thank you Aiko-san. You honor us." Tierra bowed back in turn after the hugs, and Fintan followed suit a few moments later, his own hands at his sides.

The Guild leader smiled, and moved them to several comfortable chairs in front of the large windows. Tierra took a longer look around as she walked over to the chairs. The room was airy, the windows letting in plenty of light, and showed the view that Tierra and Fintan had been looking at the day before. There were plenty of bookshelves, but also technology. Tierra saw wireless speakers, a smartphone, and a thin silver laptop open on the desk. A classic Japanese print by the artist Hokusai was mounted on the wall, but apart from the general minimalism of the office, there was little more that spoke to the energetic's human-world ethnicity.

They settled themselves into the chairs, tea on the small table between them. Tierra picked up a small cup, and took a sip. Fintan didn't touch his.

Aiko spoke. "Jeb tells me you have important information for me, to do with Cuinn Ahern's prophecies. Come, tell me your news."

After a glance at Fintan, Tierra related the full tale, holding nothing back. She spoke of Blaize's kidnapping, of Indigo, the trail to Vancouver, the dead body, Ai, and their discoveries while in Anahata Guild. Aiko listened carefully, and delicately drew out every detail from Tierra.

When it came to Ai's identity, Fintan pulled out the paper with the two possibilities on it and handed it to Aiko.

Aiko studied it, then looked out the window for a long moment. "I know who she is."

Tierra sucked in a breath. She couldn't help herself. She'd been expecting more drama. More buildup. Thank Source. At least something positive would come out of this crappy day.

"That poor girl. We'd thought she was dead, along with her parents." She showed them the paper, and her shapely nail pointed at one of the families. "It's a sad story. But nothing to do with the energetics. They were involved in a horrible accident on one of Vancouver's bridges. Something beginning with P?"

"Pattullo Bridge?" Tierra asked. "It crosses the Frazer river and joins New Westminster and Surrey."

"That sounds right. They were in their car driving home from the daughter's parent-teacher conference, and they were hit by another vehicle that was speeding. Their car spun and flipped over the barrier railings. They were incredibly unlucky. At least one of them was seen in the water after the car went over, but it was dark, and there was bad weather, and only the husband's body was found." She sighed. "He was called Ji, and was Ajna-Anahata. The woman was called Shu, and was Anahata-Svadisthana."

Tierra was nauseous. Those poor people. What a tragic death.

Aiko frowned. "But I don't understand how the girl is still alive. She was supposed to have been in the car with them. She was assumed to be dead. How did she survive? And how did we miss her?"

"Good question," Fintan said roughly. "Anahata failed that girl. It should take a good, hard look at itself."

Tierra put a calming hand on Fintan's thigh.

His rock hard thigh.

"Uhh. What matters is she's alive and well. We'll educate her around her energetic heritage and powers. Luckily we've found her before they're fully developed, so we can still help her to adjust. We intend to ask her to come and stay at Cathair Cuinn for a while in Vancouver. She's not ready for the Guild right now, and I don't think human education is right for her given her background."

She looked Aiko in the eye. "Would the Guild have any problem with that?"

Aiko smiled. "No. I'm happy that Ai has found someone with your capacity for love, but I'd be glad if you included Anahata in her education. Once she needs a Maven, Jeb can help. She needs a human education first, but you might have to home school her."

"She's smart," said Fintan. His posture was still alert, wary. Tierra couldn't understand why. There was no danger here. "She'll catch up quickly."

"You like her," Aiko commented.

"I do. She's prickly, but she's kept herself together despite a tough life. She deserves better."

"I'll assign someone to look into how we could have missed that she was still alive," said Aiko. "I find that strange. And I don't like the implications."

"Agreed. But I will look into it. There's no need to put a stranger on the case," said Fintan.

Aiko nodded. "As you wish."

Tierra squeezed his thigh again. Not that she was sure he'd even notice the limited pressure she was able to exert. "You weren't Guild leader then, Aiko. You weren't responsible."

"No. But still. I've changed a lot in the Guild in the last decade, but worms still keep coming up out of the apple. This looks like another." For a moment Aiko looked weary.

Tierra hated to burden her further, but they needed to talk to her about the information they'd gained from Jeb. "There was a second puzzle which the Anahata Guild has also helped us with. I'm afraid it's another tragic tale."

"This is in reference to the death of Aimée Fortin? I'm aware. I, and the other Major Circle members, have discussed Cuinn Ahern's dreamwalks, and the terrible situation with Blaize. However, we are divided as to the true import of the prophecies. Some believe that the situation with Blaize, and even now Aimée, could be a coincidence. His prophecies are – troubling. And there is little detail to help us to understand exactly what we should be doing."

"And you, Aiko? What do you believe?" Fintan asked. He seemed so confrontational today. So angry. Tierra's shoulders were tight.

"It seems an unlikely coincidence. The fact Jeb saw several people involved, not just one Rogue, is alarming. And I am distressed that whatever the situation, it has caught an innocent in its wake." Aiko drew in a long breath through her nose. "Do you need anything from me at this time?"

Tierra looked at Fintan. He shook his head. "No. The family may. We need to keep the fact that we've discovered the girl's death quiet for a time, as we're still hoping that those involved in this crime might come back to the house. That may be difficult for the family. Perhaps you have somewhere you could offer them sanctuary for a while until we have resolved the situation?"

"We can do that," said Aiko. "Please let me know once they have been informed of the death, and I will call them personally."

They took their leave of her. On the way back to their rooms Tierra said, "I'm going to let Jeb know what we found out."

Fintan changed direction to follow her, and she waved him back. "It's fine, I can do it. You head back to the rooms and start packing. We're done here now. Let Cuinn and the others know what's happened."

She walked off without waiting for him to protest. She needed some time away from him. And she wanted to see Jeb before she left and see if he was feeling better. And, she admitted to herself, she wanted to feel his comforting energy herself. She felt exhausted and lost.

She knocked on his door, but it took longer this time for him to answer. When he did, she saw hollows under his eyes, as if his own night had been even more troubled than hers.

After they greeted each other with an embrace, Tierra curled up on one of the armchairs and tucked her feet underneath her. She hugged one of the cushions to her chest. Jeb followed and sat opposite.

She filled him in on their meeting with Aiko. "So we've managed to find the answers to both our questions, and can head home."

Jeb nodded. "I'm glad, though I'll be sorry to see you go. But you know that."

He smiled at her and she smiled back, though a wave of sadness choked her and stopped her from saying anything.

He got up and went over to his desk, picking up a notebook. He came back and handed it to her. "This is every detail I can remember about my vision. It's mostly just a series of sense impressions, but there might be things you can use. I hope it's helpful."

She gripped it. "Jeb, thank you so much. I know how hard this was for you, and I can't tell you how grateful we are."

"I enjoyed seeing you again. And meeting Fintan." He left an expectant pause.

"What do you mean?" Tierra was cautious.

He laughed. "Tierra. Come now. Even if I wasn't an empath, your love for Fintan shines out from you."

She put her hands to her face as her cheeks burned. "Jeb. I…"

He waved it away. "It's fine. I wish you happiness with him. He may not realize it now, but he loves you just as much."

She looked out over her hands. "Thanks Jeb, but I don't think so. I mean, he does love me, but not as a partner. He loves me as a dear friend."

Shame stopped her from mentioning the night before.

Jeb gave her a long look. "Perhaps the time isn't now, but it won't be long. You deserve joy, Tierra. You give so much to others, without expectations or demands."

She turned the question back on him. On this one, he was mistaken, and it hurt her to talk about it. "And you Jeb? Do you have someone who loves you? Who you can love?"

Jeb looked away then. "That part of my life is over. I have nothing to offer a woman."

"You're wrong, Jeb." Tierra's voice was firm. "Any woman would be lucky to be with you."

He got up and walked over to the window. "I'm happy enough as I am. My life here in the Guild lets me contribute and support others in a way that keeps me content."

She got up and walked over to stand next to him, putting her hand on his arm, looking up at him. "Is contentment enough for you, Jeb?"

He laughed, and the sound was harsher than normal. "It's more than I deserve. Really." He turned and dropped a light kiss on the top of her head. "Thank you for coming to see me. I'm glad I was able to help you a little. And come back if you think there's anything else I can help you with. If I can, I will."

She knew she'd get no further. "Thank you. It's been good to see you. Keep in contact – I'd like to hear from you more often."

He nodded. Their discussion was over.

20

Somehow, Fintan and Tierra had departed the airport for different destinations – she home to Canada, he back to New York – without any further discussion of the night before. His body hummed with a constant sense of unease, as if something were out of place.

Instead of clarifying the situation the night before, he seemed to have royally fucked things up with Tierra. And he had no idea how to fix it. Every time he tried, he seemed to get into more trouble.

It wasn't like he'd started it, he thought, with a sense of righteous indignation. She'd been the one to open the can of worms that had caused all of this.

He arrived back at his apartment, the fourth floor of a walk-up in the Meatpacking District. He'd owned the place for decades, watched the area evolve from gritty to sophisticated. His neighbors used to be hookers and meat truckers, and now they were designers and hipsters. There was a sense of relief as he walked up the wooden stairs into the familiar space. Perhaps he could throw himself back into work for a while, to give himself a sense of perspective on the situation with Tierra.

Fintan had never really had a problem with women. His ability to connect with them attracted them to him in plentiful supply. He kept things light and playful, always keeping some of himself back. There weren't many he let in to the deeper parts of him, and after a while, the women got frustrated and left him. But they usually stayed friends. Occasionally, Fintan played matchmaker, using Anahata and his own intuition to find someone who was a better match for whoever he was dating. That worked even better than the commitment issues.

In his bedroom, he tipped his duffle bag upside down on the bed and shook it, his clothes and toiletries falling out into a heap. He threw all the dirty clothes onto the floor ready for the wash, and scooped up the clean ones and dumped them in a drawer in the wardrobe. He'd spent enough time in the military over the centuries that he took pleasure in being untidy at home.

He had the entire top floor of the building, the glossy modern interior a contrast to the stone it was built from. Long thin windows let in plenty of light.

Tierra … she wasn't like the other women in his life. They were friends. She did know him. He'd never hidden any part of himself from her. And he couldn't bear to lose that friendship.

What had gone wrong?

It wasn't as if he could talk about it with Adam. And he hoped Tierra didn't tell her brother. Or Cuinn. Or Blaize.

He winced and sat on the bed, head in his hands.

He was going to get his ass kicked if he didn't sort this out. Though he probably deserved the kicking if he didn't resolve the situation.

He reached for his cell and called his team in Manipura Guild to see if there was anything that needed his attention. There was nothing pressing, but enough emails and ongoing work that he decided to head into the office as soon as possible to catch up. It might be that he was needed again by Adam fairly quickly, and it would be better to be up to date on this part of his life if that was the case.

He showered and changed, and was in the office within an hour, picking up a couple of PB and J bagels on the way. One thing about the current century he loved was the diversity of food in one place. You no longer had to travel for hundreds of miles to get a different kind of food. You just switched to the restaurant on the other side of the street.

Fintan had an office to himself at Manipura HQ. The Guild owned a collection of brownstones on Washington Square Park, nestled in among New York University buildings. They were a warren architecturally, having been acquired as the Guild needed them, and Fintan loved them. It still amused him that the Americans considered them old, but the hustle and bustle of New York made it one of his favorite places to stay, and he found the mishmash of buildings, people and scents exhilarating. Let alone the secret rooftop speakeasy close by.

His space was a messy room off the bullpen where many of his colleagues worked. It was still early, and there weren't many others in. He shut his door, preferring to be alone a while longer. He worked through what felt like a million boring emails, the ones he'd ignored while away, which updated him on various ops. This wasn't the image most people had of Manipura Warriors, the fighters of the energetic world. But he stuck with it, rather than using his preferred method of 'delete all', because he wanted to see if there were any other leeching cases that had come up in recent weeks. He had a hunch that the ones they'd come across weren't isolated.

And he was right.

Several hours and hundreds of emails in, he came across something that looked promising. A report of a leeching of a teenage Ajna-Muladhara energetic across the Canadian border in Seattle. The young man was drained and killed. The police had discovered him and assumed he'd died of malnutrition, but local energetics had checked it out and had found signs of leeching.

The teen had had ligature marks on his wrists, indicating he'd been held. No prints or other useful physical evidence had been found at the scene to trace who the perpetrator might be.

It could be the work of the man, or his colleagues, who'd killed Aimée. Typically, because the taboo against killing in their society was so strong, energetic Rogues who got involved in leeching didn't kill their victims. Sometimes leechings were accidents. Sometimes they were addictions. In either case, the perpetrator wasn't in control of himself enough to clean up and remove physical evidence from the scene this well.

Fintan stared at the screen and rubbed his forehead. This was a nasty case. He frowned and went back to the report, and the date of the crime. Buried in his emails, he'd assumed it had happened a while ago. The report said the body had been found in the last three days, and the search for the perp was ongoing.

He took notes from the report. This could be the break they needed. At least it gave them a more recent location. Seattle was only about two or three hours from Vancouver. Close enough for it to be a short trip for the Rogue, or Rogues, and it also suggested that there was a reason they were staying in the area. *What was it?*

He was considering whether it was too early – or rather, late – in Seattle to call the energetic who'd been looking into the death, when his phone rang.

"Fintan."

"Adam here. We need to talk."

CHAPTER

21

Blaize met Tierra off her plane at Vancouver airport. The slender, toned redhead looked like a dancer – though a dangerous one. All muscle and lithe grace, her naturally pale skin had lost most of the tan it had had when she arrived in Canada from sunny Thailand, but she was still a striking woman. Today her expression was grim.

"What's the matter? Is everything alright?" Tierra's stomach fluttered. There was a constant sense of anxiety in her life at the moment. She was much closer to the reality of the jobs that Blaize, Fintan and Adam did daily, and she didn't like it.

"It's Ai." Blaize headed for the exit as soon as Tierra reached her. Her pace was determined, and other patrons veered out of the way as she stalked through it.

"What's happened? Is she ok?"

"We're not sure. She'd been staking out the house you found."

"The house where Aimée was killed?" Tierra's stomach lurched at the danger Ai had placed herself in, and she hurried to catch up. "How do you know?"

"When Cuinn and I went back in to check things out before they removed the body, she came in." Blaize pulled open the door to the car park and let them both through. "She had a gun."

"She what?" Tierra stumbled. "What happened?"

"I disarmed her. I think she was surprised about that." The corner of Blaize's mouth quirked. "Anyway, once she realized who we were she apologized. She'd been waiting for someone to come back to the house. I think she was trying to impress you and Fintan by catching the bad guys."

Tierra winced at the thought of the teenage Ai going up against the Warrior Blaize. "But she's okay now? And you're okay?"

Blaize clicked the lock on the car with her remote, opened the door and slid in. Tierra put her suitcase in the back and hurried into the passenger seat. Blaize turned on the engine and continued. "Not exactly."

Tierra's stomach flipped. "Tell me, please."

"We didn't realize you hadn't told her about Indigo."

"Oh." A blush suffused Tierra's face. She wanted to explain their reasons, which had seemed right at the time, but the tingling in her face and sweat on her palms were an indicator that perhaps at a deeper level she was less sure.

"It came up in conversation. We didn't know it was a secret," Blaize said.

"Oh, Source." The tingling spread down her neck and across her chest. "How did she react?"

"Not good. She ran." Blaize crossed her arms over her breasts. "We haven't seen her since."

There was a thickness in Tierra's throat. She'd had niggles of doubt at the time that it hadn't been a good idea to keep the reality of Indigo to themselves, but she'd wanted to protect Ai.

She grimaced. No, let's face it. She'd thought that Ai would run if she pegged Tierra and Fintan as part of the group that killed Ai's friend.

"We might never find her." There was a sinking feeling in her chest. "We don't know where she spends her time, where she lives. If she doesn't trust us, we might never see her again."

Tierra slumped in the seat, everything catching up with her at once. She wasn't cut out for this life. She couldn't juggle the dangers and the risks not only to herself but to others, that her friends and family seemed so comfortable with.

"I'm sure it won't come to that," Blaize said, her tone brisk. "I'll take you to the house, and maybe you can track her from there."

Tierra's brain teemed with images of Ai injured or dead, as she watched the scenery pass. Ai might be alone forever, because the first people she'd trusted in years had let her down. "What about the cell phone we got her? Adam or Fintan might have connections at Vishudha Guild with some of their comms energetics – maybe we can track that."

Blaize shook her head. "It's off. We're monitoring it, but it's dead so far. The last cell tower it bounced off was near the house. We haven't seen her since."

Tierra bit her lip. "Okay. Don't go to the house. Let's go to where Fintan and I first saw her. Perhaps she'll go back there."

"Can you put the directions into the GPS? And text Cuinn to let him know?"

By the time Tierra next looked up, they were approaching the area where they'd first seen Ai. They drove up and down the streets for half an hour. No sign of Ai.

"Okay, park anywhere," Tierra said.

Blaize pulled the car over, and loped over to two teenage boys who were playing a card game while pretending not to watch her approach. Blaize was in her work gear, which was tight jeans that had plenty of stretch so she could move in them, a black T-shirt, and a black jacket. It was sunny enough for her to be wearing a pair of sunglasses. She looked pretty bad-ass. Certainly compared to Tierra's own small frame and floaty skirt.

Blaize came back, smoothing her jacket and humming.

"What were you doing?" said Tierra.

"Paying those kids to keep an eye on the car. This isn't a neighborhood where I want to take chances. It's twenty bucks well spent."

Tierra was already searching the street around them. "Let's try the hotel first. That's where we first talked to her."

She walked quickly along the pavement, boots tapping. Blaize walked along next to her.

"We'll find her, T." Blaize's voice was firm. "I'm sorry we scared her off."

Tierra rubbed the back of her neck. "You're sorry? Fintan and I should be the ones who are sorry. It's our fault. We should have told her. It just seemed easier not to at the time."

They were nearly at the hotel doorway.

"How do you want to do this?" asked Blaize.

"He seemed to respond well to cleavage last time." Tierra wrinkled her nose.

"Eww. One of those. Let's see how he responds to a woman who can kick his ass."

Tierra trailed behind Blaize as she burst through the doors into the reception. The odious man Tierra and Fintan had met previously glanced up from behind the desk with little interest, saw Blaize, and got to his feet in a hurry.

"Can I, uh, help you?" He caught sight of Tierra, and his shoulders relaxed. *Not this time, buddy.*

"Remember my friend here?" Blaize jerked a thumb back at her. "She's looking for the girl she met when she was last here. Dark hair, skinny, teens, goth look. Where does she hang out?"

"I don't know what girl you mean."

"Listen, pal, there's fifty bucks in it if you help us, or a broken nose if you don't." She shrugged, checked her nails. "The nose is cheaper for me, so it's your choice."

His eyes widened. "I don't know. I've seen her sometimes, around this street, or sometimes near the bus station down the road. The diner, a couple of times. I don't know where she lives, I swear."

Tierra's eyebrows raised at this side of Blaize, who exuded menace as she leaned on the counter and put her face close to his. "Are you sure?"

He shot backwards, almost falling over the chair. "I'm sure. Give me your number and I'll call you if I see her. I promise."

Blaize shook her head and her lip curled. She took a leaflet from the counter and scribbled her number on it, leaving it on the wood. "Don't let us down, pervert."

Back outside in the sunshine, Tierra was open-mouthed. "Wow."

Blaize shuddered. "He was gross. And easily scared."

"You were pretty intimidating." In a way that Tierra knew she could never have been. When they had last been here, it had been like playing a role, a sex siren who could vamp information out of a guy. She wished she had Blaize's confidence. Her shoulders dropped.

"To a worm like that, sure. At least he gave us a few more places to check. Somehow I don't think he's going to call." She gave a wry smile.

They were both quiet as they made their way down the street, searching the alleys and roads they passed. It would be easy to miss Ai. At the end of the road they turned and looped back again, heading to the diner.

"When did you last eat?" Blaize asked.

"I don't know. I had some food on the plane." It wasn't important. And her sense of time was pretty messed up after the flight and with the time difference.

"Let's get something in the diner. It'll give us a reason for being there. And you need a break. We can sit in the window so you can still watch for her."

"I guess." Tierra's body was heavy with fatigue. She hadn't slept much on the plane.

Tierra's shoulders hunched at the sight of Betty the waitress, who gestured them towards a clear table.

Blaize ignored her and steered them to a different table, a booth in the window where they could see in both directions by sitting opposite each other. The plastic seat was grimy, and slightly sticky.

Blaize searched the menu for vegetarian options. Energetics were too connected to the food chain to eat meat.

"Don't have the omelet," Tierra said. "Or the coffee."

"Hmm. I might have a shake. And pancakes."

"Don't say I didn't warn you."

"You should eat something too." Blaize pursed her lips and tapped Tierra on the hand.

"I'm not that hungry."

Betty came over. "Yeah?"

"Two pancake stacks, and a chocolate shake and a strawberry one."

"Sure." Betty scratched something on the pad. "You find your cousin?"

"Yes, thank you. And one of her friends, Ai. Do you know her?" Tierra asked.

"Perhaps. What's your name?" Betty rested a hand on one hip.

"What? Why?" Tierra frowned.

"Maybe Ai left something for the right person." Betty's thin lips were pursed.

"She left something? What?" All Tierra's attention was on Betty.

"Name?" Betty's voice was obstinate.

"Tierra. I'm Tierra." *Please let that be who she was looking for.*

"Right. She said you'd give me $50 for delivering it to you." A glint of avarice shone in the woman's eyes.

"$50?" Blaize's voice was incredulous.

Betty shrugged. "If you don't want it, that's no skin off my nose. But she seemed to think it was important."

She ambled off in the direction of the kitchen, calling over her shoulder, "I'll put your order in, and you can think about it."

Tierra rose slightly, as if to go after her. "Sit down," Blaize said.

"We already gave her fifty for the information about Indigo. She knows we're good for it." And it's not like they didn't have the money.

"You gave her $50? Ah, Source. She's taking advantage of you," Blaize said.

Sure. Because everyone was. An ember of something lit for a moment in Tierra, then suffocated. "Sometimes it's easier to catch flies with honey."

"Like you did with that repulsive guy in the hotel?" Blaize reached across the table and poked Tierra playfully.

The ember flared again. Tierra flushed. "I was with Fintan. It seemed more like a game. I didn't have to threaten to break his nose and we still got the information."

"Hmmph. I like my way better," Blaize said, but when she caught Tierra's gaze she continued hurriedly, "Sorry, T. We can give her the money. It's just the principle of the thing."

"It was actually Fintan who gave her the money last time." Tierra lowered her eyes and reached into her purse. She pulled out a $50 bill. She did not want to feel ashamed for what she'd done. She had to contribute in her own way.

Blaize plucked it from her fingers. "I'll deal with it. Otherwise you'll end up giving her more."

Did everyone else think she was a soft touch? Tierra shoved sugar packets around the table while Blaize looked around to attract the waitress's attention.

The woman didn't come back for a while, and when she did, she had their shakes in her hands. She put them on the table, and paused.

Blaize slid the $50 bill across the table. "This is to cover our check," she said. "You can keep the change as a tip. How about that?"

The woman frowned, but then she shrugged and pulled out a plastic bag and handed it over. Inside there was a phone, and piece of paper, folded over and stuck together. There was no envelope, but in order to read it the woman would have had to tear it, and that didn't seem to be the case.

"Thank you," said Tierra. They were making progress, and a spark of hope ignited inside her. Perhaps they would find Ai today.

Betty shrugged again, and headed off.

Blaize ripped open the paper, and money fell out. She fanned it out on the table and frowned, then held the opened note out to Tierra. "It's yours. Can you read it aloud?"

Tierra nodded, and took it from Blaize's hand, her fingers trembling. She hoped it would tell them where Ai lived, or give some kind of clue as to where she might have gone.

She unfolded it and scanned the scrawled letters. She read them out loud as Blaize requested.

Tierra / Fintan,

You lied to me about Indigo. Did you kill her?

I guess my senses don't always give me good information. Seems like I was pretty much wrong about you. Here's your phone and money. I don't need you. I'll find answers myself.

A.

Tierra tried to read more into the stark words. Her stomach roiled.

"We didn't get a chance to tell her the whole story about Indigo. She's inferred a lot more from the conversation than we said." Blaize shifted in her seat. "I'm so sorry."

"It wasn't your fault." She didn't need to reread the note. The words burned in her mind. How could the girl think they might have killed Indigo? Tierra wrapped her arms around her body. They'd betrayed Ai's trust, and treated her like a child by not telling her. And they'd given her reason to doubt her gifts. Ah, Source. They'd really messed this up.

"I know it feels like everything's gone south, but enough of the guilt for now," Blaize said. She tapped the table to get Tierra's attention. "We're going to sort this. Let's think practically. How would she try to find the man who lived there? What could she do that we can't?"

"I don't know. We have much greater resources than she does." The guilt wasn't shifting, despite Blaize's order.

"Unless she's found something else out from her contacts. It wasn't from watching the house." Blaize frowned. "Adam's had his team watching it almost from when we left, and no one came or went. Though…they missed Ai who was also staking the place out."

"It's possible she got something from her gifts. She's Anahata-Ajna, which is a powerful combination for prophecy, even untrained. She told us she'd always had feelings about people, always had thoughts about what might happen to them, or about whether they were good or bad." Tierra bowed her head. "That's why she trusted us. Her feelings about us were good."

Blaize stretched out a hand across the stained Formica. "You are good, T. You're one of the most selfless people I know. She's got this wrong."

Tierra clutched at Blaize's hand as if she were drowning. "We have to find her. The man in that house is depraved. He killed a blameless girl, and who knows who else? If he gets his hands on Ai, she's likely to be drained and killed just as Aimée was."

Blaize nodded. "We will. I'll call Cuinn and update him. Drink your shake. You'll need the fuel." She reached for her cell and slid out of the booth, heading outside.

Tierra sat, her hands wrapped around her glass. The cold seeped into her hands. She kept them there, deliberately punishing herself with the small gesture.

Betty returned with their pancakes and slid the plates onto the table. She hesitated. "You okay?"

Tierra looked up at the previously surly waitress, her eyes overflowing at this small indication of concern.

"Shit," Betty muttered, and grabbed a handful of napkins from a dispenser on the next table. She dropped them in front of Tierra. "It's a hard world, lady. You're luckier than most. You have friends or family to help you. Lots of people don't. So suck it up and get on with it."

Tierra gaped at the woman's retreating back. It was an unexpected kindness from the hard woman, and demonstrated to Tierra once again there was good in everyone. Trying to dislodge a lump in her throat, Tierra took a swallow of the milkshake in front of her. It was a great deal better than the awful coffee from the last visit. More solid with something in her stomach, she ate some of the pancakes. It was slow going, but she'd managed one of the pancakes and half her shake by the time Blaize came back.

She set her phone on the table, and settled back into the booth. She took a sip of her shake. "You doing okay?"

"Yes." She wasn't great, but the food and the moment with Betty had helped. Now she just wanted to take action.

"I've let Cuinn know. He'll fill in Adam and Fintan. Cuinn's been dealing with the parents of the dead girl —"

"Aimée." She had a name. Her name was important.

"Aimée, that's right. They told them this morning. They're devastated, of course, but they're going to keep it quiet. Apparently Aiko, the head of the Anahata Guild, called them personally and offered them the use of one of the Guild's safe houses to grieve privately."

Ahh. Aiko had come through. More of the inner tightness that had come from reading the letter released. There was kindness in the world. "She offered. She was sympathetic – they're members of her Guild."

"You helped with that? Good work. It keeps them out of the way."

"Blaize." Tierra dropped her chin and shook her head, but couldn't help but smile at Blaize's efficient practicality.

"You know I'm right. It's for their good as well as ours." Blaize took a bite of her pancakes. "So. What now?"

CHAPTER

22

They searched the streets for hours but found no trace of Ai. Some time later, Tierra and Blaize were back in the generic hotel room with Cuinn.

Blaize sprawled on the large bed, her head in Cuinn's lap. He sat up against the headboard, absent-mindedly playing with her hair.

"The parents are on their way to Aiko's sanctuary. That will give us some time to sort this mess out." He sighed deeply. "I didn't see this coming."

Blaize twisted to look up at him. "You – we – can't see everything. We're still trying to put the pieces together."

She addressed Tierra, who sat in the room's only armchair. "Nixie's coming next week and I'm strong enough now to mentally share images of all the vision pieces we have had. She and I have a previous energetic connection that I think will enable me to do it. It will help us with finding out who all the figures standing with Cuinn and me are."

Cuinn's first visions of the prophecies had seen eleven figures standing with him. So far he'd identified Blaize, Adam, Tierra, Fintan and Cara, and Blaize had recognized Nixie, but there were six figures who were either too blurred for Cuinn to see clearly, or who he – and now Blaize – hadn't recognised.

"Great idea," Tierra said. She slumped in the chair, her mind dull. What in Source's name were they going to do? And where was Ai? Was she just in a burger joint somewhere chatting to her friends? Or had she somehow found the owner of the house and was even now being drained? Tierra shuddered. "We need to find Ai. But we don't have the first idea where to start."

"She might not have found the Rogue," Blaize pointed out. "Just because she said she's going to look for him doesn't mean she'll find him."

"She's a determined young woman, with Anahata-Ajna energies. When she spoke to Fintan and me previously she talked about having 'gut feelings' about things that came true. Perhaps she had a feeling about – or even a vision of – the man involved." Tierra bit her lip. She wanted to be out there, taking action, except – she didn't know what action to take.

"Either way, Tierra, we don't know." Cuinn's tone was gentle. "We should work with what we have, and not with 'maybes'."

Blaize nodded. "Okay, so what do we know? Let's start from the beginning."

Tierra closed her eyes and stifled a scream. She didn't want to go through it all again. She took a deep breath. "We know that there's a threat to the energetics, as per Cuinn's vision. I think we have to assume that these events are all linked."

"Definitely," said Blaize.

"The threat is undefined, but potentially to the whole race, not just us and those we love. We know that eleven energetics stand with Cuinn against this threat, and we're included in that number," said Tierra.

"The Ajna Guild leaders gave me some information before Blaize was taken, that led us to research that told us two things. First, that at the start of our history, each of the Chakras corresponded to a single Archetype. And secondly, each energetic had access to all the different gifts of a Chakra, unlike the diluted gifts we have now. If they were Ajna energetics, for example, they didn't just have the gift of prophecy. They could mind-speak, were great teachers, had drum-tight memories, and could even manipulate others' minds. This was their Archetype."

Tierra's mouth made an 'o'. She'd never heard this. Cuinn was one of the stronger energetics she knew, with several Ajna gifts, but he couldn't manipulate minds. She didn't know anyone with all the powers and gifts possible for their dominant and auxiliary chakras. "Which Archetype is which?"

Cuinn sketched out a list on the notepad by the bed.

Manipura – Warrior – Blaize / maybe Fintan

Ajna – Sage – Cuinn

Muladhara – Protector – Adam

Anahata – Healer – Cara

"Creator and Communicator were harder, but by process of elimination, we think that Svadisthana is Creator, and Vishudha is Communicator," Cuinn said.

Tierra counted in her head. "So if Nixie counts for Svadisthana, we have five of the roles covered, but no one with Vishudha? We're missing the Communicator. And do we only need one of each Archetype?"

"Maybe," said Cuinn. "We can't be sure. It's likely we need two of each though, male and female, if we go on the personal prophecy I got at Ajna guild. That makes it more complicated."

"Okay. What about the bracelets?" Tierra asked. "I thought you said each of those in the vision had a bracelet on their wrist? Only you and Blaize have them so far."

Tierra knew that Blaize and Cuinn's twin bracelets, made of entwined threads of the colors of their chakras, had appeared when they were in the dreamscape together. Blaize had told Tierra that this had happened after they'd made love for the first time.

"Yes," said Cuinn. "We don't know why. We're trying to research that too. Blaize helping has been very beneficial. I've made more progress with her working with me than I did in twice the time alone."

Blaize gave him a quick smile. "Okay, so that's the prophecies. What about the real world?"

"Indigo kidnapped you because you were an energetic match, and leeched from you. Aimée was Anahata-Ajna, and so is Ai. Which suggests, if they're leeching, that one of the kidnappers is also Anahata-Ajna, possibly the man, but we don't know how others are involved. But then we also have the Remnant stones." Tierra spoke slowly as she reasoned it out. "Jeb said that Aimée knew her attacker, and her friends said he was a family friend, which suggests he's older."

"He rented the property under false documents, so that's a dead end. And he hasn't been back," Cuinn commented.

"You didn't get any Ajna readings from the house itself?" Tierra asked.

"No. Nothing. I was impressed you were able to do an Anahata reading. Most of the house was wiped." Cuinn shook his head.

"Oh," Tierra breathed. "That makes sense. I only got a reading from the girl, not from anything else in the house. That explains why some of the details were blurred. I couldn't see the faces of her attackers at all. And Jeb said that the faces of the attackers were blurred for him too."

"We don't know if Indigo was the other woman you saw, or whether it was a third person. And there seemed to be other figures, but it's uncertain," Blaize said.

"Where does that leave us?" Tierra asked. "Do we have any leads at all?"

"We've asked the parents to write down every family friend or acquaintance they know who's an older male. However, they're each a couple of centuries old, so they've had time to accumulate a lot of people. I'll suggest they start with prioritizing the Anahata-Ajnas." He shrugged. "That might be a dead end. Or an impossible task."

"At least it's something. The parents will feel better taking action too," Tierra said.

"I'll talk to my grandmother and ask her to explore things with the other Minor Circle leaders," Blaize said. "I think it's worth tugging on any lead. She knows about my attack as she leads the Manipura-Ajna Minor Guild, and might have heard a rumor or have some suggestions."

Cuinn nodded and turned to his laptop. Tierra got up, and walked to the windows of the hotel room. The sky was clouded over, the day gray. She looked out at concrete and cars, and longed for the peace and nature at Cathair Cuinn. *But not until we've found Ai.*

"So what can we do?" She could hear the frustration in her voice.

"Adam's on his way back," said Cuinn. "A fresh pair of eyes might help."

"Really? He didn't know Ai," Tierra said.

"He knows you," said Blaize, gently. "And he trusts your opinion. Plus, you know, Protector. Looking after the innocent is kind of his job. He's going to go over the house one more time. We don't expect anyone to come back now. He can't justify the surveillance resources much longer."

"This is so frustrating!" Tierra exploded. "There must be something else we can do apart from go over old ground."

Blaize lifted her head from Cuinn's lap and unfurled to a sitting position. She took one of his hands in hers, and he looked alarmed. "What?"

"Cuinn. I know you don't want to. But I think it's time you explored the connection with your father."

He pulled his hand out of hers and stood. His tone was clipped. "I don't think that's a good idea. He won't help us, even if he could."

Tierra frowned. "What do you mean, the connection with your father? What's he got to do with it?"

Cuinn's father was a difficult man with whom none of them had spoken for decades.

"We don't know."

"Probably nothing."

Blaize and Cuinn spoke at the same time. Cuinn shook his head and squeezed out, "The last thing Indigo said to me in the ether was, 'Give my love to your father'."

"She said that? You didn't mention it." Tierra felt a little bruised. How was she only just hearing this information?

Cuinn looked even more uncomfortable. "I thought she was probably trying to get under my skin. It's no secret that my father and I are estranged."

"That's one way to describe it." How was that cantankerous old bully with the stick up his butt related to this mess? It had been a long time since they'd heard from Cuinn's father, and that was no bad thing as far as Tierra was concerned. He'd caused Cuinn a world of hurt. She accepted the man had his own burdens, but Tierra was of the opinion he'd treated Cuinn badly, and she had little time for that.

"He made it clear that he wasn't interested in a relationship with me, and he's the reason I left Ireland and came here. I can't see how he's relevant," Cuinn said.

"Why didn't you tell us?" Tierra tried to keep her voice neutral, but the idea that she wasn't Cuinn's first port of call with personal things anymore stung a little.

"Ah, Tierra. It just didn't feel like something worth sharing. It was a difficult conversation, and Indigo was mentally ill."

"Did she say anything else you didn't share?"

There was a long pause. Cuinn rubbed the corner of the duvet between his fingers while he thought. "She said she knew secrets about me, and about my friends. She said that my cousins have challenges ahead. And she said that the blond one – who I assume was Fintan, though I can't be sure – has a temper. And that there were surprises in store for all of us."

He sighed. "All typically vague and unhelpful. Nothing that could actually give us a lead, and lots that could cause people anxiety, which is what I assume her motive was."

He looked back at Tierra. "See, anxiety. I can see it on your face."

She shook her head. "No, no. Well, perhaps a little. But you're right, she was unstable, so we do need to be careful with everything she said. Cuinn, you need to share this information with everyone. Adam and Fintan especially, as it's about them as well as me."

"I agree with Tierra, my love." Blaize's face was serious. "And Fintan does have a temper, that's true. But it's rare he loses it. He has great control over his energies."

Tierra blushed. He had great control, past tense. She seemed to have messed with that, recently. She ducked her head and hoped no one noticed the color in her cheeks.

"Yes. It's time. I'll speak to Adam when he comes, and I'll call Fintan. He's back in New York, Tierra, right?"

She shrugged. "As far as I know."

"I'll contact my father, assuming I can find him. As you say Tierra, it's been a very long time. Do you know his whereabouts?"

She shook her head. "I think Adam was keeping track of him. Ask him. And if he doesn't know now, he's the person most likely to be able to find out."

"What are your father's energies? Maybe that will give us a clue as to how he can help." Blaize's tone was supportive.

"Ajna-Muladhara." Cuinn's response was terse.

"Oh … Nothing new to add then," Blaize said, weakly. These were the same as Cuinn's energies.

"I think that the best thing to do is for us to go back out and ask more questions around the streets where Ai seemed to spend her time," said Cuinn. "We'll go back to the bus station, and the diner. It's frustrating we don't have a picture, so we'll need to describe her verbally as much as we can."

Tierra nodded. "I wish I could draw."

"It is as it is. We found her in the system now that we've connected her to her parents, but she fell out of the system when she left the group home she was in at thirteen, and so there are no up-to-date photos of her there we can use. If she has any online presence in terms of social media, she's using another name."

They went back out, and spent several more fruitless hours asking questions and attempting to find any trace of Ai. Cuinn even re-questioned Betty the waitress.

But it was as if Ai had vanished into thin air.

Adam arrived early the next morning and put away a mountain of breakfast in the hotel's restaurant while they updated him, dropping bacon regularly, if clandestinely, to Argus, his husky, who sat by his feet. They arranged to go back to the Leech's house to talk Adam through everything from scratch, hoping that it might trigger some fresh insight.

Back in her room to get ready, Tierra tidied her few things, thinking ruefully she'd have to buy some new clothes if this trip continued. She'd only expected to be away a couple of nights, and it had already been twice that.

She frowned down into her suitcase at something that didn't belong to her. She plucked it out and held it at arm's length. It was one of Fintan's socks. The V between her eyes deepened. How dare it be in her luggage. And at the same time, she was flooded with a fondness and a longing so deep she crushed the sock in a fist and clutched it like a lifeline.

She wished he was with them. Then immediately wished she didn't wish it.

"Argh!" *Why is life so complicated?*

She'd thankfully regained her senses and stuffed the offending item into her dirty washing when Adam's knock came.

"I'm ready." She stepped out and shut her door behind her.

"We're not going yet. We need to go back to Cuinn and Blaize's room. Something's come up." Adam's voice was a low rumble.

"Is everything ok?"

"Not exactly." Adam set off down the corridor without explaining further, Argus trotting behind him, a faithful shadow. Tierra sighed, but, used to her brother's taciturn nature, she followed him to the other room, where Blaize paced and re-paced the few steps between bed and window and Cuinn sat on the bed, his face neutral.

"What?" Tierra stepped into the room, the churn in her stomach that had started yesterday now full-blown nausea.

"Cuinn got a message." Blaize didn't stop her pacing.

Adam pushed past her and scooped up the cell from the bed. He pressed a couple of buttons, and handed it to her. She wanted to refuse it, dread spreading through her.

She listened, and a voice came through the line, its identity obscured by crackles and computer modulation. "Blaize and Tierra for the girl, Ai. Beaver Lake, Stanley Park, midnight tonight."

Tierra wobbled and sat down hard on the bed. "Ai's been … kidnapped?"

"It seems so. If we trust this." Adam's terse voice penetrated the fog in her brain.

Argus padded over and butted his head against her legs. She put a hand down to pat him, then clutched at her usual optimism. "So… we can rescue her? It's good news?"

Blaize and Adam exchanged nonplussed glances. "I wouldn't call it good news exactly," said Blaize. "We don't know who's holding her, who will be there, and they've asked for you and me to be exchanged for her. Or if it's even real. Might be Ai pushing our buttons in revenge."

"No," said Adam. "Tierra's not going. Not Warrior trained. Or Cuinn. Team is Blaize and me, and two of my team. We'll check it out. Get Ai back, if they're telling the truth."

"My, what a long speech," said Tierra. As if she was going to stay behind. No, just no. "I thought we'd agreed I could make my own decisions."

"My op," Adam responded.

"How is it your op? You've just got here." Her body was heavy with anger. Her power throbbed deep inside her, and she wished the kidnapper, a kidnapper cowardly enough to take children, was here so she could make him or her hurt.

"Best qualified," said Adam.

"In what way —"

A crack echoed through the room.

Everyone but Adam and Blaize froze. He went to the window, and Blaize to the door. They exchanged signals, but before they could check for further danger, Cuinn raised an arm and pointed at the floor, his mouth open. "Uhhh…"

A teeny, tiny green bud had split one of the polished floorboards in two. It was very out of place.

"Oh. My," said Tierra. "Oops."

Elrian stared at the drugged and bound girl who lay on the floor in his country house.

He'd sent Dagon and Jowaki to the area where Indigo had first met Ai. When they'd found her she'd been easy prey – the girl was as untrained physically as she was energetically, despite her years on the streets.

Elrian had given the do-gooding idiots ranged against him an offer to swap the girl for other, higher value pieces, but he had no intention of swapping Ai for the other two. He wanted them all, as potential sources of energy for him and his subordinates. He had matches for all of them. Or, perhaps, they would serve to fill another Remnant stone – a harder process to manage, but where the reward was much higher.

At this point in the game, though, his priority was Tierra. She was the strategic piece. If he drained her, destroyed her, at this juncture, he would derail the prophecy.

His breathing sped. He drew in a deep breath and relaxed his hands, which had clenched at his sides.

Luckily, he knew a way to relax. There was no need for Ai to be one hundred percent healthy for the meeting. He gestured to Dagon. "Lift her up onto the bed."

The man picked up the girl by the arms and dropped her on the mattress, where her body bounced before stilling. She gave a quiet moan. She wasn't quite unconscious, wasn't quite conscious, though what he was about to do would wake her up quickly.

He sat on the bed next to her, and put a hand on her forehead.

He could only access her underdeveloped Ajna energy; her Anahata was no good to him. But it would be enough for today. He drew in a deep breath, and reached inside her with his energy.

23

Fintan's head was spinning as he raced to the airport to get to his friends. Tierra needed him. He should never have left her.

He had never been a fan of doing nothing, so the flight from New York to Vancouver was agonizing. With no business class seats left on the flight at this short notice, he crammed his broad frame into economy. He drummed his fingers on his thigh during take-off, garnering a narrow-eyed look from the business woman trying to read her book next to him. He must have checked the flight info on the screen in front of him a hundred times, watching the minutes count down.

He trusted his friends, Adam especially, though Adam didn't know Ai. But Adam would move mountains to help Tierra, and as a Protector, took the world on his shoulders for those he loved.

Fintan gripped the plastic glass the air steward had given him, then gulped some of the water in it. How could they have let Ai down like this? He rubbed at his forehead, the chill of the plane's air conditioning gnawing at him.

What if Adam missed something? Something that Fintan would have caught? Fintan would never forgive himself. Adam had talked him through the plan, and Fintan knew the two energetics he'd have as back up. As a Protector, Adam had some experience with hostage negotiations. He was better qualified than Fintan. It was better this way round, with Fintan on the plane and the big guy on the ground, but Fintan still wanted to be there. They owed Ai. He'd told Tierra they'd keep the girl safe, but his decision to let the girl come to them may have cost her her life.

An acrid scent caught his attention, and he looked around before realizing it was his plastic cup, softening under the heat of his hand. His eyes widened, and he put it down and wrapped it quickly in the napkin, hoping his seatmates hadn't noticed.

He had to keep better control of himself.

For Ai.

And for Tierra.

The day passed at a snail's pace. Adam finally relented when Tierra enlisted Blaize's support. Tierra would not miss this. Fintan had been told, and was on his way, but he wasn't going to be back in time to make the meeting.

She had missed him more that day. If he'd been there, he'd have lightened the atmosphere, made her laugh, and told her it was all going to be ok. She was a lot more intense when he wasn't around, she realized.

When she wasn't arguing with him.

They crowded into Adam's room for a final briefing. He introduced the two men who would join them, Clay and Ymir, both Muladhara-Manipura, earth-fire combinations, both Protectors who worked with Adam. Clay was short and stocky, his strength obvious in his wince-inducing handshake. Clay had a lot of search and rescue experience, and was both an experienced tracker and able to manipulate earth. Ymir had a talent for working with metal and minerals, and was taller than Clay, with hard eyes and a serious expression. He seemed to be assessing them all, and Tierra felt she'd come up wanting.

"Blaize and Cuinn, stick together. Clay, stay with Tierra, and Ymir and I will get Ai back," said Adam.

The fighters had scouted the meeting point for potential hiding places and traps that morning, but they didn't have the resources to keep a constant watch on it. And it was a big place, one of the largest urban parks in North America, surrounded by sea on three sides and connected to the city on the other.

"Beaver Lake has a park police patrolled trail around it, so we need to stay off that. We don't want any humans hurt."

Adam's a lot more talkative in mission mode.

"We believe at least one of them is an Anahata-Ajna. They may have access to empath or intuitive energies. And Indigo, the Leech who took

Blaize, suggested that they had access to prophecy. We have no idea what energies they have otherwise."

"We're going in blind," said Blaize.

"Yes," said Adam. "We focus. Go in, get Ai, get out. If we can gather information on the enemy or capture anyone, we will, but that's not our aim. We're risking enough taking two civilians with us –" he gestured at Cuinn and Tierra "– but both of you have been in battle before, even if it was a few decades ago, so I'm counting on you not to do anything stupid."

He looked at his sister, and she scowled back, but the churning in her stomach wouldn't let up. The danger ahead was sinking in, as she listened to Adam's quiet, efficient voice set out the plan. Cuinn might be a civilian, but his comfort in battle was greater than hers, and he'd been a fighter in his youth, if not for a long time. She wished she'd practised her self-defense harder. She wished she'd trained in offensive energies when she was younger.

She wished for many things to be different.

She got a hold of herself. *If wishes were horses … but they're not.*

Adam seemed to have finished. "Questions?"

No one spoke. "We leave in twenty."

They all took different routes to their assigned places in the park. Clay drove defensively, checking for tails, taking a circuitous route. Every moment tightened Tierra's nerves further.

She closed her eyes and whispered a prayer to Source that they get through this safely. She tried to use her breathing to calm herself. It didn't work. She needed to be in the park, with her element around her. She gritted her teeth. It wouldn't be long.

In the meantime, she needed to calm down. So Clay was just going to have to suck it up and talk to her. Because people helped her center herself, and she was so utterly terrified right now of what was about to happen, it was that or ask him to turn the car around.

"Sorry you got stuck with me." She watched his face for any reaction. He shook his head very slightly.

"Are you from England?" People loved to talk about themselves. Normally. But either Adam's taciturn nature had rubbed off on Clay, or Adam recruited for similar qualities.

"A long time ago. Now I'm of no particular country." He glanced at her.

"Do you have family? A home? A place you go back to after missions?"

"No. Too hard in our work." Something flickered across his face, but she wasn't at the right angle to read it.

"That must be tough. I find that for my Muladhara, home is an essential part of who I am." It really was. She longed for a day at home, baking or preparing food for family and friends. Instead, the prophecy and its consequences put her in situation after stressful situation out of her comfort zone, where she was barely managing to keep up.

"Home can be people as much as a place," said Clay. "My team are my home. I don't need to be grounded in a place."

She considered that as the city passed by the windows. Perhaps it was true for her, too. When she and Adam had moved to Cathair Cuinn, it was because family was her safe place. She loved the house, but if it was a choice between the place or the people, there was no contest.

And Fintan was as much part of that as the others.

The thought of him soothed the edges of her fear, and instead of her usual practice of stamping down on her foolish romantic fantasies around him, she let herself dream for a moment of a life with him as a lover, instead of just a friend. She sighed. The knot in her stomach eased a fraction.

They arrived at the park where the night was quiet and the abundance of earth energy soothed her further.

She followed Clay into the woods, and he stopped for a moment when they were hidden by shadows in the trees. He drew her off the path, into a wooded glade. Butterflies plagued her stomach and she was cold despite the layers she had on and the night being warm for the season.

"I'm going to connect with the earth," he said. "You might want to do the same."

She nodded and listened to the sounds around them. An owl hooted, and she followed the sound as it moved through the trees. Her attention was caught by a rustling, and her mind followed that. It was a grey squirrel, which should have been asleep in its den. Her attention swept the surroundings as she connected to the earth. To her energies. To her power.

She used the fear inside her as fuel. She was determined not to hinder the group. To do her part as best she could. She drew on the energy, connecting to the ether and pulling power so it spooled within her, ready. She could feel Clay's presence, his aliveness on the other side of the small clearing in the trees, as he too, drew in power.

He was pulling both Muladhara and Manipura, she sensed. For her, this evening, Muladhara was enough, as she'd drawn on more than she had in a long time. She would use it to scout their surroundings, to find what was hidden and to protect those she loved.

She sent her attention further through the woods, seeking what was alive there. She passed over skunks and racoons, and even a stalking coyote.

The lake was a couple of kilometers away from where they were, and she sent her attention that way. There were a couple of mounted police patrolling and moving away from the lake. She drew in a deep breath, grounding herself in the earth. She felt steadied. Connected. Energized. Her power was like a calm, deep pool within her. She only needed to draw on it when it was time. She could do this. She whispered a Muladhara prayer. *I am grateful the earth supports me and meets my needs.* It would.

She drew power over herself like a veil, hiding herself from possible trackers. She was warding herself as she would ward a property, to keep herself hidden. And protected. If she was attacked energetically, it would need to be someone who was at least Master level, like herself, for the attack to break her wardings. And even then, not every Muladhara energetic could do it. She was powerful.

She just needed to remember it.

Opening her eyes, she watched Clay come out of his own sequence.

"You sensed the police?" he asked.

She nodded. "Anyone else?"

He shook his head, no. "Are you ready?"

"I am." And to her surprise, she really was.

They walked quickly and quietly through the trees, staying off the trails. Their energies meant that they were both easily able to walk through the woods as if they belonged, making little or no noise, and leaving the smallest possible trail.

They came closer to the lake, and Clay waited for her to catch up. He breathed his words into her ear. "Go. I'll be watching. If you need me, I'll be there."

She nodded, and he melted into the trees. She was on her own.

24

Tierra crept through the last few trees towards the spot where she had agreed to meet Blaize. They exchanged nods, and Cuinn materialized from the trees beside them. The groups had split up to scout more area on their way through the park.

The three of them stood in silence, facing different ways, and scanned the area. The meeting was scheduled by the lake, but the lake wasn't small. They weren't sure which direction their adversary would come from.

Tierra could hear the gentle splashing of the nocturnal beavers, unbothered by the energetics standing close by. A sense of dread crept up her spine. What was out there?

A jarring sound came from over the water. A girl's stifled cry, cut off. Tierra spun around, and surveyed the lake, her heart pounding.

Across the other side of the water, Ai stood, her arm held behind her at a painful angle by a man Tierra couldn't see clearly, but who seemed familiar.

Oh, Source. Ai. Fear tore through Tierra, leaving her gasping. She clutched at Blaize's hand, who squeezed back, briefly, then let go, positioning her body in readiness to move, attack or defend, whatever was needed.

"Cuinn Ahern, leave us." The whisper was sibilant, an oily poison floating across the water.

Cuinn shook his head. "Return the girl."

"In exchange for the two women only."

The man jerked Ai like a rag doll, and she gave a despairing cry. Tierra bit her lip. They needed to do something. The plan wouldn't help them if Ai was half-dead.

Cuinn seemed to feel the same, as when the man across the lake had demanded Tierra and Blaize, Cuinn had drawn a huge rush of power, and the usually calm man was pulsing with his Muladhara. There was a tremor in the earth underneath them, and Blaize put a hand on Cuinn's arm. Their role was to keep the kidnapper talking until Adam and Ymir were able to take him down. If Cuinn attacked them, or even angered them to the extent that they left with Ai, or hurt her, everything up to now would have been pointless.

"Why are you doing this?" Tierra's voice was shaky, but she put a thread of power in it to make it carry across the lake, just as she presumed the kidnapper was doing.

"Come here, Tierra, and you'll learn everything you need to know."

She shivered. There were few things she wanted less in this life than to be on the other side of the lake. She extended a thread of energy, seeking to learn more about the owner of the voice. And recoiled, as her energy was thrown back at her with the force of an electric shock.

She gasped.

"What?" Blaize's gaze raked the landscape around her for the threat.

"It's the energy. Male. Nasty. Protected. Ajna-Muladhara. He's the one who was at the house." Tierra was breathing hard. She drew on her center to ground herself.

Cuinn turned to look at her, a frown on his face. That was the same as his energetic combination. He shook his head and focused back on the small figures across the water.

A soft, unpleasant laugh drifted their way. "If you're not interested in the girl, I'm sure I can find another use for her. She's truly full of life."

Ai lurched again, and another cry echoed on the water.

Tense seconds passed, the night expectant around them.

"I should go over there," Tierra murmured to Blaize. "We need to make sure he stays. If he thinks we're not going to swap ourselves for her, he might leave. Or do something horrible to Ai."

Tierra hated the idea of getting any closer to the male figure across the lake, but she would do anything to get Ai back. The ice water in her veins could not, would not, hold her back this time.

"Absolutely not," Cuinn said, his voice hushed and calm. "We stick to the plan we all agreed on with Adam. It's the logical thing to do. And that does not involve you or I engaging with the kidnapper."

Tierra opened her mouth to protest, but he continued, "However, I agree we need to do something to keep Ai and her captor there until Ymir and Adam attack."

"Clay's here. I could go. You're protected, but it looks like the kidnapper is alone." Blaize almost vibrated with energy. She had her own defensive shields in place and was ready for an attack.

Or to attack.

"We seem to be alone too, and we're not," Cuinn said. "But yes. Go. Distract them. Be ready to take Ai when Ymir and Adam attack and bring her back here."

Blaize pulled Cuinn to her in a fierce embrace.

He leaned his forehead against hers for a moment. "Thank you, my love. Stay well."

"I'm on my way," Blaize pushed the words across the water. "I need to check you really have Ai, and she's safe."

She took off at a run, disappearing round the dark edges of the lake.

Tierra and Cuinn were left standing together. Tierra searched the trees for a sign of Clay. He was out there, but she didn't want to search with her energy in case it drew the man across the lake to her somehow. She'd be happier if she could see Clay. For all her bravado, the energy of the man across the lake was so twisted, so uncomfortable to touch, she didn't think she could protect herself from him.

Thoughts become things. Thoughts become things. She chanted the mantra in her mind and tried to picture herself beating the figure. Picture herself winning in a fight. After all, she was a Muladhara Master in her own right. She was powerful. She connected to the ground again, topping up the energy she held spooled inside her.

Blaize arrived at the two figures, and Tierra crossed her fingers at her side. Blaize's power shimmered as she talked to the Rogue, her shields up and ready for an attack. They were no longer projecting their voices and Tierra strained to hear what they were saying. As the man's attention was on Blaize, Ymir, Adam and Argus appeared from the scrub to the east of the man, and the Rogue was distracted enough to let go of Ai.

But the Rogue didn't release her easily. He shoved the teenager to the ground and kicked her, hard, in the stomach while he put strong Muladhara shields up around himself and Ai.

Ymir and Adam attacked. Adam caused the earth to move, the ground mounding and flattening underneath the Rogue male's feet. Argus darted in and out to nip at the man's ankles. The Rogue stumbled but didn't lose his footing, pulling energy to make the branches and the bushes turn on Adam. Tierra clenched her fists. Adam was an earth energetic too – did that mean the Rogue was stronger than Adam? Oh, Source. What could she do to support their earth attacks from here? She'd promised to stay out of danger.

Ymir was much closer to the man, and added physical attacks to his energetic ones. He threw out a snap kick, aiming at the man's side. The Rogue retaliated and swept Ymir's other foot from under him. Ymir went down hard, then used the energy of the fall to roll backwards and up on his feet again.

It was all so fast and hard to follow. Tierra was unable to think of a way to help.

In the meantime, Blaize burned the plants and trees that had captured Adam, freeing him. As Adam leapt forward, she forced her way through the strange man's shields with a blast of Warrior fire while he was distracted by Adam and Ymir.

It was enough to give Blaize time to pull Ai away, although the girl was no help. She looked injured. She cradled her arm, protecting it as Blaize dragged her behind her. Ai struggled to keep up. Before they could get more than a few paces, the Rogue sent a blast of greasy energy at both the women, who froze in place.

Cuinn startled and shook his head. He turned to Tierra, his face pale.

"He's using Ajna on them," he said. "He's really strong. He's keeping them still with a suggestion. I need to help. Watch my back."

Cuinn sat on the ground and closed his eyes, drawing yet more power, preparing to aid them.

Tierra's limbs were so cold, she was shaking. Everyone was helping except her. But what could she do? She looked at the forest behind them again, hoping Clay was still with them, a silent watcher. Her neck prickled, and she listened over the sounds of the struggle across the water.

She saw the next few moments in slow motion.

Blaize and Ai moved again, presumably as Cuinn broke the Rogue's hold on them.

Cuinn, Adam, Blaize and Ymir attacked the man, using different energies, and he held his own.

His power must be immense – there weren't many in the energetics world who could hold off the combined powers that were focused on him.

Surely they must be able to identify him after this, at least.

She swept another anxious glance at the forest behind her, full of adrenaline and anxiety with no outlet. Cuinn was still and focused beside her. Perhaps she could give him some of her power again? Boost him by sharing? It was forbidden, but they had done it before, in equally desperate circumstances, and there hadn't seemed to be any negative consequences. She hoped.

Funny how it was easier to break a taboo the second time.

She drew in a deep breath, and glanced across the lake to check events there. She had to force the nausea down at the sight of her friends in battle.

Her side of the lake, a beaver slapped his tail on the lake as a warning, and a raft of ducks quacked in fear and outrage as their normally serene home was disturbed.

She dropped down to push her hands into the earth, to see if she could read the terrain and see what was disturbing this side of the lake. She connected with the earth, power sending tingles up her arms, her body between the forest and Cuinn, the lake protecting his other side. There didn't seem to be anyone this side of the water. All the action was over there – where she should be. Her body vibrated with power, and after another quick glance, she stood and stepped towards Cuinn. She would give him a tiny part of her power. He was more likely to be able to use it than her.

She bent, hands reaching for him, and agonizing pain seared through her skull. She tried to cry out, but a hand was over her face, stifling her, toppling her backwards, off balance.

The pain receded, and she crumpled into the arms of her assailant.

And everything was quiet.

Fintan was on a motorbike, driving from the airport to Stanley Park.

The bike was a dream to ride. Big, powerful, its throaty roar muted by the padding in his helmet. He kept his body low over the bike, reacting to each bump in the road, other vehicles and traffic signals by instinct as the wind pushed against his body. He was forced to be fully in the moment, be fully present. Air was his element, and he spared a touch of power to cloud his passing with a mist to obscure himself from any human law enforcement. He could do without that problem tonight. He was wary, though, of spending too much power. He might need it.

Which stopped him thinking about the danger his friends were in.

That Tierra was in.

She was so stubborn, so brave, and he knew she wouldn't think twice about putting herself into danger if she thought she could rescue Ai. She needed someone to protect her from herself.

The bike soared through downtown, and streaked past lights and other cars on late night errands. He flew through the entrance to Stanley Park, but Beaver Lake was in the interior, and eventually he had to leave the bike and run.

Another five minutes and he was close to the lake. He slowed his pace, and crept through the trees, being careful to keep any noise to a minimum. No energy use needed, this was woodsmanship, learned from many hard years of fighting in forests similar to these – if a lot colder – in his native Scandinavia.

He came to the edge of the trees, where a path cut around the lake. There were figures to his left. A girl on the ground. Ai. A woman standing next to the girl, her hand on the girl's head. Too tall to be Tierra. It must be Blaize.

His body was ready to fight, desperate to help, but years of training and discipline forced him to scout the situation before rushing in. He swallowed, mouth dry.

The moon had gone behind a cloud, and, in the darkness, it was hard to make out who was who. There didn't seem to be any fighting, but he could see two men, most likely Adam and Cuinn, were nose-to-nose arguing.

What the fuck was going on here? What had happened? He swept another last look, before he sprinted the last few hundred meters to join them.

Adam gave another man some kind of instruction, and he took off running into the forest. Was he looking for someone? Chasing someone?

Where is Tierra?

There should be one more man present, as well as Tierra. Perhaps they had gone back to the safety of the hotel. Source, he hoped so. He loped round the side of the lake, keeping his eyes open for anyone else as he moved.

And fell right over a body.

C H A P T E R

25

Fintan twisted in the air so as not to land on the body.

He sucked in a breath as, on his hands and knees, he stared into familiar eyes. Eyes that no longer held any light. Clay, a man he had known for over a century, and had worked with probably hundreds of times, had been killed. *Shit.* Grief stabbed his chest.

Then icy fingers crept up his spine as he realized the implications.

Clay had been protecting Tierra. Adam had promised him in his last conversation that if Tierra went with them – and Adam had implied that he wasn't going to be able to stop her – he would ensure she was protected. Not left alone. Fintan and Adam trusted Clay as a first rate fighter, and unfailingly loyal. He would protect Tierra to his last breath.

And it looked like he had.

Fintan swore again. Tierra wasn't across the lake with the others.

Then where the fuck was she?

He sprang up, refusing to consider the worst at this stage, and ran the rest of the way to where the others stood. Ai sat on the ground, eyes glazed, and Blaize crouched next to her, checking her over.

"Where's Tierra?" Despite being both naturally athletic and in great condition, his fierce sprint left him breathless and panting, desperation for air mixing with fear for Tierra clawing at his lungs.

Adam glanced at him. "With Clay."

Fintan's heart rate shot up further. *Shit shit shit.* There was no time to pretty it up. "Clay's dead. We need to find Tierra."

Adam's eyes flickered, and his mouth tightened. Fintan knew his friend well enough to understand the flood of emotion those small facial moments indicated on his normally impassive face. Argus whined.

Adam's gaze swept the others. "I've sent Ymir to track the Rogue, and anyone he was with. We couldn't identify him because he hid his face. We'll stay in pairs. Search the area, Cuinn and Fintan. Blaize stay with Ai. I'll track alone."

"Are you sure you should be alone?" said Cuinn. "We don't know if they're still out there."

"Adam's like a ghost." It was the right call. And they needed less arguing, and more action. "He's right, we can cover more ground like this."

Adam acknowledged Fintan with the barest movement of his head. Tierra was important to them both. "Phones everyone?"

They all nodded.

"Check in with me by text every ten minutes. I'll check in with Fintan. Look for any trace."

"Check in with me too," Blaize said. "And hold on a second."

Ai was shivering continuously, and tears streaked her cheeks, though she hadn't made a sound since Fintan had arrived.

"Ai, can you tell us who was with the man we were fighting? Or how many came tonight with him? Or anything about their energies?"

Fintan knew she was right to gather more information before they went hunting, but the delay was almost intolerable. He needed to be taking action. His hand burned as his energy pooled inside him, boiling to get out.

More tears escaped from the girl's eyes, and she put her hands over her face. Blaize sighed, and started to stand, but before she could, Ai's muffled voice said, "They told me their energies. The male is Muladhara-Anahata and the female is Manipura-Ajna."

Ai's distress ramped up to the extent that even Fintan, with his weak empathy from his Anahata, could feel her emotions. Ai had no ability to shield, had never been taught how to manage her feelings as most energetics were taught in their basic training, and she was broadcasting to all of them terror, horror, anxiety and more.

He wanted to comfort her, but he needed to find Tierra. The addition of Ai's emotions on top of his own heated his body further, and the damp ground under his feet started to smolder.

He needed to calm down. Or at least present a calm exterior, while he raged inside. Adding to Ai's distress wouldn't help any of them.

Because Tierra was the best of them. And she was gone.

Tierra was blindfolded, gagged with material across her mouth and nose, and her ankles were tied. Her hands were bound in front of her and to her waist, so she couldn't move them. Lying on her side, she could feel every single bump in the road.

She was nauseous, and having trouble concentrating enough to draw any energy. She was grateful she'd pulled so much in before, and was using that to heal the many injuries her body appeared to have sustained when she'd been hit across the back of the head.

She had no idea how long she'd been in the car, and she'd already tried everything she could to escape. There was nothing in the trunk with her, no handy serrated edge to cut her bindings like in movies, and her throat was sore from screaming and shouting through the gag whenever the car paused at a stop light.

Her breathing was fast and shallow, and she was close to hyperventilating. She needed to calm down. If she didn't, she'd never be in a state to take her opportunity to escape when it came.

She turned to the familiar in her mind, and composed a letter in her head.

Dear Me,

I need your help. I've been kidnapped.

Any thoughts?

Me.

The process, ridiculous though it might be, gave her comfort. She gave a sob of laughter. Writing thousands of replies to letters over the years, there was always a solution, no matter how complicated. Granted, none of the letters had involved kidnapping, but there was a way forward. Somehow. There had to be.

What she needed to do was stay away from the doubts that had been plaguing her since she'd become involved in this situation. Doubts that reminded her she wasn't like Blaize, strong, an energetic Warrior, trained in offensive and defensive magics and energies. She was a Healer. Her energies had been turned towards keeping family and friends safe within the home, providing security and a sense of comfort. She could ward a home, but her own personal shields were never up to much.

Oh. Damn. Okay, she needed to work harder at keeping away from the doubts, clearly.

She hoped the others were all okay. Had anyone else been taken? No one else was in the trunk with her, anyway. Which was a good thing.

Unless they were all dead.

Source, no.

She set her mind against the idea. It was unthinkable. *Plus, no one else is as stupid as me, getting captured.*

The road surface changed from smooth tarmac to something that sounded more crunchy. Were they on a driveway? A country lane? Would they stop?

Saliva pooled in her mouth, and she swallowed, before the foul fabric stretched between her teeth soaked it up. *Source, protect me.*

She needed a plan. She had no way to attack, but she could shield herself a little with the energy she'd drawn previously. Even on this surface, the car drove too quickly for her to be able to draw on Muladhara energy when she was feeling this ill. She could, however, draw on Anahata, the energy of air. She wished she'd spent more time building it up before the fight, but she really hadn't thought it would be useful, and there was only so much energy an energetic could cache inside themselves.

She breathed in deeply, trying not to choke on the fumes in the trunk, and her own sweat and tears. The air came thickly through the gag, but she was able to fill her lungs several times. The deep breathing calmed her, and she drew energy through her Anahata Chakra, concentrating on the space between her breasts where the Chakra was located.

The car drew to a stop, and minutes passed. She kept her breathing steady. She would remain calm, and she would look for opportunities to escape. She might be terrified, but she was also determined. She had unfinished business with Fintan, for starters. She drew on the thought of him for motivation. He would be so disappointed with her if she gave up. She could do this.

Muffled voices sounded around the car, at least two.

The trunk opened with a click.

It must now be after dawn, as light trickled past the edges of the blindfold. Not being able to see exacerbated her fear. Someone grabbed her arm and yanked her to the front of the trunk. She tried to maintain a personal shield to make herself harder to grasp, but couldn't keep it steady.

She wriggled ineffectually, and got a casual backhand across the face that left her stunned. It stopped further resistance from her, as she was pulled up and out, and hoisted over someone's shoulder like a sack of flour. She was shivering, her mind so overwhelmed it was blank. She knew she needed to try harder, but without the ability to touch the earth to draw on its energy, and with her terror blocking her capacity to draw on the air, she couldn't use her energies. Her physical body was equally useless, trussed up and draped over someone's shoulder.

Breathe. Breathe.

She concentrated on that as they moved to an area where the noise of the footsteps changed – inside? There would be a chance to escape at some point. All she had to do right now was keep herself in as good a shape as possible so she could take that chance when it came. And to try and take in any information she could about her environment.

The sound of the footsteps was dampened in some way – carpet, perhaps? She was carried up stairs, a door creaked open, and she was put down on a soft surface. Rough fingers loosened her wrist bindings.

Without sitting up, she tore them apart, and ripped off her blindfold. Before she'd adjusted to the murky darkness, the door was slammed and locked.

She rubbed feeling back into her wrists, and tried to rip the gag out of her mouth. It was tightly knotted at the back, but with some effort she was able to yank it down so it was around her neck. She'd work on removing the disgusting thing later.

Could she stand? No. Her shaky legs could use a bit more rest before she tried it.

She was in a bedroom, on a bed. A window next to the bed leaked weak morning sunshine into the room. There were two doors. She needed to try them, though she didn't hold out much hope they'd open. She pushed against the wall and swung her feet onto the floor, standing slowly, a newborn deer taking its first steps.

She wobbled to the first door. Locked. She rattled it a bit, but there was no give at all. She moved to the second door, determined. It opened, and her stomach lurched. But it only led to a bathroom. Her shoulders drooped.

She sighed. Perhaps the water would help her wake up. She ran the faucet and splashed water over her face. She rinsed out her mouth, desperate to be rid of the taste of the gag. She felt a tiny bit better, but she was glad there was no mirror.

She searched the rooms. She made slow and thorough progress, twice, and took stock of her surroundings.

A small bathroom, which held precisely one bar of soap and some toilet paper.

A large bedroom. About twenty-five square feet. A bed, with bedding. A cupboard, a wardrobe, a chest of drawers. All empty, with no hangers, or anything else she could use as a weapon.

And a thoroughly locked door.

26

Fintan, Adam, Blaize, Cuinn and Ymir spent the night searching the park. They didn't come across another living soul, apart from the park police, whose patrols they avoided.

Every moment that Tierra was missing more and more rage built in Fintan. His view was that she was long gone, but they had no other leads than the park.

The idea that Tierra might be suffering while they blundered around the park hoping to find a clue infuriated him. It might be a cool night, but his rage and energy kept him hot.

Ymir found a trail going away from the lake towards the outer edges of the park, which was likely to be from the person who took Tierra, easier to track because the impressions were deeper, presumably from carrying her. They led to a small beach where it looked like a boat might have been drawn up onto the shore. It seemed they'd left by sea – and none of Fintan's group was able to track across water, or had any affinity with Svadisthana, the water Chakra. They were at a dead end.

Fintan wanted to raze the park to the ground.

They continued searching, but eventually, an hour or two before dawn, Adam texted to say they needed to leave. They had to move Clay's body so park police didn't find it, or worse, a tourist or jogger.

Adam and Ymir undertook the macabre task, and drove out of Vancouver and back to Cathair Cuinn. Blaize, Fintan and Cuinn took Ai to their new hotel.

The girl still hadn't spoken. Blaize had asked her a few questions while they sat together, waiting while the others searched, but the girl didn't respond, staring into space without acknowledging the questions. There was none of the bravado that Fintan had seen in his previous interactions with Ai. It was as if the spirit had been sucked out of her.

Back at the hotel, while Blaize got the girl showered and changed, Cuinn sat on the bed in Fintan's connecting hotel room. "I think you need to try and talk to her, Fintan. You have some sort of connection with her, even if she doesn't trust you right now. You need to rebuild the connection and get through to her."

Fintan shoved his hands in his jacket pockets. Deep inside, he was cold. Icy cold. But his hands were hot, and they itched with the need to use his power. To find an outlet for it.

To destroy whoever had taken Tierra.

"I'm not sure that's a good idea." It really, really, wasn't. He wasn't stable right now. His energies bubbled inside him, screaming to be let out. Anyone could be a target if he let his guard down for a second. Ai was innocent, if foolhardy, and he needed to protect her, not put her in the line of fire.

"It's not the girl's fault Tierra was taken, Fintan." Cuinn's voice was gentle.

"I know that. I'm afraid for Tierra. And I'm angry. I can't afford to lose control, and I'm balanced on a razor's edge right now." He picked up the cushion from the arm chair and a smell of burning crept into the room. He dropped it on the bed, and scorch marks stood out starkly on the cream embroidery.

"You have to control it, Fintan. We need you." Cuinn sat on the edge of the bed, face equable.

Fintan breathed in deeply, and packed his energy down, wrapping it around his Manipura Chakra so the area behind his navel felt white hot. He might need the energy later – he couldn't afford to dissipate it. But Cuinn was right; he needed better control.

"It's fine," he said. "I just want to be doing something, not talking to a frightened teenager."

"She's our only lead. If we can't get anything from Clay's body, and we don't know where the boat took them, the only thing we have is Ai. She might be able to give us information on who the kidnappers were, why they wanted Blaize and Tierra, and where they're staying. She won't talk to Blaize. She needs someone she's familiar with. You have the best chance of rebuilding trust." Cuinn put a hand on Fintan's shoulder, wincing only slightly as the heat from Fintan's body penetrated though his jacket and then Cuinn's hand.

Cuinn seemed rational, reasonable. How much effort was it taking for him to stay that way, when Tierra was like a sister to him? Though perhaps it was just his Ajna, providing him with a logical, rational outlook on the world.

Lucky him, to have a reasonable energy.

Fintan shrugged Cuinn off and stood. "Fine."

He wished again that Tierra was here. She was the one best suited for this kind of emotional task, not him.

He knocked at the connecting door between the hotel rooms before pushing it open. Blaize paused in combing through Ai's dark hair, one hand on the girl's shoulder.

Ai was dressed in a pair of Blaize's jeans, which hung off Ai's sharp hips, and gave her a waif-like appearance. A T-shirt and a hoodie were also a little too big. She appeared the frightened child that she was, not like the belligerent goth she'd first presented as.

When she saw Fintan, her eyes widened, and her pupils dilated.

It awoke his protective instincts, but didn't calm his rage. If anything, it moved it from hot to cold – the sort of burning cold that blistered and burned. Now he had two people he wanted to keep safe.

Blaize stood, kept one hand resting on the girl's shoulder. "Fintan. Your energy is unstable. We don't have anyone with Anahata to help you if it twists. Be calm."

She stepped in front of Ai, who peered round her legs.

"I'm calm."

He wasn't. Not really. And he was worried what that might mean.

Ai stood and stumbled. Blaize let her step forward, but kept a hand on the girl.

"Are you hurt?" he asked. Concern for her flickered, but just stoked the rage further. It pressed on him like a physical weight.

She shook her head.

"Did they…?" He wasn't sure how to ask someone if they'd been drained. Especially a child. "Did they take any of your energy?"

A tear trickled down one of her cheeks.

Blaize shifted her hand to prop the girl up, mouth a flat line. Her eyes locked on his but he couldn't hold her gaze. He paced to the other side of the room. He was so hot.

He spun on one heel to face them. The girl stepped back into Blaize, who put a protective arm around her. "It's okay, sweetie. He's just worried about Tierra."

Blaize's eyes didn't match the soft tone of voice she'd used with Ai. "Aren't you, Fintan?"

"Where did they hold you?" The question burst from him. "We weren't able to track her. We don't know what they want with her. We don't know where she is."

So much for careful. A wave of energy spun out of him. He was parched. He knelt next to the minibar and grabbed a bottle of water, draining it in one long drink. The bottle it came in was plastic, and it gave way under the heat of his hand.

"Fintan," Blaize said. "Get a grip, for Source's sake."

His mind was filled with images of Tierra. Tierra being leeched from, drained. Tierra being harmed or intimidated to the point this girl had been. He imagined the girl's eyes were Tierra's, frightened and in pain. He took a step towards her, wanting to help. His brain was fuzzy, heated.

"Ah, hellfire," said Blaize. She darted across the room and grabbed him. She dragged him into the small bathroom and pushed him so he fell painfully into the tub, the shower curtain slowing his fall a little.

"What are you…?"

Blaize turned on the shower and steam hissed around him, as the heat in his body caused it to evaporate.

"You're on fire, you idiot." Blaize sprayed him with the shower head. Too dazed to do anything, he half sat, half lay across the bath, his clothes soaked and charred.

Cuinn was at the door, blocking Ai from seeing what was happening. Through the steam that was filling the room, Fintan caught sight of himself in the bathroom mirror. His eyes were wild, his hair slicked down to his head with water. His clothes hung off him in wet tatters. He looked a mess.

He laughed, wild and fierce.

He hadn't lost control of his energy in centuries. He'd kept it together through battles, wars, and numerous terrifying or difficult situations.

But he'd lost it twice in the last couple of weeks, and the cause had been the same in both cases.

Tierra.

Wonderful, beautiful, kind, Tierra.

Ahhh, shit.

He was in love with Tierra.

His stomach lurched at the idea, which was both terrifying and wonderful.

He staggered to his feet. What if he never got to tell her? What if before he got to act on it, he lost her?

His mind whirled. They had to get her back.

A noise woke Tierra. A woman stood inside the room with her, the door shut at her back. Why was she there? What did she want?

Tierra sat up, and put her feet on the floor. She needed to be ready to take any chance to get out of here. But right now, even if Tierra had the wit or the energy to tackle the woman, there was nowhere to go.

Maybe she could appeal to her. Tierra believed people were good at heart.

"Help me, please. Let me go." Tierra placed her hands behind her ready to push herself off the bed and take any opportunity that came to escape. The woman would have to open the door again to get out.

The woman laughed unpleasantly. "I don't think so."

The spark of optimism in Tierra sputtered out. She got to her feet, trying not to look like a threat, which wasn't very difficult given how beat up she felt.

The woman was short, plump, and seemed to be of Indian descent. She didn't look much like the 'baddie' Tierra had imagined. But then, the War had taught her that evil came in all shapes and sizes.

"Who are you?" she asked. The more information she could gain, the better.

"Jowaki, not that that really matters though, does it? I've brought you food. If you're lucky, you'll see the Maven soon. It's for him to explain what's what."

Tierra pushed a thread of Anahata towards the woman. Perhaps she could read the woman's emotions and understand more about what was happening. They tasted ugly. Avaricious, desperate, angry. Twisted, without a doubt, so another Rogue. A chill went through Tierra. It was rare for Rogues to work together, but this was evidence it was happening.

Weak Manipura-Ajna energy came from the woman. Very weak. But then, Manipuras trained physically as well as energetically, so Tierra knew not to underestimate her.

"Why do you want me? And Blaize?" Tierra tried for reasonable.

"I don't want you. But he's got a plan for you, I imagine." She shrugged. "I do what I'm told."

She put the tray she held on the chest of drawers at the side of the room.

"Who is he? Why do you do what you are told, when you must know this is wrong? Let me go, please." Tierra no longer held out much hope the woman would listen, now she knew what the woman was, but she couldn't help but try.

"Why? Because the rewards are great." The woman leaned towards her and licked her lips. "Be happy you're not my type."

"What do you mean?"

The woman laughed and turned away.

"Wait." Tierra took a shaky step. If the woman left who knew when the next person would come. Tears burned her eyes. She was so bruised and battered, every movement she made was a misery.

The woman moved closer to the door, her muscles tense.

"Please," begged Tierra. "What's going to happen to me?"

Before Tierra could get closer, the woman slipped out, and there was a click as the door was locked.

Tierra walked to the chest of drawers and pulled the tray towards her. She poked at the food on it. There was a sandwich, an unopened packet of chips and a sealed bottle of water.

Tierra cracked the water open and drank. The water quenched the thirst she'd been trying to ignore. Then she opened the chips and ate those. She was more hesitant about the sandwich. She left it to the side for the moment.

The food and the drink helped. The sun was up fully now, and the room was light, but another visual examination didn't bring up any new objects in the room. There was nothing she could do much with, even if she knew how. She was no inventor, couldn't create something out of nothing.

She swallowed over a knot in her throat. A tear crept down her cheek. She dashed it away with her palm. *Blaize wouldn't cry.*

That was a good idea. Channel Blaize. What would Blaize do? How could she tap into Blaize? Ah. She could write Blaize a letter. And have Blaize answer. Tierra's empathy was strong – it was how her answers to readers of her advice column were so popular. She'd never tried to answer as anyone else, but it was possible.

"Dear Blaize,

I'm trapped. I have no fighting abilities, and I'm in a room with very little furniture and no exits. I've seen one woman, and I don't know why I'm here. I'm scared.

What should I do?

Tierra.

Dear Tierra,

You say you have no fighting abilities. Yet you're an energetic, and you still have access to your power. You're a strong Muladhara and Anahata. What are your strengths? Use those to figure a way out.

Blaize.

She looked around the room with fresh eyes, and less emotion. Right. There was no point in feeling sorry for herself. That wasn't going to get her out of here.

She picked up the wooden tray her food had come on and swung it experimentally. Could she use this as a weapon? It was light, and her swings didn't give it much power or momentum. She put it down and went to the window.

She seemed to be at the back of the property, and on at least the third floor. There were fields surrounding the house, no other properties, and trees to the right. The garden was unkempt, as though once it had been tended, but not for many months.

Tierra tried the window. Locked. Of course.

She sat back on the bed, elbows on her knees, chin in her hands.

As she did so, she caught sight of something on her wrist.

It was a finely woven bracelet, delicate silk cords wound tightly together. The colors were red, yellow, green and white. Pretty, but she'd never seen it before. Was this from her captors? She tugged at it, but there was no end to catch hold of, and she had no cutting edge that she could rub against to cut the cords. She tried stretching it so that she could pull her hand out, but it was snug around her wrist, with little give.

What is it? She hoped it wasn't some kind of tracking device her captors had put on her. There didn't seem to be any electronics in it though. *Perhaps it was energetic?* She sent a fine thread of Muladhara in, and got an answering ping. Huh. She tried with Anahata, and got another ping.

She regarded her wrist again. It was on her left wrist, which was traditionally the feminine side in energetics. And red was the color of Muladhara, and green was the color of Anahata. What about yellow? Manipura. It was the color of Manipura. Was that relevant? She didn't have any Manipura energy, so she couldn't see if it pinged to that. Who did? Blaize. And Fintan.

The pieces of the puzzle came together so quickly that she gasped.

Blaize had a wrist band like this. Given to her by Source. And Cuinn had one too. A matching one. The colours of their wrist bands matched their combined energies. With white, the color of Sahasara running through them.

They hadn't been able to get theirs off either, or understand exactly why they had them.

She had one bracelet. Did that mean there was another? Who had it? Her stomach squeezed painfully. Fintan was a match, with Manipura to add to the mix. Did he have a corresponding band? Her breathing quickened as she realized she wasn't sure which was more terrifying – the idea that he might have the other, or the idea he might not.

She really hoped she had the chance to get out of here and find out.

27

Fintan moved between the soaked bathroom and the bedroom in a dazed, sodden state. He sat in a chair in the room where Ai was propped against one of the beds, her legs pulled close to her, her arms wrapped around them.

Blaize had thrown a towel onto the chair, and another around Fintan's shoulders, but his messy hair still dripped onto the carpet.

Cuinn and Blaize talked in low, urgent tones across the other side of the bedroom. They were all on edge. Then something caught Cuinn's eye and he came over to Fintan and grabbed him by the wrist, eyes widening.

"What?" Fintan said.

"What's this?" Cuinn shook Fintan's arm.

Fintan stopped and looked at his wrist, frowning at what he saw there. "Ow. I don't know. What is it?"

"You don't? When and where did you get it?"

"It wasn't there yesterday. Or when I got off the plane." He'd never seen it before. He gave it an experimental poke. Where had it come from? And what was it? He didn't wear jewelry. He frowned.

"What's the problem?" said Blaize from next to the bed, where she was encouraging Ai to drink.

Cuinn beckoned and she came over.

"Give me your left hand." She complied and Cuinn tugged her forward so she stood in front of the men. Cuinn turned her wrist to show her bracelet.

As he was using his right hand, the tightly bound cords around his own wrist also became visible.

Fintan's frown deepened. This wasn't good. He moved his wrist next to theirs. The bracelets were identical, apart from the colors. "Uh…"

"Fintan. Who has the matching bracelet?" Cuinn spoke urgently.

"I don't know! I've never seen it before. Maybe there isn't one." Fintan's voice was strangled. This was too much to take in. He'd known he was involved in the damn prophecy, but this took it to another level.

Blaize cocked her head as she examined him. Her eyes narrowed. "Is it possible Tierra has the matching bracelet?"

Fintan sucked in a breath, his insides fluttering. Could she? What would it mean if she did? Or, Source, what if someone else had the bracelet? The fluttering coalesced into a rock, and his stomach clenched. Another woman? He didn't want anyone else. He just wanted Tierra. Shit! He wanted her. But he couldn't have her. Or could he? Did the bracelet change things? He wished his damn brain was working properly.

"Tierra? Why would Tierra have it?" Cuinn asked.

Fintan jolted in the chair, half-naked and dripping wet. He glanced at the door, considering an exit, but there was nowhere for him to go. In his flash of realization about Tierra, he hadn't considered that he might have to face Cuinn before he told Tierra herself. He couldn't see Cuinn being that happy about it, and Fintan would understand why.

If she had the matching bracelet, that was good, wasn't it? That meant his stupid behavior hadn't put her off completely. He had a chance.

Oh shit.

He was going to have to tell Adam he was in love with his sister.

Oh double shit.

He was also going to have to tell Tierra.

Tierra eventually gave in and ate the sandwich.

She needed to get out of here, but had no idea how. Her energies were low, and the level of fear she was feeling was limiting the amount of Anahata she was able to pull.

Restless, she alternated between standing at the window and sitting on the bed. She wanted to take a shower, to see if the water might freshen up her brain, but the idea of being naked when anyone might come in made her feel sick. She washed herself as best she could in the sink.

Dusk fell, and she could no longer see out the window. There were no lights in the surrounding countryside. *I wonder where the nearest town is.* How far was she from help?

Could she smash the window and use the sheets to climb down? She'd seen it in films, or read about it in books. But when she tried to find something to smash the window with, she'd come up blank. The drawers in the chest of drawers didn't come out. The furniture was all too heavy to lift. Her energetic gifts didn't allow her the power to smash the window. Which was a shame, as the energy of air could certainly help her drift the couple of stories down to the ground.

She picked up the tray, and enhanced it with Muladhara, and made it heavier. If she could even crack the window, she might be able to use her elbow, covered in the duvet, to smash it. She was at the window, deciding on the best angle to strike, when the door opened again.

This time, Tierra was quicker. She ran to the door, clutching the tray to her like a shield. She tried to barge past whoever was on their way in, but a thick arm caught her with ease, and flung her back into the room, the tray slipping from her grasp to the floor with a thud.

Tierra fell to the floor, gasping for breath, and the door slammed on her hope of escape. Worse, the man was in the room with her. He loomed over her, smiling. "Well, now. Hello, little rabbit."

His eyes were more than avaricious, they were proprietary. This man wanted her, and looked at her like she was already his.

Tierra's bones turned to water. The other woman had scared her, true, but not like this. He took a step towards her and she shuffled further out of reach. With his second step, she hit the wardrobe behind her.

"What do you want?" She pulled a feeble shield around her, and at the same time threw out a thread to see what his energies were, and how powerful he was. If his energetic powers matched his physical strength, she was in trouble.

He was an energetic match for her, Muladhara-Anahata. Was he like Indigo? Was he going to leech from her?

His powers weren't at the same low ebb as the woman's, but they weren't as strong as her own. If she could get him to engage energetically, she might be able to beat him. But she'd need to concentrate to use her own energies.

"What I already have, little rabbit – you. My colleague has had to go into Seattle to sort out a problem, so you're all mine." His voice was seductive, silky, and yet grated like nails on a chalkboard. She scooted to her feet and darted to the side, to keep out of arm's reach.

But his arms were longer than hers. One of his hands shot out and enfolded her upper arm. He dragged her towards him, crushing her up against himself. His other hand tangled in her hair, stretching her neck out like a sacrifice. She struggled in his grip, and he laughed.

He leaned down, and licked from her collar bone up to her ear. He gave her ear lobe a painful nip. She sobbed. Her free arm tried to push him away, but that made him laugh harder.

"You won't be able to fight your way out from me, little rabbit." He watched her writhing as if she were a fish on a line, caught between the hand in her hair, and the hand which was now painfully tight on her arm.

"It's not my intention to hurt you. Oh no. Anything but. I want you fresh." He threw her with casual violence onto the bed. She bounced, winded, and started to get off the other side, but he pulled her back by the hem of her top. It strained around her neck and she choked. Her hands flew up to release the pressure, and she toppled backwards. He put a knee on her closest arm, pinning it to the bed.

She couldn't think. All the self-defense she'd learned, even that which Fintan had taught her recently, had gone.

The only thing inside her was terror.

CHAPTER

28

Fintan had finally managed to divert Cuinn from talking about Tierra and the bracelets. They were hardly a priority right now despite Cuinn's belief they were a key part of the prophecy. They had to find Tierra. Ai had finally drifted into a restless sleep, and Fintan, Cuinn and Blaize talked in low voices in the adjoining hotel room. Fintan was really sick of this hotel. He'd had enough of being caged in this bland room.

"We're getting nowhere," Fintan said. He'd been turning possible avenues over in his head, and was struggling to see a way forward. His usual dispassionate evaluation of a problem was gone, and he was all fire and energy. He needed to burn some of it off by doing something, and soon.

"I found a report of a leeching of a teenage Ajna-Muladhara energetic across the border in Seattle," he said. "We don't have much detail on it, but it might be connected. Maybe I could go there and see if there are any other leads?"

Cuinn frowned. "Leechings are rare. If we get a handful a year across the whole continent I'd be surprised. So it would be quite odd to have an unrelated leeching so close by without it being connected, but equally we have no evidence it's relevant. It could be a fool's errand. Do you really think it's the best use of your time?"

"I can't stay here and do nothing," Fintan bit out. "I need to be doing something. What else do we have here? You guys can go into the ether for leads. I can't. And it doesn't look like I'm the right person to get something out of Ai. I don't see anything I can be doing here."

"I've called Nixie to see if she can come sooner," said Blaize. "I thought if we could work out who one or two of the unidentified energetics were in the prophecy we might be able to ask them for help. Or find out if anything strange had been happening to them."

"Once Adam's dealt with Clay's body, he and Ymir will keep searching the park," Cuinn said. "I'll dreamwalk, and Blaize can question Ai."

Blaize nodded. "I can use Ajna to relax her so she can access as much information as possible."

"She should be our best lead," Cuinn said. "But she's so traumatised it's hard to know if we'll get anything useful out of her."

"I'm going to call Jeb at the Anahata Guild," Fintan said. He didn't think the man would come here, but who knew, he might have a feeling, a lead – Fintan would take anything. And if they needed him in Vancouver, then Fintan would do everything in his power to get him here. He hoped to Source that Jeb's fondness for Tierra might force him out of his self-imposed confinement in Anahata, and that his injury wasn't so bad it meant he couldn't leave.

Fintan set his mouth in a hard line. He needed to do something. The prospect of dragging Jeb here was satisfying just because it was action, but it didn't feel like it would truly accomplish much.

He would go to Seattle. He would follow the lead, and find Tierra.

I won't let her down again.

Fear clogged Tierra's throat. With her arm pinned by his knee, both the big man's hands were free. One closed over her breast, squeezing it. Pain blossomed in the delicate area. Tierra struggled harder, trying to get her legs up to kick him. Her breath was rapid and her vision blurred.

"Shhhh," he crooned. And bent down, looming over her.

There was a bang on the door, and he looked towards it, jaw clenched. Tierra writhed in his grip.

The door opened, and bounced against the wall with a crash. A tall, slender woman entered.

"Dagon." Her tone was lazy, but carried a threat. "You're wanted. There's no time for games."

She didn't spare a glance for Tierra, who tried to scream for help. The man looming over her frowned, and backhanded her in the face. "Shut up."

Pain exploded in her face, and she sobbed. She could feel the imprint of his knuckles throbbing on her cheek. Dagon ignored her whimpers, and to the woman, he said, "I'm busy."

She shrugged and turned. "Not my funeral."

She caught hold of the door handle and began to leave.

"Fine, fine. Wait." He turned to Tierra, and put one hand around her neck, squeezing a little. Tears streamed down her cheeks, but she was too frozen in fear to scream.

He leant down and put a parody of a lover's kiss on her lips. She had nowhere to go, and wanted to throw up when his mouth touched hers. A whimper tore from her throat as he pushed her into the soft mattress and got up.

Before she could move away, he gave her a final backhand across the face, snapping her head to the side. Pain thudded into her cheek on top of the last strike, hot and sore. She put her hands on her face and curled up into a ball, trembling with relief at his exit.

The woman left as well, the lock snicking shut behind her once more.

Tierra lay on the bed, and cried.

She was a failure.

All the things she'd told Fintan and the others, about being able to protect herself, were a lie. She'd been captured, and assaulted. And what had she done to defend herself? Nothing. She'd frozen with fear, and sobbed like a child and let that animal touch her. She clenched her hands, her body closed in on itself.

Had she been brought here to be raped? She shivered, the trembling increasing. Her muscles were like water, and she couldn't get her thoughts in order.

No. She shook her head. She wouldn't stay and wait for that. She would do whatever it took to get out of here. She might be scared, petrified, in fact, but she would force herself to get up, and try and think of something – anything! – that might help her get out of here.

She would not let herself, and her family, down.

And she would find out if Fintan had the matching bracelet, and what Source needed from them. She was caught up in something bigger than herself, but she couldn't play that role if she gave into the fear trying to consume her.

She pushed herself shakily up from the bed, and went to the bathroom to wash her face. She took a few moments for the cold water to bring her back to the here and now. To gather herself.

Back in the bedroom, she picked up the tray and concentrated on it. She pushed Muladhara into it, grateful that it was wood and a natural material she was able to work with. She made it as dense as she could and hefted it again. It was heavy in her hand. She might have a chance.

If necessary she'd use it to hit a person, but she would try to get away without violence first. She was in mid-swing when the door opened. The tray smashed against the window with all the power she had. There was a boom, and a thin crack appeared in the window.

It wasn't enough. She spun in place, and drew the tray back to strike at whoever had come in.

Thank the Source, it wasn't Dagon. It was a woman, all angular cheekbones and a sharp bob of ash blonde hair. Tierra gritted her teeth. The woman might not look dangerous, but she hadn't responded to Tierra's previous cries for help. Tierra glanced at the door, shut, but possibly unlocked.

She set her lips, and swung the tray at the woman's head.

The woman caught it in her right hand, a modest exhalation accompanying the catch, and wrested the tray from her. "Good. That's helpful. They'll think you left that way."

She gave Tierra a little push, so she staggered and ended up leaning against the wall, then took the tray and smashed it against the window once more. A web of cracks appeared.

"I'm here to help you. I'm going to get you out." The woman was efficiently wrapping her arm in a pillow case.

Tierra was paralyzed, wanting to try and flee, to shove the woman out of the way, but seduced by this offer of help. She had no idea what was outside the door. If there were more people like Dagon, she didn't stand a chance on her own.

"Why?" Tierra would trust her gut on the answer. There was no time for analysis. She'd go to her energies, her feelings. What did they say? What could she feel?

"I'm Cassidy." The woman drew her arm back and rammed it against the window, which shattered. Shards of glass fell to the floor. Cassidy used the pillow case to clear out the remaining glass. "It's complicated. Come on."

She moved to the door with poise, but looked back when she realized that Tierra hadn't followed.

Tierra gazed at the woman, eyes wide. She needed to make a decision. This woman was known to Dagon, at least, and able to give him orders, yet at the same time, was someone who said she would help Tierra escape. It didn't feel like a trick. Though why weren't they going out the window?

"I'll get you out of here," Cassidy said. "Don't worry. The window's not the way, though. But we need to hurry, please."

Everything had happened too fast. Maybe Tierra should go out of the window? She thought she'd be able to support herself enough with air to fall and not break something.

But she might stand a better chance with Cassidy – if she was telling the truth.

Tierra threw out a little Anahata. She didn't want to waste it, as she had precious little energy. Cassidy felt like a strong Ajna-Muladhara, and the feelings she gave off appeared genuine. She planned to help Tierra. Tierra probed a little – was the woman's energy twisted? Tierra frowned. Not really. It was…dark, perhaps, but not wrong. Emotionless, as if her Ajna ruled her with an iron fist. Tierra doubted she would have been able to sense the Muladhara if she hadn't had the energy herself.

"Quick. Follow me." The woman ordered Tierra with the tone of one who was used to being obeyed.

Tierra went with her gut, and trusted. She followed the woman, and the smallest flicker of relief crossed the woman's face. *Wow, she really rivals Adam for self-control.*

The woman slipped out the door, and locked it once Tierra was also in the corridor. They jogged along to a grubby looking staircase.

"Servants' quarters," Cassidy explained, her voice low. "We rarely use it."

Tierra followed her. Cassidy put a finger to her lips. There was little light in the stairwell, but what Tierra could see of Cassidy's skin was as pale and translucent as a pearl. They went down two flights of stairs. At another door, Cassidy paused.

"I need to tell you some things. You must take them back to Cuinn. Do you understand?"

So she knew Cuinn, too. Tierra nodded, none the wiser. The woman seemed impassive, emotionless, while a roman nose and dark blue eyes gave her a regal look, despite the jeans and shirt she was wearing.

"I believe you were taken to wound Cuinn. I didn't realize what was happening until too late."

Who was this woman? And what was she to this house? "If you're not involved in kidnapping me, who was?"

The woman hesitated. "Elrian."

Tierra gaped, staring. Cassidy had to be mistaken. "Elrian? Are you sure? He wouldn't hurt me."

Cassidy laughed bitterly. "If you think that, you don't know him at all."

She unbuttoned the first two buttons of her shirt and pulled the material back to show her left shoulder. Even in the dull light of the staircase, Tierra could see the dark yellow and browns of a deep bruise. It looked like a nasty injury.

Tierra's mind reeled. Things had just got a lot more complicated.

"Cuinn, and anyone he loves, is in danger. But I think there's more going on. I can't quite get to the bottom of it – it's already gone much further than I'd realized. He hasn't let me in on his plans for a while."

Tierra needed to get back to Cathair Cuinn. This information changed everything. "Who are you?"

Cassidy shrugged. "No one important. I've done some prophecy work for Elrian. He says the prophecy work he has done shows him heading the Major Circle. But when I dreamwalk, the prophecy slivers I see show him standing on a barren wasteland, in a future lifeless Earth. If he wins ... he'll do so at the expense not only of the energetics, but the world. If he wins, he'll somehow destroy the balance."

Her gaze drilled into Tierra. "He can't win. I've been trying to persuade him to take a different approach, and I thought it was working, but he seems to have stopped sharing his plans with me."

Elrian. Elrian was behind this? The others needed to know. She considered asking Cassidy to take her to him, so she could talk to him — because surely, surely, there was something else going on here. The man she had known had been angry, and bitter, but not violent.

Not a Rogue. And a Leech.

She shuddered. She wouldn't face him alone. She'd take this woman's help, get home, and bring the others back in force. It was time to stop being fearful, and be the energetic she used to be.

"I didn't realize he'd taken you." Cassidy hugged herself and rubbed her upper arms. "He's not going to like that I've found out, either."

"Come with me," Tierra urged. "You don't need to stay here. We'll bring others. My brother's a Protector and my – my friend is a Warrior. They can get us, you, help."

"I can't. You can," Cassidy said. "Tell Cuinn to find me in the ether. I think if we work together there we might be able to find out more. I might be able to explain your escape away, I'm not sure. My place is here, either way. I can do more good here."

"But ... he's hurting you." *Why would she stay?*

"I've told you. It's more complicated than that. And he loves me. I might be one of the few people who can stop this. Help the situation." Cassidy lifted her chin. "The other two energetics you met are Dagon and Jowaki. The latter trained as a Warrior."

Tierra was struggling to take it all in. Her cheek still throbbed, the pain distant but clear. She didn't understand this woman, who she was, why she would stay, but she would accept her help, and she would take the information home.

"Let me show you my energetic signature so you can share it with Cuinn. I'll plant it in your mind and he'll be able to see it, assuming he's as strong as everyone tells me he is."

Tierra nodded. She'd got this far trusting the woman, and her gut wasn't telling her anything different.

"Before you do, let me heal you," Tierra said. She could spare a little energy if she was getting out of here. She got the impression that the woman might take more damage for helping Tierra, which was sickening as an idea. "Have you had that looked at? You might have a fractured collarbone."

"I don't know if we have time," Cassidy said.

"Give me 30 seconds." Tierra didn't need long. She placed a hand either side of the injury, and spun power. Being underground didn't help with accessing air, but she was no novice. She fed energy into the woman's body, threading it through to first understand, and then heal. There was no nerve injury, and the slightest of fractures. Tierra increased blood flow to the area, sending energy with it, soothing the swelling and speeding the natural healing.

Cassidy stood, face impassive throughout the healing, even though Tierra was sure it must have caused her pain. But given how well she hid the injury in the first place – she'd caught the tray with her other hand, but it had to have jerked the opposite shoulder too – the woman's self-control was extraordinary.

When Tierra finished and drew back, Cassidy tugged her shirt back into place and nodded her thanks.

"Now. My turn, and let's get you out of here." It was Tierra's turn to nod, though she threw up some internal shields as best she could because she might be done being fearful, but that didn't mean she was going to be foolhardy. Cassidy reached out her hand and placed it on Tierra's cheek. Cassidy's power bled into her, and her body relaxed. She slipped into a blank, meditative state, only catching the last of Cassidy's whisper before everything went black. "But you can't bring the others back here. And before you get home, you have one more thing to do."

29

Fintan rang the energetic who'd been looking into the leeching in Seattle, and told her he was coming to meet her. The woman was evasive, and didn't seem that keen to help, suggesting there was nothing to find, but Fintan shrugged it off. He'd make his own decisions about that.

He took the bike, and it ate up the miles. The border crossing chewed up some time, but he stayed civil with the police there, despite the desperate inferno inside him that wanted to burn the checkpoint to the ground.

A couple of hours later he was met by the local Warrior energetic, Jowaki, at the door of a bland apartment in the suburbs.

She jerked her chin in hello. "Like I told you on the phone, the place was wiped clean. There's nothing to find here."

She unlocked the door and gestured him in.

"Run me through it," Fintan said.

"A homeless kid's body was found after a window cleaner caught sight of him through the window."

"Any leads?" He paced around the studio.

She shook her head.

"The place was wiped down, physically and energetically. The police have nothing. But you're welcome to try your luck." She shrugged.

Jowaki leant against the door frame, arms folded across her chest. Fintan knew the tension building up in him wasn't leaving much room for compassion and tolerance of others, but he was surprised how cold her attitude was about the death of the youth.

He focused on the main room. It was big enough for a bed, a couch, a small table and a TV, a tiny kitchenette, and a bathroom with shower, sink and toilet. The whole place would have fitted in the lounge area of the house where they had found the other dead energetic, and was quite the contrast.

If they were connected the MO for the crime had changed a lot, which would be unusual. His heart sank. He'd pinned a lot on this place bringing him a lead.

Jowaki, a trained Warrior he'd never met before, hadn't moved. She was annoying him. She was unhelpful, and he didn't have the patience for games today. She needed to change her attitude or she was going to be an unfortunate target for the anger that brewed inside him, sullen and terrible. He might not be able to influence people's emotions like some Anahatas, but he would be happy to try a little brutal honesty.

"You understand that there's a woman's life at stake here?" he said. "We think this is related to two cases we have going on in the Vancouver area, one of them being the kidnapping of a friend of mine."

"I did my best, but I didn't get anywhere," Jowaki said, shifting her weight to the other foot.

"Where was he? What was the position? Who found him?" he fired questions at her, and excavated the details, fighting her apparent boredom. Maybe this was her way of showing grief? Or guilt that the energetics had let this happen? He narrowed his eyes. It didn't seem likely.

The boy – he was seventeen – had been found propped against the couch. Jowaki produced photos when prompted by Fintan, who was quickly getting tired of her attitude.

"Neither we nor the police have found anything to identify him," she said.

The photos showed a horribly thin, white male, his body wasted as though malnourished. He'd been drained over a period of time. The bed had been stripped, so it was hard to tell if he'd been kept here, but the marks on his wrists indicated he had been held somewhere against his will.

Fintan stalked the room for clues. For something, anything, that could connect this to Indigo and the previous leeching, and help him find Tierra. He clenched and unclenched his fists as he thought about her. Where was she?

"Have you come across anything like this before?" he asked.

"No." Jowaki rubbed the back of her neck.

Fintan frowned and stepped towards her, into her space. "Why aren't you helping me? What's going on here?"

He didn't have time for this. He would probably need to talk to her supervisor when they were through this crisis, but in the meantime, he needed to find out what she was hiding. He didn't really care why.

"It's a one-off. The perp probably left town already." She continued to lean against the door frame, but her hands dropped to her sides, loose. The room was full of tension, and Fintan's energy crackled inside him. He wasn't sure if this Warrior understood what a dangerous game she was playing by not just offering up all the information she had.

He cocked his head and stared her down. Her breath sped up, and her fingers flexed. There was something here.

"It's not like Indigo's work," she stuttered. "I don't think there's anything here for you to find."

He sucked in a breath, and she realized her mistake in that instant, her gaze shooting towards the door. Indigo's name and actions were a secret known only to a select few. There was no reason for this woman to know it, unless she knew a lot more than she had revealed. Fire flowed through him, ready to heed his call, and he stopped it escaping with an effort.

"What are you hiding? What do you know?" He crowded into her space and grabbed her shirt, his hand burning hot. He held the energy inside him, forcing it to stay there by sheer willpower. It wanted, needed, to be used.

She froze in his grasp for a few moments, and his energy darkened, wanting to hurt her. Shit. His energy was on the verge of twisting. His body trembled, muscles jumping. He thrust himself away from her, and at the same time he drove his energy into the floor around her, drawing up a cage of flame. As he did so, he shielded himself. She hissed, but didn't attack – yet.

"Tell me what you know," Fintan said, "and help me find Tierra, or so help me, Source, I will destroy you."

So be it.

If it took his energy twisting to find Tierra and keep her safe, he would suffer the consequences of that.

Tierra woke up with a jolt. Where was she now? She rubbed at gritty eyes, and her head pounded. She was slumped against a wall in a corridor that looked none too clean. What was this place? An apartment block? Why was she here?

What did she last remember? Being in that horrible house…Dagon…and Cassidy. Cassidy! She had helped her escape. But how had the woman made her forget the journey? She was an Ajna …but she'd have to be very gifted to be able to blur Tierra's memory like that. Plus it wasn't exactly forbidden, but it was frowned upon. There were few circumstances considered serious enough to change someone's memories of an event. It was too close to mind control for the energetics.

Why was Cassidy protecting people who hurt her? She didn't seem to have been a willing participant in Tierra's capture. And yet she stayed there, with a man – oh, Source, with Elrian – who had abused her.

Tierra needed to get home. She glanced around the space and saw no danger. She wasn't restrained, and she could see a sign to a fire exit. She pushed herself to her feet, wobbling slightly, and went rigid at a sound behind the door next to her. She pressed herself back against the wall and listened.

There were two voices, a woman and a man. Both sounded familiar. Had Cassidy brought her back to friends? Or dumped her into new danger?

Tierra drew on her limited reserves of energy, and pushed a little through the door. She could at least taste their energy to see if they were energetics.

Her frail tendrils touched on the two energetics, and she gasped.

She couldn't understand it. Both energies were dark – one twisted, and the other one so close to twisting she recoiled in disgust.

But …one of them was Fintan.

30

Tierra didn't hesitate. Even though he didn't know it, Fintan had been her strength while she had been captured. Her gifts meant she was one of the few people who could stop his energy twisting, and she would not let it happen.

She went through the door in a rush, and threw herself to the side, away from where her investigation had told her the two energetics were. She needed to get to him and draw off some of the excess energy before he used it for anything stupid.

She took in the room at a glance, and frowned. It made no sense. Fintan had the horrible woman, Jowaki, caged, but his eyes were wild, his Manipura energy visible and sizzling along his limbs and torso. If she was captured, why hadn't he stood down? Relaxed? Released the energy that was growing inside him?

He turned at her entrance, and let out a huge breath. His energy wavered but the cage around Jowaki held.

"T! It's you? How are you here? You're safe? Thank Source," he said. He took a step towards her then hesitated, his forehead wrinkled. "Just …wait. I need to…I'm not feeling great."

His eyes were unfocused, and the flames around Jowaki rose and fell, one minute scorching the ceiling, the next tightening around the woman's waist. The cage was there, but uncontrolled, and Jowaki, sensing this, held still, eyes wide, a grey tinge to her dark skin. She had shielded to keep his power from burning her, but she wasn't a match for him if he unleashed his power without limits.

And he was losing it.

Tierra drew a shield around her, and took one more pace towards him. She had to earth him. Out of control, he could destroy not only her and Jowaki, but this whole building. He was a powerful man.

"I just need a minute or two. I'll be okay in a minute," Fintan said. He hadn't moved, but his breath was harsh, heaving from somewhere deep inside him. The sparks were more noticeable now, and static electricity surrounded his body, his hair floating around his head like dandelion seeds.

There was a bang, and the electricals in the apartment shorted, the fuse box kicking in. She winced.

This wasn't the mild reining in his Manipura had needed in the restaurant before they'd met Ai.

This was the burn of fire and the searing of wind combined. The crash of a summer storm, wild lightning and dark thunder.

If she gave him a minute, they could be caught in a firestorm. One that might not even stop at this building, or city block.

She had no time to be scared for herself. Fintan was too important.

She reinforced her shields, then darted forward to close the gap between them. He put up a hand to stop her, but she braced and grabbed it. She crumpled over it in pain as his energy crashed into her body. She gritted her teeth. She could do this.

"Fintan?" she gasped. "I need you to listen to me."

He blinked at her, the blue of his eyes darkening like the storm. "T? You shouldn't be here. It's not safe. You need to be safe. I need you to be safe."

His words came like a mantra, his eyes unfocused. His energy pulsed, and he tried to push her away, but she held on tight, providing a lifeline to him. She needed to keep touching his skin.

She drew off a little of his energy and winced. It burned. She was going to need to channel it better. She'd have to use both her energies.

She spared a glance for the cage of fire. It held, but the bars were fierce. She wanted to trust the control Fintan had built over a lifetime of practice to ensure the flames of his energy didn't destroy anything in the apartment, but it would take just one moment and everything would be gone. For carpet, floor, furniture – and people – to catch fire. And she couldn't even be sure if he heard her, saw her.

She couldn't let him destroy this place. And not just for the obvious reasons. But because it would devastate him.

No, she would not let that happen.

There was a draught, and some papers blew off a table in one corner. Her eyes flicked over to them, and then to the closed window.

She buttressed her shields once more, bringing in both earth and air. She wound them together inside herself. She needed earth for its grounding properties, but air for healing.

And air carried risk. His was clearly active, from the soft currents that had begun to swirl around her feet. Active, and not under his full control.

Because while air could help her to draw off the negative energy, help stop him twisting, air also fed fire.

If she misjudged this, she could be the catalyst for the very catastrophe she was trying to avoid.

The room was now so hot, her lungs burned with each breath. She blinked away sweat that rolled down her temple, stinging her eyes, and sent a thin thread of earth and air into Fintan, and for want of a better description, given it was happening on the metaphysical plane, tied it to his energies. She tethered herself to him, so she had a bridge across which she could draw the energy from him more quickly, more smoothly.

He staggered, and fell. She went down with him, still clutching him physically as well as energetically. They faced each other on their knees, their foreheads touching. Every part of her that was in contact with his skin stung, but she needed to focus on the energy. She drew off more.

His blue eyes were luminous, glowing. She stared into them, but he didn't seem to see her. His gaze, inhuman and numb, was focused behind her head.

With Anahata, the energy of air and love, as their common energy, the nature of the bridge transmitted to her his feelings as well as the energy.

She closed her eyes. If Jowaki escaped, there wasn't anything she could do. She had to focus on Fintan if any of them were going to survive this.

She tried to breathe into the pain of his twisted energy being drawn out from him, through her. It was like draining poison from a wound – but from a well that was being refilled almost as quickly as she could extract it.

A river of energy washed over her, the feelings almost as unbearable.

Loneliness and isolation. Disconnection. Unworthiness.

He wanted a family, loved them as a family. But never felt he fitted in. Never felt he truly belonged.

His energy battered her, and she tried to root herself in her earth energy as it rushed through her. A sob tore from her throat as the feelings came close to overwhelming her.

She had never known how lonely he had been. He had always been the joker, everyone's friend. But all those lovers had been to fill a space inside him, a space that deep down, he didn't really feel deserved to be filled.

The energy burned hotter, waves of heat rolling off him. She clutched at his hand, and pressed her forehead harder into his. He was immovable, unreachable.

The only way to bring him back now was to siphon enough off him. It was a race.

Source help me, please.

She strengthened the bridge she'd built between them, and was able to bring the energy out of him and through her more quickly. She could disperse it when it hit her, her energy dissipating it harmlessly. Well, harmless to others. Not so harmless to her.

Sweat soaked her body, dripping down her back, and her grip on his hand was slippery. She tugged harder, drawing the energy off faster and faster.

More feelings, positive this time. The love he felt for her family.

The love he felt for her.

The bracelet around her wrist shone, and from the corner of her eye she saw a mate on his wrist shimmer.

She gasped, and wobbled on her knees, managing to hold on at the last minute.

His love for her wasn't like the love he felt for Adam, or Blaize. It was strong, and friendship was wound into it, along with respect. But unlike for her family, his love for her wove in desire, and longing, and intimacy.

Oh, Source.

He loved her. He really loved her.

The realization burst over her, and gave her a boost, and she was able to increase the speed at which she bled the energy coming from him. The bracelet, whatever it was, enhanced her powers, rebounding and cleansing the energy that came from his, and adding another channel to get rid of the danger.

Malignant energy rushed through her, feelings and energy and power.

She grasped at it, siphoning faster and faster, as her own control wavered. Her head ached, her body throbbed. She was light-headed, unsure how much longer she could do this.

It couldn't need much longer though, surely. She needed to draw off a little more energy, hold on for a little more time, stay conscious and in control, and he'd be safe. Herself, not so much, but it was worth it.

She sucked in a breath, and went for another desperate effort, trying to let go of as many of her walls as possible. To open up to allow his power to surge through her.

The power smacked into her like a blow.

She held on one, two, three more seconds for it to move through her, then dissipate.

He blinked.

"T? What's going on? Why are we on the floor?" Fintan said. His eyes widened as he took her in, her nearness, their heads pressed together, almost close enough for their eyelashes to touch.

Another second, that's all she needed, for the deadly power to leave him. She didn't have the words to tell him, but she needed him to stay where he was, needed that skin-to-skin for the process to be complete.

He tilted his head, and the space between their mouths lessened as his forehead lifted off hers. She panicked. If she left any of the twisted energy inside him, the cycle could restart, and she didn't have the energy to drain it a second time.

But she was so tired. She couldn't raise her leaden limbs, couldn't form words.

She did the only thing she could think of to keep them touching.

She kissed him.

Then the last of the energy flowed from him to her, and with a low groan, she released it, harmlessly, into the air.

She slumped to the ground, exhausted, sparks dancing across her vision. She held on to consciousness a moment longer, enough time to see Fintan's eyes lose their glaze.

Then the sparks blinked out, and she lost herself to the darkness.

31

The silence in the kitchen was charged. The men were in their own private worlds. Fintan sat at the table and stared into space. Adam stood at the window looking out at the grounds, Argus occasionally whining at his side. And Cuinn kept himself busy in the kitchen, pulling together a meal from leftovers in the fridge. This was the kind of situation none of them could fight.

Adam had asked Fintan what Tierra's status was, but he hadn't been able to tell them much. Yes, she was in one piece. But somehow she'd expended huge amounts of energy, and she still hadn't woken up by the time he'd handed her over to Cara. He wasn't sure what had happened.

Because he really didn't know.

The kitchen, usually the heart of Cathair Cuinn, usually Tierra's domain, was claustrophobic with too much over-protective male energy churning with nowhere to go. Fintan's skin buzzed, and he was torn between bolting out the backdoor to get into the air, or busting the door of Tierra's room down.

Burning something down would also feel pretty good.

He'd gone to meet that Warrior Jowaki to follow a lead, and find Tierra. And somehow, instead, she'd found him. But what the hell had happened in between? The last thing he remembered was caging Jowaki, then feeling sick. Tierra came in, and after that, he lost time.

Until the moments before she kissed him.

By the time Fintan was fully himself again, Tierra in a crumpled heap next to him, Jowaki was long gone. It had taken Fintan a while to piece things together, time when he'd been trying to rouse Tierra, using his rusty medical skills to assess her, and making calls to her family. He'd taken stock of the scene too, though Adam had sent Protectors to investigate properly, when it had struck him that he had done this to Tierra. He'd been the one she'd had to save the neighborhood from. His disturbed, inadequate energy.

He had rushed Tierra, who his limited healing energies told him was stable, if unconscious, back to Cathair Cuinn. It had been a frantic few hours. He'd had to dump the bike and get a car, and install her in the back. Somehow he'd got them through the border, showing their IDs and joking with the guards about his sleeping wife. His only thought had been to get her to the safety of family, where she could be looked after properly. He'd hoped the sleep she was in was healing, but he couldn't reach her in the physical world or with his energies.

On the horrible drive back, glancing at her in the rear-view mirror every few seconds, he knew the time had come to stop messing around. When she was better – and she would get better, he would see to that – he would tell her how he felt.

He still didn't think he deserved her, but if there was even a small chance they could make it work, and she might accept him, it was worth trying.

He'd thought this crisis they were all facing meant he shouldn't distract them with emotions. That now wasn't the time for relationships, or love.

But it was the opposite.

It was with love – lovers, family, friends, love of all types – that they were stronger. The prophecy showed a connected group of people who were somehow woven together as tightly as this damnable bracelet on his wrist. He didn't know all the players yet, or how someone like Ai might be connected, but their strength was in unity – that was something he knew.

And in partnerships like that of Cuinn and Blaize.

Maybe, just maybe, he and Tierra could be their own version of that if – no, when – she recovered fully.

If not? If she came to her senses and rejected him, he'd still work with the group. He wouldn't risk them all for his pride.

It would hurt, he knew that.

But it was time for him to stop playing around, and take a risk.

His shoulders sagged. He'd rather fight a Rogue.

The door opened, and Cara came in.

"Tierra is awake, and wants to talk through what happened, and she'd rather do it just once. Then she needs to sleep. Come through to see her."

There was a sense of relief in the men as they trooped after Cara to one of the empty suites that she'd set up as a small medical bay with both Tierra and

Ai. The room was dim. Ai slept soundly in one bed, Blaize leaned down to talk to the occupant of the other.

Tierra's usually cheerful demeanor was dulled, her energy muddied and weak. Fintan ached to rush over to her. On the journey back he'd spotted her bracelet. He was desperate to talk to her about it, but knew he'd have to wait. For the moment he'd drawn his sleeve over his, unsure if she'd seen it already. With Cuinn and Adam balanced on the very edge of reason, the last thing he wanted was to discuss his relationship with Tierra. Especially before he had had a chance to discuss it with her.

The kiss … the kiss had given him hope, even though he knew it probably shouldn't. At the same time as he'd proved himself yet again unworthy of her, unable to hold his energy together, she'd saved him, taken herself to the brink to keep him together. That kiss had been her last way of drawing out the poisonous energy from him, and meant nothing more than that.

Did it?

He raked his eyes up and down her, deliberately searing her wan image into him. He had done this to her.

Tierra huddled in bed, sitting up but leaning heavily against a wall of pillows. She was wrapped in a huge hoodie. Argus threaded his way through the human occupants of the room, and nuzzled at her, and she absentmindedly patted him once, then drew her hand back. He huffed, and put his large silvery head on her thigh.

"The Rogue took me. And one of his team members let me go. I know you'll have questions, but I need you to let me talk it through chronologically before you do. Please." Argus gave her hand infrequent licks as she opened her story.

There were nods all round.

Cara put a hand on Tierra's arm and squeezed. "Whatever you need."

Tierra drew a deep breath, and talked them through the events of her kidnapping.

When she got to the part about Dagon, tears fell. The inflection of her voice never changed, but she groped for Blaize's hand, and held it while she talked.

If Fintan hadn't been so effectively grounded by Tierra so few hours before, this might have tipped him over the edge. His stomach burned as she described the assault.

Cara nudged him. "Keep it together."

When Tierra got to the part about Cassidy, Cuinn leaned forward, forehead wrinkled, foot tapping under the table. He'd have questions, Fintan knew. But they had Tierra back now. There was time enough.

"She's a powerful Ajna," Tierra continued. "She put an energetic picture of herself in my mind so you can contact her, Cuinn. The most scary thing is that I think she was able to hypnotize me. I have no memory of getting out of the house and to where Fintan was."

She shuddered. "She must be very powerful to be able to use mind control in that way. But I don't understand why I don't know who she is, if she's that strong. How can she be under the radar?"

There were deep lines of worry in Cuinn's forehead. "There are a limited number of Ajna energetics who can do that, and I know them all. Maybe twenty max. None of them are called Cassidy."

For the first time in the story Tierra raised her gaze above the floor, and looked at Cuinn. "It's what I thought. She's dangerous. She's unpredictable, but her energy wasn't twisted. I can't work out what she was doing there."

"I'll need to work with you to access the picture she shared with you," said Cuinn. I'll dreamwalk as soon as I do."

Tierra nodded. "Fine."

"She needs sleep first," said Cara.

Tierra bit her lip. "There's one more thing. I know the name of the Rogue who's behind all this. The man who fought you in the park. The man who's behind draining and leeching off innocent victims."

Progress at last, thought Fintan. At least some good would come of this. Here, perhaps, there would be something they could take action on.

She swallowed hard. "It's Elrian. Cuinn, it's your father. He's the Rogue."

There was a long minute of silence. Tierra bowed her head. She knew that it would be a shock for her friends and family, and she wished she hadn't been the one to break it to them.

Blaize broke it. "Are you – are you sure?"

Her voice was without its usual confident edge.

Tierra nodded. Her whole body ached with fatigue. "I'm sure. Cassidy used his name, and said he targeted you and me in order to hurt Cuinn. Having said that, his two goons were energetic matches for us, so I assume we would have served as energy batteries for them as well."

"My father? But …this is absurd. Ridiculous. How can he be a Rogue? And involved in something so monstrous?" Cuinn shook his head. Tierra wished she had the strength to hug him, but she couldn't make herself move from her bed.

"When did you last see him?" Cara asked.

"After World War II," Cuinn said. "We argued over my mother's death. It's why I left Ireland – we both needed space. I haven't seen him since. He always was difficult, and my mother's death triggered something in him.

Without her, something dark appeared. But he wasn't a Rogue. His energies weren't twisted. Depressed, perhaps. Angry, most certainly. Not twisted."

"If that was him in the park, he's a Rogue now. And a lot more powerful." Adam spoke flatly.

"The Rogue's energies were a match to Elrian's," Fintan said.

Tierra didn't have any doubts, however horrible an idea it was to contemplate. But she couldn't be the person who convinced them, then held them all together right now. It was all she could do to keep herself from shattering into tiny pieces. She glanced at Fintan and wished things were different. That he could hold her, be there for her. Be her strength, as she'd been his the day before.

She knew he loved her. The energetic link they'd shared had shown her his feelings. But the boost knowing he loved her had given her had gone. Because she'd also seen his fear. His fear of being unworthy, and his fear of risking his chosen family by messing things up with her.

Only he could get over that. She couldn't do that work for him. Couldn't even if she wanted to as she was tired to the bone, inside and out.

But ... still. The memory of the kiss she'd given him, to save him, was seared into her. She held on to the feeling of his mouth touching hers, a talisman.

Much like the bracelet on her wrist. She fingered it under the hoodie, then sighed and rested her head back on her knees. It was pointless to think about. They had far larger issues to deal with. Her own comfort, or her relationship with Fintan, weren't a priority now given the very personal threat they all faced. But she didn't have much to offer the discussion.

"I don't know what to do with this information." Cuinn looked blankly at the wall. "What do you do when you think your father might be a murderer?"

"It doesn't change who you are, Cuinn. We'll find him, catch him, and maybe we can rehabilitate him." Blaize, with her own father issues, spoke fiercely.

Tierra wasn't sure she could cope with this conversation any more. She'd reached her limit. Elrian's activities so far indicated he was worse than some of the most notorious Rogues in the energetic race's history. The idea of rehabilitating him didn't seem too likely. In the past, she would have been hopeful. And if Cuinn needed that hope, she understood. For the first time in her life, she thought that the execution of an energetic might be righteous.

Because the kind of man who tortured and killed children; the kind of man who let Dagon assault his own niece?

Maybe he deserved to be put down.

"I need rest." Cara nodded and ushered everyone out of the room. Ai hadn't woken during the conversation, her sleep enhanced by Cara's healing energy.

Tierra didn't wait for the door to close. She slid down under the comforter with the hoodie still on. She scrunched up her eyes, and tears leaked from beneath them.

Cara had healed Tierra's physical aches, but the emotional ones she'd have to process on her own. When Cara had told her about Clay, it was like a blow to the stomach. If only she'd been paying more attention, maybe he'd still be alive. They killed him to take her. His death would weigh on her conscience forever.

Cara came back into the room and sat on the bed where Tierra was a lump under the covers, curled up as small as she could.

Cara squeezed Tierra's hand. "Do you want to talk?"

Tierra shook her head.

She'd lost a little of her innocence this week. A little of her faith in the goodness of the world.

She needed time to mourn.

32

Tierra woke up. Morning light trickled into the room. She still ached inside and out, but there was comfort in being back at Cathair Cuinn.

And in knowing that Fintan was alive and well close by.

She pushed herself into a sitting position, and saw Ai was awake. She sat on her bed, arms wrapped around her knees, staring at the wall.

Tierra winced. She owed the girl an apology. Tierra and Fintan had really messed up there. In trying to protect her, they'd made things worse.

"Ai?" she said, softly.

The girl didn't move. Tierra lifted the pale blue comforter off herself and threw her legs over the side of the bed. The floor was cold, stone that was pleasanter in the summer than an early spring morning. Okay, so she'd take the blanket with her. She wrapped it around herself and shuffled the handful of steps over to Ai, and sat on the side of the bed.

Ai's jaw tightened, but there was no other response.

It was time to start being open with the girl. "I'm so sorry we didn't tell you about Indigo. Can I tell you the whole story now?"

Ai shrugged.

Tierra took a breath, and launched into the story, holding nothing back. She spoke of the prophecy, of Blaize and Cuinn's relationship, their bracelets, and how Indigo had kidnapped Blaize, and nearly killed her.

Ai had turned to look at her before she got far in the story, her eyes wide.

Tierra brought her up to the point where she and Fintan had met Ai. She wasn't ready to tell the rest quite yet, though she would need to soon.

"Please, ask me any questions you have," Tierra said. "I don't want us to keep secrets anymore."

Ai blew out a big breath. "I want to call bullshit. But…the stuff I saw with that guy, Elrian. He did something to me. I don't know if it was this leeching stuff or what, but it wasn't normal."

"If you want, we can hold hands, and I'll open my emotional shields so you can see what your gut says." It wasn't something done much, but Tierra owed it to this teenager, who she'd so badly let down.

Ai's brow wrinkled. "I guess? Will it hurt?"

Tierra shook her head, and offered her hands, palms up.

Ai took them very tentatively, laying her palms down on top of them. Her fingers were like twigs, so light and slender.

"Tap into that space inside you that you call your gut feel. Your 'spidey-sense'. Close your eyes if it's easier. I'll open my shields for a moment."

Ai shut her eyes, and Tierra dropped her shields, exposing her emotions to the girl, hoping Ai would be able to tap into her Anahata enough to sense them.

A long minute passed. Then Tierra felt the ripple of connection in her heart Chakra, the girl's fingers clenching around Tierra's hands.

"Oh!" Ai said, and her eyes snapped open. "I knew you and Fintan were together!"

Tierra squeaked, and slammed her shields back up reflexively, dropping Ai's hands. That had *not* been what she'd meant to share.

"Um. How do you feel about Indigo? Do you feel you can trust us?" Tierra asked.

A weight seemed to have dropped from the girl, who scooted back and rested against her headboard. "Sure. Can we eat breakfast? So how long have you and Fintan been together?"

"Er, we're not together." This was not how she'd expected this to go. She was ready for questions about possible betrayal and the tragedy of Indigo, not about her own non-existent love life. She really needed to learn how to deal with teenagers again.

"You are. You're in love with him, and even I can see he totally digs you. Also you have that bracelet thing, and I saw one on him last night that matches. Isn't that what Cuinn and Blaize have?" Ai heaved herself off the bed, and grabbed a thick robe from the side, and walked carefully to the door.

"Yes….but that doesn't mean —" Tierra, still sitting on Ai's bed, was nonplussed.

"Plus he's pretty into you. Seems simple to me. I'm going to find Cara and see if there's something to eat." Ai turned with her hand on the door.

"Thanks, though. I still don't know about all this stuff, but I'll stick around for a bit."

She disappeared out the door, leaving Tierra simultaneously relieved and dazed.

And wishing it really was that simple.

After her conversation with Ai, Tierra had slept for most of the day. Now she was in the garden. Crying.

She sat on the grass outside her window, cross-legged, deeply connected to her element of earth. She tried to ignore the tears. If ever in her life she had needed to replenish her Muladhara, the Chakra of grounding, security, and safety, it was now.

Her world had been turned upside down. Physically, emotionally, energetically, she was wounded. She'd gone out into the world, broken her self-imposed retreat, and it had cost her. It had been worth it, she thought, to have found Ai.

And then there was Fintan. She'd seen the sadness inside him, the loneliness and most surprisingly, the love he had for her.

A love that he wasn't prepared to act on. Wasn't prepared to risk losing the others as family for the chance he'd gain her as a partner, despite the fact Source, or some aspect of the energies, wanted them to be together, given their wristbands.

If he did offer her the slightest opportunity – was brave enough to even open the discussion – she'd take it, and do everything she could to reassure him that she loved him back. And that even in the very unlikely event that they couldn't make it work, and they needed some time to get over it, he wouldn't lose them as family.

Dusk was falling and she got to her feet, moving deeper into the forest that surrounded the shady bower outside her room, the spring flowers peeking through and beginning to blossom. She breathed in the smell of mulch, and more tension drained away.

A voice behind her interrupted her thoughts. "Can I talk to you?"

She turned. Fintan had showered and shaved, and wasn't nearly as unkempt as he'd been when she'd seen him nearly lose control in Seattle. She enjoyed his rugged surfer look, the stubble making him seem mischievous and non-conformist, but when his hair was tidy and his beard shaved off, the angles and planes of his face made him breathtakingly handsome. Her heart gave a squeeze. She let it mourn, and comforted it. *We'll be okay.*

"Good evening, Fintan." Her voice was soft.

He stood in front of her, hands rubbing together. "How do you feel now?"

"Better. Definitely better. Still a way to go." She sighed. "But people need to stop treating me like glass. I'm better when I'm looking after other people. And Ai needs me."

"Cara's looking after Ai. They seem to be building a relationship, of sorts."

Tierra's heart squeezed again. *Poor heart. It's okay, little one. We'll rebuild our relationship with Ai.*

Fintan cocked his head. "It'll be hard for her to trust anyone for a while. She feels like she's let us – you in particular – down."

Tierra toed some leaves. "I know. It's fine. She needs time to heal too. They leeched from her. She's okay, but her crash course in the energetics has been pretty tough."

A silence stretched between them. Tierra rolled her shoulders to ease the rigidity that appeared. She wasn't sure what to say to him. *Sorry I kissed you? But you know it was only to save you, right?*

"Do you want to take a walk?" Fintan said.

"Now? It's nearly dark."

"I can help with that." He concentrated for a moment, and a glowing ball appeared above them, bobbing up and down.

Tierra stood and took the arm he offered her. They set off at a gentle pace through the woods. Cuinn's estate was quiet, their nearest neighbor miles away. They ambled along for a while without speaking. Her shoulders relaxed. *I wish we could go back to being like this all the time.*

"Matching bracelets, huh?" Fintan said.

Heat washed across her face, and she was glad that the darkness surrounded them. Okay, not quite back to normal. "I guess."

"I think we need to talk about them," Fintan said.

She wasn't sure she did. She didn't want to have to hear how, despite the universe trying to bring them together, she still had an unrequited love.

"What's to say? We know nothing about them." Tierra dragged her feet. *Maybe I can say I don't feel well, and go back to the house.*

Fintan frowned. "We know it's linked to the prophecy. And that you and I got them about the same time. And we have the same colors, which, if Cuinn and Blaize's are a good model, are the colors of our Chakras, and the color of the Source."

She shrugged. "We don't know what that means."

He stopped, and turned her towards him. He put a hand under her chin and tipped her face up. His blue eyes were dark in the light he'd conjured.

"What were you thinking when the bracelet appeared?"

"I don't remember." It had been when she'd been captured, that she knew. There had been a lot going on.

490

"Well, I remember what I was thinking. At least, feeling. I was feeling utterly terrified that you were hurt, or dead. I was losing control. For the second time in a couple of weeks – which was also only the third time since I became a Manipura Practitioner." He paused. "Do you know when I lost control before that?"

She shook her head. The whole forest was hushed around them, the sounds of dusk faint and faraway, the two of them caught in their own tiny, intimate bubble. Her stomach fluttered and danced, the aches in her soul banished to a far corner of her consciousness.

In the dark forest clearing, visibility was reduced, which heightened her other senses. She could smell his delicious smell, spicy and smoky, black pepper and amber. She could feel the cool breath of the wind on her arms, and the warmth of his hand, which had moved from her chin to cradle her cheek. She resisted the impulse to snuggle into it.

"The last time I lost control – apart from in the bloody restaurant – was when a teacher called Maya at the Anahata Guild told me my Anahata energy was barely worth bothering with," Fintan said. "That my heart Chakra wasn't worth their time. That I should forget about it and focus on Manipura, because there was only enough energy in me to be a Warrior, and not a Healer, or any useful or worthwhile Anahata energetic."

He emphasized the last words with anger – and hurt.

Tierra gasped at this. "Really? How could any Anahata say that to you? That's awful."

And what a way to shut a young man down. Pieces flew into place. A way to create someone who never went too deep into romantic relationships, but kept them easy and shallow. Where he didn't bother with his feelings. His heart.

"I agree. But at the time, as a young, impressionable energetic, I was upset – and those damaged feelings expressed themselves in anger. And a loss of control that burned several Anahata Guild buildings down." He laughed grimly. "Unsurprisingly, it took me longer than most to be ready for the Anahata Practitioner trial, and I passed that by the skin of my teeth. I didn't have much interest in it after that. Anahata. The Guild. I dedicated myself to Manipura, to being a Warrior."

Her heart ached for him. She hadn't known him then, though the story of how he'd burned down buildings in the Guild was a legend. *But the legend was wrong.* It had never mentioned the cause of his anger and loss of control, but rather painted him as a mischief maker who wasn't serious about the Guild. Well, no wonder.

"And matters of the heart … I kept them light. Given how weak my Anahata was, there wasn't much use in trying to love one woman deeply. I told myself I fell in love all the time, but when I looked into myself – which I tried not to – I knew it wasn't real love. Seeing Blaize and Cuinn together has hammered that point home."

Tierra tried to back out of his grasp. She didn't want or need a break-up speech from someone she wasn't even dating. "I know you're not interested in a long-term commitment."

She didn't need that rubbed in right now. She was too fragile. She felt brittle, as if a casual word could smash her to pieces. And she wasn't sure how long it would take her to repair herself if that happened. It had just been too hard a week.

He caught her other hand, holding her in place. "That's not what I said. Yes, that's the way I used to think. But seeing Blaize and Cuinn together ate at me. And when you dropped your bombshell in Vancouver –"

Argh. She winced. She didn't regret that moment of being true to herself – mostly – but being vulnerable wasn't easy. She turned her cheek away from the heat of his hand. He let her, but his other hand held on.

"– I was shocked. I lost control, for the first time since those buildings burned down. I was ashamed. Ashamed that I needed you to stop my energy from getting out of control. It almost twisted in that restaurant, but you stabilized me, grounded me. And I burned you." He swallowed.

She hadn't seen shame. She'd been puzzled why he'd seemed to lose some of his control, but she'd put it down to embarrassment about her confession.

"When I got the bracelet, Tierra, I had just realized I was in love with you."

Okay. That wasn't a small opening. That was the whole dam crumbling. She gaped, unable to speak from the shock.

"I know you deserve more. Because everything that's in you is good and true, and wonderful. You deserve better. But I will do what I can to prove to you every day for the rest of our lives that I'm worth you taking a chance on."

Her mouth remained open as she stared at him. Then a sparkle caught her eye, and a thread of fire shot past her face, and looped around to encircle them, shooting sparks of gold and green. Fintan drew on the ether, and flowers of fire appeared between them, in every color. They were stunning.

"Be with me, and I'll create hearts and flowers every day for you," Fintan said.

The flowers flew up and apart in a small, contained explosion, creating a mini-fireworks show above their heads.

She finally was able to nod her head, words still failing her.

Some tension in him seemed to relax. "I'm going to kiss you now."

"Um, okay."

And it really, really was.

He stroked a hand over her hair and rested it on her neck. The other traced meandering circles down to the curve of her rear. She shifted her hips towards him. She looked up into eyes the midnight blue of desire, his pupils huge. He kissed the side of her neck as he brought her body flush to his. She put her hands on his hips.

Tentatively, still uncertain of her welcome, she stroked a hand over his hip and thigh. He was warm and firm, his muscles lean and hard. The muscles in his butt tensed under her fingers.

Her whole body tingled in anticipation of what she expected to be a gentle kiss. A follow on to the way she'd pressed her lips against his to save him.

But this was no gentle kiss.

When his mouth came down on hers, it was urgent and demanding. She opened in response to him, her tongue darting out to meet his. His groin, pressed against her abdomen, showed her how attractive he found her.

A great weight fell from her, and she returned the kiss with a vengeance. His mouth was hot and wild, and his hands pulled her tightly against him. She moaned, and both his hands scooped under her buttocks and picked her up.

She wrapped her legs round his waist, and he started to carry her towards the house.

"Wait," she said, breaking the kiss.

His breath came quickly, and the look he gave her was a mix of desire, concern and puzzlement. "Do you want me to stop?"

"Yes. I mean, no. I don't want to stop, but I don't want to go inside. I want to stay out here."

"You want to … make love … outside? For our first time?" he asked.

She nodded. Her whole body felt electric, the nerve endings on fire, a match waiting to be lit.

He gave a little laugh, and laid her on the soft forest floor. They tore each other's clothes off, and he covered her body with kisses as she writhed on the ground. He knelt above her, the flat planes of his body delighting her as his pale skin caught the moonlight. He was hard and ready, and she couldn't wait another second.

She'd waited most of her life, after all.

"Please, Fintan."

He stroked himself, teasing her. "This?"

"Yes. That."

He put his hands either side of her head and entered her. She gasped and they moved together, bodies joined, until the match was lit and the woods were illuminated once again by fireworks.

They walked back to the house hand in hand, the night still quiet around them. Fintan felt his usual sense of security and calm at Cathair Cuinn multiplied tenfold. He glanced at their hands, joined, her left and his right, their bracelets next to each other.

They only managed a few moments back in her room before there was a knock on the door. "Tierra, love? Can I come in?"

It was Blaize's voice.

"Of course."

The door opened and Blaize said, "Family meeting, I'm afraid. Adam wants to get everyone on the same page."

"Ai, too," Tierra said.

Blaize raised her eyebrows. "Is that wise?"

"We need to build trust with her," Tierra said. "That means sharing what's going on. All of it."

They picked up Ai from her room, where she'd moved from the makeshift infirmary, on their way back to a warm and inviting kitchen. She greeted them cautiously, but with a lot less anger than before.

They joined Adam, Cara and Cuinn, already at the table. Blaize sat next to Cuinn, and Ai perched on a chair next to Cara, and fed occasional titbits to a contented Argus. Tierra sat opposite Adam, and Fintan stood behind her, massaging her shoulders.

There were a few knowing glances from the women and Cuinn's lips pressed together in a slight grimace when Fintan and Tierra sat down.

Adam leaned back in his chair and he tilted his head, seeming to weigh something up.

Fintan swallowed. He probably owed Adam an important conversation. Soon. But if Tierra had accepted Fintan, then he had better get to work on proving his worth to all of them.

"Something you want to share?" Adam said.

Okay, maybe that conversation would be sooner than Fintan had expected.

Fintan lifted his and Tierra's hands, displaying the bracelets. "Yeah. I'm in love with your sister. And for some reason, she's going to give me a chance."

He kind of wanted to add "Please don't kill me," on the end, because if Adam wanted to land a punch or two, Fintan wouldn't stop him. He loved the man like a brother, notwithstanding his relationship to Tierra.

Adam's eyes narrowed and very deliberately, he placed his hands flat on the table. He stared into Fintan's eyes for a long moment, while Fintan's shoulders tensed. Argus rested his weight on his front paws, ready.

The room was silent. Eyes wide and puzzled, Ai glanced between them and tried to work out what was going on.

Tierra rolled her eyes. "He's fine, aren't you?"

"Why wouldn't I be? My sister just chose my best friend to date." Adam leaned back. "And she's free to choose whoever she wants."

Fintan let out a relieved breath. Argus huffed and lay down, head on paws.

"He probably shouldn't fuck it up though," said Adam thoughtfully, appearing to speak to the air.

Fintan rolled his shoulders, and Tierra squeezed his hand. It's not like he disagreed with Adam. Still. Their outdoor sex – amazing outdoor sex – seemed to have renewed Tierra some, so he had to be doing some good somewhere.

Cuinn brought Ai up to speed on the time since Ai had met Fintan and Tierra. The girl's posture was more relaxed, though she still had purple smudges under her eyes. It would take time for her body and mind to heal, but her acceptance of the group would go a long way to making that happen. And they would do everything in their power to support that.

"So far we have identified myself and Blaize, Tierra and Fintan, and Adam of the twelve. The rest of the faces are either blurred or Blaize and I don't recognise them. We hope that when Blaize shares the images with Nixie, who will draw them so you can all see them, we may identify more. I haven't seen you in the prophecy, Ai," Cuinn said. "You're a wild card."

Relief and disappointment warred on Ai's face. Cara put an arm round the girl.

Fintan hoped Ai wasn't involved. Because there could be another reason Ai wasn't in the prophecy, which didn't bear thinking about. Though prophecies were slippery things, never set in stone. Even if Cuinn and Blaize could work out what they thought it meant, they couldn't take any of it for granted.

Whatever happened, they would come through this, all of them. There were a lot of loose ends to tie up first – who Cassidy was, and why she was working with Elrian. Who else was in the prophecy, and what would happen when they identified them all. What the larger purpose of the prophecy was. What the bracelets meant.

At least Fintan hadn't got through to Jeb. One less person tangled in all this.

Cuinn handed out tasks. Before they would go their separate ways, they'd go into the forest and have a ceremony to remember Clay. He had returned to Source.

Cuinn and Blaize would work on the prophecies, at the same time as Blaize would work with Nixie, and Cuinn would try to contact Cassidy. Adam and Fintan would go back to their Guilds and see what information there was on Elrian's last movements. Cara and Tierra would begin to teach Ai some of the things she needed to know as a young energetic, and Tierra would look into what had happened to Ai's parents, though she'd base herself at Cathair Cuinn to do this while she recovered.

They had their roles. And they had each other.

The meeting over, back in Tierra's living room Fintan gathered her to him once more. She was feminine and warm in his arms, and despite everything happening around them, a sense of wellbeing flooded him. He was home.

She laughed as she stretched up on her toes, and he bent down, the difference in their heights making the logistics a challenge.

The kiss was worth it though. Her lips were soft, and his hands moved from her glossy, smooth hair to the roundness of her hips. She was luscious. Her body was so inviting, so womanly.

He growled, and pulled her down with him onto the sofa. Her laugh was throaty now. She straddled his hips, and he made no attempt to hide his arousal. Because, despite the fact it hadn't been that long since the time in the forest, he was very obviously still enthusiastic about her being on top of him. He moved his hips slightly, and she responded with a gasp. He stretched out an arm, and drew her head down to his. She lay along his length, her head resting on his shoulder, her feet just past his knees.

She felt so right in his arms. She belonged there. He took a moment to enjoy the feel of her, to wrap them both in love, and he used a little of his Anahata to disturb the air around her, caressing her with a light breeze as well as his hands. Something healed inside him, something he hadn't realized had been broken.

He took a moment longer to enjoy the sensation and the peace.

"Did I mention I love you?"

She blushed.

Then he closed the short distance between their mouths, and forgot everything but being with her.

Dear Me,

Next time you get in a pickle, remember this:
  Just because you're not a warrior, it doesn't mean you can't fight.
  Just because you're not an adventurer, it doesn't mean you can't explore.
  Just because you're not a hero, doesn't mean you can't be brave.
  Just because you need help sometimes, doesn't mean you can't contribute.

Just because you're looking after everyone else, doesn't mean you can't look after yourself.

Let yourself be loved, little heart. Trust, build, belong.

Me x

There had been a time when he and his son had been close. But that had been before his wife's death. Against his wishes, she had become involved in human affairs. Elrian had told her to leave them to their idiocy, but her soft heart had bled for them as they fought and destroyed each other. And Cuinn had encouraged his mother. Helped her find a place in Poland where she could use her talents as a healer, along with her sister.

Then the hospital she'd been working at had been bombed. And no healer could put back together a body in so many pieces.

He hated humans.

But he hated Cuinn more.

After his wife's death, Elrian had destroyed his relationship with his son, just as Cuinn had destroyed his father's relationship with Cuinn's mother.

Cuinn had deserted Ireland, and Elrian had retreated to the coast of Galway, and spent his days looking out on dark angry waters that crashed against jagged cliffs. The gray weather and atmospheric countryside suited his mood. His dreamscape had become full of nightmares of his dying wife, a spirit who wouldn't leave him alone.

Then decades later he'd met another woman, with unusual gifts, and his life had changed.

He'd once more been given a purpose and a plan.

He had been a dreamwalker for centuries and had worked with prophecies extensively. But he'd withdrawn from life in the Guilds long before his wife's death. Since meeting his second great love, he'd completed many dreamwalks, and the nightmares had been contained to one part of his dreamscape.

The dreamwalks had shown him his destiny. He would become the most powerful energetic in the world.

If he had to destroy Cuinn and his friends to do it?

Excellent.

Elrian turned away from the broken window through which Tierra had apparently fled and strode across the room. He ignored Dagon, who looked away as Elrian passed.

It seemed Elrian had failed again. Tierra, someone he had considered easy prey, had escaped, and if the possible futures he'd seen in the dreamscape were true, the bracelet Dagon had seen on her wrist meant she was probably even now mooning over the boy Fintan. Still. If they had coupled up, Elrian would have four more chances to ensure the prophecy went his way.

But perhaps more drastic measures were required to prevent the next couple from getting together.

Though given how unsuited they were, the wild water spirit and the dour healer locked in his tower, perhaps it wouldn't be so difficult.

END OF BOOK 2

The Guilds and Circles

The energetics' power structure is Guild based.

There are six Major Guilds, one for each of the six Chakras:

- **Muladhara** (The Root Chakra – Earth Element)
- **Svadisthana** (The Sacral Chakra – Water Element)
- **Manipura** (The Navel Chakra – Fire Element)
- **Anahata** (The Heart Chakra – Air Element)
- **Vishudha** (The Throat Chakra – Ether (Space) Element)
- **Ajna** (The Third Eye – The Mind)
  (Sahasara, the Crown Chakra, does not have a Guild.)

Each energetic has two activated Chakras, one Dominant and one Auxiliary, and it is the combination of these that influences their power, and to some degree, their personality.

Because of the huge differences between an energetic like Blaize, who combines her Manipura Dominant with Ajna Auxiliary, and one like Fintan, who combines Manipura Dominant with Anahata Auxiliary, a system of Minor Guilds also developed. There are thirty Minor Guilds representing each combination of powers (for example, Manipura-Ajna is a separate Guild from Ajna-Manipura).

Each individual energetic therefore belongs to two Major Guilds, and one Minor Guild.

For example: Cuinn has Ajna Dominant, and Muladhara Auxiliary. He therefore belongs to the Ajna Major Guild, the Muladhara Major Guild, and the Ajna-Muladhara Minor Guild.

The Major Circle is the highest form of government with one powerful energetic representing each Major Guild, making decisions on behalf of the race. The Minor Circle, the second tier of government, is made up of the thirty energetics who lead each of the Minor Guilds.

List of Minor Guilds:

- Muladhara-Svadisthana
- Muladhara-Manipura
- Muladhara-Anahata
- Muladhara-Vishudha
- Muladhara-Ajna
- Svadisthana-Muladhara
- Svadisthana-Manipura
- Svadisthana-Anahata
- Svadisthana-Vishudha
- Svadisthana-Ajna
- Manipura-Muladhara
- Manipura-Svadisthana
- Manipura-Anahata
- Manipura-Vishudha
- Manipura-Ajna
- Anahata-Muladhara
- Anahata-Svadisthana
- Anahata-Manipura
- Anahata-Vishudha
- Anahata-Ajna
- Vishudha-Muladhara
- Vishudha-Svadisthana
- Vishudha-Manipura
- Vishudha-Anahata
- Vishudha-Ajna
- Ajna-Muladhara
- Ajna-Svadisthana
- Ajna-Manipura
- Ajna-Anahata
- Ajna-Vishudha

What's Next?

The story of the energetics continues in Nixie and Jeb's story, **Nixie and the Healer**.

To get it, and for updates, giveaways and inside information, visit my website:
EllenBardAuthor.com/sign-up

Discover Your Energetic Profile!

Want to know what your Dominant Chakra would be? Which Guild you would belong to? What your archetype is?

Take the Chakra Quiz, and find out!
EllenBardAuthor.com/chakra-quiz

Share Your Thoughts in a Review?

If you loved the book and have a moment to spare, I would hugely appreciate it if you had time to leave a short review where you bought the book, and/or on goodreads. For instructions, go to the link below.

EllenBardAuthor.com/how-to-leave-a-review

Your review will help other readers discover the series, and is greatly appreciated in spreading the word. Authors like me rely on amazing readers like you to share their love of books with others.

Thank you!

About the Author

Ellen is an author who writes paranormal romance full of enchantment, intrigue and action. Her writing blends a background in psychology and her experiences traveling the world, with a love of magic, fantasy and a happy ending.

She's a Chartered Occupational Psychologist with the British Psychological Society, and continues to work as an international management consultant, which she has done for the last 17 years. She's worked all over the world in countries such as China, Saudi Arabia and Malaysia. She writes non-fiction under Ellen M Bard.

Her passion for other lands and cultures helps inform her writing, as does her desire to try new things – from art classes to Krav Maga, the self-defense system.

She's a passionate and dedicated reader, speeding through 100 or so books a year – find her on goodreads to see what currently has her hooked.

Born in the UK, she currently lives in an apartment nest in Bangkok, Thailand where she (almost!) never has to feel the cold.

Connect with Ellen:
Facebook: facebook.com/EllenBardAuthor
Twitter: twitter.com/ellenbard
Goodreads: goodreads.com/ellenbard
Instagram: instagram.com/ellenbard/

Acknowledgements

This book wasn't easy to write. I adore Tierra and Fintan, but getting their story right, and showing Tierra's journey, took time.

I am so grateful for the support and love I have in my life which meant I managed to slog through the hard bits instead of giving up. My mum, Mary Bard, and my sister, Sarah Bard, have acted as cheerleaders and amazing alpha readers, and have never wavered in their confidence this book would get done. I also have a wonderful extended family, the Dunnes and Bards who are always there when I need them.

Whilst writing, I went for the second time through the book The Artist's Way, by Julia Cameron, but with a group. That amazing knot of women, Eleanore (who was also an amazing beta reader), Liza, Dani, Laura and Paige helped me process a lot of bumps as well as sharing the joys of progress.

Anna Charbonneau has acted as beta reader, friend, coach and supporter, and her love of the series has helped me to keep going and help Tierra's story live.

Thanks also to Katie Bullas, another brilliant beta reader, and my writing friend Nyla Nox. Other wonderfully supportive friends include the stalwart Graham Morley, Justin and Ed (and Honey!) and Helen Clark.

Thanks also to Peter Bainbridge (there helping both at the start of the book, as well as when it was done!) and my aunt, Ellen Dunne, who helped do the final proofs of the book.

I listened to the first two albums by 'Oh Wonder' pretty much on continuous repeat while writing Tierra. Their gentle energy, connection-focused lyrics and acoustic melodies are very Tierra.

Finally, thanks to my Fox. In real life, the story doesn't end when you say "I love you", and I'm delighted to be creating our story with you (and tinyfox). Thanks for helping me get Tierra past the finish line. We both know this one wouldn't have happened without you.

Ellen Bard, July 2018

THE ENERGETICS, BOOK 3

NIXIE AND THE HEALER

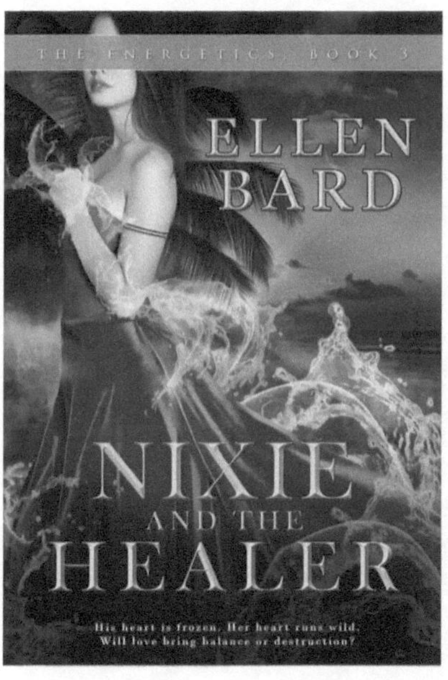

ELLEN BARD

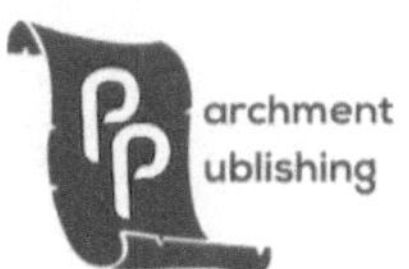

Dedication

For my Fox,
for all your support.

The Chakras and their Energies

Muladhara: The Root Chakra – Earth Element
The energy of nourishment and home, family and safety.

Svadisthana: The Sacral Chakra – Water Element
Fluid and adaptable, the energy of movement and connection, of practical and physical creativity. The energy of pleasure, sexuality and sensation, and emotions.

Manipura: The Navel Chakra – Fire Element
The energy of the individual; of confidence, of proactivity and of drive and passion. Playful and proud.

Anahata: The Heart Chakra – Air Element
The energy of healing, and of balance, located in the middle of the body and the seven Chakras. The energy of love, of relationships, of devotion. Of compassion and empathy.

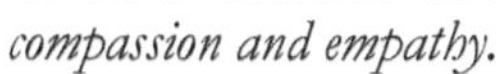

Vishudha: The Throat Chakra – Ether (Space) Element
The energy of communication, of conceptual creativity, and of truth. Of expression, and of listening.

Ajna: The Third Eye – The Mind
The energy of imagination, of visualisations, and insight. Of clarity and wisdom. Of dreams and intuition.

Sahasara: The Crown Chakra – None*
The purest of all the energies. Only experienced through the Grace of the Source (the energetics' name for the creator, the divine).

*Neither a dominant nor auxiliary Chakra for energetics

Jeb came to on the wooden floor of his office. His muscles cramped and his body burned with pain. He retched. The energy rose again and he fought to suppress it, but it was strong. He'd had a hold on it for decades, but recently it was harder and harder to keep it bound.

His body spasmed as he fought the internal battle to keep his auxiliary energy, Svadisthana, locked down. It was too dangerous for him to use. He'd learned that the hard way.

He tried to pull on Anahata, his dominant energy, to bind it. The energy wouldn't stay contained. His pulse raced as some energy escaped and found a nearby source of liquid, the water glass on his desk – which exploded. Shards of glass shot across the room and a few embedded themselves in the arm he'd thrown up to protect his face.

As Jeb was senior Maven for the Cairo-based Anahata Major Guild, the study was warded against all energies getting in, and his students' Anahata energies getting out. But the wards were less effective against other energies. His mistake.

Another pulse of energy wracked his body, and he had to grit his teeth against a shout of pain. What was going on? Why was it so much harder for him to keep his Svadisthana energies bound? He lost the thought as more energy leaked. As fast as he drew on his dominant energy from the ether, the auxiliary burned it away, a war between two opposing sides within his flesh.

Anahata, the healing energy of air and of love. An energy Jeb was at peace with – unlike his Svadisthana energy.

Which disgusted him.

The energy of water, of practical creativity – and of sex. Once, he'd used all aspects of that energy assuredly. And then, he'd used it to murder innocents.

He'd vowed never again.

Had bound the energy, with help.

And had considered that part of him, that despised energy, gone.

It had taken a will of iron, a will that he drew upon now. He used his Anahata to create a glowing shield around his body to contain any further energy leaks. Then he went inside himself. He spun Anahata energy into a second shield tight to his skin. When it covered him, and he had the two shields in place in addition to his regular shields, he relaxed a fraction.

All hell broke loose.

Svadisthana exploded from inside him, and raced around the room. He felt as though he'd been punched in the abdomen, the area where Svadisthana Chakra was located, and he curled up in a ball to lessen the pain.

The energy sought to ground itself. With no other humans in the room, it couldn't find a sexual outlet, so it found the drops of water from the glass, as well as the beads of blood that had been created by the glass breaking Jeb's skin, and it worked with those.

A fine mist of blood and water began to form around Jeb, while the energy continued to shoot around the room. The walls and floor had a spray of blood misted over them. But worse, the energy was calling to the weather outside. Egypt was a dry land – one reason why Jeb was happy to stay in the Guild's headquarters here – but there was water, with the Nile so close. When Jeb raised his head, groaning, to look out the window, he could see a cloud forming outside, tiny drops running down the glass.

Jeb lay on the floor, his body convulsing as energies that had been kept inside him for decades escaped. He managed – just – to keep some shields up, but he wasn't sure how long he could maintain it. If he stopped balancing the destructive Svadisthana with Anahata, the scales could tip, and the energy he'd tried so hard to keep hidden would be loosed. Done in an uncontrolled manner, it could pose a danger to all the Guild buildings – and everyone inside them.

There was a knock at the door. A soft voice came through the wood. "Jebediah-san? May I enter?"

Source. It was Aiko, the Head of the Guild. This was a blessing and a curse. On the one hand, Aiko was exactly the person to help him. On the other hand, if she came through that door without knowing what she was walking into, his escaping energy could slam right into her, which could have some nasty consequences. He could enthral her sexually, or hurt her physically with his energy wild and uncontrolled in the room.

Another knock.

The moisture at the window ran down in rivulets, blurring the view of the sky. A couple of books were dislodged from the shelf, and thudded onto the floor.

The door opened cautiously, and Jeb made a heroic effort to draw on Anahata in order to strengthen his Svadisthana shields. Cold sweat bled through his shirt onto the wooden floor, only to be immediately swept up in the mist around him.

He opened his mouth to warn her, but only a croak came out, his throat parched.

"Jeb?" Aiko peeked around the door, caught sight of the room, and stepped inside smartly. She shut the door behind her, and studied Jeb.

Closing the door on the rest of the Guild was a wise move, though from Jeb's perspective she was now on the wrong side of it. He felt her draw on Anahata to protect herself from the sexual energy he was exuding, and he rasped a sigh of relief.

He curled into himself, trying to focus, trying to find his voice to ask for her aid, but more energy escaped, and called to the water outside. The window shattered, and glass flew. A piece sliced across Aiko's arm and she cried out, her hand flying to the wound, blood sliding down the arm to stain the white top she wore. Her shields wavered and Jeb's stomach tensed.

He needed her help, and he needed it urgently. But what if she became lost to his water energies, and two of the most powerful members of the Guild lost control?

There was going to be a hell of a lot more damage than a broken window.

Nixie stretched, cat-like, and purred in satisfaction. Life on her Thai island was good. She rolled onto her back. "Mmmm. Thank you."

The tousled-haired youth beside her was still breathing hard, and nodded weakly, his body sprawled inelegantly beside hers.

They'd been seeing each other for a week or so, and Nixie was thrilled that they'd finally slept together. She tried to keep a little discipline, and rarely had sex with anyone on a first date. She loved the buildup, the intensity, the butterflies in her stomach as she anticipated what their physical connection would be like. To make it last she had a personal target of waiting at least a week.

Okay, sometimes six days.

She shrugged internally. It wasn't her fault that she liked sex. A lot. She glanced back at the lean, long-limbed twenty-something she'd just very much enjoyed a couple of hours with. He stared up at the ceiling, eyes wide. She'd made sure he'd had a good time too. Sex was something she was passionate about in all the ways, and she was skilled in bringing pleasure to her partners. White, with dark hair curling around his ears, he wasn't that much younger than her – she was in her early thirties in human years – but in life experience, given she was a part magical being who was likely to live for hundreds of years, they were worlds apart.

Nixie's energies were Svadisthana and Vishudha. The first was where her love of sex stemmed from, in addition to a love of swimming and her creative talents. But Nixie was a romantic at heart, despite the fact that she had no Anahata in her energies. She blamed her parents. Marius and Fai had been together centuries – true soulmates.

Nixie wanted that. She wanted someone as strong and as fearless as her father, a bear-like man, who made his tiny but fierce wife Fai look delicate by standing near her. They were strong individually, but even stronger as a couple.

Nixie had bathed in their love all her life, sharing that love with her cousin Blaize who had moved to Thailand and joined their family as a child when her parents died. Blaize was a best friend and sister in one.

Nixie propped herself up on an elbow, and ran a finger down the man's flank. She liked the play of his muscles. They would look good sculpted in a pale stone, perhaps. She tipped her head, idly considering his body.

Nixie had never thought that Blaize would find her perfect partner before she did. Blaize had reluctantly gone to be trained in her auxiliary energy by a Maven called Cuinn, and then fallen in love with him. Nixie scowled briefly, then shook it off. She was pleased for Blaize, she was. She just…wanted to find her own soulmate sooner rather than later.

In the meantime, she told herself, she was auditioning men for the part. After all, you needed to spend time with someone to really decide whether they were right for you.

The guy lying next to her was human. It was possible for energetics to fall in love and marry humans, but it was rare as the human had to pass your Guild's approval to share their world's secrets.

She looked at Ben, the man in bed beside her, and sighed to herself. He probably wouldn't pass muster. And Nixie didn't think she could live her life with a secret that huge from her partner. She wasn't big on secrets. They were too much like hard work. Much like sculpture. She saved those for only the most interesting models.

Ben would make a fine subject for a life drawing, however.

"What's up?" he asked.

She smiled.

"Nothing. Unless…?" She looked suggestively down at their tangle of naked bodies.

He grinned back. "Sure. Give me a minute or two. And in the meantime, why don't we talk?"

Nixie's forehead creased. "Talk?"

That's not what they were here for. She ran a hand down his back, kneading the muscles there, reminding them both of their physical connection.

He lifted a shoulder. "You know, talk. I don't feel like I know that much about you. What's going on with you?"

Nixie recoiled a fraction. She couldn't help herself. She wasn't a fan of sharing. She was a realist, and knew men were usually attracted to her for her looks. She was fine with that. Her deep relationships were with her friends and family, not her various lovers. They came to her for fun, and sex, and she made sure all parties had both. He caught her expression, and hurt flashed across his face. He spoke quickly. "Or not. It's fine."

"It's not that, I just…I don't know what to say." She couldn't exactly tell him that her plans for the future were currently suspended, as she'd been included in a prophecy which potentially foretold the end of her race's world.

That was the problem with humans. Things got complicated quickly.

"What do you do for a living?" he said.

"Business graphics," she said. She had set responses for questions like this, designed to be as boring as possible, to stop this type of conversation developing into something too personal. Not that many pursued conversations with her. They were usually too swept up in the physical pleasure she could provide, a mutual connection that was more than enough.

"Okay. What do you like to do when you're not working?" he said.

She was impressed – and surprised – at his tenacity. But what could she say? That she practiced what he would see as magic in her spare time, using the energy from water. Huh, water. That would do it. "I like swimming."

"I guess you do live on an island. Makes sense." He was a traveler to Koh Somdun, the island where she lived off the west coast of Thailand, there for a few months to enjoy life in paradise on his way round the world. Another reason it wouldn't last.

He was looking at her expectantly. Apparently he needed more.

"I sometimes do archery. And I like art. Drawing, painting, that kind of thing." She had a sudden feeling of panic. Talking of which – she was supposed to be driving her parents' car down to the dock to collect Blaize and Tierra. Her parents were away travelling and calling on friends in Europe, and Nixie was looking after their house.

Blaize was here so Nixie could use her artistic skills to help with some of the details of the prophecy, and Blaize could have a break. Plus it was well past time for Nixie to catch up on Blaize's love life.

She felt a brief flicker of unease about the prophecy and she quickly stuffed the feeling down inside herself. She was involved, but not really *involved*, in the same way the others were. She knew Blaize wanted to discuss that with her too, but Nixie saw herself as support, a friend, for those who were the main actors.

Talking of which, she rolled over to the bedside table where her phone was lying and picked it up. *Shit.* She was cutting it pretty fine. Nixie tended to operate on 'Thai time' – after all, she was half Thai – but Blaize most certainly did not. Blaize would not be happy if Nixie left her standing on the dock in the sun for half an hour.

"Now what?" There was a touch of irritation in Ben's voice.

"I forgot I have to pick up my friend from the dockside, and I need to go home and get the car." She'd ridden her scooter to Ben's house. She should have brought the car, but she hadn't thought of it. Nixie was more of a big picture girl than someone focused on the details.

"Right," he said. She couldn't figure out what his tone meant, but she didn't have time to explore it. She bounced out of the bed and scrambled into her clothes. She should probably shower, but there wasn't time.

Ben lay on the bed watching her. She couldn't interpret the expression on his face either. Never mind. She tended to keep things flexible. Casual. He was fun in bed, and she'd like to see him again, she was sure of that. Ben had had a great time, she'd seen to it. He didn't need to know her deepest self to enjoy sex with her again. And who knows, maybe things would develop.

After all, she knew her soulmate was out there somewhere, and she was willing to do a lot of experimentation to find him.

Nixie sped home on her bike, grabbed the keys to the car and drove as fast as she dared to the dock. As she'd thought, Blaize was already there, frowning, green eyes stern. Her red hair gleamed in the sun, porcelain skin indicating she'd been away from Thailand a while in the cold Canadian spring.

Both Blaize and Nixie were in their mid thirties, but neither had chosen to fix their age yet, something all energetics were able to do through a ritual. It could be changed again with effort, but most of them opted for more sleight of hand tricks like type of clothing, hairstyles and make up to change their age for the humans around them. Or moved location and started again.

Blaize, Tierra, and a surly girl Nixie didn't recognize, who must be Ai, stood under the only bit of shade on the dockside, and as there were no other people waiting with them, Nixie had to assume the boat that they'd come in on had docked a while ago. Nixie squirmed as she drew the car up next to them. She hadn't meant to be late. She knew it frustrated Blaize. Luckily Blaize could never stay annoyed at her for long, and especially not when they hadn't seen each other in an age.

She bounced out of the car, and threw her arms around Blaize, who stiffened before she sighed and put her arms round Nixie in return. "Hey, Nix."

Nixie exhaled in relief and dropped her arms. "Sorry, B! I got caught up."

Blaize put out a hand and tugged on Nixie's jade-colored top. "Oh yes?"

Nixie looked down and flushed.

"Oh." She'd put her top on inside out and back to front. Blaize had the label between her fingers, underneath Nixie's chin.

"In a rush to get dressed, were you?" Blaize's tone was dry.

Nixie grimaced. "Sorry, really. I lost track of time."

"Mm hmm." Blaize rolled her eyes. She likely had a good idea of what Nixie had been up to. "Anyway. Let me introduce Tierra, Cuinn's cousin."

A woman as short as Nixie, but a great deal curvier, stepped forward. She had dark hair and brown skin, and with her near-black eyes sparkling she gave Nixie a sunny smile.

Nixie made a noise of delight. "Tierra! So wonderful to see you."

"Oh, I forgot you knew each other," Blaize said. "Great."

Blaize gestured to the girl on her other side. "This is Ai. She's hanging out with us for a while, and she's never been out of Canada before, so we thought she'd enjoy the trip."

Ai was an Asian teenage girl already taller than Nixie. Tierra and her Manipura Warrior partner, Fintan, had met her when they were tracking a Rogue in Vancouver as part of the prophecy. The girl was an energetic – but had had no idea of her heritage, as she'd been orphaned young, and ended up in the foster system and then homeless for most of her teens. She was streetwise, but wary. Right now she looked somewhat sweaty in skintight black jeans and a black T-shirt with a skull on it, a cell phone welded to her hand.

Nixie smiled at her. "Hey, Ai. Welcome to Thailand."

Ai looked up briefly, and nodded stiffly. "Yeah. We've been here a while already."

Nixie's shoulders tightened. She usually got on well with everyone, but perhaps she hadn't made the best first impression. She glanced at Ai's cellphone screen. "Crystal Bust, I play that sometimes. Nice."

"Crystal Bust is so three years ago," Ai said, scorn lacing her voice. "This is Sonic Caverns. It came out last week."

Nixie's cheeks heated. She suddenly felt old, which was not a feeling she was used to, as she spent time with younger men all the time. And it wasn't like she was old herself. Okay. She'd try again later. She could build rapport with a teenager, it was no problem. One of Nixie's gifts was supposed to be charm after all. She was just tired.

"Now we're all caught up, can we go home?" Blaize said.

"Of course," Nixie said, and opened the trunk of the car for their luggage. They packed the cases and themselves into the sporty little Mazda, and Nixie drove them home.

Set back in the forest on the island, the three traditional Thai-style wooden houses were clustered in a clearing – close enough to walk between them, but far enough for a little privacy, important given the fact that the heat was such that windows and doors were rarely closed.

Nixie loved living here, with nature and the sea so close by, and her parents within walking distance. Nixie was excited to have Blaize back. She wanted to tell her all about the art pieces she had on the go.

She hadn't had anyone to share her art with for a while now, and Blaize, while not appreciating art in quite the same way Nixie did, always listened. In turn, Nixie had always listened to Blaize's goals and whatever she was focused on achieving next, and been her cheerleader.

This trip, Blaize had given up her two bedroom home, closed up for the months she'd been away, for Tierra and Ai. These latter pair had formed a close bond, and Ai was still fragile, though she would never admit it. Blaize would sleep in Nixie's spare room.

Which Nixie was thrilled about. Blaize wasn't only her cousin, but her best friend, and she had sorely missed her in recent weeks.

Plus, Nixie really really wanted to hear about the sex Blaize was having with Cuinn. He sounded hot.

Jeb uncurled his body and began to drag himself over to Aiko, worried about her slashed arm, wanting to heal her, but she threw up a hand to stop him.

"A minute," she said, tightly. Blood trailed down her arm, but she ignored it.

Ah. Yes. If he came closer his escaping energy could affect her more. He shook his head to clear it. She closed her eyes and the room shivered with energy as she rebuilt her shields. Thank Source she was so powerful.

A box fell from a shelf with a bang. Papers fell and scattered across the floor. He jolted in reaction. What could he do? How could he help Aiko?

Distance. Right. Distance, so she could focus and regain control. She wouldn't leave him while he was like this. She knew what was happening with him. He managed to get up onto his hands and knees, but he wasn't strong enough to fight the energy and to stand at the same time. He slumped against his antique desk, holding the energy, no longer trying to stop it.

The energy that had already escaped still bounced around the room. The cloud of blood and mist followed him, and soaked the side of the desk he leaned on. He simultaneously drew the moisture from the desk – and heard the wood creak and crack.

"I need you to – to hurry," he managed to grind out, his jaw aching with the effort of keeping the energy under some semblance of control.

Moments later there was a snap, and the desk split across the middle, the wood as dry as bone. His possessions – pens, notepad, laptop – fell to the floor in a crash. He grimaced. He'd been fond of that desk.

Dark clouds gathered at the window. He heard a soft patter and rain hit the glass, falling into the room where the pane was broken. Jeb's stomach tightened. If he didn't get a handle on this, it wouldn't take long for the rain to get torrential. His power was thirsty.

Aiko's delicate figure stood above him. He heaved a sigh of relief. He was lucky he could count on her. "Aiko. Please. Help me lock it down."

She nodded sharply and dropped down next to him. Ignoring the rain of blood that soaked her tan skin and her pin-straight dark hair, and the not insignificant slice on her arm, she put a hand either side of Jeb's head, and cradled his chin and cheeks in her small hands.

Aiko's power ripped into him, and he welcomed the pain with relief. Her Anahata healed his shields even as it drew the errant Svadisthana back into Jeb. It wasn't an easy process for either of them, and sweat beaded on Aiko's skin while Jeb's jaw clenched and unclenched as Aiko's energy tore through him. The cramps were back, and his body felt as if it was being turned inside out. He squeezed his eyes shut and stars burst inside his head. It probably took only minutes, but Jeb felt as if he were back in a war zone, bombs exploding around him, as his head filled with noise and light.

And then there was blessed silence as Aiko drew her hands carefully back.

He threw up.

Aiko didn't flinch. She moved her body out of the line of fire, and pulled some tissues from a pocket. After Jeb had heaved everything out of his stomach onto the floor he leaned back, blank, onto the side of the desk. Which was no longer there, as the wood had fallen in on itself when the desk split. He toppled over.

Aiko grimaced as she stood up and dragged him to prop him against the wall.

"You're okay." She knelt next to him. "May I check you over?"

He nodded, too miserable to speak. Aiko touched his arm and he felt a tendril of her Anahata energy, a healing balm this time, thread its way around his system. She was checking to see there was nothing else wrong with him. Wasn't what she'd seen enough? *What could be worse than the psychic wound he'd been bearing for so many decades?*

After a minute or so Aiko opened her eyes and settled back on her heels, at ease. For an energetic with so much air, she was surprisingly grounded. "There's nothing wrong with you that some healthy sex wouldn't fix."

Jeb spluttered.

Aiko waved a hand. "Or another appropriate use of your Svadisthana. It's gone far enough. Something's shifted in you. The energy was harder to bind this time. It doesn't want to stay locked down, and it's fighting you and the bindings to be free. It's not natural. My advice both as a Healer and your friend is for you to re-integrate the energy as soon as possible in a controlled way."

It had seemed worse than previous leakages. And he had no idea why.

She rested her hands in her lap, her shoulders back. "It doesn't set a good example. Energetics are about balance. If a student doesn't suspect that you're holding your Svadisthana in check, rather than that you are weak in that energy, as you claim, another member of the Guild will. In fact, anyone who knew you before the war must surely wonder."

They'd had this discussion before.

"No one but you sees this," he rasped out. "It has to be this way."

She shook her head, the straight drop of hair that framed her face rippling. "It really doesn't. This is something we do to punish people, or to restrain Rogues. Not to normal, healthy energetics who could be using their energy for the good of the race."

He didn't answer. What was there to say?

She helped him wash up in the bathroom, then physically locked and energetically warded the door behind them while she escorted him to his quarters. They didn't want anyone else seeing his room after what had happened. He was going to have a lot of cleaning up to do tomorrow.

She briskly helped him into bed. His body sagged against the pillows, and guilt permeated his being.

She paused at the door on her way out. "This isn't a sustainable solution, Jeb. One day, you're going to want to leave the Guild. Or to have a relationship again. If it's the former, then I might not be around to help you. If it's the latter, unless you're careful, you're going to release decades of pent up Svadisthana energy onto one woman all at once. And that could easily overwhelm her system. If she's not someone you have a connection with or a strong energetic, at best you could end up influencing her to do something she doesn't want to do. At worst, you could kill the both of you."

3

Long after Nixie had grilled Blaize about Cuinn – until Blaize had finally thrown a pillow at her and ordered her out of her room so she could nap – Tierra, Nixie and Blaize gathered on Nixie's balcony. Ai was sleeping.

"We don't have to do this now," said Nixie. "If you guys need to rest, it's fine. Jet lag can be a bitch."

"The sooner the better," said Blaize. "We need to work out who the twelve people are in Cuinn's vision. If we can identify them, we can talk to them. We can find out if anything weird's been going on with them, and warn them."

Cuinn had started everything when he'd received some disturbing prophecies. As part of Blaize's Ajna training, he'd shared the images with her through their minds, and then taught her to be able to project them into the mind of someone else, as to this point only the two of them had seen the faces in the prophecy shards.

Nixie would start with faces. It wasn't a beginner level task for Blaize, but luckily she was powerful, if new to training in her Ajna energy, the energy of the mind.

Blaize lay in Nixie's hammock, which was strung across a corner of the broad balcony surrounded by wooden balustrades. Tierra chilled comfortably on a pink beanbag, watching, and Nixie sat on a cushion on the floor.

Nixie nodded. "Okay. How's it going to work?"

"I don't think it should be too hard. For you, anyway. We'll need to touch," said Blaize. "I'll use Ajna to project a figure into your mind, and then we need you to draw it."

Nixie patted the sketch book and pencils next to her. "No problem."

"Sometimes it can be a bit blurry. I'm still learning how to do this, but it's a priority."

"I could've come to you in Canada, you know," Nixie said.

"I know. But Ai needed a break," Blaize replied.

Blaize and Tierra exchanged glances and Tierra continued. "She's never really spent much time in the countryside, and she was getting spooked really easily at Cathair Cuinn. She might have grown up on the streets, but it was an urban landscape, and even the tough lifestyle she's had to deal with hadn't involved people trying to kill her with magic till now. She's been in some shock. We thought a change of scene, and getting her out of Canada, might help her settle into our world. Plus Cara's helping Cuinn, and Adam's in the area if he needs him."

Adam was Tierra's brother, and a Protector with Muladhara Guild, and Cara, one of Tierra's closest friends, ran a Rehab Centre off the west Canadian coast. Both were included in the prophecy along with the others.

"Alright," said Nixie. "How'd you want to start?"

Blaize swung her legs over the hammock to sit up, and planted her feet on the floor, about half a yard between her feet. "Bring your cushion here. How long do you need me to hold the image for?"

"I'm not sure. Depends on the quality. It's not like drawing from a still life, I can't quite tell how I'm going to switch between the image and the paper." Nixie shrugged. "Let's try it and we'll see."

She went and sat between Blaize's knees, facing away, her sketch pad in her lap. Blaize put her hands on Nixie's shoulders.

"Relax," Blaize ordered.

Nixie laughed. "I'm not sure the best way to help me relax is to boss me about."

Blaize gently bopped her on the head. "Whatever, nong sao."

It was the Thai for little sister, and was a term of affection she had used for many years.

They both closed their eyes. Nothing happened for a few minutes. Nixie began to feel sleepy. She'd had a busy day.

Nixie didn't have either of her energies in common with Blaize, so couldn't tell if Blaize was doing anything or not, until suddenly an image appeared in Nixie's mind.

Nixie jumped and opened her eyes, jerking forward and breaking the connection between them. "Oh! Sorry."

Blaize looked at her flatly. "Nix! Concentrate. I'm not as good with Ajna as Manipura."

Nixie bit her lip. "Sorry. Really, I am. It was just a surprise."

"I didn't think I'd ever say this for real," Blaize said, "but if we don't work out what is happening, and why, and stop it, then it could truly be the end of the line for the energetics. I need you to concentrate."

Nixie's eyes widened. *Shit.* That kind of pressure was definitely not going to help her relax, which was when her best drawings came. Though Blaize had never had a tendency to exaggerate. Nixie flexed her drawing hand. This wasn't quite as fun. On the other hand, the sleepy feeling had been entirely chased away.

They settled back into position, and Nixie tried to focus. She did tend towards the distractible, it was true. But drawing was something she loved, and she wanted to help.

It took another minute or so, but the image appeared again, small at first, as if it was at the end of an out-of-focus telescope. Nixie concentrated. She could tell it was a male figure, but that was all so far.

The figure flickered, and slipped away again. Nixie took a breath to speak but Blaize said, in a tight voice, "Stay still."

Okay. Patience. Nixie did as she was told, and within a few more moments, the image was back. Blaize's fingers were digging into Nixie's shoulders, and it was clearly taking a great deal of effort on her part.

Nixie focused on the man as the image stabilized. *Hmmm.* Nice enough looking, she supposed, though nothing special. He was slender, but his shoulders were filled out, and his body was toned.

His chin was covered in stubble, but not the well manicured beard that her lover of this morning, Ben, had had, but more the sort of beard that suggested that the figure had a tendency to forget to shave. In fact, the man generally was sort of scruffy.

Under the stubble though, the guy had some killer cheekbones. Nixie studied the picture. Whoever he was, he was not making the best of himself. She looked at the image again, past the scruff and the bland clothes.

And then she raised her eyebrows, as the image wavered and shifted, and when it came back into focus, the pure, unadulterated carnality in the man's eyes had her gasping for breath. Suddenly his scruffy look had her panting.

"Woah," she muttered.

Blaize's hands squeezed down hard.

"I know, I know," responded Nixie. She hadn't moved, had she? She hadn't even opened her eyes.

The image shifted again, and his eyes changed. The sex had gone, and now his dark blue eyes held a deep sorrow, and the almost-hobo look was back.

She was confused. It was the same man in both images, and yet he was so different. It was as if there were two versions of him. In one, you'd pass him in the street without noticing him. He blended in, unless you caught his eyes and saw how sad he was. Something terrible had happened to this man, she was sure of it.

And then there was the other version. The version that smoldered and could stop traffic if he chose. But which was the real him? She knew which she preferred.

For now, she was ready to start drawing. She opened her eyes slowly, wondering if she'd still be able to see the image at the same time, but it disappeared. *Oh well. That would have been too easy.*

Blaize kept her hands in position on Nixie's shoulders, and all Nixie needed to do was close her eyes to remind herself of the face as she drew. She picked up the pencil and sketch pad and began.

She first sketched out the man's proportions with faint pencil marks. She blocked out the head, his torso and the top of his legs, and then his upper arms. No detail yet, just the outline of his shape, and then the lower legs and lower arms. She would close her eyes every ten to twenty seconds to catch another glance.

She nibbled on the end of her pencil, considering. She'd leave the clothes for later. The face was the important thing as they were trying to identify the figures first off, but they'd discussed it being worth doing the whole scene in case there might be other clues the wider group could piece together. Which version would she draw? She closed her eyes for a longer look.

Nixie was all business now. She concentrated, seeing the detail, the lines on his face, the mixed colors in his hair, the angles and planes of his face.

But the image was like a flipping coin, changing every handful of seconds. Sexy. Sad. Sexy. Sad.

Which version?

She went for sexy.

Well, duh.

She sketched for thirty minutes, Blaize's hands on her shoulders the entire time, the image ready and accessible for Nixie whenever she shut her eyes. After that time, Tierra, who had moved to the table to work on her laptop, intervened. "I think you should take a break."

A faint crease appeared between Blaize's eyes. "Why?"

Tierra smothered a smile. "Because you have smudges under your eyes that weren't there an hour ago, and because I think Nixie has something for us."

Nixie nodded absently, gazing down at the paper in front of her. She had scratched away with the pencil until she was satisfied that the sketch pad held a reasonable representation of the man from the image.

She wasn't sure going for the sexy version of the man had been the right decision. Because she couldn't stop staring at him. He wasn't at all her normal type – even the sexy version seemed much more serious than she was usually drawn to – but there was something magnetic about him. He had depth, she decided. As if she could spend time with him, and never be bored. And Nixie was quite often bored. She had a need for variety and for new experiences, and that went double for relationships. This man seemed like someone who might be both interesting, and also interested in sticking around for something in addition to the incredible sex she could provide.

"So?" said Blaize.

"Hmm?" said Nixie, her eyes not moving.

Blaize put out a foot and gave Nixie's leg a shove. Nixie looked up to see Tierra and Blaize both looking at her.

"Oh. Sorry." Nixie handed the pad to Blaize, a little reluctantly.

Blaize took it. Her hair was sweaty, and her breath came a little quicker than normal, as if she'd run a hard race. "That looks pretty good. Well done, Nix. Now we need to distribute it to our friends and see if anyone knows who it is."

Tierra got up and stood behind Blaize, and she gasped. "We don't need to. I know him. It's Jeb. Jebediah Gale. He was my Maven for Anahata, a century or two ago."

Tierra craned her neck over Blaize's shoulder to get a closer look. "I saw him a couple of weeks ago – he helped us with finding Ai's parents. But there's something odd about the drawing. Can I see?"

Blaize handed the pad up to her, and Tierra took it out of the shade of the balcony into the sun. "Huh. That's odd."

"What?" said Nixie. There was nothing wrong with her sketch, she was confident. It looked like the guy in the image. The not-miserable version, anyway.

"Well…" Tierra hesitated. "It looks like Jeb used to look, when he was my Maven, and before World War II."

"World War II?" said Blaize. "Why? What happened to him?"

"The details don't matter. But what does matter is that after the war, he sequestered himself in Anahata Guild, and he hasn't been out of there since."

Nixie drew in a breath, shocked. "Never? How can he live like that?"

"There's more. Jeb's auxiliary energy is Svadisthana."

"Well that makes sense," said Nixie. "I mean, look at him. He's not that attractive, but he's very, very sexy."

Blaize tipped her head to the side. "I guess."

Nixie poked her in the leg. "You're distracted. Cuinn's all you can think about. You don't count."

"Anyway," said Tierra. "After the War, for various reasons, he decided that he would ignore his auxiliary energy. Bind it."

Blaize and Nixie's heads snapped round at that.

"What?" said Nixie. "What does that mean?"

"He swore off relationships, and all that comes with them," said Tierra.

Nixie's mouth fell open. *Wait, what?!* Surely Tierra didn't mean what Nixie thought she meant. "Everything?"

"Uh huh," Tierra said. "Everything."

Nixie goggled. Enforced celibacy was hard for anyone. Harder still on an energetic, and harder again on a man, surely. In fact, if she'd had to say, she'd have considered it physically impossible for Svadisthana energetics. Especially male ones.

So, wow. She had to ask. "What kind of guy doesn't have sex?"

After a restless night Jeb was up early. He needed to clean his workspace as quickly as possible so rumors didn't spread. In a Guild, especially within the teaching areas, strange things often happened, but blood-spattered walls weren't typical of the Anahata Guild. He'd cancelled his first few lessons, but it was still possible for people to drop by unannounced.

His body felt weak, but under his control again. Whatever Aiko had done had bound the Svadisthana energy again, thank Source. *But would it last?*

He had already borrowed a new, simpler table from the Guild's stores before he opened the door to his study. He'd get a replacement desk later. He shuffled the table inside the room, then rubbed a hand over the back of his neck as he looked around. It was worse than he'd remembered. The floor was covered in a fine mist of blood, and the wild energy that had escaped before he had controlled it had knocked things off the wall.

While he lectured in the larger halls, he spent much of his time in these rooms, and seeing his personal space like this was almost physically painful. His gaze caught on the broken wooden box that had fallen from the shelf, and the breath went out of him in a whoosh, his stomach clenching. He stepped over the debris and squatted next to it. Cards and photos had fallen out in a heap. This cedar wood container was one of the most precious things in the office to him, filled with the photos and notes from people he had helped since his actions in World War II had caused so much devastation. The contents didn't balance out his actions, but it soothed him a little. He gently scooped up the papers and laid them back inside the box, putting the box back where it belonged. He rested a hand on it for a moment, his head bowed, then swallowed and went into his attached bathroom to fill the bucket he'd swiped – along with a mop and cloths – from a cleaning supplies cupboard on the way to his study. He began to clean.

He'd tried so hard to make the right choices. To not make any further mistakes, or bad decisions. It seemed, however, from the havoc he'd caused in his study, he was no longer able to do even that right. He felt powerless.

By mid-morning, he felt that the room was decent enough. He cleaned the older, broken desk, and got help from a passing student to take it to the garbage room. A couple of hours later, showered and in fresh clothes, he decided to go into the grounds of the Guild for some air.

Jeb was used to the pollution and the intense heat, over 100°F at this time of year. He hadn't left the grounds since he'd come here after the war to recover from his energetic and physical wounds.

He walked to one of his favorite places in the grounds, a shady garden with wrought-iron benches, surrounded by palm trees.

He sat on one of the benches, rested his elbows on his knees, and propped his face in his hands, deep in thought. *How can I prevent last night from happening again?*

There was a buzz from his pocket, and his phone rang. He straightened, and took the phone out. Seeing it was Tierra, he answered it. After exchanging greetings, Jeb frowned. Something was off. "What's up?"

There was a beat or two of silence before Tierra spoke. "I'm so sorry to share this with you Jeb, but Cuinn's seen you in the prophecy. You're one of the twelve energetics involved."

Jeb stood up in one swift movement, the phone clutched to his ear. *That's ridiculous.* "He's wrong. He's never met me, how would he know?"

"He and Blaize have shared the images, and Blaize was able to project it into her cousin Nixie's mind. Nixie's an artist, and she drew you."

He was shaking his head over and over, despite the fact she couldn't see him. The implications of what she was saying, if it was true, were not something he was prepared for. "Tell me exactly what she drew."

"Your figure, with detail on the face. You're one of the twelve. There's no doubt. You're standing along with the rest of us."

He didn't want to ask the next question, but he had to. "Am I on my own?"

If he was in a romantic relationship – a full, true relationship, with love, sex and all the things those entailed – then there would be no way for him to keep his Svadisthana bound any more.

"It's hard to tell. Obviously Blaize and Cuinn have come together as a couple, as have Fintan and I. But we don't know that all twelve of those we can see are romantically linked. We still have several blurred figures, though we do know that there are six men and six women."

Something tight loosened around Jeb's chest. "There's been no clear indicator that the prophecy needs six couples?"

"No. It's a possibility, but there's nothing to say it has to be like that."

Well, that's something. Although being involved was bad enough. Jeb was happy to support Tierra and her friends, but he wouldn't – couldn't – leave the Guild. This was the safest place for him to be. He probed further. "Are there any clues about the physical location?"

"Not that we can work out so far," Tierra answered. She understood what he was asking. "And it might not even be that we need to be in the same place as a group. The image might be a metaphor for us working together."

The band around his chest loosened further and he took a deep breath. "Okay. I'll have to see what I can contribute from here. Which I would do anyway, you know that."

"I know," Tierra said, her voice soft. "Though when you feel ready, we'll help you acclimatize back into the world. If you need it."

"I'm not –" he stopped, realizing how sharp his voice sounded. He tried again, matching her tone. "I'm not leaving the Guild. I need to be here, where Anahata is strongest, and I can keep my other energy under control."

Although it wasn't, was it? He shook that thought off, and began walking back to his room. He had a meeting with a student scheduled, and he should prepare. "Is there anything else I should know? Or anything I can do to help?"

"No," said Tierra. "We'll let you know if you can. Thank you."

They ended the call.

What did it all mean?

He'd aided Tierra and Fintan when they had come to the Guild for information on a teenage orphan they'd come across as part of the search for answers around the prophecy, and they had also asked him to identify the murder victim. The latter, especially, had taken it out of him, as he'd had to use his telemetry on a photo of a dead girl, and from that photo he'd re-lived her death, a traumatic and draining event. But it had been something he could do. And he'd continue to do whatever he could to help, of course.

But there were two things that the prophecy could ask of him that he could never do.

Form a romantic and sexual relationship, and leave the Guild's grounds.

And if they needed him to do that?

They'd already failed.

Elrian gripped the shoulders of the thin young man at his feet, and dug his fingers into the scarce flesh there.

The bland surroundings of the guest bedroom they were in were an odd contrast to what he was about to do. It had the benefit of isolation, however. The Seattle safe house was out in the lush, cool forest that surrounded the city. Orderly and clean, this house wasn't as nice a place as he had had in Vancouver, the place he had had to abandon when his son's friends found it. Elrian preferred more luxurious quarters. But it would do. After Tierra's mysterious escape from his main home, and the work he'd had to do to remove the incident from Cassidy's memory, he'd decided not to bring subjects there any more. He was reluctant to spend too much time in Vancouver.

Not that it was easy to find leeching candidates. There were never that many energetics in an area, and the American Pacific Northwest was no different. He tried to take runaways, or other energetics who wouldn't be missed, and the information he'd been getting from his lover had helped with that. Energetics were such a clannish race that they tended to have strong family ties and cluster together.

He had had to send Dagon, one of his enforcers, all the way to Portland to capture the youth. Aeros, he was called. White, with untidy, shoulder-length hair and nondescript blue eyes, he wasn't especially remarkable in any way as far as Elrian knew. A loner by nature, the young man's energetic family was in New York, and he hadn't been in Portland long enough to establish a routine and friends who might miss him.

He was perfect.

Dagon stood to the side, patient and motionless. Elrian let Dagon take energy sometimes, but his enforcer was more interested in the captives for other reasons. Elrian didn't ask – as long as Dagon didn't damage their energy too much, Elrian didn't care what he did with their physical bodies. It tarnished their energy a fraction if Dagon played with them too close to Elrian's ritual, but it was worth it as payment for loyalty.

Sitting on the edge of the bed, Elrian centered himself and closed his eyes, preparing himself to siphon the other man's energy. Weak and already drained, Aeros struggled momentarily in place on the floor, fear widening his eyes. He was bound and gagged, and there was nothing he could do about what was going to happen. By now Elrian had come to enjoy the fear a little. What had started as a practical exercise had become delicious in more than one way.

The energy of another energetic helped Elrian overcome some health issues he'd been experiencing. Yes, it was a forbidden use of energy, but only fools obeyed the rules when there was power and bounty there for the taking.

Leeching wasn't all he wanted from his victims. He needed them so that he could create remnant stones. Without these, he wasn't going to be able to ensure that the prophecy went his way.

He gritted his teeth as he remembered how he'd had both Ai and Tierra in his hands, and both had slipped through his fingers. He could have leeched from one or even both of them, and their deaths could have provided the basis of a remnant stone each, if he'd had sufficient strength and control. Now, this youth was the only victim they currently held.

However, his latest prophecy dream had indicated that one of the energetics on the opposing side was sick, and there was a strong possibility that they would die. He bared his teeth. That might be enough, but now there were two established couples, Elrian was concerned the death of only one of them might not be enough.

At some point soon he was going to need to invest some serious time and effort into seeking prophecy in the dreamscape. There were so many gaps in what he could see ahead. A new energetic couple would be likely to meet soon. He still had four chances left to ensure things came true in the way he wished, but he was not happy that he'd already missed two opportunities.

In the meantime, he had dropped his focus on the twelve and was concentrating on himself. He'd finally admitted to himself that he needed the energy that leeching provided. Not as badly, perhaps, as his former Adherent, Indigo, had needed the energy. He hadn't sunk that low. He shuddered. She'd practically been a junkie.

He reached inside Aeros's body, delicately. Today he wanted to draw from the boy's Ajna, to replenish Elrian's own store, but eventually he might use up Aeros's auxiliary energy, his Vishudha, to create a remnant stone. Elrian also needed to replenish the remnant stone ring he wore, that had been a gift, and worked as an emergency back up external store for energy.

He had to be careful, and take things more slowly. Siphon the boy's energy, and keep him alive as long as possible, unlike the last victim whom Elrian had killed accidentally by taking too much, too fast. That had drawn attention he hadn't wanted, the Guilds' top people hearing about it, not only those ranged against him in the prophecy. It couldn't happen again.

He tried to keep his own consumption limited, sipping at the energy of those he captured like fine wine, until he was ready to use their death for remnant stones. He also gifted his people, like Indigo and his bodyguards, with energy in this way, but that meant more energy was needed.

Perhaps it had been best that Indigo had been killed by Blaize. Indigo had became a little peculiar at the end, and he had needed to feed her a great deal of energy. He may have pushed her too far. He was glad he was stronger and wouldn't have that issue. Her own weaknesses led to her demise.

He took in a breath and tugged on the incandescent streams of energy that he could see in his mind's eye. The boy's struggles were irrelevant now.

Elrian clamped down and tore the energy out of him.

Aeros' eyes bulged as he tried to cry out, but the cotton scarf stuffed in his mouth prevented him from making too much noise. Not that there was anyone to hear.

Elrian barely registered the youth's muffled screams.

4

Nixie had been glad to help Blaize, but it had soon been time for the new arrivals to crash. The next day, Tierra had declared they should start the day with some relaxation, so they'd all gone down to the beach. Tierra was so friendly everyone wanted to please her.

Nixie's friends had opted to lie on the sand, though they approached it in different ways. Blaize, unselfconscious about her body, stripped off to a skimpy bikini, and basked in what was left of the day's sun. Tierra had said she was tired, and had decided that lying on a towel was preferable to any kind of exercise in the sea, and Ai had joined Tierra on the beach, unwilling, it seemed, to be separated from her for the moment.

"It's a lot hotter than the last beach I lay on," Tierra said. "That was on Vancouver Island, Canada, with my friend Cara, and the best you could say for the weather that day was…almost warm. We definitely didn't go in the water."

She smiled, though she seemed subdued.

Nixie loved water. Her energy of Svadisthana was linked with that element, in the same way as Blaize's Manipura was linked with fire, and Nixie adored the peace of being underwater. She was a PADI certified Divemaster – easy enough to achieve on the islands – and had also done a lot of free-diving.

She floated on the surface of the sea, and bobbed up and down with each wave, trying to quell the disquiet that she felt. While Tierra had called this Jebediah guy, Blaize had filled Nixie in on all that had happened since she'd gone to start her training in Vancouver in the last few months. Not the details about Cuinn – well, okay, some of those – but details about how much danger Blaize and her new friends had been in. Danger which apparently was now coming for Nixie.

Nixie didn't take life too seriously. She was likely to live for a long time, and didn't have Blaize's ingrained sense of duty and responsibility, which probably came from the tragic start Blaize had in life when her father, Aden, killed her mother, Aria.

Nixie wanted to enjoy life. What was the point of it otherwise? And while she searched for her perfect mate, she wanted to have fun.

This situation did not seem like fun.

A hand pressed on her shoulder, and Nixie slipped under the water and came up spluttering. Blaize floated in front of her, smirking. They had a definite tendency to regress to a younger age when there was any chance of playing a joke on the other. Nixie was usually more of a brat though, naturally taking the younger sister role in their relationship over the years.

Nixie swiped her hands over her hair to stop the water flooding her eyes.

They chatted for a while, treading water and luxuriating in the sun. Blaize was happy to tell Nixie all about Cuinn and their relationship, which sounded sexy and intense. Nixie loved it.

"How's Cuinn doing given Tierra's discovery that it was his father behind the attack on you, and Tierra's kidnapping?" Nixie asked. She couldn't imagine. She knew she was lucky to be so close to her parents.

Blaize's mouth twisted. "Not great. He doesn't like to talk about it. They were estranged a long time ago, but I can see it still hurts him."

That seemed eminently reasonable to Nixie. She couldn't imagine what pain would drive someone to go to the lengths Elrian, Cuinn's father, was going to. She nodded, then tilted her head. "Why is he doing this? Elrian?"

"We don't know," Blaize said. "Power, we think. But we don't know how, exactly."

"Tierra seems quiet. Is she always like this? Or is it part of what she went through?" Nixie asked. Tierra had been taken by Elrian, held captive, then released by a mysterious woman called Cassidy in Elrian's household, who had wiped Tierra's memory of where the location was.

Blaize fingered her bracelet. "She's not great. She puts on a brave face, but she's been having headaches, and I've caught her staring into space several times. She's usually more grounded. Fintan and Ai have helped. Fintan keeps an eye on her, and given his role as a Warrior, he knows a lot about dealing with the aftermath of trauma. Ai gives her someone to look after."

Fintan's dominant energy was Manipura, and he'd been a Warrior for a hundred years, perhaps more. His current role was as a troubleshooter, someone sent in to solve problems that might also need some muscle, or to capture more unusual or difficult Rogues when he might also take a team with him. Nixie liked him. He rarely took life took seriously, and enjoyed jokes and pranks.

She and Blaize swam in silence for a while. It felt like a lot. So much had happened in a short time. But what could Nixie contribute?

"What's up?" Blaize said. She was well attuned to Nixie's thoughts. This was awkward, though. How did you gracefully back out of a potentially world-changing prophecy?

"I'm not a Warrior," Nixie blurted. Alright. Less on the graceful side, so far. She kicked her legs in agitation, and circled Blaize, who followed her with her gaze.

"Okay? I mean, I'm aware," Blaize said. "Why are you telling me this now?"

"This prophecy. Are you sure you saw me?"

Blaize frowned. "Of course I'm sure. You're my best friend, and hardly someone I'm going to mistake for someone else. I'll show you, if you want. Once we've identified a few more of the unknown figures, we can do you. We should get everyone on paper in case there are clues in the visions that Cuinn or I have missed."

"I'm not sure why I would be involved. I don't have special skills, like you or the others." Nixie ducked her head under the water to cool down, then broke the surface.

"You can fight well enough when you can be bothered," Blaize pointed out. She lay back in the water, floating gently. "Or when you're not distracted by the beauty of an ant on a dead leaf or something."

"If Mum and you weren't Warriors and hadn't made me practice with you, I wouldn't have gone anywhere near it." Nixie was too agitated to relax and float. She wasn't an intellectual, a fighter, or even a healer. She was an artist. And how could that help?

"The prophecy seems to want all kinds of skills and energies, not simply fighting," Blaize shrugged, water cascading over her pale shoulders as she moved them in and out of the water.

"It's hard to see how being an artist is going to prevent the end of the world," Nixie said.

Nixie had studied art rather than academic subjects, and her only ambition was to be happy, and to find love. Her motto in life was 'go with the flow,' and she liked it when she was able to do that. Rules, structure, boundaries – none of these excited her.

She frowned, and brought her legs into her chest in the water so she could execute a gentle forward roll, turning in the water. She popped up for a breath, and then dived back down into the underwater silence.

When she came up again for air, Blaize was still floating in the same place. She cocked her head and looked at Nixie.

"What?"

"You're part of this," Blaize said. "It's not something you can pretend isn't happening. It's too dangerous to ignore."

Nixie pressed her lips together, and tried not to sound as surly as she felt. "Sure. Maybe I'm the light relief."

Nixie was better at cheering people up than serious stuff.

"I love you, Nix, you know that, but maybe, just maybe, it's time to grow up a little." Blaize's tone was gentle, but she had fixed Nixie with a look that said arguing was pointless. This certainty was typical of Blaize. It had got Nixie – a follower more than a leader at the best of times – into trouble on numerous occasions when they were younger.

Nixie was cut by Blaize's words. Nixie was an adult. She made an income through her graphic art, and she was helping with the prophecy.

"I don't think there's anything wrong with living lightly. With not getting too attached to things. With fun." Nixie thought about the image on the sketch pad, which wouldn't leave her alone.

"That guy I drew today, seemed like he could do with cheering up." Nixie wrinkled her nose. "Imagine deciding not to have sex. Or relationships."

"Yeah, okay. I mean, it's not a path I'd take, and you wouldn't last more than ten minutes. He must have good reasons, though. Maybe his Svadisthana wasn't that strong to begin with?" Blaize didn't sound convinced.

Nixie shuddered. It was almost unthinkable for any energetic, a race much more relaxed about sex than your average human. But for someone with Svadisthana energy to decide that was unheard of. What did he do with it all?

Maybe she could help him with that too. She grinned. She wasn't sure about the serious version of this Jebediah, but if he was the sexy version, she could definitely help him with his sexual energy.

"Nixie! I know what you're thinking," Blaize said, laughing. "He's a real person, who obviously has issues. Sex isn't the answer to everything, you know."

Nixie blew out a breath and mock-pouted. "I don't know what you mean."

To be fair, for most Svadisthana energetics sex *was* the answer to many things. She scrunched her nose up. It was one of the key ways they contributed to the balance. When energetics used their magic, they brought energy into the world from the ether, energy that helped the world function and was part of their race's duty for Source.

"Race you back!" Nixie kicked her legs, and tore off through the water, strong strokes of her arms bringing her back inland. Blaize groaned but launched into the waves behind her.

Nixie was ready to start drawing again. But in the meantime, she'd enjoy being, um, creative with her mental vision of Jebediah, daydreaming about how she might persuade him to own his sexual energy once again.

Now that might be an adventure she could get on board with.

Nixie hit the beach a few seconds ahead of Blaize, and they staggered over to their towels, laughing and dancing over the hot sand so their feet didn't burn. Nixie was ahead, but stopped short at the sight of Tierra, head in her hands, eyes closed. She'd moved to the shade of a tree.

Ai hovered protectively, and glared at Blaize and Nixie. "Tierra's not well. She needs help."

"What's up?" Blaize asked.

Tierra shook her head vigorously, then grimaced. "It's fine. I need more sleep, that's all. I'll skip lunch and head back to the house for a rest."

"What's wrong?" Nixie said.

"I'm not sure. I feel exhausted, and achy." Tierra shrugged. "It's probably jet lag. I haven't done much travel outside Canada in the last few decades. My body's adjusting to being away so much recently."

Blaize looked unconvinced. "You never complain about your health. And you're really pale."

"It's time for us to go in, anyway," Nixie said. "We can eat, then Blaize, you and I can have another session and Ai can tell us if Tierra needs us."

Ai nodded. "Alright."

"Let's see how you feel after some rest. It's unusual enough that you might need to see a healer if it continues," Blaize said.

Tierra looked rebellious, but given the slow way that she got to her feet as they packed up, Nixie thought she probably didn't mind that much. Nixie didn't know Tierra that well, but she liked her. Tierra was a kind person, with a tendency to put others first.

Nixie felt a stab of guilt. She didn't always remember to put others first. She meant to, she really did, but sometimes she got distracted. She'd make plans with friends or family, then go off for the day and paint, and lose track of the time. Her auxiliary energy, Vishudha was partly the cause. It was the energy that linked to the element of space, and its energetics tended to be abstract and not great with time – time was a relative construct after all. Nixie's Vishudha wasn't strong, and she hadn't started her training in it yet, but it was definitely there. She tried, she really did, she was just so distractible.

A couple of weeks ago she'd gone to pick her mother herbs, telling her parents she was popping out for ten minutes, and hadn't returned for five hours, having gotten caught up in the charm of a flower she'd seen and wanted to capture in her sketch pad. There were so many objects of beauty in the world. She wanted to encapsulate them all in her art.

Nixie trailed after the others up the beach. She'd admit, she was worried about the danger they all seemed to be in. Physical danger was fairly alien to her. She'd have to refresh herself on updating her bungalow wards. Nixie hadn't done that for a while. She grimaced. She'd rather be drawing.

Tierra headed back while the others stopped for a quick late lunch. Blaize led the conversation over their food, grilling Ai about what she had read so far in the energetic texts Tierra had set her. The girl had a quick mind, Nixie would admit. And despite the fact she seemed to be playing games on her device the whole time, somehow she was also learning about her new world.

Sated, they walked the rest of the way home. When they reached the cluster of houses, Ai went in one direction to sit with Tierra, while Blaize and Nixie headed back to Nixie's place. Nixie slipped her arm through Blaize's.

"I missed this," she said. And she had. Blaize had been a constant presence in Nixie's life, and even when they'd been far away from each other, at university, or when Blaize was working in a different country, they'd emailed or texted pretty much every day.

But since Blaize had left for Canada and met Cuinn, things had changed. Blaize hadn't been in touch as much, and Nixie had missed hearing about the small things in her day. Nixie was glad Blaize had met Cuinn, but she wished it hadn't impacted her relationship with Blaize. Nixie's relationships had never come between her and her friends and family.

Blaize squeezed her arm back. "It's good to be home, Nix."

Nixie felt lighter as they got to her balcony. Blaize's words earlier had been hard to hear – Nixie was used to being the little sister bossed around by Blaize, but her criticism had gone further than that. Nixie knew it was because she cared, though, and usually Blaize's words didn't cut quite as deeply. But Blaize had had a lot on, after all. Not just the romance, but the prophecy, and Blaize's own part in it. It was understandable.

They got into position on the balcony, both sitting on the floor cross-legged this time. Nixie picked up her sketch pad and pencil again, ready. Instead of turning to a fresh page, she turned back to the picture of Jebediah. "Would it be possible to see the image of Jebediah again? I want to fill in more detail."

Blaize put a hand on one hip. "Why? We know who he is. We can move onto the next person."

"I think there's more in there. Don't be so task-focused." Nixie poked Blaize in the stomach. "It's good practice for both of us. We can start on a new figure tomorrow when you've had some sleep."

It was good practice. But she also wanted to make sure she'd got all the details of Jebediah down first. There was something about him, something that she was missing.

And she wanted to try drawing the sad side of him. Just his face. She'd start with the eyes. Those sorrowful, spellbinding, midnight blue eyes.

"We have another eleven to do," Blaize said.

"Please? In case there's a detail I've missed." Nixie flicked to a new page, ready to capture the darker side of the man.

Blaize shook her head and then, at Nixie's pleading look, reluctantly relented. "Fine."

They began the process, and after a minute or so, Blaize was able to project the image of the man back into Nixie's mind.

Nixie shivered as she took in the sad version of Jebediah. She opened her eyes, and her pencil flew across the pad. Time rushed past as she and Blaize worked together, until eventually Nixie came out of her creative trance enough to notice that Blaize was shaking.

"Oh!" Nixie's hand shot to her mouth and she dropped the pad on the floor. "I'm so sorry."

Blaize shook her head, though the fine trembles continued. "I'm fine. Are you done?"

Blaize wasn't fine. She was exhausted. Nixie had a hollow feeling in the pit of her stomach as she realized that without Tierra to keep a check on things, Nixie had pushed Blaize too far.

"Yes, I'm done. Go inside and wash up. Do you want food before you sleep?

Blaize shook her head.

"Okay. Then get ready for bed. Let me clear up here. I'll be right behind you," Nixie said.

Blaize staggered to her feet and went inside.

Nixie bit her lip and stared after her. *Shit.* That's why she needed someone like Tierra as a spotter. Nixie adored Blaize, but Nixie got lost in the flow sometimes. And she was doing this for Blaize. Being focused was her way of doing a good job for her cousin.

She sighed, and looked back down at the pad in front of her. Jebediah was complex, that's for sure. On the one hand, the only thing that was different about this version of him was the eyes. But he seemed like another man. Abject. Despairing almost. *What's his story?* She'd like to ask him.

She flicked back to the first page, and traced a finger over the picture with the tip of her forefinger, then stopped abruptly. It wasn't only the eyes that were different.

Huh. I don't remember drawing those.

The first version of the man had two details that didn't appear in the version she'd drawn most recently. In the first – the sexy – version, Jebediah had a plaited bracelet on his right wrist, and in the far distance of the picture, there was a bird of some sort freewheeling across the sky.

She jumped up and ran into the house. "Blaize!"

Blaize came out of the bathroom in a hurry, her toothbrush still in her mouth. "What? What's happened?"

Nixie showed her the two pictures, excited. "Look!"

Blaize looked at them, one at a time, blankly.

"See?" Nixie said. "I saw two versions of him, like the two sides of a coin. Did you see him like that too?"

Blaize frowned. "No. What do you mean?"

"I saw a very, very sexy version of him, with the bracelet, and then the sadder version of him without."

"That's strange," Blaize said. "If I'm the one transmitting the image, how can you see something different?"

Nixie considered. "Artists often see things others don't. Just because you didn't see it doesn't mean it wasn't there all along."

Blaize's forehead creased even more. "That doesn't sound very logical."

"Does it have to be?" Nixie said. She paused for a moment. "The bracelet. The bird. What do they mean?"

"Huh. Well, it means that Jeb was probably wrong about him never having another relationship," Blaize said around the toothbrush, then held out her left hand to show Nixie a very similar plaited bracelet.

"What do you mean?" Nixie went to look.

"Hold on," Blaize mumbled round the toothbrush, and disappeared back into the bathroom. Nixie flopped onto the bed in Blaize's room, holding the pad above her head and looking up at it. She'd felt a twinge of – what? Something, anyway – at Blaize's words. Was Blaize saying the man in the picture would look like this again? Sexy and sensual? Which of these pictures was the future, and which was the past? Or were they both possible futures?

Blaize came back into the room without the toothbrush. "Cuinn and I have paired bracelets, that are the colors of both our Chakras plus white for Source. So do Tierra and Fintan. We don't know why they appear, or what they do, but they are gifts from Source. Cuinn thinks there are powers in them we need to unlock somehow. Either way, they have indicated a romantic relationship so far. Everyone in the vision is wearing them, though they're blurry enough we can't tell whose matches whose."

Nixie rubbed at her left wrist. So she had a bracelet in the vision too? Did that mean that her soulmate was one of the men in the vision? Her chest felt tight at the idea. She suddenly had a lot of questions. She needed to see the vision of herself, and soon.

Before she could ask more, the thud of someone running up the wooden outside stairs startled them both.

"Blaize!" It was Ai, and she sounded terrified. Blaize ran outside to meet her, Nixie hot on her heels, her stomach churning.

"What's the matter?" Blaize spoke quickly, but she was in control. She was good in a crisis. Much better than Nixie, who wanted to go and hide under a blanket.

"There's something the matter with Tierra. She's having some kind of fit." Ai ran back down the stairs, beckoning them, and they all flew across the scrub between the bungalows.

"What were her other symptoms?" Blaize demanded. Then she tossed over her shoulder "Nixie, are there any healers on the island?"

"I don't think so," Nixie stuttered. "I can call people and check."

"Do it."

Nixie pulled out her cell and rang round the two or three other energetics on the island. There was no healer visiting any of them, and a human doctor would bring the risk of exposure, and would be very unlikely to be able to help if it was an energetic illness, which it almost certainly was. Energetics rarely got human illnesses – from colds to STIs, they were resilient to most diseases and infections.

Blaize had disappeared into Tierra's bungalow, and as Nixie followed her, she gasped at how ill Tierra appeared. She was unconscious, her breath coming in heaves. Sweat dripped off her. Blaize sat on the bed next to her, holding her hand and talking to her, but Tierra wasn't stirring.

Blaize looked up, swiping her free hand across her forehead. "She's stopped fitting, but there's something seriously wrong."

Nixie felt helpless. What could she add in this situation? Poor Tierra. She looked awful, her usually brown skin pale and clammy-looking. She'd like nothing better than to flee, but she could never leave Blaize alone to deal with this. Tierra, too. Nixie would do what she could.

Blaize's hand clenched into a fist, and Nixie realized Blaize felt as impotent as Nixie. Blaize was trained to fight her enemies, but this wasn't something she could fight with fists or feet.

Nixie stepped across to Blaize and put an arm round her waist.

"She's going downhill far too fast, and her vitals are thready. We need to call Fintan, and we need to get a healer. We don't have the abilities between us to diagnose her, let alone cure her." Blaize swallowed. "The only one of us that could have helped her? Is her."

"It worries me," the Guild's elderly Records Keeper, Feng, said. He'd been in the position since Jebediah had first visited the Guild hundreds of years before. Of Chinese ethnicity and slender, he was vague in everything apart from his work in the archives, where he was laser-focused. As he spent more time with records and books than people, it worked okay. "As a race, we're already stretched thin. A number of the Rehabilitation Centers have asked for more staff."

Jeb nodded grimly. The birth rate of the energetics was down, and the number of Rogues was increasing, putting strain on Rehabilitation Centres that looked after Rogue energetics and restored them to health. It was also a problem because too much dark energy upset the world's balance, the maintenance of which was part of the energetics' purpose from the Source.

Jeb had ample experience in the field dealing with Rogues, imbalanced energetics whose energy had twisted, and who had been taken over by the dark side of their emotions and Chakras. One such case had been where Jeb's journey into espionage had begun. An Anahata's love energy had twisted to hate, and he had become so destructive that he had become involved in human affairs, finding ways to express his energy in horrific ways. Living in Constantinople during World War I, the energetic had denounced some Armenians who had been in hiding, leading to their deaths as part of the

Armenian genocide. He'd been caught by Protectors in the Muladhara Guild, who had handed him to the Rehabilitation Center Jeb had been working in.

Jeb had been horrified at what the man had done, while it had also brought the frightful acts that were being committed by the humans to his attention. He'd asked if he could do more to help the efforts of the Guilds to end the War, and that had led to him becoming a spy.

Had he done any good in that role? He'd thought so, at the time. But the final consequences of his acts hadn't been worth the rest.

These days, Jeb advised Rehabilitation Centres on their Rogues remotely, as one of his many roles in the Guild. He was also in charge of the Maven-Adherent pairings, and of the education of Anahata energetics, lecturing and teaching in the classroom and one-to-one. As one of the senior members of the Guild, he supported Aiko on special projects. Today he was working on one such activity. Aiko, who oversaw all the Rehabilitation Centres, had noticed trends in the data from recent decades and asked Jeb to look into the issue. For all the energetics' sophistication and knowledge, there were some big gaps in what they knew. Like how Rogues came about in the first place. They knew what happened, but not why.

Jeb pulled the first of the pile of texts Feng had found for him towards himself. Moments later, Jebediah realized that Feng had continued to hover. "There is another option, if our research doesn't help."

Jeb cocked his head. "Yes?"

"You could go and see Damir." Feng flinched as he said it, as if expecting a negative reaction.

Jeb caught it, but while he was able to stop himself hitting the table with his forehead, he wasn't quite able to suppress a groan. "I'd really prefer not to do that if at all feasible. The man is impossible."

They called Damir 'the Hermit', as he'd chosen for the past several centuries to live in the Cairo Necropolis, the Egyptian city of the dead, away from other energetics.

The man was clear-sighted and knowledgeable, but was rarely prepared to share his wisdom and insights with those from the Guild. He preferred to live humbly in the slums with some of the poorest humans in the country, which would be admirable if the man wasn't such a huge pain in the ass.

"But he knows such a lot!" Feng exclaimed. The man really did love knowledge in all its forms. Despite living alone, he remained well-connected with other energetics, exchanging frequent letters with those he thought were worthy, and had a constant stream of rare texts delivered for scholarship purposes.

Jeb hadn't been out to deal with Damir since World War I, but the memory of the last time was seared into his mind. In exchange for the knowledge that Jeb had wanted, something about a specific way of purifying water to prevent the dysentery that plagued the armies of the allies, Damir had lectured him for an hour on why the Guild system was doomed, how energies were being used wrongly in the modern age. Damir had derided Jeb for his work helping the allies, suggesting that his efforts would be better placed helping the non-military personnel affected by the war, rather than their armies. At the time, Jeb had thought his own efforts critical, and considered himself, if not a hero, then something close.

That hubris had brought a tragic end to innocent lives.

Facing Damir now, nearly a hundred years later, would bring that up, and if the man knew anything about what Jeb had done – and damn the man, he always seemed to know everything – then it would reopen all Jeb's emotional wounds. Jeb didn't feel that would be good for anyone. The Hermit was better left alone.

"The man is graceless and purposely offensive, and is as likely to hold back the information out of spite," Jeb said. "We have plenty to read through. This library is second only to Ajna's in terms of the texts we have. There's bound to be information that can help us here."

Jeb's phone buzzed, and he wandered outside to take the call. It was Fintan. Jeb had liked him when Tierra had brought him to the Guild. He'd had a playful air despite the difficult topics they had consulted him on.

He wasn't playful now.

"Tierra's sick. She had a fit for no reason, and lost consciousness," said Fintan, at the end of the phone. "We need your help urgently. There's no healer on the island, and something's very wrong. You need to get on a plane, now."

Jeb felt cold. Tierra, sick. His mouth was dry as he forced out the next words, knowing Fintan would react badly. "I can't come. You know that. I don't leave the Guild. But I'll find someone experienced to come and examine her."

It wasn't even a question. After his recent loss of control, the Guild was the only safe place for him, and for anyone near him. But he would do whatever he could to help Tierra. She was as dear to him as a sister.

"How many Anahata energetics are as powerful as you?" retorted Fintan. "I don't want to waste time with someone else. We need you. You're one of the best. And we need you now."

Fintan's breath came quickly on the other end of the line. Jebediah rubbed a hand over his chin and closed his eyes.

"I can't leave the Guild. But I'll find you someone, I promise. I'm sorry."

"What would it take?" Fintan asked. "Name it."

"It wouldn't help. You don't understand what the consequences could be."

"You're right. I don't understand," said Fintan, flatly, the sound of an airport public address system in the background giving out the last call for a flight. "You know where we'll be if you change your mind."

Elrian shuddered. Energy came from the captive in a rush, and Elrian drank it in greedily, feeling his own stores replenish. The energy circled through his body, and with some effort of will, he released the boy's head. He mustn't take too much. He needed to save the kill for when they were making a new remnant stone, a process which took great effort and preparation. The youth slumped to the floor, tears leaking from his eyes.

Pathetic.

Elrian wiped his hands on a pristine handkerchief from his pocket, and pointed at the boy. He addressed Dagon. "Clean him up and put him back."

A hint of a smile appeared on Dagon's face. "Sir."

"Don't damage him."

"Of course." Dagon made a little bow. Elrian turned away, absentmindedly smoothing a crease from his pressed white shirt sleeve. He went into the room he used as a study here in Seattle. He settled into an armchair, and decided to use the energy he'd gained to dreamwalk.

Like his do-gooder estranged son Cuinn, Elrian was Ajna-Muladhara, and was able to dreamwalk in the ether to gather and interpret prophecy.

Elrian himself had been senior in the Guild for much of his long life, until he'd gone off the radar after his wife, Cuinn's mother, had been killed in World War II.

That death had confirmed in him a hatred of humans, and also been the last nail in the coffin in his relationship with his son. The son that had encouraged his mother to help the weak humans, using her gifts in a hospital – a hospital that was bombed, so his beloved wife died along with the useless humans she was trying to heal.

His lips tightened as he remembered. But now was not the time for that. He lay back in the chair and put his feet up on a stool. He took several breaths and closed his eyes.

He went through the usual relaxation process fast, and in a short while he was in his Haven, his personal safe place in the ether, or the dreamscape.

Elrian had updated his Haven several times over the years. These days it was a slick and modern monolith of concrete, glass and steel. He didn't need all twenty floors; only the top two were built out, the rest empty space.

His work space was on the nineteenth floor, and his living space was on the twentieth, where he also had an outdoor area with gardens. The Haven, with its manmade-looking exterior, was in part a show of power – not many Muladhara energetics would enjoy being so high up, without access to earth, even in the dreamscape. But Elrian wasn't a coward. The dreamscape was a place he could make and remake around him. He influenced it, not the other way round.

He took the lift down to the ground floor and walked out of the glass doors. His Haven extended far into the distance. But now he needed to hunt.

He drew on the energy of the dreamscape, created a bow and arrow, and jogged into the forest. When he was surrounded by trees, he paused. He walked forward a few paces, then stopped.

He wanted the rabbits he was hunting to hear him, and be startled from the ground and bolt. They weren't real, exactly. They were parts of the wild ether, drawn into his dreamscape by his desire and shaped by his requirements. A way of seeking prophecy.

He walked a few more paces, paused. He looked closely at the ground for signs of movement, or the telltale glisten of eyes.

He stalked through the forest, pacing, pausing, pacing, pausing. Watching.

He enjoyed the hunt. The knowledge that there was a creature out there who would soon meet their end through his actions. But not through the ease of a gun. No.

There was a rustle off to his right, and he turned his head silently.

There.

He raised his bow and arrow, and drew his arm back slowly. If the rabbit bolted, he'd probably miss it. They were fast.

He could see the dark glint as he loosed the arrow, and the rabbit, catching the sound, streaked away. But not fast enough. The arrow caught it in the hindquarters, and the rabbit faltered and dropped to the ground, screaming in pain.

When Elrian got to it, he picked it up by the ears, its pulse fluttering. It dangled in front of him, its belly heaving with panic and pain.

He wrung its neck.

It took him a few minutes to jog back to his building, rabbit in hand, and take the lift up to his workspace.

He was skilled in haruspicy, or the reading of animal entrails. There were other ways to discover prophecy in the dreamscape, but this was his current preferred method. Understanding the future demanded a sacrifice. He knew Cuinn, his ignorant son, preferred to go outside the safety of his Haven – building and lands – into the wild energy and gather prophecy shards himself. But why risk it?

There had been a time when this was Elrian's approach too, but no longer. Now he let prophecy come to him.

He put the rabbit on the clean, wide steel table he used for this kind of activity, and filled his lungs. He drew on the dreamscape, activating his Ajna energy. He relaxed his shoulders.

He took a sharp silver knife from a leather sheath, and raised it, pausing for a moment with the tool in his hand. Then in a smooth movement, he brought the knife down and slit the rabbit's belly, letting the entrails fall out onto the metal table.

He put his hands into the entrails, careful not to disturb the arrangement, closed his eyes, and opened himself to their message.

He saw images flicker across the inside of his head. Jebediah and the girl Nixie dancing around each other, with a strong sexual chemistry, but their personalities so different they had no way to connect. His lips flattened as he saw them with matching bracelets as part of the twelve who ranged against him.

He asked the entrails what he could do to change this image of the future. He saw the man and the woman naked, wrapped around each other. He was puzzled. Surely this was what he was trying to avoid?

But the image developed, and the orange of Svadisthana surrounded the couple, who writhed and moaned, their bodies pressed tightly together. But the energy grew and grew, feeding on the sexual activity of the couple, and feeding it in turn.

The moans changed in tone from sexual to anguished, and a huge burst of sexual energy was unleashed. The female slumped in the male's arms, her heart stopped.

And Elrian understood what he needed to do. Instead of splitting this couple up, as he had tried with the others, he needed to encourage them to be together. He needed the death of two energetics, the entrails told him, but it was achievable. Jeb's attempts to dam his auxiliary energy – a stupid thing to do – would create a pressure that his growing attraction to the girl would shatter when he finally gave in to the attraction, destroying her in the process.

Elrian smirked, well pleased.

Because the death of another innocent would finally devastate Jebediah's spirit, and ultimately, Jebediah would destroy himself.

6

Nixie sat on the floor, head in her hands, next to Tierra's unresponsive body. It had been a long twenty four hours for them all. She'd tried to help where she could, but she couldn't offer much. They hadn't had time to invest in sketching more of the twelve figures when Tierra was in crisis.

Blaize had spent a lot of time on the phone to Cara, also involved in the prophecy and Tierra's friend. Given her role managing a Rehabilitation Centre, Cara was a good choice to consult about medical matters, but she hadn't been able to give them much more help than in dealing with some of the symptoms.

Fintan, Tierra's partner and a scruffy surfer-type, had arrived in the morning, and told them someone was coming to help. He'd tried to get the man that Nixie had drawn to come, but despite the fact he had been Tierra's Maven, and Nixie's picture had shown he was part of this, he'd refused to join them. Perhaps she'd been wrong about his kind eyes.

Nixie heard a car draw up, its headlights cutting through the night outside. With everyone else occupied, she headed out to meet the visiting healer. Sounds from one of the regular jungle parties drifted through the night, and Nixie peered through the trees to see if she could catch a glimpse. At around nine p.m. it was early for a party, and if it was anything like usual, it would only get louder from this point on. She bit her lip. For a moment, she longed to be there, to shed the responsibilities of the prophecy and Tierra's illness, and lose herself in the music. *No.* She brought herself back to reality and turned back to the man who had disembarked from the taxi.

The healer Jeb had sent was a delicate man, with the olive skin and dark eyes of Egyptian heritage, and he smiled warmly at Nixie, greeting her with an embrace despite the fact they'd never met.

"I'm Heka."

She greeted him with her name. "Do you want to wash up? Or have something to eat?"

"I'm fine. I'd like to see the patient," he said.

Nixie nodded and led him to Tierra's room, where Fintan sat vigil, and Ai was slumped against the wall in a corner, almost blending into the shadows due to the black clothes she always wore.

The healer came over to the bed and politely asked Fintan to step back. "I need a little space for diagnostic work."

Fintan scowled, but stepped back into the corner of the room with Nixie, who stayed to see what he would do.

There was a screech and the music outside was cranked up. It was as loud as if it was coming from a speaker inside the room.

Heka pressed his lips together but gently folded the sheet back from Tierra, who was wearing her panties and a T-shirt, and ran his hands slowly from her feet to her head.

Nixie didn't know that much about Anahata, but it was Fintan's auxiliary, though he didn't have enough skill with it to heal Tierra from such a serious illness himself.

"What's he doing?" she whispered to him.

"He's scanning her. Using his Anahata to probe inside her physical and her energetic bodies to see if he can find out what's wrong. An infection, a break or tear, her immune system, anything."

Nixie nodded and squinted, trying to see if she could spot any of the Anahata energy. She saw nothing. Heka was no inexperienced teenager, energy leaking everywhere.

The music swelled, techno beats drumming through the room. This must be a spontaneous gathering, because Nixie didn't know of any parties that were regularly held this close to her home.

"It could be a while," Fintan said quietly. "Jebediah told me this guy's very skilled, but he's going to need to do a thorough exam."

But moments later Heka stopped and said to them, "The noise is distracting. Could one of you see what's happening? If there's anything you can do? I'm going to need you to step outside anyway and give me some space as I'm getting traces of other energies as well as Tierra's own Muladhara and Anahata, and I think your energy might be mixing in with hers. I don't want the diagnosis confused."

"I'll go," Nixie tried to subdue her eagerness. She wanted to help, and she was a lot more suited to going and checking out a party than she was sitting in this room.

Nixie hated waiting. She wasn't a patient person. She tended to gratify her desires immediately. After all, why wait? You could be dead tomorrow.

Fintan looked mutinous, but nodded. "Alright. Nixie can go check the party. Ai and I will be with Blaize next door. Let us know when you're ready, Heka, or if you need anything."

Nixie slipped on her sandals at the bottom of the raised bungalow's wooden stairs, and headed towards the music. She had only gone a few hundred meters through the humid forest before she started to see blurred shapes writhing and twisting around each other. She got closer and could see they were dancers. A cornucopia of noise, sound and light assaulted her senses.

The revelers had set up a portable sound system and she could see fire dancing, hula hooping, and participants with fluorescent paint on their bodies and faces, a popular trend at the island parties. It gave the gathering a tribal, earthy feel, but the dancing was rhythmic and sexy, and her Svadisthana thrummed at the sight of so many bodies enjoying their sensuality.

The scene was the polar opposite of the serious, tense sickbed she'd left behind moments before. People twirled and spun in front of her, whooping and chanting along to the music and beat. Bodies rubbed against one another and it was hard to tell where one person ended and another began.

She'd use an abstract style to represent it, oil paints, wild curved brush strokes of bright colors curling around each other and swirling around solid trees, depicted more naturalistically. The strokes would represent the people, but also the music, and the primality of the scene.

Oh, she wanted to join them so much. The natural energy of the humans captivated her, made her want to lose herself in the gathering as she had so many times before. It was easy for an energetic like her to become a center of gravity in such a group, and she had never, ever failed to take a man home when she'd decided to. The pounding primal music called to her, the jungle by the sea, the wild celebration of life her natural habitat, the temptation of escaping for the rest of the night hard to resist.

She wrapped her arms around herself and stood watching. She could talk to them, to ask them to turn it down, but she couldn't get distracted. Couldn't give in to her desire to lose herself in the music, even for a moment.

Another handful of people spilled out of the other side of the forest and joined the group, which was up to about thirty. She spied drink, and given the joy and abandon on faces, it was likely some other less-than-legal substances were involved. It was pretty unlikely even her powers of persuasion were going to get them to turn the noise down.

What else could she do? What did the healer actually need? Did he need the party to stop? No. He just needed quiet. And though she wasn't highly experienced in her auxiliary energy, Vishudha, with some effort she could create a small silent zone for him to work.

With a long exhale, she turned her gaze from the party, and jogged back to the house, where she updated Fintan and Blaize. When she suggested she would work with her Vishudha to mute the sound for the healer, Blaize looked doubtful.

"Are you sure you can?" she asked.

Nixie winced internally. "Mai benn rai." *No problem.*

She went inside the house, and told Heka what she was going to do.

"Alright," he said. "I can account for more of your energy when I diagnose. I'll pause while you get it set up."

She nodded. She folded herself into a cross-legged position on the floor, her back to the bed. She didn't train with her energies much. She had a tendency to be a little leisurely in her practice. She had completed her training to be a Practitioner in Svadisthana, but she hadn't had Blaize's drive to start training for her auxiliary energy yet. There would be plenty of time for that.

She closed her eyes and felt for her connection to the ether, the place where Source provided infinite energy, energy that was bounded only by the amount the energetic in the physical world could contain.

As an artist she loved color, and the strong orange of Svadisthana was her favorite, with the bright blue of Vishudha close behind. It was easy for her to draw the latter from the ether, sculpting it with her mind into a smooth ball inside her.

She made the sphere dense with energy, the sides smooth, until it was almost heavy inside her throat, the seat of the Chakra. Once she was satisfied with it, she took a handful of deep, deep breaths. Now was the delicate bit. She put her hands on her throat, and she sang out a long, clear note.

As she did, she increased the size of the energy sphere, which expanded around her. It took some effort. She really should practice more with her energies. When the sphere covered her body entirely, silence fell, as if she was in a padded tomb. She sucked in another breath, a bead of sweat at her temple, taking a moment before she was ready to expand it further. Another breath, and she gritted her teeth. She wasn't going to let Blaize and the others down. She saw blue flickers in her vision, and she shook her head to clear it. She pushed again, to encompass the bed, Tierra, and the healer. She opened her eyes to peek and check that it was working.

Heka's eyebrows twitched, and he gave Nixie a nod. Okay. Good. It was working. She considered the size of it. She should make it a little bigger, so Heka had room to work. Another deep breath, and she expanded her chest and diaphragm. She used the large exhale to inflate the sphere to cover most of the room.

There was nothing but hush.

It wasn't a state that Nixie was especially familiar with, and after only a few minutes she became uncomfortable, left alone with her own thoughts. She preferred to live in the now. When she reflected on the hundreds of years she might live, and the expectations she, as part of her race, should live up to, she became overwhelmed. Better to live in the present, and experience life through the senses, not the intellect. Though her 'now' was equally full of responsibility, it seemed, with the prophecy looming over her and her friends.

Heka continued to examine Tierra, but there was no one else in the room to distract Nixie. She held the bubble of silence for another forty-five minutes, an age, until Heka finally gestured. It was a test of emotional as well as mental and energetic prowess, and she'd heard that holding silence like that for several days was part of the Practitioner test for Vishudha. She could see why. Left alone with nothing but your own thoughts, no other sound or input to distract you, was disorientating. She'd heard that when their eyes were also covered, some energetics almost tipped into madness from the solitude. More practiced energetics had more control, and were able to shut out external noise without dampening the sound inside the orb, but she didn't have the training for that.

She dropped the bubble gratefully, and the sounds of the jungle rushed back. Animals, night birds, the party, music, Heka's footsteps, Tierra's breathing, Nixie connected to them all and bathed in them.

Heka had called the others, who filed in around Tierra. Heka cleared his throat and cracked his knuckles. "There's something very strange going on here."

He addressed Fintan. "Tierra's energy is Muladhara and Anahata, correct?"

"Yes," said Fintan, tightly.

Heka rubbed the back of his neck. "I found traces of all six energies in her."

They all stared at him.

"You mean…like everyone else?" Nixie asked. The Chakras were present in every living thing, including humans and animals. But usually they were only activated in energetics, and only ever two, a dominant and an auxiliary.

"No. All six are active," said Heka. He gazed down at Tierra, and tapped a finger against his lower lip.

"What are you talking about? That's not possible." Fintan's arms were crossed, his jaw clenched.

"Her dominant and auxiliary as you describe them are there, very strong, but the other four are also there. Active. Very weak, but there. It's…peculiar."

It was more than peculiar. Nixie had never heard of such a thing. It wasn't supposed to be possible.

"Is this causing her illness? How can we stop it?" Fintan asked.

"I don't know why this is happening," Heka admitted. "I can stabilize her, give her a healer's shield, and I think I can bring her out of unconsciousness, but I don't know if this energetic anomaly is what's causing the issue or whether it's something else. So I still need to talk to colleagues at the Guild once that's done and see if anyone has come across this before."

"Do it," Fintan ordered.

Blaize laid a hand on Fintan's arm.

"Please," she added.

The healer nodded. "Can you lift her up? I need to sit with her head in my lap so I can concentrate."

Blaize put an arm underneath Tierra's back and lifted the other woman's limp torso, steadying her head while the healer got on the bed and crossed his legs. He gestured and Blaize rested Tierra's head in his cupped hands.

"Do you need us to go?" Blaize asked.

Heka shook his head. "As you like. But I will need quiet so I can concentrate."

He raised an inquiring eyebrow at Nixie.

She breathed deeply. It wasn't an easy magic. But she nodded, and raised the sphere of silence again.

The healer's eyes closed and his face went blank. Nixie couldn't see what he did for the next thirty minutes or so, but she figured Fintan, who had Anahata as his auxiliary, could from his eyes, which moved up and down Tierra's body as if following something.

But when Heka created the shield, they could all see it. A glowing green light surrounded Tierra, at first in a bumpy ovoid, then moving to cling tightly to her skin. It shone brightly for a few minutes and then disappeared into Tierra's body, leaving a dark afterimage.

The healer slumped a little, then opened his eyes, which were blurry with fatigue. "It's done. The shield I have created is a general one, to protect against illness and the symptoms of what she has. She should wake up naturally in a few hours. I brought the materials for a glucose drip, and I'll put one of those in too to prevent dehydration in this heat. But it's not over. Whatever this odd infection of energies is, her body can't defend against it. It's simply not used to all six energies being activated, and it's going haywire trying to deal with what it considers an attack. And because I don't know the cause, I can't create a shield that defends against that."

"So what do we do?" demanded Fintan.

"We get more help. Or it's going to happen again."

C H A P T E R

7

"I have information," Imogen said. The attractive blonde wore a pencil skirt, heels and a white blouse, her heavy blue-green pendant hanging between her small, high breasts and contrasting with skin the color of milk. She'd chosen to look in her early thirties, but she was centuries old, a Master in one energy and a Maven in the other.

She'd entered the room at the safe house without Elrian noticing, and he raised his head wearily. He'd drained a little too much of the energetic that Dagon had brought him, and his system had felt the overload. After his trip into the ether, he was letting it settle within him before he did anything else. He'd have to take less next time. The energetic had survived, perhaps more through luck than by judgement. And that was very unlike Elrian, whose judgement was always level.

"What is it?" he asked. He didn't rise to his feet. He was too tired. He was devoted to her, but she was unpredictable, while it was his nature to be careful. She shouldn't be here. She should be at the Guild given everything that was happening.

They didn't know her as Imogen there. She'd long since taken another identity while she re-climbed the Anahata power structure after her first fall from grace, and subsequent retreat. As far as he was aware, he was the only person who knew her true name and her dark past. A hidden Rogue in the heart of Anahata. What sweet irony. More so when you considered the double meaning of the name she'd taken.

She had said she'd come to check on him, and take care of him, but there were times when she added to his work rather than helped. She had access to great power, and while it took a lot out of her she was somehow able to use it to transport herself instantly between locations, though she hadn't revealed the mystery of how to him yet. She was full of secrets, and she was hard to predict, both in action and mood. He sighed. Having said that, he wouldn't be on this path without her.

"It's about Jebediah," she said. "The Anahata-Svadisthana energetic who's the next in the prophecy to couple."

"Yes?" The back of Elrian's skull rested on the armchair he sat in. Study was too grand a name for this room, but it had a desk, a chair, a lamp and the armchair. There was little decoration apart from a five foot dragon tree in a terracotta pot that stood in the corner of the room opposite the armchair. Elrian's Muladhara energy needed something growing around him.

Imogen stalked to the chair at the desk and swung it round so the seat faced Elrian. She sat gracefully in the chair, her ankles neatly crossed, her hands loosely clasped.

"Do you know Jebediah's story? Why he's stuck in the Guild?" she asked Elrian.

He shrugged. "Something about a woman and his Svadisthana? An inappropriate use of his energy? He contravened their rules about the use of influence."

She nodded. "Correct. But I have new information."

He waved a hand for her to go on.

"The woman Jebediah influenced was the person who then gave the Germans the location of the hospital where your wife was working. The information that led to its bombing."

Elrian stiffened. "What?"

She smoothed a hand over her already perfect hair and settled back with an exaggerated casualness. "Jebediah is the person who got your wife killed."

All tiredness left Elrian, his system electrified. Rage sang through him and he jerked upright. He was dedicated to Imogen, and she was his lover now, but his wife was the reason he had started on this path in the first place. The reason he craved revenge on the humans. The reason he wanted power, to cleanse the world.

"You need to do better this time," Imogen said. "The prophecy needs to turn our way. So I will help you. Together we will ensure the deaths needed."

Elrian swallowed. That was … a mixed blessing.

"What is your plan?" she asked.

He mentally shook himself. He needed to put fatigue and fury aside and focus.

560

"My dreamwalk tells me the male is unsteady, easily shaken, and has a great deal of pent-up sexual energy waiting to explode. I need to get the couple together. The female is wild, out-of-control, and has no boundaries around sex. Once they're in the same place, they will only need a small push to get them together, and then –" He waved a hand. "Boom."

"Good." She recrossed her ankles carefully. "I have hired a mercenary to help us. I want you to talk to him about what he can do on the island. I've also been jabbing holes in Jebediah's Svadisthana wardings for weeks. It's causing his control to slip, and he has no idea why. It's getting worse, and he thinks he's losing his mind. A couple of days ago I was able to push him to a point where he nearly razed his study to the ground."

Elrian's pulse quickened. She was taking action without him. That wasn't part of their plan. They were supposed to work together, to be a co-ordinated team. "Alright."

"And it's time to get Cassidy involved. I talked to her on the phone yesterday, and she still seems to be resisting your influence on her. Would you like my help?"

"No," he said, quickly. He had been so careful to keep the two women apart. After Imogen, Cassidy was the most important person in the world to him. She wasn't resisting the influence because he wasn't really using much influence on her. She was a powerful Ajna influencer herself, and he told himself it was because she was a difficult target, but really it was a line he hadn't wanted to cross with her. She still had most of her free will, and he'd worked around her, nudging her only when he really needed to, or when the time came to hide things from her. "I'll manage her."

"She's an asset, my love," Imogen reached out and stroked his cheek. "We can't be sentimental when we have so much to do before our power base is settled."

Hellfire and negativity, no. "I'll keep her in line. It's not a problem."

He loved the beautiful, hard-edged woman in front of him, it was true. And he was confident that by the conclusion of this prophecy they'd rule the Guilds together.

But if he used too much influence on Cassidy she might end up losing her sense of self, her personhood. And he wasn't ready to let go of Cassidy quite yet.

Jeb was concerned that Heka, an experienced healer, hadn't been able to restore Tierra to health. He went down to the archives to research the issue to see if other Anahata healers had encountered anything similar in the past.

He walked to Feng's desk. The slight Asian man smiled at his approach. "I don't have anything new for you on the Rogue issue yet."

"I'm not here for that," said Jeb. He explained the situation to Feng, whose long face fell as Jeb told the story.

"Poor Tierra. She's such a wonderful woman," Feng muttered. "That's very unusual. Very unusual indeed. If it's in the archives, we will find it."

Jeb nodded. Tierra made a positive impression on most people she met. "She's important to me too."

Feng was already walking into the stacks. "Do you want me to ask anyone else for help?"

Jeb hesitated. Given all that was going on, he thought not. Though he would tell Aiko when he got the chance. He'd already asked Heka to stay quiet about it for the moment. If it was connected to her breaking the energy sharing taboo with Cuinn, they needed to keep it quiet as long as possible. Cuinn and Tierra could face consequences if others knew.

"No. Unless there's something specific we find, or you think someone has information that would be helpful, let's keep it between us."

The next day, Fintan stayed with Tierra. Nixie and Blaize had made him and Heka up a bed in Marius and Fai's house, as Nixie's parents were away visiting their in-common Guild, Svadisthana, but Fintan wouldn't leave Tierra's side, preferring to sleep on a mat on the floor next to her. Heka was grateful for the bed, and took rest after his work.

Tierra thus safe under watch, Blaize asked Nixie if she would spar with her. Nixie made a moue of distaste, but agreed despite her usual reluctance. Blaize was taller, more muscular and better trained than Nixie, and these bouts never went well for her. But even Nixie could see that Blaize was worried about her sick friend, and Nixie wanted to cheer her up. And not much cheered Blaize up more than kicking someone's ass.

Blaize was also more comfortable with the odd bruise than Nixie, who tried to avoid pain wherever possible. This time Nixie lasted all of fifteen minutes before she pulled on her Svadisthana energy and drenched Blaize in the equivalent of a bucket of water.

Blaize stood in front of her, her auburn hair dripping down her neck, and actually growled. Nixie burst out laughing.

Blaize bared her teeth, which made Nixie giggle harder. Blaize swiped out an arm, which Nixie "eeep"ed at, and jumped backwards. Then she slipped on the water, and ended up flat on her back on the training mat, still laughing.

A slow smile spread across Blaize's face even as she shook her head. "Nong sao, you can be a pain in the ass."

"It's why you love me, right, pee sao?" Nixie gasped for breath even as her body continued to be wracked by giggles. The laughter had released tension she hadn't even known was there.

Blaize shook herself off, and used a flare of Manipura heat up and down her body, which evaporated the water in a puff of steam. Then she stepped carefully around the puddle, and threw herself down next to Nixie. They were in a shared outside gym area between the three houses.

Nixie lay on the floor and looked up at the blue of the sky. *Like an upside down ocean.* Perhaps she would go for a swim later to clear her head. The two of them lay in a companionable silence, both looking up at the sky, their heads close together, bodies pointing away from each other.

"How's Cuinn?" Nixie said.

Blaize's lips twisted. "I spoke to him yesterday. I miss him. He's been having nightmares recently, and we don't know why."

"Something to do with the prophecy?"

"We don't know. They actually seem like more ordinary nightmares."

"From what you've said, there's a lot of stress. Could it be that?"

Blaize shrugged. "There's a lot we don't know in this situation, and not much we do."

Nixie wriggled on the floor, and let the blue above her fill her up. She tried to think of nothing, but her mind kept turning over everything Blaize had told her, as well as the situation with Tierra.

"Blaize?" Nixie asked.

"Hmm?"

"I'm frightened. I don't think I'm cut out for this kind of adventure."

"It's not an adventure, Nix. We're fighting for our lives here. And perhaps more."

Nixie felt cold. "That's what I mean. I'm not a fighter. I'm an artist. I don't see what my role is."

"You're already helping with the identification. We'll work on that some more until we have pictures of everyone who Cuinn has seen clearly so far, and also any important images he's seen. It's a good use of time, as I can't dreamwalk for prophecy like Cuinn, so he's trying to find more pieces while we do this."

"And then what?" Nixie said.

"How'd you mean?"

"How else can I help?" Nixie persisted. "You're used to danger from your Warrior training, but I'm not. I'd freeze if someone attacked me."

Nixie felt a thickness in her throat, and moisture prick the back of her eyes. She didn't like admitting to this, but she didn't want Blaize to rely on her when Nixie knew she couldn't deliver. "I'll help where I can, like with the images, but I can't fight. I'd panic."

Blaize pushed herself up to lean on one arm, and stroked Nixie's hair. "It's okay. I know you. The real you, not the side you show to most people. You've always been there for me when I needed you. This won't be any different."

A tear leaked out of Nixie's eye. She'd do what she could. But Blaize was wrong.

"What're you going to do next with your life, Nix?"

Nixie blinked at the change of topic. "What?"

"You did your initial training in Svadisthana, but what about Vishudha? Are you going to stay on the island, living next to your parents? What's next for you?"

"Why does there need to be a next? I like my job, I like my house, I like my life. There's plenty of time for more training later. People are always looking at what the next thing is, they never enjoy what they have now. Then when they reach the next thing, they move the bar again. I want to enjoy the beauty of the moment. To be present right now, here." The heat of the day suddenly felt stifling, rather than comforting, and the ground underneath her was hard and unforgiving, no longer cradling.

"I love the island, you know I do, but right now we have a problem a lot bigger than this moment." Blaize half sat up and rested on one arm, contemplating Nixie's prone form. "I can see you're frightened. Me too. But we – I – your friends need your help. You can't just coast past this one and expect it all to work out."

Ouch. What was this, lay into Nixie day? She wished Blaize would stop. Nixie had forgotten this side of Blaize, the persistent, moral, driven person whose total faith in Nixie was a double-edged sword.

"I guess I got used to living down to people's expectations." Nixie sat up and wrapped her arms around her knees. "Tired of people judging me on my appearance."

Nixie was attractive, she knew, by the current standards of society, but she had no control over that. She was so much more than her body and face. Getting others to see past them had been exhausting, and eventually, she'd given up. She dressed to please herself. She'd pursued graphic art, a human career that didn't involve people seeing – or judging her on – what she looked like. She worked from home, kept her gender hidden from readers, and kept her work boxed off from the rest of her life. She'd been so discouraged by jealous hints that she wasn't serious enough for study at her auxiliary Chakra Guild, Vishudha, she'd put her energetic studies on hold indefinitely.

"Let's try more sketches while Fintan looks after Tierra," Nixie said. "We can do whichever you find easiest so it doesn't drain you too much."

Nixie would offer what she could to help her friends. Blaize knew about her past, but also knew Nixie had no interest in talking about it these days. She was happy as she was. Nixie accepted herself, and had no need to chase anyone else's acceptance.

But dammit.

Blaize's words had opened up an unpleasant possibility. If Nixie hadn't been skating along on the surface of life for the last few years, if she'd bothered to bite the bullet, weather the storms, and start her Practitioner training in Vishudha?

Maybe she'd have some help to contribute right now, more than the odd drawing. Be a useful chess piece, rather than a pawn who had no skills or abilities better than a hundred others.

But she hadn't. And now it might cost her friends their lives.

CHAPTER

"I need you to tell me what is happening to Tierra." Fintan's voice was gruff with emotion. "Please, Jeb."

Jeb and Feng had spent the day searching deep in the stacks of the archives, following references like breadcrumbs from one to another. Now Fintan wanted an update.

"We haven't found much" Jeb said. "A reference in the diary of an energetic from the fourteenth century, the leader of a small energetics community in southern France during the plague they called the Black Death. She was able to protect herself from the sickness, but didn't have enough power to save the humans around her."

"Alright. And?"

Jeb continued. "She was an Anahata energetic living together with a small community of other energetics and running a human orphanage. She was married to a human, and their own children died in infancy."

"She'd watched the spread of the plague and realized how bad it was – in some places in Europe, sixty to seventy percent of the people died from the disease. She wanted to protect the orphans but she wasn't strong enough on her own."

"So what happened?" Fintan was becoming more and more frustrated.

"When she saw the plague nearing her community in 1349, she asked her brother, also an Anahata dominant but without the same healing powers she had, to break the taboo and share some of his energy with her."

Could Fintan see what was coming? When Feng had told him earlier, this had been the *oh shit* moment for Jeb.

"Tierra told me about breaking the sharing energy taboo with Cuinn, to save Blaize." Jeb had been uncomfortable, shocked even, but he'd understood her motives. For Tierra, rules were important, but people came first.

"Yeah," Fintan said, winter bleak. "I tried to stop her. But you know what she's like."

"They shared energy, and at first, everything was fine. Ninety percent of the children survived the plague. However, she became very sick after a few weeks."

"Why did it happen? What caused it? And more importantly, how did they cure it?" Fintan asked.

Jeb ran a hand through his hair and stared at the wall of books. "They didn't. And they didn't know why."

There was a silence. "Fix this. Please, Jeb. She looks so small in that bed."

Fear for Tierra had crept into Jeb's heart. If he couldn't find the answers they needed, what would happen to Tierra?

Feng hastened in.

"I'm on the phone to Fintan," Jeb said, his brow wrinkling in puzzlement. The refined Feng rarely rushed anywhere.

"I have something to share with you both," Feng said.

Jeb put the handset down, put the call on speaker and gestured to Feng, who introduced himself.

"It's a case study written up by an Anahata Rehabilitation Centre in 1902. A Muladhara-Anahata energetic was captured by two Manipura Warriors because of serial leeching. He was caught because the last of his victims had been his lover – who had been willing when they were together, but when she'd found him cheating on her, she'd reported him to the Guild," Feng said.

Leeches were a type of Rogue. Feng went on to describe the rest of the story. The Leech had been taken to a Rehabilitation Centre. These weren't like human prisons. In them, Healers worked to untwist the energy of Rogues that had become tangled and used in a dark way. They also gave Rogue energetics the opportunity to repent, but this Rogue had shown no remorse for his actions.

Jeb pinched the brow of his nose, thinking. How did all this connect?

"He was powerful, and appeared to have access to other energies," Feng said. "He told the Healer that he'd taken energy from six people. The first time had been an accident, when he took energy from a lover during sex. It felt good and he chased the feeling again, but the next woman sickened and died. He'd travelled to areas where no one knew him, and experimented on other women, siphoning off different amounts of energy and noting the results."

Feng's tone was hushed, and horrified. "The Leech worked out how much he could take on a regular basis without killing his lovers, and then met the woman who had eventually turned him in. He told her what he was doing, and together they'd turned outside their relationship to other energetics, leeching from victims and having sex with each other while their victims looked on."

Jeb's stomach turned.

Feng continued. "It was only when the Leech slept with someone outside the relationship that the lover had turned him in, perhaps hoping to be seen as another victim."

"But what happened to him? Did he live?" Fintan said.

Feng hesitated before speaking. "He got sick. And his symptoms seem to echo Tierra's. He fitted and lapsed into unconsciousness. They didn't know how to help him, and he died six weeks later."

"I found the case study in the sealed, classified papers of the Guild," said Feng.

There was a long silence.

Jeb's stomach churned, and he rubbed his upper arms. He felt a chill that was from more than just the air conditioning of the temperature and humidity controlled archives.

"Tierra has the same mix of energies as the killer," stated Fintan.

"Yes."

"But she wasn't the recipient of the energy when she shared it with Cuinn, she was giving," Fintan said. "So how can it be the same?

His tone was desperate, pleading. Jeb didn't have the answers he wanted.

"Somehow, in opening herself up, she seems to have triggered something. She's activated her other Chakras," Jebediah said slowly. He was working it through as he talked.

"How can this be possible?" Feng asked.

Jeb was too busy reeling from the information to answer. If it was possible for energetics to have more than one Chakra activated, then it put into question everything they knew. The fact that energetics had one dominant and one auxiliary Chakra wasn't only a core part of what energetics were, it was a fundamental truth.

"I don't know," Jeb said. His mind raced. He needed to take this to Aiko. This fundamentally shook his understanding of the Chakras and how they worked in energetics. It was overwhelming, and he needed her counsel.

"You need to get here," Fintan said, his voice cracking. "Do not let Tierra down."

He hung up. Jebediah rubbed his forehead, talking to Feng. "Put this somewhere safe, away from others' eyes. I'm going to talk to Aiko."

When he arrived at her office, he knocked and walked in. She sat on one of the armchairs in the corner of the room, a headset on. When she saw Jeb she pulled it off, looked him up and down, and cocked her head.

"What's the matter? More trouble with your Svadisthana? Or is it Tierra?" She gestured to him to sit in the other armchair.

He sat and leaned forward. "My energy's fine, and Tierra is stable, though I am worried. Even more so now."

He filled her in on what Feng had found in the text. Her eyes widened as he talked her through it, the only sign of her shock.

"Never have I come across this," she said, when he finished. "This could change everything we know about our energy and our power. It brings up so many questions. Is it possible for everyone to access all six Chakras? Or only some people? And if it's possible, why don't we see more energetics who have access to all six? I will admit, Jeb, I'm worried about Tierra."

"And can it be done without negative side effects?" Jeb asked grimly. "So far, people have either died, or the energy has been too much for them and it has twisted."

Aiko leaned forward and put a hand on Jeb's knee. "I'm sorry to ask this of you Jeb-san, but you need to go to Tierra. She's not the only factor involved here now. We need to know more about the situation. How was it triggered? And how can we keep her alive and untwisted?"

Jeb reared back. "Don't ask this. It's too dangerous for those around me. What if I make things worse simply by being there? There must be someone else."

Aiko's face softened.

"I'm sorry. We cannot let others know about this yet. The Guild seems unsettled at the moment – Maya came in only last week with a complaint about a decision I had made, and seems to be stirring things up. She's already Guild leader for her Minor Guild Anahata-Ajna, but it's not enough for her. I think she wants my job." Aiko sighed.

Jeb's eyebrows drew together. He hadn't heard that. Maya could be a challenge, true, despite the Anahata being the Guild associated with love. There were as many politics here as in any other Guild. "You should have said. I might be able to help smooth things over. Maya and I get on fine."

"It's just one of the challenges of running the Guild. I wouldn't even mention it but it means I don't think it's a good idea to share the information you've discovered until we know more. Maya and others like her may use it to stir people up because I don't know the answers," Aiko said.

Jeb tried once more.

"Is there no one else?" The stress of leaving the Guild made his entire being tighten, and he could feel a dull ache between his shoulders. How would be protect others from his energy if he left the Guild?

Aiko shook her head.

"What about my Svadisthana energy? What if it…" he trailed off. They both knew the risks.

"We'll work together now to bind it again. You're very disciplined, and you have iron self-control. You come into contact with new people all the time here, and you've kept it locked down for decades. You've proved you can do this. Why would going outside the Guild be different?" she asked.

Jeb pursed his lips. He looked out of the window and thought, breathing deeply, trying to center himself. Why was it different?

When he'd first arrived at the Guild, he'd been angry and guilty, and devastated at the loss of innocent life his actions – his use of energy – had caused. He no longer felt quite so angry, but he would never get over the guilt at what he had done during the war. His Svadisthana wasn't safe, and he would not use it again.

But perhaps Aiko was right. Perhaps there was no difference between being here and being outside. Now his energy was bound, and he'd controlled it for so long, he no longer needed the safety of the Guild. If he and Aiko could be confident that his energy was locked up tightly, then being outside might be no different from being here.

Plus, he'd be among friends. It was a good place to be, Koh Somdun. He'd never been before, but he knew it was small, with a tiny population, and he'd have plenty of space. He tried to visualize it in his mind, to see himself safe, his energy locked down, and on the island.

He knew if Tierra didn't survive and he hadn't tried to help her, and he truly was the only one for the job, he would never forgive himself. Perhaps it was the right thing to do, despite the risks.

Source, am I actually considering this?

"I need more time to think," he said.

"We don't have that time. It's a flight or two away, and we don't know how long Tierra will stay stable. You need to talk to her to make sure you have all the information you can extract in case anything happens. If we don't take care of her, she may become a Rogue."

Jeb's heart jolted.

"I'm sorry, Jeb. I hope very much that you will be able to help Tierra, and Feng will continue the research here in the meantime – I will give him support for his other duties. But if she dies, we need to ensure we know everything that has happened, down to the last detail," Aiko said.

Jeb shook his head. "I won't let her die."

"If you are with her, that is more likely to be true," she said. "It's time to leave the Guild."

Cold eyes met Elrian's. There was plenty of confidence in them. Elrian tried not to sneer at the Rogue mercenary-for-hire his lover had sent him. Called Trent, a Svadhistana-Ajna energetic, he had an angular face and strong jaw. Muscular and rugged, he was the epitome of tall, dark and handsome.

He was also chewing on a toothpick, which to Elrian's mind was disgusting. It wasn't even disposable, but made from eighteenth century carved bone. Trent had told Elrian matter-of-factly it had once belonged to a pirate king. Trent had murdered the most recent owner for it. Elrian thought it likely the only time the toothpick was out of the man's mouth was when he was actually consuming food. The idea made Elrian shudder in distaste. Why was good hygiene such a difficult concept for people?

"How do you want me to proceed?" Trent asked. They sat across a table from each other in the bar in Seattle. It was raining outside, and Elrian felt the cold in his bones. He tried to smooth down his white shirt, which, usually immaculate, had become creased on the trip into town.

He ached with exhaustion. This journey he and Imogen were on was supposed to be more energizing than this. When only one or two couples had formed, he'd only needed to destroy one person from among them. Now he had three couples bonded, he would need to kill two of the energetics from their ranks to thwart them enough for his version of the prophecy to win through. If, Source forbid, there became five or six couples, he would need to kill three individuals.

That would not happen.

He was focused on killing both members of this couple to be sure, and perhaps killing Tierra, his niece, who'd just been the bait at first, might also be worthwhile. There was safety in contingency planning. So much power was within reach.

"Follow them, and look for an opportunity when they are alone together," Elrian instructed. "If you see a chance, weaken his shields. He thinks he's protected, that his sexual energy is locked down, but the vision I saw indicated that she can break through them. Help it happen."

"Understood," said Trent. He had shown no emotion. No pleasure, displeasure, enthusiasm, nothing. Simply stared at him with those coal black eyes.

"I will also give you a carved jade charm to place near Tierra," Elrian continued. "It doesn't need to be in the room with her. Within about ten meters should do it. This will speed the draining of her energy. It's tied to her, so it won't affect anyone else."

Trent nodded.

"The money is in your account." The man was paid well for his services, paid for his loyalty.

What was Trent's relationship to Imogen anyway? How did they know each other? If it came to it – and Elrian was sure it never would, but, still, he couldn't stop the thought from worming into his mind – whose orders would Trent follow? Elrian's? Or hers?

He shook it off. Trent was a tool to be utilized, nothing more. The tool that Elrian needed to tip the already vulnerable Jebediah over the edge.

Whilst Jebediah thought it was Tierra who was the sick one, it was actually Jebediah who was most at risk.

Because with the right trigger, Jebediah would destroy both himself and Nixie.

9

Jeb stepped off the boat and into the clinging wet heat of Thailand. He was used to hot weather as he'd lived in Egypt for seven decades. But Thailand was humid, and within moments of leaving the air conditioned boat his shirt was sticking to his chest and a rivulet of sweat ran down his back.

The journey had been tiring, exposing Jeb to new technologies that he'd only seen on television. Usually, energetics were used to the world changing around them, and learned to adapt quickly to social and technological changes, taking the progressions – and regressions – of the human world in their stride, just as the elements ebbed and flowed around them. This much change at once, however, was draining. He was grateful for the island's gentler pace.

The dock was pretty basic, and brightly colored traditional fishing boats were moored opposite where the commercial passenger boats drew up. Beyond them lay the clean white sands of the beach, and then the changeable blue of the sea.

Jeb had missed the sea. He might have locked down his Svadisthana, his water energy, but it was still part of him.

A motorbike pulled up. Not the usual low cc scooters you saw on this sort of island, but a proper sports bike. Jeb had never learned to drive a car, sequestering himself as he had before cars were common, but he had learned to drive a motorcycle around the time of World War I. He'd always enjoyed the speed and the feel of the road underneath him.

The male rider got off the bike and without saying anything handed Jeb a helmet he produced from underneath the seat. He lifted his own plastic visor and turned cool blue eyes on Jeb.

"Fintan," said Jeb. Right. It would be him who came to pick him up.

"Thanks for coming. Get on." Fintan steadied the bike, closed his visor, and waited for Jeb to do up his helmet. There was no sign of the lightness that Jeb had seen in Fintan when he'd visited the Guild. The man was closed up tight.

They weren't going to catch up first then. *Lucky I only have a rucksack.* Jeb pulled the straps over his shoulders and hopped onto the bike.

Fintan gunned the engine and drove the length of the dock, past stray dogs, children fishing and street food carts selling everything from corn on the cob to unidentifiable meat on a stick. They drove through the small town that was bunched around the dock: cafés, hotels, travel agents, and the ubiquitous 7-11. A few miles and they were onto a sandy road edged with coconut palms, where few scooters and fewer cars passed them.

After about twenty minutes they turned down a track that Jeb would have missed if he'd been looking for it alone. The lane was not much more than a couple of ruts in the sandy earth, and Fintan had to slow the bike as it bumped along. A clearing came into view with a cluster of traditional Thai bungalows spaced for privacy. Each was raised on thick wooden posts.

Fintan parked his bike underneath one of them, and Jeb got off.

"Thanks for the lift," Jeb said. He and Fintan had got on well when he had come to the Guild with Tierra. And Jeb was here now, wasn't he? Not that he was sure he could help. He pushed that thought away.

Fintan looked at him, his fists clenched by his sides. He was angry, that was obvious. But he wasn't only angry at Jeb.

"I'll do everything I can to help. I know you're worried," Jeb said, his voice soft.

"Don't read me!" Fintan was a tinder box looking for a spark.

"I'm not. I'm worried too. Tierra is important to me." Jeb felt as if he was talking to an injured wild animal.

"Not so important you came sooner. What if that was the difference between her being well and —" Fintan broke off and looked away.

"I wouldn't have known any more than Heka did. If Feng hadn't found the information on past cases, I wouldn't have known what this was either. We haven't come across it in the modern age."

Heka had left for another emergency elsewhere once Jeb had made it known he was on his way. They'd spoken on the phone so Jeb could understand what had happened so far.

He stepped forward. "Take me to her, and let's see what we can do."

Jeb followed Fintan up the stairs, stepped onto the large wooden balcony, and stumbled when he saw what at first his addled brain took for a fairy sitting on the floor.

A very sexy petite fairy in a white summer dress that set off liquid brown eyes and black hair.

Jeb's Svadisthana energy roared into life, and smashed against the bars of the cage of shields and wardings that he had created with Aiko. There was an orange flash as a little energy escaped before he could clamp down on it, and Jeb staggered and fell to his hands and knees, the wood grazing his skin where he hit it.

He clenched the energy inside him like a tight fist, and swallowed. It took a few moments, but he got it under control, patching the gaps in his shields. *It must have been spending that time on the boat. Too much exposure to wild waters.*

He got up slowly, carefully. The journey had tired his physical body, but also his energy, as he'd been hyper-vigilant the whole way. This was exactly what he had been worried about.

"Are you okay?" Fintan asked. There was a crease between his eyebrows. He stuck out a hand to help Jeb up.

"Fine," said Jeb, taking the hand and pulling himself up. "I tripped on the step."

That excuse would hold unless they had seen the orange flash. He wasn't going to think about it now. Tierra was his priority.

The black-haired woman rose to her feet, and bit her lip. "Can I help?"

He shook his head. "I need to see Tierra."

"Come in," she said. Her voice was musical, seductive. This was a lot to deal with on top of Tierra. He needed some rest, and to work through what to do about this, and who to tell, if anyone. He rolled his shoulders to soothe the ache there. He missed the peace of his study.

All three of them went inside the house, where Tierra was propped up in bed on several cushions, conscious but wan-looking. A fan stirred the heat of the day into a cool breeze onto her face, which disturbed her dark hair so it moved gently. She talked in a low voice to Blaize, who sat next to her, their heads close together. At the sound of the door, they both looked up.

"Jeb!" said Tierra, obvious delight in her voice.

There was a twist in Jeb's belly. He had already let her down – and she didn't hold it against him. He came over to the bed and dropped a gentle kiss on her cheek. She held her arms out for a hug.

"I don't want to hurt you," he said.

"Don't be silly! I'm fine. Well, I'm not squashable, at least. Give me a hug, then tell me what you've discovered so far."

He sat next to her on the bed and wrapped his arms carefully around her small curvy body. He would fix this.

Fintan and the dark-haired woman stood behind him, and Blaize sat in a chair the other side of the bed. There were a lot of people in the room. "Am I telling everyone here?"

Tierra nodded. "All of us here have been featured in Cuinn's prophecy. It's hard to believe this illness isn't connected in some way. But we really don't have any idea of how at the moment. Tell us what you know."

He gestured them all in, and the fairy dropped to the floor and sat with her legs crossed, while Fintan went over to stand next to Blaize, his arms folded across an intimidating chest.

"I don't know –" Jeb gestured politely to the woman he didn't know.

"Oh!" said Tierra. "This is Nixie. She's Blaize's cousin. They grew up together."

He put out his hand to shake Nixie's, but she'd already given him a Thai-style wai, the palms-together bow that Thais used to greet each other. His hand stayed awkwardly in front of him until she realized and grabbed for it. But by that time, he'd already begun to pull away.

He colored under his stubble, heat washing over his face. "Sorry. Hello."

He was usually better than this. Empathy was one of his gifts. He needed to start paying attention to the people around him. He was so wrapped up in keeping his auxiliary energy locked down, he was missing the things that would normally come naturally to him.

Nixie stared at him. Her sitting posture meant her skirt had ridden up to show perfectly proportioned legs that ended in tidy feet with toenails painted shell-pink. He rubbed his face, and the feel of the rough bristles on his chin brought him back to the moment.

She probably thought he was an idiot. *He was an idiot.* He took a deep breath and addressed the room. Since he'd left the Guild, Feng had found one more case, which had given them enough information for a tentative hypothesis. Normally it would be too early to share without further research to back it up, but they didn't have the luxury of time.

"Here's what we've discovered so far. We have found three recorded cases in the Anahata records of what seems to be wrong with Tierra. There are likely to have been more, but given what we think causes it, they may have been kept quiet or even suppressed."

"How did they treat it?" Fintan asked.

Jeb gritted his teeth. He hadn't wanted to share this information this early. "They didn't. They all died."

The room was silent for a few moments as the energetics absorbed Jeb's horrible news. Nixie's hand had gone to her mouth in shock, Blaize paled, and Fintan's hands balled in fists at his sides. Nixie swallowed, and then as was her wont, she stepped back in her mind, withdrawing, and viewed the room as art. A black and white sketch, perhaps. The color leached from them all, strong pencil strokes, jagged lines. It would be striking. Affecting. Painful to view.

She'd call it Stricken.

Only Tierra stayed remarkably steady. "What do you think caused it?"

"We think it's to do with the fact that Tierra shared energy with Cuinn to help him find Blaize when she was kidnapped," Jeb said.

"What?" said Blaize. "Cuinn's fine."

She glanced around the room, frowning. "Isn't he?"

Nixie and Blaize had worked on the image of Cuinn, easier while both of them were distracted by Tierra's illness. In his image he held some kind of bound book, and a mist surrounded him. Blaize had thought the mist represented the ether, or the dreamscape, and they had sent the sketch over to Cuinn for his review. That had been hours ago, and his response hadn't indicated any issues.

Blaize swiftly pulled her phone out of a pocket. She checked it, and her face relaxed a little when she saw no messages. She tapped out something even as Fintan said, with steadying hand on her shoulder, "He's fine as far as we know, Sparks."

Blaize looked up again. "Then why Tierra?"

"Because she's never been a Maven. Cuinn is. When an energetic becomes a Maven it's accepted that they will share energy with their Adherent, you in this case, Blaize. Whatever the Maven-Adherent ritual and link does, it seems to protect Mavens from any kind of ill effects."

Nixie shuddered at the idea of energy sharing. The taboo against it for energetics was as strong as that against eating meat was for the energetics. Tierra must have been truly desperate to try it.

"So the taboo about sharing energy is based on something real," Nixie said, softly.

"It seems so," agreed Jeb.

She observed him, comparing him to her prophecy sketch. It had been accurate, but to her dismay, it was the sorrowful version in front of her. Her back had been turned when he'd come in and fallen, and she had been certain she'd felt a flash of Svadisthana, but it had been gone as quickly as it had arrived. If she hadn't been so conscious of him, she'd have missed it.

He had a depth and presence that many of the men she dated lacked. Part of that was his age and experience, but there was more to it than that. But she felt that there was a wound there of some kind.

"But why did it take so long for anything to happen?" asked Tierra. "We shared energy weeks ago, but I didn't start feeling like this until I came to the island."

"Have you felt at all ill since then? Felt anything at all unusual?" Jeb said.

Fintan and Tierra exchanged a glance.

"Perhaps. Some headaches," Tierra admitted. "Nothing like this."

"Feng – that's the Anahata archivist – and I think it might be because you were in contact with people with all six of the energies at once when you came here. At Cathair Cuinn, you were missing Svadisthana and Vishudha, but with the addition of Nixie, you were in the presence of all six energies. That seems to have triggered something inside you," said Jeb.

Nixie hunched her shoulders guiltily. It wasn't her fault, she knew, but that didn't make her feel much better.

"What do we do about it?" asked Fintan, urgently. "How do we fix it?"

Jeb took a deep breath. "We're not sure. But we'll work it out. Now, I need to examine Tierra without any other energies nearby. I need to get a read on what's happening inside her, and what might be overspill energy from the rest of you nearby," said Jeb.

There was a silence, but no one moved.

"It's fine," said Tierra. She was speaking directly to Fintan, who looked sick.

"We're experienced energetics, you know," Fintan muttered mutinously. "It's not like energy is leaking out of us."

Fintan's strong Manipura, the energy of fire, meant that he was quick to anger, but Jeb appeared calm. Centered, if sad. But Nixie thought the wilder emotions and feelings, the *passion* that was the vitality and motivating force for many Svadisthana energetics seemed to be missing.

"I'll take care of her," he said to Fintan. "It won't be long."

Blaize opened the door, and Nixie got up to follow the others out, sneaking a quick look back at Jeb as she did. She'd had an idea.

Nixie might be powerless to help Tierra, but she might have thought of a creative way to contribute. Nixie was good at bringing lightness to others, at helping them lose themselves for a little while in sensation rather than having their brain switched on the whole time. Svadisthana was the energy of desire, of the soul's longings, of aliveness and sensations. She danced through life with joy, and if she avoided the more difficult aspects of the world, who would blame her? Too many people lived in the past or the future, and didn't experience the present fully.

Jeb seemed to be living in the past, and Jeb was the man who was going to make Tierra better. Nixie, then, would give him a wonderful experience in the now. She would bring out the sexy Jeb, and bring a little fun into his life to ensure he was operating at his best when healing Tierra.

Nixie would help Tierra, indirectly. She would help Jeb. And she might even help herself.

10

They all traipsed out of the room. Fintan was last out of the door, and shot Jeb a fierce glare as he did. Jeb hoped that someone would help him calm down before he came back into the room. That kind of emotion wouldn't help Tierra heal.

He turned back to Tierra. "I'm so sorry this has happened."

She nodded. "I'm glad you're here. But how are you?"

Tierra knew Jeb's story. Knew this was his first time out of the Guild in decades. And despite her illness, the first thing out of her mouth was to check on him.

"I'm okay. Really. It's strange being out of the Guild, but I'm okay," he responded. For the moment, he spoke the truth. The pressing anxiety that he'd had about leaving Egypt hadn't materialized into anything more. Perhaps the chains he and Aiko had put on his energy would work, and he could finish his task here in peace.

Then he thought of Nixie, the strange fairy creature, and his response to her, and the anxiety was back.

One thing at a time.

Tierra cocked her head to the side. "Are you, Jeb? Really? I saw Svadisthana energy flash when you came in. Have you decided to stop locking it down?"

Jeb felt his cheeks heat. "No. Aiko and I put extra wardings on it before I left the Guild."

"Maybe now's the time to let the wardings go a little," said Tierra. "Where's the harm? It's time to be a whole person again. What happened during the War —"

"It's not an option." He interrupted her before she could go further. Tierra was a true model of Anahata forgiveness. His actions in the war had the direct consequence of both her mother and aunt's death, and Tierra had managed to forgive him.

He would never forgive himself.

"Anyway, I'm here to help you, not the other way round," he said. "Let me examine you."

She nodded, and gestured to her bed. He helped her to sit up, cross-legged, and lean back against the headboard. He mirrored her position. She put her hands out palms up, and he covered them with his own, palms down.

She was the receptive party, as he would use his energy to probe her system and energies. They both closed their eyes and he got ready to work.

He felt the familiar and almost indescribable sense of energy within. It was a sixth sense to energetics, another part of themselves, another limb or function. He simply reached out with his Anahata into Tierra, as he might touch his friend with his hand. But with the energy, he could enter her system, and he didn't stop at the barrier of her skin.

He touched her energetic body, where all the other senses mixed into a synesthesia, and as he'd expected the energy of Muladhara sounded like the smell of fresh earth. That was Tierra's primary energy. He tried to separate the feel of that energy from the next strongest, Anahata, the energy of air and the heart. This was as familiar as home to Jeb, and tasted like blue and clouds.

He separated this last out too. As the energetic who had been her Maven, he was familiar with her energies, unusual in that she was almost equally strong in both. Her dominant and auxiliary energies were prevalent in her energetic body, but Jeb could sense something more.

He breathed in deeply. He centered himself and reached deeper into Tierra's energies. *Are there others?* Perhaps Heka was wrong and he was sensing the other energetics in the area.

And at first, he couldn't feel anything else. But then he caught, at the edge of his senses, a flash of the smell of heat. A little Manipura and fire. Strength and rage and willpower flowed over him, and he sucked in a breath. This was an alien energy to him.

But he'd worked through his rage many years ago. He could handle this. He gritted his teeth and moved past the Manipura.

Ajna, the energy of the mind, and Vishudha, the energy of space, washed over him and he felt as if he was falling into a great emptiness. For one moment, his mind was clear, and he saw a vision of the fairy, naked and lying on her back in front of him. Her straight hair was mussed, her back slightly arched, and her small breasts cried out to be touched.

Then the image was gone, and in his mind he tumbled over and over, losing his sense of self as his consciousness zoomed out to see the world as if from space. He could see tiny pinpricks of light, connected to each other by fine spider silk threads of energy, and he zoomed in again onto the Thai island to realize that the pinpricks were energetics scattered around the world, all joined.

Then finally his etheric body was drenched in the last, horribly familiar energy of Svadisthana. His pulse hammered in his ears. The energy of water, creativity and sexuality combined with the picture of the naked fairy to arouse his physical body.

He drew back and fled from Tierra's energetic body, and dropped her hands, breaking the connection between them. Tierra's eyes snapped open, and she caught her breath. He stumbled off the bed and sat on a chair, his head in his hands. The panic crushed him. What if he'd lost control and hurt Tierra? What had he been thinking, letting himself leave the Guild? What if he made things worse?

Tierra hugged herself and rubbed her upper arms, leaning back on the headboard. She was shivering despite the heat. "Tell me what happened there, please."

"Heka is right. You have all six energies activated. I touched all of them with my energy." He didn't mention the vision of the naked Nixie. Image, rather. It wasn't a vision. It hadn't come from Ajna, it had come from his sneaky Svadisthana energy trying to find a way out of his body. It wasn't a true glimpse of his future, and it wasn't relevant to the discussion at hand.

It was just his bloody Svadisthana trying to escape. He would take some time alone once he'd finished here, and check his wardings. He'd work out what was happening with Tierra, and keep her safe not only from that, but himself.

Tierra nodded, her face set. She looked wan, worse than before his examination. "I felt them as you moved through them. As if you were plucking strings inside me. Each one set off vibrations. But I don't know what to do with all those energies. How to handle them. My two main energies have always been part of me, always stood out. They increased as I grew, but they were always there. These feel alien. Wrong."

She paused and picked at the pillow she sat on. "Can we reverse it, Jeb?"

He wanted to reassure her, wanted to tell her this was temporary. That she wouldn't suffer the fate of any of the case studies they'd found. But he couldn't lie to her.

"I don't know. I think I can stabilize them enough so that you don't have any more fits, and so that your body is able to handle all six of them active inside you. But reversing them," he winced, "right now we don't have any information on that."

He smiled, but it was a weak effort. "Perhaps it will be a good thing. Imagine if we had access to all the energies. You could be powerful."

A crease formed between her eyes. "I'm already powerful. I don't need more. I'm happier than I've ever been."

Tierra was a strong energetic. Jeb should know – he had been her Maven for her auxiliary energy, Anahata. Tierra had proved stronger than many who had Anahata as their dominant energy. But she had no pride, no ambition. She loved to help and nurture others, never seeking positions of power in the energetics' structure.

For some, the activation of the other four Chakras within them would engender aspirations for power. But for Tierra, it meant nothing.

He sent a prayer of gratitude to Source that it was Tierra who had to bear this issue and not other energetics he knew. If – when – she came through this, and somehow ended up with all six active, she would find a way to remain steady.

"How do we fix it?" She leaned her head back against the headboard, arms wrapped around her upper body, but kept her gaze on Jeb. "We need a plan."

He nodded. "Feng is researching at the moment. He sends his love by the way."

Tierra smiled. "Thanks. He's a sweetheart."

"He's very fond of you. As am I. And, of course, so is Fintan. I'm glad the two of you got together." He glanced at her wrist, where the twin bracelet to Fintan's wrapped around the slender column. They were some kind of mysterious gift from Source, connected to the prophecy somehow, though he wasn't sure how far their research had gotten in determining what they did.

Tierra's smile turned into a beam. "Me too. I had a crush on him for the longest time, but it wasn't a real thing, a true thing. Now? The love that I feel for him, that's real."

Tierra and Fintan seemed to bring out the best in each other. Another stab of guilt assaulted Jeb. He was supposed to be one of the most powerful healers in Anahata, and he had no idea how to cure her.

"I want to talk to Heka," he said, "and then I'll find a way to stabilize you further. I have a lot to think about."

He took her hand. "But we will sort this, Tierra. We will get you back to normal."

He needed to believe it as much as she did.

Nixie came into the room where Ai was slouched on her bed, fiddling with a cellphone. The girl looked up for a moment, jerked her head in acknowledgement, then went back to the screen.

"How're you doing, Ai?" Nixie asked. Tierra had asked about Ai, and Nixie had said she would check in on her. It was something she felt she could do. She didn't know the girl well, but Nixie didn't need Anahata energies to read the sullen anxiety coming off her in waves.

Nixie would try and keep it light.

Ai snorted. "Been sent to babysit?"

Nixie's eyebrows rose. Cranky much? Nixie didn't really have the energy for this. "Something like that. Better if you're not a baby though, and talk to me like an adult. How are you?"

Ai looked at Nixie with a disbelieving sneer. Nixie tried to soften her tone. "Really. I care. And I'm concerned about Tierra too."

Ai shrugged. "Tierra's cool. She doesn't deserve this."

Nixie nodded. "Do you want to talk about it?"

"Nuh, uh." Ai shook her head emphatically.

"It's going to be okay," Nixie said. "Blaize is good in a crisis."

As much as Nixie had got them into trouble over the years, Blaize had usually got her out of it. Nixie just needed faith in her pee sao, or big sister.

Ai didn't reply, but her shoulders loosened slightly. She got up and went to the wardrobe in the corner of the room. As she opened the door, a tokay gecko, one of the little lizards that frequented most houses on the island, fell out and hit Ai's arm on its way to the floor. She screamed, and it shot off into the corner of the room.

Ai gave another yell of frustration, and slammed the door shut again. "I hate this place! There are creatures everywhere. What the fuck is it with Thailand's nature anyway? Why can't it stay outside?"

Nixie winced. She liked the geckos. "It's harmless, really. They help to keep the insects down."

"I don't give a shit! I want to go back to the city," Ai snarled.

Uh. Oh dear. She was trapped with an angry teen. What was she supposed to do? She didn't love the idea of being the 'adult'. It wasn't a role she felt she played especially well. She'd never been drawn to parenthood, and had little experience with kids of any age. Maybe it was time for a different tack. "Have you ever drawn?"

Ai's brow crinkled. "What are you talking about?"

"When I'm upset, art helps me to settle myself. We could try it, if you like." Nixie wasn't exactly feeling calm and relaxed at the moment. She could do with some time in 'flow', drawing. She wasn't a huge fan of doing art with others, but maybe it would help the girl chill out. An olive branch, of sorts.

Ai squinted up at Nixie. "Really? You want to finger paint our feelings while Tierra's sick?"

The girl was a nightmare.

"I don't want to finger paint." It came out more sharply than she'd meant. "Think of it more as a form of therapy."

That went down like a lead balloon.

"Therapy," said Ai, flatly. "I've tried that. In the group home they put me in when my parents were killed. It didn't work out."

Nixie ground her teeth. This was uphill work. The girl had had a rough life, sure, but Nixie hadn't caused that. She was trying to help.

"Fun then. A distraction. You and I can't help Tierra right now, and she'd hate to think of us brooding." She'd hate to think of Ai brooding, anyway. Nixie certainly wasn't brooding. She could entertain herself fine.

Alright. One more try to explain how art could help. The teen probably hadn't had much exposure to the idea, after all. When would she have had a chance, spending most of her teenage years on the streets? "When I was a Svadisthana Adherent in the Guild, I missed home a lot. I spent a lot of time working in the sculpture room. Creating in that way helped me process what I was feeling and move past it."

One of the pieces of art she'd created had even won a Thai national art prize, though she'd given both prize and sculpture to her parents as a thank you for all their support.

"I don't want to have fun while Tierra's sick," Ai said.

"Don't be such a martyr," Nixie snapped. The child was thankless. Art was something Nixie lived and breathed, and if the kid couldn't appreciate it, that was her problem. "I'm asking you to draw, not to party. Tierra's worried about you, and I want to be able to tell her you're doing okay."

Okay, so Nixie didn't really know how to treat kids. She was going to leave her to Blaize and Tierra in future.

The girl was huddled on the bed, her face pale. Nixie had gone too far.

"At least you had parents to miss," Ai said, her tone derisive. "It's all about you. What do you do? Blaize and Fintan are Warriors, and Tierra looks after everyone else. Even that new guy has dope healing skills. But you're just hanging out drinking coconut shakes while the rest of us are trying to survive."

Nixie felt winded, as if the wounded young woman on the bed had punched her in the stomach.

It was all she could do to stumble out the door, across their wide balcony and down the stairs of the house. She threw a leg over her bike. What *did* she do? She'd even failed at the simple task of checking in on the teen.

Nixie's go-to when emotions raged inside her like this was usually sex. Today, though, when she thought about her options, the only face that came to mind was Jeb. With Jeb, though, she was the one who was meant to be providing the solace. The lightness. Right now, her frustrations were swirling inside her needing grounding, and she wasn't about to take that out on a guy who hadn't had sex in decades.

Ai had issues, she knew that. Nixie was just indignant the girl had taken them out on her. For some reason, something in Ai's criticism had shaken Nixie's usual self-confidence. She knew she couldn't be angry with the teenager, so she needed to channel her feelings elsewhere.

If it wasn't sex, then there was only one place that would do.

The sea.

A swim would help relax her, and bring her back to herself. A storm was coming, and the sands would be empty. Arriving, she parked, stripped down to her skin, and walked into the water, where she let the salt water of her angry tears blend with the warm embrace of the ocean.

11

Jeb walked along the beach and looked longingly at the sea. He didn't dare go in the water this soon after leaving the safety of the Guild, but he'd missed the wild waters of the ocean, rivers, lakes. Swimming pools, baths and showers didn't measure up to the feeling of being surrounded by water in nature.

It was too soon. The Guilds were steeped in the energies of their members, the very bricks and mortar supporting any magics done there. Out here in the real world using Anahata with Tierra at the same time as keeping his Svadisthana in check was a small but constant drain, wearing him down.

His temples ached, and pressure built inside his head. His energy told him a storm was coming, so he'd stripped to his shorts to walk along the quiet golden beach, hiphop from his phone in his pocket keeping him company, the music he preferred to relax to. The skies were darkening quickly, the tropical storm coming in faster than he'd expected. Should he risk it and stay outdoors for the storm?

He took in lungfuls of the ozone in the air, relishing the empty horizon in front of him and the breeze that was building and tossing the beach's natural debris onto the sand. He felt invigorated, like something inside him was waking up.

His eyes narrowed. The view in front of him wasn't completely empty. There was a shape far out to sea – some sort of fish? No. And it was too small for a boat. He shaded his eyes with his hands, straining to see. Was it a person? They were a long way out, and taking a risk as the waves were increasing in height and frequency. It wouldn't be long before any person out there would struggle to come inland.

Rain started to fall, light at first. The figure was moving towards the shore. He was a few feet back from the water's edge, wary of it touching him. He'd need to be a damn sight surer that someone was in trouble before he went in the water.

There was no point trying to save someone, only to endanger them more.

Nixie's tears had been lost to the ocean, and she was more settled. She could feel the storm coming in, and she delighted in the air pressure building up. She loved the rain on her skin – it was a pleasure only second to swimming for her.

She ducked and dived, playing with the increasingly large waves. Her freediving experience meant she could hold her breath for many minutes so she would alternate swimming under a wave to bodysurfing on top.

The rain fell harder, and she bobbed up and down, putting her hands in the air to feel more of its punishing patter on her skin.

She loved this.

The storm built momentum, and thunder and lightning crashed through the sky. She should go back in. It was unlikely she'd be hurt by the waves, but there was always a chance for Svadisthana energetics they'd get too caught up in a storm and meld with it, losing their selfhood. She should go inland, and get back to the others. They'd wonder where she was.

She lit out for the shore. It wasn't sex, but a swim in a storm was almost as good.

She dived in a graceful ripple under the waves, and powered back with strong, sure strokes. She cut through the water, then flipped in a full roll to place her feet on the sand beneath the sea as she surged out of the water at a run, laughing.

Only a few steps out and she slammed into something solid. Dazed, she wobbled in place, then found her shoulders gripped by dry, warm hands. *What the hell?*

She blinked to clear her vision, and brought her hands up in front of her, groping the air to try and understand who was holding her. Male. A chest with a light dusting of rough hair, slick in the storm. Lean, but well-muscled.

Finally, her eyes adjusted to the dusk.

Her mouth fell open in shock as she realized who it was.

Jebediah let go and took a step back as the fairy bared fierce white teeth up at him. She might be many inches shorter than him, but in that moment he felt a sharp spike of adrenaline as to what she might do next. He turned his palms up to show he meant her no harm. He wasn't sure he could say the same for her.

It was then he realized that she was naked, her lithe light brown body showing no tan lines. His eyes were caught by a drop of rain that fell from her hair onto her small right breast. It followed that curve until it slid between her breasts, over her belly, and down into a tiny patch of trimmed hair.

He swallowed, and the adrenaline was joined by a wash of arousal so strong that his groin was filled with blood in seconds. *Shit.*

He took a step back, his hard dick obvious through the wet shorts that clung to his body. Who was this woman?

She glanced down, and her look of anger turned to one of consideration. She tipped her head to the side, and stepped into his body.

"Jebediah," she breathed. "I saw you in Cuinn's vision, you know."

He nodded. He was a fly in a spider's web. Stuck fast in place. Whoever she was, it wasn't safe. He thought about research and dusty books, about Feng and Fintan, anything to calm his sexual energy down. He could feel it hurling itself against the wardings and locks inside him.

The warm rain hammered down, and lightning flashed in the distance. They both ignored it.

"I saw two versions of you," Nixie said.

He cocked his head, his interest caught. He'd take the distraction. "What do you mean?"

"I saw lonely eyes, as if you'd spurned your Svadisthana … " she put up a palm to his cheek and he closed his eyes as her hand reached him. She touched each eyelid lightly, and put her hand on his chest, running those featherlike fingers between his nipples, and along the planes of his stomach, stopping a little above the waistband of his shorts. He stifled a groan. "…And I saw your eyes burn when you'd let go of your control."

"I can't – I don't do that."

He stepped backwards again, but she followed him, her toes pressing into the wet sand, leaving shallow footprints that the sea washed away with each new wave.

Still the rain beat down.

She put one hand on his hip, and her other slid around the back of his neck. She drew him down towards her and he was ensnared. Her mouth touched his like a brush of petals and he groaned again, but made no move to touch her. Her fingers on his cool wet skin were like a burn.

His Svadisthana energy swirled and looped inside him, looking for a way out. He needed to get away. To find a safe place away from this delicate-seeming sprite, till he figured out what she wanted.

But while it might have been what he needed, it wasn't what he wanted.

Seven decades of discipline cracked slightly, as personal desire surged inside him, and he longed to let himself free.

Instead of taking another step back, he opened his lips a little, enough for her to probe between them with a soft tongue, one that entwined with his oh-so-gently. She was wearing him down, not with a flourish of her own Svadisthana, which she could easily do, but with a serene and gradual assault on him that was making him lose his mind.

He broke the kiss with an effort, pulling his head upright and out of her reach. She really was a tiny thing. Surely he could disengage from her gracefully. "I can't do this."

She slid her arm around his waist, and then over his buttocks. "Of course you can."

She was matter-of-fact, an energetic in harmony with her Svadisthana energy. She had no issues around sex.

But her energy hadn't caused the death of innocents.

That sobering thought was enough for the hardness in his groin to subside, and he reached behind him to take her hands and detach them.

She looked up at him, those damn drops of water still falling from her hair as the rain pummeled them both. Rivulets of water drew his gaze over and over the graceful curves of her naked body.

"You're putting too much importance on sex," she said, her voice seductive. "It's just like a massage. Don't be like the humans. Don't attach shame or other issues to it. Don't make more of it than it is. And we're both Svadisthana. I can take what your energy gives, even if it's been a while."

Perhaps she was safe in that way from STIs and pregnancy, but he didn't think she quite realized what his energy might do to her.

She walked him backwards another step, and then one more.

"Sex is a gift. We can lie here on the beach, water all around us, and you can bury yourself inside me. Stroke by stroke, the pleasure will build. I can help you reclaim your Svadisthana energy. You no longer need to cut yourself off from half of who you are. You can be yourself fully once more."

The words were dangerous. Because part of him would love that. Wanted it desperately. But he knew that was a fantasy. He could never return to the lighthearted way he'd treated sex and his energy before the war.

With each sentence, she pushed him another step backwards. At the end of the last few words, he smacked into something solid, and his breath 'ouf'ed out of him. He'd hit a palm tree, and there was nowhere else to go. It broke her spell for a moment, and he tried to explain to her the danger she flirted with.

"You're desirable, Nixie, but sex with me wouldn't be safe. My energy is locked up and it needs to stay that way. My control could easily break and you could be destroyed." His body was as rigid as the tree behind him, tension in every muscle.

She put slim arms around him, and pressed her belly into his hard dick.

"What's sex without a little risk?" she whispered.

He groaned again and fisted her hair. He wrenched her head backwards, baring her neck. He leant down and kissed it, as he slid the other hand down her back to her small firm butt. He squeezed hard as he bit her neck lightly, and she moaned.

As he did, a thread of his Svadisthana slipped out and mixed with her own sexual energy. The two energies embraced each other in a shower of bronze sparks, and she gasped. He palmed her naked sex roughly as he slid two fingers inside her.

She tipped her hips up to encourage him, and he massaged her with his hand, the skills he'd learned as part of his Svadisthana training coming back to him despite the length of time since he'd last used them. Her breath came in tiny gasps, and he lifted and spun them both so she now pressed against the uneven surface of the tree. He had one hand inside her, and the other held her neck, pinning her in place.

He leaned her hard into the tree, and moved his palm and fingers, fast and light, quick and deft, following the urgent rhythm of her body and breath, until she came with a sob, her body quivering, held upright by his hands.

As the pleasure wracked her body her energy released in a rush, and swept through him in a surge.

He slammed more shields into place as his fingers curled in reflex, and stretched her neck taut as the fingers of the other hand brushed her g-spot. She cried out again.

He concentrated and kept his body a rigid fortress, while her energy and her pleasure battered at the wardings on his Svadisthana energy. He would not let go. He hadn't been able to keep all his own energy inside him, but the curls and twists that had escaped were limited, and had been mostly absorbed by Nixie as she'd writhed on his hand.

His dick throbbed in his shorts as he held his body a little away from hers. She was limp and relaxed against the tree, but he sensed she wouldn't stay that way for long.

The storm raged around them, the waves now nothing you could swim in. *Even this water sprite would have difficulty.*

After a few moments, she opened her eyes, and he removed his hand from her sex and bent slightly to scoop her up. She was as light as she looked, her skin hot.

"Where are your clothes?" he asked.

"In my motorbike." She trailed her hand over the exposed skin of his chest, face and neck. "No need for them yet. We can go to one of the beach huts."

She met his eyes. "I want you inside me. Then you'll see what letting go really means."

Lightning flashed and lit her body up. It glistened with fat drops of water that slowly gathered until they became too heavy to stay in place, and then made their leisurely way down her body until they detached themselves for the leap to the wet sand beneath them.

He carried her easily over to her motorbike a few hundred yards away, and set her gently on the ground.

"I'm sorry," he said. "You're beautiful. Wonderful. You can see that from my body's response – your skin on mine felt amazing. But I can't risk my Svadisthana. There are good reasons I no longer use it."

He stepped back to gain a little distance between himself and her still naked, still delightful body. He felt his statement would have had more weight if his cock hadn't been visible through his shorts, the rainsoaked material clinging to it so it stood out in stark relief.

Her emotions whirled around him: surprise, disappointment, disbelief. She turned and crouched, and picked up her bike key which had been hidden beneath the wheel. The view of her curved back didn't do anything to help his dick subside. He looked away and focused on the sea behind them. Concentrating on the waves, he took deep breaths and thought about anything other than sex.

She unlocked her bike's storage compartment, and pulled out a dress that she dropped over her head. She turned back to him. "Fine. But you're missing out."

She slid a leg over the seat, the size of bike making her seem even more fragile, and shoved the key into the ignition. She turned the engine on, and with a twist of her hand, accelerated off into the night.

He was left with nothing but the sound of the rain, and a body that ached with loss and lust.

"I'm starting to realize that," he whispered into the storm.

12

Nixie drove like Diana during a hunt. Her body tingled all over, and she had to swallow repeatedly past a lump in her throat. She wanted to drive and drive until she was as far away as possible from that … that bastard. Unfortunately, you could drive round the whole of Koh Somdun in less than a few hours, so it wasn't an option.

She skidded onto the little road that led to her place, the combination of sand and water untrustworthy under her wheels, and jammed her brakes on to stop in front of her house. She ran up the stairs and flung herself into her hammock on the balcony. She wasn't ready to go inside yet. She wanted to be surrounded by the sound of the storm's wrath which echoed her own.

Her sobs were muffled by the sound of the weather, but after a few minutes Blaize appeared in the doorway.

"What's the matter?" Blaize asked. She pulled a chair over to the hammock and sat next to Nixie, putting a hand on her hair and stroking it gently. Being friends with a water energetic meant Blaize was no stranger to Nixie's tears.

"I had sex with Jeb," Nixie burst out.

Blaize's hand paused momentarily. "Jebediah? Isn't he celibate?"

"Apparently so." Nixie gulped back more tears.

"Wait, what? I'm confused. Did you have sex or not?" Blaize asked. "In fact – hold on."

Blaize got up and went back into the house, and returned moments later with a cool damp flannel which she handed to Nixie. Nixie swiped at her face until she felt calmer.

"Okay, continue," said Blaize. "What are you talking about?"

Nixie filled Blaize in on what happened on the beach. By the time she was finished, ending with her rush to get back home, Blaize's eyebrows were up near her hairline.

"Huh," she said. "How'd you feel? What are you going to do?"

"I don't know," Nixie admitted. "Not good. Even a bit stupid. Especially because he made me come, but never let go himself. And that's where the meaning is in Svadisthana sex, in letting go to each other."

She swallowed hard. "Actually, I feel like crap. I'm struggling with all this prophecy stuff, and sex is supposed to be the thing I am good at, but I missed something important there too."

Nixie hadn't mentioned her interaction with Ai to Blaize, though two rejections in quick succession were weighing on her.

Nixie continued. "I thought that sex with Jeb might be fun. Usually sex with another Svadisthana energetic is out of this world."

Blaize raised her eyebrows.

"I thought I could help him with his weird thing about not using Svadisthana by reminding him how great Svadisthana sex could be," Nixie continued. "And I thought if we had sex, he'd be out of my system too."

"You thought you'd forget about him after you'd had great sex?" Blaize said.

Nixie shrugged. "It happens. Sometimes I enjoy the buildup more. The flirting. The potential. Then once we actually sleep together, although the sex is mostly great, I'm less interested."

"Maybe your current approach isn't working," Blaize suggested. "Try getting to know people a bit more. Maybe if you let yourself care about them, they'd hold your interest longer."

Nixie huffed. "I do care! In general, the guys who have sex with me aren't interested in getting to know me."

She thought for a moment about Ben, who'd seemed to want something else from her, and her panicked response. She'd probably misread him.

"Anyway, thanks for listening. I appreciate this isn't a priority."

Blaize got to her feet. "I'm always here if you need me, Nix. You know that. I'm going to go and check in on Tierra before I sleep. I'll catch you in the morning. We can try another sketch."

Nixie nodded and lay back in the hammock as Blaize walked off. It had probably been a mistake to try and seduce Jeb. He was a reclusive introvert, not her type at all. There was plenty of fun, light-hearted sex available on the island. She didn't need him, and wouldn't pursue him further.

Though dammit. There was something about him.

The thunder and lightning that had surrounded Jeb and Nixie's encounter was over. She hoped that was the only storm she'd have to weather concerning him, but she worried there'd be more bad atmospheric conditions to deal with before he was gone.

It took Jeb an hour to walk back from the beach. The rain stung his bare skin every inch of the way.

He enjoyed the rain, though it wasn't comfortable. There was something else, too, some darker emotions from the night, almost a sense of being watched. He scanned the terrain around him frequently, but didn't catch sight of anyone.

He tried to open himself up to sense what was around him. His headache intensified. The encounter with Nixie had thrown him, and his energies were unsettled. He struggled to get a read on anything.

He tried instead to repair some of the damage to his wardings as he walked, building up his shields in layers. He felt a sense of urgency to talk to Nixie and apologize for his behavior. Truth was important to Jeb. Truth, and integrity. Nixie was owed more explanation as to why he couldn't be with her. Why he needed to keep his sexual energy bound tightly.

Arriving at the house, he walked upstairs to where she lay in the hammock on her house's balcony. Her balcony faced into the privacy of the forest, and wasn't overlooked by the other houses, which were all at least fifty yards apart.

It looked as if she had fallen asleep. He rocked the hammock slightly. "Nixie?"

"Hmmm?" She sounded as though she was having a nice dream.

"I'd like to talk," he said.

She opened her eyes blearily, and shook her head when she saw him standing there.

"You," she said.

"Hello." It wasn't his most scintillating conversation starter, but he was a bit thrown by the sleepy version of the fierce fairy he'd met on the beach. She looked like something from a painting, curled up in the hammock, her hands tucked under her head. She rubbed one eye with a fist and yawned. She had a perfect mouth.

"Why are you here?" She didn't sound that interested in the answer.

"To apologize."

She gave him a searching stare. "Really."

He was going to have to work harder. "I wanted to explain."

She had both eyes open, but wasn't giving anything away. Perhaps she really didn't care. But his intuition told him she did. He'd hurt her on the beach by saying no, and he wanted to explain why.

"Go on," she said. She didn't sit up.

He walked to the corner of the balcony and picked up a cushion from one of the chairs. He dropped it in front of the hammock and sat on it, facing towards her.

"I can't let my Svadisthana energy out," he said.

She tutted and waved a hand. "I know that. You mentioned it. Is that all?"

Jeb held back a frown. "No. I wanted to tell you why."

She watched him, her expression steady.

"During World War II, I used my energy to help the Allies gain information about the enemy. I was focused on saving the most lives possible. It was an adventure. I was a 'Raven' – I would seduce women collaborators for intelligence purposes. I would make sure they had a good time, and then share the information with my handler. We were careful not to burn the women as assets, and I only chose those who would have willingly slept with me anyway."

Nixie hadn't moved a muscle.

Jeb gazed off into the distance at the stars over the forest that surrounded the house. He could hear geckos chirping, and other sounds of the Thai night that surrounded them just as the warm blanket of night air did. He was grateful the humidity wasn't too bad this evening. The storm had freshened the atmosphere.

"So I thought, anyway. I fell for one. A Parisian collaborator, she ran a jazz club where she would pass on gossip to the Germans in exchange for being left alone. She was very beautiful." Men had flocked to Lucie, her infectious presence and her bewitching looks.

"We spent a week in bed, and she told me everything. I thought she cared for me in turn, that she trusted me." He shook his head. "I passed on the information to my handler after the week, and moved on. It turned out the Germans were seeking a mole. They'd passed out misinformation to find the leak. My allies used the information Lucie had provided, and she was outed."

Nixie's eyes were wide, and he could see the white surrounding her dark brown irises.

"She was executed," Jeb said.

Nixie made a sound of distress. Jeb continued on grimly. "It doesn't end there. They tortured her, and initiated reprisals in the form of collective punishment of innocents in her area. They executed another ten people, and burned businesses down. They destroyed hospitals."

Nixie took an intake of breath.

"You couldn't have known what was going to happen. I don't understand how you can blame yourself," she said, her forehead creased, her eyes soft.

598

He didn't deserve the look she was giving him. He needed to make her understand.

He rolled his shoulders, trying to stop the muscles tightening. "After she died, I received a letter she'd written the day I left that week."

A letter that had shattered his illusions.

"What did it say?" Nixie breathed.

"It was a letter that asked me not to visit her again. That something about me clouded her judgement. That she found me arousing, but she didn't understand why. And that when I was around her, it was hard for her to think straight."

"Oh, no." Nixie understood. Any energetic with that energy would.

"Yes. Not only is all that blood on my hands, but somehow I let my Svadisthana energy manipulate her. I had convinced myself she wanted it, I wanted us to connect so much. She didn't. I might as well have forced her."

"You didn't do it on purpose," Nixie said. "It's not the same."

He shook his head. "Does it matter? I was supposed to be a Master in my energy, and I got carried away. I thought she was in control of her actions. I thought no woman could resist me. I was way over the line."

He'd stopped his actions immediately, withdrawn to the Guild. In the long months that followed, had wondered how many of the women he'd seduced had been influenced by his energy. Been manipulated into sex, which was anathema for those with his energy.

"It was War. Your work saved lives, right?" Nixie said. "You were already lying to the women."

He shrugged. "I went back to that area, and I walked around. The smoke from the burned out shops got into my nostrils. I watched children who'd had a parent taken play in the street. And I felt the pain of every person in that neighborhood. I walked around like a ghost, and realized I had a responsibility to be different. That things weren't as black and white as I'd thought, and that the great adventure was more about shades of grey than being on the 'right' side." Jeb sat up straight on his cushion. His neck felt stiff, and he rolled his head to try and loosen the kinks.

"Tierra speaks very highly of you."

He snorted. "She deserves better. Her mother and aunt were working in a Polish hospital the Germans destroyed because of information that Lucie gave them. She knew I had important connections at a hospital in a particular area, and the Germans bombed both to make sure they killed them. Tierra had to hunt for her family's bodies in the rubble. I have no right to her friendship." Yet he was grateful every time he saw her that he had it.

"I'd offer to help you with a massage, but you'd think I was coming on to you again," said Nixie. Her voice was dry, and Jeb had trouble reading her. She was still interested in him, certainly, but he also got a sense of empathy from her. He wasn't sure he could take her kindness.

"I wasn't trying to get your sympathy," he said. "I want you to understand why I chose to lock up part of myself. I wasn't able to control and channel that energy in a positive way. I wasn't in control of it. Anahata is a purer energy."

Nixie snorted. "Thanks."

"I didn't mean —"

"I know what you meant. You mean, in fact. But you're wrong." Nixie said. "Every energy can be used for good or ill. This is basic energetic teaching. I don't understand how you can be so senior in your Guild and have this giant blind spot."

She twisted so she sat up in the hammock and faced him dead on. Her feet touched the ground lightly and she pushed with the balls of her feet to make the hammock rock a little.

At one end of each oscillation, she swung over his lap. Her dress lifted with the air, and he felt a rush of arousal remembering her putting it on at the beach – with nothing underneath. He shifted on the cushion. It was fine. It was dark out here. She couldn't see.

There was a thickness in the air, almost like a syrup. Which was strange, because it wasn't humid. That darkness he'd sensed earlier was present – perhaps he was oversensitive to Tierra's illness? She was in a house not far away. He couldn't think what else it could be. His brain was so fuzzy.

He bent his head towards each shoulder, and stretched his neck out more.

She jumped off the hammock and darted round behind him. "I can't bear to see you like this. Hold still."

She put her hands on his shoulders, and he jerked a little. "The pain will help, in the long run."

She dug those slender fingers into his trapezius muscle, and squeezed and massaged and rubbed. He grimaced as she worked out kinks and knots in his shoulders and neck, and then began to dance her fingers over his skull, her body against his back.

He had to stifle a moan of appreciation at that. It was a hurt that felt good.

The thickness of the air had intensified, and he felt lightheaded, almost dizzy. Her touch slowed, her movements more languorous.

He put a hand back on one of hers and held it. "I think you should stop."

She paused in place, which was fine until he realized it meant that her small breasts rested against his back.

Her nipples dug into his back like pebbles. He drew her round, but instead of sitting in front of him on the floor or the hammock, she circled his body like a pole, and ended up sitting in his lap facing him, her legs either side of his.

He swallowed. The air was so heavy now he could barely breathe. He tried to blink away the sluggishness that pervaded his body. He wasn't sure he could move if he tried.

He needed to try. Something wasn't quite right here, but he couldn't work out what it was. All he could think about was the woman in his lap. His mind was clouded.

Her legs were loose around him, but it meant that her sex was exposed, her dress having ridden up to her waist.

He put his hands on her back to move her, but instead of encouraging her to move, his hands slid of their own volition down to her buttocks, and he cupped them, kneading and squeezing them gently. The material still covered the hot flesh, but when she tilted her butt back, his hands slid between her legs and met with the smooth slick flesh there.

She looked him in the eyes. She was as serious as him. There was little of Svadisthana's play in either of them. The dark wrapped around them on the wooden floor, him on the cushion, her on him.

He sucked in a breath, his chest expanding, and her hands came down to his nipples. She scratched his chest lightly, tracing the contours of his muscles, and he realized that he was hard. This time, though, he found it more difficult to remember why he needed to stop. He couldn't think straight. *I do need to stop though. Don't I?*

He wasn't sure. It was so hard to breathe. He felt as if he was made of thick treacle, his body hot and malleable, responding to her heat and her massaging hands. He couldn't think properly, couldn't clear his mind. It had been so long since he'd done this, he couldn't remember if this was normal. There was something at the very back of his consciousness that pinged, warning him this was a mistake, but it was a weak signal, easily ignored.

She pulled herself in tighter towards him and rested her head in the crook of his shoulder. As she did so, her hips came towards him too, and her sex met his cock, with only his shorts between them.

He lifted her up with one hand, and created enough space to unzip his pants with the other, freeing his hard dick so he could slide it in the next movement into her still slick channel.

He held himself still, lost inside her. He shouldn't move, he knew. Couldn't let himself go. Couldn't lose control.

He had enough wits about him to remember her pleasure. He slipped a hand between them and touched the area where they joined, finding her most sensitive place and tracing it, over and over and over.

Such a subtle movement.

Both of them still and silent apart from his hand working her gently, building her pleasure.

And still his head felt murky and confused.

The only thing he knew was that he wanted this woman. She liberated something inside him. He felt more free than he had for decades.

She was still nestled against him, his free arm wrapped around her. Was he holding her in place, or supporting her?

Repetitive movements.

Flesh touching flesh, softly, gently, persistently.

Her breath fluttered over his chest, warm even in the tropical night that cloaked them. It sped.

He increased the tempo of the small movements of his finger. Her clit was firm, and her orgasm was close.

The temptation to move, no, to thrust inside her, and to let go, was fierce.

He couldn't. Mustn't. Wouldn't.

Why, again?

He blinked and tried to clear his head, but as he did, she threw her head back and climaxed with a soft outbreath. Her walls clenched around his member, squeezing.

i need to keep control

Hot flesh surrounded him

dontletgo

as she contracted

controlhehadtokeepcontrol

he was almost delirious with the pleasure

control

of her tightening around him.

He tried to heed the tiny voice at the back of his head, tried to focus on what it was saying, knowing it was important, a part of him trying to reinforce his shields and keep his wards strong – even as the world exploded.

His Svadisthana energy cracked his shields, so energy escaped and rolled over hers, then spiked out into the night. He held onto the shields as much as he could, kept control in the center of the storm, but it was a battle. It tore at him, and he wrestled with the leash, trying to keep the energy in whilst his body let go. He spilled himself into her in a handful of rippling movements.

The physical was understated compared to the energy. Their Svadisthana energies entwined with each other, touching the insides of their bodies just as their flesh met outside. He tried to keep it between them, cycling between their bodies, and to keep the flare to a minimum. To ensure she, and anyone else nearby, wasn't damaged.

But he couldn't bear it. The release of pressure whilst trying to retain control was too much for him. As he came, his member jerking inside her, his energy ripping through her, his body shut down. He slumped backwards, pulling her down, and passed out into darkness.

13

Nixie slept badly, and woke up earlier than normal. She rubbed her eyes and sighed. She was going to have to face Jeb today. The night before, he'd come so hard that he'd passed out. Well, perhaps not only from his orgasm. There was also the unleashing of his sexual energy. Some of it, anyway. He'd held back most, though the encounter had been a lot more satisfying than the beach, and a lot less one-way.

Her mouth twisted. She'd had an effect on him, she knew that. So why wasn't she enough to make this man truly let go? His story had been sad, certainly, and he had a somewhat tragic past, but why was he still living in the past? Why not live for today? What he'd done had been bad, certainly, but these days he appeared to have developed iron control over his energy. He wasn't going to be influencing anyone accidentally.

Once she'd poked him in the side hard enough to wake him up, his reaction hadn't been quite what she'd been hoping for. Whilst she'd felt a tentative hope that this man might actually be someone she could connect with, and the sex had left her energized, he'd appeared horrified. Okay, perhaps horrified was a bit strong, but it had been like having drunk sex with a twentysomething guy, who'd woken up in the morning to regret it.

It wasn't a feeling she'd ever had to deal with, and she didn't like it.

While she could – and sometimes did – have sex with anyone she was attracted to, sex between two energetics with Svadisthana energy was something special. They had the potential to galvanize or soothe each other through their sexual energy. Sex with her should have made him feel good, relaxed. She knew she'd taken in some of his energy, cleansed it. She was disappointed she hadn't made him feel better. Why wouldn't he let her help him?

She sighed again. She'd get up, eat breakfast, and see if there was anything she could do to help Tierra. Nixie might as well be of some use – she'd pissed off Ai, messed things up with Jeb – who else could she upset while they were around?

She sat up in bed and wrapped her arms around her legs. Then stopped dead as her left wrist caught her eye. Wrapped tightly around it was a bracelet. A bracelet she'd never seen before. She tried to get it off, but there was no clasp, no opening, no easy way.

"Oh, shit," Nixie breathed. This looked a lot like Blaize's. And Cuinn's. And Fintan's. And Tierra's. *Shit shit shit.*

She ran a finger over it. It looked as if it was made of satin embroidery thread, with a glossy luster on each of the four colors: burnt orange, cobalt blue, fern green and a pure, bright white. It was a heck of a lot stronger than thread however, as no amount of pulling or tugging was making any difference.

She stared at her wrist for an age before she jumped out of bed and went over to her dresser. She rummaged around the jewelery scattered in heaps on the surface – she loved pretty things – until she found a large stylish silver cuff, which she put on over the bracelet. She gave her arm an experimental shake. The new bracelet was hidden, and would stay hidden until she understood properly what it was. She wasn't in a rush for bad news. She couldn't think about this right now, whatever it was.

She showered and dressed, and checked Blaize's room to see if she was up. There was no sign of her, so Nixie went across to the other house and into Tierra's room, where Nixie figured Blaize was most likely to be.

Nixie knocked softly on Tierra's door, and opened it slowly. In the room, Jeb sat on a chair next to Tierra, his fingers on her pulse. *Ah, shit.* The person she least wanted to see. Tierra looked pale and weak. There was no sign of Blaize.

Jeb rose when he saw Nixie. She saw bags under his eyes, and wondered how his sleep had been. Was it petty to wish that he'd had bad dreams too?

"I came to see how things were with Tierra," said Nixie. "I'll leave you alone."

"It's okay," said Jeb. "I need to talk to Blaize and Fintan anyway. Come walk with me."

Nixie couldn't think of anything she'd like less.

Nixie held the door for Jeb, and followed him out of Tierra's room, which led directly onto the balcony. Tierra's eyes were already closing as she shut the door.

"She needs to rest," said Jeb, walking down the stairs that attached this side of the house to the ground. He was worried about her. This morning Tierra had seemed worse again. Apart from a reduction in symptoms, nothing he had done seemed to have got to the root of the issue, and Feng hadn't come up with anything new.

"Sure," said Nixie. She was subdued.

Jeb waited for Nixie to catch him up as they walked across the land between Nixie's house and where Tierra and Ai were staying. Nixie had opened up her parents' house for Jeb to sleep in last night. Not that he got much sleep. She didn't look him in the eye, but he caught her looking at his wrists several times. Eventually, he cracked.

"Everything ok? Are you looking for the time?" He held up his bare wrists. "I don't wear a watch."

"Huh," Nixie said, and her nose wrinkled. She had a pretty nose.

They found everyone eating breakfast at the shaded tables outside. Fintan half-rose to his feet as they came into view, and only Blaize's hand on his arm kept him in place.

"What's happened?" he asked.

Jebediah wasn't looking forward to this. He could feel a mix of emotions coming from the group, and few of the emotions were positive. He went for direct. "Tierra's worse."

"What? Why? I thought you'd stabilized her?" Fintan's voice rose at the end of the sentence. Jeb could feel how worn the man was. He and Tierra had barely been together for a week or two and she was sick. It was a tough burden for the man to bear.

"I thought we had. I don't know what's changed, I'm sorry. I need to go back to the Guild. If I thought Tierra was well enough to travel, I'd take her, but she should stay here. I'll be back as soon as I can." Or he'd send someone else, if necessary.

Blaize looked concerned. "Was it something to do with the energy spike I felt last night?"

"What do you mean?" said Jeb, tilting his head.

"I felt something in the air last night, a burst of something. And a strange atmosphere before I went to bed. And my dreams were —" Blaize coughed, "er, more explicit than usual. It felt like it might be Svadisthana."

Jeb's face heated while his stomach froze. Had he caused that? Had the unleashing of his sexual energy affected people who were fifty yards away?

There could be no doubt he was attracted to Nixie – and that was why he needed to get away from her as soon as possible. Not only had she got through his wards, so that some of his Svadisthana energy leaked out when he'd come, he'd been up most of the night trying to repair the damage.

His body ached, and his head swam. He had a horrible feeling that his own energetic instability might be one of the reasons why Tierra had taken a turn for the worse. She was sensitive to others' energy when she was well, let alone in the kind of situation that was happening now.

"I don't know why, Fintan," Jeb said. "That's why I need more information."

And he also needed to get away from Nixie's influence. He had let his cock get the better of him for the first time in more than half a century.

He needed to get the hell out of here.

"What happened?" Elrian got straight to the point. He paced up and down the study of his Seattle safe house. It would be time to replenish his energy again soon. He needed the boost. No, wanted, he didn't need it. He could get on okay without it, but would perform better with a top-up.

Aeros was weaker now, having served as a battery for Elrian on a number of occasions, but he was still potent enough for Elrian to drain him and benefit. Imogen was suggesting it might soon be time to make another remnant stone with him, but Elrian wasn't ready to let go of the youth until he had another energetic to replace him.

"I influenced them as discussed, and they had sex," Trent said, his voice cool even down the phone line. "The male passed out when he came."

Elrian grunted. "Excellent. Did he lose control?"

"His shields are powerful. They didn't splinter, they simply fractured, and he kept the majority of his wardings in place. He is likely to have repaired them already."

Elrian clenched his jaw. "That is…disappointing."

Elrian needed that energy to be ripped out of Jebediah, to engulf him and his lover in an ecstasy-filled feedback cycle so they had sex until they were both drained lifeless husks.

Normally, when Svadisthana energetics had sex, they energized each other. But Jebediah's moratorium meant his energy was potentially more malign than benign, pressure having built up as the energy had nowhere to go for decades, and it wasn't cleansed or filtered. He and Nixie could be consumed by it when he finally let go fully – at least that was what Elrian anticipated.

"Do you think he noticed you? Or your influence?" Elrian asked.

"I do not. However, he's going back to Anahata Guild."

"Hmm." Luckily, Elrian had Imogen inside the Guild; powerful, deadly and hidden. He ran a hand through his hair. It could do with a trim. Usually Elrian was on top of his personal grooming – outer order produced inner calm – but recently it had fallen by the wayside.

He now needed to get Nixie to the Guild along with Jeb, and Elrian could hand the problem over and focus on creating the stones. It wouldn't be long before there was one less couple to worry about. The thought brought a thin-lipped smile to his mouth.

"Do you want me to stay here?" Trent said. A faint scraping sound came through the phone. Elrian grimaced. That toothpick. Revolting.

Elrian considered what to do. The mercenary wasn't cheap, but his loyalty was assured through cold, hard cash. The Healer wasn't likely to leave the perceived safety of his Guild in a hurry for a second time, but there were a number of other…problems on the island. Perhaps it was worth investing in destabilizing those further. His whiny niece was sick, dying probably, but he needed Trent to keep hurrying things along.

"Keep the charm draining Tierra and hasten the illness. Her death will destabilize them all. Avoid any wards they have, and ensure you are not seen." That would remove one of them, and then he only needed to take Jeb or Nixie, and wouldn't need both. The risk of failure would be lowered.

"Not a problem," said Trent. "She'll be dead within the week."

C H A P T E R

14

Nixie pushed the silver cuff to the side and stared dully down at the multicolored strands around her wrist. She was in the bathroom, where she'd tried to cut the bracelet off with no success. It seemed to be resistant to energy and to human-made tools.

Normally the artist in her would be fascinated by something like this. But not this time. She hadn't mentioned it to Blaize. She didn't want to take the focus off Tierra, and she wasn't ready to explore what the bracelet might mean for herself. Was it a hope, that she might soon connect with her soulmate, or a snare where she might be trapped with someone for external reasons that weren't her own choice?

Jebediah had left the island soon after breakfast that morning, catching the first boat out to the nearest island with an airport. Which was fine, because, apparently, he didn't have the matching bracelet. If there was a matching bracelet. Just because it had worked like that for the others, didn't mean it would work like that for her.

Despite the fact she actually wanted a relationship. Wanted a lover. A soulmate.

Don't I?

She was starting to think that she'd been chasing a fantasy. She loved the sex, and the thrill of the chase, and she'd felt she needed to meet a lot of men in order to find the right one for her. But perhaps the reason no one ever measured up was that it wasn't destined to happen for her.

Perhaps she wasn't relationship material. Perhaps people were right when they'd said men were only interested in Nixie for her looks, and that what was inside her was irrelevant – or worse, a turn off for guys.

She stared into the mirror, eyes narrowed. Her usual confidence in her appearance, and gifts when it came to sex and relationships, had taken a hit. She was uncertain, a feeling she hadn't experienced much in this area. Her looks and effect on men had been a problem, sure, in her life, but not the kind of problem she was having now.

Jeb was several hundred years old. Despite the last seventy years of celibacy, he would have had a number of relationships, with all kinds of interesting women.

Whereas what could Nixie offer him? Blaize was right, Nixie had been coasting. She wasn't ready for a life of responsibilities, of adulting. It hadn't taken Jeb long to realize that. He seemed to be a man with only responsibilities, but while she'd thought to bring him some joy, she'd seemed only to bring him more difficulty.

For some reason, Jeb's leaving hurt, even though she'd only recently met the man. She winced. She didn't want a guy affecting her this way. She wanted fun, lightness, joy and delight. Great sex and play. Relationships didn't have to be serious to be meaningful, surely?

She picked at the bracelet again, frustrated. Yeah, it wasn't going anywhere. She slowly slid the large metal cuff over it again and hung her head as she rested her hands on the sink, gripping the porcelain.

She really wasn't sure this bracelet was going to lead to anything good.

"I can't believe he deserted us," said Blaize. She was oiling one of her knives, methodically and carefully running a rag up and down the blade. "He was barely here twenty four hours."

She, Fintan, Ai and Nixie were together in Tierra's room. Tierra was no longer propped up in bed, but lay, eyes closed, her dark eyelashes stark against cheeks that were no longer butterscotch but a dark vanilla. They'd opened the curtains and the shutters, so at least the air and the light streamed in and the room wasn't as claustrophobic as it had been when Tierra had been unconscious.

Nixie was doodling in her sketch pad, her pencil moving without her really thinking about it, laying lighter, darker, thicker, thinner strokes upon the page.

Tierra spoke without opening her eyes. "He's a good person. He's gone to see what else he can find."

"Why couldn't someone else do the research? Why did he have to go?" said Blaize. "I know you like him Tierra, so I'm trying to give him the benefit of the doubt, but I'm struggling. He shouldn't have run off when you're still sick."

Fintan paced up and down the room, stopping every few laps to stroke Tierra's brow, squeeze her hand, or stare down at her. Several times Nixie itched to pick up her pencil and sketch his face as he did so. She'd call it 'Devotion.'

"We needed him here," Fintan ground out.

Ai watched them all from the floor where she lay on her front, leafing through a text that Cuinn had lent her about energies.

"He has so much experience. If he reads through the research with Feng, we're much more likely to get a cure sooner," murmured Tierra.

"Can't he get help from the Guild? There's enough of them," Fintan said.

"Aiko says it's too risky to talk about until we understand more about it, and what the consequences are. It's something that no one can remember happening in living memory," Tierra said.

Nixie's stomach was like a small rock. Was she part of the reason Jebediah had left? Of course she was. He hadn't wanted to be around her. That and the comments at breakfast that indicated the sex she'd had with Jeb had loosened his energy in a way that had made Tierra worse, meant now Nixie was partly responsible for Tierra getting sicker. Should she tell them? She couldn't see how it would help, especially as Jeb had removed himself from her vicinity, and he hadn't mentioned it as far as she knew. He was a far more experienced energetic than her, and he must have had a good reason to keep it quiet. Another couple of rocks joined the first inside her.

"Why is it so wrong to share energy?" Ai asked, quietly. "Why wouldn't it be a good thing to have access to more Chakras?"

All the adults stared at her. The taboo against sharing energy was so ingrained in the energetics' culture that Nixie, certainly, had never examined it. From the looks on the others' faces, neither had they.

"In answer to the second question, I didn't think you could," Fintan said. "It doesn't happen. It's supposed to be impossible."

Ai sat up and crossed her legs, and shoved hands into her black cargo pants' pockets. "Okay. But why is sharing energy seen as so terrible? When Tierra shared energy with Cuinn, she helped him to have enough energy to find Blaize and save her life, right? How could that be bad?"

Nixie continued doodling, her hand working without needing her mind, which was partly on Jeb anyway. "I always thought it was too dangerous to share energy. Though I'm not actually sure anyone ever said what the danger was."

Blaize tapped the flat of her blade on her leg a few times. "Did we actually learn this? Or is this something that everyone just knows? I've never really considered it before."

"Is there a punishment?" Ai said, rubbing a lock of her hair between her fingers and glancing at Tierra.

"I don't know," Blaize said. "Do you, Fintan? You're closest to what's considered law around here."

Ai was asking some interesting questions, Nixie thought.

Fintan scratched his chin. "There might be. I've not heard of a case though."

"I think keeping this aspect of the situation quiet is a good plan," Blaize said. "I doubt Cuinn and Tierra would be punished in a formal sense, but there would be a lot of disapproval."

She hesitated. "Even disgust, I think, from some."

There wasn't much conversation for a while after that.

They were all on edge. Blaize spent a lot of time on the phone to Cuinn and Cara, trying to support their progress, and researching what she could with the books she'd brought with her. Blaize also dealt with talking to Tierra's work colleagues. Tierra was a syndicated columnist and was organized enough to have columns written in advance, so all Blaize needed to do was send them on. Ai looked after Tierra or helped Blaize.

Fintan reported that Adam was chasing leads in the Pacific Northwest, and had put his Protector duties on hold while he did. They were all doing what they could. More strokes joined the initial lines on her pad.

Nixie wished she could take action. Do something. The pictures, the reason the others had come here in the first place, had stalled while they dealt with this crisis. Then a thought struck her.

"Why don't...I go and help Jeb?" Nixie spoke slowly. "I'm not doing much here while Blaize is busy, but I could help with research there easily enough. I read several languages, which might be helpful, including Cappotian."

Her auxiliary Chakra, Vishudha, was seated at the throat, and an affinity for languages sometimes came as part of it. Nixie was fluent in Thai and English, and had good Mandarin, and a smattering of romance languages. Her Latin was fairly good, and she had taken to Cappotian, the energetic's ancient language, fairly well when she'd studied it at her Guild.

Fintan stopped and stared at her. "You'd do that?"

"I want to help," said Nixie. "And I can do my graphic design from anywhere."

Going to the Guild seemed pretty safe, something that would keep her out of the line of fire, and stop her messing things up further for Tierra.

"They won't let you in on your own. Well, they probably would if Jeb accepts you as his guest, but he'd be responsible for you," said Fintan. Fintan was a member of Anahata, though his trip to see Jebediah with Tierra a few weeks before had been his first trip back there in many decades.

"Can you go with her?" asked Blaize. She angled her knife to the light and studied the blade.

"I'm not leaving Tierra," said Fintan. "She needs me here more than there. Anyway, we know research isn't my best thing."

"Nixie can be Jeb's guest," said Tierra. "He'll be fine.

Nixie added a few finishing touches to the detail she'd sketched and considered it.

"Then you're up, Nix, if you really don't mind," Blaize said.

Fintan grasped Nixie by the shoulders. "And if you find out any answers? Bring them, and him, back here as soon as you can."

Nixie nodded absentmindedly, still staring down at her sketch pad. Perhaps she would bring him back. For Tierra's sake.

In the meantime, she was wondering why she'd drawn a strong male wrist. A bare one.

Jeb sat in Aiko's living quarters, head in hands. The journey back from Thailand to Egypt had passed in a blur, and once back in the relative safety of his room, he'd wearily begun rebuilding his wards. But after only a few hours, he'd realized he was struggling to put the Svadisthana back in its box, and he'd come to Aiko.

But he couldn't bring himself to tell her everything.

"It's not sustainable. The wards are going to keep breaking down," Aiko said, gently. "The only other thing I can suggest, if you must keep doing this, is that you go to Svadisthana Guild. Perhaps they have a better way of keeping the energy suppressed."

Jeb took his head out of his hands and looked at her. "No. I haven't been back there since before the War, and I don't think the atmosphere there would be beneficial."

Aiko considered him for a moment. "Perhaps you're right."

"It's awash with sexual energy. I'd step through the door and be swimming in it – I'd never keep my shields up. At least here in Anahata Guild I don't come into as much contact with that kind of energy." Jeb said. His stomach felt like lead, and his eyes were gritty. Holding the energy in wasn't easy. It was like trying to hold back the tide. Exhausting.

"I'll help you, both in my Guild capacity, and as a friend. But this needs to end." She pursed her lips. "You're sick. And I think it's because you're only half of who you are."

Jeb shook his head vigorously, and then regretted it as his temples pounded. "Please. Just help me."

She sighed. "Come here."

She walked over to one side of the room. With wooden flooring and several windows, it felt spacious and airy. The only items in that part of the room were a couple of mats on the floor and a small altar. She lit a candle, and placed it on the altar, bowing her head for a moment. Then she directed Jeb to lie face up on one of the mats, and she sat at his side, her hands outstretched over his body.

"Relax," she said. "I'll try and make this as painless as possible."

It wasn't.

She was trying to force his energy back inside him, when it wanted out. He'd been keeping it stable, but it wanted to be used. He felt comfortable with Aiko, even with this dangerous energy, as her sexual interest was women, not men. It wasn't that his Svadisthana couldn't affect her, but it was much less likely to than if she had a sexual preference for males.

He lay with his eyes closed and his teeth gritted, and attempted to keep his muscles lax. Which wasn't easy when spasms of cold fire chased around his energetic and physical body.

After what seemed like hours, Aiko paused in her ministrations. "Jeb. Something's not quite right."

Jeb felt a spurt of adrenaline. From the understated Aiko, that was tantamount to an admission that a catastrophe was about to happen.

She continued. "Don't move, please, but I want to try something."

He lay rigid. The cold fire started again, this time accompanied by a feeling of someone riffling through his body, as if he was a pack of cards being flicked through. It was a disturbing feeling.

After a few moments, Aiko spoke. "Did anything…strange happen while you were away? Was there a trigger for your shields breaking again?"

Jeb was glad his eyes were still closed. He really, really didn't want to admit this. But this was Aiko. They went back centuries. She had been there for him as a long-term friend. Plus, she was his physician in this context. He'd be a fool not to tell her everything.

"The sea affected me. So much wild water…" He swallowed. "And there was a woman."

She nodded with a grave expression. "And what happened?"

He talked her through the experience on the beach and on Nixie's balcony.

His cheeks were hot, and he was glad his eyes were closed. It wasn't shame at the sex. Energetics didn't have the same shame culture as humans about sex, and Svadisthana-trained energetics least of all. It was self-loathing at his lack of control.

"I don't know how this all connects, Jeb, but there are traces of influence in your aura. A sort of sticky energetic residue. If you'd waited much longer before coming to me, they'd have disappeared completely, but it looks to me like someone was exerting their Svadisthana on you to make you lose control."

He felt her light touch on his arm. "How much do you really know about the woman you slept with?"

Once Aiko had finished helping Jeb to lock his energy back down, they had further discussed the possibility of someone tampering with his energy. They'd discussed Nixie, and Aiko, knowing her family well, agreed it was unlikely that it was she who was influencing Jeb, but not impossible.

When he'd looked at the parts of his aura she'd pointed out to him he'd seen the taint. Where normally a healthy Anahata-Svadisthana energetic would have an aura of orange and blue, his had been tainted by subtle traces of silver-grey, as if someone had swirled cobwebs through it.

Jeb's skin crawled at the idea of anyone influencing his free will. Yet part of him wondered if this was some kind of cosmic payback for his actions during the War. Karma.

He was struggling to believe, having touched Nixie's energy, that either incident had anything to do with her directly. Someone was using them both, surely. But, why?

He sat in his study in one of the armchairs. He'd worn his favorite loose sweater today, needing the comfort of familiarity. He stared at the stained glass panel in his window. The bright sun and blue sky behind it made it pop with color. It normally soothed him, but not today.

When he thought back to a couple of nights ago, he thought about the syrupy feeling of the air, which he'd put down to humidity and sexual arousal. It had been such a long time since he'd felt either that he'd never even considered the idea that it might be a Rogue who was twisting energy to use it in such a dark way.

But Nixie was not that Rogue.

Jeb had been dealing with Rogues for centuries, and his empath energies had felt no trace of that kind of energy from her. And she didn't appear to have much guile or artifice about her. Much of her charm was in her natural allure. She had an unconscious and unaffected way of moving through the world that exuded sensuality without her appearing to make much effort. Could she really maintain that kind of deception around people like Blaize, and Fintan, who had known her for years?

Once Aiko was confident he believed her, she'd burned away the remaining traces of alien energy, and reassured him that what had been left had stopped influencing him, most likely after the sexual encounter. She'd also congratulated him for not losing his control entirely. She'd questioned him more about Nixie. He'd shared a little more detail, but he'd also told Aiko he was confident that the woman he'd had sex with – he couldn't call it making love given this new information – hadn't been the one who'd influenced him.

He was, wasn't he? She hadn't even seemed that interested when he'd come onto her balcony to apologize. Was she? He shook his head. And he had come to her, of his own free will. Or had he?

Damn it. He was tired emotionally, mentally, energetically. He needed to rest before he could sort this out in his head. Meditate, perhaps. Ground himself somehow so everything that was going on wasn't such a snarl in his brain.

Was Nixie caught up in someone else's mind games, or was she the one playing him? And what on earth would someone have to gain from making the two of them have sex?

And if it wasn't her, he probably needed to tell her. What if she was in danger?

Since his discussion with Aiko, he'd been umming and ahhing about whether to call Nixie, and he'd had his cellphone in his hand for an hour. It had grown warm from being held.

And then it rang. He almost dropped it, before he fumbled to answer it.

"Hello?" he said.

"It's Fintan. We're sending you some help. She'll be there tomorrow."

"What? What are you talking about?" said Jeb. Fintan. Of course it was Fintan. The man was relentless. Jeb had barely arrived back at the Guild.

"You need to find out answers and get back here. We're sending Nixie to the Guild to help you."

Jeb's stomach crashed to the floor.

"There's no need for that," said Jeb. He needed distance from Nixie until he worked out what was going on. When he was around her, with or without energetic influence, he was clearly susceptible.

"You can use all the help you can get, Jebediah," stated Fintan flatly. "Tierra needs you to find out answers as soon as possible. If Nixie can support you in that, that's great."

"She and I didn't resonate," said Jeb, then felt bad as soon as the words were out of his mouth. It was mean-spirited, and more than that, it wasn't true. They'd resonated far too well on some levels, that was part of the problem. He liked the woman, but she was bad for him. Possibly really bad, if Aiko's worries turned out to be true. He hurried on. "Anyway, she's an artist, not a researcher, correct? I'm not sure that she's going to be able to help. Perhaps someone else would be better?"

Please, Source, let there be someone better.

"Blaize says for all her apparent spaciness, Nixie's good at seeing the big picture. Her Vishudha isn't as strong as her Svadisthana, but it's there. Perhaps she'll see patterns that you and Feng don't see."

He needed another tack. "Is she trustworthy? There's delicate material in the archives. We can't have someone who's more, say, impulsive or capricious. She'd have to keep what she reads between us."

Fintan laughed, though there wasn't a lot of humor in it. "It's true she can be a bit fickle. But she's steadfast when it comes to loyalty to family and friends."

"I'll have to get permission from Aiko to have a guest who's not Anahata in the Guild," Jeb made one more attempt. Maybe he could get Aiko to veto the idea. He didn't want the woman here. Really. He didn't. Given the effect on his control she'd already had, he wanted to stay as far from her as possible. "She might not be comfortable with the idea."

"Cuinn has already spoken to her. She's fine with it. So tough luck, there's no problem," Fintan said. Jeb knew he'd pushed the other man far enough, especially with their already prickly relationship. Jeb rubbed his forehead. He needed to sleep. "She'll be with you first thing in the morning. Deal with it, and put her to work."

15

Nixie looked up at the entrance to Anahata Guild in some trepidation. What had seemed like such a good idea a day ago in Thailand was seeming a lot less sensible now.

The Guild was the same pale yellow that all buildings in Egypt seemed to be. She'd never seen such a yellow and blue country. The sun shone as brightly as in Thailand, but here there weren't the lush green rain forests of Thailand, or the bright colors Thais loved generally. If you went to a market in Thailand, it was a riot of color. Here, dusty yellows and bright blue dominated.

She already missed the sea. No wonder Jeb's Svadisthana had dried up, so far away from real water. Whilst the Nile would certainly count, he'd have to actually visit it. Tierra had told her that Jebediah hadn't even left the Guild in decades until his trip to Thailand last week. Nixie shook her head.

She stepped up to the door and pushed it open. A young female receptionist sat behind a counter. The entrance was neutral, with no hint as to what was in the building – it could be academic, research, an office, anything. "Can I help you?"

"I'm Nixie Lynch. I'm a guest of Jebediah Gale," she said. At least, she hoped she was.

The receptionist nodded and made a soft-voiced call. At the end, she looked at Nixie again, a more considering look this time. "Jebediah's busy. In the meantime, Aiko, our Guild Leader, asks for the pleasure of your company."

Nixie pressed her lips together. "Oh. Really? Are you sure?"

The receptionist's eyebrows drew together. "Yes. Her assistant, Sajan, is on his way down. We'll make sure your luggage gets to your room while you talk."

Nixie slunk back to the seating area, until a few minutes later a snappily dressed male energetic appeared and greeted her. He led her through a maze of corridors until he brought her into the plushly furnished anteroom of the office. "Wait here for a moment while I check she's ready, please."

Nixie kept her sigh internal. She wasn't great with bureaucracy, or pomp and circumstance, and with her recent run of pissing off everyone around her, she wasn't sure meeting one of the six Major Circle members, who was in part responsible for the political governance of the energetics race, was a good idea after such a long journey with little or no sleep.

The door behind which Sajan had disappeared opened again, and he gestured her in. She glanced at his wrists as he did. Because you never knew. Another petite Asian woman, though Japanese rather than Thai, stood to greet her. Jasmine tea in a beautifully decorated teapot with matching cups was on the table. The room was decorated in a minimalist style, with several Japanese artworks on the walls from both well-known and lesser-known artists. If Aiko herself had chosen them, she was cultured. They weren't a style Nixie favored, but they showed taste and discernment.

"I welcome you to Guild Anahata, Nixie," she said. "I am Aiko, Guild Leader."

Everyone knew the six Guild Leaders, even energetics like Nixie who didn't do politics. Whilst the Minor Circle, that is, the energetics who headed each of the thirty Minor Guilds, such as Nixie's own Svadisthana-Vishudha, weren't all known to Nixie, the six who headed the Major Guilds were.

"Svadisthana-Vishudha greets Guild Anahata," Nixie said, giving the ritual greeting of an energetic meeting any of the Guild Leaders. "May we bring balance."

She'd heard good things about Aiko. Nixie followed up by putting her hands together in a respectful wai that was all hers. "I want to help however I can. Tierra, of all people, doesn't deserve this."

They sat down at the low table, and Aiko poured out the tea. Nixie picked hers up and cupped the warm ceramic in her hands.

"I agree," said Aiko. "But it's not Tierra that I want to discuss with you."

Why else would the leader of the Guild want to talk to her? Nixie had assumed it was something to do with keeping their secrets, if they were about to let Nixie into their archives.

"Yes?" she murmured, non-committal.

"I want to talk to you about Jebediah."

Nixie's tea cup wobbled in her hand, and she placed it carefully on the table, not meeting Aiko's eyes. "Oh yes?"

What did she know? Nixie wasn't entirely innocent there. She'd tried to seduce him, and at the end of the day, he was a senior member of Aiko's Guild. Nixie had also promised Fintan she would drag Jebediah back by any means possible if Tierra needed him. Neither of these seemed like something to mention to Aiko in their first interaction.

"You may know that many decades ago, Jebediah renounced his Svadisthana," said Aiko.

"He mentioned it," said Nixie. "But even if he hadn't, it's obvious that he's not using his full powers."

That seemed safe.

"Yes," said Aiko. "With my help, and that of other senior members of the Guild, he bound his auxiliary energy. He's a strong enough Anahata energetic that he's still been a highly functioning member of the Guild."

Aiko paused and took a deliberate sip of tea. Nixie feigned polite interest, but her gut churned.

"But when he came back from his visit the to the island, his bindings were in tatters. As if he'd exploded them from inside out. We've put many of them back, but I don't think they'll ever be the same."

"Oh, dear. Is he okay?" This wasn't exactly news to Nixie. She'd been there when his bindings had cracked after all. Was it her fault? Or his? He'd acted like it was something that had happened before, and had seemed to have it under control. Perhaps the fact he had immediately left had indicated something different, though she had thought it more of a reflection of his feelings about her.

"He is, to a degree," Aiko said. "However, I understand you're the only Svadisthana energetic he had contact with."

How was she supposed to reply to that? Was it a statement or a question? Or an accusation? Was Aiko saying it was her fault?

"Possibly," Nixie said. Short and factual seemed the way here. Aiko was polite but hostile, and Nixie had no idea why. Anahata were supposed to be a Guild more welcoming of outsiders than most.

"Did you access his energy?" Aiko asked.

Nixie blushed. Was Aiko asking her about their sexual interaction? Or something else? Nixie felt there was more than one level to this conversation, and some of it was passing her by. This was definitely not her Guild, where charm, flirtation and lightness was more common than this earnest civility.

"I don't believe so," Nixie said. Not on purpose, anyway. Her ears felt hot. She'd been willing, eager, even, to have sex, but so had he. Should she mention the bracelet? Her impulse was to confess everything to Aiko, but what would she say? 'I have this weird bracelet, I don't really know what to do about it so I'm pretending it doesn't exist until I can work it out.' Yeah, that didn't seem a great idea.

"I see," Aiko said. Nixie tried not to squirm. She wasn't entirely sure what she was being accused of, but her behavior wasn't exactly of the non-guilty variety. "While you're here, Nixie, I'll be checking in with you regularly."

Did the woman mean what Nixie thought? She was going to check up on her? Spy on her, even? It wasn't as if Nixie had any ulterior motivates apart from to get some kind of cure – and, Jeb, if necessary – back to the island.

"Alright," Nixie said, "though I'm not sure why."

Nixie was tired of getting it wrong recently, tired of people disliking her, rejecting her or disapproving of her.

"It's important for me to look after my Guild members," Aiko said. "Thank you for your time, and I hope you find what you are looking for in the archives."

Nixie did too. So she could get out of here as soon as possible. She'd barely arrived – and she already wanted to leave.

Jeb was in the library concentrating on a text when Aiko's assistant, Sajan, appeared. Feng bustled over to him. "Can I help? Do you or Aiko need anything?"

"No, it's Jeb we're here to see."

We?

Sajan stepped aside, and revealed the fairy. She looked a little lost amongst the stacks of books that surrounded them. She wore a short, loose skirt in a dark orange, a white short-sleeved shirt, tied over a flat stomach, and a huge silver bangle on her left wrist.

"Hi," she said. He nodded, a little at sea himself. He felt, well, something. Hmm. It was unlike him not to be able to identify an emotion. Was there any of the thickness in the air that he'd felt last time they'd, um, interacted? He took a breath, but the archive's dehumidified air felt as dry as ever. Though he was looking for it, he saw no trace of any influence magic being used.

Feng stepped over to her and gave her a little bow, and she wai-ed in return.

"Welcome to Anahata Guild," he enthused. "I hear you're going to help us. We appreciate it."

He drew her over to the table where he was working, and showed her the heap of papers he was ploughing through. Sajan disappeared silently, leaving the three of them alone.

Feng's energies might be best used in the library, but he had empathy like any other Anahata. Jeb could tell Feng had picked up on Jeb's discomfort, and stepped in. Jeb was grateful to his friend.

On the one hand, Nixie was a likely candidate for using the influence magic, if he thought about it rationally. On the other, what would her agenda be? And how could she be so trusted by Fintan, Blaize and the others if she wasn't what she seemed? Were they all taken in? She confused Jeb's emotions, it was true, but he had never picked up any negativity, or twisting in her energies, so if she was a Rogue or similar she was very well camouflaged. And she didn't seem that experienced or capable. Jeb's substantial experience with Rogues didn't align with her being one.

Feng outlined their research so far to Nixie, and Jeb went back to his text. Though he couldn't refrain from looking up every now and then to see what the fairy was doing. She seemed to be paying close attention to what Feng was saying, a serious look on her face.

They were adults. There was no need for any awkwardness, whatever his body thought of her. He'd be able to keep his energy under control. As long as they kept a polite distance between themselves. He was glad she wasn't wearing a dress. Because the thought of her in a dress, perhaps without any underwear on…

His groin twitched, and an orange spark fell from his body onto the desk in front of him. It came perilously close to setting light to the centuries old text he was reading.

"Source!" he yelped, and frantically patted the surface in front of him. It had mostly survived intact.

Nixie and Feng looked up. "What happened?"

"Nothing. A bug or something." Though not the insect kind. More like a sickness inside him. Was he still being influenced? Was she doing it? It had been harder than ever to lock down his energy this time, and Aiko had warned him once again that it wasn't going to last.

It had to last.

Although, being with Nixie hadn't felt as…wrong as it should have. There had been a sense of rightness, of completeness, when his energy had exploded and he'd once more been able to reach out and touch his Svadisthana.

Was it real?

"It's working," Trent said. "The woman, Tierra, is fading fast. She's a very strong energetic, a Master in both her energies, so it's taking a little time, but it's in progress. You don't need to check in on me like this."

They were on the phone again. Elrian was too tired to pace. He sat watching the rain through his study window. It was relentless, but it made the area very green. His Muladhara felt nourished in the woods around the house, the damp earth boosting him to some degree. But it wasn't enough. He needed to siphon energy more and more often, burning through the energy he took from Aeros in a short time. He was finding it harder to draw energy of his own from the ether, and becoming more reliant on the external sources of energy from his victims.

Trent's flat tone held a chill. "Being subtle is important in this situation. You told me you want it to look natural, part of the illness. Trust my judgement."

Elrian bit his tongue. This employee should absolutely not be talking to him like this. He was a paid worker, nothing more. Right now Elrian would tolerate it because he needed the man, and getting someone else at this stage would pose a number of risks. Afterwards, however, they would have a very different conversation.

"Fine," Elrian said. "Get the job done."

He put the phone down without further discussion, and his door opened. He looked across the room, scowling at the fact the person hadn't knocked, but his face softened slightly when he saw it was Cassidy.

She was tall for a woman, with ash blonde hair cut below her ears, and an imperious look. She had dark blue eyes and strong angular features, and she was as elegant as Elrian was dignified.

"Cassidy, good. I want to talk to you," Elrian said.

"What is it? I came to ensure you ate something," she said.

"Sit down," he gestured to one of the armchairs, and when she sat he came over to join her, sitting in the armchair next to her.

She reached out to remove some fluff from his sleeve, then put her hands in her lap and sat patiently, waiting for him to speak as he had trained her to do over the years. She was always pale, but recently her skin seemed almost translucent, thinner. Perhaps he was asking too much of her. Perhaps even the mild influence he was using on her to keep her docile was too much. He pursed his lips. There was little he could do. She had a role to play in his plans.

"I need you to dreamwalk for me again," he said.

Cassidy's eyes flickered, but other than that she did not show any reaction. "Why is that? What is it that you need?"

She had been in there before for him, perhaps more times than she realized.

"There is some information that I seek," he said. "I can brief you later. In the meantime, take the day to rest so you are in good shape, and don't forget to take your special drink. It will help you be strong."

He had trained Cassidy as an energetic himself, as her Maven, but kept her out of the Guild system. It hadn't been easy, and he had had to use persuasive methods to ensure she did not ask too many questions. She was a tool that he used, and nothing more, though one he would admit to having a soft spot for. The drink helped her to be more suggestible, and made influencing her easier.

She nodded. "Is everything okay?"

He frowned. The last thing he needed was her suspicion. "Fine, my dear. Why?"

"You seem tired. And you're still wearing yesterday's shirt," she said.

Elrian's head snapped down and he realized she was right. That was unthinkable. He nodded tightly. "Thank you. Please have dinner prepared for seven p.m. as normal. It will just be the two of us."

She nodded and stood, then glided away.

If only everyone in his life could be so agreeable.

16

Nixie spent the day with Feng. Jebediah had acknowledged her with a grunt when she came in, and then ignored her for the rest of the day, apart from another grunt of surprise when she mentioned she could read Cappotian. Feng was lovely, and had given her a good overview of where they were up to, but she could acknowledge to herself that she was hurt that Jeb hadn't paid her any attention.

Meh. He was an older energetic. Age differences between energetics weren't the issue they were between humans usually, but perhaps he was more set in his ways than most. Okay, who was she kidding? He'd been out of the Guild once in seventy years. He was the personification of set in his ways.

It was strange being in a Guild when you didn't have that energy. It felt a little bit uncomfortable. Part of it was not fitting in, that was certain, but there was also something about being surrounded by so much alien energy. Her shoulders felt stiff, and the usual grace with which she navigated the world was affected.

At dinner time Nixie went down to the dining hall. She'd thought about going out somewhere for dinner, but if she was honest with herself, she was hoping to encounter Jeb. Casually. To bump into him at the buffet perhaps. But when she went into the large hall, filled with chattering Anahata energetics, there was no sign of him, though Sajan, who she'd seen a number of times throughout the day, sat where he could see her. She wondered, paranoid, for a moment or two, if he was following her, the eyes and ears of Aiko, but this wasn't a huge Guild, and he must get around to do errands for the Guild Leader. She was sure she was imagining things. She wasn't important enough to follow.

She sat at a table on her own and forked salad into her mouth. She wished Blaize or Tierra were here. Or she'd even take Ai. Nixie's usual brightness was dulled, and she needed to get her spark back.

She finished the last few mouthfuls, and decided to get some ice-cream to take away with her. Perhaps she could befriend Sajan? Ask him to sit with her in the Egyptian night and look at the stars. Perhaps she'd feel a little more connected to her beloved island that way, and she could chat with him about the Guild. Information gathering was always useful. Or gossip. She loved gossip. Perhaps he'd know about Jeb, even. She wouldn't mind finding out more about the man.

She walked over to Sajan's table, where he sat alone. "Hi. I'm off to sit outside for a bit, and I'd love to pick your brains on the Guild. I don't know much about it."

She beamed at him, a smile that few were able to resist, though the stiffness in her shoulders had spread to her whole body and her neck was starting to ache. She rolled her head from side to side while she waited for him to answer.

"Thank you, no. I have work that I must do after dinner." He inclined his head and went back to his meal.

Ugh. What is it with this place? This was supposed to be the Guild of Anahata, love, of connection, but she was finding no emotional intimacy here at all, no inclination from any of the Guild members to reach out, or even accept her friendship advances. Her strengths of connecting to others should work well here, and yet she hadn't felt this alone for months.

She gave up. She chose a strawberry cone, and asked one of the energetics she passed to suggest a good place to sit outside. He pointed her in the right direction, and she went down several corridors until she found the external door. She pushed it open and the warm breeze, smelling of the desert, cocooned her.

She walked along a path, enjoying the well-tended hanging plants and the hint of jasmine that reminded her of home. She licked her ice cream carefully, trying to make it last. She happened across a bench that looked over a water-feature that trickled water down and along a path, a ribbon of silver in the night. She sat and looked at it as she finished her dessert.

She'd paint this in the style of van Gogh's later works, all swirls and thick paint. She rested back on her hands and looked up at the sky. So many stars. It was beautiful. But she still felt like an alien.

She'd work on the research until they found something. But in the meantime, one question wouldn't stop circling her mind.

What am I going to do about Jeb?

Jeb watched Nixie sit on his favorite bench. He'd come out for a little air, but when he'd seen her there he'd stayed in the shadows. She'd proceeded to kick her legs and lick her ice cream with apparent enjoyment, her gaze shifting between the stars above and the water feature in front of her. At first she'd appeared a little preoccupied, but by the time she seemed ready to head back inside, she'd cheered up.

He wished she hadn't had an ice cream. The sight of her small pink tongue working its way around the cone had been troublesome.

Why had she gotten under his skin? What was it about her that he found so damned attractive? He didn't know. She'd been a distraction all day, and he couldn't have that. They needed to find a cure for Tierra. He'd spoken to Fintan earlier, and Tierra was stable, but she hadn't gotten any better after her recent relapse.

Jebediah's phone buzzed in his pocket and he drew it out and answered it without looking. "Yes?"

"It's Fintan."

Jebediah winced. He should have checked it. "We haven't found anything."

"That's not why I'm calling," said Fintan, his tone a bit more upbeat than Jeb had heard since Tierra's illness began.

"Oh. Why then?" said Jeb.

"Because Cuinn's been dreamwalking, and we have more pieces of prophecy."

"Tell me," said Jebediah. Anything that might point him and Feng – and, he supposed, Nixie – in the right direction, would be helpful.

"He wants you to look into remnant stones further. Anything you can find on how they are created, and what they can be used for. He's also found a name. Iskander. You need to find any references to a man called Iskander in your research. Cuinn thinks it will help."

"I don't think I've ever come across that name," said Jebediah, disappointed. He'd hoped for more.

"It's relevant somehow," said Fintan. "Find it, and get back here."

"I –" Jebediah started, but Fintan had rung off. Was the word goodbye not in the man's vocabulary?

Back to the library Jeb went.

17

At first when Jeb had mentioned the new lead, Nixie had been excited. A message had found her, and she'd come back down to the archives, ready to put in a couple more hours.

But with no results and after working with dusty books all day and half the night she was ready to call it quits. Jeb had sent Feng — who hadn't stopped even when the other two had taken a break — to bed already. Now it was just Nixie and Jeb, alone in the library surrounded by books and a portentous silence.

She wasn't a books person. She was ready to admit that. She liked things to be more…juicy. She threw the book she was working on down on the table.

Jeb looked up. She met his eyes.

"Careful. The books can be fragile," he said. Polite. Distant. She wanted to go over there and wreck his control.

Okay. Grow up, Nixie. She'd try helping instead.

"Do you want to talk about your Svadisthana?" she asked. "Aiko told me your shields are failing. Was it to do with us?"

"I.. don't know. I don't think so. It started before I met you."

"Can I do anything to help?"

He rubbed the back of his neck. "Ah, no, I don't think so."

Gah. That was enough with trying to help the man. She picked up the next book on her pile and turned away. She was in a whole new Guild of potential partners right now, and could be socializing with interesting men, trying on possibilities for the person who had the matching bracelet to hers, and instead she was stuck with Jebediah. A guy who had rejected her.

She checked the list for why this text was in the pile. There was a reference to several prophecies that included all the energies. Which wasn't as common as you might think. She scanned the text to find it, carefully paging through the delicate sheets. This was a handwritten notebook from an Ajna-Anahata, which was how it had ended up in the Anahata library.

Cuinn, who was back in Canada, continued to look through the Ajna texts, and had drafted in Cara, as an Anahata-Manipura, to make sure he didn't miss anything from the Anahata side of things. But he hadn't mentioned the text she was holding. Perhaps this was the only copy. It certainly seemed old.

She'd gone a couple of pages more when she stopped. *Was that...?* She flicked back a couple of pages, a spark of excitement kindling in her stomach. She found the page, and traced a finger down the lines, looking for the name.

"Nixie, I'm not –" Jeb started.

"Ha!" She had it. Now to hope that it actually gave them something useful.

"What?" Jebediah demanded.

"Give me a minute." She was reading the full passage and needed to concentrate. After a few lines, she swallowed.

Oh.

Fuck.

It seemed to Jeb that Nixie was unable to focus on something for more than a few minutes, switching between books and jotting notes down in some kind of shorthand he didn't understand. Then she stopped dead, and slumped in her chair. She really was very expressive.

"Tell me what you've found." For all he knew, it could be some ancient piece of gossip. But the way she raised huge eyes up to look at him, he very much doubted it. He could feel waves of distress coming off her. He sat in a chair next to hers. He scooted it round so he sat opposite, their knees a hairsbreadth away from each other.

He reached out his hands and took her empty hand between his, the one not holding the book, and gave it a rub. Her flesh was soft, but not as much as he'd expected. Perhaps she needed a little distraction. "You have callouses on your fingers."

A look of disbelief crossed her face. He winced. Perhaps that wasn't the right distraction. Though it had worked. "I was just surprised. I didn't realize you did manual work."

She shook her head slowly, her brow still scrunched up, and pulled her hand back out of his. "I play the guitar, and I sculpt. I like working with my hands. But I'm not out digging the fields if that's what you were thinking. Nothing so worthy."

Jeb hunched his shoulders. Back to the matter at hand then. "What did you find?"

The book hung limply from her hand, but she rallied. She passed the open page to him. The book was a bound note-book, hand written in ink in beautiful flowing penmanship. "It's a translation from the original Cappotian."

He read:

From the House of Iskander
When the Twelve shall gather

Each shall have a role
But on each the work will take a toll

Twelve bracelets will give them power
Activated by pairs or all at the final hour

The pair joined in the element of mind
Will fight tooth and nail but eventually find
Dreamscape defences must be breached
If their love be found and reached

The pair joined in the element of air
Will seek far and wide for something right there
Will locate puzzle pieces made of flesh and of bone
Then find heart-magic begins at home

The pair joined in the element of water
Will battle control that has to falter
Sacrifice made and offering given
Will help ensure both are truly living

The pair joined in the element of fire
Will uncover secrets, ancient and dire
Wild energy transmits, affects and enhances

Finds solutions and increases love's chances

He frowned. "What's the gap?"

She raised empty hands. "I don't know."

There was a smudged area before the last couple of stanzas of the prophecy, as if drops of water had fallen on the page. He measured the space against previous verses. "It looks like there's room for another two verses. Which would make sense, as we have four verses about the energies, which would leave, hmm, earth and ether."

"Okay, that makes sense," Nixie said. "I wonder if it happened naturally or someone has erased them."

"We take two steps forward and one step back every time we find more information," Jeb muttered. He continued reading.

Twelve bracelets, twelve stones
Together, not alone,

In pairs they will be
And only then will they see

Without the support of them all
The Circle, the Guilds — our race — shall fall.

Jeb expelled a puff of air. It didn't relate to Tierra's illness, that was true. But it sounded worryingly as if it related to Cuinn's wider prophecy. And it didn't sound that cheery for those involved – which included both him and Nixie.

He quickly dismissed the bit about pairs. He could only worry about one thing at a time. "On each it will take a toll. That doesn't sound good."

She shook her head. "Um, understatement?!"

"Do you think that the couples joined in the elements of mind and air are Blaize and Cuinn, and Tierra and Fintan? They have bracelets, which this seems to refer to, and those are the elements they have in common."

"Perhaps," said Nixie, scratching the skin underneath her large bangle. "The verse seems to fit their stories, but we'd have to ask them."

"We should get a copy of this over to Cuinn as soon as possible," said Jeb.

"I agree. Shall I take photographs and email them to the others now, while you keep looking through the texts?" Nixie asked.

She was being very polite. Jeb wasn't sure he liked it. Usually she was more of a wildcat, spitting and hissing at him. The verses must have really affected her. What did she see in them? How did she interpret them? He nodded and walked back to where he'd been working. Perhaps Cuinn and the others would be able to fill in the gaps.

It was the first reference to this Iskander after all. Who was he? Was the use of Circle, rather than Circles, a mistake? If not, there was a minor and a major circle – which one was the prophecy referring to?

And, he thought, with a sinking heart, which verses were he and Nixie in?

It seemed the prophecy expected both of them to be in a pair, though with whom was unclear. The use of pair, not couple, suggested the pairing didn't have to be romantic, surely? Two connected energetics in some way helping each other?

He kept paging through the texts, scanning as he went, looking for more mentions of Iskander, sharing energy and the consequences, all six energies being used together, the Twelve, or really, anything that might help. His head felt fuzzy, and he needed a break. He was starting to miss things and having to catch himself and go back.

He sat back in his chair and stared into space, his eyes looking at but not really seeing the many texts around them. So many books. And yet there were many more – did they need to look in the other Guilds' libraries? Cuinn had visited Ajna, which contained most of the prophecies, if not all, that had ever been recorded, and the Anahata records contained information about Healing. But what if, like the diary Feng had found the day before, it was solely in the daybook of some ancient energetic? Not a manual or a formally written text?

They were looking for a needle in a haystack. He groaned and rested his head in his hands.

Nixie looked over. "What's the matter? Did you find something else?"

"No," he mumbled, directing his voice at the desk. "Just realizing how big the task we have is."

"Don't have such a defeatist attitude. If you think like that, we'll never find the answers. Tierra's counting on us."

Jeb's body sunk lower in the chair. "I know. That's what I'm afraid of."

"Let's lay out what we have," suggested Nixie. "That might make you feel better. Because we have made progress, whatever you think."

Jeb sat up. "Fine. Talk me through it."

Nixie got up and began to pace. "Everything started when Cuinn saw a prophecy about himself and eleven other energetics protecting our race against some great evil, which could cause the end of the energetic world. The twelve include a bunch of people he knows, and some he doesn't, but so far my drawings have helped to identify you, and once Tierra is better, Blaize and I will work together to identify the others. The prophecy snippets he has so far seem to talk about six pairs, which so far could be seen to correlate with Cuinn and Blaize, and Fintan and Tierra, but we don't have any guarantee of that. But we've sent the snippets to them to see if it resonates as a description of their relationship." She looked over at him. "Sound correct so far?"

He nodded. It was a concise summary, he supposed. In all honesty, he was fighting a little bemusement at the fact she seemed to have such a good overview of the situation. She always seemed so distracted. He blinked when he realized she was continuing.

"We seem to be fighting against what is so far a small group of Rogues, which is unusual because Rogues rarely band together. At first we thought it was Indigo working alone, but now we believe the leader seems to be the man who is Cuinn's father and was Indigo's Maven, Elrian." She stopped. "How's Cuinn doing with that, do you know?"

"I don't. I don't know Cuinn really, apart from through Tierra. It must have been a shock, although I understand they haven't talked in a long while."

"I can't imagine." Nixie shuddered. "Are your parents, or family, still alive?"

"No," he said. She waited. "But we got on fine, thanks. No dark secrets in that part of my life."

She rolled her eyes. But curiosity had come off her in waves. Perhaps he should remind her he could read emotions, even though she was a surprisingly difficult signal for him to decipher.

"So, anyway. We don't know their motives, or what, exactly, they're trying to achieve, apart from the fact it's dangerous, and risks our race, somehow. And they think we can stop it, in part by potentially killing one or more of us on our side of the prophecy." She shifted in her seat at that, which was fair. It wasn't comfortable for him to think about either. Especially as Elrian's wife, who was also Tierra's aunt, had been one of the casualties of Jeb's actions in the war. If Elrian knew that, he might be a little keener to hurt Jeb than the others involved.

"Elrian's the leader, and there's also some blonde woman involved called Cassidy, who helped Tierra escape, but wouldn't leave herself. We don't know who she is, or what her role is, but we know she was a powerful energetic because she was able to influence Tierra and cause some memory loss, which is a strong power."

Jeb frowned. "Maybe that event was part of Tierra's illness. I'll email Fintan to ask. I think she was injured afterwards though, as she and Fintan fought a Rogue, so it might be hard to disentangle."

"Perhaps. We haven't considered that, have we? So far we think Tierra's ill because she shared energy with Cuinn, and she's not a Maven level energetic. Something about being a Maven seems to protect energetics from sharing energy, as Mavens and Adherents are the only group who seem to do it both ethically and safely." Nixie commented.

"That's correct. And we've never looked into Leeches before as they've never been that common." Jeb leaned forward. "We rehabilitate some, but many of them die. But I've never seen any information on what the ones who survive have in common, if anything."

He made a note. That would be a good thing to follow up and see if there was any research on. He'd ask Cara to check the Anahata Healers' database, and he'd also see if Feng had any thoughts.

"Tierra had some symptoms before she got to the island, but we're not sure when they started. And then we think that the fact that she was on the island with energetics with all six energies triggered a reaction in her, which then sparked the full blown illness. Whatever it is." Nixie paced up and down the small area, weaving in and out of the tables. She waved her hands around to illustrate her points as if she was lecturing. He was enjoying watching her. She was impressive.

She turned to him. "How does all that sound?"

"Good. Shall I summarize our research?" he asked, needing to contribute.

She nodded and perched on the edge of a table, the tiny skirt she wore sliding up her legs to show off an expanse of smooth tan thigh. He raised his gaze firmly up to her face.

"We've found a small number of cases where energetics have shared energy, and have been triggered by being surrounded by all the energies into whatever this illness is. Once triggered, they have – admittedly unstable – access to all the energies, unlike every other energetic alive, who only has access to a dominant and an auxiliary. And finally, we haven't found any cases where the energetic has survived unless they were a Maven." He stopped. That didn't seem like much when he put it like that.

"And then there's the name Iskander, which Cuinn also thinks is important," said Nixie.

"Yes. And also the archetypes. Cuinn thinks that snippet of the prophecy means each of the energies will be represented – Muladhara is the Protector, Svadisthana is the Creator, Manipura is the Warrior, Anahata is the Healer, Vishudha is the Communicator –"

"– and Ajna is the Sage, I know, I know."

He eyed her. He could be considered a Healer, he supposed. As could Cara. What would that make Nixie? A Creator. Again, it fit. But what could a Creator contribute to a fight? Then again, what could a Healer?

Nixie had jumped down from the table and was pacing again. "What can it be like to have access to all the energies? It must be overwhelming. How could you learn to control so many different aspects of power?"

"We don't know that anyone has. It's an anomaly, that's all. I agree, it's too much power for one person," Jeb said.

She turned on him. "But you think even two energies is too much for some people."

He gave her a sad smile. "For me, Nixie. Just for me."

18

Nixie glared at Jeb. "Why are you like this? How can you bear to close off such a big part of you?"

"I told you why." He turned another page in the text he was examining.

"Sure. You betrayed a woman. Yada yada. It was during the war, and you were working for a greater good. Your use of influence was accidental, and in quite a pressured situation." Nixie had been talking to Feng, and he'd confided in her that what Jeb was doing to his energy was almost always damaging for the individual. Nixie got up and once again prowled around the room. She was restless.

He stared at her, his face neutral. "It was more than a simple mistake, Nixie. It got innocent people killed."

"But that was never your intention." She was stomping rather than prowling now. "What kind of hubris does it take for you to believe that you're such a big deal?"

He started. "Hubris?"

"Yeah, hubris. It's arrogant to believe you're so important that you need to shut part of who you are away. Didn't you come from Source, like everyone else?"

A slight crease was forming on that poker face. Good. Maybe she was getting through to him. Finally.

"Who are you to believe that Source made a mistake? Why would you have access to Svadisthana if you weren't meant to use it?" She slammed her palms down on the table in front of him to emphasize her point, bending a little at the waist. Her cultured Thai mother would have a heart attack if she saw her now. Nixie was definitely channeling her Gaelic father's temper. "And what's wrong with Svadisthana, anyway? Or the energetics who have it? And actually use it?"

He put his hands over hers, and his covered hers completely. She looked down. He had strong hands, with long, nimble fingers. Good in a Healer; better in a lover. She shivered, and felt her nipples harden very slightly through the thin cotton top she wore. She wasn't wearing a bra, because no need.

She raised her head again. He hadn't moved his hands. She brought her face closer to his, and peered into his eyes, her head tilted to the side very slightly. Her back arched.

Did he feel at home in the Guild? He seemed to. "How could you hide here for decades? Didn't you miss the outside world?"

His hands tightened on hers. "I didn't."

She persisted. "And now you've been outside? Seen the sea again? How do you feel now?"

"I…" He shook his head.

He was a puzzle, that's for sure. She licked her lips. Their faces were only a handful of inches away from each other.

"You were inches from the ocean. You made me orgasm in a storm, dammit! Sexual contact surrounded by water and air, both your elements! You must be made of stone to be able to keep your control and your shields going through that kind of stimulation." She made a "pah" of disgust, and began to stand.

His fingers convulsed over hers, and she nearly lost her balance when he stopped her pulling away.

Jeb's control broke.

He cuffed both her wrists in one of his hands, put the other hand on her neck and drew her mouth to his. He did it before he'd even realized himself what he was going to do. He just knew he needed to do something. All that talk of wetness had pushed him over the edge.

The speed he'd moved at meant she gave a surprised 'ouf', and her lips stayed closed for a moment, her eyes wide, before she realized what was happening. But when she did, she gave a satisfied hum against his mouth, and returned his kiss enthusiastically.

After a few moments, she drew back for a second to look into his eyes. "Well, finally."

He growled, and pulled her back to him. She came willingly, and gave a nimble hop over the table in front of him to land in his lap. He slid a hand underneath her to cup her backside, and massaged the firm flesh there. His groin ached with need.

She skimmed her hands over his shoulders and down his upper arms, before threading her fingers through his hair. His skin felt ultra-sensitive to her touch. Or perhaps it was that it had been so long since he'd let himself enjoy a woman touching him like this.

After spending time with her, watching her, he knew she wasn't the one who had influenced him. There was no sign of the thick feeling in the air that had affected him in Thailand. Here the air around them was cool from the air conditioning, but his head also felt clear. And he had warded his shields to warn him if any trace of that energy hit him again.

He checked in. No sign. This was all him. He needed to show Nixie, who he knew he hadn't treated especially well, that he was a generous lover both in giving and receiving. He wouldn't lose control. Didn't need to. He knew he was flirting with danger, but he had confidence he could do this. He would need to tell her about the influence soon, but now wasn't the time.

He stood and took her with him. She wrapped her legs easily around his waist, adapting to their change in position. He held her in place with one hand still underneath her butt, while he walked them both over to a table that was clear of texts that were hundreds of years old. He would have her, but even in this madness, he wasn't going to have sex on texts that Feng considered priceless.

The thought of Feng gave him pause for a second, and his lips stopped moving against Nixie's. She broke their kiss, but kept a hand on the back of his head. "What? Really. Don't stop now. For Source's sake. You need this – I need this."

"I'm not stopping," he said. He pushed thoughts of anyone but Nixie firmly from his mind, and put a finger against her mouth. Her tongue darted out, and she licked the length of it.

He groaned, and pulled it away to lay her body on the table in front of him. Her legs dangled off the side. He stepped between them and hooked his fingers into her underwear and pulled it down her legs. He pushed the little skirt she wore up, and she was naked from the waist down in a moment.

He squatted and put his hands on her inner thighs and pushed slightly, enjoying the resistance as he opened her up wider. He brought his mouth to her sex and blew a little. She quivered in front of him. He breathed in the fresh smell of her, and licked along her soft folds. Her hands came to his head and massaged his scalp.

He found her clit and sucked lightly, and she gasped. He licked with a combination of zeal and finesse, and her hands convulsed in his hair, pulling him in tighter.

There was a sexual charge in the air, but he was determined to keep his Svadisthana energy reined in. He would use it – it would be almost impossible not to if he was having willing sex with another of the same energy – but he wouldn't completely let go of control. It would take finesse and some restraint, but he could do it. He would walk that line for her.

He danced his tongue along and inside her, until he focused almost entirely on that sensitive nub of flesh, taking long, slow, rhythmic licks. He paused for a moment to adjust his pants, and her hands clenched in his hair. He laughed softly into her sex. He was glad she was enjoying herself.

He was as hard as iron, his dick aching, but he was determined to bring her pleasure with his mouth. It wasn't a hardship, after all. She tasted … wonderful. Slightly more comfortable, he resumed his activity, and ran one hand up her torso, under her top, to stroke across her breasts and belly. He'd noticed her erect nipples earlier, though he'd tried to ignore them. She had tiny and perfect breasts that he could cup in a hand. The nipples puckered again as he ran his palm lightly over them.

He put his hand up to her mouth, and brushed his fingers over her lips. She nipped at his fingers, and he thrust one inside her mouth. She sucked on it hard, and he moved it in and out of her mouth in time with the movement of his tongue on her clit. She moaned.

He throbbed in his now uncomfortably tight pants.

He pulled a little Svadisthana energy, and drew his finger reluctantly out of her mouth. He wanted her to come, but he also wanted it to be memorable. He put his left hand on her belly, and stroked along her velvet folds with the fingers of his right hand. He made the strokes of his tongue a little faster, and she writhed underneath him.

Faster still.

Soon.

He lined up his first two fingers at her entrance, and then at the same time, he flooded her system with Svadisthana energy and thrust those two fingers inside her. She arched up on the table, her hands clamping his head so his mouth was pinned to her sex, and she came long and hard. He kept the energy circulating, and continued to thrust his fingers in and out in forceful strokes, whilst his tongue lapped at her clit. She throbbed and pulsed around his fingers.

After several long moments, her grip on his head relaxed, and he slid up her body to kiss her. She returned his kiss enthusiastically, and her taste was in both their mouths. She reached down to his pants to undo them, and, freed, he guided himself into her. He gasped at the hot silken sheath that surrounded him, and had to pause for a moment, his arms locked in a push up position over her, to remind himself to take it easy. He was not a boy of scant years' experience.

He began to move, gliding in and out of her as she bucked her hips to encourage him. She put her arms around his neck, and pulled him down to kiss her again as she wrapped her legs around his hips, her heels digging into his buttocks.

She broke the kiss and her head dropped backwards, and he took the opportunity to kiss her neck. She was clinging to him, only her butt and lower back on the table, and his thrusts had speeded up.

The tiniest hint of Svadisthana energy came from her, a trickle, as if her entire body had become a low level pleasure emitter. He growled, and put one arm around her back to hold her in position so he could go deeper. She let out a cry on the next thrust, and it pushed him over the edge.

His shields cracked, and orange flashes of Svadisthana sparked from him as his whole body tensed, and he came inside her with his own rough cry.

After several more hard thrusts, he squeezed her body tight, then lay her carefully down on the table. He opened his eyes, and swore.

"What?" she said sleepily, stretching like a cat with him still inside her, clearly luxuriating in the energy she'd absorbed from him.

"The energy!" He was batting at the sparks that they'd given off that had turned into water and now covered the table around them, despite leaving them in a dry circle.

Nixie turned her head to the side and bit her lip. "Oh, shit. Feng's going to be really mad."

19

The next morning Jeb got up early to swim in the Guild's pool. He ploughed up and down the length of the warm water, the pool at its best early in the day before the heat kicked in. The small, artificial body of water had been a saving grace while living here, as it didn't have the same effect as natural bodies of water.

The night before he'd asked Nixie if she wanted to come back to his rooms to stay there with him, but to his relief she'd refused. He wasn't sure why she hadn't wanted to, but on his part it was guilt that he hadn't told her about the energy that had influenced them in Thailand. He would discuss it with her this morning.

He swam faster, cutting through the water with a smooth front crawl that ate up the meters. It wasn't the same as the sea, it was true, but there was a peace in the clear blue water that he didn't find in many places.

His Svadisthana energy was escaping, and he couldn't bear the idea of going back to Aiko so quickly to rebind it. He was starting to wonder if she was right. Should he loosen the ties that kept it contained? He felt healthier since the night before, which was strange, and unexpected. He sped through the pool and did another length, diving under the water to rebound off the wall at the other end in a fluid turn.

Perhaps he could have his energy be dormant, rather than locked. Though that wasn't realistic. He was a Master energetic in Svadisthana, which had been part of the problem all along. He was powerful, and had too much energy to pretend it didn't exist. It either had to be locked up or used. There was no in-between.

But if he was going to open himself up again, he would need to have regular sex. Nixie last night had taken in some of the energy that he had leaked and made it safe as part of their sexual activity. Being with another Svadisthana energetic was a powerful experience, though he had kept his energy under control as much as he could. Of all the energetics to start having sex with, a Svadisthana was certainly the safest.

Now he had allowed himself to think about sex again, his body and his mind remembered how much he enjoyed it. Another dive under the water and another flip as he swam another length. The exercise distracted his body's attention away from exactly how much he enjoyed it, if not his mind.

And then there was Nixie. Had the sex with her been so wonderful because she was the first in decades? Or was it the influence of the energy that had ignited their sexual encounter in Thailand? Or was it her?

He didn't know. He ducked under the water again and as he came up for air he stood in the shallow end. He slicked his hair back from his face so he could see, and lounged against the side of the pool, his back to the concrete, leaning back on his elbows. Jeb's energy meant that emotions were usually an open book to him. Others' and his own.

But when it came to Nixie, he felt cloudy. As if the radar that usually meant he could pick out emotions was broken. Off.

Her emotions came through, sometimes. But not always. He'd been surprised, for example, by how much he'd appreciated her optimism the day before in the library. Sometimes she wore her emotions on her sleeve, and sometimes they were a puzzle to him.

He just wasn't sure how safe it would be to solve that puzzle.

Nixie ran along the corridors of Anahata to find Jeb. After much searching, she'd been told he was probably swimming.

She pelted towards the pool. She stumbled through the doors that led to the bright blues of the water and sky, and saw him at one end of the blue rectangle. His skin was pale – much paler than hers – but his shoulders were broader than they looked when he was wearing clothes. His hair was pushed back from his face, showing off the sharp angles of his cheek bones. There was something fragile and angelic in his handsome face.

Drops of water on his eyelashes drew her eyes to his, and finally she realized that the smoldering gaze from the second picture she had drawn had come to life. She felt a pulse between her legs and skidded to a stop, then slipped on the water on the tiles that surrounded the pool, and had to wave her arms frantically to prevent herself from falling in.

"Shit!" she said.

He was standing in the pool, but he didn't get out. She stood with her hands on her hips and looked down at him.

"Hi," he said. "Everything okay?"

She was distracted by how handsome he was for a moment, until she remembered the reason she'd come to see him. "No. Everything's not okay."

He tilted his head slightly. "What's happened?"

"Blaize called. It's Tierra. It's bad."

His eyebrows went up, and he turned away from her to heave himself out of the water, his hands on the side. Muscles corded in his upper arms.

He walked over to her, and she watched water stream down his body to pool on the floor at his feet. She really, really wanted to touch. But now was not the time.

"Tell me what she said," he asked. His voice was gentle, but there was an urgency in his tone, and the sexuality that she'd seen in his eyes had been shut down. She felt a pang of loss.

"Tierra's unconscious, and they can't wake her. Fintan's best guess is that something is draining some of Tierra's energy. They've warded her, but they can't work out how – or where – the energy's going."

Jeb walked towards the locker room. When she made no move to follow him, he beckoned her. "Come, talk while I get dressed."

That sounded like a very distracting idea indeed. She'd have to keep her eyes closed.

She followed him into the men's changing rooms, empty at this time of day. He went directly to the shower, where he turned on the water and stripped off his shorts. Nixie's eyes widened before she turned away. Yep, distracting.

"That's new information," said Jeb.

"What?" said Nixie. Her voice echoed in the changing room, bouncing off the tiles. She could hear the tap of his wet feet on the floor and him rubbing soap on his skin. She imagined her own hands helping and then shook her head.

"That she's being drained. That suggests there is something out there which is making this happen. Or at least taking advantage of it. Which tells us a lot."

"It does?" said Nixie.

"Yes. The fact that someone else knows enough to take advantage of it means that someone else is likely to know how to fix it. Given that Elrian is leeching from other energetics, and someone is trying to drain Tierra, it indicates he could be involved. He tried previously to hurt her, and failed."

"We don't know how she got away last time, do we?" Nixie asked.

"No. She was kidnapped, and then she turned up at Cathair Cuinn with massive memory loss." The noise of the shower shut off. "Can you throw me my towel?"

She opened one eye but continued to face away from him. "Where is it?"

"On the bench to your right."

She walked over to it and picked it up. The room had taken on a masculine scent of ozone and wood, and she shivered. She turned back to him and kept her eyes downwards. His feet – nice feet, for a man – came into view. She stuck a hand out with the towel.

A tug and she let go. *Is it safe to look yet?* She raised her eyes slowly, running her gaze from his feet up muscled calves with just enough hair, firm thighs, and then, thankfully, the blue towel around his waist. The planes of his stomach were clearly outlined, and she moved her gaze more quickly up to his face.

He was watching with an amused smile. "I won't ask if you like what you see, because I think we're beyond that. I didn't expect you to be shy."

She flushed. "I'm not shy. At all. But sometimes my priorities get muddled. Tierra's our focus now, and we still don't know how to help her."

The laughter lines in his face fell away. "I know. No, we don't, but every piece of information helps us. I can cross reference what we've already found with information on leeching and energy drainage. It gives us more pieces of the puzzle."

Nixie nodded, then bit her lip. "Yes. But Jeb, Blaize said that Tierra might only have days left."

Nixie didn't add how guilty she felt that they'd been having sex while Tierra got more and more ill. Nixie started. Did that mean each time they had had sex, something bad had happened to Tierra? She ran her hands up and down her upper arms. That was a crazy thought, right? Her sex with Jeb couldn't affect Tierra on another continent? That was ridiculous, right? Yet she wanted to be told it was okay, and that her focus on her own needs hadn't hurt Tierra.

"We'll have to work harder today. We both needed the break last night. I believe you were at the throwing-ancient-texts-around stage." Jeb replied as he used a second towel to dry himself off, thoroughly rubbing his hair and patting odd droplets of water from his arms. "So I'm clear, what you're saying is that Fintan thinks Tierra is being attacked psychically, and he and the others are putting energetic shields round her, but her energy's still being siphoned off. Right?"

He pulled on his clothes, which had been folded in a pile on the bench between them. His outfit included one of the casual baggy sweaters he tended to wear in the air conditioned parts of the Guild, and something in her chest squeezed at the sight. It was so ... so him.

She nodded. "Heka is on his way back. He was only in Malaysia, working with some energetics there."

Fully clothed, he strode towards the door. When she didn't immediately follow, still trying to process everything going on, he turned.

He smiled, but she could see the strain in his eyes. "Come on. We have a puzzle to solve."

Nixie hurried along the corridor after Jeb to the archives. He seemed more relaxed than yesterday, which she was glad about. And last night had been good, really good, and he'd retained some of the control he wanted to. They seemed to be finding a way to satisfy them both, for the moment. His personal wards had fractured, but not shattered, and she'd managed to absorb some of his escaped energy as part of the natural Svadisthana sex process. Which was lucky, because Feng would have been heartbroken if they'd flooded his archives, and she'd come to be quite fond of him.

But damn.

Jeb's wrists were still bare.

Her heart shrank a little as she thought about it. She'd been making more of an effort to connect with Jeb. She'd found she was genuinely interested in what he thought about things, and wanted to share her own deeper thoughts and ideas in a way that was new to her with a man. She'd always saved that sort of emotional intimacy for Blaize.

Did he not have a bracelet because he was still suppressing his energy? Or did she get her drawing wrong, somehow, and he wasn't in the prophecy at all? Or was it Blaize's image that was wrong, and he wasn't one of the twelve, but more tangentially related? Or – and to her surprise, this one hurt her heart the most – was he going to be part of a couple with another woman? Perhaps his bracelet would turn up once he met the right woman – but that wasn't her.

She tried to shake the mood off. It was just sex between them. And hey, if there was a man that was out there who was an even better match for her than Jeb, she was excited to meet him.

She followed Jeb into the archives, where he threaded his way between shelves.

She'd managed to remain friends with most of her lovers over the years. Most Svadisthana energetics did. She and Jeb would develop a friendship, a different kind of relationship, eventually, without this heavy sexuality between them. *Right?*

Or perhaps they had this whole thing wrong, and the prophecy's use of the word pair had been very deliberate, and there was no need for romantic couples. Maybe it was each pair of the Archetypes that the prophecy referred to.

And maybe she wasn't destined to meet any kind of soulmate soon.

Perhaps that was a relief. Her brow furrowed, uncertain as she was about the idea that if it wasn't to be Jeb, she'd rather have no one. That did not seem like her at all.

Jeb paused to turn back to her, studying her. Then he pinched the brow of his nose, massaging it. It was a cute action. "Huh."

"What are you doing?" she asked. He had turned back to a section and was studying the spines.

"Your comments made me think of something I read years ago. I'm going to try and find it. You carry on with the pile from yesterday."

Nixie stifled a groan. It was going to be another long day. Then she thought of Tierra, and rolled up her sleeves.

"I need to tell you something," said Jeb.

Nixie looked up from the text she was reading. She'd made some progress in the last couple of hours, but there were still many more to read. "What?"

Jeb hunched his shoulders. There was no good way to say this, but it had been on his mind all morning. He couldn't keep it in anymore. He had quite the knot of tension between his shoulder blades from thinking about it. "Aiko found traces of influence energy on me when I came back to the Guild."

Nixie's eyebrows shot up. "Influence energy? What do you mean? And to do what? Are you okay?"

His shoulders curved a little more. "Ah, around sex. She, er, thinks it happened on the island."

Light dawned in Nixie's eyes and her mouth dropped open. "You were influenced to have sex with me?"

He shrugged helplessly. "I don't know. Maybe. It was out of character for me."

Out of character then, certainly. The times since then? Out of the character he had been for the last half century, but perhaps more of a return to the person he had been for the rest of his life.

"Okay," Nixie said, slowly. "Then… you didn't want to have sex with me when you came to visit me on my balcony?"

She pushed her chair back from the table, putting space between them, face pale. "What about last night?"

"There hasn't been any influence energy since the island. Last night was all me."

"Why didn't you tell me?" She wrapped her arms around herself.

He knew he should have told her earlier. He had been selfish. His relationship with her, whatever it was, felt so fragile he hadn't wanted to damage it.

But he had.

"You didn't tell me, and you slept with me again last night anyway," she said. "Did you really sleep with me thinking I might use my energy in that way?"

Her cheeks were flushed, and he could see her skin pale where she dug her fingers into her arms.

"No, I didn't, I don't…that's not what I think," Jeb said. How could he explain it to her?

To himself?

She opened her mouth to retort, but before she could say anything, Feng hastened towards them. She snapped her mouth shut and glared at Jeb.

Feng glanced between them, confusion on his face. He took a step back. "I didn't mean to disturb you. Is all well?"

"It's fine," Jeb assured him, hurriedly. "We can finish this later. Tierra can't wait."

He regretted it a moment later when Feng said, "You need to go and see the Hermit."

Jeb wanted to groan. How could a day that had started out so pleasantly turn thunderous so quickly?

"We've had this discussion. I don't think there's a need," Jeb said.

"Oh. No. I mean, yes, we did. But now there is," Feng said, still looking between the two them as if he could taste their emotions on the air.

Nixie's eyes were still narrowed, but she'd cocked her head to the side.

"Who's the Hermit?" she asked. "Why don't we want to see him?"

"A very annoying Anahata energetic," Jeb replied.

"He can be irascible, it's true," Feng agreed. "But he can also be very useful, if the mood strikes him."

"Which is rare. Mostly he's an arse," Jeb said.

Nixie gave a surprised giggle which she quickly tried to hide. "What?"

Jeb sighed pointedly, but in his chest, his heart turned over. Perhaps, he thought, there was hope he hadn't destroyed things entirely. "I see you didn't get a proper British education."

"An arse is –" Feng stopped mid-helpful explanation as Jeb put a hand over his mouth.

"She knows."

Poor Feng. He looked really confused now. Jeb took pity on the man. "Why should we see him?"

"Well, there is the matter of the Rogues, of course. But in addition, this morning I found some of his notes with a text on remnant stones, which suggests at some point he was doing research into them. It's possible he may have discovered how they are made."

"We know how they are made. An energetic is killed for them," Jeb said.

"We know what they are made from, but not the ceremony or ritual, or what it takes," Feng corrected. "And his research was connected to some expertise he had around healing those who had been leeched from." Feng was almost hopping in place with excitement. "Plus, I remembered that many centuries ago, he used to teach on the darker side of energy healing. I really think he could be hugely helpful."

"How can there be a darker side of healing?" Nixie asked.

"Using Anahata magic to destroy inside the body, or to take, instead of to heal," Jeb said, face grim. Dammit. That was quite a good rationale to visit the Hermit, but by Source, he really didn't want to. Plus, he'd have to leave the Guild. "Hmm. That's actually given me an idea. What if there's more than one thing happening. What if the illness was triggered by the energy sharing, but someone is draining her as well?"

Nixie pursed her lips. "Wouldn't Fintan find them? He has everything warded, and he or Blaize are on constant guard. They're barely sleeping."

"It depends how powerful they are. Elrian doesn't have Anahata, but he may have an associate who does."

"You warded her, though, right? You protected her?" Nixie said. "From that, I mean."

"Yes. Yes I did." Jeb stared at the table. He'd thought he'd had something there, but perhaps not.

"Damir, then?" Feng said, politely.

Jeb groaned.

Nixie raised her eyes to his, defiant. "When do we go?"

20

Nixie wasn't entirely sure who they were going to see. She'd been so furious with Jeb about hiding the influencing energy issue from her, that as soon as she'd seen he didn't want to go, she hadn't been able to stop herself, despite the fact it would only be his second trip out of the Guild in seventy years. He seemed to be handling it okay so far, she thought. Not that she cared.

Alright, maybe she cared a bit. She snuck a glance at him. His hands gripped his thighs, but other than that there were no external signs of tension.

They'd taken a taxi, and she hoped her silence was frosty and dignified.

"I'm sorry I —" Jeb started, but Nixie cut across him.

"Why were you really so reluctant to go see this guy?" she asked. Let's see how he liked his motives being questioned.

"He's difficult, and quite unpredictable," Jeb said. "Unpleasant, crotchety, and not one who likes to share information. It's not going to be easy to get anything out of him."

Okay, this Hermit didn't sound a lot of fun. It was too late to back out now, however. Plus, the scenery was stunning. She hadn't been to the Middle East before, and was enjoying the washed out feel of the city, and the strange juxtaposition of old and new. This was a city that had seen a lot.

A horn blared, and Nixie winced as someone tried to overtake on a two lane road that already had four lanes of cars jockeying for position. She couldn't believe how many vehicles Egyptians could cram into a small space. Nixie was used to traffic flowing like water in Thailand. Sure, there weren't a lot of turn signals or warning given, but drivers rarely used their horns. That wasn't so much the case here.

It was a fascinating place. And the seat of the oldest known energetic Guild, as it had been the first to be refounded after their civilization had sunk to the bottom of the sea when Atlantis drowned.

Her attention flicked from point to point outside the car, drinking it in.

"This is such a different Egypt to mine," Jeb murmured.

"Hmmmm?" Nixie said, eyes trying to absorb everything she could. She couldn't even choose what she might paint, there was so much inspiration around her.

"When I sequestered myself in the Guild, British influence was still very strong. Now the British legacy is mainly in crumbling architecture."

"And looted artefacts," Nixie said absent-mindedly. Poor Egypt. So much heritage, stolen by other more 'civilized' countries.

"I am sorry," Jeb said quietly. "I should have told you earlier."

"It's alright," Nixie said. "You wouldn't be the first to sleep with me because of my outsides even though you had a problem with my insides."

Usually, she didn't mind, as long as the experience was enjoyable for both parties. Perhaps she kept a little more distance from men because of it, but here today was a good example of why letting her guard down, and entertaining the possibility of a deeper intimacy was a mistake.

There was a sharp intake of breath from Jeb. She turned, puzzled.

"That is not what happened," Jeb said. "Aiko spotted the traces of influence when I got back to the Guild. It's true I was a little uncertain at first, but it didn't last."

"So why didn't you mention it?" Why hide it from her? It affected her, too.

"You're the first woman I've been with in a long, long time, Nixie." He twisted in his seat and took one of her hands in both his. The air conditioning wasn't powerful in this old car, and his hands were warm. "I don't know what this is, but I wasn't ready to mess it up so quickly. And truly, I'm not sure I'm good for you. For anyone."

Okay, that was a good speech. A little of the ice inside her melted.

But only a little. She was going to take a bit more time than usual before she decided whether he was worth her letting it go. In the meantime, she should really find out what they were doing.

"Why did this guy leave the Guild?" she said. "Are there other energetics there? And where exactly is there?" Nixie said.

Jeb was aware of Egypt's progress while he'd been in the Guild. He had a television, and was an enthusiastic history and culture buff who was as happy to watch the odd documentary as he was to read a book. But the TV wasn't the same as the sights, smells and sounds of Egypt up close and in person.

In this modern age the streets were as busy as they had been in the past, but now it was cars that thronged the road rather than hawkers and market stalls.

"I'm not sure why he left, but he lives on his own," Jeb said. Which was unusual. Most energetics liked to live within easy reach of others of their race. "We're going to the Necropolis, the City of the Dead."

Sitting next to Nixie in the back of the dilapidated, dented car was surprisingly soothing, despite the fact she was clearly, and quite reasonably, angry with him. On his first trip out of the Guild the week before he'd been in a daze of stimulation, all his focus as he travelled through the city to the airport on holding in his energy. He hadn't left the airport in Bangkok, had flown through to a smaller airport where he'd taken the boat. And Koh Somdun was nothing like this teeming city.

"Seriously?" Nixie said. "What is it?"

Once, Cairo had been a rich center of culture, a modern metropolis. Now, while still one of the biggest cities in the Islamic world, it felt like a faded grande dame, its revolutions and instability damaging its place on the global stage. There were fewer tourists on the streets than he had expected, and buildings and cars tended to be older and more worn.

He mourned a little for the city he had given up by isolating himself in the Guild. He had blinded himself to how insular he had become, his attention centered on his energy and the mistakes he had made in the past. He hadn't considered having a future – had felt that causing Lucie's death, and the death of the many innocents, had also been a type of death for him.

"It's a giant cemetery that dates back thirteen or fourteen hundred years," he said.

Was he ready for that to change? Being out of the Guild was uncomfortable, but he was managing so far. Was Nixie helping, or could she hinder him given her propensity to impulsiveness?

"He lives there?" Nixie said, eyebrows inquisitive. She had pretty eyebrows. Very fine and dark.

"Over half a million people do," Jeb said. So he understood, anyway. When he'd been active and out of the Guild, it hadn't been nearly that many, but migration into the city, an earthquake and poverty had increased the population greatly. "Many people live in family tombs, but I understand these days there's a medical centre, post office and even some apartment blocks.

Damir lives in a large mausoleum, but Feng says he still keeps it in pristine condition."

"Okay. That's … different," Nixie said. "Um … who does it belong to?"

Jeb grimaced. "His human wife. She died a very long time ago. He never got over it."

"I can't decide if that's incredibly romantic or incredibly ghoulish." Nixie's face was hard to read. She shivered. "I really hope this guy can help. He sounds quite the character."

"He's hugely experienced. Feng's right. I just wish he wasn't, because it's never pleasant. But when his information's relevant, it's invaluable."

It took a while longer, but eventually their car dropped them off, and they picked their way through the dusty, dirty streets to the Hermit's house. They passed plenty of washing hung on lines, some goats, and a cluster of old men watching two even older men play dominoes on an upended plastic crate with a board laid on top. Jeb was impressed Nixie didn't comment on the filth and garbage they had to walk through to get to the house, a small, single story rectangle of grey, though not crumbling to quite the extent of some of its neighbors.

At the door, Jeb went to knock, though no one locked their door in this area as few had anything worth stealing. Anything that the Hermit did have would be under a magical lock and key that wasn't going to be something a casual thief could find, let alone steal.

As he touched the door, he knew something was very wrong. It wasn't the fact that it drifted open, but the flash of violence he got from the object. Someone had forced their way in here recently.

"Stay here," he said to Nixie, and slid in through the door. It had been a long time since he had needed any combat or stealth skills, but they were there, dormant inside him.

He needn't have bothered. It was a one room building, and Jeb was able to take the whole room in at a glance. He swallowed.

It included a very dead Hermit slumped on the floor cushions, a bloody wound slashed across his neck.

Nixie was still too annoyed at Jeb to be left out, and had followed him in, albeit quietly. She was fascinated to meet a man who could so annoy the usually even-tempered Jeb. Plus, she wasn't keen to be left alone in a giant graveyard.

When Jeb stood stock-still a few steps into the room, she peered cautiously round him, puzzled, then let out a little cry. She ran over to the body on the floor, hoping she could help.

Jeb cried out a warning, but before she could react a man in a suit stepped out of the shadows next to a bookshelf, a grim look on his face, and threw something at her.

She lurched back, already off balance as she'd been going towards the man on the floor, and Jeb caught her arm before she fell. Before either of them could react further, the man, limping, vanished out of the back exit of the simple structure.

Nixie clutched Jeb, breathing hard. She was frozen in terror. She'd never seen a dead body before. And she was pretty sure that that was what was in front of her. At the same time, she'd been attacked. Breathe. She needed to breathe.

Adrenaline winged around her body like a pinball machine ball, her system on high alert. Jeb touched her cheek. "Nixie? Stay with me. I need to check the back exit, but I don't think there's anyone here anymore."

She gestured, vaguely, weakly. "Don't you — don't you need to follow that guy?"

Her stomach gave a squeeze as she said it, as the idea of him either leaving her, or her having to go with Jeb to fight materialized in her mind.

No. She could do it. "We should. We should follow him, c'mon."

But to her huge relief he shook his head, and moved catlike towards the back door and carefully checked outside. He stepped back in. "There's no one close, and we need to understand what happened here. I'll set up a warding in case he comes back."

He placed a hand either side of the doorframe, and to Nixie's eyes it shimmered. Then he went quickly to the body, which he examined, even checked for a pulse, using the wrist — which merely had a few drops of blood spatter on it — rather than the neck. Even Nixie, with no healing knowledge, could tell that no charms or healing magic were going to bring this man back.

"It is him? Damir? The Hermit?" Nixie stuttered.

"Yes. Can you look around?" Jeb said to her. "He's dead, I'm afraid. I need to call Aiko, and then I'll study the body a little more."

Yes. A task. She could do a task. She stood in place, her eyes flicking from the threadbare rug in front of the sofa to the sink unit and single plate in the drying rack, to the well-stocked bookshelves that filled one wall. The color seemed to have been drained from everything.

She registered a marble rectangle slab at one end of the room, close to the sofa. She gulped. It was a tomb. The space was clean, that was something. Her focus skated over Damir's body, refusing to acknowledge it for the moment.

"You can move, it's okay," Jeb said.

She realized her feet had been stuck to the floor, only her gaze moving. She stepped carefully to the bookcases which dominated the room's decor. Books were piled on books, neat, but over-stuffed onto the shelves. It was almost homely, if you didn't think about the idea that the inhabitant's dead wife's tomb was at the, um, heart of this home.

She tried to work out where the man had been standing, and what he could have been looking at. Some books had been pulled out and were on the floor. She snapped a few photos with her cell before bending down to look at the titles. None seemed immediately relevant, but she might not be the best judge.

She scanned the floor around her, before catching sight of a few loose pages of handwritten script that looked like they might have fallen from a folder or notebook. She squatted next to them, afraid to move them in case she damaged them. The writing was spidery and compact, and though in her panicked state she found it hard to focus on any one part, it seemed to be in several languages. She thought she could pick out some Cappotian, and perhaps some Latin, but much of it was incomprehensible to her. She reviewed the entire page she could see, and then, with a pen from her bag, poked that page to the side to review the second.

One word jumped out at her.

Iskander.

"You shouldn't have pushed him," Elrian snapped. He and Imogen were in his hotel room in Cairo. Sweat had soaked through his shirt, and it clung to his back and underarms in an unpleasant manner.

He flicked on the air conditioning and paced the room. *Damn heat.* A cold blast cut through the close air. Blood trickled down his lower leg from a nasty slash Elrian had taken from the Hermit before he had killed him. It had been a long time since Elrian had been the one doing the dirty work in this kind of situation.

She shrugged. "I didn't expect him to be prepared to die for the knowledge. It only shows how important it is. We'll find it somewhere else."

She had fled before Elrian, as soon as they'd heard voices outside. Elrian hadn't wanted to leave without gathering more information, and had stayed, hoping they wouldn't enter. Once they'd interrupted him, already weakened, and without Imogen, he'd escaped rather than engage, but he wasn't happy about it.

"The remnant stones are critical, we know that. But we need more information about what we do with them when we have them." Elrian ran a finger over his ring. He no longer took it off. There was a palpable absence when he did, and some … discomfort. There was no need to suffer that when all he had to do was leave it on.

"We know we need to create two stones for each Chakra, draining to death an energetic who is dominant in that energy," she said. She stood by the window, leaning against the wall, watching him rage. "You need to spend more time in the dreamscape, searching for the answer. Or send Cassidy. Did you talk with her?"

He jerked his head in the affirmative. "It's getting harder to find new information in the ether at the moment. There may be something more that needs to happen for me to be able to divine new prophecy shards."

Imogen frowned. "I'm counting on you in this area. Don't neglect it."

Elrian balled a hand into a fist, then released it and ran it through his hair. He was hot and agitated. The interaction with the old energetic had been unpleasant, and, frankly, much too close for comfort. He shouldn't have been a challenge for Elrian and the woman. They were far more powerful separately than the Hermit, let alone together.

"We should have stayed and fought those two idiots. I could have taken at least one of them out, I'm sure of it," he said.

"The warding that that old fool did as he died locked my Anahata. I couldn't have fought, and I couldn't take the chance they might recognize me and survive," Imogen said, her lips flattened in displeasure. "I still need to be in Anahata Guild. There's work to do there yet."

She was right. He knew it. But he had been so close. The next couple had appeared right there in front of him, and she had called him away. Given Elrian had a wound on his leg and was hardly in perfect shape, retreat had been wise, but … Source. He slammed a fist into the wall beside him.

"We were lucky I heard Feng talking to Aiko about him at lunch," said the woman. "At least we got his notes."

She gestured to the blood-spattered thick book stuffed with pieces of paper. "There should be something in here. You will need to begin reviewing it immediately. I can't take it back to the Guild, and I need to get back quickly because all hell will break loose once news of his death gets back there."

"Your power is unlocked again?" Elrian said in surprise.

She laughed scornfully. "Of course."

She tapped the blue-green jewel around her neck. "The kind of power I have in here is far superior to his. He was lucky, that's all."

In the end, Elrian thought, remembering the limp body falling to the floor, and the sticky, hot blood that had covered his hands, not really that lucky at all.

21

Nixie and Jeb were back in the Guild a few hours later. Aiko had taken charge of the problem, liaising with Muladhara Guild and their Protectors to clear the scene of the Hermit's many non-human artefacts and make it ready for the Egyptian police. She was trying to decide what kind of warning to put out to her people, and how to share the information with the other Guilds. This was going to get out soon enough. The Hermit was known by many, and the energetics, though spread across the globe, were a small community who loved gossip.

Jeb didn't envy Aiko. Politics and leadership wasn't something for which he'd ever had any desire himself, and this was a good example of why.

The Guild was in chaos. Clusters of energetics stood in the corridors and halls talking in hushed voices. Given the looks that he and Nixie got as they walked to her room, it seemed many knew that they had been involved.

He led her to the sofa and sat next to her, taking her hand. She had barely said a word on the journey home. He had been disturbed by the scene, of course, but he hadn't been shocked in the very visceral way that Nixie had been. It's not that he didn't have faith in people – be they energetics or humans – but that faith was tempered by the knowledge that both light and dark existed in the world. He had caused darkness. Could he do more if he released himself from his need for penance and restriction? Or would it create more damage? He sighed.

Nixie started at the noise. She'd been in her own world, her hand limp in his.

"I'm sorry you had to see that," Jeb said. He truly was. Nixie was all lightness. Not very serious, perhaps, but the world needed butterflies and rainbows as much as anything else. More, maybe.

She shrugged. "I guess I needed a wake-up call."

Jeb cocked his head. "Why?"

"I was enjoying the adventure a bit too much," she said.

"Finding joy in difficult moments isn't a weakness," Jeb said. "You saw a horrible, terrible thing today. You didn't deserve it."

He put a finger under her chin and lifted it so he looked into her eyes. Tears glistened at the corners. She reached out a hand and stroked his cheek. "Thank you for that. I'm not sure you're right, but thank you."

Jeb placed a gentle kiss on each tear.

"I saw the man's face. I can draw him," she said, as he pulled back.

"That could help us a lot," Jeb said. "It has to be connected to everything else. It's too strange he would be killed on the same day we went to see him otherwise."

He'd been turning it over in his mind. "He must have known something important. I wish we knew what."

Nixie had seen a new side to Jeb today. He'd taken charge in that horrible room. And this evening, it had hit home quite how senior he was in the Guild as he'd interacted with the other members. He certainly didn't hide his Anahata energy, that was for sure.

She will still a bit pissed at him that he'd kept the knowledge of the worrying influence energy from her. They needed to find out where it had come from. She was starting to realize that he was juggling politics and responsibility as well as his own feelings.

Right now, comfort was what she craved. He had been kind to her this evening, and she'd treasured that. Unusually, she didn't feel interested in sex, so she thought she ought to let him go back to his rooms. His kisses had been gentle, but it would be understandable if he was hoping they'd lead to more.

Likely they'd get back to that tomorrow.

She let herself touch him for another moment, and then pulled back. "I'm going to have a bath, I think. I need to let some of the adrenaline inside me subside."

"That sounds like a good idea. Do you want me to stick around?" He gave her hand a squeeze.

"I'm not feeling very sexual this evening," she admitted.

Jeb scratched a cheek. "That seems quite reasonable, given the day we've had. I meant, can I make you some tea, or chat to you from either inside or outside the door. Whatever you need to make you feel better."

Nixie stared at him. Her relationships with men tended to be focused on the physical. There were emotions, certainly, but they were the highs and lows of lust and love, not this sense of, well, intimacy that Jeb seemed to be offering.

She swallowed, overcome at the idea of him caring for her, caring about her, in that way. She wasn't sure exactly what to do with it.

"You're welcome to talk to me while I have a bath," she said.

He showered while she ran a bath, using bubbles she'd brought with her, and sunk into it. He wrapped himself in a towel and perched on the toilet seat, diagonally across from her. The water was warm and the scent of roses and vanilla permeated the air. Tension began to flow from her muscles.

Jeb asked her questions about herself, from her art to her guitar playing to her relationship with Blaize. Source, the man really paid attention. He pulled her out of the dark thoughts from the day with a feeling of normal conversation. At least, the kind of conversation that was normal for her to have with Blaize or her family. Not the sort of conversation she usually had with the men in her life.

His words were an anchor for her while she felt so ragged from the day's events, and her black thoughts tried to suck her down like a whirlpool. When she got out of the bath, he pulled a towel down and tucked it around her. And cradled her for a long moment.

"Will you hold me?" she said, from the protection of his embrace. "I know I shouldn't ask, that it's unfair. I want to feel safe." She looked down at the floor, and her bare toes. "I don't feel very safe."

He squeezed her tight. "Of course I will. And it's not unfair to communicate honestly what you want or need. I'm an adult. I can say no."

He scooped her up, and carried her to the bedroom, turning the lights off on the way so the moon was their only illumination. He laid her tenderly on the bed, then shuffled into place behind her so she was propped up on his chest. He stroked her hair and his masculine, fresh scent wrapped around her like a blanket.

"I'm not saying no, Nixie," he whispered into her hair. "I'll look after you tonight."

He traced up and down her arms, the touch sensual but not quite tipping into sexual. The touch soothed her. She wanted to give something back to him.

"Jeb?"

"Hmmm?" They were in more of a reclining position now, coasting towards sleep, and Jeb sounded like he, too, was relaxing. She was glad. His day had been as tough as hers. More. She'd seen him feel responsible for the death, heard him ask one of his team for a second opinion on how much earlier they would need to have been there to make a difference. She couldn't help with that.

"I've been thinking a lot about your wards, and your auxiliary energy."

Jeb tensed.

"No, hear me out," Nixie said. "You made a mistake, and you went too far. You put a limit on yourself while you learned how to deal with that mistake."

Jeb grunted. *Damn the man and his grunts.* She pressed on.

"But we only grow if we learn from our mistakes." She twisted in his arms, and rested her chin on his chest, looking up at him. "At this point, surely it's more of a punishment than a protection?"

His hands had stilled on her body, but he didn't tell her to be quiet, yet.

"I wonder if, perhaps, your shame prevents you being who Source created you to be, so that now you've caused yourself a different issue, where your energy has built inside you, stale and destructive, and it needs letting out in a way where you can manage the release healthily."

Another grunt. She ran a hand over his chest. Up close like this, the silvery light of the moon cast shadows that she could almost imagine as shallow valleys and hills. She'd paint them as a miniature fairytale landscape, watercolor brushstrokes a mix of fine and striking.

"When you're ready to release your energy fully, I'd be privileged to help you. And in the meantime, thank you for today," she said, laying her head back down on his chest.

She liked him a lot, just as he was. But it would be nice if he liked himself, too.

Nixie didn't sleep well. She couldn't get the scene they'd walked in on the day before out of her mind. She'd drawn the man as soon as she'd gotten up. It was Elrian, of course.

The body, the blood, the vivid fear inside her when Elrian had thrown what had turned out to simply be a book at her. She relived the moment over and over, until she'd considered going to one of the Healers in the Guild – and of course, there were many – to help her calm down some.

She could have asked Jeb, but for some reason that felt too intimate. She wasn't ready for him to realize quite how frightened she had been, and still was. She would keep her cowardice to herself, for now. He had been grounding for her last night, but they weren't in a relationship, he'd been clear about that. She couldn't rely on him in that way.

Today Jeb had invited her to attend one of his lectures. She'd asked about his day-to-day duties in the Guild, and he'd replied he'd been getting substitutes to fill in for his lectures the last week, but this current crisis meant both he and Aiko felt he should show his face to reassure the students.

Thankfully, Aiko seemed to have forgotten about Nixie for the moment.

She walked into the lecture room one minute before the lecture was due to begin. It wasn't huge, perhaps able to hold fifty students. Jeb had told her he expected it to be quite full today, given recent events, and he was right. There were no seats left by the time Nixie arrived, and she had to perch on a step near the back.

Jeb was already at the lectern, arranging papers and setting up some slides. He looked good; his stubble tidy, hair washed and brushed, wearing a grey shirt and khaki pants, with a loose navy woolen sweater over the top. The color that suited him well. She liked the look, and this version of him. She was beginning to understand that he was more than the sexy and the sorrowful she had drawn. He was a healer, and a spy, and a Maven, and a member of the Guild Leadership team. Not to mention a man who gave really good cuddles.

He began speaking at one minute past the hour, welcoming the students, and acknowledging the events of the day before, which were an open secret at this point. There was rustling in the room in response, but no one raised a hand to comment. Then he introduced the topic.

"Today, I'm going to discuss what happens when an energetic's energy twists. One way that we can tell this might happen from a medical-energetic standpoint, is through the lymphatic system."

Jeb used the computer to click through to a diagram of that system. "A couple of decades ago we realized that the Chakras have a strong energetic connection to the lymphatic system, despite the fact that in general the Chakra points in the body are not physically directly correlated to these areas. Research showed that the five hundred to six hundred lymph nodes in the body, and the waste products and cellular debris it transports and drains, change as an energetic's energy twists. Measuring this gives us a good understanding of how far along an energetic might be in terms of going full Rogue."

Nixie didn't follow much of the lecture for a while after that, as it went into more technical details. She watched Jeb's hands as he shared his information, and how he used them to emphasize points. There was a sense of musicality to it which she enjoyed, as well as his voice which she loved listening to, whatever he was saying. She began to sketch him while she watched and half-listened, feeling calmer than she had for a while.

The last part of the lecture was a case study. She wasn't sure, but she thought she picked up that Jeb had been part of the team that had discovered a way of diagnosing the connection between the Chakras, the lymphatic system, and energy twisting, though it was downplayed enough she wasn't sure. He'd certainly been one of the earliest to experiment with it.

"In this situation, an Anahata-Svadisthana woman came to me to get help for her husband, a Manipura-Svadisthana energetic, who was having jealousy issues. She could see there was something wrong, and wanted a more precise way to know when to use Anahata to soothe him, so she wasn't influencing him without cause. We'd been working on the diagnostic and I was able to share the methodology with her." Jeb then described more technical detail on how they did this, and Nixie could see pens scribbling notes all around the lecture hall. The ending of the story wasn't so happy, however.

"It worked well, until the time she went on her yearly retreat. She'd done what she could to steady him before she went away, but unfortunately he refused to see anyone else for similar treatment, and his jealousy exploded. He found her in her retreat, and killed them both."

Nixie sat up straight, shocked. That sounded horribly, terribly familiar.

Jeb had been aware of Nixie's presence in the lecture hall, and had tried to ignore his tendency to want to study her. He had made a conscious effort not to look at her, but his gaze was drawn to her repeatedly. It was as if she sparkled with an inner light.

His head was full to bursting right now. He'd had to block others' feelings temporarily, as his empathy energy teetered on overload. The politics of the Guild, the death of the Hermit, Tierra's illness, the research he desperately needed to do, the prophecy, all pressed on him tearing his attention in different directions when all he really wanted to do was put his head in Nixie's lap and rest. Despite the fact he was supposed to have been comforting her last night, she'd been something he, too, had desperately needed. That sense of connection and intimacy in the dark had created a bubble around the two of them. The content of her words he couldn't deal with alongside everything else, but her voice had been pacifying.

Today, however, he needed to manage his attention better. At the end of the lecture, when the students had gone and he was packing his things, she walked over to him. He couldn't decipher the look on her face. She seemed paler than usual, and there were taut lines on her forehead, while her lips pressed together so they seemed almost bloodless.

"Are you alright?" he asked. Had something in the lecture bothered her?

She nodded. "The case study you talked about today, who was it?"

He shook his head to clear it, uncertain of what she was talking about. She seemed very different from the woman he'd left that morning. He rubbed his forehead, pressure building in his temples. Why would she ask about that?

"I try to keep the case studies anonymous," he said. It was part of Anahata's promise to its patients, and it didn't add anything for his students to know the people. It wasn't relevant.

"Was it Aria McCarthy and Aden Blackfire?" Nixie said. She clutched a sketch pad tightly to her chest.

How did she know that? She should have been a child when the incident happened. Although he supposed it was relatively well known in some circles. "It's not really appropriate for me to confirm or deny that."

"It was a long time ago, and you said they're both dead, so how can it hurt?" Nixie said.

"I can't tell you," Jeb said. Though she was right, they were dead, so his duty of care wasn't the same as when they had been alive. Why was she so focused on this? She must know he wouldn't usually give that kind of information out. Her pressing for this right now was too much. His head throbbed, pain blossoming and spreading. He squeezed his eyes tight, trying to clear it, then blinked them open again.

"I want to know more about what happened. It's them, right?" she said.

Perhaps if he confirmed that, she'd drop it? He needed a break. He needed to rest. If he didn't take some time to ground himself, he'd struggle to hold his Svadisthana in check. He was worn out from the energy it needed from him. He was confused about why she was prying about this, it wasn't her business, and it was a strange side of her to see. His role in that episode hadn't made him particularly proud.

He packed up the last of his things and straightened. "Yes, it was them. Now I need to go to my office."

He gave her a nod, then walked out of the room – while longing to be back with her in that bubble in the dark, no matter what uncomfortable ideas she might plant in his brain.

22

Nixie stormed to the library. She didn't understand why Jeb had been so patronizing. There was a big hole in her family history that he could potentially fill, and he was refusing to. He had no right.

Obviously, she hadn't actually told him, or reminded him, rather, that they were her aunt and uncle. She'd thought he'd make the connection himself, and when he hadn't, she'd decided to leave it. Though on reflection, she wasn't sure quite why. Was she annoyed he wasn't interested in her enough to know?

She didn't have many connections in this Guild, but the one she did have knew Jeb quite well. And she and Feng had got on well so far, as the fussy, precise man was also kind and helpful.

She found him in the stacks, still researching the Tierra issues. He smiled in welcome, and she launched in.

"In Jeb's lecture just now, he mentioned helping Aria McCarthy and Aden Blackfire. Do you know what he did?"

Feng blinked. "Yes, I do."

Finally, Nixie thought. Answers. "Okay. Can you tell me? He said something about a diagnostic tool that he used."

"He didn't just use it, he invented it," Feng said. "And it has saved lives. The Anahata Rehabilitation Centers use it now to monitor the Rogues they are rehabilitating."

Huh. Jeb had never mentioned that. That seemed like a big deal. She'd seen he was important in the Guild, but that kind of contribution seemed like something her friends, or those she'd met in the Guild, might have mentioned.

"What happened with Aria and Aden?" Nixie said. Her stomach hurt thinking about the aunt and uncle she had only known as a small child. Aria had been loving and kind, coincidentally with the same energies as Jeb, but with full access to both. With hindsight Nixie could see she had been a very sexy woman, but at the time it had been sitting on her lap reading together, with the little Blaize in one of her arms and Nixie in the other, that made the most impression on Nixie. Aria had also been quite happy to play hide and seek with the children, either in Thailand or in Europe where her family was based.

Aden had been a more difficult man. It had been a prophecy, as far as Nixie knew, that had sown the initial seeds of jealousy that had eventually turned him into a Rogue. They had been told if they married, their union would cause both great good and great harm in the world, and a man would come between them.

"Aden was suffering, his energy flaring and twisting because of his jealousy. He lost control several times, though didn't slide into being a Rogue. Aria was worried he might be a danger to their daughter. As a healer she consulted Jeb for help. He taught her how to use the diagnostic, and use her energy, with Aden's permission, of course, to soothe him." Feng had a faraway look in his eyes. "She would come to the Guild to see Jeb, because he wouldn't leave even then, and they would spend intensive time together. What she was doing wasn't easy, especially because it was her lover she was trying to save."

He continued. "Such a use of energy drained Aria, and Jeb became her physician as well as her teacher. He kept her going during that time, which in turn kept Aden going. He gave the family a few more years together."

"But Aden still died," Nixie said, flatly.

Feng nodded, his face drawn.

"It shouldn't have happened. Aria went on a yearly retreat of several weeks, which she had done for decades. She'd been the year before and Aden was fine, because they'd spent time beforehand preparing. They prepared as usual that year, and Aden even stayed at a Rehabilitation Center for the first couple of days, so that others could keep an eye on things." He sighed. "We don't know what happened. He checked himself out without permission, and something triggered him. And you know the rest."

She did. He'd killed himself and Aria, leaving Blaize to grow up an orphan and as Nixie's surrogate sister.

Nixie rubbed her forehead. It was puzzling, to say the least, to think of Jeb playing such a role in her personal history. He had gone to so much trouble to try and save a man with a lot of problems, and his actions had probably given Blaize more years with her mother and father than she might have had otherwise.

She hadn't seen Jeb as a mystery. She'd seen him as a distraction from her own problems. As a lover, without question. But the complex man she was uncovering, who juggled political issues, invented healing practices, and saved lives, was so much more. She wondered if he'd even got any recognition or credit for what he'd done with Aria and Aden. She doubted it. He was an introvert to her extrovert.

She glowered. It seemed that Jeb was not only hot, he was a hero.

And the damn man still didn't have a bracelet.

Sitting in his office, Jeb's eyes were gritty and he was exhausted from the parade of colleagues, students and others in the Guild who wanted to extract the gory details from him as to what had happened, what it meant, and what would happen next. The care with which he needed to handle which details he gave to who made his head hurt.

He hadn't enjoyed politics before, but this current incident had stirred the pot considerably in the Guild. Incident. Source, not incident. It was a tragic death. A murder. Sanitizing it by calling it an incident was falling into a politics mindset indeed. He rested his elbows on the desk, and put his head in his hands.

He hadn't seen Nixie since after the lecture. He knew he'd been short with her, but the pressure was getting to him. He should go and talk to her. Taking her in his arms at this moment was quite the desirable goal. He needed to be careful, though. He was feeding more and more energy into his shields yet they still seemed to be weakening. He had managed to hold them through the times he and Nixie had been intimate so far, but if the trend continued, he wasn't sure what might happen. He'd injured enough people already.

He still didn't know what to think of the Hermit's death. Harrowing, certainly. But why had he been killed? And why now? The pages that Nixie had found were from some kind of notebook, presumably the Hermit's, and the variety of languages Damir had used so far also included modern Arabic, ancient Aramaic and Vietnamese, of all things. The pages were being translated as quickly as possible to see if they contained anything useful. Jeb really wished they had the rest of the pages, or the notebook that they came from. Who knows what the murderer of the Hermit had taken from the scene?

His door was pushed open without warning and he snapped his head up, shaking it to try and clear it. He felt muggy, and his brain was slow. Ah, Source. It was Maya.

"Jebediah," she said. She looked crisp in a white pant suit and matching blue jewelery. He felt creased and grubby next to her, the clothes he'd lectured in now the worse for wear after the day he'd had.

"Hi. What do you need?" he asked. He kept his tone polite, as he felt they'd always got on in the past, no matter how difficult she seemed at times. She always seemed to be laughing at her own private internal jokes, usually, he thought, at the expense of others.

"I wanted to give you advance warning that you need to prepare the information on your students for the database," Maya said. "I'm letting all the staff know."

"Okay," Jeb said, though his heart sank at yet another task going on his list. He cocked his head as a thought struck him. "How's it progressing? Is this latest release nearly ready?"

"Yes," Maya said. "I have a guy auditing the beta release right now."

"Oh, yes," Jeb said. "The audit. It seems to be taking a while? Is there a problem?"

"Not at all," Maya said, as smooth as honey. "I find technology often takes longer than planned. The modern world's conveniences can also be its downfall."

Jeb shrugged his shoulders. "Sure. Email me a reminder and I'll have the information ready for when you need it."

"My thanks, as always, Jebediah," she said. "How are you feeling today?"

"Fine, thank you," Jeb said, politely. "Busy."

"Of course," Maya said. "I'll leave you."

He could feel his internal shields and wardings stretched thin, and the pressure was getting to him.

He needed rest. Alone.

23

After supper, as Nixie still hadn't seen Jeb she decided to visit him. She'd missed seeing him that day, and at random intervals she had been struck by visions of the murdered body of the Hermit. Several times she found her eyes welling up for no reason, and had had to excuse herself from Feng and the research she had been doing with him for a moment alone.

Jeb didn't seem thrilled to see her. There were dark circles under his eyes, and he ran a hand through his hair as he let her into his living space. The revelations from Feng made her see Jeb differently. There was so much more to him than she'd realized.

She sat at the table with him. The lights were gentle, a warm breeze drifting through the room. It was simple, yes, as living quarters went, but it was calming. Peaceful. His body language was cautious. She supposed their last interaction had been a little brusque considering how intimate they had been.

She didn't beat around the bush. She needed to clear up why she'd needed to know. "Aria and Aden were my aunt and uncle. They were Blaize's parents."

Jeb looked stricken. "Nixie, I'm sorry. I was so focused on Tierra, and drained from everything that happened, it didn't occur to me to make the connection. I've given that lecture a hundred times. I wouldn't have…"

She stopped him, flushing. She could have told him what they were to her earlier. It was on her as much as it was on him. "It's fine. Feng told me more. He says you gave them extra time together, that Aden could have turned Rogue earlier had it not been for your intervention and teachings for Aria."

It was his turn to redden. "I happened to be their healer. It was a good opportunity for the diagnostic to be field-tested, and Aria was a great student. I can't take credit there."

Hmm. He really wasn't feeling very Svadisthana. Apart from Manipura, they tended to be the energetics who were least bashful about their achievements. All those artists.

She was grateful to him for what he had done for her family, however much he played it down. She stroked his hands, which were clasped loosely on the table. He didn't pull back.

"Thank you for what you did." She locked gazes with him, and ran her hand up his arm. She wanted to wipe away the tired from his eyes. The last twenty four hours had been pretty shit all round, and they both deserved cheering up.

She stood and walked over to his music system, fiddling until she found some Bach. She wound her way back across to him, and drew him out of his seat by the hand. Words weren't useful now. It was time for touch.

She wrapped her arms around his waist and swayed against him as the music changed the tone of the room to something more intimate. Her head barely came up to his chest, but she liked hearing his heartbeat as she lay her ear against it.

He stroked a hand over her hair, and she tilted her head so she could look up at him. She sighed. She enjoyed the touch, smell and look of him. He bent to kiss her, a gentle touch of the lips, a brush of the tongue.

Not to mention the taste of him.

"Let's go to bed," she said.

He hesitated a moment, then leaned to scoop her up under her legs and around her waist. She giggled in delight. He walked them both to the bedroom, and laid her on the bed reverently.

They gazed at each other, drank each other in.

They luxuriated in each other's bodies, touching without a goal. He kissed her everywhere, and she eagerly did the same.

He made her come more than once with soft licks of the tongue, and the gentle pressure of his fingers.

When he put his cock inside her, it was a tight fit at first, and she had to breathe to relax and accommodate him. He took the on top position over her – a way of having sex she'd often thought quite boring, but the intense eye contact they made with each other that night made it anything but.

She trembled underneath him, and wrapped her legs around his waist. He took long, slow strokes in and out, building the pressure inside her slowly,

slowly, while she urged him on with her hips, but he was consistent, his pubic bone grinding against her clit each time he was fully inside her, and she was stimulated inside and out by his body.

He kissed her, his tongue sweeping inside her mouth as his cock did the same to her body. She wriggled underneath him, encouraging him, and moaned as his stubble rubbed against her face. Her ass cheeks clenched as she met his thrusts, and he increased the pace very slightly, driving her crazy with need. The man certainly had stamina.

It didn't take much longer before she felt that white heat between her legs. Orgasms were funny things, never the same thing twice, their final strength often difficult to predict from the way they were built. The hot ice grew inside her, his strokes kept going, until finally, finally, she crested the peak and exploded, the cold fire licking out from her core into the rest of her body.

He caught it happening, and sped up, letting go a little of his control — control that she was starting to see fade, thank Source. Moments after she came, he followed suit, burrowing his head into her neck and biting her shoulder as he did.

She saw stars on the inside of her eyelids, her orgasm prolonged by the delicious little bit of pain. He slumped, then rolled so she was on top, sprawled on his chest. She enjoyed the warmth of his body, the loose feeling inside her, the scent of sex around them, for a few minutes, then propped her elbows on his chest, and looked down at him.

"Ooof," he said. "You have sharp elbows."

She grinned. "Don't fall asleep yet."

He shook his head, eyes still shut, and drew himself out of her, nestling her onto the bed beside him. She was a perfect fit in his arms.

The sex they had that night wasn't the desperate passion they'd shared before. It was soft, gentle and connected.

She turned so she was on her back, and he on his side, one leg over her hip. "That was wonderful. But you can let go with me Jeb. I'll hold the space and keep your energies in check. You can't harm me. I'm stronger than I look."

He shook his head and slowly opened serious eyes. "I'm not ready, and anyway there's no need. I'm finding my balance with you. The place between control and release. If I keep back some energy, it's safer."

She waved her free hand, raised herself onto an elbow, and drew some Svadisthana energy, letting orange sparks leap up and down her arm. "I don't have the opportunity to use it much, but I'm a creator. I can create illusions and make fantasies come true."

She concentrated and pulled the energy through herself, and Jeb sucked in a breath. As far as she knew, he didn't have these energetic talents, despite his Svadisthana. She grinned. "Arabian princess?"

She concentrated again. "Or sexy librarian?"

Each time she created an illusion around her looks, so Jeb saw a version of her that fit the role she suggested.

Her smile faltered as he didn't look very enthusiastic. She didn't have much opportunity to practice these skills as most of the men she slept with were human, but she'd built up reasonable strengths in the area as part of her training. Her auxiliary energy helped with the illusion part.

He brushed some errant hair off her face, ignoring the illusion she had created of her wearing glasses. "Nixie, it's you I like. I don't need a fantasy. You're already enough of one of those. Do you have any idea how sexy you are?"

She glowed, and lay back down and nestled in his arms.

"Alright," she said.

Jeb watched Nixie doze in his arms, her fairy energy quieted for a change. She was usually all movement and action, chattering away to anyone they passed, though the Hermit's death had damaged that some.

He was a fool for not remembering that Blaize was the daughter in the case study from his lecture. He'd sleepwalked through the day, and the lecture had been one he'd repeated so many times over the years he hadn't thought about the content at all. Most of his mind had been on everything else that was happening.

Once again he'd held onto his control while having sex with Nixie, but his grip on it was tenuous. The strong shields he and Aiko had built were eroding, and he didn't know why. Was it Nixie? Was it simply exposure to this woman and everything she was that meant his body wanted to forego the protection he had put around it? At the same time, she felt like the safest person for him to be with – even as he cracked his shields around her, she took in his energy and cleansed it, the dangerous buildup inside him relieving slightly, the pressure diminishing.

The magic and energy in the Guild should protect him, but even that wasn't helping. He was having to invest time and energy in re-warding himself regularly through the day, and it was taking a toll on him. His whole body ached.

He put a gentle hand on Nixie's heart Chakra and felt her chest rise and fall. This woman was something, whatever else was happening.

Cuinn's prophecy surfaced in his mind. Both Jeb and Nixie were in it. Were they a pair? No. They couldn't be. They had no idea, really, how they might each be involved in the prophecy. Seeing energetics standing together had no real meaning without more interpretation, and he hadn't heard any of that from Cuinn or Blaize so far.

He ran a hand over Nixie's soft, straight hair, and her eyes opened. She sleepily stretched and then turned to hug him like a koala bear.

Should he continue this liaison? There was no real question. He shouldn't. His shields were weakening, and she was probably part of that, albeit not on purpose. She was encouraging him to use the energy he'd put away for good reason. And there were moments when he had certainly been tempted.

Being with her, feeling her Svadisthana energy, was like coming home. When she'd played with the illusions, not only had he been turned on despite just having come, but the feel of her energy had been sublime. He wanted to bathe in it. But that was a dangerous path.

He carefully disentangled himself from her grasp. "I need to go and check something with Aiko."

Her face fell, then stiffened into a mask. "It's late. Can't it wait till morning?"

"You can sleep here if you like. I might work through the night. I'm not helping enough with the Hermit investigation. The Guild's in chaos." He wanted to explain, but he knew if she tried to talk him out of it, while the room had the faint scent of sex in the air, and her lithe body lay there offering warmth and tenderness, he'd stay. That wouldn't be good for her, in the end.

She nodded, and shrugged. "See you later."

He needed to cool things off, at least until he'd worked out how to ensure his shields weren't draining as fast as he made them.

He glanced back as he dressed and exited his rooms. She lay in his bed, carnal and wicked, tan nude skin stark against his grey sheets. He wanted to run back inside and shut the door against the world.

Staying away from Nixie might not be as easy as he thought.

Cuinn's body lay on a mat in his work room in Cathair Cuinn, but his essence, his soul, was in the dreamscape. Cara was helping him with research while the others were away, was coming to see him for a couple of days here and there to slowly, patiently, fill in the gaps in the prophecy. Her no-nonsense attitude and driven nature were helpful.

They now had more information, and Nixie and Blaize had identified Jeb, a new member of the twelve, but there were still so many gaps. There were four faces missing, and several verses of the interesting Iskander document Nixie and Jeb had found were obscured.

And now Tierra was sick. She'd already been through so much. Fintan and Blaize had told Cuinn to concentrate on the prophecies rather than come to the island, but it was a hard burden to carry. Cara was a good friend and he was glad she was with him. She was close to Tierra, and worried sick.

Adam, Cuinn's cousin and Tierra's brother, was attempting to hunt the enemy here in the Pacific Northwest. As a Protector, he had skills in hunting and tracking, and he was looking into another case of leeching in the area which Fintan had found. Fintan had promised to let them both know if they needed to come to Thailand, but it seemed they could all do more from where they were. Though Adam, Cuinn and Cara were all questioning whether they should go to Thailand now. Recent reports from Blaize said Tierra was deteriorating. It was hard to know the best way to help her.

Cuinn walked out of his Haven, his safe place, in the dreamscape, into the wild energies. He wrestled with the taffy-like energies for a moment before shaping them into a place where he could open himself to the energy of prophecy. It was wearing, he'd admit. He'd done this so many times now. Sometimes information came, and sometimes nothing. But he had to hold back the wild energies each time, which wasn't easy. Only a Master level Ajna energetic could seek out prophecies like this. Other Ajna energetics could only receive what came to them.

He released the energies he'd gathered, and asked his question. *What happens now?*

His environment flickered and changed. He stood on a rock, looking out to sea. A beach was below him, with two figures who looked to be yelling at each other. A storm raged around them. They looked familiar. Were they part of the prophecy?

The smaller one gestured, and he realized it was Blaize's cousin, Nixie. He wracked his brains. If what Fintan and Blaize had told him about Nixie was correct, that might make the other figure Jebediah. Cuinn squinted. Yes. It was him.

The figures kept arguing. Cuinn could see that the man, Jebediah, was fighting an internal battle. Something was wrong with his energies. Very wrong.

The storm was right above them. Lightning cracked down like a whip. They needed to get off that beach. Cuinn resisted the urge to call down to them. This was just a potential projection of the future. Not only could he not do anything to save them, right now, there was no one to save.

The argument was reaching its peak at the same time as the storm was. If they didn't get off the beach, they were going to drown.

A huge wave was coming out of the sea. As the wave crashed over them, Nixie screamed, and the energies in Jeb exploded as he lost his final vestiges of control over his auxiliary energies.

They disappeared beneath the waves.

Blaize was on the phone, and wanted to talk to Nixie and Jeb together. Nixie had put her on speakerphone in the privacy of Jeb's study. Nixie had begun to find the books that surrounded them in there comforting rather than intimidating. Perhaps it was a form of Stockholm Syndrome.

Nixie felt a bit awkward because she'd told Blaize some of what had happened with Jeb, but nothing since she'd been at the Guild. She needed to catch her cousin up, but clearly, not right now.

Nixie sat in the chair at Jeb's desk, using a foot to push herself round in small circles. Jeb leaned against the wall. If he'd looked tired last night, now he looked shattered. His posture was slumped, the dark circles under his eyes were huge, and he could barely keep his eyes open. He must have stayed up all night. She'd gone back to her own room soon after he'd left. She hadn't slept well, but she'd done better than him.

Blaize cut to the chase. "Cuinn's received a prophecy which involves you both."

Nixie stopped, and her heart raced. Not more prophecies. She glanced down involuntarily at the silver bangle that she now never took off. "What? What was it?"

Blaize described the scene, the beach, the storm. "But it could be a metaphor. It doesn't have to happen exactly as shown. But there are two things Cuinn thinks. One is that you need to get off that beach if you ever find yourself in a similar position. And two, if you find yourselves in that situation, Jebediah needs to keep control of his energies. Cuinn thinks that given your energies, your loss of control powered the storm to rage as it did."

Nixie felt sick. Jebediah was never going to trust himself now. This was exactly what he'd been afraid of. She'd thought they were making progress — he'd opened himself up a little to his auxiliary energy, and had even used it during their lovemaking. He'd yet to use it outside the bedroom, but she'd been hopeful he might, if the opportunity presented itself.

"Nixie, we don't know what your role is here. Cuinn couldn't tell if your presence helped or hampered Jeb. Still, it's worth reminding you that prophecies are twisty," Blaize continued. "They give us hints about the future, but as I'm learning, they're a lot easier to interpret afterwards. Which doesn't really help us."

Blaize talked for a few moments more, giving them an update on Tierra's condition. Things weren't good. But Nixie and Jeb still hadn't found any answers that might help. They needed to do more, work harder, to bring something back to save Tierra.

When Blaize rang off, Nixie addressed the elephant in the room. "Using your energy again, slowly, will mean it doesn't build up so dangerously to create the problem Cuinn saw. It doesn't mean you should stop using Svadisthana again, but the opposite. You need to rebalance to be safe."

Jebediah had turned to look out the window. Nixie got up and went to him, putting a hand on his forearm, which hung loosely by his side. He put a hand over hers briefly, then moved away. The rejection hurt, but Nixie tried to hide it.

"I won't put you in danger Nixie. Or anyone else, ever again. If that means I need to go back to the way I was before, so be it. It's a small price to pay for the safety of those I love."

Jeb's heart was heavy, but Cuinn's prophecy was all he had needed to cement the decision he knew he should have made last night. Jeb should never have become involved with Nixie. He didn't deserve a relationship with her, and the call had shown him that his small attempts at happiness with her came at too high a cost. He had to let Nixie go, for her own good.

He circled his neck, trying to get a crick out.

"There's something between us. I'm not sure what, exactly, but something," Nixie put her hands on the desk and leaned forward urgently. "And it's worth exploring. Source tells us we are responsible for balance. That means within us, as much as within the world. This is an opportunity to heal."

"I've been playing with fire," Jeb said. "I need to strengthen my shields, and that means we can't be together sexually anymore."

He felt contemptible, but this wasn't about his feelings for her. This was about the danger he posed to others.

She walked around the desk and stood in front of him, hands on hips. She had to crane her neck to look him in the eye, but the force of her gaze almost made him take a step back.

"Haven't you felt better since we've been together? Hasn't your energy felt calmer?" she asked.

"Well, yes, but my shields are crumbling," he said.

"You've developed high levels of control since the War. There's no chance anymore of you influencing people by mistake. And if that's the case, the only problem is that your energy is building up inside you in a negative way, looking for a way out." She studied him. "But if your energy is in balance, you don't need the wardings, Jeb. Think about that."

It was tempting. Source knew it was tempting. He couldn't take that risk though, especially now with Tierra's illness, the prophecy, and everything that was going on. He needed to be in control of himself, and his energy, and to be able to function around others without the fear he was going to hurt them.

"I can't, Nixie. I'm so sorry. You have no idea how sorry," Jeb said, brokenly.

Nixie nodded slowly. "All right. I think you're wrong about this, and you still have a mistaken need to punish yourself, but I accept you feel the need for it and I'm not going to try and change your mind anymore."

Jeb felt a strange mix of relief and was that – regret?

She hadn't finished, however. "I'll help you with the research, and work on the prophecy, but once this thing is done, I can't see you again."

"Of – of course," he stumbled over the words, but she had already turned away from him.

She went out of the door without looking back.

He groaned, and went to sit at his desk. The faint scent of her hung in the air and he closed his eyes and breathed it in.

Was she right, and the only reason to keep his energy bound was because he felt he needed punishing? Or was he too dangerous to others to ever let his auxiliary energy free again? He had no idea.

In the meantime he had enough to occupy him. Tierra was still deteriorating, though at a slower rate. They needed to understand and reverse her condition as soon as possible given what the research had netted them so far.

And why had the Hermit been killed? Why now? He must have known something important, presumably connected to the prophecies. But he was ancient, and his store of knowledge was huge. They were assuming it was connected to the prophecies but they didn't have proof. The mention of

Iskander seemed important. But what other notes had been in that book? He needed to hurry the translation along, but part of it had been found by the linguists they were using to be in a kind of personal code of Damir's they had yet to work out.

It felt like there were a million open loops right now, and it was impossible to close them. And at the same time, he felt an ache in his chest.

At this rate, he'd have to put his heart back together as well as his shields.

25

Nixie, pacing her rooms, called Blaize and filled her in on what had happened. Nixie had managed to stay calm and mature in her engagement with Jeb, but she was a lot less chilled out now. Blaize listened and made sympathetic noises.

"The man's an idiot. An idiot!" Nixie said. She ground her teeth in frustration.

"It seems like he's trying to be responsible, Nix," Blaize soothed. "Cuinn's prophecy seemed to show a cataclysm of epic proportions if he releases his Svadisthana. You don't want to get caught up in that. Maybe after things have settled down you and he can try again with the balance thing you suggested."

Maybe. Nixie was missing the sea and wild open spaces. The Guild walls were pressing on her, and she hungered for freedom. She'd swum in the pool when she could, but it wasn't the same as the sea. "I feel like I'm going to explode into a million pieces. We're not making much progress here."

They talked about Tierra for a while and threw around various theories and ideas, mostly repeating themselves to see if anything new came up. It didn't.

"How does the bracelet thing work?" Nixie asked, trying for casual.

"What do you mean?" Blaize said.

"When you got yours, how long did it take for Cuinn's to appear?"

"They came at the same time, actually. But I think Tierra and Fintan's timing was different."

"Why?" Nixie said. She threw herself backwards on the bed, bounced once, and lay on her back.

"We don't really know," Blaize said. "We think they're from Source, but we don't understand much else about them."

She sighed. "There's really a lot we don't know right now. It's like we're drowning in questions."

Nixie shook her arm so the silver bangle slid up and stared down at her bracelet, thinking once again of Jeb's bare arms. Yeah, she knew about frustration.

She and Blaize chatted some more, then Nixie left her rooms. She needed some distraction from thoughts of Jeb which haunted her every moment.

She was full of pent up tension, and needed to do something with it. She'd checked out the Guild's training facilities, and seen they had a space for archery. It had been a while since she'd picked up a bow, but there was a point in her life when it had been one of her interests. She'd had a lot of those, she supposed. Definitely more of a jack-of-all-trades type.

She'd go to the range, and lose herself in the flow of firing arrows at a target. And she most definitely would not imagine anyone's face on that target. Nope. No matter how pissed off she was.

Jeb was back in the archives. The translation still wasn't complete, as they needed to find energetics he could trust who first recognized, then read, the various languages, some of which were dead, and some of which were in code. So far the parts Nixie had been able to read seemed to focus on some kind of tool, which was puzzling. She was poring over the Cappotian now, though it was apparently incredibly archaic, with many possible meanings. Her closest translation so far was 'tools of the conduit'.

In the meantime he was back on research.

It seemed strange that Nixie had only been in the Guild for a few days. It seemed like so much longer. He glanced across the table. She'd barely said a word to him. Feng, sensitive enough to pick up on the tension, had given Jeb an admonishing glance before being quite solicitous to Nixie's needs.

Jeb didn't like seeing Nixie upset either. Knowing he was the cause made it all the worse. There was an ache inside him despite knowing their relationship was both a distraction from what was important right now, and also hazardous to her and everyone else. He'd spent time meditating and working on his Svadisthana wardings that morning.

At one point, when Feng was off in the stacks, Jeb leaned over the desk to Nixie and said, "We can still be friends, you know. You don't have to stop talking to me."

She looked up and stared at him with such pain he almost recoiled. Without a word, she looked back down at the book she was consulting.

His heart squeezed.

They weren't getting far in the library. He leaned back in his chair and gazed at the ceiling above him. They needed a new angle, to find a different perspective.

Aiko walked up to their table and Jeb stood, surprised to see her. "Is all well?"

She nodded and sat in a seat close to him, her posture upright, her hands neatly on top of each other in her lap.

"Jebediah-san. My heart tells me you will at some point need to go back to see Tierra. If you truly wish to persist in holding your shields, you need to practice being outside the Guild."

Jeb's heart sank. Despite newly reinforced shields, and stamping down the sexual energy circulating between him and Nixie, he didn't feel ready. He opened his mouth to protest, but Aiko continued.

"I want Nixie to accompany you." Nixie, who had been studiously examining her text, snapped her head up. "She can help you to test your shields."

As both Nixie and Jeb opened their mouths to protest, Aiko held up her hand. "Carefully."

She left them. Jeb groaned. "Looks like we're going for a walk."

26

Despite her mixed emotions about spending time with Jeb, Nixie's feeling of being trapped had eased some by getting out of the Guild.

Given the attack on Damir, Jeb was alert to the possibility of being followed, and she, in turn, was alert to Jeb. She tried not to glance too often at him as they walked.

"We're going to stick to quiet areas," Jeb said. "In case of problems with my energy."

She nodded. There was a tension between them, and yet at the same time she was glad to be with him. She was also enjoying looking at the local shops they passed, even if the streets were dusty. There was more greenery than she'd expected, though she wasn't used to the dry heat.

"Are you ready for me to test your shields?" Nixie said, tentatively. She saw the muscles in his neck go taut, and there was a long pause.

Nixie was wondering what else to say when a woman in dark pants and a fitted polo neck, with a hijab drawn across her face stepped out from the shadows and swept a low leg at Jeb, who avoided falling, but staggered.

The woman was tall and slender, but strong, and clearly experienced in both hand to hand combat and energy fighting. Jeb regained his balance, and defended himself as the woman continued to attack.

After her experience at the Hermit's residence, Nixie had been reminding herself about her shields, and though there had been no use of energy as yet, she pulled on her own energy to create one. The woman seemed to see Jeb as the harder target, and while she wasn't wrong, it wouldn't do for her to underestimate Nixie, she thought grimly.

Jeb was holding his own for the moment, but Nixie wondered if the binding of his Svadisthana would hinder him. Surely he would be more effective with access to both his energies?

Nixie sought a source of water in order to draw on her creator magic. Why were there no fire hydrants? Her energies discovered a stone cistern, containing enough water to support her. She pulled Svadisthana through from the ether to create a bow and arrow. It took a great deal of energy to manifest something physical, and it would take a toll, but close quarters fighting was something she was lousy at. Plus, she was terrified. Her stomach was a ball of ice, and she was shaking.

Jeb and the masked woman still fought.

Nixie's bow and arrows were basic, made from her element of water, but it was something she was practiced with. As soon as they appeared in her hands she felt lead weights land on her, as the exhaustion from the energy work hit her. At the same time, adrenaline flew around her body and kept her upright.

Energy was flashing between the two but it was hard for Nixie to work out exactly what was happening. Energetic attacks happened inside the body as well as outside.

She needed Jeb to move back for her to be able to shoot at the woman. She notched an arrow, and sighted, waiting for an opportunity. Source, she wished she'd trained more with Blaize.

Her eye followed the other two's movements. It was a quiet time of day because of the heat and there were no others about, which was lucky.

Jeb fell back against a street lamp, and cried out in pain as his ribs hit the hard surface. Before the woman could close the gap between them, Nixie let her arrow fly, then notched another one and released that.

Her first went wide, but her second scraped along the woman's left arm, tearing her sweater and opening a sharp cut which immediately produced a line of blood. The woman clutched at her arm and hesitated. She muttered something under her breath, then with a pushing motion towards Nixie, palm out, she shoved energy in her direction. Jeb yelled, and flung himself at the woman. He caught her in the side with a fist, and she let out an ooff. She shook him off, then ran, her flat shoes slapping on the concrete until she disappeared into the distance.

The energy she'd thrown had hit Nixie. Much of it had been absorbed by her shields, but the bow and arrow had fallen to the floor and disappeared, and Nixie had been caught across the top of her chest and shoulder. She had what felt like a nasty burn, and along with the energy she'd already expended to manifest the weapon, she could barely stay upright.

Jeb ran over to her and caught her as she was crumpling to the ground. His warm, strong arms coming around her and lifting her off the floor were the last things she remembered before she passed out.

Jeb took Nixie back to the Guild as fast as he could find a taxi, assessing her injuries on the way. She wasn't in critical danger, but the manifestation had taken a lot out of her, and the nasty second-degree burn the masked woman had given her had shocked her system into unconsciousness.

It wasn't far, though the driver eyed them cautiously in the mirror frequently during the trip. Jeb had given the driver money hoping he wouldn't be asked questions, had covered Nixie's upper body with a coat and had briefly mentioned they'd been out for a drink.

He should have protected Nixie better. He knew she wasn't a fighter. But despite his desire to stay in the safety of the Guild, he'd seen the sense in Aiko's suggestion. He didn't plan to leave again if possible, but he should be better prepared next time if he did.

He'd been surprised to find being out with Nixie had felt restful. His Svadisthana energy had quieted. He wasn't sure what that meant, if anything.

She groaned, and opened her beautiful eyes. Her lashes fluttered as she worked out where she was. She reached up and touched his cheek.

"Are you okay?" she said.

He nodded, relief flooding his body. "I'm okay. I'll have some bruises. You have a burn, and you need rest, but you're going to be fine too."

She nodded, and lay back in his lap. "Thanks."

"I'm sorry I didn't do more," he said.

She tilted her head to the side. "What are you talking about?"

"I should have taken better care of you."

"Why? You're not in charge of me. Or responsible for me. I'm an adult, and I know what's going on. We worked together, as a team," she said, deep lines scoring her forehead and between her eyes.

Jeb knew he should have felt relief at her words, yet that wasn't what he was feeling. He had a lump in his throat and his body was heavy.

He sent word to Aiko they'd been attacked as he carried Nixie back to her room and checked her over more thoroughly. Using Anahata on her was confusing. Their energies had been so closely linked through their intimacy that it was harder than usual to get a clear reading, and he could feel his Svadisthana awake and writhing at the connection.

He slathered her burn with Anahata energy to encourage it to heal more quickly. It was possible she might end up with a faint scar in the area, but he'd done what he could.

Her cellphone rang and she gestured from the bed where she was resting. "Could you?"

He picked it up, and his heart sank when he realized it was Fintan.

"Just the man," Fintan said.

Jeb's stomach dropped to join his heart on the floor. He sat on the edge of the bed next to Nixie.

"Can you put it on speaker?" Nixie mouthed.

He nodded and did so. "Nixie and I are both here, Fintan. What is it?"

"Someone got through our outer wards. Ai saw them outside Tierra's window, but when she yelled for help, they ran away."

Nixie lifted her head, alarm on her face. "Is everyone okay?"

"Yes," Fintan said. "But I did a search and the person dropped something. We need to send Jeb an item to read. Tierra is getting sicker again, and we think the intruder did something, but we don't know what. She's lost weight, and her vitals aren't great. I'm worried she's going downhill, and fast. I don't know what to do. This item is our only current lead, and I don't know anyone else but you who can do telemetry, Jeb."

Fintan spoke in a rushed, jittery way, most unlike his normal laid-back self.

"What's the item?" Jeb asked.

"We're not sure. It looks like a small stick made of bone. We don't get any energy off it."

Jeb blew out a breath. "You can't send it. If it goes through the post it will pick up more memories and experiences and the reading won't be as clear. I would have to come to the island to read it. I need to think."

At every moment there was a new blow.

"I'll call you back. Let us know if anything changes." Jeb hung up the phone before either Nixie or Fintan could say anything more.

Nixie spluttered. "So?"

"What?"

"You know what. Are you going?" Nixie said.

Jeb ran a hand through his hair. The fight, such as it was, was something he hadn't been involved in for decades. His rusty skills had come back to a degree, but his body was battered and bruised, and he needed to recharge his Anahata to heal himself, having expended so much energy on Nixie.

All he wanted to do was go to bed and sleep for a week.

Ideally with this water fairy by his side.

He blew out a breath. That couldn't happen. He hadn't managed to keep Nixie safe from harm, but she was okay. Was he really going to leave Tierra to die, because he was frightened of what was inside him?

No. He was better than that. The trips outside the Guild into the city hadn't been easy, but Nixie was right. They'd been made less difficult with

Nixie by his side. He wasn't going to explore why at the moment, but he was aware of it.

He wasn't going to let Tierra get worse, and he wouldn't let Nixie down. He would control his energy as best he could. But it was time to let go of some of the fear and self-hatred he'd lived with for more than half a century.

"I'm going. Will you come with me?"

27

Jeb and Nixie were back in the room with Tierra, who slept restlessly. She looked terrible, her eyes shadowed and sunken, her cheekbones more pronounced. Jeb spent some time feeding healing energy into her, but as fast as he supplied it she seemed to burn through it, her system devouring it. He'd increased the wards, yet still she was sickening.

He needed a break to think and recharge before he read the object that Fintan had found. He needed all the energy he could get right now.

He blew out a breath and turned to Nixie. She'd said she would avoid him when things were over, but they were still in the thick of things. He'd chance it. "I heard Blaize mention a lake on the island. Will you show it to me?"

There was a long pause. "Alright. Is everything okay?"

"I need a breather before I read the object." He'd have preferred the ocean, but given Cuinn's prophecy, that seemed too risky.

Nixie nodded, and she showed him the way to the lake, their walk one of companionable silence. He appreciated Nixie's quiet.

At their destination he scooped up a handful of flat, smooth stones, putting some in his pocket and rolling a couple in his palm. The water was calm, and perfect for something he hadn't done in decades.

They meandered to where the water met the shore. He didn't hesitate to shuck off his shoes and stand in the shallows. He dug his toes into the sand

and let the warm water flow over his feet and ankles as he sucked air into his lungs. His auxiliary energy was under control, but he was alert.

"What were you doing that day when we met on the beach?" Jeb said.

Nixie looked puzzled for a moment, then comprehension crossed her face. "Oh. I was free diving. Well, not really, but that's why I can go under for such long periods. I was playing with the waves."

"How long have you been doing that?" Jeb asked.

Nixie shrugged. "Since I was a kid. A fisherman on the island taught me when I was young. I love going deep into the water. I scuba dive as well, but the freedom of being without equipment in the deep is amazing."

"I see," Jeb said. Though he wasn't sure he did.

Nixie seemed amused. "You don't like it? How do you like to enjoy your element, when you do? I've seen you in the pool, at least."

"I prefer to float. When I'm in the water, I love to float on the waves and stare up at the sky. It feels like I'm at one with the water."

"I don't like to be passive," Nixie said, and waved a hand. "I want to dance in the sea, to be part of the life underneath it."

Jeb grinned. "Yes, you're not the submissive type."

She really wasn't. She was vibrant, radiant, and filled with life. Even when quiet, she radiated a type of exuberance. They didn't need to have sex to enjoy each other's company. Her energy, though spirited, comforted him somehow.

"Did I hear you listening to some kind of rap on the plane?" Nixie asked.

Jeb winced and scuffed a foot, creating a small wave that he watched disappear quickly into the wider body of water. "Yep."

Nixie's brow furrowed for a moment.

"Oh-kay?" She drew out the word, and examined his face, peering at him. He kept his eyes on the lake.

She touched him on the bare arm, and his skin tingled at her touch, a light ripple going through his wards. He tried not to jerk back. He needed to watch that.

"I like it," he said.

She stepped into him, looking up into his eyes, her body not touching him, but close, so close. His groin stirred. She had dark and merry eyes.

"I'd have you pegged more for classical music," she said. She traced a finger along his arm, a gossamer touch. "I have a thing for Bach. I can listen to the cello for hours."

He needed to distract her, and him. "I don't listen to anything from before World War II. Music is a powerful trigger for me, and can bring back the horrors I saw."

Her hand covered her mouth, and her striking eyes widened. He shrugged, and hurried to move them on. "I've learned to deal with it. But that's why."

He stepped away from her, and tossed one of the stones he'd picked up in his hand. "Did you ever skim stones?"

"Sure," she said. She put a hand out and he placed a couple in her palm. "How many can you do?"

"I'm not sure," he admitted. "It's been a long time. I used to manage about eight."

She raised her eyebrows, turned, bent her knees slightly and with her arm low to the ground, let her stone fly.

He watched as it skipped once, twice, and eventually five times before it sank beneath the waves.

She beamed. "Your turn."

He only managed four the first time, but by the time they'd worked their way through the stones he'd picked up they were both on six, and laughing.

They walked back slowly.

"What is it you do in the human world?" Jeb asked.

Nixie glanced at him, eyes narrowed. "I'm a graphic artist."

She tilted her chin up, as if ready for battle.

"Okay," he said. "Comics and so on?"

He wasn't exactly sure what a graphic artist did.

"I do graphic design, and yes, I do some art work for graphic novels."

"Okay," he said. "That's how you use your Svadisthana creativity?"

She scowled. "Yes. It is."

He couldn't understand why she was being so defensive.

"Okay," he said.

She spun to face him, and he stopped short as words burst out of her. "Art and creativity are a lot more than oil paintings in a gallery chosen by some old white man in the nineteenth century. Art can be anything that expresses our thoughts, desires, feelings, ideas to others. And creativity can be applied anywhere, anyhow."

He nodded, bemused, unsure where this was coming from but interested. "My education around art was a long time ago, and more formal."

"Exactly!" she wagged a finger at him. "But that's only one aspect of art!"

"I'm not an artist," he said. "My energy, even when I used it, never came out that way."

"Huh." She dropped the finger, but put her hands on her hips. "Beauty and good design can be used anywhere. Art can be graffiti on the street, a child's pencil drawing, or a sculpture in a gallery. People's definitions are too narrow. It pisses me off."

"I see that," he said, dryly.

"Aesthetics are important. Art can make the world a better place. It ignites our imagination, creates shared values, and is a way to explore and question the world around us." Her face was alight with an earnest passion.

"I've never really thought about it that way before," Jeb said. She certainly made him look at the world in a different way.

On the way back she talked about some of her projects, creating brand images for NGOs and sculpture projects for large organizations. She had works inside some major buildings in New York, London and Vancouver. He was impressed. She was diverse, that was certain, in her creativity, but there was a coherence and vision behind it all that he hadn't expected. She truly wanted to create things that inspired people.

And he realized her enthusiasm had kindled yet another part of himself that had been quiescent. It had engaged the part of him that enjoyed intimacy and connecting with a woman. Building a true relationship.

He'd enjoyed talking to her. Watching her passion and animation. Initially, he'd thought they hadn't much in common apart from the sexual tension that simmered between them, but perhaps they could be friends after all.

He could use a friend.

Back in Tierra's room Fintan looked almost as bad as Tierra, his hair wild and unwashed, his usual stubble now an unkempt scraggle.

Jeb felt refreshed by his time at the lake, and was ready to work.

"I'm going to need to do this outside. I don't want to do it around Tierra, just in case," Jeb said.

Fintan, Jeb, Blaize and Nixie trooped outside, leaving Ai to stay with Tierra.

"How can we help you?" Fintan said. The man was desperate for action and running on empty. Jeb would try and handle him with kid gloves, though he didn't have a lot to spare when he was doing telemetry as it was very wearing.

"I have it under control, though we'll go a bit further from the house. Don't touch me while I'm reading the object," Jeb said.

Fintan had watched him do this before, and had brought a traditional-style straw mat with him for them to sit on.

Jeb arranged himself into a cross-legged position on the mat and breathed deeply. He needed to center himself before he touched the object. He put his hands on his knees and deliberately relaxed his muscles, maintaining an upright posture.

He pulled Anahata energy through from the ether, and felt his heart Chakra tingle. This kind of energy work was difficult, because it carried risk. When you touched an object to read it, you never knew what might have happened to that object. As you lived through those experiences, albeit in a flash, when you were reading it, you had no idea what you were inviting into your psyche.

"I'm ready. Can you drop it into my hands?" He held out cupped hands in front of him, eyes still closed. A touch from someone else would confuse things, and he wanted a clean reading.

He pressed his tailbone into the ground and wriggled slightly so he was solid in place.

Then something light and cool fell into his hands, and he opened himself up to it in a rush of sensation.

He jerked, and images and scenes hurtled through his mind.

He was on a nineteenth century pirate ship, the toothpick — because that was what it was — between the captain's teeth. He'd carved it himself out of the penis bone of a racoon, and he loved the look on pretentious ladies' faces when he told them what it was made from.

Blood. A lot of blood. The pirate rarely took it out of his mouth, even when murdering his victims.

Rape.

Death.

Destruction.

Arson.

Jeb took a breath, his heart racing, his chest heaving, face full of disgust. But this wasn't what he wanted. These were images from the first owner. The pirate was not an energetic, and would be long dead. The challenge with telemetry was that it had a tendency to pick up more easily on events with high emotion, and this toothpick apparently had seen more of that than most objects.

He dived back into the swarm of emotions and scenes that were connected to the toothpick.

A safe being opened by a terrified man. Twentieth century dress. A more recent scene, but not current day.

The toothpick is spotted by another man, who is methodically clearing out the safe, and he puts it in his mouth to chew on while he takes money, bonds, jewelery.

In the doorway a woman is slumped, arterial blood splattering the walls.

The terrified man is on his knees.

The new owner of the toothpick grabs him by the hair, lifts his head so his chin is up, and with a swift left-to-right movement, slits his throat.

Murder.

Many murders.

But strange. From here on in, all the emotion was from the murder victims. The owner of the toothpick was cold and impassive, even when he slaughtered his victims. It was rare for anyone to show no emotion. A psychopath? A sociopath? And yet, an energetic, because in the scenes, the murders that the man had committed sometimes involved energy use. Jeb thought Svadisthana-Ajna, though the latter energy was slender.

Jeb was sick to his stomach at the visions passing through his senses.

The iron tang of blood in the back of his throat.

The rattling gurgle as a victim died.

The feel of hot blood gushing down a chest.

The harsh smell of urine and worse as a victim released their bladder and bowels in death.

Ah ha.

The sight, from the victim's perspective, of a tall white man, with dark, neat hair, and a relatively unprepossessing face. Not unattractive physically, he clearly trained his body to be in peak condition. Watching the murders he committed, Jeb could see death in his eyes, combined with indifference.

Jeb's gorge rose.

But he needed more information.

He drew energy harder and faster, trying to find the more recent emotional memories on the toothpick, something that would tell them where the man who was trying to hurt Tierra was hiding.

Prickles ran up his arms and legs as magic raced around his body. He focused it on his hands where he cradled the toothpick.

There had been no murders on the island as yet. Which was a blessing, but it also meant that the emotional memories here were harder to trace. The psychopath emitted very few feelings of any kind, and so Jeb's only chance was where others had had emotions he could 'catch'.

That meant increasing his sensitivity, which meant the deaths that the toothpick had seen pressed in on him, crowding his mind with images of brutality and nightmares. His head pounded. He couldn't keep this up much longer. But he needed to find something. Anything. Some kind of clue to find this bastard and bring him down.

Ah, here. A faint – compared to all the blood and executions – emotional sense memory which was recent. The man with the toothpick had rented a house here, and Jeb suspected the woman he'd rented from was a sensitive of some kind, given her reactions to the man – reactions which Jeb experienced for himself.

Cold fear. Ice in her veins. She froze when he walked up, asking for rentals on the island.

Which was less dangerous? Telling him she was fully booked? Renting to him?

Showing any kind of fear was dangerous with this kind of predator.

An evil man.

Casually threatening though his words were sweet.

She'd rent to him, as the easiest option.

She hoped she wouldn't regret it.

Jeb shuddered, and released the toothpick to the ground. He had what they needed, the image of where the psychopath had rented his accommodation. All they needed to do was find it.

He staggered to his feet, lurched a few feet away into the bushes, and threw up.

Nixie had watched Jeb read the toothpick with her heart in her throat. The distress on his face was evident as he read the object and pushed out words. She jotted down notes as he did so, glad to have a task.

When he threw up, she jumped up and grabbed a bottle of water. He unbent and stood, scrubbing an arm wearily over his face. She offered him the water carefully, not touching him. She hated herself a little for checking his wrists yet again, covering the big silver bangle with her hand when his were still bare.

Was there someone out there with a matching bracelet? She'd really thought Jeb might wear the corresponding one. It had the right colors, after all – her own orange for Svadisthana, and blue for Vishudha, white for Sahasara, which was the color of the energy of the Source, or the divine, and then one final color. Green. The color of Anahata. Which Jeb had.

And yet.

The walk by the lake had been intimate in a way she wasn't used to. After he'd taken sex off the table she'd expected him to be less interested. She was perplexed, but intrigued, by this interaction. She was a bit embarrassed about the intensity with which she'd shared her views about art, but she'd wanted to explain, to show him, how important it was to her.

She had found it was nice to be listened to. To be really heard.

He took the water from her, swilled it round his mouth and spat it out. "Thanks."

"What do we have?" Fintan demanded. He'd been silent for long enough, but was bursting to do something.

"I saw the place he rented his lodgings." Jeb looked as though he might collapse at any minute.

"Where is it?" Fintan said.

"I don't know. It seemed familiar, like something I'd passed in town, but I can't remember exactly."

"Right," Fintan said. "Let's go. I'll drive us round until you see it."

He hesitated, then met Jeb's eyes with his own. "Thank you."

Jeb nodded, and the men drove off accompanied by the throaty roar of Fintan's bike.

Nixie looked at Blaize. Jeb set an example that was hard to live up to, but she could show him she too could contribute.

"I'm ready to do more sketching," Nixie said.

Blaize tilted her head from side to side and stretched. They'd done little on the sketches while Tierra was ill, as both Nixie and Blaize struggled to focus with everything going on.

"I don't know," Blaize said. "I'm not sure I can hold an image for long. And we don't have a spotter."

"We'll set an alarm," Nixie said, more confidently than she felt. "Small periods, with breaks. I need to be doing something, Blaize."

Nixie wanted to throw herself into helping. Blaize nodded slowly and Nixie felt lighter.

She'd told Jeb art could change the world. This could be an opportunity to prove that.

Elrian reviewed the Hermit's papers, but couldn't concentrate. The words swam in front of his eyes. He sat at a desk in the dusty apartment he was currently inhabiting. There were plenty of empty apartment buildings on the outskirts of Cairo. It was an excess of housing created by a country where high inflation and limits on sending cash abroad meant the Egyptians had needed internal, local investments that would maintain their value. But most were priced outside the ordinary Egyptian's means.

Whole streets stood half-built, or built but empty, waiting for better times. It had been simple for Elrian and Imogen to find a quiet place for him to heal from his wound after the fight with the Hermit, while she went back to the Guild.

Elrian needed more energy to heal and complete the task she had set him. He tried to draw from the ether, but his connection was sticky, blocked. He needed an external source.

His head was in a fog. He left his papers and he went out.

He needed energy.

Elrian wandered aimlessly in the streets near the Guild. Not too near, he had some sense of self-preservation, but in the places Guild members frequented.

A youth crossed his path. A younger energetic, with no Adherent markings, the single stripe an energetic gained on their shoulder when they were bonded to a Maven. He seemed to be on some sort of errand, an empty bag in his hand. He was a higher risk abduction, but Elrian needed what he had.

Elrian stalked him, purpose infusing him. He could impress Imogen. That morning he had found a suggestion about a shortcut to create a remnant stone. This youth would be perfect to try it on. Elrian would gain energy for himself, and he would show Imogen he had power, that he was able to create the stones as she did, on his own. The papers had seemed to show him a way.

He stalked the prey till he crossed to a quiet street. Elrian came up behind him, placed a hand on his shoulder and began talking. His prey was weak, easy to influence. It took only a minute to have the boy under his control.

Elrian brought him home. He didn't waste time. He leeched enough energy to heal his wounds and find clarity through the murkiness that kept clouding his mind.

Next was to show Imogen he could create a fifth stone on his own. As far as they knew there were only five or six people in the world who had the knowledge to create new remnant stones – one fewer since they'd killed the Hermit – and perhaps only he and Imogen who were able to combine that knowledge with the power and the will to create them.

She'd had to go back to the Guild to maintain her cover. He had plenty of time before she returned.

The boy was unconscious from the leeching, so there was no issue there of him trying to get away. He lay the boy on the floor and set up the ritual around him, preparing him as a sacrifice.

They needed twelve remnant stones for the final ritual. Each one took a great investment of power to create. So far, they had the original stone, the one that had started everything. Then she had created two more, and they had created one together. That last stone Indigo had had charge of, and had been lost. They would need to find it, or create another to replace it, but that was a problem for Canada, not Egypt.

He breathed in deeply, and opened the channel. He poured himself into the ritual, ready, eager to offer the youth in exchange for the power of another stone.

The energy built up inside him, painful in its intensity. He guided his energies as they cascaded into the ritual, and he grew ready to draw the energy out of the boy to create the stone.

A flash. The boy screamed, long and loud, then slumped back, his eyes burned out.

Elrian's gorge rose, and shaking, he stared down at the corpse.

He'd failed.

And wasted another source of energy.

He'd failed.

Time passed as he stood there, frozen in place.

He'd failed.

A blow hit him across the face and he staggered, his head snapping back. He blinked, and Imogen came into focus. He lifted his hands in front of his face, palms out. How much time had passed? How was she back already? He must have been standing there for hours. The eye sockets no longer smoked, which was a blessing.

"What have you done?" she snarled.

Failed.

"I wanted to show you – to create – I wanted to make a new stone," he stuttered.

"The Guild is in uproar, and you abduct and kill a member? What is wrong with you?" She was furious, eyes cold, lips curled, her body taut, as if she was keeping herself under tight control. "What if you were seen? What if they use a Tracker? You're going to have to get out of town."

His head was muddled again, the clarity of the energy rush draining in the face of her fury.

He'd failed.

They'd have to create the next stone together. Somehow she was more powerful than him. He needed her. Did that matter? He didn't want to be without her, after all. They needed each other, surely?

Or perhaps he could still make one without her. Perhaps he'd got the shortcut wrong. He'd study the notes more. He'd been tired when he'd tried today. He should have spent longer preparing. He straightened, and tried to pull himself together. His hands dropped to his sides. He had no need to defend himself from her. She'd slapped him to bring him back to himself. He'd needed it.

Perhaps Cassidy and he would have enough power to create one together? Though it would cross a threshold with her he wouldn't be able to reverse, involving her in that. He might not be able to hold her under his influence while managing such a tricky magic. Cassidy was something else he was worried about. The balancing act of protecting her from the blonde and yet using Cassidy's still growing powers to help their cause was a strain.

His cell phone beeped, and he glanced reflexively at it. Imogen hissed, but he snatched it up gratefully.

"It's Trent." He read the message. "The charm is working. He's checking it twice a day, and he doesn't think she has much longer."

"Good. That will help. Then we still need to deal with either the healer or the flighty chit." She stepped across the body that lay on the floor between them without appearing to notice it. She put a hand flat on Elrian's chest. "Perhaps it's time for you to go there. The girl is hardly a rocket scientist. She's not a fighter. Separate her from her friends, and she should be easy to pick off. She's vain, proud, and emotional. And Source knows we need to get you out of here."

He didn't know the girl well, but perhaps Imogen was right. He put one hand on her shoulder, and texted Trent with the other.

Get Nixie to the beach at midnight in two days. I'm coming.

The response was fast. *Roger that. How?*

Elrian's jaw clenched with irritation. Wasn't that his problem to figure out?

Tell her we want her bracelet in exchange for Tierra's life. She will believe she is giving up the chance for true love.

The prophecy slivers he'd seen indicated Nixie was ready for some kind of self-sacrifice. He might as well play to that. While in fact, he'd end up with the two energetics he needed to end the prophecy at this stage, Nixie and Tierra.

"It's done. I'll burn this place and leave." He bent down and kissed her, threading a hand in her hair. She tasted of honey and lemon, sweet with a bitter aftertaste. It was addictive.

He'd read and research more in the Hermit's papers, he'd center himself, and next time, he'd make the remnant stone correctly. He'd show Imogen he was as valuable as she was. That they were equals.

He wouldn't fail again.

28

Nixie hopped on her bike to get fruit smoothies for those at the house. There was a woman with a bamboo stand who made them a kilometer or so away. Nixie could have walked it, but she'd been in creative flow, and didn't want a long break. She was keen to get back to her sketches as quickly as possible. They'd completed Fintan, an easier image for Blaize to hold while tired, as they'd known each other a long time. He had a long sword of fire sheathed on his back. Nixie wanted to see herself, but they'd realized they should focus on Tierra next, in case her image provided any clues to her illness. Nixie was annoyed at herself for not thinking of it before.

With four drink orders and only one blender, she'd be at the drinks stand a while. She wandered a few meters from the woman while she worked, and gazed into the green of the jungle. Home.

Her skin tingled, and she turned. A man stood there, sunglasses propped on his head, neat and handsome, yet there was something off about him. Something unpleasant.

She shifted her body and decided to walk back to the fruit shake stand.

He shook his head. "Uh uh. I have a message for you."

"I'm not interested." She tried to push past him, but he grabbed her wrist. She broke the grab by jerking her wrist through the weakest part of his hold, between his first finger and thumb, and backed out of reach.

He sighed in an exaggerated fashion and gave a forced smile. "Just stay there. All I want to do is talk."

She gestured. "Talk. Then fuck off. Or fuck off first. Either way."

She feigned indifference, but inside she felt sick. She was barely preventing her whole body from shaking from the massive adrenaline dump caused when he grabbed her. Who was this guy? The one Fintan and Jeb were out looking for? He matched the limited description Jeb had shared. Or was there more than one enemy on the island?

She shot a glance over to the fruit stall to check the woman was still there. She was, unconcernedly working on drink number three. At least there'd be a witness, she thought. But to what?

"A friend of mine wants to offer you a trade. Your bracelet for Tierra's life." The man was a kind of bland handsome, yet managed to exude menace. He was overdressed for the island, a shirt and chinos. A predator in smart casual clothing.

"Why would I do that?" she asked. She was proud that her voice didn't waver.

"Because Tierra is only one or two nights away from death. And because the only reason Jebediah wants you is because I encouraged him through Svadisthana influence. Whereas your feelings for him … " he shrugged. "Well, those I didn't touch. Your bracelet doesn't have a match."

Nixie felt tears prick her eyelids. She knew it. That was why she had a bracelet and Jeb didn't. The answer was as simple as that. Jeb had been manipulated.

She'd hoped after all this hellish situation was over, she'd be able to persuade him that they were good for each other. She'd wanted to believe that their growing relationship was somehow more real than other relationships she'd had with men.

When in fact, it was the most fake of them all.

She wouldn't cry in front of this jerk. "And what would it mean to give the bracelet up?"

"You'd come with me. Willingly. We only need one bracelet. We'll remove it in a ritual, then you can go. It won't be pleasant, but once we have it, we'll leave Tierra – sweet, warm Tierra, who has contributed so much to the world, with a partner who loves her – alone."

"When do I have to decide?"

"You have till sunset tomorrow. If you're not with me by then to go through the ritual, Tierra will go downhill quickly. But we'll leave her alone for now, as a show of good faith." He took his sunglasses off his head and cleaned them diligently, then handed her a white card with a phone number on it. "Text this number to confirm. I hope, for her sake, you make the right decision. Personally, I have no problem killing you all, including that man you wish was yours. The bracelet seems an easy trade for the lives of those you love."

He put the sunglasses back on. "I suggest you keep this conversation to yourself. Don't think we're not listening. If we hear you tell your friends about it, it will be easy enough for us to end Tierra."

He slashed a hand through the air in front of her, sharp and fast. Then turned on his heel and stalked off, leaving her clutching the paper, eyes wide and pregnant with tears, her heart cracking inside her chest.

Nixie waited till he was out of sight before she went, mechanically, to collect and pay for her drinks. She hooked the little plastic bags they came in to her bike, then drove a short way away before pulling over to the side of the dirt road. She walked into the trees that fringed the road, and sank to the dry, sandy dirt as if her legs had stopped working.

The tears she had held back overflowed down her cheeks, and she swallowed compulsively to try and rid herself of the burning lump in her throat. She rubbed at her eyes angrily. She didn't have time for this. *What am I going to do?*

She was the weak one in their group. She'd thought she'd spent her life searching for love, but she was beginning to realize love wasn't what she'd thought. The bracelet had offered her hope that might change, and now she needed to give it up.

What did she have to offer? She was a quick study with a pencil. It was hardly a talent that was needed to prevent the end of the world.

It was better for Jeb they weren't a pair. If she got rid of the bracelet, and stopped being so attached to him, perhaps he'd finally shake off the traces of the influence energy, and choose someone for himself who he could really let go with. Who he'd feel comfortable enough to loose his Svadisthana energy with, confident his partner would be there to hold the space for him.

Tierra was good, and kind. And at the heart of the group of energetics who had been called to this great task. If she died, it would tear them all apart. You only needed to see Fintan and Blaize right now to realize that they would be devastated by her loss. And Ai. Tierra was the closest thing to a mother that the girl had ever had.

She knew it was probably a trick, but she couldn't live with herself if she didn't try. These people had tried to kill Blaize already, and had kidnapped Tierra. It was likely they didn't simply want Nixie's bracelet, but her energy, or her life. And yet, what if it wasn't a trick, and she could save Tierra?

If something happened, while Nixie wasn't so stupid as to think she wouldn't be missed, the loss would be bearable. She knew that she wasn't as reliable a friend as she could be. She was impulsive and self-centered and easily distracted by the world around her.

She laughed grimly. A week ago, Nixie had been full of herself. This has been one of the longest weeks of her life. She stood slowly, wobbling, and walked back to her bike in the darkness. She rubbed at her eyes with her sleeves, and ignored the aching lump in her throat.

She got out her cellphone and the white card. She texted the number written there with a simple: *Yes*.

She knew what she needed to do. She just hoped she was brave enough to go through with it.

29

Jeb and Fintan had driven round the small harbor town where the ferry docked for a couple of hours before Jeb had been so exhausted he'd nearly fallen from the bike. Fintan had driven them back to the house for rest and food.

Jebediah had slept for an hour, then they'd all gathered for food in Tierra's room.

She'd seemed to rally this evening, and he hoped it had been the energy he'd poured into her earlier. It was so frustrating not to understand what was going on with her.

He sat on the floor with Ai, Nixie and Blaize on Thai-style cushions, with the food on several low tables Blaize had brought in. Fintan sat on the bed with Tierra, feeding her as much as she would let him.

Nixie seemed withdrawn, her usual sparkle dimmed. She'd been polite to Jeb, but the solicitude she'd shown earlier wasn't present. Fair enough. He hadn't exactly covered himself in manly glory by puking in the bushes. He grimaced. It had been a long time since he'd cared what another thought of him in that way.

"Thank you for reading the toothpick, Jeb," Tierra said. "I know how much it takes out of you. I wouldn't have asked."

She shot a look at Fintan, who shrugged innocently.

"It was impressive," Blaize said. "And useful. If I'd known I'd have brought something Tierra found in the remains of Indigo's house."

"The remnant stone?" Tierra asked.

Blaize nodded.

Jeb shook his head. "That's not something I could read. Well, I might be able to. But it would almost certainly send me mad. You know what has to happen to make them?"

"A death," Fintan said.

"The negative emotional potential in them is so great that even low level, prolonged exposure to them would drive you slowly out of your mind," Jeb explained. "An intense, active engagement like the kind I do with telemetry would dump the experience of that death into me, not just into my brain as a thought, but as a sense memory – I would literally go through that experience of dying."

Blaize grimaced. "Got it. No reading the stone."

With a meaningful glance at Ai, Tierra turned the conversation to lighter topics. There was a little more color in her cheeks, and Jeb could see the relief in Fintan's posture as he nagged her to eat more food.

"How will you stand up to all that ravishing I'm going to do to you when you're better if you're not properly fed?" Fintan said.

"You won't be doing any ravishing unless you trim that caveman beard," Tierra retorted, though she ate another few spoonfuls of tom yum soup.

The room's shutters were open, and the night breeze, along with the occasional light-seeking moth, blew softly through. Six in the room was a bit of a squeeze, but there was a warmth and connection in the group that felt good. He wished Nixie wasn't on the other side of the room. She alone seemed a bit off, and he would have liked to have checked on her, but didn't want to draw attention to her if she wasn't feeling good.

They were a very diverse set of individuals, with energies that were quite different, despite the various ones they had in common. The way Tierra's Muladhara-Anahata was very different from Fintan's Manipura-Anahata, or his own Anahata-Svadisthana, despite the heart energy in common. Such was the way with combinations of energies. And even then, there were different abilities within each Guild.

His brow furrowed as something tickled his brain. He'd had the inkling of something, there, something relevant. But he couldn't quite catch it.

Jeb was glad of this respite, but he knew he'd done nothing that was likely to have cured whatever was wrong with Tierra. All he'd done was slow the symptoms. And unless the illness was something that spontaneously resolved itself – possible, but unlikely given the pattern so far and the evidence they'd found in the archives – they still needed to understand what was happening and solve it.

He might have bought time, but he still needed to work out how to use it.

After the meal, Jeb paced the beach with a manic energy. He could protect Tierra, he knew it. He could save her. He would. He was wracking his brains to try and come up with ideas that might help her. And there was something – something that might help that had tickled the edge of his brain earlier when they'd been talking and eating, family and friends gathered together. Something that would help, Source damn it.

He couldn't grab it. Couldn't make it surface from his tired-wired brain. He was pacing because it helped him to think, and the noise of the sea soothed him. The closest beach wasn't far from the houses, and he had his cellphone so he could be back in under ten minutes if there was a problem. He'd needed some silence to think.

Fintan had agreed to wait till first light to try to find the rental place again, while Jeb's brain worked on Tierra's illness. Jeb felt the weight of expectations and hope pressing on him, his stomach tight, his body fizzing with nervous exhaustion as it ran on fumes.

It was strange being here, where Nixie had been brought up. He'd like time for her to show him around at some point. When all this madness was over. To talk to her parents, when they came back from their current trip, and learn more about who Nixie was.

What he and Nixie had was valuable. He'd thought it was merely a sexual connection, but even when he'd paused that, he had still enjoyed being around her more than any woman in decades. Had found himself wanting to share parts of himself that hadn't seen the light of day in forever, but which he wanted to dust off and offer to her.

And, like a miracle, he seemed to be able to be with her without unleashing his Svadisthana completely. He did feel better with some of that energy present once again in his life.

However, he couldn't, wouldn't release it entirely. Cuinn's prophecy had reinforced that. Source knew his self-control could manage to hold back. But there was the possibility that perhaps, after this period was over, he could have his cake and eat it too, although he planned never to unchain that energy fully. He didn't trust himself.

Still. He felt a sense of optimism about his personal future for the first time in a long, long time.

He stopped and looked out to sea. The squid catchers were out there, with their strange fluorescent lights that apparently brought the squid to the surface, ready to be caught. Poor creatures. Going to their deaths happily, without realizing they were chasing their own mortality.

He turned away from the water and began to walk once more, his bare feet sinking into the damp sand and leaving a trail of footprints behind him.

Elrian had been heading to the Thai island when he'd received Trent's text that Nixie had confirmed she would hand herself over in exchange for Tierra's life.

Elrian had been beside himself with relief and anticipation.

Once their adversaries in the prophecy were taken care of, that would leave them free to create the rest of the remnant stones, and once they found the place required for the final ceremony, power would be within their reach. So much power.

Then Imogen and he could remake the energetics into the race they had once been. And prune the humans, teaching them their place.

Thinner, perhaps, than he used to be, he had taken care to dress for the travel in a well-cut bespoke suit and shirt, top button undone.

The girl had agreed to sacrifice herself as the shards of prophecy Elrian had gathered predicted. Tierra would die either way.

But the best part was, Nixie was both prize and bait. Elrian's reading indicated a willing sacrifice made a stronger remnant stone, and it would help him get round the issues he'd had without Imogen there to support him with her energy. He knew if circumstances stopped working against him, he could make this stone alone.

They needed two individuals from the prophecy to die at this point. Elrian planned for Tierra to die anyway, but this time, he was putting in place a contingency, and aiming for the deaths of three of his enemies.

When Nixie volunteered herself, Jebediah would almost certainly come after her.

And when he did, given the instability of his energies, and the storm that was predicted, they would both die.

A romantic death, true, as they'd die together. And with two of them removed, the prophecy would be ruined and he would be able to continue with his activities unchecked.

It was perfect.

30

Jeb's walk hadn't worked. He knew – knew – there was something that could be done, but it kept slipping through his mind, a fish through water that he couldn't catch. He'd come back into Tierra's room to watch her, to see if he could work out what it was by monitoring her symptoms. And perhaps a small part of him thought that he could prevent her from being drained if he was in the room. Though it was strange, she did seem to have stabilized.

He stood, his hands clasped in front of him. Tierra lay, her normally vibrant energy dimmed, her body small in the middle of the bed as he studied her. She opened her eyes and stared at him. "What's wrong?"

He gave a strangled laugh. "You're asking me what's wrong? While you lie there, being drained? And we can't find who's doing it? Everything is wrong, my friend."

They both spoke in hushed voices. Fintan was asleep on the mat next to her bed.

"Pft." Tierra waved a hand weakly. "I hear Nixie has been helping with the research."

He gave a small nod. Tierra was empathic enough to be able to read more than he'd like from him. *But perhaps she was too ill to notice?*

Tierra cocked her head to the side and narrowed her eyes. "How are the two of you getting on?"

Perhaps not. "We're fine. We just met."

Tierra shook her head. "No. The two of you are meant to be. I saw the spark – the literal spark – when the two of you met. You practically fell over when you first saw her."

Jeb came close and gripped the end of the wooden bed frame. "Something had been happening with my Svadisthana for weeks. It was a coincidence."

She gave him a direct look, calling him on his attempt at self-deception. "I don't think so, Jeb. She calls to something in you. You haven't been a whole person for a long time. None of us can suppress our true selves for so long – energetic or any other part of ourselves – without consequences. You've been as sick as I have in your own way. Nixie is a gift. She's helping you to be the person you were before the war."

"I can't erase what happened in the war. I have to live with it. And I don't want it to happen again. I have to be careful. Cuinn's prophecy shows that." He walked over to the large open window, covered with the mesh screen that let the air circulate around the sick room without the insects getting in. The air was sultry today. There wasn't much of a breeze. Tierra had a fan in the room, and the hum of it felt loud.

"I know I'm dying," said Tierra. There wasn't any emotion behind her words, rather, it was a statement of fact, as if she'd said 'I know the sky is blue.'

Jeb spun round and walked over to her side. He perched himself on the side of the bed and took one of her hands in his. "You're not dying."

Not if I can help it, he added silently.

"You haven't got any worse today," he said.

She shrugged. "It's the calm before the storm. It happens, sometimes, with patients before the last, we both know that. I've accepted it. But if I'm going to die, I don't want my friends missing their chances. And you might have been my Maven once, but now you're my friend. You deserve happiness. You did what you felt was right after the war, and I know that you needed time to heal. But that season has passed. You need to be back out in the world."

She looked out the window. "And Fintan is going to need friends. You and he can be friends, I'm sure of it."

Jeb struggled to get his words out past the thickness in his throat. "We need you for the prophecy."

"Perhaps. Perhaps not. Perhaps I've served my function, or perhaps there'll be someone who will take my place in the prophecy. I've been around Cuinn and Adam and their Ajna long enough to know that no prophecy is set in stone, or we wouldn't have so many interpretations of each one by different Sages."

She coughed, and lifted a hand to her mouth to cover it. When she brought it away, Jeb saw the brightness of blood on her palm. He took in a breath. She hadn't been drained any further, but damage had already been done to her body.

"I can heal that." He pulled Anahata and putting a hand on her chest, closed his eyes. He drew on his energy to heal the blood vessels that had ruptured in her lungs.

She swallowed but didn't cough again. "It's like giving blood to someone who's bleeding out from an artery. You can't just keep healing me while I'm drained elsewhere."

"Yes. I can." And he would.

Early the next morning Nixie came into Tierra's room and found Jeb holding Tierra's hand. He looked broken, and she looked pale and fragile. The man at the beach was right. If Nixie didn't act, Tierra didn't have much time left. It made Nixie fiercer in her resolve to go through with it.

She'd always avoided pain. She was a sybarite. A pleasure seeker. And that had served her well for many years, while she thought she had been looking for her soulmate.

But now, finally, she'd learned what real love was. It was about compromise, and sometimes, choosing to put someone else's needs before your own.

It was Jeb leaving the safety of the Guild to come and help Tierra. It was Cuinn risking madness searching for Blaize in the dreamscape. It was Fintan sleeping on the floor by Tierra's bed. It was Nixie's parents, who she'd called before she came into the room to hear their voices one last time, living together and creating a life out of small, everyday moments of connection.

It wasn't Nixie's grand romantic notions of love. Of flowers and candlelit dinners and sex. That might be part of it, but it was just the surface. Love was kind, and it didn't ask, it gave.

Love was also brave. Which she wasn't, really. But perhaps she could be brave when it was for someone else, not for herself.

She knew that at the very least she might be giving up the opportunity for love with the bracelet. The prophecy hadn't guaranteed a match, and if it wasn't going to be Jeb, there could still have been someone else. Without the bracelet, she might lose that, forever. Even if she lived, Source might not give her a second chance.

She stepped up close to the bed and stroked Tierra's hair. Tierra smiled, a true smile, as if she was genuinely pleased to see Nixie, with no thought for her own illness. Nixie fought back tears. "Hello, love."

Jeb didn't look up at Nixie, but he did rest a hand briefly on her free arm. She nodded at him.

"No news," Nixie said. "Thought I'd come say hi."

"Thanks for coming," said Tierra. "Nothing to report here either."

She laughed, but neither Nixie or Jeb could raise a smile.

There was a grunt from the floor, and Fintan came to a sitting position. "What happened?"

Tierra turned her head towards him. "Nothing. Get more sleep."

He rubbed his eyes, and pushed himself to his feet. He pressed a light kiss to Tierra's palm before stumbling over to the coffee machine in the corner of the room. Something twisted inside Nixie's stomach at his gentle gesture.

"No need," Fintan said. "I'm up now. We can go search again once I'm properly awake."

Jeb glanced over at that other man. "We'll leave you alone."

Fintan waved a hand back at them, still focused on the coffee. "S'fine."

Tierra looked up at Nixie then across at Jeb. "No. Fin and I should have some time alone. You two go and get some food. You must be starving."

Nixie couldn't remember when she last ate, and she wasn't interested in food now, but she also realized that Tierra probably wanted some time together with her man. And Nixie and Jeb weren't doing anything useful here.

Nixie stroked Tierra's hair back from her forehead one more time. "We'll see you later."

She hoped so. But there was no guarantee.

When Nixie drew him out of the room, Jeb was annoyed at first, as he was still trying to remember his idea. But when she had looked meaningfully between Fintan and Tierra, he'd realized why. It was strange, his sensitivity to emotions really must be confused by Nixie, because he'd missed that entirely.

He followed Nixie out after a final squeeze of Tierra's hand and a sympathetic slap on Fintan's shoulder, who'd jerked his head in acknowledgement.

They stepped out into the warm day and went down the bungalow's steps to the scrub and sand. He was grateful Nixie still seemed to be talking to him, and hadn't followed up on her threat to not interact with him. He'd try and enjoy her company while he could.

"I got close to an idea last night," he said. "Something that might help. But I can't remember it."

It was giving him a headache trying to work out what it was.

She looked up at him, the shade making her dark eyes luminous. "Can you remember what was going on when you thought it? Maybe that will remind you."

He shook his head and rubbed his temples to relieve the ache there. "Something triggered during the meal last night, when everyone was together."

She gave a stifled snort. "Yeah. It was pretty awful. Like a wake. And people taking it in turns to spend time with Tierra. The poor woman was probably worn out with all our visiting."

"Everybody cares, and wants to do something for her," he murmured.

Nixie nodded, and they walked aimlessly in a companionable silence, though Nixie seemed distracted. It was rare she didn't chatter at him.

Tierra's words about Nixie and him nagged at him. Perhaps it wouldn't hurt to touch each other.

He put a hand out to capture her hand. She didn't pull away.

They walked until they came upon a hammock slung between two trees. She tugged him into it, and after some shuffling and a little inelegance – mainly from him, Nixie was as graceful as a cat, as always – they were both nestled together in the hammock. He yearned for the warmth of her body against his. He gazed upwards at the blue of the sky and took a deep breath, grounding himself. This felt … right. She connected him to the now.

And, he realized, her presence no longer automatically pushed at his wards. No longer shook his control. Carefully, he focused on his Svadisthana. He examined his shields as best he could. There were cracks, but nothing was leaking. However, there was some kind of link between him and Nixie. Some of her energy was entwining with his, and soothing his wards, a balm, of sorts. Somehow, they had become attuned to each other. Her energies seemed to complement and support him.

Source. He felt a thrill of something down his spine. Fear? Excitement? He couldn't tell.

"I'd really like you as a friend," he said. He needed her to stick around until he worked this out. And, of course, until they'd solved the deadly and mysterious threats hanging over all of them. "Don't bail on me yet."

She didn't say anything.

He tried not to beg. He really didn't want her to leave him alone. "Maybe, one day, once this prophecy is done, we can be something more."

He knew, now, he wanted that, though who knew what the future held. He wasn't convinced about her argument about balance, but he would try whatever it took to both keep her, and keep his energy in check.

She shrugged in his arms and twisted in the hammock so she could kiss him. It was a soft kiss. Gentle. Caring. On the edge of friendly and, well, not. He returned it just as carefully.

"Sometimes I can inspire other people's creativity. I can spark them," she said. "You want me to give you a little of that energy? Maybe it will help you to remember or to find a solution. It's not my strongest gift, but it might help."

He tried to sit up and failed, as there was no purchase in the hammock. "Yes! Yes. I haven't come across that very often. I don't have it and my Svadisthana Maven didn't have it. I didn't realize you could. Usually those who have it are teachers, or muses for other artists."

"Like I said, it's not a strong gift. But it can't hurt, right?" she said.

"Definitely. How do we do it?"

"Can you sit up in the hammock? It might be stronger if we were near water, but I'm pretty sure I can do something where we are. We don't want to waste time."

They shuffled around until they were both sitting cross-legged in the hammock, facing each other. She took his hands in hers. "Close your eyes, and wait. You should feel something, I think, and then you need to go and work on the problem straight away. Just head off, no need to talk to me. See what happens. I've been told it's like a shot of caffeine, or those smart drugs, what are they called – nootropics?"

"Okay," he said. She was over-explaining – was she nervous? "It doesn't matter if it doesn't work. I'll keep working anyway."

She nodded, and they both closed their eyes. He could feel a ripple of something, presumably as she drew on her Svadisthana, and the greenery seemed to still around them.

Out of nowhere, her emotions smashed into him. He hadn't been expecting that. He tried to pick them apart, to distinguish all that she was feeling, so they didn't engulf him. The emotions hacked at his hard-won control, and he wavered in the stream, not so much a rock as a bit of flotsam caught in the weeds, that any moment could be torn loose and be lost forever.

He caught hope, sadness, fear, love and altruism before his whole body was hit by the next phase, a shockwave of energy that drenched him from head to toe. He felt electrified, and a flood of thoughts, ideas, inspiration and visions galvanized his brain. He could feel that the answer was in there. He just needed to find it.

She squeezed his hands and let go.

"Write it out," she advised. "Go back and write everything down you can think of, and connections might come. Or take a shower. Sometimes a shower helps – it's weird but whatever works, right? Good luck."

She closed the short distance between them and kissed him. He couldn't concentrate on her perfect mouth right now. It was almost a sensory overload. He broke the kiss before her, and fell out of the hammock, leaving her swinging.

"Thank you. I'll see you later." He ran his hand over her silky hair once before he turned and ran back to the house. The solution to protecting Tierra was on the tip of his tongue. He could taste it.

Nixie was amazing. Her 'spark' might have saved Tierra's life.

31

The day passed surprisingly quickly. Nixie lay in the hammock a little longer, savoring the last kiss she and Jeb had shared, before gathering her courage. She'd been glad to give the spark to Jeb, to leave him with a positive memory of her. She wanted to know there would be another option for Tierra, if this didn't work.

She really hoped it would.

She had drawn on the sense of security and strength that Jeb had provided, one last boost of courage before she left. She was a constantly moving creek, and he was a pool, still and deep.

She and Blaize had completed the image of Tierra that afternoon, while Jen and Fintan continued to scour the island. Tierra's sketch showed her with an olive branch wrapped around one arm and the faintest smear of color at each of her Chakra points.

Blaize had frowned at this. "This wasn't in the image Cuinn passed to me. Are you sure you saw it?"

"Yes," Nixie said. "It's there. And the colors correspond to each Chakra. But they're not the wheels you would usually expect if they were representing Chakras. They're more like paint splodges, or splashes, uneven with torn edges."

It seemed that Nixie's creative Chakras saw more in the image than Blaize and Cuinn had. They hadn't come to a conclusion as to what it might mean, and she had left the drawing for Blaize and Cuinn to argue about over the phone.

As the day waned, and shadows started to grow longer, she drove to the meeting point Trent had given her. It wasn't quite sunset, but she wasn't rushing. She left her bike by the road and walked the last few hundred meters onto the beach.

She wasn't sure how they would take the bracelet – Source knows she had tried to cut it off herself – but it was unlikely to be easy. She wondered why they wanted it. It felt like the lesser evil, compared to Tierra's death, but could they use it as a weapon? She paused a moment in her walk then resumed. She had to have faith that her friends were strong enough to overcome any negative side-effects of her actions.

It was strange, but she felt calmer than she would have expected once she'd made the decision. Being surrounded by water would help with whatever came next.

A wind arose, whipping dry leaves and sand past her legs. She smelled ozone on the air.

A storm was coming.

The man had asked her to meet him at an outcropping of rocks on the beach that jutted into the water, where several sturdy coconut palms stood.

Her feet dragged as she got closer. She realized there were two men, the cold one she'd met, who stood, feet planted apart, solidly watching her approach, and another thinner, older energetic, who was drawing with chalk on the bare rock. He was incongruously well-dressed for a man crawling on his hands and knees.

She swallowed. He was setting up some kind of ritual. It was overly complex if they were simply removing her bracelet. There were symbols written on the floor, and physical totems that she couldn't make out, though they likely represented the Chakras, amongst other things. Fire was easiest to spot, and there were several torches stuck into the ground, their light flickering wildly.

"Good," the cold man said.

"I want you to heal Tierra," Nixie said. She kept a couple of meters away, out of arms' reach. The other energetic glanced at her, but kept on with his work, his mutters drifting away on the wind.

"After. We gave her a reprieve. You must have noticed," he said.

She nodded. She needed more. "It's not enough."

"We'll stop the illness once we're done here," he said. "Still. I thought you might ask, so as a token of good faith, your friend should be a little better now. Text your friends, and ask."

Nixie fumbled for her cell, and texted Blaize for an update on Tierra. The answer came quickly.

She's looking better. I think she might have turned a corner. We're chatting, it's nice. Come join us!

Some tension left her body. It was real. She could do this.

So Tierra didn't lose her life.

So Fintan didn't lose his lover.

So Jeb didn't lose his friend.

So Nixie's friends would be able to resolve the prophecy, and save their world, and their lives.

"Throw your cell into the water," the man said.

She bounced it in her hand a couple of times, then flung it as far as she could. It sailed over the rocks and dropped into the sea.

She was alone.

Jeb ran back to the tiny bungalow where he was staying. He would take a cool shower first, given he needed waking up rather than relaxing, and let the ideas percolate.

Nixie had seemed subdued today. Jeb's empathy was still off, but he thought it had been sadness that he'd sensed from her most clearly. She must be worried about Tierra.

As was he. Tierra didn't have much time. She'd rallied some, but if her illness continued and she was also drained remotely, and he wasn't able to protect her, she would fade away within days. He swallowed. He couldn't let that happen.

He'd go sit with her after the shower. Perhaps that would help trigger his memory.

He reached his place and bounded up the steps and inside. He stripped off and went into the shower, turning it to cold.

He reached out a hand to grab the soap, and paused.

What is that?

Oh, no…

His heart sank, and for a moment he felt trapped, unable to breathe as he stared.

A bracelet was wrapped around his wrist, the twin to the ones he'd seen on Tierra, Fintan and Blaize, though with different colors.

But – it was a bracelet he hadn't seen on Nixie, the person who'd finally opened his heart again. She tended to wear a big silver bangle on her left wrist, which must have some sentimental value, as she never seemed to take it off. But he'd seen no sign of a Source-given bracelet.

He stared at the plaited cords on his wrist for a few more moments before he made a decision about what to do. He'd meditate and ask the Source for answers, on the off-chance it was related to Tierra.

He finished in the shower in less than three minutes, and roughly toweled himself off. He dressed in loose pants and a long-sleeved shirt and went out onto the balcony, where he sat cross-legged on the wooden floor.

He took a deep breath and closed his eyes. This was a form of prayer for him. Energetics didn't have a religion, as such, because there was no need. Source, their divine, was an easy and self-evident part of their lives. They were connected through energy. Every time they pulled energy from the ether, the energetic plane, they were connected to Source.

But that didn't mean they understood it. Or her, as Jeb liked to call it. Each energetic connected to Source in their own way. For a dominant Ajna energetic, it might be through a dreamwalk in the ether. For a dominant Svadisthana, it might be through a piece of art. For Jeb, as a dominant Anahata, it was through the embodiment of love.

For him, he personified Source as a feminine figure. Divine, loving and always there.

He took another breath from his diaphragm, and connected to Source. He pulled both his energies, Anahata and Svadisthana, and held them inside himself. The energies bounced around his body, and he felt wired, alive. They mixed inside him and he addressed Source as if she were there with him. As if she were a person.

Source, I ask you. What is this bracelet you have given me? Who has the other?

He waited. He stayed still, and kept his breathing steady. He opened himself up to receive as much as was possible, while still holding both the energies within him. His cracked shields were more of a hindrance than a help at this stage. Was he going to have to let go of them completely? *No.* He shut that thought down. He could use a little of his Svadisthana, but not all of it. He wouldn't open himself to temptation again.

There wasn't always a response from Source. And even when there was, it was hard to tell at times if it was from one's own subconscious, or from the divine.

This time, after twenty minutes of meditating, holding his question and Source in his mind, a cryptic answer came back to him.

Embrace your full self. Then help the others to understand their bracelets' gifts.

That didn't really help him. He had embraced his full self. Hadn't he? Then he thought about his Svadisthana. Surely she didn't mean for him to fully open himself up around that? He shook his head. And what could the bracelets do?

He considered it a moment more, then boxed the whole problem up for later, sliding his sleeve over the bracelet. He couldn't deal with it now. They all had enough to worry about. Tierra first, then the bracelets.

He got to his feet. To try to recall his earlier idea, he'd sit in the room with Tierra and free-write, to see what came. His brain felt alive. He grabbed a paper and pen before he walked across the yard between houses to where Tierra was. As he entered the room, Fintan glanced over at him before he turned back to Tierra. He was talking to her in a soft voice, their heads close together.

They weren't alone. Ai was here, her arms wrapped around her knees so she took up as small a space as possible in the corner of the room, listening to something on her cellphone, earbuds in. Blaize paced backwards and forwards, her energy barely contained. With this many upset energetics in the room, the air was thick with power.

His mind bubbled with thoughts and ideas, the creative energy that Nixie had sparked still lively inside him. He got out pencil and paper and jotted down anything that came into his head, while keeping an eye on the room.

Fintan was amusing Tierra by playing with a flame that he made flicker over his hands and dance up and down his bare arms. She chided him and he grinned. She asked for water, and Fintan walked across the room to refill her glass.

Jebediah frowned. Something wasn't right about what he was seeing. He shook his head to clear it. Was he seeing an after-image?

He narrowed his eyes. It was still there.

A flame, rippling with oranges and yellows, rested on Tierra's palm. But Fintan, the fire energetic, wasn't anywhere near her. Yet the fire didn't seem to be hurting her. She stared down at it, a confused look on her face.

"Uh, Fintan?" Tierra said.

He turned, and nearly dropped the water. He ran over and smoothed a hand over hers, and the flame went out.

"Um. I don't think I should be able to do that," Tierra said, weakly.

"You really shouldn't," Fintan said.

They both looked at Jeb.

And it came to him, finally, that last click as the thing that had been tantalizing him slid into place.

That was it. The solution to keeping her protected. They'd only been warding her with Anahata, the usual healing wards and protection. And Tierra had her own Muladhara wards and protections which he knew were active.

But Tierra was something new. She needed protection across all the energies. That's what he'd thought of the night before, when the handful of energetics had been present and all the energies had been represented.

At the moment the energies that were new to her were loose and unbound within her, and the Leech, whoever it was, was able to siphon energy from her from a distance. Maybe he was Ajna – which of course, if it was Elrian, he was. And Tierra now had Ajna too, so that could explain how he was able to take her energy from a distance.

He could test this. "Fintan. Use energy to see if you can see Tierra's new Manipura energies. What can you sense?"

Fintan looked at him, his forehead creased. "I don't —"

"Just look," Jeb urged.

Fintan shrugged and closed his eyes. After a couple of long minutes, he opened them again, wide. "I can see it. She has Manipura energy like a Dormant. It's there, but not active, not really."

He puffed out a breath of air. "She's going to need training."

Jeb nodded and turned to Blaize. "Can you do the same for Ajna?"

She stepped over to the bed and closed her eyes in the same way, touching her fingers to Tierra's forehead. After another few tense minutes, she breathed out "Oh, shit."

"What?" Fintan and Jeb said at the same time.

"She's a Dormant in Ajna too, but there's a gaping tear there where someone's draining energy from her. We need to get shields and wards up around her asap."

When Tierra had shared energy with Cuinn, she'd somehow both awakened her other Chakras, and become a Dormant in all the other energies, but it had also left energetic weaknesses in her that someone had been able to exploit. He could kick himself for not thinking of this earlier. He could ward her to some degree across all energies, but ideally they needed a stronger energetic in each specific energy to help her with the new energies that she was Dormant in.

Jeb nodded grimly. "She needs warding for all the energies. Not the usual healing Anahata, or her dominant and auxiliary. She's open through them all."

Blaize nodded decisively, clearly happy to have a task. She glanced around the room. "We can cover everything apart from Vishudha. We need Nixie for that."

"Ai, could you go find her and bring her back?" Jeb asked.

The teen sprang to her feet like a colt and shot out of the door.

Jeb felt something that had been tight inside him relax. They'd done it. They could have Tierra warded in an hour. She'd be safe.

On the plane Elrian had pored over the Hermit's notes, revising, cross-checking and reviewing the information against what he already knew about remnant stone creation.

He'd had the chance to begin his preparations for the ritual as soon as darkness fell, on this isolated part of the island's coast away from the tourist hot spots. He was taking her Svadisthana, so completing the ritual on the beach, near her element of water, would strengthen the final stone.

He was impressed Trent had managed to get the girl here of her own accord. All his notes said a willing sacrifice would create a much stronger stone. It was also likely to be less difficult for him.

He'd try and keep her willing, but he'd planned to restrain her anyway, in case she changed her mind. Either way, she'd make a stone.

Currents of air lashed at him, and he had to grab the dried flowers he'd put out and place a stone on them to hold them down. The storm was natural, but Trent's energies, which included an affinity with the weather, meant he could influence it to some degree. They'd agreed rain would shelter them from prying eyes further, and was to their advantage.

At the moment, it was still dry.

Elrian was prepared, but he didn't feel well. Pulling energy was much harder than it used to be these days. He had always been a strong energetic in both his energies, Ajna and Muladhara, and at points in his life had been a Maven in both. He had a lot more inner resources to draw on than the average energetic.

He wanted to show Imogen that he was equal to the task of making a stone on his own. Did the fact she'd let him come alone mean she believed in him? Or was she playing some kind of twisted game where she set him up for failure? He was never quite sure where he stood with her. Which made her all the more alluring. Plus, the power she wielded was an aphrodisiac indeed. But that was why he needed to make a good showing himself.

He flicked a glance over to where Trent and the girl stood. She was quite tiny next to the mercenary. Her power, happily, was a lot greater than her stature might indicate. He shot out a thread of his Ajna, assessing her power levels, tasting her. She shivered, but it was unlikely she knew what he was doing. Yes. With the right training, she could eventually have been a Master in Svadisthana, and a Practitioner in Vishudha. That was fine for his purposes. It was the former he was interested in harvesting for the stone. It was a shame he couldn't leech from her first, but with no energies in common, that wouldn't work well.

Trent, however, had Ajna as his auxiliary energy. Elrian assessed the big man. Clearly, Elrian had no chance against him physically, but energetically – could Elrian take from him without him noticing? Siphon a little from him. The man wasn't a talker. He was more than muscle, but he wasn't an intellect. Given the weather, and the need to influence the storm, Trent's attention would be on his Svadisthana, not his Ajna. It would be an extra service the man could unknowingly provide for his exorbitant fee.

It might work. A dangerous balancing act, tonight was another step forward in their plan to ensure the prophecy went in their direction.

And the eventual rewards?

He'd remake the world.

32

Ai came back into the room ten minutes later. Tears streaked her face. She thrust a piece of paper out in front of her, biting her cuticles and staring down at her feet.

"Nixie's gone."

"What?" Jeb took the paper from her, while Blaize put an arm around the distraught girl.

It was a note.

Jeb

A man offered me a trade, my bracelet for Tierra's life, down by the water. I took it. She's worth a lot more than I am to the prophecy. I hope to be back soon, and Tierra will be well again, but if not, for what it's worth, I'm glad I met you.

I think I even loved you a little.

Nixie.

He read it out loud, blinking at the idea she had a bracelet. Why had she hidden it from him? And what the hell did she think she was doing?

Ai buried her head in Blaize's shoulder. Blaize comforted her, but at the same time, her eyes were hard and flat. Blaize and Nixie were like sisters.

"Where has she gone?" Blaize snapped out. "What has that crazy girl done now?"

Jeb turned the note over to see if there was anything else. He shook his head.

"Call her," Blaize ordered Jeb. He fumbled for his phone, and did so. It went straight to voice mail.

"The phone's off," he said.

Jeb pushed a hand through his hair and squeezed his eyes shut. They had two serious problems now. They needed to find Nixie urgently, but Tierra was also in danger.

Without Nixie, they had no Vishudha energetic to help complete the protection and warding of Tierra. And he was also the only Svadisthana energetic. They could ward four of her Chakras without him using his Svadisthana, or five if he was prepared to open his wards further, which posed a different sort of risk.

Thunder cracked close by. There was no rain yet, but a storm was on its way. That wasn't going to help.

"We need Nixie to keep Tierra safe," Fintan said.

"We need Nixie because we need Nixie," Blaize stated. "Battle plan?"

They were all looking at him, despite the fact two of them had more military understanding than him, being Warrior-trained. Jeb was the one with the healing knowledge. His war days were long behind him.

He tried to tap into the Jeb of old. The devil-may-care, confident spy. The supposedly wise guru of the Guild.

The person who got people killed.

He shook that thought away.

This was a chance to do things differently. To use his energy carefully, appropriately.

To save, rather than to slaughter.

Tierra had rallied this evening. She had more color in her cheeks than she'd had since he'd been back.

"We're going to ward Tierra in all her Chakras apart from Vishudha. I'll use Anahata to give her a patch in case the draining starts again while I'm out. You'll stay with her to keep her safe." His jaw clenched. "Then I'm going to bring Nixie home."

It wasn't that simple, and they all had questions. But there wasn't that much time to lose. He chopped through all their initial arguments and focused them on warding Tierra. Her biggest danger areas were Ajna, where the tear had been, and Vishudha, where all he could do was give her an Anahata patch, which anyone with the right energy could probably rip through pretty fast.

Tierra was sitting up by the end of the treatment. Without the drain, she was able to pull her own Muladhara from the ether and boost herself.

"Right," she said. "Blaize. Go get me something important to Nixie. I'm going to track her. Jeb, you can't go off half-cocked. You never found the landlady, so you need a place to start."

Blaize darted out of the room. Tierra was an expert tracker. She was also ill. Jeb put a hand out then dropped it to his side. "Tierra, you're not well enough for that."

"Don't be silly," she said briskly, and for all his worry, he was pleased to see a little of the old Tierra back. "How will you find her otherwise? She hasn't been gone long, it's a small area, and I have a good connection with her. Conditions for me being able to narrow down the area she's in are good. We know she's by the water, so it's either one of the lakes or the coast. Plus, the sooner you bring her back, the sooner you can complete my wards and I'm safe."

Blaize came back in with a slim, elegant lighter in her hand and gave it to Tierra.

"What's that?" asked Jeb. "Nixie doesn't smoke."

"No. She uses this for her art," said Blaize. "It was part of a gift from her parents when she won a national art prize in her teens. It's part of her finishing techniques for many of her pieces. She loves it. Also, I'm coming with you to find her."

"Perfect," said Tierra. "Now everyone give me some peace to work with the energy. I don't have a lot to waste."

They tied her to the rough bark of one of the palm trees, facing out to sea. She didn't resist. It was her choice to do this.

Elrian had examined her bracelet initially, and bound her so her arms were in front of her, and the bracelet accessible.

The ritual seemed to involve a lot of stuff. The two men had very different roles. The cold one, the younger one, Elrian had called Trent. He was some sort of guard or soldier. Less interesting if she was to draw him. Handsome, but somehow blank.

The older one had introduced himself as Elrian, but she'd known who he was as soon as she'd seen him. The man from the Hermit's house, who'd thrown the book at her.

The heavens had opened not long after they'd tied her. It seemed to be causing Elrian some challenges. His torches fizzled out, and as neither of the men had any Manipura, he struggled to relight them.

There'd been some weirdness between the men, she'd thought. Something strange that she couldn't quite make sense of. The dynamic between them wasn't exactly friendly.

She wondered about using her own power on them, but Trent had told her that Tierra's life was on the line for her compliance. For perhaps the first time in her life, she'd obey all the rules. Slivers of doubt slid through her mind as she wondered if she was doing the right thing, if she was in over her head, but she crushed them.

To calm her nerves she considered how she might paint the scene. A sort of Andromeda chained to the rocks. Not in the classical style though, too dull. Cubist? Perhaps she'd take inspiration from the region and try some Malaysian-inspired batik. She'd seen some beautiful examples there last year when she'd gone for a weekend break to Kuala Lumpur.

Focusing on the way she'd create art from the scene helped her to ignore her racing heart, flickering pulse, the metallic taste of fear in her mouth and the very real fact that the two men in front of her appeared to be preparing to kill her.

"Why are you doing this?" she asked Elrian.

"I'm going to take your bracelet, and use your death to create a remnant stone," Elrian said.

Despite the fact she had considered the possibility they might do this as well as taking her bracelet, her blood ran cold and her pulse sped up, fluttering inside her. She had hoped she was wrong, it seemed. She wriggled her torso, checking how secure her bondage was. Was she still prepared to die? To sacrifice herself, not simply her bracelet?

Elrian was less elegant now, with his hair plastered to his head from the rain, but he was studiously ignoring it. Nixie, with water in her blood, reveled in it. With the sea and the storm, power washed through her veins, begging to be used. It would take her a moment to pull power, she thought. Just a moment.

Elrian caught something in her eye, and reached up and slapped her in the face. Pain smashed through her, and she froze for a second, then blinked, her eyes watering. Her jaw snapped shut, her cheek throbbing. Ouch. Her body shook, and her tears mixed with the rain.

Could she paint pain? She'd never experienced anyone deliberately causing her that level of physical pain before. What would it look like? A red smear? Black tones?

Her head swam. She was going to die here on this beach. She would become one with her element, and her soul would roam the waters. She chided herself for her romantic notions, even in death. She'd never really thought much about the afterlife, only that she'd somehow go back to Source. It had always seemed so far away, when energetics could live hundreds of years.

Whatever Elrian needed to complete his preparation seemed to be done. He was pulling in a great deal of power. He bent to squat inside the circle he'd created, and placed his hands on the runes and symbols he'd drawn.

They lit up with power. And that power shot straight to her, at the center of it all.

Fuck, the pain.

She'd never known such pain. White-burning-ice-fire-intense. A laser beam installation so bright that viewers couldn't look at it directly. That would be interesting, to create a piece that couldn't be seen.

It hurt so much.

She kept up the narrative in her head, even while her body bent in cramps from the agony that Elrian was inflicting on her. It gave her strength to disassociate from what was happening, to see it as art.

She didn't feel as powerful anymore. He was draining that from her. Taking her energy. Leeching. But the pace was fast, faster than she'd expected.

She wished she'd had the chance to tell Jeb he'd taught her about real love. That love was made up of a thousand tiny touches, not just the flash and bang of the sexual peak. That she didn't only love the sex they had – although she did – but she loved the way he pinched the brow of his nose when he was thinking. That she adored the baggy wool sweaters he wore, which had a touch of old-fashioned about them, whilst his torso was slender but as well-muscled as any athlete. That she loved the way his body cut through the water when he swam.

That she loved him. All of him.

She held onto the thought of that love as the pain burned through her, and weakness began to enervate her system.

Something small and orange glowed on the floor in front of Elrian, and all the lines from him to her and around them led to it.

It was beautiful.

It was her death in the sand.

Elrian's exhaustion had fallen away as the runes he'd made on the sandy rock lit up.

It was working.

His knees and shoulders ached as he held his position on the floor, the conduit of the energy from the girl into the stone, but it was working.

He was exultant. He could do this. He needed to hold until the girl was fully drained, which could be four minutes or it could be forty. It seemed to be happening quickly so far.

But the pace was taking a toll on him. He'd taken the merest touch of energy from Trent before starting the ritual. Trent had shuddered, but hadn't seemed to catch what he was doing. It had been helpful, that boost.

Elrian consciously slowed down the rate at which he was draining the girl into the stone, unsure he could take the flow of energy for much longer at the same rate.

With things more under control, he glanced around him. The sea heaved behind Trent now, the waves high. They were above beach level, and their rocky outcropping had some shelter, but occasionally spray reached them, adding to the constant rain.

Elrian frowned. He needed to keep the pace up if he was going to drain her before the storm caught them. He shifted his gaze to Trent. The man stood at ease, but his eyes ranged around the landscape for threats. He was alert and ready in case of an attack. Trent checked in on Nixie too, infrequently, but he rarely looked down at what Elrian was doing.

Good.

Maintaining his position as the channel for the flow of Nixie's energy to the stone, Elrian put out the merest thread of energy towards Trent, aimed at scraping more off the surface, like a cat skimming the cream.

It was a delicate balancing act. Lightning cracked through the sky and lit up purple clouds, and the rain sheeted down harder.

"Can you take the edge off the storm?" he shouted to Trent.

Through the energy wisp, he felt Trent pull energy from the ether and feed it into the storm. His face had a wild joy on it, an expression Elrian hadn't seen before. Actually, he'd barely seen any expression from him before.

The rain was cut by perhaps ten percent, and the next gap between thunder and lightning was longer.

Elrian kept holding the connection. The girl, despite her natural skin tone, was pale and bloodless, and he wasn't sure what was rain and what was tears as water poured down her face. She was limp in the wet rope, but she was still conscious, the whites of her eyes stark and vivid. She glared at him, but her power was dimmed.

There was a rumble in the earth, far, far away, and Elrian's Muladhara pricked even with everything going on. Trent shouted something, but Elrian couldn't hear.

Then Trent was at his ear, yelling urgently. "A tsunmi's coming. We have maybe fifteen, twenty minutes. We need to get the fuck off this beach, now."

"Calm it!" Elrian shouted back.

"I can't. Come on. We need to go."

Elrian shook his head. "I don't need long. Calm it."

He needed more from Trent though, if he was going to speed up. He reached to take a little more from him, but he was clumsier, his tiredness tripping him, and Trent's eyes widened.

"Tell me," he said, "that you didn't leech from me."

A shiver ran through Elrian at the very matter of fact way Trent said it.

Trent leaned down, and spoke very close to Elrian's ear. "I could kill you in a heartbeat. And it would not be an easy death."

He stood straight again. "I'm going. Come with me, or you'll die here on this beach. I've earned my money, so I'd prefer it if you were still breathing tomorrow to pay me."

Elrian was so close. So close. He shook his head.

Trent shrugged. "Leave, or die. Personally, I'm leaving."

"Then we need to take her with us! I might be able to finish the ritual later," Elrian said, desperate.

"No time," Trent said. He began to jog inland. "I suggest you leave her, and you do it now."

Inside Elrian's head he was screaming, screaming with rage at the disrespect, and at the opportunity loss. Trent was correct. The girl's bonds were sodden, getting her out would take precious minutes he no longer had.

He couldn't believe he'd failed again. He'd been so close.

He disconnected from the runes with a hot wrench, scooped the topaz from the floor, and lifted Nixie's hanging head by the hair. He hissed into her ear, "Leave here, and I will drain Tierra. Nothing's changed. Your life, for hers."

The tsunami would take her. He might not get a stone from this debacle, but he would get a death. He would be one step closer to stopping the prophecy.

And when he drained Tierra, they would be impotent to stop him, and all he would need to concentrate on was the stones.

33

It had taken longer than he'd wanted, but Tierra had narrowed down the area that Nixie was in. Jeb and Blaize had split up, she starting inland at a freshwater lake, and he starting on the coast, and they planned to work their way towards each other.

There was an ominous feel to the air, the rain pouring down, thunder booming and lightning cracking down far out to sea. But the storm was coming in.

Where was she, damn it?

Jeb got to the beach and ran along it, his gaze raking the wild and empty expanse of sand.

He ran until his lungs burned. Finally, up where the shore rose to a low platform, he saw the first person since he'd hit the beach. Only a silhouette at first, but when he was within a hundred yards it resolved itself into Nixie's petite form, slumped against a palm tree. There was no sign of anyone with her, though as he got to her he saw the signs of a ritual disturbed.

He intended to lift her over his shoulder and take her back. But when he got to the tree, he realized she was tied to it with rough ropes that were wet and swollen from the spray of the sea and the rain. The waves were already higher than the usual tide line. And the tide wasn't going out.

He tugged at the ropes ineffectually, trying to release her, but they were stiff and unyielding. Damn it. Why wasn't he the sort of man who carried a knife? He bet Fintan carried a knife. He shouted her name. "Nixie! Wake up! We need to get you out of here."

He barely noticed the water now, though it thudded into his body like a hail of tiny spears. He cupped her head in his hands, and she groaned.

"What…?" She opened her eyes and looked around her, her eyes going wide and then squeezing shut as she drew in several rasping breaths.

"We need to get you out of here," Jebediah said urgently. "But I don't know how to free you. Any ideas?"

She shook her head and swallowed. Her voice was breathy with fear and she was trembling. "We need Blaize and her fire. I don't think any of our energies are going to help here, are they?"

"No. But we'll get you out. I'll get you out." He promised. He looked around the beach. What could he use? How could he help her?

"Wait, no! You can't!" Her eyes were huge, pleading. "They'll drain Tierra. I promised I'd stay here so they wouldn't. You need to go."

The waves were higher, and the sea washed around their feet as it teased them by coming in, and then retreating. It had crested the rocks, and the spray was up to her calves. They didn't have much time. He ignored her words, focusing on the problem at hand. He could solve this.

She was bound around the tops of her arms, above the elbows, her hands in front of her. She reached out as far as she could, and he reached back towards her even as he continued looking around for a way to free her. The silver bangle caught in her drenched clothes, and he pulled it off her wrist and shoved it in one of his pockets. He might be able to expand the loops of the rope enough for her to pull her wrist through, but not with that giant bracelet on it.

He cupped her face in his hands, briefly, to comfort her, and she closed her eyes for a second and leaned into them, then shook her head. When she opened her eyes, she caught sight of something and stopped dead.

Jeb's head pounded, the pressure and exhaustion of the last few days pressing on him.

What new danger was happening now?

She'd taken the comfort of his hands, and was ready to tell him to get out of there and leave her to die.

And then she'd seen his wrist, and had frozen.

When Nixie realized that Jeb's bracelet was the twin of her own, she didn't know how to react. To laugh at the ridiculousness of seeing it now, as all they were and could have been was about to be destroyed, or to cry because of all that they could have had, could have been.

"Look," she urged, and used her head to indicate their wrists.

His mouth dropped open, and wonderingly, he put his wrist next to hers so they touched. She clasped his right hand in her left.

She felt her Svadisthana and her Vishudha rise up in her. She wasn't even drawing on them, but out of nowhere she knew that both were inside her, ready to be used.

Her energies had somehow been amplified by the bracelets.

"Do you feel that?" she yelled over the noise of the storm.

He had his eyes closed, fighting something inside him. Fighting his own energy, she guessed.

"You need to go!" she yelled. "Leave me!"

"I won't until you come." He didn't open his eyes. "We can protect Tierra. I worked it out. We need your energy to do it though. The way to save her is to come with me, not stay here."

Something rigid inside her relaxed, and hope flooded her. Perhaps…there was another way? Her impulsive nature surged and she made a split second decision.

"Get me out of here!" she shouted.

His body shuddered, and his grip on hers tightened. "Are you sure?"

She knew that Source wouldn't have given him a bracelet if his feelings for her hadn't been his own, and not the product of influence. And if Jeb was able to save Tierra without her death, there was no need for her to give up.

"Yes!" she said. "Yes."

She felt a touch of his Svadisthana. What remained of his wards, the last remnants, were being assaulted by an energy that wanted to be fully free. Would it help them, or kill them faster?

Cuinn had seen them like this in his vision, but he hadn't seen that she would be bound. *Did the fact that I chose this willingly change anything?* Had Cuinn been right that Jeb needed to keep control? Some primal instinct deep inside where her sparks of inspiration came from said he was wrong. And what did they have to lose?

"Let go!" she screamed. The sea pooled around her knees now, and the spray hit her chest. "You would never hurt me! I trust you! You need to trust yourself!"

"There has to be another way," Jeb said, vehemently. "Otherwise, I'm going to end up killing you myself."

34

She was wrong. He couldn't trust himself. Didn't. He needed to keep her safe, and he wasn't safe. But the words of Source came back to him. 'Embrace your full self.' Did she mean now? What would happen if he let those last pieces of control go?

He could feel his energies inside him, battering him on the inside as the sea was battering his physical body. The storm was elemental, made of air and water just as his own energies were. He felt almost as if he could take the storm and make it his own. He could become the storm. What would happen to him if he did? Would he lose himself? What would happen to Nixie?

Everything was unknown. But he had no other ideas. If he could control the storm, if he was one with the storm, maybe he could direct it back out to sea. Away from Nixie. But it would take more power than he'd ever had before. It had been many decades since he'd experimented with influencing the weather.

But this surge of energy throbbing inside him made him feel powerful. As if he could do anything. If only he was prepared to let go, and embrace all his energies.

And if it destroyed him and left Nixie alive? It was a sacrifice more than worth making.

He leaned in and cradled her head in his left hand, his right still holding hers, and kissed her mouth. Water ran down their faces. The sea was up to

Nixie's waist, and every other wave sprayed their faces with the sting of sea water. Their touching hands and wrists were under the water.

It was now or never. He'd run out of time.

With a roar, Jeb finally tore down the last of his wards, and released his Svadisthana from its bonds. His shields exploded into shreds.

His long suppressed energy flooded his whole being, both agonizing and invigorating, but his scream was lost to the crash of the storm that pounded the beach around them. Nixie clung to his hand, her hair plastered against her head, her hand in his like a tether. She gripped his forearm so their bracelets still touched.

"Focus on me," she yelled. "Don't lose yourself!"

He tried, but the energy that he'd freed was almost too much to bear. It ran up and down his body in a pleasure-pain combination that was on the wrong side of too sensitive.

He was fading in and out of consciousness. A pain in his hand brought him back to the moment. Nixie was digging her nails into his palm. The surf pounded on the beach, the waves rising and rising.

"We need to get you to higher ground," he rasped. He leaned against the tree next to her. He didn't think he could move, but she needed to get away. He should have broken her bonds first. He couldn't control the energy. It came through him from the ether without him pulling it. He was merely a conduit. He had the fleeting thought he should have cleared away the remnants of the ritual, as who knew how they were interacting with the energies. He had no idea what the ritual was for, but he wanted to be sure they didn't feed it further.

How would he halt the energy exploding within? A dam inside him had burst. All the suppressed wants, needs and desires from the last seventy years had exploded at once.

Nixie, who still held his hand tight, stretched out her arm as much as the ropes allowed her to. The sand was gritty underneath his feet. They were both soaked to the skin. Lightning cracked across the sky in the distance, and the thunder came quickly after. The storm was almost directly over them.

She dug her nails in again. "Focus! Take control of the storm!"

Could he? The energy could destroy him. Consume him. Could he find the strength to dominate it, and save them both? If he didn't, when the storm was above them, the energy and the storm would become one, and he would be annihilated. A crack of thunder and barely two seconds later, the lightning came, and indicated he didn't have much time left.

He blinked and her face wavered in front of him. He needed to keep her safe. If she was here she'd be destroyed along with him. And she was still tied up. The beach was otherwise deserted, but she needed to get out of here.

Her voice came into focus again. "Take control of the storm! Or we both die!"

It was the 'both' that did it. The energy spun through him, out of control, but he had to fight it, and control it, if they were going to live.

If she was going to live.

"Don't let go of my hand!" he shouted. She nodded. Her face was pale, silver-lit by the moon and each strike of lightning, strikes which were coming more and more frequently.

He closed his eyes, still propped against the tree, one hand in hers. He was going to try and command the storm.

He reached inside himself to connect with the energy. To become the energy. He'd never felt his energies as powerfully before, and given he was already one of the most powerful energetics in the Anahata Guild, that was a terrifying thought. He took the energy of air and water and expanded his consciousness outside his physical body.

The storm had no personality, no agency, but nonetheless, he could feel the weight and power of it in the air. He searched blindly to find the point at which the temperature differed – where the heated air rose, cooled, and the moisture fell back to earth.

His physical body told him the sea was up to his waist now. Up to Nixie's chest. They didn't have long.

He found it. He drew on all his energy and calmed the sea breezes that had caused the air to lift. He thrust his energies out into the unstable warm air that kept rising, causing the storm to continue. He felt a shift and the storm calmed.

But it wasn't enough. The waters, the tide, kept rising.

And a giant wave was coming. His connection to the sea and storm showed him a tsunami on its way, a growing wall of water that would not simply take him and Nixie, but destroy much of the coast here, smashing into it at high speed and dragging houses, cars, bikes and people back into the sea.

No.

He needed to calm the tsunami, then the storm. He pulled energy from the ether to add to the huge wellspring of power he felt inside him, and with an enormous effort of will, threw up a gigantic wall of water in front of the wave, mimicking the sea walls the Japanese used to protect their ports from the same. It was over fifty feet tall and a hundred miles long. It took tremendous effort.

The wave smashed against his wall instead of the coast, and he waited for the drawback, the wave's trough, which lowered the sea level in that area by meters for minutes. The wave built into another ridge, and once again smashed into Jeb's wall.

He clutched Nixie, her touch and the connection with the bracelet somehow amplifying his power. He needed it. It was the biggest single use of energy he had ever undertaken. He was burning through energy at a shocking rate, his body electric with the energies flowing through him.

Dissolving the tsunami took time, but eventually it was done, he released – gently – his wall of water, and he was left with the storm, still wild and savage.

He focused on the wind. He coaxed it and soothed it, the energy in him thick and plentiful. It was like spreading balm onto a burn. The balm cooled the waves, and they began to drop. He sighed in relief. He could do this. A few more minutes and the storm was dying down. The lightning whipped, and the thunder cracked, but it was further out to sea.

It was done.

He had a moment where he hovered between the energetic world and the physical one. He could follow the storm. Become the storm. He could leave his physical body and chase it, and he would no longer be bound to the physical plane. He'd be free of the guilt and the shame of his past actions. As the storm, he could take the pain of the war and be part of the cycle of natural disasters that affected the world, and forget all about control. He could let go entirely, and dissolve. Become a natural force of destruction.

He wavered, his senses alert to the disappearing storm, his energies still part of the wind and the waters, poised, ready to be assimilated and subsumed.

But he could feel the heat of Nixie's hand in his, their bracelets still touching, tethering his physical body to the world. If he left his physical body, he would be leaving Nixie. She'd asked him to stay.

It was hard, living in the world. Vanishing into the elements might be easier.

But, Nixie. Beautiful, light, fun and talented. With a depth most didn't see. If he faded away, he would never have the opportunity to experience love with her.

Her hand went limp. Their connection broke, and the decision was made. He needed to ensure she was okay. She wasn't saved yet.

He flew like an arrow, his essence hitting his physical body in a rush. The power was still there, coiled inside him, but he was in control of it. His Svadisthana was no longer a liability.

Moreover, there was something missing inside him. The guilt and emotional pain he'd been carrying for decades had been left out in the ocean with the storm. His body was light, despite the pain from the power use.

He opened his eyes and saw Nixie slumped over the ropes that tied her, her eyes closed. The waves were now back at his thighs as the tide began to go out. He had no way to judge how long it had taken, but for Nixie to have breathed in water, it must have been more than a few minutes.

"Nixie!" he shouted.

He couldn't give her mouth-to-mouth standing up, but she needed it now.

He had a crazy idea. He threw his energetic essence out again and called a part of the storm back. He drew the smallest lightning strike he could from the clouds and aimed it at the tree. A tingling and a hiss, and he threw shields around both himself and Nixie. This was going to sting a little.

The lightning struck her bonds at the back of the trunk, and chunks of the tree exploded outwards as the moisture in the bark was super-heated even by this small lightning strike. The tree provided a path for the lightning to hit the ground, and it would have left a scar on the tree. But the ropes were burnt through, and Nixie fell into his arms.

He carried her several hundred yards inland, her body light in his arms, to where there was no longer any sea, and laid her on the ground. He checked her pulse, but her body was limp and lifeless. He administered CPR, willing her to breathe again. Nothing.

She was so pale. He tried not to panic. He kept up the CPR, and drew on his energy. This time, instead of rescue breaths, he put his hand in the air above her mouth, squeezed his hand into a fist, and threw his healing energy into her body. He jerked the water out of her lungs, and used his energy to increase the oxygen flow through her blood. Then went back to rescue breathing.

He blended human and energetic methods of lifesaving, willing her to live, to breathe.

He needed her.

An eternity passed. An eternity considering a life without her.

He'd braved the storm for her. She couldn't leave him now.

Her body jolted, and she coughed and spluttered, water coming out of her mouth. He turned her head to the side, until she was ready to sit up. She was shivering.

He put his arms carefully around her to warm her. The skies were clearing, the seas receding, and they were finally safe.

35

Nixie faced Jeb over a supine Tierra, who Jeb had made lie down on the bed. She was much recovered since she'd been able to draw on her own energy from the ether, but her new Vishudha needed warding, and for that they needed Nixie's energy. He'd already removed the Anahata 'patch' he'd put over it.

They hadn't rested since the beach, where Blaize had found them, bedraggled and staggering to Nixie's bike. They'd come directly to Tierra's room. Nixie was still dripping wet, but thankfully, the island was warm.

She didn't have much left in her at this point. She was ready to collapse into bed and sleep for a week.

Jeb placed Nixie's left hand on Tierra's lower abdomen, and put his right hand over the top so their wrists, and bracelets, touched. She felt him draw on his energy, and she opened herself up, sending the blue of her Vishudha to mix with the greens of his Anahata. Together, they warded Tierra's last Chakra, weaving their energy together into something that would last until it became second nature for Tierra to do it herself, as any new energetic coming into their powers would be taught as a child or teenager. Tierra herself had taught Ai only a couple of weeks ago.

"It's done," Jeb said. Nixie nodded, tired to her very bones. She slumped into a nearby chair.

Tierra sat up, energized. "I'm going to track down whatever was draining me."

Nixie cocked her head. "You can do that?"

Tierra nodded firmly. "It might take me a while, but I think I can."

"She's a tracker," said Blaize without looking up, as she read through some material Cuinn had sent on her phone. "Now we know more, she'll find it."

"Don't overdo it," Jeb warned, stretching. He yawned, and beckoned to Nixie. "Let's go."

She shuffled over to him and he held out an arm. She tucked herself under it, and burrowed her head into his warm chest. He smelled divine.

"Wait, we need you to tell us what happened," Blaize protested, finally looking up. "We need the details to send to the others."

Nixie almost cried. She needed to rest. She could barely stand.

"We'll tell you later. We need to sleep first. This one –" Jeb gestured to Nixie, who was using him to stay upright, "– needs rest."

"You too," Nixie mumbled, not bothering to move her head from where it nestled against him. Rest sounded nice. In fact, for perhaps the first time in her life, it sounded better than sex.

There was no longer any rush. She had all the time in the world with him.

Jeb and Nixie retired to her bed, and, exhausted, slept wrapped around each other. He loved holding her in his arms. She felt so right there. They slept a long time.

They got up to eat, and Nixie worked with Blaize on another sketch while Jeb filled Aiko in on what had happened. Neither of them had the energy for much more, withdrawing to her hammock after only an hour or two.

She lay between his legs, both facing forward, her back resting on his stomach, his legs outside hers. He stroked her hair in wonderment, the texture lustrous. He loved to touch the thickness of it.

Though at this point, despite having slept the night and much of the day away, he was so worn out he could barely move a muscle. The gentle sway of the hammock was soothing, lulling him into a semi-doze.

The air was sweet and clear around them, stars sprinkling the sky above. There was little light pollution on the island to cloud their view. There was a hint of lemongrass in the air, a scented candle Nixie had lit to keep the bugs away. Noisy crickets kept them company.

Nixie ran a hand up and down his thigh. They touched as much as possible, their bodies stacked on top of each other. He was shirtless, and her top was half a shirt only, stopping a fraction below the smooth swell of her breasts. She wore no bra.

He wrapped an arm around her, and traced circles on her bare, flat stomach.

"You nearly went with the storm, didn't you?" Nixie said, eyes shut.

"Hmmm?" Jeb said. It was hard to concentrate on her words when he had her body in his lap like this.

She turned, and his body stirred in response as her breasts pressed against his legs, his groin, and she crawled up his body to sit on his torso, her legs either side of his chest. His arms were free, and he rested his hands on her thighs. She had dug her toes into the hammock netting to keep herself in place.

She was as agile as one of those geckos she loved so much.

"I felt the call of the tempest through the bracelets. I thought you might leave. Did you want to?" Nixie said. She looked down at him, her dark eyes serious.

He thought about lying to her. Did she need to know the truth? He lifted his hands, palms up, let them fall and blew out a breath.

"There was a moment when I did, yes," he admitted. "It would have been so easy. I've never been so at one with the elements."

Nixie dropped her head for a moment, then gazed at him directly. "Do you regret the choice you made?"

He raised his eyebrows. "Not for a second. I came back for you, and I will never mourn anything I lost because of that. Besides, there's nowhere in the world I want to be more than in this hammock, with you."

She cocked her head and then jerked it in the direction of the bedroom, suggestively. "Nowhere?"

He grinned. "I want to be wherever you are."

She had no idea that she'd liberated him far more than losing himself to the storm would have.

She nodded and bent and dropped a swift kiss on his lips. "And your Svadisthana?"

His lips twisted, rueful. "It's as much part of me as anything else. My wardings are all gone. It's time to remember how to use it, and to put it to good use in the world."

Nixie gave a short laugh. "It looked to me like you remembered how to use it pretty well on the beach. I've never seen power like that."

He shrugged. "I think it was a one-off, a combination of circumstances. The buildup of my power and me letting down my shields fully for the first time in decades, the ritual and runes that Elrian left, and —" he hesitated.

"Yes?" she said. She was kneading his chest.

"Our bracelets. Did you feel anything?" He was fairly certain some of Source's message to him had been untangled in the use of the bracelets, but he wanted external confirmation.

"Sure," she said. "Connecting them makes us stronger. It's obvious, really."

She made it sound so simple. She shifted her left hand to his right, and interlocked their hands, then pressed her wrist against his. An instant shock of energy invigorated Jeb, and he jerked in the hammock, setting it swinging. Nixie almost purred.

His energies twanged inside him like plucked strings, his Svadisthana finally as free as his Anahata.

"We're stronger together,' Jeb said. He'd been alone so long, he'd forgotten the power of having someone in your corner. Someone on your side no matter what. Someone who believed in and accepted your, good and, well, less good bits.

"You don't have to fight yourself anymore," Nixie said. "You're fine as you are, a man who's made mistakes, like everyone else. You have dark and light in you, as I do, as everyone does. Our mistakes help us choose the light the next time."

Nixie was a source of light for him, that was certain. He'd misjudged her initially. She had a personality that was light, and fun, and the sensual fairy was part of her, but that didn't mean she couldn't be serious or thoughtful.

Watching her concentrate while drawing as she'd completed another sketch with Blaize that day, and get lost in the flow of putting pencil strokes on a page, had made him realize she had stronger powers of concentration than most. It was a time he'd enjoyed, when he could study her without her realizing given how absorbed she was in her work.

The damage from the war hadn't gone, but a burden had been lifted from him, and this amazing woman was part of that. He couldn't believe how lucky he was that she was his.

He drew on his Svadisthana and sent a pulse of it through their bracelets. She shivered delightfully and his groin responded.

He suddenly found he wasn't quite as tired as he'd thought.

Nixie wanted to roll herself on Jeb like he was catnip. Wanted to nip and nibble, to rub herself on his scent, and generally stay as close to him as possible.

She'd grown up a lot in the last couple of weeks. Her entire outlook on love had changed, as she'd realized what she'd previously been chasing in love was selfish, a mirror for her own vanity, rather than something more solid and selfless.

She responded to his pulse of desire by running her hands down his bare chest, using the merest touch as she skated her fingers over his nipples. He let out a groan.

Jeb wasn't the kind of man she'd been looking for. He was serious, damaged, scholarly, steady, much more experienced in the world, and involved in highlevel Guild politics.

Yet his solemnity complemented her more mercurial temperament. He grounded her, and she uplifted him.

She bent down and licked along the shell of his ear, then bit the lobe very gently. He sighed and she felt his cock harden between them. She moved her hips slightly, rubbing, encouraging, daring.

And Source, the man had power. Exhilarating, impressive, terrifying power. When he'd taken control of the storm, she'd thought she'd lose him. Or that he'd lose control and destroy the island. She'd seen the possibility in that moment.

He'd stayed with her though. With his matching bracelet. Source had paired them together. Through good times and difficult ones, she'd be there for him now. Whatever else this prophecy threw at them.

He scooped his arms around her and swept her into a horizontal kiss. She wriggled on top of him, and got her hand between them, deftly undoing his pants. He spluttered and laughed through their kiss, but didn't stop her. She shoved them down and he kicked them off. They ended up in a heap at the end of the hammock, but she didn't care.

She shimmied her shorts and underwear off, writhing against him delightfully as she did. He skimmed hands over her naked ass.

She was wet for him, ready, and she sat up, gazing down at him. His hair was as unkempt as usual, but his mostly-dark stubble was neat, around a mouth that curved up a little either side. She ran a finger down his neck and along the lean muscles on his shoulders and arms that must come from swimming.

It was his eyes that caught her, though. Blue like a storm, blue like the sea, they held a world of promise and desire for her.

The heat and thickness of his cock was gratifying.

She lifted her hips, and, slowly, without dropping eye contact, she slid him inside her. It wasn't easy, and the effort showed in her face, and she could see the idea pleased him. Men.

His smirk dropped once she'd sheathed him fully inside her, and began to roll her hips. She rode him, bit him, scratched him, and he met her action for action, deed for deed.

Their energies danced between them, enhancing sensation, curling around each other, twisting and winding until they melded completely, and there was no separation in their Svadisthanas.

The pleasure built and built in her, and she squeezed her pelvic muscles, spurring him on, and he met her thrust for thrust, despite the limited purchase he had on the hammock.

The hammock swung faster, side-to-side just as they moved up and down. The movements complemented each other, hypnotic and primal, until with a howl she came, and her pussy contracted around him, her nails digging into his shoulders. Mine, she thought. Mine.

The orgasm went through her like waves on the sea, taking its time to calm. When it had finished, she was hyper-sensitive, and his movements inside her felt disproportionately huge.

His eyes had darkened as he'd watched her come, and he reached two fingers down to stroke her clit gently as she continued to circle her hips.

"Again," he said, insistent, and she linked her hands behind her head, her small breasts thrust out, and rode him harder, harder, till the perfect and continuous pressure he was putting on her clit pushed her over again, and she clenched and squeezed and asked and took and he came inside her, while their gazes stayed as locked as their energy was.

36

Elrian stalked through the dawn in Seattle, cold wet rain running down his neck. He'd lost more weight, and he'd had to tighten his belt a notch. He was shaky. He needed energy.

He had been livid about the beach, and losing Nixie. Worse still, Imogen had told him the Guild's latest gossip. Tierra and Nixie had both survived, and Nixie and Jeb were a couple. He'd failed again.

Three couples down.

Three to go.

A man and woman, clearly on a date, blocked his way, and he covered a sneer by stepping aside to let them pass. He turned the collar of his long black raincoat up as he did.

He'd spent a great deal of the last couple of weeks in the ether, searching and seeking as to who the next couple would be, determined not to fail again. He'd decide then whether it would be easier to focus on one of this couple and one of those already bonded, or simply kill both members of the next pair. He still only needed to kill two of the twelve, but if he somehow bungled this next two, and his adversaries managed to have four couples together, he would need to kill three of them.

Inconceivable.

Cassidy had been worried about him, and forced food and drink on him that were irrelevant. The only thing he needed was energy.

It was so hard to pull energy from the ether these days. So much easier to take it from someone else.

He'd kept the stone that he'd part filled from Nixie, and tasted a little of her energy now and then. It kept the edge off. But he needed another victim. And he needed to show Imogen that he was a capable partner. She had responded with disdainful silence to the disaster at the beach. He wondered what Trent had told her. He'd had to pay Trent extra, as the man had noticed Elrian's leeching from him, despite the fact he had no proof. Elrian supposed he was lucky Trent didn't murder him in his sleep, but the other man was unlikely to cross Imogen.

He strode on, passing endless coffee shops and anonymous office buildings.

Happily, the male of the next potential couple worked right here in Seattle. Some kind of tech geek, he didn't seem likely to cross paths with Cara, the female, anytime soon. Especially as she lived on some godforsaken island off Canada, managing a Rehab Center.

Elrian had time, but he wanted the man. He would use him for a remnant stone, as the man was a strong Vishudha-Manipura. Elrian had let go of the need to find energetic matches to drain energy from. While his own energies were Muladhara-Ajna, and energetics with these nourished him the best, Nixie's Svadisthana had still given him something worthwhile. So he'd kill two birds with one stone, and take this male for both purposes.

He'd been shadowing the man, Archer, for days, watching his habits. He was a runner, and every other day he did a three mile loop around the city at dawn. Elrian planned to grab him at the end of this, when he was tired and off-guard. Elrian would use his influence energy to move him, and had prepared a space for the ritual in a hidden spot nearby.

Archer always parked his mountain bike in the same place at the edge of a park. He'd head off, do his three miles, run back to the bike, do a couple of stretches, take out an energy drink he'd stashed on a clip near the handlebars, drink it down, then hop on and cycle the two miles home.

Routine could make you stronger, but could also make you sloppy.

In this case, Archer being sloppy would make Elrian stronger.

Nixie dropped a kiss on Jeb's palm, then flicked on the video call, and her friends' images slowly came into focus on the laptop screen.

Despite the constant sense of menace and threat they lived with, the connection between the different members of the team — for Nixie had begun to think of them that way, though, perhaps, family was a better word — was strong. There was even back channel chatter in the text chat scrolling along, with Blaize messing with Fintan, who messed with everyone, while Tierra scolded him, and worried about her brother and cousin.

Nixie had taken a lot of scoldings and recriminations herself from everyone for her actions. For the first few days, Jeb had flickered between anger and an inability to leave her side. It had worked out, but Nixie had learned she wasn't alone, and the value of real connection. There would be no more superficial hook-ups for Nixie. She had found her match. Her soulmate.

It had been a couple of weeks since the events on the beach, and the group had scattered to the winds.

On screen the video boxes lined up.

There were Blaize and Cuinn, both now at Cathair Cuinn, outside Vancouver. They were back to the research, dreamwalks, and trying to put everything together. They were looking into Iskander, what Elrian might be doing with the remnant stones, why Atlantis burned, and the many other mysteries that were still unresolved. Cathair Cuinn was still HQ, no matter how dispersed they all were.

Nixie had been able to draw the majority of the twelve energetics from Blaize's mind-pictures. Eight energetics they'd already identified, there was one male she'd drawn who none of them yet recognized, and there were three she, Blaize and Cuinn were having trouble with. In the meantime, she was part of the small team finishing the translation of the Hermit's notes, which Jeb was convinced held some kind of key.

Back on the screen, she saw Adam, Tierra's big brother, in Seattle, investigating a recent leeching in case it was connected. He was also checking with his human contacts in the various governmental agencies around the world to see if they had any knowledge of Elrian's whereabouts.

There was Cara, at Vancouver Island's Rehab Center, with Ai hovering behind her, the girl staying with Cara for her first lessons in Anahata energy.

There were Tierra and Fintan in Cairo, at Anahata Guild, where Tierra was healing and being examined by Feng and Aiko, and Fintan was keeping a worried eye on her. Something bigger was going on at Anahata, Jeb felt, and he'd sent Tierra on ahead to check it out.

Cuinn began to speak, and everyone hushed. Nixie smiled. Jeb would nudge her if there was anything she really needed to pay attention to.

She sat curled up next to him as he watched the screen intently, the tinny voices of the others coming through their laptop's speakers and fighting with the sounds of birdsong and gecko on the island, where she and Jeb were taking some time to recover before they went to visit Svadisthana Guild. Jeb wanted to spend a few days there to refresh himself now that his energy was in harmony again.

She smiled, capturing the scene in her mind, another group of contrasting portraits, full of color, light and love. She was looking forward to it. There was a hell of a lot of sexual energy around the Guild. And she intended to take full advantage of that.

END OF BOOK 3

Glossary

Adherent – Once an energetic is taken on by a Maven, they are called an Adherent as they train for their Chakra trial. As part of the ritual when they bond with their Maven, they receive one thin black band around the top of their arm (left arm for females, right arm for males)

Ajna – The Third Eye Chakra, associated with the element of the Mind and the color indigo. The energy of imagination, of visualizations, and insight. Of clarity and wisdom. Of dreams and intuition.

Anahata – The Heart Chakra, associated with the element of the Air and the color green. The energy of healing, and of balance, located in the middle of the body and the seven Chakras. The energy of love, of relationships, of devotion. Of compassion and empathy.

Auxiliary Chakra – Energetics have two Chakras activated in them, that is, energy they can draw upon and use as power. Their auxiliary Chakra is the weaker of the two.

Chakra Trial – When an energetic wants to move up a power level, they are trained for several years by a Maven, and then tested by a Chakra trial (e.g. From Adherent to Practitioner, or Practitioner to Master).

Dormant – When an energetic is born, their energies are Dormant. At birth, their strongest Chakra is almost always identifiable and they are named after this.

Dominant Chakra – Energetics have two Chakras activated in them, that is, energy they can draw upon and use as power. Their dominant Chakra is the stronger of the two.

Dreamscape – Another name for the ether, where Ajna energetics can create their Haven and use Ajna to search for prophecy shards or do other activities related to their energy. The ether is also the place where raw energy is drawn from by energetics, so all energetics have some kind of internal connection to it.

Dreamwalker – An Ajna energetic who can go the dreamscape and gather prophecy.

Ether – Also known as the dreamscape, where Ajna energetics can create their Haven and use Ajna to search for prophecy shards or do other activities related to their energy. The ether is also the place where raw energy is drawn from by energetics, so all energetics have some kind of internal connection to it.

Haven – The space in the ether/dreamscape that an Ajna energetic creates for her or himself that is 'safe'.

Guild Leader – The energetic who is the leader of either a Major or a Minor Guild. A Guild leader has to 'balance' a Guild's energy so it takes an energetic of some power.

Practitioner – Once an energetic has passed a Chakra trial, they are a Practitioner, and receive a second thin black band around the top of their arm (left arm for females, right arm for males). This is the most common level of power for energetics.

Leech – An energetic who has turned into a Rouge, and is draining other energetics of the energy (not all Rouges are leeches).

Major Guilds – The six Chakras have one Guild each (e.g. Muladhara, Svadisthana etc.).

Major Circle – The Major Circle is the highest form of government with one powerful energetic representing each Major Guild, making decisions on behalf of the race.

Manipura – The Navel Chakra, associated with the element of Fire and the color yellow. The energy of the individual; of confidence, of proactivity and of drive and passion. Playful and proud.

Master – If an energetic passes a Chakra trial at the end of their Practitioner training, they become a Master energetic, and receive a third thin black band around the top of their arm (left arm for females, right arm for males).

Maven – This is the name for those energetics who take on an Adherent to train in an energy. An energetic has to be at Master level to become a Maven, but Mavens are outside the power structure. Their symbol is an owl on their robes, but there is no tattoo as it can be a position only taken once in a lifetime, or a Master can take on many Adherents consecutively.

Minor Guilds – These represent each dominant-auxiliary Chakras. There are thirty Minor Guilds representing each combination (for example, Manipura-Ajna is a separate Guild from Ajna-Manipura).

Minor Circle – The Minor Circle is the energetics' second tier of government, and is made up of the thirty energetics who lead each of the Minor Guilds.

Muladhara – The Root Chakra, associated with the element of Earth and the color red. The energy of nourishment and home, family and safety.

Remnant Stone – A stone that can store the energy of an energetic who has been drained to the point of death.

Rogue – An energetic whose energy has 'twisted' into the negative version of the Chakra.

Sahasara – The Crown Chakra, not associated with an element. The purest of all the energies. Only experienced through the Grace of the Source (the energetics' name for the creator, the divine).

Svadisthana – The Sacral Chakra, associated with the element of Water and the color orange. Fluid and adaptable, the energy of movement and connection, of practical and physical creativity. The energy of pleasure, sexuality and sensation, and emotions.

Vishudha – The Throat Chakra, associated with the element of Ether (Space) and the color blue. The energy of communication, of conceptual creativity, and of truth. Of expression, and of listening.

The Guilds and Circles

The energetics' power structure is Guild based.

There are six Major Guilds, one for each of the six Chakras:

- **Muladhara** (The Root Chakra – Earth Element)
- **Svadisthana** (The Sacral Chakra – Water Element)
- **Manipura** (The Navel Chakra – Fire Element)
- **Anahata** (The Heart Chakra – Air Element)
- **Vishudha** (The Throat Chakra – Ether (Space) Element)
- **Ajna** (The Third Eye – The Mind)
  (Sahasara, the Crown Chakra, does not have a Guild.)

Each energetic has two activated Chakras, one dominant and one auxiliary, and it is the combination of these that influences their power, and to some degree, their personality.

Because of the huge differences between an energetic like Blaize, who combines her Manipura dominant with Ajna auxiliary, and one like Fintan, who combines Manipura dominant with Anahata auxiliary, a system of Minor Guilds also developed. There are thirty Minor Guilds representing each combination of powers (for example, Manipura-Ajna is a separate Guild from Ajna-Manipura).

Each individual energetic therefore belongs to two Major Guilds, and one Minor Guild.

For example: Cuinn has Ajna dominant, and Muladhara auxiliary. He therefore belongs to the Ajna Major Guild, the Muladhara Major Guild, and the Ajna-Muladhara Minor Guild.

The Major Circle is the highest form of government with one powerful energetic representing each Major Guild, making decisions on behalf of the race. The Minor Circle, the second tier of government, is made up of the thirty energetics who lead each of the Minor Guilds.

List of Minor Guilds:

- Muladhara-Svadisthana
- Muladhara-Manipura
- Muladhara-Anahata
- Muladhara-Vishudha
- Muladhara-Ajna
- Svadisthana-Muladhara
- Svadisthana-Manipura
- Svadisthana-Anahata
- Svadisthana-Vishudha
- Svadisthana-Ajna
- Manipura-Muladhara
- Manipura-Svadisthana
- Manipura-Anahata
- Manipura-Vishudha
- Manipura-Ajna
- Anahata-Muladhara
- Anahata-Svadisthana
- Anahata-Manipura
- Anahata-Vishudha
- Anahata-Ajna
- Vishudha-Muladhara
- Vishudha-Svadisthana
- Vishudha-Manipura
- Vishudha-Anahata
- Vishudha-Ajna
- Ajna-Muladhara
- Ajna-Svadisthana
- Ajna-Manipura
- Ajna-Anahata
- Ajna-Vishudha

Want More?

The story of the energetics continues in Cara and Archer's story, **Cara and the Hacker**.

To be the first to hear when it's out, visit my website:
EllenBardAuthor.com/sign-up
for updates, giveaways and inside information,

Discover Your Energetic Profile!

Want to know what your Dominant Chakra would be?
Which Guild you would belong to? What your archetype is?

Take the Chakra Quiz, and find out!
EllenBardAuthor.com/chakra-quiz

Make a Difference with a Review

If you loved the book and have a few minutes, I would hugely appreciate it if you had time to leave a short review where you bought the book, and / or on goodreads. For instructions, go to the link below.

EllenBardAuthor.com/how-to-leave-a-review

Your review will help other readers discover the series, and is greatly appreciated in spreading the word. Authors like me rely on amazing readers like you to share their love of books with others.

Thank you!

About the Author

Ellen is an author who writes paranormal romance full of enchantment, intrigue and action. Her writing blends a background in psychology and her experiences traveling the world, with a love of magic, fantasy and a happy ending.

She's a Chartered Occupational Psychologist with the British Psychological Society, and continues to work as an international management consultant, which she has done for the last 18 years. She's worked all over the world in countries such as China, Saudi Arabia and Malaysia. She writes non-fiction under Ellen M Bard.

Her passion for other lands and cultures helps inform her writing, as does her desire to try new things – from art classes to Krav Maga, the self-defence system.

She's a passionate and dedicated reader, speeding through 80-100 books a year – find her on goodreads to see what currently has her hooked.

Born in the UK, she currently lives in an apartment nest in Bangkok, Thailand where she (almost!) never has to feel the cold.

Connect with Ellen:
Facebook: facebook.com/EllenBardAuthor
Twitter: twitter.com/ellenbard
Goodreads: goodreads.com/ellenbard
Instagram: instagram.com/ellenbard/

Acknowledgments

The character of Nixie is, of the heroines so far – Blaize, Tierra and even the next in the series, Cara – the one who shares fewest traits in common with me. She grew from experiences with acquaintances on the Thai islands, and from a desire to embody a character who was a lot more relaxed and enthusiastic about sex than many of the heroines I read about in romance. I want my heroines to display a diverse set of women, who show up in the world with strength from all kinds of sources.

That also means I struggled a lot more with getting her character right. My sister and alpha reader, Sarah Bard, and my editor, Claire Taylor Nelson, helped a lot here – and in many other places! – and I'm very grateful for their notes on this and other aspects of the plot and characters. My mum, Mary Bard, was another great alpha reader, spotting a lot of my consistency errors and typos, and bringing her own unique commentary to her editing notes.

Eléonore Chaban Delmas, friend, writer and beta reader extraordinaire, turned round a reading of this book – with more than a hundred useful comments and notes – overnight. For that, and her generosity and constant warmth as a friend, I have immense gratitude.

My friends Anna Charbonneau and Graham Morley have provided much cheerleading and support, and I'm lucky to have them in my life whether we're in the same country that week or not.

Thanks also to Peter Bainbridge and my aunt, Ellen Dunne, who helped do the final proofs of the book.

The soundtrack to Nixie and Jeb's story was Jasmine Thompson, whose many covers and original songs I had on loop while writing. Her haunting voice and danceable beats were of great help in getting me in the right mood for writing the book.

Finally, as ever, thanks to my Fox. Life-partner and accountability partner are just two of the ways that you show up in my life, providing inspiration and motivation and so much more. Thank you for all the support, encouragement and pad thais, not to mention sharing an office with a coworker who has all the questions, all the time, and expects you to be able to answer.

Ellen Bard, May 2019